W9-BKS-493

M

M

Son of the Century

ANTONIO SCURATI

Translated by Anne Milano Appel

HARPER

An Imprint of HarperCollins*Publishers*

This book is a work of fiction. References to real people, events, establishments, organizations, or locales are intended only to provide a sense of authenticity, and are used fictitiously. All other characters, and all incidents and dialogue, are drawn from the author's imagination and are not to be construed as real.

HarperCollins books may be purchased for educational, business, or sales promotional use. For information, please email the Special Markets Department at SPsales@harpercollins.com.

Originally published as *M Il figlio del secolo* in Italy in 2018 by Bompiani.

First published in Great Britain in 2021 by 4th Estate, an imprint of HarperCollins Publishers.

FIRST U.S. EDITION

Library of Congress Cataloging-in-Publication Data has been applied for.

ISBN 978-0-06-295611-8

22 23 24 25 26 LSC 10 9 8 7 6 5 4 3 2 1

"I am a force of the Past"
Pier Paolo Pasolini

CONTENTS

1919 1

1920 151

1921 275

1922 409

1923 567

1924 647

Principal Characters 763

1919

MILAN, PIAZZA SAN SEPOLCRO, MARCH 23, 1919
THE FORMATION OF THE FASCI DI COMBATTIMENTO

WE STAND FACING out over Piazza San Sepolcro. Scarcely a hundred people, all men of little worth. We are few and we are dead.

They are waiting for me to speak, but I have nothing to say.

The set is empty, submerged under eleven million corpses, a tide of cadavers—reduced to sludge, liquefied—rising from the trenches of the Carso, Ortigara, the Isonzo. Our heroes have already been killed or will be. We love every last one of them, without distinction. We sit on the sacred mound of the dead.

The reality that follows every deluge has opened my eyes: Europe is now a stage without actors. All gone: the bearded sages, the monumental, histrionic fathers, the whining, magnanimous liberals, the grandiloquent, cultured, florid orators, the moderates to whose common sense we have owed our ruin from time immemorial, the bankrupt politicians who live in terror of imminent ruin, each day pleading to put off the inevitable event. For all of them the bell has tolled. The men of old will be overrun by this huge mass, five million soldiers bearing down on the territorial borders, five million returning veterans. We must get in step, lockstep. The forecast is not about to change, bad times still lie ahead. War is still on the agenda. The world is moving towards two big alignments: those who were and those who will be.

I see it, I see it all clearly in this audience of fanatics and derelicts, and yet I have nothing to say. We are a populace of ex-soldiers, a humanity of survivors, of dregs. On nights of carnage, hunkering in foxholes, we are seized by a sensation similar to the ecstasy experienced by epileptics. We speak in volleys, briefly, tersely, forcefully. We fire out ideas we do not have, then immediately sink back into silence. We are like ghosts of the unburied dead who have yielded the floor to those behind the lines.

Yet these, and these alone are my people. I am well aware of it. I am the misfit par excellence, the protector of the demobilized, the lost drifter searching for the way. But there is business here that must be run. Nostrils flared, in this nearly empty room, I pick up the century's scent and reach out to feel the crowd's pulse, and I am certain that my public is there.

The first rally of the Fasci di Combattimento, trumpeted for weeks by *Il Popolo d'Italia* as a momentous event, had been scheduled to take place at the Teatro dal Verme, with its 2,000-seat capacity. But the vast venue was canceled. Given the choice between an immense desert and a lesser disgrace, we chose the latter. We resorted to this meeting room at the Association of Traders and Merchants. This is where I must now speak. Inside four walls covered in a drab greenish-brown, overlooking the bleakness of a desolate parish square, with gilding that unsuccessfully tries to brighten the dreariness of the Biedermeier armchairs, amidst a few scruffy hairy heads, bald pates, and stumps, emaciated veterans breathing the mild asthma of ordinary trades, age-old circumspections and scrupulous budgetary avarice. At the back of the room, from time to time, a member of the association looks in, curious. A soap dealer, a copper importer, that sort of thing. He glances in, puzzled, then goes back to smoking his cigar and drinking a Campari.

Why should I speak?!

The presidency of the assembly has been assumed by Ferruccio Vecchi, a fervent interventionist, captain of the Arditi, placed on leave for health reasons. Dark-haired, tall, pale, skinny, with sunken eyes: the stigmata of pathological degeneration. An excitable, impulsive tubercular, who preaches violently, without substance or moderation, and at key moments during public demonstrations gets carried away like a man possessed, seized by a demagogic delirium and then . . . then he becomes truly dangerous. The role of secretary of the movement will almost certainly be given to Attilio Longoni, an ignorant former railwayman, as eager and foolish as only an honest man can be. To him, or to Umberto Pasella, born in prison with a jailer as a father, later a business agent, a revolutionary trade unionist, a Garibaldian in Greece, and a juggler with itinerant circuses. The other principals will be chosen at random among those who made the most noise in the front ranks.

Why should I speak to these people?! Because of them events have exceeded anything imaginable. These are men who take life by storm like commandos. I have before me only the trenches, the spume of days, the sphere of combatants, the arena of madmen, the furrows of fields plowed by cannon rounds, rioters, misfits, felons, erratic eccentrics, idlers, petit bourgeois bon vivants, schizophrenics, the neglected, the defeated, the irregulars, fly-by-nighters, ex-convicts, convicted offenders, anarchists, incendiary union leaders, desperate hacks, a bohemian platform of veterans, officers and non-coms, men skilled in the handling of firearms or blades, those who have proved themselves violent on re-entry to normal life, fanatics unable to clearly define their ideas, survivors who, thinking they are heroes committed to death, mistake mistreated syphilis as a sign of destiny.

I know, I see them here before me, I know them by heart: they are the men of war. Of war or of its myth. I desire them, the way a man desires a woman and, at the same time, I look down on them. I scorn them, true, but it doesn't matter: one era is over and another has begun. Debris accumulates, the wrecks call to one another. I am the man for "afterwards." And I am determined to be that. It is with this shabby material—with this human wreckage—that history is made.

In any case, this is what I have before me. And behind me, nothing. Behind me I have October 24, 1917. Caporetto. The death throes of our era, the greatest military defeat of all time. An army of a million soldiers destroyed in a weekend. Behind me I have

November 24, 1914. The day of my expulsion from the Socialist Party, the hall of the Società Umanitaria where the workers who idolized me up until the day before cursed my name and fell all over one another for the honor of attacking me. Now I receive their death wishes every day. They wish it upon me, upon D'Annunzio, upon Marinetti, upon De Ambris, even Corridoni, who perished four years ago in the third battle of the Isonzo. They wish death upon those already dead. At this point they despise us for having betrayed them.

The "red" masses foresee the imminence of their triumph. In the course of six months, three empires collapsed, three dynasties that had ruled Europe for six centuries. The "Spanish flu" epidemic has already infected tens of millions of victims. Events correspond to apocalyptic tremors. The Third Communist International met in Moscow last week. The party of global civil war. The party of those who want me dead. From Moscow to Mexico City, throughout the entire terrestrial orb. The age of mass politics has begun and we, here in this room, are fewer than a hundred.

But that doesn't matter either. No one believes in victory anymore. It already came and it was mired in slime. This fervor of ours—*giovinezza, giovinezza!* ah, Youth!—is a suicidal form of despair. We are with the dead, they respond to our call by the millions in this half-empty room.

Down in the street the workers' shouts invoke a revolution. It makes us laugh. We already had a revolution. By dragging this country kicking and screaming into war on May 10th, 1915. Now everyone says the war is over. But again we laugh. We are the war. The future belongs to us. It's no use, it's hopeless, I'm like an animal: I can smell the times ahead.

Benito Mussolini has a sturdy physical constitution despite the fact that he suffers from syphilis.

This robustness enables him to work tirelessly.

He sleeps until late in the morning, leaves the house at noon and doesn't return home before three in the morning. Those fifteen hours, minus a short break for meals, are spent in journalistic and political activities.

He is a sensual man, as demonstrated by the numerous relationships he's had with various women.

He is emotional and impulsive. These traits make him stimulating and persuasive in his speeches. Though he speaks well, he cannot properly be described as an orator.

He is basically a sentimentalist, and this wins him much popularity and many friendships.

He is without self-interest, generous, and this has earned him a reputation for being altruistic and philanthropic.

He is very intelligent, shrewd, measured, reflective, and a good judge of men, their qualities and their faults.

Prone to form quick likes and dislikes, capable of making sacrifices for friends, he is relentless when it comes to enemies and those he hates.

He is courageous and daring; he has organizational skills, and is able to make decisions quickly; but he is not tenacious in his convictions and objectives.

He is extremely ambitious. He is driven by the certitude that he represents a considerable force in Italy's destiny and he is determined to assert that force. He is a man who is not content with second place. He wants to surpass all others and dominate.

Within the ranks of official socialism, he quickly rose from obscure origins to a position of prominence. Before the war, he was the ideal editor of *Avanti!*, the newspaper that guides all socialists. In that capacity he was much esteemed and much loved. Some of his old comrades and admirers still admit today that there was no one better than he was at understanding and interpreting the spirit of the proletariat, which was grieved to see his betrayal (apostasy) when in a matter of weeks he went from being a sincere, fervent advocate of absolute neutrality to being a sincere, fervent advocate of intervention in the war.

I do not believe that this came about for reasons of self-interest or personal gain.

Then too, it is impossible to determine to what extent his socialist convictions, which he never publicly repudiated, were sacrificed in the financial dealings indispensable for continuing the struggle through *Il Popolo d'Italia*, the new newspaper that he founded; in his interactions with individuals and factions of different persuasions; and in friction with his former comrades, subject as he was to the constant pressure of indomitable hatred, bitter ill-will, accusations, insults, and incessant slander by his one-time followers. But if these innermost changes occurred, swallowed up in the shadow of more pressing matters, Mussolini will never let it show and will always want to appear to be—perhaps will always delude himself that he is—a socialist.

This, according to my findings, is the moral figure of the man, in contrast to the opinion held by his former trusted comrades and followers.

That said, if a person of intelligence and high authority were to find the path of least resistance in his psychological makeup, if he were first of all likable to him and were able to worm his way into his heart, if he could show him what is truly in Italy's best interest (because I believe in his patriotism), if he were to very tactfully offer him the necessary funds for the agreed-upon political action, without giving the impression of a brash attempt at rigging, Mussolini would gradually be won over.

But with his temperament one would never be certain that, at some turning point along the way, he might not defect. He is, as already mentioned, emotional and impulsive.

Of course, on the offensive line, Mussolini, a man of thought and action, an effective, incisive writer, a persuasive, dynamic speaker, could become a commanding leader, a formidable intimidator.

Report of the Commissioner of Public Security
Giovanni Gasti, spring 1919

Action Fasci Among Interventionist Groups

In a room of the Association of Traders and Merchants, a meeting was held yesterday for the formation of regional fasci among groups of interventionists. Speakers at the gathering included auto manufacturer Enzo Ferrari, commander Vecchi of the Arditi and several others. Mr. Mussolini outlined the cornerstones on which the action of the fasci should be based, namely: validating the war and those who fought the war; demonstrating that imperialism, of which Italians are accused, is an imperialism desired by all peoples, not excluding Belgium and Portugal; opposing foreign imperialisms that are detrimental to our own country; opposing any eventual Italian imperialism against other nations; and finally accepting an electoral battle on the war "issue" and opposing all parties and candidates that were contrary to the war.

After numerous speakers had taken the floor, Mussolini's proposals were approved. Various Italian cities were represented at the meeting.

Corriere della Sera, March 24, 1919,
"Le conferenze domenicali" column

Three Tons of Soap Stolen

Several thieves broke into the warehouse of Giuseppe Blen on Via Pomponazzi 4, and managed to carry off no less than sixty-four cases of soap weighing over one hundred pounds each.

Clearly there must have been a sizeable number of perpetrators to handle such a heavy, cumbersome load of goods, and to move over three tons of merchandise they had to have had horses and wagons or trucks at their disposal.

The fact is that such a lengthy, noisy, visible operation was carried out without a shred of useful information gathered on the brazen culprits. The value of the stolen goods is said to amount to approximately 15 thousand liras.

Corriere della Sera, March 24, 1919,
"Le conferenze domenicali" column

BENITO MUSSOLINI

MILAN, EARLY SPRING 1919

ONLY A FEW streets separate Via Paolo da Cannobio, where the editorial offices of *Il Popolo d'Italia*—the so-called "number 2 lair"—are located, from the Milan section of the Arditi Association at 23 Via Cerva, the "number 1 lair." They are fetid, squalid, dangerous streets in the spring of 1919, when Benito Mussolini leaves his office to dine in a trattoria.

The Bottonuto is a slice of medieval Milan subcutaneously entrenched in the twentieth-century city. A warren of narrow passageways and shops, early Christian churches and brothels, taverns and dives, teeming with peddlers, whores and vagrants. The origin of the name is uncertain. It perhaps comes from the postern that once opened on the southern side, through which armies passed. Some say that the word, reminiscent of swollen glands, is a mispronunciation of the patronymic name of a German mercenary who had come down as a follower of Barbarossa. In any case, the Bottonuto is a putrid bog just behind the Piazza del Duomo, the geometric and monumental center of Milan.

To pass through its streets, you need to hold your nose. Filth oozes from the walls, Vicolo delle Quaglie is reduced to a public urinal, the people are as fetid as mold in cellars, everything and anything is sold there, robberies and beatings take place in broad daylight, while soldiers cluster around the doorways of the bordellos. Everyone, directly or indirectly, gets by on prostitution.

Mussolini eats late. It is after ten o'clock in the evening when he emerges from his editor's den—a cubicle overlooking a narrow little courtyard, a sort of vertical passage connected to the editorial office by a shared balcony—lights a cigarette, and sets out briskly, contentedly, through the pestilential sac. Gangs of barefoot urchins point at him excitedly—"*el matt*," the lunatic, they take turns shouting—beggars sitting in filth at the street curbs stretch out their hands, pimps leaning in doorways greet him with a respectful but familiar nod of the head. He acknowledges their greetings. With some he stops to exchange a word or two, arranging things, making appointments, minor agreements. He hears cases at his court of miracles. He passes those caged men like a general in search of an army.

Haven't revolutions always been started this way: by arming the dregs of society with guns and hand grenades? What's the difference, after all, between a maladjusted veteran, demobilized long-term, who for two liras acts as watchman for the newspaper, and a "*rachetè*," a habitual criminal who lives by exploiting prostitution? All skilled labor. That's what he always says to Cesare Rossi—his closest collaborator, perhaps his only true adviser—who is appalled by his indiscriminate association with those people. "We are still too weak to do without them," he often tells Rossi, to appease his indignation. Too weak, unquestionably: the *Corriere della Sera*, the newspaper of the arrogant liberal bourgeoisie, devoted a brief news item of only a few lines to the formation of the Fasci di Combattimento, the same space it gave to the theft of sixty-four cases of soap.

Be that as it may, Benito Mussolini, on this evening in early April, contemplates his court of miracles for a few more moments, then, jutting his neck out, he clenches his jaw and searches for breathable air, his already nearly bald cranium tilted up to the sky. Turning up the collar of his jacket, he crushes the cigarette under his heel and picks up his pace. The darkened city, the alleys of depravity, trudge along behind him like a huge depleted organism, a gigantic wounded predator limping towards its end.

Via Cerva, on the other hand, is a calm, quiet, aristocratic old street. A touch of romance is conferred by the two-story patrician homes, with their spacious architectural courtyards. Every step echoes in the night on the lustrous asphalt, disturbing the cloistered atmosphere. The Arditi occupied a space with a shop in the back owned by a Mr. Putato, the father of one of them, right in front of the Palazzo dei Visconti di Modrone. It wasn't easy to find lodgings for those feverish veterans, who upset civilians by going around in winter with their uniforms undone to expose their bare chests and a dagger at their belts. Formidable soldiers when it came to attacking enemy positions, prized in wartime, but loathsome in periods of peace. Now, when they aren't sprawled out in a brothel or camped out in a cafe, the Arditi bivouac in those two empty rooms, getting drunk in the middle of the day, ranting about future battles and sleeping on the floor. That's how they get through the interminable postwar period: they mythicize the recent past, elaborate on a pending future and glaze over the present, smoking one cigarette after another.

It was the Arditi who won the war or, at least, so they tell you. They mythicize themselves to the point that Gianni Brambillaschi, one of the most hotheaded twenty-year-olds, went so far as to write in *L'Ardito*, the new association's official organ: "Those who did not fight in the assault battalions, even if they were killed at war, did not fight the war." Certainly, however, without them the Piave front would not have been breached with the counteroffensive that in November 1918 enabled the victory over the Austro-Hungarian armies.

The Arditi's fierce epic began with the so-called "Death Squads," special companies of sappers charged with preparing the terrain for assaults by the trench infantry. At night they severed barbed wire fencing and blasted unexploded mines. By day they advanced crawling forward on their bellies, protected by utterly useless armor, dismembered by artillery fire. Then every corps—infantry, Bersaglieri, Alpines—had begun forming their own assault squads, choosing the bravest and most experienced soldiers of the line regiments to be trained in hand grenades, flame-throwers and machine guns. But it was the provision of the dagger, the Latin weapon par excellence, that made the difference. The legend had begun there.

In a war that had annihilated the traditional concept of the soldier as aggressor, in which it was the stinging gases and the tons of steel shot from a remote position that left men unmoving in the trenches, in a technological slaughter owing to the superiority of defensive fire over the mobility of the soldier bent on assault, the Arditi had brought back the intimacy of hand-to-hand combat, the intense clash of physical contact, the dying man's convulsion transmitted to the killer's wrist through the blade's vibration. Trench warfare, rather than producing aggressors, had shaped a defensive personality in millions of soldiers, modeled on an empathetic identification with the victims of an ineluctable cosmic catastrophe. In that war of sheep led to the slaughterhouse, the Arditi had restored the self-confidence that only skill in quartering a man with a short-blade weapon can provide. Under a sky hailing volleys of steel, in the midst of anonymous mass death, of slaughter as a large-scale industrial product, they had restored an individuality driven to the extreme, the heroic cult of ancient warriors and the singular terror that can only be inspired by a slasher who has come in person to your hidey-hole to kill you with his own hands.

In addition, the Arditi had cultivated all the advantages of schizophrenia. The elite units were not subject to the discipline of the troops, they did not march, they were not assigned to grueling shifts in the trenches, they did not break their backs digging burrows or chiseling passages in rock, but lived free and easy behind the front lines, where on days of battle military trucks picked them up and deposited them at the foot of the positions to be captured. Those men could slaughter an Austrian officer for breakfast and, the same day, enjoy *baccalà mantecato*, creamed codfish, in a Vicenza trattoria for supper. Normality and killing, morning till night.

After his expulsion from the Socialist Party, having lost the armies of the proletariat, Benito Mussolini had immediately, instinctively, recruited the Arditi. Indeed, on November 10th, 1918, the day of celebrations over the victory, following the speech by senator Giovanni Agnelli at Milan's Monument to the Cinque Giornate, the editor of *Il Popolo d'Italia* had sat among the Arditi on the truck flying the black flag with the skull. At the Caffè Borsa, raising glasses of spumante, he had toasted them in particular among the millions of soldiers:

"Comrades-in-arms! I defended you when the cowardly philistines defamed you. I sense something of myself in you and maybe you recognize yourself in me."

And they, those valiant combatants, who in those very days of glory were humiliated by high command with long marches on the Venetian plain between the Piave and the Adige—marches that served no military purpose other than to make use of troops who had suddenly become inconvenient and useless—they had identified with him. He, hated and a hater by profession, knew that their rancor was mounting, that they would soon be castaways dissatisfied with everything. He knew that at night, in the tents, they cursed politicians, high commanders, socialists and civilians. The "Spanish flu" was in the air, and on the low plains, towards the sea, malaria. As an honorable death faded from their thoughts, the Arditi, already outcasts, languished with fevers and passed around a flask of cognac as they read aloud the words of the man who from his office in Milan exalted their "life without languor, death without dishonor." For three years they had been an aristocracy of warriors, a heroicized phalanx on the covers of children's magazines: collars turned up, grenades in hand and a dagger between their teeth. Back to civilian life, within weeks they would become a bunch of misfits. Forty thousand loose cannons.

The Trattoria Grande Italia is a modest, greasy, smoky place. The atmosphere is unassuming, the price modest, the clientele habitual but alternating. At this time of night, mostly journalists and actors, authors, comedians, no dancers. In the gloom only the red-and-white checkered tablecloths stand out, set with flasks of *Gutturnio dei colli piacentini*, the wine from the hilly vineyards south of Piacenza. The customers are all male and almost all quite drunk.

Mussolini makes his way to a corner table where three men await him. It is a secluded table, away from the windows, from which it is easy to keep an eye on the entrance. On the right is a private room in which a table of socialist printers are making quite a racket.

When Benito Mussolini takes off his jacket and hat and sits down, it quietens for a moment. Then the excitement grows. He's been recognized. Suddenly he is the center of the conversation.

His table companions are also well-known individuals. On his right is Ferruccio Vecchi, an engineering student, from Romagna like Mussolini, an exponent of the Futurist movement, an interventionist and highly decorated captain of the Arditi. In January he founded the Cassa di Mutuo Aiuto (mutual aid fund) and the National Arditi Federation of Italy. A black musketeer's goatee, emaciated, sunken eyes, tubercular, a relentless seducer. Unbelievable and extraordinary stories are told about him: wounded more than twenty times, he is said to have stormed an Austrian trench with nothing but hand grenades, and to have fucked his colonel's wife at night as she lay beside her sleeping husband.

The sanguinary side of the table, however, is the one opposite him. Sitting there is a short, stocky man, his bullish neck making his head look like it's set directly on his trunk. The moist lips and idiotic smile on his chubby face recall the utter cruelties of childhood. From time to time the bull-child raises his head, holds his breath and stares into space as though in front of a photographer's lens. In addition to the posing, his clothing is also theatrical: under a gray-green military jacket he's wearing a black turtleneck sweater adorned with a white skull clutching a dagger between its teeth. Another dagger, a real one, with a mother-of-pearl handle, hangs from the belt holding up his pants.

He is Albino Volpi, thirty years old, a carpenter, enlisted in the Arditi. Multiple charges for non-political crimes, convicted by the civil courts for insulting a public official, theft, breaking and entering, and aggravated assaults, and by the military court for desertion. His extraordinary deeds are not spoken aloud, they are whispered in a low voice. There are two legends surrounding him, a heroic and a criminal one. Possessed by violence, apparently during the war he would venture out on his own initiative at night. Sneaking out of the last trench, in total silence, armed only with a dagger, he would crawl on all fours to the enemy lines, and, for the pure joy of hearing the hissing of arterial blood in contact with the air, slit the throat of the sleeping sentinel. They say he had his own unique way of gripping the knife. Without doubt he was a "Caiman of the Piave," one of the elite commandos who specialized in crossing the river at night to assassinate the lookouts on the bank held by the Austrians. Naked, their bodies smeared with muddy clay to blend in with the vegetation along the shore, the Caimans swam across the current of icy October floods to bring inconsequential savage death into the enemy's camp. They served practically no purpose, either on a tactical or on a strategic level, yet the Caimans had been indispensable in winning the war. Legendary creatures—maybe even non-existent, perhaps created by propaganda—they guarded a secret handed down from the beginning of time: that the night is dark and full of terrors.

"Close combat no longer exists," he'd said to himself, regretfully, about the Great War. "No criminal has ever been a war hero," the righteous officials, the honest ones, always used to say. The man who sits in front of Mussolini and buries his head in cabbage stew seasoned with pork rinds, pig feet and boar heads, the way an animal would sink his bloody snout into his prey's entrails, would seem to belie both statements.

At Mussolini's table no one speaks much. The meal is consumed in silence, glumly contemplating the bottom of the glass. Everything is already known. But a loud, corpulent guy approaches the table, black tie loosened, wide-brimmed hat askew, and starts babbling vaguely about serious accidents, explosions, bloody fights. It's not clear whether it's news or a threat. Mussolini motions him to be quiet. The ranting, menacing individual is left standing there, open-mouthed, displaying a crater where the two upper incisors had been before they were broken by a rock thrown during a rally in the piazza. His name is Domenico Ghetti, he too is from Romagna; an exile in Switzerland with Mussolini as a young man, he is anticlerical, turbulent, and violent, a conspirator and outcast.

Then, however, Mussolini motions for him to sit down and orders him a bowl of lasagna with tomato sauce. If the editor of *Il Popolo d'Italia* is able to walk home alone at night, it is partly thanks to the fondness that, despite everything, he earns in the circles of violent Milanese anarchy. Ghetti starts to eat and silence returns to the Arditis' table.

By contrast, the din mounts in the private room next door. Wine is downed and songs are raised. The staff of *Avanti!*, the socialist newspaper that has its offices on Via San Damiano, just behind Via Cerva, intone "*Bandiera rossa trionferà!*" (the red flag will triumph!) at the top of their lungs. Now a toast is made to February 17, the day when Milan and Italy, having sobered up following the nation's victory over its historic Austrian enemies, had discovered with dismay that there was a new enemy in its future: the Bolshevik revolution.

That memorable day forty thousand striking workers had marched to the arena accompanied by the sound of thirty bands, waving thousands of red flags and holding up signs cursing the victorious war that had just ended. A sadistic saraband in which the wounded were displayed as horrific living proof against a war willed by the "*padroni*" in command. The socialists spat in the face of the uniformed officers who until the day before had ordered them to attack, called for a division of land, and demanded amnesty for deserters.

To the other Milan, the nationalist, patriotic, petit bourgeois one, which in 1915 had given ten thousand volunteers to the war, to Benito Mussolini's Italy, it had seemed as if "the monsters of decadence had been resurrected" in that crowd of demonstrators, as if the world newly restored to peace "had succumbed to an illness."

Mussolini and those like him had been particularly struck by the fact that the socialists had made women and children march at the head of the parade. Political hatred shouted from the sensual mouths of females and kids still wet behind the ears was shocking, disconcerting and unsettling to the kind of adult male who'd wanted the war. The reason was very simple. To that type of authoritarian, patriarchal and misogynistic individual, the anti-militarist and unpatriotic shouts of women and children presaged something terrifying and unheard of: a future that did not include him. As the parade wound through the streets, the bourgeoisie, tradesmen and hoteliers had hastily shut the windows, lowered the shutters and barred the doors. Faced with that future, they walled themselves up in the prison of the present.

The following day Mussolini had written a strong editorial, "*Contro la bestia ritornante*" (Against the Returning Beast). The paladin of military intervention had solemnly promised to defend the war's dead, whom he said had been affronted by the protesters—to defend every last one of them "even at the cost of digging trenches in the streets and piazzas of our city."

At the socialists' table they have now moved on to liqueurs and grappa. The noisy party is in full swing. Sharpened by alcohol, their hatred is becoming more explicit. The name of Mussolini, the "traitor," can be clearly heard, shouted by a hoarse voice.

At the corner table, Albino Volpi, busy cutting up pork rinds, instinctively changes his grip on the knife. Mussolini, pale, offended by the insults of his old comrades but prudent, stops him with an imperceptible shake of his head. Squeezing his eyes shut, he parts his lips slightly and breathes between his teeth, as though pained by the slow gangrene of an old affliction, a youthful love affair, a brother who died of smallpox.

Then the "traitor" pulls himself together. He turns his head to look for his accuser. His eyes meet those of a small young man—he must be barely twenty years old—with red hair and freckles on his fair skin. The boy holds his gaze with the bold pride of someone contributing to the redemption of an oppressed humanity.

Mussolini grabs his hat. He briskly refuses an escort from the Arditi. As he heads for the door, he seems to see from the corner of his eye that Albino Volpi has again changed his grip of the knife.

Mussolini turns his head and goes out into the street. "Arditi against pacifists, socialists against fascists, bourgeoisie against workers, men of yesterday against men of tomorrow." Milan's night enfolds him like a field of two mixed forces that exist alongside one another in his arteries, with a clear, constant feeling that one of the two must kill the other.

At home, in Foro Bonaparte, Rachele, his wife, and their two children await him. But it's still early. He decides to go back through

Bottonuto, to make a stop in Vicolo delle Quaglie, to pour out the toxins of the day into a prostitute, one of those women, desired and scorned, that he and the veterans like him love to describe as "flesh and blood urinals."

As Benito Mussolini walks back up Via Cerva, he thinks he can hear a harrowed scream coming from the restaurant. But he isn't sure. Maybe it's only the city screaming in its sleep.

To you, Mussolini, our good man, for your work; but continue hitting hard, by God, for there is still so much "old thinking" blocking our way. We are with you in spirit but soon we will be standing alongside you.

Telegram from the officers
of the 27th assault battalion
published in *Il Popolo d'Italia*,
January 7, 1919

All the dregs of society armed themselves with revolvers and daggers, muskets and hand grenades . . . Joining these lowlifes were young students, imbued with militaristic romanticism, heads full of patriotic hot air, who see us socialists as "Germans."

Giacinto Menotti Serrati,
leader of the maximalist wing
of the Italian Socialist Party

AMERIGO DÙMINI

FLORENCE, LATE MARCH 1919

EVERYTHING IS GOING badly. They haven't got a cent. Sometimes they even go hungry. What did they fight for?

The man leaving the military hospital on Via dei Mille has a slight limp. His lopsided gait looks out of whack because of his bandaged left arm that hangs suspended from his massive neck. He's wearing the open jacket of the Arditi, with the black flames on the collar and the side slits designed to quickly extract grenades. On his left arm, hidden by the bandage, a shield-shaped badge bears the design of a Roman *gladius*, a short sword with a sphinx-head handle. The real dagger hanging from his belt is clearly visible. His stocky, heavy build, off-centered due to his infirmities, takes up the entire sidewalk on the railroad side. Passersby who encounter him on Via dei Mille swerve to avoid him. Some even cross the street.

At the military hospital all the veterans of the assault battalions repeat the same furious litany: it's a disgrace, they were discharged just like that, out of the blue, the way you fire a servant. First the generals humiliated them by making them march in the rain and mud for months, after the war was over, to impose some discipline on them which no one had ever dared subject them to when they conveniently attacked the enemy trenches. Then the politicians humiliated them by demobilizing them at night, in silence. "Not to provoke anyone," they were told. And who was it who shouldn't be provoked? The draft dodgers, the defeatists, the socialists who had demoralized the troops causing the rout at Caporetto, those like Claudio Treves who in parliament had shouted "never again a winter in the trenches," the papal bigots who had termed the massacre of their comrades "useless slaughter." And to satisfy those scumbags they had been discharged without ado, in the dark, not an anthem, not one flower, no street full of flags. The heroes crept back to civilian life as furtive as thieves in the house of the Lord.

The man trudges along Via degli Artisti, in borgo dei Pinti, towards the center of Florence. He'd been told that maybe they could help him at the Confraternità della Misericordia. They have a public transport service for the disabled there. Maybe there's something for him too. Right, because, while they were risking their lives for their country, the deserters at home stole their jobs and now the shirker is all set while the soldier goes hungry. In France the victorious veterans marched under Napoleon's Arc de Triomphe, in every country they were greeted with songs of praise, whereas Italy's veterans, who destroyed one of the greatest empires in history, who went all-out in a gigantic epic struggle, were sent packing in the dark and on tiptoe. No march on Vienna, no parades, no colonies, no Fiume, no compensation, no nothing. Everything is going badly. Living from hand to mouth. What did they fight for?

The Duomo's facade in polychrome marble gleams in the spring sunshine. Brunelleschi's immense cupola, the largest masonry dome ever built, seems to celebrate the glory of a people who, after Caporetto, found the strength to triumph. But now Italy is plunging back into the abyss, into strikes, sabotage by the "reds" who want to sign it over to Moscow, as if they too weren't Italians, as if glory were something to be ashamed of. To atone for. Atone for the spirit of the war. That's what deputy Treves shouted in parliament. And now they would like to make those who have already paid with their own sweat and blood, the interventionists, the veterans, the wounded, the brethren who resisted during those nights on the plateaus—now they want to make them pay for the victory. The Nitti government endorses the fraud. It humiliates the young men of the Piave by granting amnesty to the deserters, it wants to dismiss the victorious war as a failed endeavor. It even asked veterans to leave their uniforms at home, so as not to "provoke." *Avanti!* echoes this, proclaiming that Italians are "the losers among the winners." And it's right. Everything is falling apart in this never-ending retreat. Everything is going badly.

"Down with capitalism!" The shout comes from a group of masons who are paving the piazza in front of Santa Maria del Fiore's side entrance. They have it in for him, they insult the brazen soldier in uniform who hobbles along, an arm suspended from his neck, towards the head office of the Misericordia. They accuse him of having supported the imperialist war of the padroni. They yell "killer," "traitor."

The entrance to the charitable association is only a few steps away, there are probably half a dozen pavers, the soldier is alone, in bad shape. But he is also pale with rage. He had voluntarily enlisted in Baseggio's "Death Squad" not to avoid hard work but because he liked adventure, as when he was a boy in America, the continent whose name he carries. He took part in the battle of Monte Sant'Osvaldo, in Valsugana, where the entire battalion was destroyed in a frontal attack on enemy positions. In the days of Vittorio Veneto, on Monte Pertica, an impregnable peak of Mount Grappa over 4,900 feet high, fighting the Austrians hand-to-hand, he was wounded by a barrage of machine gun fire from enemy aircraft but refused medical care and went back to the front line where, three days later, he was wounded a second time by a fragment of a shell case that exploded in the battery. He was publicly praised by Baseggio in front of General Grazioli for the conquest of a stronghold in Valsugana, and was awarded a silver medal and a military cross in the war whose effects he still bears in the stiffened bones of his left hand. He used his special leave for an anguished trip to Albania, together with his fellow soldier Banchelli, to search in vain for the grave where his brother Albert lies, a lieutenant in the 35th battalion of the Bersaglieri regiment who had fallen in combat the previous year. He, this man who carries the name of an adventurous continent, is called traitor by those cowards.

It's intolerable. He would have been better off staying up there, fertilizing the soil among the dolines of Mount Grappa.

The soldier plants himself in the middle of the piazza. "Draft dodgers!" he yells. He puts a hand on his dagger.

They are on him in an instant. A short, thickset guy in shirtsleeves leaps in front of him and punches him twice in the teeth. The medal-winning soldier is already on the ground, spat on and kicked. He remains silent, doesn't cry out, doesn't plead, but his powerful adult body, having regressed twenty-five years in a few seconds to now huddle in a fetal position, proclaims his unmistakable, pitiful appeal to the Basilica of Santa Maria del Fiore. No one answers it. The first paver who attacked him rips the Arditi insignia off his jacket and stuffs them in his mouth.

The Misericordia's stretcher-bearers find him like that, still curled up like a fully grown fetus. They load him on the stretcher in that position. He is not seriously injured—only bruises, abrasions, some broken teeth—but in this man's world there no longer seems to be one good reason to get back to an upright position. Only later does he begin to speak again, to clarify a question of accents with the policeman who takes down his particulars in order to draft a report.

"Dùmini," he states clearly, "Amerigo Dùmini. With the accent on the first syllable. Tuscan style."

FILIPPO TOMMASO MARINETTI, BENITO MUSSOLINI

MILAN, APRIL 15, 1919

TODAY EVERYTHING IS silent. Milan is holding its breath.

Tram drivers and night-shift gas fitters haven't been back to work since midnight. None of the lines north of the city are operating. Public services are suspended. The hundreds of factories that employ the huge population of Italy's most industrialized city are all closed. With no exception. Not a single worker showed up at work.

The proletarian masses lie entirely in the outskirts but this time the strike has also affected the center. All the shops, the gathering places along Corso Vittorio Emanuele, the Piazza del Duomo, and the Galleria are closed. As is everything in every district of the city. The banks are guarded by the police or the army, but they are closed. The municipal offices are closed. Business offices are closed.

Two days ago, on the morning of April 13, a socialist rally on Via Garigliano ended with several people injured and one dead after an exchange of fire with the police. Filippo Turati was supposed to give a talk, but for some reason the old leader of reformist, humanist socialism did not show up. Ezio Schiaroli then took the floor in his place. The revolutionary anarchist violently attacked Mussolini and incited the workers, urging them to use violence to seize power. When the mounted police brutally charged the demonstrators along Via Borsieri, the crowd reacted for the first time. Rock throwing, vandalism, bludgeoning. The melee was intense.

Police and carabinieri were stunned. They were forced to retreat, pushed back by the mass of rabble-rousers who would not give up. At that point they resorted to the artillery division: the agents opened fire on the crowd, as they had been doing for nearly a century. The people countered by proclaiming a general strike on September 15th. Now everything points to the possibility that more blood will be shed. As usual the spiral of violence escalates from one proletarian massacre to another.

For forty-eight hours Milan has been experiencing an uninterrupted battle vigil. No one breathes anymore. The nervous tension has become unbearable. An "imbecilic panic" has spread, Mussolini comments in his newspaper, similar to that which takes hold when an enemy offensive is announced. But for months now the agonized waiting has become the dominant, almost constant, state of mind. *L'Avanti!*, edited by Giacinto Menotti Serrati—a former Leninist stevedore who unloaded coal, and who in 1914 replaced Mussolini as editor of the socialist daily—keeps the proletarians in a daily state of alarm over the imminent revolutionary wave. The wave that is already submerging Europe.

In November, in Munich, Kurt Eisner declared Bavaria a socialist republic. In February, Anton Graf von Arco auf Valley, a Munich aristocrat rejected by extreme right-wing secret lodges for being the son of a Jewess, shot him. On April 6th, the socialists fighting with the communists for the vacant supremacy proclaimed the "Bavarian Soviet Republic" governed by Ernst Toller, an utterly incompetent playwright. His foreign affairs appointee, already treated several times in a psychiatric hospital, declared war on Switzerland because it refused to lend sixty locomotives to Soviet Bavaria. Toller's government collapsed after six days, replaced by the communists, led by Eugen Levine, hailed by workers as the "German Lenin." A few days earlier, on March 21st, in Budapest, Sàndor Garbai and Béla Kun had proclaimed the Soviet Republic of Hungary; having formed an alliance with Lenin's Russia, to recover territories that were lost as a result of being defeated in the war they had invaded Slovakia and attacked Romania.

In short, for months each day has been a vigil. As they listen to the inflammatory words of their tribunes, the tens of thousands of proletarians who have flocked to the rally at the Milan arena on this morning of April 15, 1919, sniff the faint smell of blood in the air and feel the revolution, its terror, approaching. In everyone, absolutely everyone, there is the expectation of some cataclysm.

In the early afternoon, with no preordained plan, as if attracted by the magnetism of disaster, an avant-garde made up of several thousand demonstrators breaks away from the enormous procession and marches into Via Orefici, heading for the Duomo. The protest overflows from the stadium to the piazza, advancing towards the revolution. The postwar period is in a hurry. You can't live each day with an apocalypse on the horizon.

In Piazza del Duomo, beyond the cordon of troops which the socialist procession immediately engulfs, a man is heatedly addressing the small crowd of civilians, officers, university students, Arditi and fascists, while clinging to the marble lion sculpted at the base of the equestrian monument to Vittorio Emanuele II, the first king of Italy. The man is a poet, his name is Filippo Tommaso Marinetti, and in 1909 he founded the first historical avant-garde of twentieth-century Italy. His manifesto for a Futurist poetic movement has resonated throughout Europe, from Paris to Moscow; he proposes destroying museums, libraries, and academies of all kinds, "murdering the moonlight," "singing the great masses shaken with work, pleasure or rebellion," and glorifying war—"the world's only hygiene"—militarism; patriotism; the destructive acts of liberators; beautiful ideas for which one dies; and contempt for women.

After using words to celebrate war as a civilian, in 1915 the poet came to personally know the war he so extolled. Leaving behind the bourgeois luxuries of his Corso Venezia home, furnished in neo-Egyptian style, he voluntarily enlisted in the Alpines, fought and was wounded, and then returned to the front; he got a taste of defeat at Caporetto and savored triumph at Vittorio Veneto behind the wheel of a Lancia model 1Z armored car.

Now, after climbing down from the lion at the foot of the king's equestrian monument, Filippo Tommaso Marinetti, with a commanding tone, orders the bystanders, looking at him perplexed in their gray frock coats and bowler hats, to join the column of counter-demonstrators. The struggle makes no allowance for third-party stances, there is no room for neutrality. "No spectators!" the founder of futurism shouts to the neutral civilians walking through the Galleria. "No onlookers!"

Around the monument, meanwhile, everyone feels the socialists' attack is close. "Here they are! Here they come!" someone shouts. False alarm. Chemical industrialist Ettore Candiani, who takes over from Marinetti, starts talking. Nobody listens. "There they come. They're here!" The Arditi pull out their revolvers.

For a moment the two factions face one another on either side of the cordon of carabinieri which has blocked the outlet from Via dei Mercanti. At the head of the socialist column are once again women, holding high a portrait of Lenin and the red flag. Unrestrained and joyful, they are singing their songs of liberation. They're calling for a better life for their children. They still believe they've come to march in their parade, to dance their minuet of revolution. At the head of the other cortege, much less numerous, are men who for the last four years have coexisted with killing on a daily basis. The discrepancy is grotesque. A different association with death creates an abyss between the two groups.

The carabinieri's cordon opens up. On the Piazza Duomo side, the uniformed officers and the Arditi advance in twos and threes, randomly, as if everything were normal, revolver in hand. The actual battle lasts about a minute.

From the socialists' side, thousands of them, rocks go flying, a few clubs. From the side of the officers, Arditi and Futurists, who amount to hundreds, gunshots erupt. They are first fired into the air, then at the socialist column. For a few moments the marchers persist, then stunned, fall silent. In that brief interlude there is no more singing. Confused, women and men stare at the monsters in uniform arrayed before them. The Arditi burst on the scene like unexpected actors.

Another instant and the socialist column falls apart. The collapse is precipitous, driven by a demented panic. Two thousand men and women, who until a minute ago were singing the praises of the revolution, are on the ground. From there, terrified, they watch the enemies who, on their feet, advance slowly, in no particular order, calmly reloading their revolvers. Many flatten themselves on the ground, huddled between the arches of the Loggia dei Mercanti. The officers on their feet, however, put away the regulation firearm issued for their military rank and grab a weapon they consider more appropriate for menial retribution. Now they start running. The masses of terrified workers are bludgeoned. Blood runs down the steps. As they club the demonstrators, the officers and Arditi ridicule them: "Let's hear you shout viva Lenin, now. Shout viva Lenin!" A young man on the ground, distraught, holds out a few liras, as if he could buy their mercy.

Marinetti, scuffling with a burly worker, ends up in the window of a porter's lodge. Two Arditi grab the guy from below. The poet has to intercede so they don't kill him.

Now all of them, revolvers in hand, march down Via Dante, walls on either side of them, shooting into the air. Wielding clubs. The street empties. The brother of Filippo Corridoni, an interventionist martyr who fell in the first year of the war, returns from Foro Bonaparte with his right arm bloody. Over there, 200 yards away, the socialist demonstrators are still crowding around the marble monument to Garibaldi. A speaker, atop the base, is still rallying. Still shouting the ritual "viva Lenin!" as if hypnotized by a mantra.

An Ardito draws his dagger and, on his own, tears through the deserted street like a speeding bullet. He clambers up the monument, stabs the communist. Suddenly the monument blanches. The rally is over.

Returning triumphantly to Piazza Duomo, the aggressors again gather round the monument from which they'd started, the one with the king on horseback. Marinetti is bushed, done in, his chest bruised. They insist that the poet speak again. None of his words will be remembered.

After the enemy is trounced, his home must be burned down. And the home of the socialists is their newspaper. The Milanese headquarters of *Avanti!*, the flagship of Italian socialism, is located on Via San Damiano, through which a *naviglio* (canal) still flows. When the assailants arrive towards evening, they find it defended by a cordon of uniformed soldiers. Their opposition is half-hearted, however: many of the activists had been their commanders during the war. The defense soon turns into a siege.

Then all of a sudden a rifle shot, almost certainly fired by the socialists inside the building, most likely triggered by terror, brings down one of the military guards. His name is Michele Speroni, he is twenty-two years old, and he is hit from behind. Blood gushes from the back of his neck. One of the officers steps away from the group of Arditi and fascists, bends down and raises the helmet of the soldier killed by the socialists. The officer speaks, shouts, but here too nobody listens. A small opening appears in the cordon to allow the stretcher carrying the victim to pass through. The aggressors move in through it.

Still more gunshots from inside before the windows are scaled by Arditi using the ground-floor iron grilles as footholds. Once inside, they find no one left to defend the home. The socialists have all cleared out through the back door. The looting begins. Methodical, competent, unchallenged.

They smash everything. They drizzle flammable liquids in every room, empty the cans on the bound volumes, overturn desks, wreck typewriters and file cabinets. The archive of historical material is attacked with a hammer. Everything crashes to the floor, the plaster starts peeling from the ceilings due to the incandescent heat, thousands of lithographed photographs of Lenin, ready to be shipped all over Italy, fly out the window. Everything trashed. Coolly, with precision, like skilled experts of destruction. There is no hand-to-hand combat in the assault, no contention. There are no thoughts, not even brutal and vindictive ones. Pure devastation.

The only obstacle is posed by the rotary presses. The heavy typesetting machinery doesn't lend itself to being grazed by the clubs or daggers of the Arditi circling around the printers, spellbound, like big apes around a meteorite dropped out of the sky and fallen to earth.

After a few minutes of uncertainty, a gigantic young man steps forward, pushes the soldiers aside and conspicuously brandishes an iron bar. The pipe conveys a lesson. The young man, whose name is Edmondo Mazzucato, is wearing the Arditi uniform with the black flames on the jacket lapels and various medals under the insignia. Orphaned, propertyless, shut away since childhood in a Salesian boarding school, Mazzucato lost his first job at fifteen for joining the general strike of 1904. Intolerant, rebellious, and violent, after moving to Milan and embracing the ideas of anarchy, he was imprisoned several times by both civil and military authorities. In 1909 he brutally beat a corporal who, out of pure spite, had denied him leave. The antisocial outcast worked as a warehouseman, salesman, clerk, and sales representative from the time he was a boy, then found his calling by learning the trade of typesetter-typographer, continuing to work for anarchist, libertarian and revolutionary publications. When the war broke out, he also found his vocation: having enlisted as a volunteer, he was promoted and decorated several times for distinguished service in the field.

Like many other fascists, Mazzucato has also defected from the socialist camp to go over to that of its opponents. Now he evidently has one last exemplary lesson for his fellow soldiers: raising the iron bar, he shows it clearly to everyone, shoves it through the gears of the printing equipment with scientific expertise, then starts the rotary presses. The blunt force of the machine destroys itself. The young ex-printer of the revolutionary press destroys his own past.

Half an hour later the whole building is in flames. On Via San Damiano, the police watch the spectacle of the blaze shoulder to shoulder with the men who ignited it. Firefighters are prevented from stepping in to allow the fire time to burn itself out.

It is already night when, at *Il Popolo d'Italia*, Marinetti relates the events of that memorable day to the editor who did not take part in them. Actually, there had been a secret huddle with the activists on the evening of the 14th, but afterwards Mussolini had not moved from his tiny office for the entire eventful day. He didn't even go out to eat. At noon lunch was ordered in from a nearby trattoria.

The editor ate it sitting at a small table on the landing of the staircase, constantly checking, between one bite and another, that his short-barreled revolver with the reserve cylinder was working. But he never set foot outside the newspaper.

Now he listens, seated behind the desk of his dismal office. Hanging behind him, on the wall papered in a yellowed, flowery pattern, is the Arditi flag. On the desk, among the jumble of papers, days-old tabloids and a crank phone, are three SIPE grenades and a revolver. On the left, a five-shelf étagère holds a tea service; beside it stand a wastepaper basket and a stool, both unsteady on the uneven, filthy old terrazzo tile floor with white and magenta hexagons.

As Marinetti talks, Mussolini nods his head. His gaze, however, is fixed on the small wooden board that Ferruccio Vecchi has been holding since he entered the room. It's the sign that was torn off the door of the *Avanti!* office and it's clear that in a few minutes, once the poet has completed his *chanson de geste*, the war trophy will be presented to him with ritual homage. Benito Mussolini will have to take the slain enemy's scalp and display it from the balcony to the Arditi who are clamoring in the courtyard. The editor's tiny office is filled, in fact, with goliardic songs coming from the street: "Hey, hey . . . *Avanti!* is no more! Hey, hey . . . *Avanti!* is no more! Hey, hey . . ." Mussolini listens and strokes his bald head, with its fuzzy gray-blue skullcap of regrowth. Five years ago he was the editor of *Avanti!* Much loved by his readers, he had elevated the paper to a circulation never before achieved. Now he is about to trample on its corpse.

Marinetti has finished. Vecchi hands him the wooden sign. For an instant Mussolini recoils, in a sudden urge of refusal. His guts loosen, his viscera spill out, yard by yard, onto the terrazzo tiled floor. There are two men and two editors sitting in that one chair under the grotesque flag nailed to the flowery yellowed wallpaper. There are fathers and sons.

"This is a day of our revolution," the editor of *Il Popolo d'Italia* proclaims after a few minutes to the Arditi crowded into the filthy courtyard.

"The first episode of the civil war has taken place."

The decree is pronounced. From that moment on, a small patrol of armed veterans will bivouac in the basement to guard the newspaper. An old Fiat machine gun will be installed on the roof to scour the street, along with *chevaux de frises* in barbed wire at the entrance to the alleyway, in order to defend a nationally circulated newspaper as though guarding the command center of a war zone.

Tonight, however, Mussolini insists on returning home alone. After the pages are typeset, at three in the morning, he hails a public conveyance drawn by an old nag. Directs it to Foro Bonaparte, at the corner of Via Legnano.

As the worn-out beast trudges along the cobblestones, the passenger's solitude is complete. An unbridgeable distance separates him from humanity.

On the day of April 15 we had absolutely decided, with Mussolini, not to hold any counter-demonstrations because we envisioned a clash and the idea of shedding Italian blood horrifies us. Our counter-demonstration came about spontaneously by invincible popular will. We were forced to react to the premeditated provocation of the draft dodgers . . . Our intervention is intended to affirm the absolute right of four million victorious soldiers, who alone must and will lead the new Italy at any cost. We will not provoke, but if provoked, we will add a few more months to our four years of fighting . . .

Proclamation affixed to the walls of Milan, April 18, 1919,
signed by Ferruccio Vecchi and Filippo Tommaso Marinetti

We sincerely deplore the fact that blood ran through the streets of Milan, bloodshed that was more painful to us than losing a battle; but *Avanti!*, promoter of "red terror," promoter of civil war, has no right to lament, no right to protest. Did those on Via San Damiano perhaps believe that they could liberally sow hatred against interventionists and patriots, did they think they could draw up proscription lists, believe they could extol the dictatorship of the proletariat as *redde rationem* for those who had loved their country, without an immediate and imperious reaction?

Pietro Nenni,
founder of Bologna's Fasci di Combattimento
Il giornale del mattino, April 17, 1919

To the long list of our dead others have been added. Our newspaper—*Avanti!*—has been silenced for one day only, because tomorrow, thanks to our efforts and yours, it will arise more fiery and rebellious in its defense of our rights. Proud of the solidarity shown by the entire proletariat of Italy, of that discipline that is essential at given historical moments, we recommend that work be resumed tomorrow, Friday.

Manifesto of the Milan Section
of the Italian Socialist Party,
April 17, 1919

It is therefore our duty not to react to premeditated provocations . . . but to reinforce the initiatives of the proletariat with tenacity and fervor . . . in preparation for the general strike which, following the by now fateful international proletarian movement, must be the supreme goal of the dictatorship of the proletariat for the economic and political expropriation of the ruling class.

Motion of the leadership of the Socialist Party
assembled in Milan, April 20, 1919

We are here to tell you with a serenity that is certainly not in the hearts of your enemies: you will fail. You will fail with violence in the streets as you will fail with magisterial and judicial violence.

Avanti!, Rome edition, April 22, 1919

On April 15th, Milan's maximalist socialists revealed their philistine, pusillanimous soul in broad daylight. Not a single act of retaliation was planned or attempted . . .

Benito Mussolini,
Il Popolo d'Italia, April 16, 1920

GABRIELE D'ANNUNZIO

ROME, MAY 6, 1919

THE HUGE CROWD assembled in Piazza del Campidoglio is stock-still, as motionless as the equestrian statue of Emperor Marcus Aurelius around which it's gathered. They are all waiting, heads thrown back, eyes upturned, for Gabriele D'Annunzio to appear on the balcony of Rome's city hall. There are tens of thousands of men, mostly young, vigorous, physically intact, yet this man is able to make them feel maimed. Thanks to the metaphor of the "mutilated victory," coined by the poet, twenty thousand young men, sound and robust, now feel as if they're missing a limb or an organ. And they worship him for it.

Most of them are veterans of the Great War, the greatest war in history, who had fought and prevailed against the ancestral enemy of the Italian people less than a year earlier on the banks of the river Piave, yet D'Annunzio manages to make them feel defeated. And they revere him for it. They worship and revere the magician capable of the miracle of psychopathic alchemy that is transforming the greatest victory ever achieved by Italy on the battlefield into a humiliating defeat.

By the time the immense crowd stands motionless at the foot of the equestrian monument to Marcus Aurelius on the morning of May 6, 1919, waiting for the alchemist of defeat to speak from the balustrade of the Campidoglio, the sense of humiliation, failure and injustice has, in fact, become universal throughout Italy. It took only two weeks to make it so.

On April 24th, Prime Minister Vittorio Orlando and his foreign minister Sidney Sonnino abruptly walked out on the Paris Peace Conference. The Treaty of London, which in 1915 established the conditions for entering the war alongside Russia, France and Great Britain, had promised Italy Dalmatia, for centuries a possession of the Republic of Venice, in the event of victory. According to nationalists, moreover, the new doctrine of a people's self-determination, promoted by Woodrow Wilson, should now also give Italy Fiume, a small border city with a large Italian majority, excluded from the London agreements. The slogan is: Treaty of London plus Fiume. But the president of the United States of America, ruler of the diplomatic game, doesn't seem to want to concede either to his Italian ally.

On April 23rd, Wilson, bypassing and humiliating Italy's representatives, even addressed the Italian people directly through a long letter published in a French newspaper, in which he affectionately explained to the minor ally the reasons for his double refusal: neither Dalmatia nor Fiume. They might well have been good reasons, but what prevailed over the whole affair was contempt. A contempt that oozed from the paternalistic tone with which, in his letter to the Italians, the new indulgent master of the world instructed those whom Mussolini calls the "schoolboys of his victory." It is even rumored that in private the French president Clemenceau, in agreement with Wilson, describes his Italian colleague Orlando as "a vegetarian tiger."

After the walk-out from the negotiation at Versailles, disappointment in Italy immediately took on a dramatic tone. Yesterday's comrades are refusing what they promised Italy at the cost of 600,000 deaths. The peace conference, notes Ivanoe Bonomi, "appears cast in the light of an ambush."

The Italian delegates' departure from Paris was a proud, resounding gesture. Sonnino is said to have replied to the diplomat who threatened grave economic consequences as a result of Italy's falling-out: "We are an austere people and quite familiar with the art of starving to death." That populace welcomed its spokesmen with a blaze of proud self-pity. In the last week of April, piazzas throughout Italy were ignited with demands for an Italian Fiume and Dalmatia. As never before, the Italian people rallied round their leaders in a common feeling of deprivation. The entire stake was played on the universal appeal of defeat, on the intense pleasure of disaster. A decidedly dangerous wager.

In parliament, Filippo Turati, the undisputed head of the reformist wing of the Socialist Party, warned about the risks of such a chancy bet, vehemently attacking Orlando and Sonnino: "Either you know with mathematical certainty that an accord is possible . . . In which case what good is this huge buildup of the country's opinion? . . . Or else you aren't certain of the result and in that case the buildup, which you have incited, imprisons you, cutting off any way of going back that is not one of deep humiliation." An easy prediction.

In fact, at the peace conference Wilson and the other masters of victory calmly continued negotiating and determining the world's new borders without the Italians. For fifteen days of orgasmic patriotism, while Italian liberals, nationalists and fascists are hypnotically focused on some shoals in the Adriatic, the Allies in Paris divvy up the German colonies in Africa and the Turkish Empire in the Near East. Only two weeks after the proud walk-out, Orlando and Sonnino are thus forced to return to Paris with their tails between their legs. The moral damage is enormous. A people who had deluded themselves that they could alone stand up to everyone is plunged into despair. Millions of peaceful peasants, ignorant of the world, who for four years fought a wide-reaching war in the trenches without even really knowing on which soil they'd been dug, are told that they opened their veins for nothing, that their wounds bleed in vain. Disappointment explodes in them like an agonizing pain.

The train on which Sonnino and Orlando have traveled all night, breathless, repentant, eager not to miss the meeting with the German delegations, enters Paris just as Gabriele D'Annunzio finally appears on the balcony of the Campidoglio. It is immediately clear that the magician intends to keep the edges of the wound fully open. His attendants spread a large tricolor flag over the railing of the Campidoglio.

D'Annunzio's delicate, jewel-laden hand caresses the tricolor wrapped around the corpse of infantry captain Giovanni Randaccio, his close friend, who, instigated by the poet, fell in the tenth battle of the Isonzo during a suicide assault on a hill at the mouth of the Timavo river. The wound must continue to bleed. As a symbol of the "mutilated victory," the infantryman's clotted blood is a dark red stain on the vermilion red of the flag that gleams, struck by the Roman sun. The men crowded at the foot of the balcony, still motionless, contemplate the flag and covertly finger their bodies searching for a missing limb.

Gabriele D'Annunzio, in the white uniform of a high-ranking cavalry officer, grips the railing with both hands from which the flag-shroud hangs. The man is a living myth.

Born in 1863, Gabriele D'Annunzio has spent the first fifty years of his life trying to become Italy's foremost poet. He has succeeded. His verses and his prose—in particular the novel *Il piacere*—have influenced the tastes of a generation and resonated internationally. He arrogantly claims to have "brought Italian literature to Europe" and he is right. The major intellectuals of the continent read, admire and publicly praise him. Meanwhile, his life is lived as a work of art: an incomparable dandy, a militant hedonist, a triumphant, histrionic, sensual, imaginative seducer, he devotes his boundless erudition to the obsessive search for sensual pleasures and unbridled carnal appetites. Then, at the height of the Belle Époque, almost overnight, the cult of aestheticism in him transforms into that of violence, the era's anxiety takes on bloody overtones. His insatiable desire for female conquests becomes a desire for territorial expansion. The lyricist of infinite yearning becomes the wordsmith of slaughter: he first celebrates colonial enterprises in the *Canzoni d'Oltremare* (Songs from Overseas), then he pushes Italy into war with his speech at Quarto; the decadent aesthete transfigures into the *Vate*, a sacred Bard, the prophet of national glory.

Not satisfied, at the outbreak of the Great War, rounding the fifty-year mark, at a point when men of his years enter old age, D'Annunzio, the connoisseur of glaze and gloss, decides to become Italy's most notable soldier. And he succeeds. Having secured authorization to enlist as liaison officer in the lancers of Novara, and having obtained a pilot's license, he participates in air raids on Trieste, Trent and Parenzo, and takes part in the attack on Mont Saint-Michel on the karstic front. Wounded during an emergency landing, he loses his right eye. He uses the period of convalescence to compose *Notturno*, one of his most enigmatic and inspired works; then after returning to the front against all medical advice, during the tenth battle of the Isonzo he conceives the risky assault at Quota 28, a hill across the Timavo river. It is there that Giovanni Randaccio dies. As if to avenge his friend, the poet plans a series of sensational war exploits: he attacks the port of Kotor in Montenegro; he flies over Vienna with his squadron, dropping a hail of propaganda posters urging the enemy's capital to surrender; he violates the Austrian naval blockade in the bay of Buccari with small assault boats in a scornful raid that raises the morale of Italian troops after the defeat of Caporetto. His name is rightfully inscribed in the list of victors and heroes.

At this point, however, at the height of glory, the poet-warrior again sinks back into melancholy. Driven by incurable romantic despair—Mussolini notes—after the Italian army's triumphant counteroffensive at Vittorio Veneto, D'Annunzio feels a sense of his own sudden uselessness. On October 14th, 1918, during the final month of war, he wrote to Costanzo Ciano, his comrade in the Buccari escapade: "For me and for you, and for those like us, peace today is a curse. I hope I at least have time to die as I deserve . . . Yes, Constanzo, let's take a shot at some other great exploit before we are pacified willing or not." Ten days later, when the war is already won but the armistice has not yet even been signed, the Vate, writing from the columns of the *Corriere della Sera*, is already sounding the alarm against the danger that Italy may be defrauded. "Victory of ours," he writes, "you will not be mutilated." The expression already begins to circulate among soldiers who have not yet been demobilized, and within a few months, like a disquieting self-fulfilling prophecy, it becomes reality.

This man who has had everything from life and has been everything, who by becoming a soldier, sailor, and aviator has been the only Italian literary figure for centuries able to fuse poet and warrior, literature and life, salons and piazzas, the individual and the masses—this man abandons himself to premature, cosmic disillusionment. And so here he is, gripping the balustrade of the Campidoglio, preparing for one last fusion, that between the people and its leader.

"Romans, yesterday marked the fourth anniversary of the Sagra dei Mille. Yesterday was May 5, a date doubly solemn, the date of two fateful departures."

These are the first words that D'Annunzio pronounces from that balcony. They allude to Garibaldi and Napoleon. The crowd listening to him raptly remains stock-still. The oration proceeds, as usual, in high-flown language, through successive waves of Latin sayings, erudite and arcane references, indecipherable allusions, solemn proclamations, elaborate metaphors, sublime ecstasies, affectations, archaisms, aestheticisms. The common people don't understand it but they follow the oratorical rhythm, keeping time with an undulating motion of the head, the way one absent-mindedly hums the catchy tune of a popular song.

After several minutes, however, the orator seems to finally notice the flag. The poet lightly traces it, then caresses it, strokes it with his fingertips as if wanting to certify his own existence through its tactile consistency.

"Here it is. I have it here. At Quota 12, at the Stone Quarry, folded, it served as a pillow to the dying hero. This, Romans, this, Italians, this, comrades, is the flag of this hour."

D'Annunzio's eyes travel over the flag as if hoping to see the face of his lost friend. The sublime image of the infantryman who, as a cadaver, rested his head there has remained imprinted—he says—like the Holy Shroud of a lesser Christ. The miracle is not surprising: all those who died believing in the nation resemble one another.

The speaker asks for silence. Hear me now. The soul of the nation is once again poised in the unknown. We wait in silence, but on our feet. Randaccio's flag will be draped in mourning until Fiume and Dalmatia are returned to Italy. May all good Italians, in silence, drape their flags in mourning until that day.

Then, abruptly, even the speaker falls silent. No human voice can any longer be heard in Rome's Piazza del Campidoglio. D'Annunzio strains his neck to the left and upward. He listens intently for a distant echo.

"Do you hear them?!" he shouts to the crowd. No reply.

"Do you hear them?" he repeats. "Out there, on the streets of Istria, on the streets of Dalmatia, that are all Roman, don't you hear the stride of an army on the march?"

Yes, now the crowd hears them, those marching steps of ancient victorious legions vanished in time, of mythical forebears who strode out to conquer the world. The men packed into the Piazza del Campidoglio hear those steps and, under the equestrian monument to the emperor Marcus Aurelius, instinctively, unconsciously begin marching in place, matching the archaic tempo of those steps and swaying their bodies left and right like bearers under the weight of a coffin. The dead move faster than the living. Crowds, D'Annunzio knows, must be stirred up.

This, Romans, this, Italians, this, comrades, is the flag of this hour. The sublime image of the infantryman who rested his head on it has remained imprinted there. And it is the image of all those who died; because all those who died for their country and in their homeland resemble one another . . . Hear me now. Be as quiet as possible . . . Once again poised in the unknown is the soul of the nation, which in harsh solitude had regained its discipline and its strength. We wait in silence, but on our feet . . . So that the waiting may be votive and the focus vigilant and the oath faithful. I, unmoving before the sarcophagus of Aquileia, will drape my flag in black until Fiume is ours, until Dalmatia is ours.

May every good citizen, in silence, drape his flag in black, until Fiume is ours, until Dalmatia is ours.

Gabriele D'Annunzio, Rome, May 6, 1919

What is happening is so huge that . . . I could punch the wall. Shoot them, shoot them all: I can't find other words to describe my thoughts.

Letter from Filippo Turati to Anna Kuliscioff
regarding the D'Annunzian demonstrations in Rome,
May 1919

BENITO MUSSOLINI

MILAN, MID-MAY 1919

THE HAT. IT'S just an ordinary bowler bought at Borsalino in the Galleria for 40 liras, yet that black felt bowler draws his eyes like a magnet attracts iron filings.

The tolling from San Gottardo's bell tower fills the small, dreary room already permeated with the acrid odors of sex. The woman lies on her back, her thighs still spread, sprawled out yet sovereign in her shameless nudity. The bell tolls the hours and the quarter hours. He goes back to looking at the hat.

She's already forty but she's still beautiful. Gray-green eyes, coppery blond hair, the full, pendulous breasts of a mother who's nursed. In terms of apparel, she is certainly the most elegant and refined dresser that the doorkeeper of that dump has ever seen enter the hotel during working hours. Now though she is naked, it's six forty-five—nine strokes toll from San Gottardo's tower—and she is reviewing aloud the speech that her lover will have to give on May 22nd at the Teatro Verdi in Fiume.

Italy has a mission in the Mediterranean and in the East. A look at the map is all it takes to understand the axiomatic truth of this statement. Equidistant between the equator and the pole, Italy occupies the center of the Mediterranean, which is the most important basin on earth. The configuration, the littoral development, the exactitude of lines place it in a privileged position for which Italy is destined to be the dominator of the Mediterranean; and it is certain that, once the great rampart of the Alpine wall has been reconquered after two thousand years, Italy will again return to the sea from which prosperity and greatness came to her in every age. Africa is her second shore. One might say that the Mediterranean imperative represents the right of forty million Italians to be free to pursue their natural expansion. We must be strong, though. Italy's time has not yet sounded but it must inevitably come. With regard to internal order, Italy must first master herself. This is the task of fascism. A greater imperial destiny. A millenary tradition summons Italy to the shores of the black continent.

She nods her head approvingly, she likes the word "dominator." Then she crosses out a few expressions with decisive pen strokes and concludes that he must meet Gabriele D'Annunzio. The air in the room becomes unfit to breathe. The hat again.

Margherita Sarfatti and Benito Mussolini met in person in February 1913 when he, just thirty, had been appointed editor of *Avanti!* She, the socialist paper's art critic at the time, had appeared before the new editor to offer her resignation, as was customary with every change of political stripe. What she would remember from that first meeting were his feverish, yellow eyes, his animal energy, his thinness. He'd given her the impression of a man struggling to hold shut a door that he wants to open at all costs. She had already heard of him previously, however. The first to name him had been her husband, Cesare Sarfatti, a distinguished attorney, an exponent of the reformist current of Milanese socialism. On July 13th, 1912, Cesare had written his wife, who had remained home, an enthusiastic note from Reggio Emilia, where the Socialist Party conference had just ended: "Benito Mussolini. Mark that name. He is the next man." And Margaret had marked it.

In Reggio Emilia, the young, obscure delegate from the Forlì section had shown up at the rostrum as somber as an executioner—black jacket and tie, pale face, shabby clothes, a scrawny body, haunted eyes, and a three-day-old beard—and had spoken a language that had never been heard before. Disjointed, peremptory, the pounding sentences almost always preceded by a hypertrophic "I", punctuated by menacing silences, unequivocally militant connotations, and hysterical, memorable assertions. In a few minutes

Benito Mussolini, the obscure delegate of the provincial section of Forlì, swept away centuries of sonorous, cultured eloquence, gesticulating like a wild man, mangling his wide-brimmed Mazzinian hat, and cursing God from the people's pulpit. The audience was divided: the blind and arrogant laughed at him as if he were bizarre, the others were all fascinated and appalled.

The targets of his fury were the old, distinguished, gentlemanly notables of the reformist wing. What had happened was this: a stonemason in Rome had fired a revolver at the king and they, led by Leonida Bissolati, a great elder of moderate socialism, had been guilty of visiting the sovereign, going to the palace in slouch hats and straw-colored gloves. So Mussolini had rolled up his shirtsleeves and put their backs to the wall with a direct slap in the face. "I cannot approve your obsequious gesture. Tell me, Bissolati, how many times have you gone to pay your respects to a mason who fell from the scaffolding? How many times to a wagoner run over by his own cart? Well? What is an attack on the king, if not a work-related accident?" Applause. "For a socialist, an attack is a news item or a historical fact, as the case may be. The king's personal qualities don't enter into it. For us the king is a man, subject like any other to the comic and tragic whims of fate. Why be moved by and weep for the king, only for the king? Between an accident that strikes a king and one that injures a worker, the former should leave us indifferent. The king is by definition a useless citizen." Applause. Cheering. A hit.

At the end of the day, Bissolati, Bonomi, Cabrini and Podrecca—the leaders of the moderate wing—would be expelled from the party; Benito Mussolini, the primitive revolutionary from the provinces, would be elevated as its new idol; a few more months and Margherita—captivating issue of Venice's Jewish grande bourgeoisie, raised in Palazzo Bembo on the Grand Canal, wife of attorney Sarfatti, cultured intellectual and champion of socialism, *rentier* of 40,000 liras a year, refined art critic, benefactor of painter Umberto Boccioni and patroness of futuristic artistic avant-gardes—would become his lover.

Now, however, it is no longer 1912. Seven years have passed, along with a world war. The socialists have even expelled Benito Mussolini from the party, though before the war he had been its rising star; they branded as traitor the man who suddenly went from the pacifist to the interventionist front, they deposed their young revolutionary idol in shame as he had ousted the old reformist patriarchs. After four years of war constantly opposed by mainstream socialists, on May 1st, the working class that despises veterans and interventionists celebrate their Workers' Day with lavish demonstrations. Intoxicated by their power, the masses stream by in large numbers under the red flags. The fire at *Avanti!*, started by the impetuous fascists, doesn't seem to have affected them. In less than a month they have collected more than a million for reconstruction. For Mussolini, however, that fire burned all the bridges thrown out to his old comrades. Every attempt to create a constituency of leftist interventionist factions has failed. Moreover the Fasci di Combattimento were also a fiasco. A few hundred adherents, scattered throughout Italy.

On certain cold evenings of damp fog he must walk up and down Via Monte di Pietà waiting for Marinelli or Pasella to arrive and open the door to the section. In just a few months, Trotsky in Russia has assembled a huge Red Army of socialist workers and he hasn't even been able to set up shifts of squads to defend the newspaper for weeks. And besides that the paper keeps losing circulation. Morgagni, the managing editor, bends over backwards but sometimes he can't even pay for the newsprint. And then there's the president of the United States of America who at the Paris Peace Conference persists in humiliating Italy. Not to mention that crazy vindictive woman Ida Dalser who is publicly dragging him through the mud. She gave the son born from their clandestine relationship his name—Benito Albino—and now she has taken 700 liras from Frassati, the editor of *La Stampa* in Turin, to accuse him of having founded *Il Popolo d'Italia* in 1915 thanks to French gold. And then there's Bianca Ceccato, the "baby girl" who wants to be his little mistress. She quit her secretary job at the newspaper and now she's crying about the fact that people call her a kept woman. At first he took her to furnished rooms on Via Eustachi, but now she makes him take her on romantic getaways. They've been to Lake Como, and in April they went to Venice. They took a souvenir photo in Piazza San Marco, with pigeons on their heads. Hotel porters think she's his daughter. She's nineteen years old. A babydoll face under the lace nightcap. She says her prayers before going to bed.

"You absolutely must meet D'Annunzio."

Margherita Sarfatti tells him that the Vate is a dear friend of hers, that she can introduce him. The sweep of that woman fills the room: the dynamisms of the century, bohemian Paris, the city that rises, the rice weeders of Novara who after striking for seventeen days get an eight-hour working day, Umberto Boccioni, the greatest painter of his generation, a volunteer in the National Cyclists Battalion, who dies at the front at only thirty-three years of age due to a banal incident. That obscene body of a woman in control sums them all up, the century vibrates in her breasts, in her belly, in her naked, shameless thighs. He, Benito Mussolini from Predappio, son of Alessandro, slams against those genteel thighs like a crazed fly slams against the glass of an overturned goblet. He could mount her like a horse. And that's all. He doesn't know anything else.

The smell in the room has become vile. San Gottardo tolls seven o'clock. Seven tolls exactly.

He gets up, knots his tie, then lets himself flow into the magnetic current that attracts him to the bowler. No, no woman can boast of being satisfied by his intimacy. As soon as he has possessed them—an act which in itself is very swift—he feels an overpowering urge to put the hat back on his head.

Mussolini, Benito, son of Alessandro, deceased, born in Predappio on July 29th, 1883, residing in Milan at Foro Bonaparte 38, revolutionary socialist with a police record, elementary schoolteacher certified to teach in secondary schools, was formerly secretary of the Camera del lavoro (Labor Chamber Union) of Cesena, Forlì and Ravenna, then from 1912 editor of the newspaper *Avanti!* which he stamped as a violent, rousing and intransigent organ. On October 20th, 1914, after taking a stand in opposition to the leadership of the Italian Socialist Party, advocating Italy's "active" neutrality in the war of nations against the PSI's stance of "absolute" neutrality, he resigned as editor of *Avanti!*

He then, on November 15th, began publication of the newspaper *Il Popolo d'Italia*, with which, in antithesis to *Avanti!* and with bitter controversy directed at that newspaper and its chief supporters, he promoted the idea of Italy's intervention in the war against the militarism of the Central Powers.

For this reason he was accused of moral and political unworthiness and expelled by his socialist comrades . . .

He was also the lover of Dalser Ida from the Trentino area . . . with whom he had a son in November 1915 recognized by Mussolini with a certificate dated January 11, 1916 . . . Abandoned by Mussolini, she badmouthed him to everyone, even saying that she had helped him financially, though never referring to her political history . . . While she was interned in Caserta, she spoke to an official of this Office (February 1918) and accused Mussolini of having sold out to France, betraying the interests of his country; in this regard she reported having known that on January 17th, 1914, a meeting took place in Geneva between Mussolini and Caillaux, the former French prime minister, following which the latter supposedly paid Mussolini the sum of one million liras . . .

Dalser, however, is a hysterical neurasthenic driven by the desire for revenge against Mussolini and her declarations do not merit belief.

Nevertheless, our investigations show that in effect Benito Mussolini was in Geneva, at the Hotel d'Angleterre to be exact, not on the date indicated by Dalser but on November 13th, 1914 (note: two days before the appearance of the first issue of the *Popolo d'Italia*).

Report of the Commissioner of Public Security
Giovanni Gasti, June 1919

BENITO MUSSOLINI, CESARE ROSSI

END OF JUNE 1919

As regards the political problem, we want: non-submissive foreign policy, electoral law reform, abolition of the Senate.

As regards the social problem, we want: an eight-hour working day, minimum wages, union representatives on the boards of directors, workers' management of the industries, disability insurance and pensions, the distribution of uncultivated lands to farmers, efficient reform of the bureaucracy, and secular schools funded by the state.

As regards the financial problem, we want: a progressive special capital tax, partial expropriation of all wealth, seizure of 85 percent of war profits, seizure of all the assets of religious congregations.

As regards the military problem, we want: an armed nation.

The platform of the Fasci di Combattimento is published in *Il Popolo d'Italia* on June 6th, almost three months after the meeting in Piazza San Sepolcro, following thousands of discussions and modifications. Full-page coverage, screamed out over six columns, with banner headlines. Apart from a revolution, it is almost the same program as that of the revolutionary socialists, more to the left of the reformists. A program conceived by socialist exiles to attract former comrades.

Cesare Rossi, however, thinks it's hopeless. He doesn't say so openly but he gets the point across. As he sees it, and he knows the proletariat well, it is impossible by now to separate the masses of workers and peasants from the bourgeois socialist party leaders—inept and ineffectual though they may be—as Mussolini still deludes himself of being able to. And Cesarino Rossi is perhaps the only political adviser whom Mussolini listens to. He too has a square jaw like Benito's, round eyes and an already deeply receding hairline. He often arches his thick black eyebrows, which practically link his brow to his ears, and he has a bushy mustache under a pointy nose.

Born in Pescia, in Abruzzi, like D'Annunzio, a fatherless orphan, Rossi was a militant socialist and anti-militarist, and worked as a printer from the time he was a child. He later left the Socialist Party because its leaders got lost in scholarly disquisitions, and together with Alceste De Ambris founded the Italian Trade Union, the revolutionary union of direct action. After he too moved on to interventionism like Mussolini, he fought the war as a simple soldier and wrote excellent news reports from the front; he knows politics and he knows newspapers. He is the only one Mussolini pays attention to.

The others whom the Founder of the fasci has around him at *Il Popolo d'Italia* are of little use, they're either brilliant but corrupted or untarnished and imbecilic, they are either dangerous or completely innocuous. Michele Bianchi, despite being loyal and politically savvy, is a fanatic who can't live without thinking about plans for revenge and without a cigarette between his fingers; Mario Giampaoli is a criminal who still exploits women at Porta Ticinese; Pasella doesn't have a single idea in his head and for that reason is an excellent speaker, good for sending to the provinces to conduct rallies; Arnaldo, Benito's brother, stout, honest, easy-going and docile, with a bovine look, is an invaluable support, a good Christian, a good family man, and a good friend. Rossi, in contrast, has the black corneas of a wolf. And Rossi maintains that there is no going back.

Crowds of angry socialists continue to obstruct fascist public rallies. The Arditi, meanwhile, continue to knife labor leaders whenever they get their hands on them. There's no passing over that. A wall of hatred, contempt and bloodshed has been raised between them and the past.

According to Rossi, the popular riots over the rising cost of living, which broke out at the beginning of the month throughout northern Italy, won't achieve anything either. The explosion of popular rage is genuine and spontaneous, but it lacks any political substance. People are starving, that's all. Inflation is skyrocketing, the millions of soldiers back from the front after four years of war have no food. They had been promised prosperity, land, and those are not promises that are made in vain.

At their afternoon meetings, Rossi insists on downplaying the importance of the riots: the housewives who assault the stands at the vegetable market and steal tins of rolled anchovy fillets are gentle, simple, happy to finally enjoy a flask of two-lira wine, people who amiably go home, looking forward to an enjoyable family evening. These insurrections that so terrorize the bourgeoisie are certainly not the harbingers of a revolution, it all comes down to an uproar over jugs and chickens. Italy, for that matter, has forever been a country where uprisings have always begun in front of bakers' shops.

Mussolini is quite aware of this as well. He too shouts "let the rich pay!" from the columns of his newspaper, acts like a demagogue, calls for "holy popular vengeance," shows solidarity with the people "rebelling against those who starve them." Then, however, he too sees that the strikes, the riots, are becoming purely an epidemic disease, a chronic, delirious fever. Forges and fields are abandoned, nurses forsake the sick and gravediggers refuse to bury the dead, without any real imperative. The chaos is universal, growing, indistinct, but it's only chaos. Revolution is quite another matter and the socialist leaders are utterly unable to channel that spontaneous revolt into a conquest of power. They demonstrated it with the fire at *Avanti!* The feeling aroused in the country by that devastation had been enormous. The socialist leaders, however, did nothing more than launch a fundraising campaign, which in a few days collected the huge sum of one million liras from their immense base, united around the fallen flag. Then they urged those masses of militant enthusiasts to return peacefully to work. Those incompetents preach patience while awaiting the fateful revolutionary day of reckoning, openly proclaimed but continuously postponed. Those "evangelical" socialists will never mount a revolution, Rossi insists. And on this point Mussolini agrees with him.

Cesare Rossi, however, is convinced that they must look in another direction. In Bologna, the agrarians formed a federation of large landowners. It is there, to the right, that they should look, Rossi keeps repeating to Mussolini. The San Sepolcro program is not working, they must rewrite it. Enough of nostalgia and the dregs of their leftist past. They really need to ask themselves once and for all: who are we?

On this point, however, Rossi is mistaken. Mussolini, when Rossi reaches this turn in his argument, usually stops listening to him. Who are we? Wrong question, pointless, even detrimental. A superfluous question because it overestimates the importance of soul-searching.

Who are the fascists? What are they? Benito Mussolini, their creator, considers it an idle question. Yes, of course . . . they are something new . . . something unheard of . . . an anti-party. That's it . . . the fascists are an anti-party! They engage in anti-politics. Very well. But then the pursuit of identity must stop there. The important thing is to be something that allows them to avoid the encumbrances of consistency, the dead weight of principles. As for dogmas, and the consequent paralysis, Benito Mussolini gladly leaves those to the socialists.

Cesare Rossi is correct in his analysis: the fasci have no idea about the future, they don't know where they're headed. But Cesarino's prognosis is incorrect: this inadequacy will be their salvation, not their condemnation. You have to consider reality in broad terms. In the end, every life counts as much as another life, every blood as much as another's blood. The fascists don't want to rewrite the book of reality, they just want their place in the world. And they will have it. It's all about fomenting factional animosities, exacerbating grievances. Nothing, therefore, will be precluded. There is neither left nor right anymore. All they have to do is nurture certain states of mind that emerge in this twilight of the war. Nothing more. That's all.

The San Sepolcro program? Just a piece of paper, an embarrassing preamble. They threw in a lot of alarming demands, but then, they are the Fasci di Combattimento and their real program is entirely contained in the word "combat." Therefore, they can and must afford themselves the luxury of being reactionary or revolutionary, depending on the circumstances. They promise nothing and will keep their promise.

Rossi is wrong to want to rewrite the platform by positing a shift to the right. Gabriele D'Annunzio, on the other hand, doesn't give a damn about programs; in his view the emphasis must instead be placed wholly on action. This seduces young people who "go towards life," as in D'Annunzio's motto: action. The theoretical problem of the political program is solved by eradicating it like an invasive weed: the fascists must only take action, any kind of action. Everything, then, becomes simpler. At those times when thought is discharged into action, the inner life is miniaturized, reduced to the simplest reflexes, and shifts from the central nervous system to the periphery. Such a relief . . .

Left alone in his office, on an unspecified day in June 1919, Benito Mussolini takes up pen and paper and writes to Gabriele D'Annunzio:

"Dear D'Annunzio . . . When will you be coming to Milan? Or must I come to Venice? Drop me a line. I am at your disposal."

D'Annunzio and Mussolini meet in person for the first time a few days later, on June 23rd. The poet, who arrived in Rome from Venice, stayed as usual at the Grand Hotel. That same day, he met with the king. Before going to the Quirinale, he had to deny certain rumors of a conspiracy to overthrow the government that he supposedly plotted with Mussolini, with the head of the Federzoni nationalists, with Peppino Garibaldi, the hero's nephew, and with the Duke of Aosta, the sovereign's cousin. The denial will remain among his celebrated phrases: "My action is so plain and so pure that it has nothing to fear from either enemies or friends, neither today nor ever. *Ardisco non ordisco*, I dare, I do not plot."

Simultaneously, in an interview with the *Idea Nazionale*, the Vate hastened to launch a subversive proclamation: "A new popular faith must prevail, by any means, against a political caste that by any means seeks to prolong impaired and despised forms of life. If there is a need to sound the charge, I will sound it. And all the rest is putrescence." Within a few hours, the image of the political class as a privileged "caste" removed from society begins to take root on the trunk of popular discontent with the same rapidity as that of the "mutilated victory."

Mussolini, meanwhile, appeared at the first assembly of the Roman fascio formed on May 15th at the initiative of futurists Mario Carli and Enrico Rocca and of Giuseppe Bottai, a young lieutenant in the Arditi and would-be poet. Just a handful of people there as usual.

Afterwards Mussolini attended the first national congress of Combattenti, inaugurated at the Campidoglio, and phoned the newspaper with a commentary. It seems that the names of Francesco Saverio Nitti, the new prime minister who replaced Vittorio Emanuele Orlando after yet another crisis, and of Giovanni Giolitti, the old statesman who maneuvers parliamentary games behind the scenes, were loudly booed. Some maintain that the name of Mussolini, defender of the veterans but traitor of the socialists, was also booed. This detail, however, doesn't appear in the column of *Il Popolo d'Italia*.

In any case, the conversation between Mussolini and D'Annunzio takes place in the afternoon, at the Grand Hotel. Accompanying Mussolini is journalist Nino Daniele. The meeting, which is said to have lasted an hour, had no witnesses. Its only testimony, the specter of a woman: Margherita Sarfatti who, though admiring D'Annunzio immensely and remaining a friend, has rebuffed the poet's advances since 1908. It was she who interceded for the meeting and it was she who extolled the idea of an air raid to Mussolini: according to the plan conceived by Giuseppe Brezzi, director of Ansaldo in Genoa, the poet was to carry out a Rome-to-Tokyo flight on one of the planes already piloted during the war. An aviation enthusiast, Margherita has, in fact, been begging D'Annunzio to be included in the exploit since word of it began circulating. Mussolini too, urged by his lover, has recently begun taking flying lessons, emulating D'Annunzio. But he's just a novice. Not even in that field, the conquest of the sky, can he compete with his rival.

In addition to sharing those fantasies, carnal and aerial, it seems that the two men agreed on the need to accord Italy a government of fighters and to oppose head-on the great strike that socialists across Europe have proclaimed to show solidarity with Lenin's red armies. It has already been nicknamed the "*scioperissimo*," the super strike.

"An interesting man, that Mussolini," D'Annunzio apparently tossed out, finally free to devote himself to his jubilant, adored pack of borzois after saying goodbye to his old friend Margherita's lover.

The problem is clear. The Italian nation is like one big family. The coffers are empty. Who is supposed to fill them up? We, perhaps? We who do not own houses, cars, banks, mines, lands, factories, capital? Those who can, "must" pay. Those who can, must shell out . . . One of the two: either the fortunate men of means self-expropriate in which case there will be no violent crises—because we are the first to abhor violence among people of the same race who live under the same sky—or they will be blind, deaf, tight-fisted and misanthropic, in which case we will direct the masses of combatants towards those obstacles and crush them. It is time for everyone to make sacrifices. Let those who have not given blood, give money.

Benito Mussolini, Milan, June 9, 1919.
Speech in the schools of Corso di Porta Romana
on popular riots against the high cost of living.
First public rally of the Fasci di Combattimento.

Given the fact that their platform has no stability, any agreement with the Fasci di Combattimento is impossible. Benito Mussolini, moreover, is a man who can't give any guarantees.

Mario Gibelli, a leading exponent of the republicans,
June 1919

I am ready. We are ready. The greatest battle is beginning, and I tell you that we will have our fifteenth victory.

Letter from D'Annunzio to Mussolini, May 30, 1919

BENITO MUSSOLINI

JULY 19, 1919

TEN MINE BOMBS.

Cesare Rossi was so furious with his former comrades that he personally went to the Central station to retrieve the explosives from one of the storerooms where they had lain hidden since before the war, when they were intended to be used for acts of sabotage during a railway workers' strike. Rossi knew the hiding place very well because at that time he was in charge of the most violent wing of their union. Now, after only a few years, out of hatred for yet another strike by the socialists announced for the following day—this time actually baptized "scioperissimo"—even a reasonable man like Rossi risked sneaking into the equipment area at night with a trusted friend. There a fascist guard handed him ten bombs, one at a time, and he, one at a time, carried them to his accomplice, who was waiting for him with a suitcase on the station square. If they had stopped him he would have pretended to be a traveler who couldn't afford to go to a hotel and was unable to continue his trip because of the disturbances. A poor traveler with ten bombs in his suitcase. His absurd plan intended to take advantage of the confusion to mine the offices of *Avanti!* and the labor union headquarters.

Mussolini was able to stop his managing editor's madness just in time. When he disputed the savagery of a plan that did not take innocent victims into account, Rossi replied that all the printers at *Avanti!* were militant socialists and that only enemies of fascism frequented the Labor Union. The bombs were still in the home of his accomplice on Via Durini, a few steps from the newspaper offices.

When even someone like Rossi plans an attack, there is nothing to be done. Things are headed towards tragedy, no matter what. The expectation of cataclysm aroused by the "scioperissimo" of July 20 is so intense as to make even ten mine bombs deposited in a flat in the city center plausible. This put an end to the feeling of living on the brink of a new era. No capitulation by the parties. Between socialists and fascists—Rossi insists—there might be periods of more or less lengthy truce but, in the end, they will nonetheless be at each other's throats.

Mussolini tries to keep events afloat. He steers a middle course between nostalgia for his old comrades and the need to find new ones. On July 17th, the first conference of the fasci of Central and Northern Italy, held in Milan, he pronounced the most resolute opposition to the "scioperissimo." No more than a dozen cities were represented out of a few hundred registered members, yet for the first time the fascists decided on adopting a hard line against the "red" agitators, the "bastard race that dishonors Italy" and takes Lenin's Russia as a model instead of their homeland that had been victorious against the Austrians.

Besides dealing with the movement, Mussolini, to stay afloat, doesn't overlook the institutions: Michele Bianchi, on his order, has already reached agreement with Milan's prefect to make the fasci available to him for the job of maintaining public order. The prefect informed him of an explosive new development: a confidential government circular that for the first time called for and urged the fascists' collaboration in the effort to repress revolutionary attempts, even violently, provided they agreed to be commanded by the authorities. In short, the liberal state, in order to curb the advance of the "reds," allows itself to be assisted by the fascists who, in an unprecedented move, will spearhead the opposition to a strike by the popular masses.

However, immediately prior to the "scioperissimo" Mussolini also relaunched the idea of a pre-electoral committee in conjunction with all the factions of left-wing interventionism that only two months earlier had seemed to be definitively foundering. The leaders of the socialist faction who fought for Italy's entry into the war in 1915, in opposition to the official party line, assemble on the very eve of the 'scioperissimo' in the great hall of the Liceo Beccaria in Milan. All the exiles from official socialism and the radicals of the patriotic left are there.

Mussolini is among the first to speak and delivers a skillful address. Imagine a social and economic reorganization that puts workers' welfare at its center but is free of any Bolshevist influence. For a moment they all seem fervent and in agreement. They are told that, perhaps, by overcoming old divisions and personal biases, they could even run together in the November elections. The ship finally seems to be heading out to sea. They can, perhaps, hope for smooth sailing close to shore, which could also lead to a seat in parliament, despite the proclamations against the "caste."

But it is difficult to keep afloat with inshore cabotage when revolution is battering at the gates. The "scioperissimo," which was officially proclaimed by workers' organizations throughout Europe as a show of protest against foreign interventions in Russia in support of counterrevolutionary forces, is meant to be a simple demonstration, yet the situation still seems destined to disintegrate into a head-to-head confrontation. Even the honorable D'Aragona, a moderate socialist deputy, declares: "News of bloodshed and a revolutionary attempt should not be surprising. The results may not be significant but insurrection is almost inevitable." On the opposite front, the young British war and aviation minister, Winston Churchill, echoed him from London. According to Churchill, the Bolsheviks were actually "enemies of the human race" who from Moscow headed "a world conspiracy aimed at overthrowing civilization." In short, the "Asian plague" is upon us. The ten mine bombs remain hidden in a coal stove on Via Durini.

Returning to the editorial office late that night after the assembly at Liceo Beccaria, the editor of *Il Popolo d'Italia* must push aside the barbed wire fence that protects the entrance. Beside it, Albino Volpi is killing time meticulously unloading and reloading his pistol. The smell of blood is everywhere.

We are at a time when the authorities cannot remain isolated, counting solely upon state efforts and the police force . . . In cities where fasci and Combattenti associations exist . . . if they intend to cooperate in maintaining public order and repressing violence and revolutionary attempts, they will be performing a patriotic act, voluntarily making themselves available to those authorities with a disciplined spirit and accepting their direction, which must be the only one.

Francesco Saverio Nitti, prime minister,
in a confidential circular to the prefects, July 14, 1919

Mattina reports that he had a talk with authorities who had previously met with Bianchi, managing editor of the *Popolo d'Italia*, Mussolini being in Rome. Agreement between Bianchi and the prefect was absolute, partly due to Mattina's intervention. Therefore it can be assumed that local Fasci di Combattimento will be available to the authorities for any eventuality.

Telegram sent to the Head of Public Security
by the prefecture of Milan, July 15, 1919

This proletariat needs a bloodbath.

Benito Mussolini,
meeting at the Liceo Beccaria in Milan,
July 19, 1919

NICOLA BOMBACCI

MILAN, JULY 20, 1919

RED FLAG WILL TRIUMPH.

THAT IS THE headline of *Avanti!*'s Turin edition, on July 19th, 1919. Spread over six columns in block letters. Echoing it, *La Difesa*, the Florentine socialists' paper, leads with three exclamations in a single line: "Proletarians! Action is imminent, make it decisive! Let's rise up!"

In Russia, in October 1917, the red flag has already triumphed. Now it flies on at least sixteen war fronts, from Vilnius to Samara to Vladivostok, from the Baltic to the Volga to the Pacific Ocean. And it will triumph there too because in less than a year Leon Trotsky created a Red Army out of nothing, which has revolutionized the way we conceive of war. It is inspired by a new relationship between space and the array of forces, for a fluid war, of planetary motions, of universal brotherhoods, able to think conceptually on a grand scale, in a theater of operations as vast as the Earth. Its example has already been followed. In the spring of 1919 the red flag triumphed in Budapest where communist worker Béla Kun established the Hungarian Soviet Republic. And in Milan too, where on the morning of July 20, 1919, at 11:00 a.m., in front of the Labor Office on Via Manfredo Fanti in premises made available by the Humanitarian Society, a tide of red flags flies over the crowd.

Claudio Treves, the cultured, refined leader of the reformist faction, has already spoken; Giacinto Menotti Serrati, the combative head of the maximalist section has already spoken. Everyone, however, is waiting for Nicola Bombacci to speak. The French General Labor Union backed out of the "scioperissimo" at the last moment, the British trade unions did the same, and Italian workers have been left alone to support their Russian brothers. The atmosphere is more festive than mutinous, the workers are enjoying the luxury of being idle, smoking a pipe in the middle of the morning, the troops on horseback glumly patrol the perimeter streets without encountering any armies to contend with. But none of this matters because Nicolino Bombacci is about to take the floor. The workers love him, they are waiting for him.

As soon as he appears on the platform, the crowd falls silent, a silence full of respect, of paternal love, the quiet that protects the sleep of young children. Nicolino is very thin, small, gentle—the slender frame is lost beneath a black cassock of raw linen. His ethereal body is offset by a thick head of shiny dark hair and a bushy brown beard that seem to ballast him. Beard and hair give the impression that they are increasingly expanding, as if wanting to devour his gaunt face, the protruding cheekbones, the angelic blue eyes.

The red flags wave in front of the son of a humble family of farmers, born in Civitella di Romagna, in a remote province, a former seminarian, a failed priest, declared unfit for military service due to health reasons, who afterward became an elementary schoolteacher, a trade unionist and finally leader of the maximalist faction that took command of the Socialist Party after the war. Bombacci made it to the top preaching evangelical socialism, always on the side of the poor, for whom he helped create the leagues of farm laborers and workers, as well as women's organizations in the cotton mills, always diverging from the salon intellectuals—whom he describes as "manufacturers of ideas for those who have none"—constantly preaching the firm credo of revolution. They nicknamed him "Lenin of Romagna," and Mussolini at the time of shared socialist militancy called him the "Kaiser of Modena," but the nickname that suits him best is that of "Christ of the workers." A Christ recently taken down from the cross, held in his mother's arms.

When Nicolino begins to speak, with his slow but passionate voice, Hyperborean mists descend on Milan's summer:

"The red flag has triumphed in Russia."

These are the first words that Bombacci pronounces. In their simplicity, they offer an indisputable reality, a simple statement of fact. Then the speaker immediately follows with the natural conclusion:

"We want Russia to be here as well."

The crowd explodes in cheers of relief. Here is something that everyone can understand.

The continuation of the rally is apocalyptic and consoling at the same time. As if announcing a catastrophe that has already occurred a thousand times, one that is already behind us. A gentle cataclysm.

From the Humanitarian Society's platform, in the patient tone of an elementary schoolteacher, Nicolino explains to the striking workers that, signaled by the war, Marx's sixth power, revolution, made its entrance into Old Europe. We can therefore hope that the old world is finally on the verge of collapse. The symptoms of its decomposition are everywhere. The era of socialism, the doctrine of liberty and integral democracy, is in sight. In Russia it has already arrived, it will arrive in Italy as well. The leaders of the party are the vanguard of the revolution and the General Confederation of Labor their army. United, they will charge to the attack to bring down the Bastille of the bourgeoisie.

That's all. Simple and crystalline. No need to add anything more. The crowd of strikers is in ecstasy. Excited by the idea of having to reinvent the world in the next fifteen days but also uneasy, frightened, like a young boy on his first visit to a brothel. Will this really be the first day of a new life? Is the old one actually over?

Then, however, after a brief pause to recharge himself with a sip of water, Bombacci adds that the strike of July 20, 1919 is meant to be a demonstration, not a revolution. It paves the way for but does not constitute the expropriating strike. Even so, revolution is imminent. A historical necessity. It will be spontaneously triggered by the evolution of economic and political conditions. It's only a matter of being patient a little longer.

The crowd relaxes, nerves unwind, like after a few glasses of grappa. The final battle isn't today, it will be tomorrow. The spines of those hard-working, worn-out men get some relief, the lumbosacral contractions loosen up. The workers' wrath is soothed because Bombacci is on their side. The pain is sedated, the time is not yet ripe.

BENITO MUSSOLINI

SENIGALLIA BEACH, END OF AUGUST 1919

"FLY! HIGHER AND higher: in a prodigious tension of nerves, of will, of intelligence, which only man's small mortal body can offer. Fly above all the everyday battles of this terrible ongoing trench that is life today." Mussolini wrote this on August 20th to publicize the air raid on Mantua organized by *Il Popolo d'Italia*.

He's quite content to plant himself on the scorching sand of Senigallia Beach, legs spread, hands clenching his thighs, his body naked under the sizzling sun, pubes thrust forward to outrage bathers. He likes to swim and then feel the cool water evaporate from his skull in the Mediterranean heat. Everything vaporizes in that steaminess, the sultry heat is omnivorous.

The "scioperissimo" came to nothing. Two reasons for its failure: its leaders were rabbits, Italy is a wretched country. The only country in all of Europe that in two thousand years of history has never had either a revolution or a true religious war. A country where nothing ever happens and where nothing ever lasts. And, despite the reckless proclamations of socialist leaders, revolution can't be reduced to a spree or an illness, a St. Vitus dance or an outbreak of epilepsy. It takes much more than that. Misery can't be socialized.

And so, even on the occasion of the long-awaited "scioperissimo," the revolution had been adjourned *sine die*. Go back to your houses, comrades, we were wrong, this was not the fated day. Italian socialists had once again put off the assault on the palace of power. In

Russia in 1917 they had conquered a winter palace. The Bolsheviks, without a moment's hesitation, had rushed into the tsars' winter residence, surrounded by three-feet-high icy snowdrifts, to topple tyranny. But in Italy summer reigned. So in these parts, everything that might have happened was swallowed up in the laughable deferment: "Next time, comrades, next time."

Take Bombacci. Nicolino owed his fortune to his Christ-like beard and porcelain blue eyes. Nothing more. He's known the "Christ of the workers" for a lifetime. Since the beginning of the century when Bombacci was a schoolteacher at Cadelbosco di Sopra, in the province of Reggio Emilia, and the young Benito Mussolini taught in nearby Gualtieri. The first time they'd met was almost twenty years ago, at a teachers' conference in Santa Vittoria. And since that time Mussolini had never changed his mind about his friend's revolutionary fantasies: only the deficient mind of a failed seminarian, like Bombacci, could delude himself about the possibility of transplanting the Russian revolution to the shores of the Mediterranean. Instead of preaching and preparing an "Italian revolution" suited to our climate, that obsessed incompetent wanted to outfit Italy in a Russian peasant's shirt. Deep down he felt sorry for Nicolino Bombacci and he was fond of him. Nicolino wouldn't hurt a fly.

Even the Soviet Republic of Hungary that Bombacci and his comrades had so lauded had collapsed in a few months. In Ukraine, meanwhile, Denikin, commander of the counterrevolutionary armies, had allied with the Germans against the Bolsheviks and was at the gates of Kiev with his Cossacks. The tsarist general had already abolished the decree by which the communists had distributed land to the peasants only a few months earlier.

All that clamoring, so many deaths for nothing. The endless trench warfare. Pointless slaughter. That's what this senseless era was like.

It's getting hotter. People are leaving the pier pavilion, the pride of Senigallia Beach. Soon his wife Rachele would send little Edda to call him for lunch. He was fond of her. She was born at a time when they were eating bread and onions. He called her poverty's daughter.

The "scioperissimo" had scored an empty round for the fasci as well. During the days of turmoil they had entered the fray essentially on their own against the socialist masses. But they were still few in number, perhaps fewer and fewer. In Bologna the section founded in April by Pietro Nenni was already defunct by the beginning of August. Internal strife, ideological diatribes, unexpected attacks and then . . . everyone off to the beach. And so, left to oppose the "scioperissimo" with those few, they'd been reduced to putting on a show for the benefit of the bourgeoisie they so despised. That handful of pathetic fascists had only managed to operate a couple of trams and sweep some sidewalks with brooms abandoned by street cleaners waiting for the revolution. Italy is like that: all a farce, always a farce. That's its destiny: a happy ending. That's why it had no destiny. Comedy or tragedy. Almost always together. Seriousness, never.

Even the aerial exploits ended up entangled between those opposites. The first propaganda raid organized by *Il Popolo d'Italia* on August 2nd to ease the political oppression had ended in disaster. On the return flight from Venice, the plane piloted by Luigi Ridolfi, a wartime ace, crashed in Verona near the Porta Palio, 500 yards from the airport. Seventeen died.

He had persisted in organizing more raids to raise morale. On August 8th and then on the 22nd. Certainly not grandiose feats like D'Annunzio's long-distance flight from Rome to Tokyo. Nearby destinations, regional routes: Mantua, the lakes in the Alpine foothills. The director had dragged the entire editorial team on board. But unfavorable weather conditions, mechanical failures, and lack of fuel had again held them up to ridicule. For three days they had been forced to go back and forth between Brescia and the Ghedi airfield. They also had to buy lunch for the soldiers who transported them in a caisson.

Tragedy, comedy, controversy. The latter was never lacking. The results of the government's inquiry into the military disaster in Caporetto had just been published and, even after many years, even after the triumphant final victory, those documents regarding the responsibilities of the army's high command had revived the opponents of the war. And so it had started all over again, as if the war had not already begun and ended long before. Giacinto Menotti Serrati, leader of the maximalist socialists who, when he was a young penniless emigrant, had given him a roof and a job, was now relaunching the old accusation of his having founded *Il Popolo d'Italia* thanks to secret funding from France. Mussolini, in response, had raked up the old insinuation that Serrati had been a spy. They'd moved on to insults, dug up old events, sunk low. Malicious remarks, grudges, bad faith. The trench as always. Absurd, never-ending.

Now he has completely dried off and he is starting to sweat. The beach is deserted.

Even the interventionist left's electoral alliance for next November's elections had foundered. The reason was predictable and cruel: the comrades of the left who had been in favor of the war accepted the alliance with the fasci, but they did not want him on the ballot. They'd been intransigent on that point. No Mussolini.

The bathing season is drawing to a close on the beach of Senigallia. September is moving in. Yet the oppressive heat persists.

At the end of this first summer of peace, the Fasci di Combattimento are reduced to worthless trash. A few hundred soldiers, about a dozen units, no political prospects.

Luckily there is too much sun in Italy. Too much sun, the Russian revolution can't come here.

Volare! Fly! Ever higher, in a prodigious effort of nerves, will, and intellect that only man's small mortal frame can support.

Volare! Fly above the ghastly, continual trench skirmishes that are the stuff of daily life.

Volare! For the beauty of flight, virtually art for art . . .

Volare! Fly because although Icarus died, it was man's first bold act when he stole a little of heaven's glory, and because Prometheus taught that the human heart can be stronger than any adverse fortune.

Benito Mussolini,
Il Popolo d'Italia, August 20, 1919

GABRIELE D'ANNUNZIO

SEPTEMBER 11, 1919

He got up from his bed, feverish, and put on the white Novara lancers' uniform with the raised collars. Lieutenant colonel. No civilian has ever risen so high in the military hierarchy for distinguished service. He is fifty-six years old and can barely stand.

A covered motorboat awaits him at the landing of the *casetta rossa*, the little red palazzo at the corner of the Grand Canal. It's the house in which he spent a lengthy period of time, blinded after the plane crash in which he lost an eye during the war. Dawn is breaking over Venice.

It's low tide. When they go out into the lagoon, they can smell the putrefaction of the slimy muck emerging on the exposed sandbars. Day enters from the harbor inlets of Lido, Portogruaro and Malamocco. A streak of pale light spreads in the east beneath low clouds. The damp released by the stagnant waters of the shoals exacerbates the stiffness of his knees and the empty socket of his missing eye. His whole body is a wreck. Venice, instead, seen from Mestre, is a fish. A fish that's been gutted and reassembled.

Waiting for Gabriele D'Annunzio on the mainland is a flaming red Fiat Tipo 4. The open vehicle revives the fever. In addition to the driver, there is a lieutenant of the Sardinian Grenadiers, who have secretly vowed to seize Fiume from the international military garrison and return it to Italy even at the cost of sedition, and Guido Keller, eccentric rising star of the Italian air force. A highly decorated war hero and ace of the legendary Baracca squadron,

Keller is also a nudist, bisexual, and vegetarian. A man who loves to appall the bourgeoisie who spawned him by walking around with an eagle on his shoulder.

It is shortly after sunset when the poet and rebel grenadiers arrive in Ronchi, a village near the border, where their co-conspirators await them. By midnight, however, the trucks requested by phonogram at the Palmanova car park and promised by the commander of the piazza still have not arrived. The company has been betrayed.

D'Annunzio, exhausted, sleeps on a makeshift bed assembled by nailing a few wooden planks together. Guido Keller wanders off into the night with Tommaso Beltrami, an adventurer devoted to cocaine. Several hours later, as if by miracle, about thirty 15 Ter trucks, war surplus, are waiting on the square.

When the column starts out, there is still no light from the east, beyond the border. Only the vast starry night, then the thrill of dawn.

The grenadiers keep their guns hidden and the collars of their capes raised to conceal the insignia. They are part of the battalions expelled from Fiume in late August, after clashing with soldiers from the French contingent who had ripped the Italian tricolor off women's clothing. By attempting to return to the city on their own initiative they are disobeying the orders of the Italian high command, which is opposed to any "coup"; they are siding against the forces of the inter-Allied command that controls Fiume with French, British, American and Croatian contingents; they are rebelling against the will of US president Woodrow Wilson, who intends to hand the city to the Yugoslavs, and against the absence of will on the part of Italian rulers who are prepared to go along with him. All the grenadiers have on their side is a legion of volunteers from Fiume's civilian population, mostly Italian, ready to rise up. Against them, the entire modern world. They number 187. An old wounded poet precedes them in a flame-red sports car. During those same days, another writer, Franz Kafka of Prague, hospitalized not far from there in an Alpine sanatorium, notes in his diary: "In the struggle that pits the individual against the world, always bet on the world." The

187 rebellious grenadiers, instead, bet on the individual: his name is Gabriele D'Annunzio.

The convoy meets its first opposition at Castelnuovo. Four armored cars surrounded by Bersaglieri. D'Annunzio approaches, and parleys with the Italian officials. Whatever the poet tells them to convince them, within two minutes the armored cars are prepared to protect the column they should be stopping. The Bersaglieri join the rebels with shouts of enthusiasm.

Shortly afterwards, at the intersection of the road to Fiume: the first halt. All officers report to the Commander. D'Annunzio stands on a small mound.

"Officers of all forces, I face you squarely."

The poet speaks to them of oaths made on flags and handguns, of swordbreaking daggers that the duelist wielded desperately in his left hand, of damages that add up, of demons and human aspirations, of faith and violence, of a meadow surrounded by rubble. We will break the barrier.

The column sets out again. On the trucks, the grenadiers are singing. A few miles from the Cantrida roadblock they meet the assault units. Their commander, Lieutenant Colonel Raffaele Repetto, has been directed to stop D'Annunzio at any cost, the order having come directly from his superior, General Pittaluga, who threatened to have him shot on the spot if he disobeyed. Instead, as soon as Repetto sees D'Annunzio, he rushes to embrace him. The Arditi jump onto the trucks. There is no more room on board. The number of insurgents increases mile after mile. The column proceeds at a crawl to avoid wrecking the wheel hubs.

At the border barrier General Pittaluga himself, commander of the Allied forces of Fiume, confronts D'Annunzio. Given the insubordination of the troops under his orders, he personally strides up to the column with two colonels from his retinue, and with rifles fitted with bayonets, they advance among the Arditi. He orders D'Annunzio to turn back, warning him not to set himself above the authority of the state. He accuses him of ruining Italy. He castigates him for believing himself to be omnipotent.

The poet, at that point, is entranced by a recollection. For a very long moment, the old one-eyed man with ankylosis goes back in time, to his school days, to the classroom desks: he opens the coat covering his feverish body and repeats the gesture that Napoleon made, one hundred years ago, after fleeing from Elba and landing in France near Lake Laffrey, offering his chest to the French general, his former orderly, sent to stop him. The emulator nervously strikes his chest in the Napoleonic gesture for which he has been waiting a lifetime.

"Go ahead, fire on these medals," he enjoins the general who came to stop him.

Captivated by the blue ribbon of the gold medal on D'Annunzio's chest—he too seduced by that adventurous sense of life and the world, at whose flame the soldier becomes one with the insurgent, the man of arms one with the rebel—General Pittaluga replies by quoting his father and his grandfather, both followers of Garibaldi. At that moment, on the border between two nations and two eras, at the crossroads of resonances, history is reduced to a rhetorical figure, metaphor leads to metaphor, the power of symbols moves through the centuries, everything becomes a blur, the armored car accelerates, the barrier across the border shatters into splinters.

Fiume, with its ships anchored at port, set against the backdrop of the mountains, appears to D'Annunzio like a "bride dressed in white." At the turn of the road, a gleam of desire lights up the pupil of his one remaining eye: the poet has a city below to take. The man of letters finally knows the lust for siege felt by the condottiere about to send his mercenary troops off to pillage. Nitti will say of D'Annunzio that Italy is but one of many ladies the poet-soldier has possessed by this stage of his life.

D'Annunzio's troops enter Fiume shortly after eleven in the morning. The population welcomes them with delirious jubilation. The women of Fiume, wearing their finest clothing, offer themselves to the liberators. Laurel leaves rain down from the rooftops.

Arriving at the Hotel Europa, D'Annunzio immediately goes to bed. He has been guided by a lucky star. He is his own star. He's never had another. It's eleven forty-five in the morning. Not a single shot was fired.

"Who, me?! Governor?"

D'Annunzio is awakened late in the afternoon by the ringing of the bells that summon the population to assemble in the main piazza. Guido Keller informs him that while he was sleeping he took the initiative a second time and proposed that the city council give the poet full civil and military powers. Antonio Grossich, the council president, a luminary in the field of medicine—creator of tincture of iodine, a pioneer in the sterilization of surgical instruments, awarded the Order of the Crown of Italy, an irredentist and patriot—availing himself of his clinical eye, received Keller with the consideration and wariness due to a madman. Then, however, the members of the council surprisingly agreed to entrust the administration of a city contested by three nations, at the center of a diplomatic controversy of worldwide import, to Gabriele D'Annunzio, a man notoriously incapable of even administering his own finances, a notorious, ardent spendthrift, pursued by creditors throughout Europe for having frittered away more than one fortune, his own and that of others, in reckless expenditures on frivolities such as precious stones, enamels, lacquered objects and lavish home furnishings.

The poet, however, recoils when faced with that incalculable equation. Him, administrator? Unthinkable.

When D'Annunzio, escorted by a group of Arditi, arrives at the government building at six o'clock on the dot, as promised, the piazza is packed with a euphoric crowd. The scene that awaits him is unforgettable. The Liberator's car can barely manage to make its way through the crush. Everyone wants to hug him, everyone wants to kiss him. He can barely stand up. He is visibly drained, very pale, staggering. Grossich, who is himself over seventy, has to support him.

As soon as he reaches the building's balcony, the unbridled love that rises from below revitalizes him. When the great Casanova appears, the women instinctively smooth their hair and, straightening their skirts, stroke their thighs. With an imperious gesture, almost a wave of irritation, the people's champion takes the floor:

"Italians of Fiume! In the mad, vile world, Fiume today is a symbol of liberty; in the mad, vile world there is only one pure thing: Fiume; there is only one truth and that is Fiume! There is only one passion and that is Fiume! Fiume is like a dazzling beacon that shines in the midst of an abject sea."

It is colossal nonsense, but the crowd is swept up in it.

D'Annunzio goes on, recalling the anxious moments of that morning's march and the days in Rome the previous May. Only four months have passed since the nationalist demonstrations that spring, yet they are already projected into an epic past. The living poet, cheating time, celebrates himself as a mythical forefather. His is already posthumous glory.

Gabriele D'Annunzio unfolds Giovanni Randaccio's tricolor flag, taking it from the infantry rucksack he keeps it in. It is already a relic. The fine connoisseur of rich fabrics divests the banner of the black crepe band with which he had draped it in mourning.

So far it's all theater. Fiume the setting of a marvelous adventure. The hero, the poet and play-actor tread the boards simultaneously. Then, however, something unheard of happens. D'Annunzio—exalted by the roar that surges from the piazza, quivering from the vocal effort to rise above the clamor with no microphone to amplify his voice, his jugular bulging with the blood coursing through his tense neck—D'Annunzio, from the balcony of the building that for centuries had served Hungarian emperors reigning over a people kept at absolute distance, addresses the crowd directly:

"Here before the Timavo flag, do you confirm your vow of October 30?"

Antonio Grossich, at his side, turns sharply. No speaker until that day had ever directly addressed the audience. The scene has suddenly changed, the fourth wall has fallen. The public has been summoned on stage, the people have been called to participate in the Kingdom.

The population of Fiume breaks out in an impassioned roar. "Yes!" they shout three times, "yes!", "yes!", "yes!". Gabriele

D'Annunzio proclaims Italy's annexation of Fiume. It took him only four months to fulfill the promise. The Campidoglio vow has been kept. The members of the City Council all approach to kiss him. He allows them to.

Next morning, awake at 5:00 a.m. contrary to his customary pattern, D'Annunzio writes to General Pittaluga: "General, it is necessary that I immediately assume the military command of Italian Fiume. It is a measure to ensure order." Since there was no response from Rome to the gauntlet thrown down by the march, the poet assumes power. The aesthete steps aside. The lawmaker enters the scene. From here on, he will be the one in charge. His first provision will be the temporary closure of the brothels to prevent brawls between the Legionnaires of Fiume and the French troops. For D'Annunzio, an insatiable sensualist, it is a huge renunciation. The Commander, however, is willing to set an example. He deprives himself of those pleasures that throughout his life he's considered unrenounceable. He has his room hung with flags instead of the inevitable tapestries. He allows himself only a bouquet of flowers in a crystal vase and a handful of chocolates in a hefty silver goblet.

BENITO MUSSOLINI

VENICE, SEPTEMBER 20–22, 1919

SINCE THE EVENING of September 20, Mussolini has been spending a few days in Venice. Police files register his presence in the company of Margherita Sarfatti. It is feared that the director of *Il Popolo d'Italia*, like thousands of volunteers from all over Italy in those days, might also join D'Annunzio, violating the fragile embargo that President Nitti has imposed on the rebellious city.

The lovers are tailed. Two plainclothesmen are breathing down their necks. At every turn of every narrow Venetian street, every *calle*, *calletta*, waterfront promenade, dead-end *ramo* or stone-paved *salizada*, at every opening to a *campo* or square, at every *campiello* or *fondamenta* bordering a canal, the fugitives see the agents reappear behind them. Unrelenting. Margherita, however, appears amused by the quixotic adventure. To the woman in love, being followed seems romantic.

There would be numerous means to evade them, by air or by sea—motorboats, airplanes, watercraft—but the labyrinthine city tightens around the couple like a fishing net. D'Annunzio set sail at dawn on September 11th, racing through the open lagoon on a speeding launch. Only ten days later, on September 21st, Mussolini's Venice is, instead, a maze, a twisted bowel, a city of entrails. Sarfatti, being Venetian, guides him through the stone viscera. After reaching Ponte delle Tette, so-called because in the past the whores had displayed their *tette*, breasts, from the windows of the brothels, the lovers turn abruptly into the tiny Calle de la Madonetta. The police bloodhounds do not lose them.

Since the poet initiated his venture, relations between Mussolini and D'Annunzio have been intense, worrisome, epistolary. Mussolini received the first letter on the very night of September 11. He had gone to the theater with Rachele, on one of the rare occasions when he offered his wife a break from her domestic duties. As they were leaving the playhouse, he had been given a message:

"My dear comrade, the die is cast. I am leaving now. Tomorrow morning I will take Fiume by force of arms. May Italy's God help us. I got out of bed feverish. But it cannot be put off. Once again the spirit will conquer the miserable flesh. Recap the article that the *Gazzetta del Popolo* is going to publish, and print the end in its entirety. And support the cause vigorously during the battle. I embrace you." The Vate addressed Benito Mussolini affectionately, embraced him on paper, he kept him aware of things (even if after the fact), but he was publishing his proclamation to the world in another newspaper. In essence, the message was a dispatch in which instructions are issued to a subordinate.

In the following days, Mussolini, as a disciplined lieutenant, had acclaimed the shining hero from the columns of *Il Popolo d'Italia*, pledging obedience to him; he had insulted Nitti, who in a parliamentary speech threatened to repress the rebels; he had upheld both the nobility and rationality of D'Annunzio's action, but he had not launched an appeal for general insurrection, as D'Annunzio would have liked and, above all, he had not moved from Milan's sidelines. The meeting of the fasci committee on September 16th had ended without any plan to violate the government blockade around Fiume. To make things difficult for the blockaders, they had merely proposed sending women and children to the border.

A week later the second letter from the Commander had arrived from Fiume:

My dear Mussolini, I am astounded by you and by the Italian people. I risked everything, I gained everything. I am the ruler of Fiume . . . And you are shaking with fear! You are allowing the most abject charlatan ever represented in the history of universal scum to put his swinish foot on your neck. Any other country—even Lapland—would have overthrown that man, those men. And you stand there yakking, while we struggle from moment to moment . . . Where are the Arditi, the soldiers, the volunteers, the Futurists? You don't even help us with fundraising and collections. We have to do everything ourselves, impoverished as we are. Wake up! You should be ashamed . . . Is there really nothing to hope for? What about your promises? At least stick a knife in the belly of your oppressor and deflate it. Otherwise I will come and do it myself once I have consolidated my power here. But I won't give you a glance.

A real whipping for the unfaithful servant. Mussolini had had to censor the letter, as Nitti the "cop" did with all the news coming from Fiume, before publishing it in *Il Popolo d'Italia*. Then the fasci's founder had had to grin and bear it: he had licked the wounds of his injured pride and obeyed. The fundraising for Fiume was launched on September 19th. Even then, however, Mussolini did not leave Milan. The reason was simple: Nitti's government had faltered but it had not fallen. The "swine," the "cop," the "ambitious cold-hearted despot," the "callous bootlicker of the Anglo-American plutocracies," the slave to bankers and industrialists, the "ragpicker," had traded heroism for ignobility, but he had not fallen. Mussolini, therefore, at risk of being crushed by raison d'état for serving as underling to D'Annunzio's visions, had preferred his lover, a gondola, Venice.

Now, in a dark votive chapel behind the church of San Lorenzo, under a narrow portico, Sarfatti shows him a pink marble paving stone, worn smooth and gleaming. Four hundred years earlier, popular devotion had considered that massive *masegno* of Istrian stone the spot where the merciful mother of God is said to have ended the plague. There had been a hecatomb: a third of the population wiped out. Doctors went around protected by monstrous masks with a hooked beak. Pyres of cadavers burned in front of baroque churches.

He, superstitious as always, touches the paving stone with the sole of his shoe. A shiver of worlds ending is transmitted to his syphilitic body, radiating up through his calves. Why doesn't he go too? Why not offer everything he has to the Commander? Why not send the young generation? Why are there still pestilences?

Because the army has not moved, because Nitti has not fallen; because the Anglo-American plutocrats, the bankers, the steelworkers whose feet Nitti was licking were indispensable; because if he sent his limited number of fasci to Fiume, there would be none left in Milan; because he was still struggling to reconcile with the interventionist left; because the navy sided with D'Annunzio but the army was divided; because its median ranks certainly sympathized with the rebels, but the high commands were hostile to them; because there were still four hundred thousand steelworkers on strike shouting "down with D'Annunzio!"; because the "march on the interior" that D'Annunzio was yearning for would likely pave the way for a communist revolution and because, even if he led them to Rome, he, Benito Mussolini, would only have figured in the unacceptable role of supporting actor to the glorious Commander. And so for all these reasons Benito Mussolini was not going to Fiume, and for a hundred others, but above all because D'Annunzio excited the bored young idealists, the decadent scions of a sated, exhausted bourgeoisie, who might well be willing to risk their lives but not to make their own beds. The Vate, with the magic of those hysterical, bewitching inspirations of his, elevated them to something superior and ineffable, magically uniting the orator and his listeners in a category of chosen ones that soared in a kind of first-class festive spirituality above the filthy combat trenches in which ordinary men lived, slaughtering each other in a perennial feud whose origin they had forgotten, dehumanized by drudgery, dulled by the slow digestion of pitiable meals, addicted to wine, only eager to loot, drink themselves into a stupor and fuck. He did not leave for the highly vaunted gulf of Carnaro because, ultimately, D'Annunzio was a poet, and the biggest letdown that reality has in store for us is that it never resembles a poem. Mussolini, on the other hand, the son of Predappio's blacksmith, preferred reality. The coarse, steely, brutal kind, the unyielding type. He knew no other pleasure than that.

On the extreme edge of the labyrinth, at the Celestia landing, Venice opens onto the inner lagoon. Sarfatti points out the graceful cypresses of San Michele cemetery. Further on, Murano is already disappearing in the season's first fog, while Burano and Torcello are just a thought, hearsay. Farther out still, the Adriatic sea, Trieste, Fiume, Dalmatia.

Yes, it would be nice to wake up at dawn, drop everything, climb into a red spider and march on Rome at the head of the young generation, leading a column of soldiers, of twenty-year-olds, of Arditi. The poet's fierce delirium is fantastic, extravagantly so—it brings tears to your eyes—but it's not politics. Politics requires the gritty, ruthless courage of street brawls, not the breezy boldness of cavalry charges. Politics is the arena of vices, not virtues. The only virtue it requires is patience. To get to Rome, he must first perform in this senile parody, be heard by the council of elders, that handful of doddering, naive good-for-nothings who rule the world.

BENITO MUSSOLINI

FIUME, OCTOBER 7, 1919

THEY CLIMBED TO an altitude of 5,300 feet in a caliginous sky. They took off without notice from Novi Ligure airfield aboard an SVA, headed east. In misty haze, with a barely sufficient amount of fuel, they flew 190 minutes as the crow flies over the Adriatic to Grobnik airport. Waiting for them is a car sent by the Commander.

Benito Mussolini arrives in Fiume on October 7th, 1919, almost a month after the "sacred entry." The city where he lands is already cloaked in legend and enveloped in a fog of rumors. It is said that D'Annunzio intends to make it a base for a larger operation of conquest aimed at the east, towards Zadar, Dalmatia, Split. It is also said, with greater insistence, that the Commander is instead preparing a "march on the interior," towards the west, to Pula, Trieste, Venice and then up to Rome to terminate the Albertine Statute, topple the monarchy and establish a military dictatorship with the complicity of the Duke of Aosta. It seems he had concocted this plan with his collaborators as early as September 19, and that he disclosed it at the end of the month to the officers of the first armored squadron at whose table he was hosted. Edmondo Mazzucato immediately informed Mussolini of it in Milan. Others maintain that the Vate's sole purpose is to bring down Nitti's despised government and support the rise of a new executive committee made up of soldiers that will immediately proclaim Italy's annexation of Fiume.

What is certain is that until now the Commander has not moved.

The army, apart from individual defections of men and units, hasn't made a move. Nitti, stolid and calculating, hasn't abandoned his post either. Instead, he reacted to D'Annunzio's coup by convening the Consiglio della Corona, the Crown Council, composed of eminent politicians, former presidents and heads of the armed forces. The assembly of old has-beens preferred to stall; no one spoke in favor of annexation. Nitti, therefore, chose his only option: he dissolved the parliament and called for new elections. His tactic is an age-old one: overcome the enemy by starving him. The embargo around Fiume barely allows the city to breathe, tightening a rope around her neck. The country, as usual, is deadlocked, going aimlessly in circles. The poetic raptures of D'Annunzio's men, on the other hand, require constant movement, hot blood passionately pumping through their hearts.

In broader circles, the Fiume venture has earned the enmity of Wilson, the president of the United States of America, the new great world power, the only true victor of the Great War. Wilson considers Fiume the caprice of an aged little boy that threatens to undermine the construction of the League of Nations, the grandiose juridical, diplomatic and humanitarian edifice which, in his vision, is to give the world a century of justice and peace. He despises D'Annunzio with the fervent indignation of a mature, responsible man towards a puerile pipedream that endangers the laborious work of a lifetime. Worse yet. Wilson abhors D'Annunzio. Son of a reverend, son-in-law of a cult minister, chancellor of Princeton University, an academic and puritan, a rigid, austere, captive of integral evangelism, a prophet of good tidings that will triumph over evil purifying the earth, Wilson is the type of man who has probably never cheated on his wife. In his eyes D'Annunzio is a hardened sinner, a destroyer of bourgeois morality, sowing sin is his only calling. It is said that Wilson considers the Italians' enthusiasm for the invocations to the "god of all men," with which for years D'Annunzio has been inaugurating his public prayers, to be an expression of the total lunacy of the Italian people. It is said that the American president erupts into fits of horror when his advisers summarize the contents of the poet's licentious works for him, albeit in a toned-down version. It is even said that the stroke which afflicted him on October 2nd was the result of rage over the man who dares to defy him boasting of having fornicated with hundreds of women.

D'Annunzio, meanwhile, swings between sublime ecstasies and apocalyptic fervor. He renamed Fiume "Holocaust City," a name of biblical tragedy for a small, sleepy Middle European port renowned for its patisseries. On October 5th he wrote to Mussolini with this threat: "If the city is not returned to its conditions of normal life, in ten days I will cast the die again. If the martyred city is still martyred, I will avenge her with a massive retaliation."

Mussolini also vacillates. At the end of September, having returned from his trip to Venice, he seemed to have unreservedly embraced the wild fanaticism. He wrote of a "revolution underway" which, launched in Fiume, could be concluded in Rome. He advised parliament to vote for annexation. He threatened them in turn: "Either annexation very soon or civil war between the soldiers' Italy and that of the parasites." Then, however, at the beginning of October, he sent Michele Bianchi to Fiume to restrain the Commander. In the continuous temperature changes, there is only one thermometer impossible to ignore: since D'Annunzio has been in Fiume, the newspaper's sales have continued to rise steadily.

Wilson is right: Fiume is a delirium. The car in which Mussolini enters the city for the first time on October 7th moves slowly through the crowds' enthusiastic demonstrations. It's Tuesday but it seems like Sunday, it's autumn but it seems like mid-August Ferragosto, it's already evening but it seems like high noon. The whole city appears orgasmic. The human climate is like an open-air orgy. The unbridled lust of the seducer pervades it. Soldiers, sailors, women, townsmen, variously clustered, eddy about to the rhythm of military fanfare. At every corner, groups of Arditi ardently vow on their unsheathed daggers; girls parade by decked in garlands like votive statues or dressed up like boys in borrowed uniforms; the walls are scrawled with graffiti declaring "I don't give a damn!" Even regimental decorum has vanished. Infantrymen go around with their uniform jackets open, collar gaping, neck exposed. Some have the front fastened by black frogging, the jackets trimmed with braid, but they've adorned the fezzes with silver stars and use the colored ribbons of the medals of valor in odd ways, like polychrome glaze adorning nothing. Everything is bizarre, unusual, exciting. But there's something grim about this celebration. The youth of the century, having escaped death for four years in trenches throughout Europe, rather than returning to thrift, family, religion, ancestors, virtue, day-to-day life, seems to have drifted to Fiume, prey to an obsession to put an end to this stupid, pointless life.

The talk between Mussolini and D'Annunzio lasts an hour and a half. This second meeting, like the one that took place in Rome on June 26th, has no witnesses. On the threshold of the command center, however, before announcing him, D'Annunzio's orderly officer, with his one arm, detains Mussolini for a few seconds. His name is Ulisse Igliori, an infantry lieutenant, maimed in the Great War, and interned for ten months in Mauthausen; he was decorated with a gold medal for heroism demonstrated on May 16th, 1916, in an assault on Austrian positions on Mount Maronia, where the enemies picked him up dismembered but still alive on a pile of bleeding corpses. The one-armed hero, future founder of the A.S. Roma, wants to know what the visitor thinks about the prospect of a march on Rome. Mussolini is still wearing the white outfit of an amateur aviator. From under his visored cap, he replies that Rome is the ultimate goal but the whole matter depends on choosing the moment:

"Italians are not yet prepared for this event; the initiative, if immature, could degenerate into an immense tragedy. We must feel the pulse of the nation, and I will do it when I return."

It's the same cold water that Mussolini threw on the Commander's fire in a letter of September 25: march on Trieste, declare the monarchy ended, appoint a directorate with D'Annunzio as president, form a constituent assembly, declare the annexation of Fiume, send trusted troops to disembark in Romagna to provoke a republican uprising. That is the plan that Mussolini proposed to D'Annunzio. Then, however, he added that it was necessary to postpone everything until after the November 16 elections. This, therefore, was his advice: a laughable postponement to defuse the drama.

Towards evening, Fiume is completely bedecked with flowers.

The "Holocaust City" is preparing to bury its first dead. Their names are Giovanni Zeppegno, a carabinieri brigadier, and Aldo Bini, a lieutenant observer. They crashed in a reconnaissance flight to Sussak. Bini, recovered still alive but with burns on virtually the entire surface of his body, died shortly thereafter; Zeppegno, thrown from the cockpit, died on the spot, impaled on the spike of a fence surrounding a cottage.

Since morning, in preparation for the ceremony, the residents of Fiume have been frantically searching for flowers. They'd worked all night, hands folding leaves and braiding laurel wreaths. Flower vendors were sold out before noon. Greenhouses were looted. When supplies were exhausted, people moved on to parks and private gardens. Not in living memory—a local reporter notes—has Fiume seen so many garlands in a mortuary chapel.

The funeral procession is resplendent with colors. Flowers, flags, uniforms. It's endless. Two platoons of sharpshooters lead the march, followed by city organizations and a band. Immediately behind the marksmen and the band, a formation of children. And behind the children, the hearses, completely covered in wreaths. On either side of the hearses march the wounded and decorated war heroes. Behind the marksmen, the band, the children, the war veterans and flowers, comes the Commander. Surrounded by his staff officers. At the end, two more large vans heaped with flowers to be placed on and around the graves. Finally, people from all walks of life: soldiers and railwaymen, politicians and teachers, firefighters and musicians, workers and gymnasts, thousands of Fiume residents. The entire city population of Italian bloodline.

The procession culminates in Piazza Dante, filled to capacity; the scene is solemn. Mussolini is present, mingling with the crowd. Everyone is wearing his Sunday finery, while he still has on his comical aviator suit. It's clear that the entire populace is at the theater, though the theater has poured into the streets. He, a spectator, looks on and notes every detail. When D'Annunzio starts to speak, the whole city of the living suddenly turns into a graveyard:

"Glory to the winged pair that has offered the first holocaust of liberty to the City of Holocaust!"

The speaker is alone on the balcony, minute, remote. But his words resound clearly in the large square, wrapped in a sepulchral silence. D'Annunzio speaks without any amplification system, only the air from his lungs thrust by the diaphragm towards the trachea and then the larynx. The effort gives his voice a metallic resonance, almost a falsetto. Yet it reaches the immense piazza, holds it spellbound. The thousands and thousands who are listening seem almost not to be living and breathing. He's made them a people of wraiths. The poet speaks under a luminous full moon. Some weep. It is an intense weeping. He praises the evening for its pure death.

"Glory to the two heavenly messengers, who in the span of brief hours taught our spirit how this life we live may be eternal life."

A lie. Colossal, shameless, pronounced at the solemn ceremony. This life, incinerated by fire, in a crash caused by an inept maneuver, impaled by accident on the tip of a spike adorning the gate of a cottage, this is supposed to be eternal life!? A poison monger. The poet's words make their way through the air, like nerve gas, into the crowd's pulmonary alveoli. People give in to it, numbed, poisoned by the lie as if by a systemic toxin.

Then the poison monger veers and awakens them all from the spell:

"Citizens of Fiume, bare your heads. Soldiers of Italy, present arms." And they do it. All the men take off their hats, all the soldiers hold up their rifles.

"My pilots, cloak the two coffins." And they cloak them.

"People of Fiume, gentlemen of the council, we consign these first of our dead to the sacred earth, to the free earth. Watch over them." Now the Commander is no longer speaking to an audience, he is engaging with the crowd. At every word of his, the piazza responds, with actions or with words. The theater is in the streets, the whole city is at the theater but it went there to watch itself.

"*A chi la morte*?" the poet shouted, who is ready to die?

"*A noi!*" We are! A corresponding, huge roar echoes him from the piazza.

The novice aviator takes note.

AMERIGO DÙMINI

FLORENCE, OCTOBER 10, 1919
TEATRO OLIMPIA

THEY HAVE BEEN waiting for him for hours in front of the station of Santa Maria Novella. Benito Mussolini, however, wasn't on the midnight train either.

But for Amerigo Dùmini, waiting has never been a problem. Waiting and being still. It's easy for him. He stands stock-still inside that massive body of his, a stocky, solid figure, slightly bent, his thick, black hair slicked over a low forehead; his eyes are fixed, opaque, as if focused on just one thought. He stands there, silent, for hours even, and if he really must talk, he speaks in a low voice. He smokes and drinks. As he did in the dolines of the Karst under fire from the howitzers, he takes out his flask, holds it with his rigid left hand, unscrews it with his good hand and downs a couple of sips of grappa. Many criticize him for not talking much. They tell him that people are afraid of men like him, capable of going into a cafe and not saying a word for hours, staring into space. Men like that are killjoys.

His drinking and brawling buddy, Umberto Banchelli, known as the "Mago" (wizard), smoked and drank like him, but he fidgeted the whole time, incapable of being quiet even though he stutters painfully. While they waited for Mussolini to arrive on the midnight train, the Mago couldn't help telling his war stories yet again: at sixteen he went with the Garibaldians to fight against the Turks in Epirus, at twenty he was a colonel in Serbia, at twenty-five a non-commissioned officer of the Italian army rotting away with malaria in Albania. He never once stopped talking about his wars, and cursing God for the train delays.

Not Dùmini. He gladly keeps quiet. If a man has something to drink and smoke he's never bored. A man can wait his whole life even, as long as he can drink and smoke. That's what life is for Amerigo Dùmini: the period of time in which we are alive. That's it. Waiting and not talking. Since the war ended, he feels like he's done nothing else.

Nothing good is happening in Florence. Eleven contingents were demobilized between March and October and there's no work. In the countryside the strikes are so violent that the carabinieri have to rush in. Incidents are on the increase in front of factories closed for lockout. Children are begging at the open-air market of the Cascine and in the streets of Careggi. Of the comrades who had wanted war in 1914, not many are left. Those few have come back shattered: wounded, emotionally disturbed, reduced to begging. They are split among dozens of patriotic associations. Some have founded the "Futurist Political Fascio." A lot of noise, a few weird notions. Patriotic education for the proletariat, an assembly of young people under the age of thirty in place of the Senate, compulsory gymnastics with penal sanctions for slackers. That's the political program. In November those fanciful futurists launched out against a demonstration of thousands of "reds," then held a rally in Piazza Vittorio Emanuele. There were thirteen of them.

Other disgruntled veterans gather at Via Maggio 38, at the home of a wounded aristocrat, a former infantryman at the Karst. There is talk of an armed organization to stem the tide of red leagues. The machine gun is the favorite topic of discussion. Or there's the Countess Collacchioni's association, "Italy and Vittorio Emanuele," that meets with Count Guicciardini, Marquis Peruzzi de' Medici and Marquis Perrone Compagni in the contessa's living room. The countess is very kind in welcoming even agitated commoners to join those composed, elegant, cultured gentlemen. Banchelli gladly goes there. The countess calls him "my golden squire." The Mago waddles into the rooms of those palazzi, feet shuffling, and, serious as can be, babbles about his war exploits to those peers and marquises. But it's all talk. Of that there's plenty.

There is the National Servicemen's Association that wants to take back the jobs performed during the war by wives ("Away with the women! Let the women knit!"); there's the Association of the Arditi, the volunteers of despair, and the Association of the Wounded and Disabled, sprinkled with charlatans, impostors, and blind seers; and then there's the Liberal Union, the Anti-Bolshevik League, not to mention the "Citizens' Defense Alliance," financed with money from the agrarians. There attorney Francesco Giunta was able to organize gangs. During the July riots over the high cost of living, they protected the merchants' fabrics and other products against communist workers on the one hand, while on the other hand looting them with the excuse that the merchants were profiting from the prices. Giunta himself, waving a pair of shoes for which he paid as much as 48 liras, led the looting of the Ploner shoe factory. Never before had so many people been seen in the streets of Florence armed with flasks of wine as in those days.

In Florence, in short, everyone rants and raves, no one keeps quiet, and a growing feeling of betrayal is widespread. When emboldened workers hear a dapper gentleman in an officer's uniform with a monocle in his eye boasting about his exploits on his way out of the Café Paszkowski, they are convinced that the war was merely an opportunity to profit on the backs of the poor, and they spit in his face. On the other side are the petite bourgeoisie, who had perhaps commanded a platoon at the front, bringing home a ribbon of valor or a medal, and who now in civilian life, unemployed and worthless, spat upon by their former subordinates, feel even more betrayed. When all is said and done, the disillusionment is mutual and universal between bourgeoisie and proletarians. The victorious war has left everyone tasting the bile of defeat.

Now hopes are on Mussolini, the herald of interventionism. After waiting for him in vain the whole evening at the station of Santa Maria Novella, Dùmini, Banchelli and the other Florentine ex-Arditi are still waiting for him the following morning at the

Teatro Olimpia, on Via dei Cimatori, for the first national assembly of the Fasci di Combattimento.

The Fasci di Combattimento in Florence don't amount to much. The first meeting took place at the end of April in Piazza Ottaviani, at the Association of Servicemen. The founding members were quickly forgotten. The reconstitution of the fascio took place at the end of June, again in Piazza Ottaviani. A group of twenty-seven people took part. A directorate of three members was appointed, proportionate to the number of participants: one board member for every nine persons.

The meeting started half an hour ago. The room is small, adorned with tricolor flags, Tuscan regiment banners, black pennants, and signs hailing Fiume's liberation; the first rows have been reserved for delegates from the other parties. They haven't come either. The public consists of a few hundred people. It's already ten o'clock and there's still no sign of Mussolini. But the Founder wouldn't miss the event and besides he, Dùmini Amerigo, knows how to wait. He lights another cigarette and knocks back a swig of grappa.

On stage Umberto Pasella, secretary general of the movement, pudgy and prosaic, dressed in shades of gray, called upon to entertain the audience awaiting Mussolini, suddenly shifts from a business-like tone to a more emotional one. He stops, looks up and raises his arms to a blind, wounded war veteran, Carlo Delcroix, who with his military escort, is watching from a balcony box next to the stage. Everyone stands. To accept the audience's applause without losing his balance, the veteran lets his caregiver lift him up: in addition to his sight, he's missing both forearms. Waving without arms, Delcroix speaks, vowing to his fascist brothers that the wounded "will sign the death sentence for cowards with their stumps." Ovation. Everyone sits down again. Pasella resumes the inane tone of a salesman.

Then, however, another round of applause explodes in the room. Pasella falls silent again. From the back of the theater, Benito Mussolini is making his entrance. He takes long strides towards the stage. He is followed by the leader of the Futurists, Filippo Tommaso Marinetti, wearing a bowler on his head; then comes Ferruccio

Vecchi, in a black shirt and gray-green military coat, his chest covered with decorations, and a tall, hefty young man in civvies.

A single chorus of general elation rises in the hall, another of D'Annunzio's many slogans adopted by the fascists: "Long live our Duce! *Eja, eja, eja, alalà*, hurray for Benito Mussolini!"

Despite the enthusiastic reception, the fasci's founder appears tired, unshaven, wearing an odd white jumpsuit covered with grease stains and a comical visored cap a cyclist might wear.

Pasella steps aside. Mussolini goes up on stage. He smiles indulgently, jokes with those in the first rows. He purses his lips as if he wanted to send kisses from afar. He sways on his legs, hands on hips. He has to ask for silence several times with quick jerks of his outstretched hand. Then, finally, he speaks:

"Forgive me for the delay. I just landed. I was in Fiume yesterday, the city of miracle and portent!"

Hearing him name Fiume, the city of D'Annunzian legend, the Jerusalem promised by the poet-warrior to all patriots and adventurers throughout Italy and Europe, the few hundred fascists gathered in the Teatro Olimpia burst out in thunderous applause. Everyone applauds. Even Amerigo Dùmini applauds, smacking the palm of his good hand on the back of his rigid one.

When the applause dies down, Mussolini talks about evading the government blockade by flying at high altitude with a war ace, about speaking for three hours with D'Annunzio, about being forced to make an emergency landing near Udine on the way back, about being arrested by the carabinieri, about resuming his flight after a meeting with General Badoglio. And now here he is, having just climbed out of the cockpit, having come straight down from the sky to the stage of this small local theater on Via dei Cimatori. The audience cheers ecstatically.

BENITO MUSSOLINI

FLORENCE, OCTOBER 10, 1919
TEATRO OLIMPIA

IT WAS A really brilliant idea to show up in his aviator's suit. The audience at the rally seems to be thrilled by it. A small solitary blessing.

The evening before, when he arrived at the station of Santa Maria Novella on the last train of the night, there was no longer anyone waiting for him. Finding himself alone, he was able to conveniently make his way to the Hotel Baglioni and get a good night's sleep. The following morning Marinetti arrived to wake him, insisting that the assembly, which had already started a while ago, wanted to see Mussolini at all costs, and he, instead of putting on clean clothes, had a flash of inspiration and wore the grease-stained white flight suit again.

His flight back from Fiume had ended at the Aiello airfield, near Udine. The pilot, Lombardi, to avoid being stopped by the carabinieri, had dropped off his passenger and resumed the flight without ever turning off the engine. Mussolini had been led to General Pietro Badoglio, military special commissioner for Venezia Giulia. Although publicly everyone proclaimed they were ready to die to assert Fiume's *italianità*, in private to the general—who had had his share of infamy in the defeat at Caporetto and his taste of glory in the victory at Vittorio Veneto—Mussolini had said he was in favor of a compromise, even suggesting that D'Annunzio himself could have accepted solutions other than that of annexation; he also recommended that censure be relaxed and that the rebellious city be given economic support. After that brief talk between reasonable men, Badoglio, reassured, had let him go with no problem and the fasci founder had been able to catch the last train to Florence.

Now the fascists in the theater are hypnotized by the grease stains on his suit. The spellbound way they stare at it gives the impression they're trying to divine the geography of an unexplored continent. There aren't many of them. Pasella publicly declares 137 sections, 40,000 members. It is a ridiculous lie. Mussolini declares 56 sections, 17,000 members. But that's a lie too. The Founder knows it: the sections probably number a few dozen and the members a few thousand. In any case, a far cry from the 1,000 fasci predicted in March as well as from the 300 hoped for in July. They are few and they are surrounded by hostility. The socialists hate them; the republicans would like them to be more decisive on the anti-monarchy question; the monarchists would like to drop it, the bourgeoisie smile, pleased at their violence, but curse them under their breath when they read about the decimation of wealth in their programs; the nationalists value their patriotism but denounce their residual socialism; the democrats consider them extremists. The only ones the fascists get along with are the Arditi and the war veterans.

His adversaries are many, the enemies few, and Benito Mussolini does not intend to preclude any possibility. To the audience at the Teatro Olimpia, mesmerized by his grease stains, he declares that the fascists are "antidoctrinal, problematist, dynamic." Their watchwords are those of futurism: synthetic, cheerful, swift, presentist, practical, modern. The fictitious aviator just back from Fiume emphasizes what the fascists are not: they are not republican, socialist, democrat, conservative, nationalist. Instead, they are a synthesis of all affirmations and all negations. We fascists, he concludes, have no preconceived ideas, our only doctrine is action.

On one point Mussolini is adamant:

"We do not intend to be considered a kind of bodyguard for a bourgeoisie, particularly the nouveau riche class, that is simply undeserving and vile. If these people cannot defend themselves, they should not hope to be defended by us."

Cesare Rossi and Michele Bianchi are now openly urging him to shift to the right, to forget any pipedream of forming a bloc of leftist interventionists, but he persists. We must maintain our ties to our old comrades, he counters. At least to those who were for the war. Isolation must be avoided at all costs. The people are not lost, we just need to unseat the bourgeois hot-air blowhards leading them and jump onto the saddle. The people are better than their leaders. The people loved Benito Mussolini and will do so again.

Marinetti speaks after him. He demands nothing less than the "de-Vaticanization of Italy," the replacement of the Senate with a "stirring body" made up of twenty-year-olds, the acclamation of intellectuals, and free entry to art exhibitions. The bizarre Futurist program entertains the audience but the political rally already ended a while ago. Outside, waiting for them, are the people, the people that Mussolini deludes himself he hasn't lost. And they are armed with stones.

At aperitif time Mussolini is with his men at an outdoor table of Gambrinus. A scuffle breaks out among workers returning from the job on tram number 15. After the banquet at the Servicemen's Association, the fascists have stopped for one-for-the-road at the Café Paszkowski. All the other bars in Piazza Vittorio, anticipating riots, have already lowered their shutters. The police crisscross the streets on patrol, personally led by the police chief. Mussolini and his men have not yet sat down at the outdoor tables when revolver shots are fired. The group of socialist workers begin booing them. Wicker seats go flying. Chairs, blows, punches are thrown. In the confusion, an anarchist who at one time had been an admirer of his, manages to get close to Mussolini's table and hurls a handful of copper coins at him, the price of betrayal. He has to be escorted to the Hotel Baglioni. The group of fascists closes ranks and sets out with the Founder in the middle, acting as his shield. Leandro Arpinati, a tall, hefty young railway worker, an ex-anarchist from Forlì, who accompanied his Leader to the Teatro Olimpia that morning, watches his back. In front of the Hotel Baglioni, more pursuits, more brawling, more beatings. The fascists finally manage to enter the hotel. They have a few drinks in the salon. The piazza is strewn with rocks.

On the morning of October 11, Mussolini is finally able to leave Florence, driven out, in fact, by the hostility of "his" people. He leaves by car, headed for Romagna, for the paternal home. Driving the vehicle is Guido Pancani, a pilot famous for his exploits as an aviator during the war. In the passenger seat is Gastone Galvani, Pancani's brother-in-law, and in the back, along with Mussolini, Leandro Arpinati of Bologna.

He and Arpinati have known each other since the young man was a defiant boy and Mussolini the head of Romagna's socialists. Sitting side by side, they recall the days when the eighteen-year-old anarchist went to challenge the secretary of the federation of Forlì. It was 1910 and in Civitella di Romagna, Bombacci's same town, they were opening a covered market named for Andrea Costa, the patriarch of Italian socialism whom the anarchists considered a traitor because he had been the first to agree to being elected to the king's parliament. The mob crowded below the stage of the prestigious orator from Forlì. Arpinati and his pals, dressed in black from head to toe, waited against a wall, ready to trigger a fight. Mussolini had looked them up and down, eyes blazing, then held the briefest rally of his life. "Imitate the example of Andrea Costa," was all he'd said, "the carrion-eaters don't count." When he stepped down from the stage, however, he and that gang of eighteen-year-old "vultures" had become friends.

Now, as they reminisce, the car speeds past Faenza. Florence's protesting workers, the same ones who ten years earlier had acclaimed him when he headed the socialists of Romagna, are behind them. The travelers stop for coffee, then resume their journey. The man they threw copper coins at dozes off. The wartime pilot shifts into high gear. The trail of betrayal fades in the engine's roar. Hurtling along at top speed, the car crashes into the lowered bars of a grade crossing.

The passengers are thrown several yards away, like rag dolls. It could all end here, in a moment of distraction, in front of an overlooked grade crossing. Pancani and his brother-in-law, lying in a ditch, cry out in pain. Arpinati is bruised. But Mussolini comes through unscathed. Treated at a nearby hospital, he resumes his journey with his old friend. He will tell himself that his enemies' hatred served him as a lucky charm.

Re your 27644. Mussolini back from Fiume landed today Aiello airfield. Accompanied here had long talk with me that he promised to keep quiet. He expressly told me that if planned solution meets no D'Annunzio opposition he will vigorously support it in his newspaper. As for D'Annunzio's intentions re said plan, Mussolini made no declaration, but I seemed to see signs he is convinced D'Annunzio is also not adamant about annexation as sole solution.

Telegram from General Pietro Badoglio
to Prime Minister Francesco Saverio Nitti,
Udine, October 8, 1919

We have no allies. The Fasci di Combattimento only get along with the Arditi and the war veterans.

Benito Mussolini,
Il Popolo d'Italia, October 6, 1919

BENITO MUSSOLINI

MILAN, LATE OCTOBER 1919

THEY FORCED HIM into looking pathetic. In front of hundreds of people. At a public assembly, at the Via Rossari schools.

He had convinced everyone that they could not vote for the governing parties bloc in the upcoming elections, not even as anti-socialists. He had talked himself hoarse. Fascism, he'd said, is a progressive movement, dynamic, youthful, spirited, born to rejuvenate Italian politics and open it to the participation of the masses. It could not support liberals, democrats, nationalists. Those were antiquated ideas to be "put into liquidation," the continent of has-beens. Fascism was the refuge of all heretics, the church of all heresies. The bigots of all churches should be spurned, without regard. Fascism was a unique mentality of unrest, intolerance, boldness, which seldom looked back at the past and which used the present as a springboard for momentum towards the future. And the future takes no prisoners.

Then, however, Umberto Pasella had stood up, and with his usual way of beating around the bush, had made it clear that the possibility of the fascists forming an electoral bloc with the leftist interventionists was once again chancy. The reason was the same as always: they did not want Mussolini on the ticket. They were afraid it would enrage all the socialists.

The outcast, who until then had fought with all he had for that alliance, had then had to try to convince everyone that it had become unfeasible. Benito Mussolini, with an acrobatic twist, made a 180-degree flip and shouted himself hoarse again, this time against the alliance. More contortions, spasms, more frenzy. He could also have agreed not to run on a fascist ticket, but he couldn't tolerate being banned from an interventionist list because he himself had been the prophet of intervention, he had endured beatings from the police, during the war he had taken fifty-six mortar fragments over his entire body. It was unacceptable. The interventionist left was incarnated in him, scarred in his flesh. And besides, they were fooling themselves: the socialists would certainly not stop him if they presented a list of unknowns.

But this time he did not persuade them. The personal circumstance was too obvious. Someone, taking advantage of an oratorial pause, stood up and challenged him: "Why didn't you come and tell us these things at the assembly two days ago?" At that point he had been forced into sounding pathetic.

"Because my son was dying!" he'd exclaimed, clenching his fists.

Every adult man in the hall had then stood up and applauded the distraught father. A good half of them would no longer dare vote against him. That's how it went at those meetings: you had to take advantage of whatever feeling was needed wherever you found it. Always theater, even when the feeling was sincere. Indeed, especially then.

And his anguish truly was sincere. For two whole days, his wife Rachele had seen him devastated, his face unrecognizable. He stood there, frozen in a convulsive spasm over the cradle of his son Bruno; the man of action, feared, admired or hated, completely crushed by the threat looming over that tiny creature, barely eighteen months old, his infant face livid, asphyxial, nearly strangled. The baby had been struck by a severe form of diphtheria, his tonsils reddened, swollen, a very high fever quickly complicated by bronchopneumonia, and his father stood there stock-still, paralyzed with anguish, mentally contemplating the bacilli that have penetrated the upper respiratory tract, the false membranes that, hour after hour, had formed on top of one another on the tiny larynx causing the child's asphyxiation. The difficulty in breathing progressed, until it became noisy, choking into a whistle, and he, the Founder of the Fasci di Combattimento, could do nothing more than stand stooped over watching the small gasping mouth that was barely breathing.

It was always that way with illnesses. The internal enemy's assaults terrified him because they were not projected out in the open in any theater of war. You could not face them bravely because they did not allow for any audience, any stage, because with them there was no theater.

It was Rachele who made a difference. She was an uneducated woman. She was twenty-nine years old and was just learning to read and write. She incorrectly signed her notes "bachi" instead of "baci" for kisses, and insisted on specifying on the back of her letters that she was the sender, writing "*spedisse Rachele Mussolini*," gliding over the sibilant "s's" of the Romagna dialect. He had wanted her, seized by the irresistible urge of sexual desire. She was his stepmother's youngest daughter. Girlish, blonde, shapely. One evening he'd dragged her before his father and his second wife, through the tables of the tavern they kept in Forlì, and had threatened to kill her and then kill himself if they didn't give her to him. They'd given her to him.

Rachele Guidi was an ignorant woman, having never gone to school. She hadn't even understood that little Bruno might die. She'd downplayed it, only a little bit of a cold. It had been Sarfatti, his lover, not his wife, who realized it. As soon as he'd described the child's symptoms to her, to excuse his being late for a secret tryst, she pronounced: "It's diphtheria! Take a taxi, hurry and call a doctor." Dr. Binda—an old family friend who had previously treated Mussolini for war wounds—had put a tube down the baby's throat and urged both parents to hope that the child wouldn't dislodge it. In a family of professed atheists, in fact, one couldn't even pray. He, the anguished father, then, had simply hoped, turning to the wall.

Rachele, however, despite her ignorance, had held her son in her arms for twenty-four hours, pacing back and forth in the dark corridor, to give him a breath of relief. She was a good woman, a good mother. She had already given him three children. In her arms, Bruno had begun to breathe again. Only at that moment, as if by magic, had breath returned to him as well.

But it was black magic, evil. A spell for loss, a circular deception. All it took was one invisible bacillus to settle on the pharyngeal mucosa and a newborn infant was already dead. The slightest thing was all it took to carry them away. The "Spanish" influenza was suffocating millions in their cradles. This tenuous life of theirs was all a deceitful pretense, all show, even this farce about elections, this waiting for a messiah to come out of the ballot box. As if a mountain of cards checked by a pencil mark could make up for history's violence.

He, deceitful in turn, had even written to D'Annunzio, who was itching to march on Rome, and advised that they wait for the result of the elections. The fasci's founder continued telling the Commander that they absolutely had to wait until November 16, because that day—he was sure—they would get a huge plebiscite for Fiume, that day new people would emerge from the electoral rallies.

In actuality he was just stalling for time. The elections were only a mousetrap, camouflage. Nothing would come out of the electoral rallies—of this he was certain—the ballot box would come up empty. Tough weapons had to be readied again. Rather than voting, whoever gathered around this flag had to prepare for a different victory, a bloody one.

Now he had decided. If the socialists hated him, if the comrades from the interventionist left didn't want him on the ticket, if the traditional governing parties were "antiquated" bodies to be disposed of, the fascists would run as candidates on their own. Backed by the Combattenti and the Arditi. Nobody else. He would head the ticket.

Sarfatti would mock at him. "What!? Until yesterday you said that you would never be a candidate in this electoral circus!"

Yes, of course, yesterday . . . But tomorrow is another day.

My dear D'Annunzio, Pedrazzi will have already told you what I think about the situation in general. Here we are sinking into a paper quagmire. It's sad but inevitable. The elections are a magnificent pretext for shrill, filthy socialist opportunism. For us they are a means of rallying and camouflage. I was finally able to put something together. We are organizing squads of twenty men each, armed and in a kind of uniform, both to demand our freedom of speech, as well as for other events, for which we await your orders. Overall, the situation is difficult and lacks coordination and synchronicity of movement. In the big cities, we will be easily overwhelmed by the socialist surge.

Letter from Benito Mussolini to Gabriele D'Annunzio,
October 30, 1919

GABRIELE D'ANNUNZIO

FIUME, OCTOBER 24, 1919

After sailing from La Spezia, then stopping in Messina to take comestibles on board before making for the open waters off the coast of Sicily—a sea smooth as glass populated by tuna and swordfish—the crew of the freighter *Persia*, instead of heading towards the Suez Canal and from there turning the prow towards the Far East, in the direction of Vladivostok or, perhaps, towards some Chinese port, suddenly changed tack. After sailing back up the Adriatic, the precious cargo of mountain artillery batteries, rifles, ammunition and provisions—intended to support the counterrevolutionary armies of the Cossack generals in Russia who had remained loyal to the tsar—therefore ended up arming the rebellion of the free city of Fiume.

Legend has it that the *Persia* was diverted by "Uskoks," D'Annunzio's pirates who have revived the exploits of the corsair wars in the Adriatic, raiding food supplies, boarding vessels and creating myths, in order to feed the city blockaded by regular troops of the Italian army. The truth is that the command to change course and sail to Fiume was issued to the crew of the hijacked steamer by Captain Giulietti, the powerful head of the Seaman's Federation, who allied with D'Annunzio on behalf of people's liberty and an elaborate face-off with the Italian government aimed at obtaining concessions for the workers of his union. The fact is that, as of the evening of October 14, with the *Persia* anchored in the port of Carnaro and the weapons intended for the White Army in the depots of D'Annunzio's legionnaires, the small town of Fiume entered the arena of global conflict between oppressed fledgling populations and the old lords of the world who insist on shaping the postwar scene without them.

On the other hand, in just over a month Fiume has already become a world of worlds, a free port for rebellion of all political sides, nationalist and internationalist, monarchist and republican, conservative and syndicalist, clerical and anarchist, imperialist and communist. Political, social and artistic avant-gardes throughout Europe are flocking to the wonderland of wonders: dreamers, libertarians, idealists, revolutionaries, nonconformists, adventurers, a horde of heroes and misfits, restless, eccentric talents, men of action and ascetics, down-and-outers with nothing to lose and millionaires in search of passion, violent youths and Parisian-style writers, vegetarian artists and reformed priests, Amazonians in military uniform and servicemen dressed up like ballerinas, Casanovas looking for female conquests and pederasts for boys. The amalgam is exciting, the bacchanal orgiastic, licentiousness the norm, excess absolute; the spectacle is continuous, the party uninterrupted. Individualism, piracy, eccentricity, transgression, drugs, sexual freedom, cosmopolitanism, feminism, homosexuality, and anarchism rank Fiume out of this world and, at the same time, above it. A single world is not enough. In the corridors of Rome's palazzi of power, politicians resort to the usual intrigues, plotting schemes, temporizing, proposing compromise solutions. That's the underworld. Fiume, in Gabriele D'Annunzio's vision, is the supra-world. There's no topping that.

Nitti's government, through his foreign minister Tittoni, proposes a diplomatic stratagem to the rebels: the city under Italian control, the port and the railway under that of the League of Nations. It is a pre-war ruse but Nitti can do no better. The politics of the masses is completely foreign to the interests of men of traditional power. For them, the people must be kept at a distance, at bay, in the doghouse, in a perpetual state of minority. The old has-beens have no clue as to what to do with popular consent, they don't understand it, they don't seek it, they don't find it. For them power is a canasta game played among old acquaintances at the table of an exclusive club somewhere on the hill.

D'Annunzio, on the contrary, is entirely committed to shaping the masses to his will. Confident in the assent of the people of Fiume to deal with the crisis resulting from the stalled negotiations, on October 16th he dissolves the city's municipal representation by imperium, calling for elections for a new City Council on October 26th. His plan is simple: October 30 marks the first anniversary of the proclaimed annexation of Fiume to Italy, which took place at the end of the war in the name of the city's Italian population. One year later, the election result will renew the solemn vow of the Fiumani by popular acclaim. The masses, if you pay attention to them, if you don't ignore them, are like that: you just have to lead them and they will follow.

The electoral propaganda culminates in a grandiose rally at the Teatro Verdi. On the evening of October 24, the theater is already packed two hours before the start. When the Commander appears at 9:00 p.m., he has a hard time getting silence. An overwhelming round of affectionate applause persists for at least fifteen minutes despite his repeated signals. When the poet finally manages to speak, it immediately becomes clear that something new has happened.

D'Annunzio begins by extolling Fiume's will to be Italian, a free city of free Italy. He dwells on the boundaries that the free nation should have with a cartographer's precision, meticulously listing regions and villages, islands and archipelagos, down to the last insignificant reef. So far it is the usual pedantic, impassioned nationalist speech. Then, however, it suddenly soars and veers towards a second take-off. The oration is entitled "Italy and life" but Fiume this evening is no longer just an Italian city, Fiume has magically become the beacon that will light up the world, the "spark of a new fire that would illuminate the West." Fiume, moreover, is no longer the "holocaust city"; like a priest who has again found God after a mid-life crisis of faith, D'Annunzio has now discovered a second vocation, the most difficult one: Fiume has become the "city of life."

As its administrator, D'Annunzio knows that the economic situation is worsening, that the port is a disaster, that basic necessities are becoming scarce, that the new currency is accelerating inflation, yet the gambler in him raises the stakes. The aviator pulls the control stick towards himself and proclaims that the great cause is the cause of the soul, of immortality. The speech climbs higher, gains altitude.

All insurgents of all stripes will gather under our insignia. And the defenseless will be armed. And force will be met with force. From Ireland's indomitable Sinn Féin to the green flag that in Egypt unites the Crescent and the Cross, all the insurrections of the spirit will be rekindled at our flame against the devourers of raw flesh. A new crusade is announced, of all indigent, free men against usurping nations that monopolize all wealth, against predatory races. Therefore our cause is the greatest and noblest that today stands in opposition to the insanity and vileness of this world. It is time to dive into the future.

As D'Annunzio speaks at the Teatro Verdi on October 24th, 1919, time hangs suspended, expanded to the point of tedium or condensed into an instant. It is not a tactical plan, it is not a strategy, it is not a man speaking to the Fiumani: it is an event. Its consequences are incalculable. Its charge has no objective, it is consummated in the gap between historical venture and puerile caprice; Fiume, the city of life, rotates forevermore on the axis of its backbone, like a dervish.

The elections mark a triumphant plebiscite in favor of the poet and his future.

BENITO MUSSOLINI

MILAN, NOVEMBER 11, 1919

IT HAS BEEN decided that the only Milan-based electoral rally of the Fasci di Combattimento will be held in Piazza Belgioioso, the elegant heart of the city, surrounded by stylish neoclassic buildings, a sort of outdoor salon of the aristocracy. Mussolini personally chose it during an on-site inspection a few days earlier: "This will be just fine," he decided within five minutes. He chose it because the square is open on one side only, making it suited to being defended in case of aggression.

The electoral campaign is unfolding in an atmosphere of danger and messianic expectation that has taken on the fanatical fervor of prayer. Socialist workers are attacking the rallies of anyone who had spoken in favor of the war in 1915. They attack them with the passion that the tormented have towards their tormentors. When interventionists of various kinds appear in the piazzas, the proletarian mob doesn't see political opponents in front of them, it sees enemies. Bissolati, the prestigious, upright leader of the moderate socialists, was prevented from speaking in the province of Cremona, only because he had stated his support for the war in 1915 and had then gone to fight himself, enlisting voluntarily at age sixty. The rally of republican Pietro Nenni in Meldola, Romagna, was interrupted by gunshots. In Sampierdarena the rally of socialist interventionist Giuseppe Canepa was cut short by bludgeons wielded by maximalist socialists.

To defend against probable attacks, Mussolini had a group of old republicans and anarchists brought from Romagna. He says he wants them beside him as an "Honor Guard and Death Squad." Among them is Leandro Arpinati, again assigned to watching his back. D'Annunzio sent sixty legionnaires and authorized Mussolini to employ others using funds raised for Fiume. Groups of fascists have come from nearby cities. Reimbursement for expenses was set at 30 liras for travel and an overnight stay. Roberto Farinacci, a railway worker who started the fascio of Cremona, demanded 100 liras instead of 30 for four of his men. He claims that they are felons ready for anything. Specialized personnel. Albino Volpi and other Arditi filled some backpacks with iron bars and grenades. Mussolini has given precise instructions: members of the fascist bloc are to pledge the utmost silence if asked to identify any disruptors; in case of any clashes, the uninvolved public will have to clear out quickly by way of Via Morone; no women and children; the rally will be brief. It will be held even in the event of rain.

The selection of candidacies was also swift. Once it was decided that the fascists would enter the race with their own ticket, it took no more than ten minutes. Some of the usual crew and a few illustrious names, all Combattenti. Of the 19 candidates, 18 fought at the front, including 7 volunteers, 5 silver medals, 8 wounded and 2 disabled. The prominent names, in addition to the one heading the ticket, are those of Filippo Tommaso Marinetti, the anticlerical Podrecca, labor leader Lanzillo, and industrialist De Magistris. Also on the ballot is Arturo Toscanini, the celebrated conductor and diligent member of the Milanese fascio. The maestro learned of being a candidate during an assembly in a school gym as he stood aside, leaning against a coat rack. Marinetti persuaded him to accept. Toscanini also financed the list to the tune of 30,000 liras. The platform is the same as that of San Sepolcro, cushioned in the socialist cocoon that Mussolini does not want to leave: abolition of the Senate, tax reform, decimation of wealth, confiscation of ecclesiastical assets, accommodation of the wounded, disabled and veterans, and an armed nation. The electoral symbol is a French-manufactured hand grenade, issued to the Arditi by the Italian army. The electoral manifesto promotes the "Thévenot Bloc" grenade, urging people to pin their vote on it.

The rally is scheduled for nine. At eight o'clock in the evening Piazza Belgioioso is still deserted, already dark. The residents who live in the buildings of the city center have stayed home. Then, little by little, a small crowd trickles through the cordon of Arditi stationed on the Corso Europa side, the only open side, and gathers below the improvised stage. It is a truck used for troop transport, covered with pennants and parked sideways to block access between Via Morone and the house where Alessandro Manzoni lived and died: the house where in 1848 young insurgents against the Austrian occupiers formed a delegation and went to implore Italy's greatest writer to come down to the streets and lead them to the barricades, and where the writer, instead, prematurely aged, drained by neurosis during long sleepless nights, sent them away, missing the day he had waited a lifetime for. In the glow provided by wind torches illuminating the scene in front of Manzoni's house, the profile of the fascist truck looks like a rostrum, the hooked beak of a huge bird ready to demolish the delicate facade of pink terracotta. Around it, on all sides, are sparse formations of armed men in closed ranks.

The small piazza has gradually filled up. The crowd waits in silence in the darkness dotted by torchlight. It is completely dark now, the gloom funereal. In addition to the torches, only a faint oblique moon. The far corner, that of Via Omenoni, is weakly lit by an arc lamp.

Suddenly, however, from behind the stage, a luminous tracer, used to light up the "no man's land" during the war, hisses through the darkness. For a few instants, before silence returns, the white light of a sighting flare traces a milky parabola in the sky above Milan, which is unexpectedly projected into a war zone. At the end of its trajectory, the illuminating rocket goes tumbling down, clattering off the roof of a neoclassic palazzo. Everyone in the piazza follows its iridescent foam, spellbound like children, the great emotions of primitive humanity. It is a Very rocket, the falling star of nights in the trenches. And it's the starting signal.

Ferruccio Vecchi, Captain of the Arditi, goes up to the stage.

He addresses the crowd with his usual fanatical vehemence. He rants and raves about assaults, about moments when war is bloodiest and darkest, about soldiers blown apart, about infantrymen scorched in the karstic blast furnaces, of rebel souls transformed into daggers. The Arditi, disinterested apostles, are sworn enemies of that obscure tangle of interests, frauds, and dishonest parliamentarianism, of banks denying credit to the dispossessed and small businessmen, of perpetual bourgeois betrayal, of moldering away. I would not decimate wealth, but the wealthy. The tide is rising, good people. We the dispossessed will get justice. Even the calmest lagoon has risen in delirium. Step aside, the black banner is passing!

Vecchi shouts himself hoarse, piles on the delirious metaphors, his jugular swells with blood but his words are nothing compared to the Very rocket. Everyone keeps searching the sky for the diffused glow of its silent magnificence.

Benito Mussolini steps up on stage. The small crowd acclaims him. Major Baseggio, founder of the "Death Squads," demands silence by raising a club. A torch is moved closer. The crowd falls completely still: the speaker, perhaps to protect himself from the drizzle, is wearing an eerie balaclava.

Mussolini begins philosophically:

"Life in modern societies is formidably complex." Its many urgent needs require technical skills, men who are free and daring. They require "the downfall of the past." A clean sweep must be made of that inert, parasitic bourgeoisie that flaunts an ill-acquired wealth and twice as much impotent imbecility. He is not against the proletariat. That's a lie. He has always fought for an eight-hour day for steelworkers. He is against tyranny, even by proletarians. That's all. It is also untrue that fascists are violent. If attacked they respond, but the fascists are not bloodthirsty. He, personally, is against violence. Nor does he even care about being elected, the badge of office isn't important to him.

Like Vecchi before him, Mussolini also shouts himself hoarse, but not even he can compete with the fascination of the sighting rocket. As for the socialist hordes, not a trace of them. The crowd listens in silence, still enchanted by that starting signal. People sigh.

It's true, life in modern societies is formidably complex, and it's all allayed, it's all put to rest with the Very rocket, the comet tail that marked the beginning and end of the rally. Never before in the postwar period has the simplification of the war been so present.

After the event, on Via Manzoni, Marinetti climbs up on a fascist's shoulders and contemplates the crowd marching through the night in a column through the elegant streets of the city center; a disciplined, tightly packed, vibrant crowd, bristling with flags, clubs and torches.

Give the splendor of violence to these citizens of an inscrutable modern metropolis with its dense, murky darkness, these men bowed down by an existence they do not understand, give their sanguine desire for light a luminous tracer, give them a destiny and they will follow you.

What is happening was to be expected. The proletarian crowd is reacting to its abusers and tormentors with the unstoppable vehemence of long-suffering, passionate outrage. It would be nice to hope that debates on the current political issues might take place in an atmosphere of serenity and tolerance, but such an appeal falls on toxic ground . . . The crowd does not see political adversaries before them when interventionists of various stripes show up, it sees enemies. It sees those who wanted, imposed, and exploited the war.

Avanti!, November 1, 1919

Instructions for tonight's Rally.

At the appointed time, Fascists, Arditi, the Demobilized, War Volunteers, Combattenti, Futurists, and Futurist students will assemble at their headquarters to go to the site of the Rally.

The Rally will be held even if it rains . . .

In the event of any clashes, the general public must quickly clear out by way of Via Morone, towards Via Manzoni . . .

At the end of the rally, with the cry of "Eja, Eja, Alalà" the fascist crowd will march in tight formation down Via Morone, Via Manzoni, Piazza della Scala, Via Silvio Pellico, and will disperse without incident in front of the Fascist Electoral Committee Headquarters.

Other meticulous measures that cannot be made public have been taken, so that the fascist rally may—and will—turn out to be undisrupted and solemn.

Il Popolo d'Italia, November 10, 1919

NICOLA BOMBACCI

BOLOGNA, EARLY NOVEMBER 1919

In Piazza del Nettuno, crowded around the god of the sea's statue, there must be a hundred thousand people. Maybe two hundred thousand. Maybe even more. Everyone is waiting for the "Lenin of Romagna" to say *the* word. He hesitates. He has been talking for twenty minutes but has held back. Restraining him is a reluctance in the face of sacred things.

Behind the crowd, facing Nicola Bombacci, the serpentine figure of the bronze giant rises majestically above the fountain's marble-covered stone basin. The Neptune who lends his name to the piazza towers over four dolphins, symbolizing the Ganges, the Nile, the Danube, and the Amazon rivers, the four regions of the known world. The sea god, with great vertical élan, extends his left hand to the wind, as if he too wanted to calm the tempests. But the pontiff who had him sculpted in the sixteenth century, as a symbol of his papal power, no longer dominates the world. The twentieth century has a different god: the word "revolution" cannot wait.

The XVI congress of the Socialist Party that was held in Bologna in early October decreed it. The maximalist majority adopted a platform inspired by the Bolshevik revolution, hailed as "the most auspicious event in the history of the proletariat." In view of a revolution, the party's magna carta was even rewritten, a charter that dated back to the nineteenth century, the heroic era of the first workers' struggles. But times have changed and now is the time for revolution. To accelerate its maturation, the congress appointed Nicolino Bombacci himself secretary. The "Christ of the Workers" who preaches the advent of the Soviet republic in Italy: all power to the proletariat amassed in his counsel. Those who don't work, don't eat. And he immediately adopted the symbol of the Russian proletarian committees: a hammer and sickle surrounded by two ears of corn. A magnificent symbol, brand new and yet eternal, a perfect circle, the entirety of the redeemed world, history that begins again after reaching its end. And yet he, in front of his crowds of workers and the god of the sea, hesitates to pronounce that word: revolution.

With his left hand, Neptune calms the storms, but in his right he holds the trident. A three-pronged spear capable of eviscerating a seven-ton cetacean. Violence, that's the problem. It was discussed at length at the socialist congress, it's discussed daily, but the more it's discussed, the more it continues to be deferred. Gennari deemed it "historically necessary," Lazzari warned that we must wait for "mathematical certainty," Serrati that "before attempting the supreme move it is necessary to at least test the terrain," Turati considers it folly. The old patriarch of humanitarian socialism says that for now the fascists don't take them seriously, but when they do, their call for revolutionary violence will be met by fascist squads a hundred times better armed than they are. Turati is right, as always. None of the socialist leaders was at the front. Between them and their adversaries the chasm dug by the Great War is unbridgeable. The hammer and sickle will never frighten the dagger.

Also of that opinion is Vladimir Degott, representative of the Communist International in Italy, who behind the scenes at the congress conspired to prepare the revolution. In his view, Serrati, the party leader, is a careerist, a politician who occupies two chairs and agrees as needed, at times with the left, at times with the reformists, a common Menshevik who could write good things about the revolution but is afraid to call for one; Gennari is a "brilliant Marxist but he lacks the spirit of initiative" and Gramsci "has understood the Russian revolution better than all the other comrades but he cannot influence the masses." Degott, and through him Lenin, are pinning their hopes on Bombacci, placing their trust in the “Christ of the Workers.” They are certain that, when it becomes necessary, Nicola Bombacci will side with the vanguard of the advancing proletariat. But the former priest studied in the seminary; he was declared unfit for military service for health reasons; he knows he couldn’t hurt a fly. And so Bombacci continues to hesitate. The crowd in Piazza del Nettuno who came to celebrate the liturgy of that word is left empty-handed.

Turati is always right, of course, but the future doesn’t recognize his arguments. The future exists to redress wrongs. Violence shouldn’t scare them, they are well acquainted with it. Handcuffs, jail and, when that isn’t enough, a bullet in the gut. That and only that is what the bourgeoisie, landowners or industrialists, have always shown the people, both in the days of their fathers, when they were Bourbonist, papalist, pro-Austrian, and now that they say they are liberal, democratic, even republican. The people crowded in this square know violence better than anyone else: being victims of it has made them experts.

Dozens of examples can be counted. On October 11th, after the first six days of a general strike in the Piacenza countryside, in Mercore di Besenzone, the Bergamaschi brothers defended their property, weapons in hand, from a mob of strikers who had invaded it. Repeated gunshots, from both sides. Five dead. On October 26th, in the piazza of Stia, in the province of Arezzo, the commander of the local police headquarters, feeling overwhelmed by the crowd of socialist demonstrators, fired at point-blank range. Two women severely wounded, one of whom, Rosa Vagnoli, died the following day. She was eighteen years old. On November 11th, in Turin, socialist tram driver Giovanni Cerea was attacked with clubs and whips by two police officers just because he was putting up his party’s electoral posters. He tried to get away, fell, and they trampled him as if he were the discarded inner tube of a bicycle tire, a cigarette butt, or whatever. They left him in a pitiful state, dead before reaching the hospital.

All those murdered comrades knew violence all too well. And besides, the word “violence” had already been written in black and white in the winning motion passed at the congress in Bologna that had elected him, Nicola Bombacci, secretary. Then too, the war never ended, this peace has all the characteristics of a truce. Furthermore, there are a hundred thousand comrades in Piazza del Nettuno, maybe two hundred thousand, maybe more. It can't all be hallucination, all an illusion. Certainty in the decisive nature of events is indubitable, faith in the party's imminent triumph absolute. The times are ripe.

And so Nicola Bombacci, on behalf of the victims, of the Bergamaschi brothers, of the eighteen-year-old peasant girl Rosa Vagnoli, of socialist tram driver Giovanni Cerea, of the party, of certainty, faith and the future, shows some courage and says it:

"Go ahead and chop my head off if within a month I haven't forced the king to pack his bags, by God. You can chop off my head if within a month we haven't had a revolution even here in Italy!"

The Congress is convinced that the proletariat will have to resort to the use of violence in order to defend themselves against bourgeois acts of violence, to acquire power and to consolidate revolutionary gains . . . that the violent acquisition of power by the workers will mark the transfer of power itself from the bourgeois class to the proletarian class, thus establishing a transitional regime of dictatorship of the whole proletariat.

From the program of the Italian Socialist Party,
Congress of Bologna, October 8, 1919

BENITO MUSSOLINI

MILAN, NOVEMBER 17, 1919

A CORPSE IN A state of putrefaction was fished out of the waters of the *naviglio*. It appears to be Benito Mussolini.

Two lines in the local news section. *Avanti!*, the socialists' paper that he directed for years, has given his demise no more than a couple of lines in passing. Two venomous lines at that. Instead, on the front page, in block print, the headline proclaims their triumph: "Revolutionary Italy is born!"

From the street the clamor of the crowd that has rushed to his funeral reaches the minuscule office of *Il Popolo d'Italia*'s editor. Mussolini's body is carried in procession through the filthy streets of Bottonuto. Funeral hymns are loudly chanted over strident frequencies of jubilation. Whores, temporarily unemployed because of the brouhaha that is discouraging clients, stand openly in the doorways of the brothels.

In his miserable little workspace the living Mussolini's thoughts go round in circles like a caged animal. He's gone over it from all angles but he can't find any breach in the wall of universal hostility. Every time someone knocks at the door, he ducks his head and hunches his shoulders to reduce his body surface and turns quickly, driven by the instinct of prey under attack. Then, as soon as he realizes that he has an audience, even if it's just an errand boy, he regains his self-control and feigns nonchalance. To anyone who comes by to verify the well-being of the living cadaver, he blusters: "We didn't get many votes, it's true, but on the other hand, we fired off quite a few revolver shots." Or something like that. He even laughs heartily when they tell him the joke with its play on words that is already going around Milan: "With an orchestra conductor like Toscanini on the ticket, the 'sonata' could only be exceptional."

The truth is that the setback was deadly for the fascists, the personal blow stinging for the man who had already imagined himself "deputy from Milan." The election on November 16th was a "red" vote. 1,834,792 votes were showered onto the socialists, equivalent to 156 elected parliamentarians. A triumphal result, a harbinger of revolution. In inverse proportion to that, the failure of the fascist ticket was absolute: out of approximately 270,000 voters in the district of Milan, the fascists garnered only 4,657 votes. Mussolini obtained only 2,427 preferential votes. None of the fascist candidates was elected. Not a one. Not even him. It was a complete fiasco.

He lies to the others, but to his wife he admitted it: "A total defeat. We didn't even get one seat. In the Galleria, the people raged against us." He was forced to call Rachele to try to reassure her when they told him that the mock funeral procession staged by the socialists had even stopped at their home in Foro Bonaparte. People were shouting: "Here's Mussolini's body" and banging on the front door. Behind "his" coffin, two more empty caskets hypothetically held the corpses of Marinetti and D'Annunzio. Rachele, in turn, confessed that she had taken refuge in the attic with the children. It seems that little Edda suffered an anxiety attack.

Visitors keep showing up at the newspaper offices, just like at a funeral. No use trying to keep the door locked. When they're burying your ghost in the street, people come looking for you.

To show that he is himself, he has them bring him a glass of milk. He sits at his work table in the stark room and sends for Arturo Rossato, one of his editors, to have him write the addresses of Milan's socialist mayor Caldara and Cardinal Ferrari by hand on two spherical parcels wrapped in newspaper. The setting around the desk gives the impression of an imminent move. The only thing on the wall is a map of Italy with a tricolor flag marking Fiume.

The writing table holds only the big glass of milk and an old monumental quartermaster's pistol. The shouts of the socialists rise threateningly from the street. Mussolini stirs the milk with studied leisureliness, sips it, drop by drop, sets it back down and stirs it again. The viscous white ripples contrast with the inert dark metal of the gun:

"They may yell, shout, and make a hell of a racket, but eliminate the ascots, the flags and what's left is a bunch of idiots. They'll never carry out a revolution. If these revolutionaries with their empty talk don't honor their promise, the masses will protest and then they'll be in deep mud . . . as they used to say in the trenches. There are victories that are equivalent to defeat."

Arturo Rossato, the editor who came to deliver the parcels with the handwritten addresses, can only agree with his boss's bluster with an imperceptible nod of his head. From the street the socialists' shouts rise another octave.

"And don't think they'll come up here because I'm dead, see. I am now a man without a shadow."

Benito Mussolini pauses a few seconds to give the editor time to be shocked. He stirs the milk, then resumes: "They passed me off for dead, but that's exactly why they know that if they come up here, I'll wipe out at least a couple of them with this gun. And in Milan, in case you don't know, there isn't a single member of the Socialist Party, I mean, not one hero, who can stand up to danger. A bunch of idiots. They're a bunch of idiots. So . . . I'll just drink my milk."

Arnaldo Mussolini comes up from the administrative offices. Usually mild in temperament, he is uncharacteristically furious with his brother:

"So now you're a murderer, an actual criminal!" Arnaldo shouts, not worrying about being heard by the entire staff, then puts his head in his hands. The two parcels addressed to the archbishop and the mayor of Milan contain two SIPE grenades. Benito Mussolini decided to send the explosive devices as retaliation for the defeat he suffered. The addresses, written by the editor's hand, are meant to thwart the detectives' investigations.

"A bomb is worth more than a hundred rallies."

It's the slogan that the young spirited agitator fired off in the heated piazzas of Romagna at the time when he preached socialist revolution, an old battle cry of his. Now—while down in the street his old comrades spit on the puppet of his corpse—the mature man, editor-in-chief of a national newspaper, utters that same old slogan in a flat voice, with not a hint of emotion, for the benefit of the entire editorial staff and the Arditi guards summoned by Arnaldo's shouts. Then Benito Mussolini, the bomber, slowly resumes stirring his milk with the aluminum spoon. There is nothing more to see. The show is over.

As the small crowd drifts back down the balcony stairs, Albino Volpi draws Arnaldo aside. There's no reason to worry, he reassures him. Because of its type of fuse and detonator, a SIPE grenade sent by mail presents no danger.

ALBINO VOLPI

MILAN, NOVEMBER 17, 1919, 8:00 P.M.

THE SIPE IS a fragmentation hand grenade. To trigger it, after removing the protective cap, you have to rub the head against the igniter or light it directly from an open flame. In war a cigar was usually used. Since its range of impact is greater than the thrown distance, it is a defensive weapon. It is generally used to stop an enemy attack. The Thévenot petard, on the other hand, is an offensive weapon. Its limited range of impact, always less than the distance thrown by a good launcher, allows you to blast the enemy while leaving him unharmed, even if launched in an open field. When it's time to employ it, you simply remove the safety pin. The impact with the ground or with the target will do the rest. Moreover it is a bomb of great psychological effectiveness: the powerful detonation stuns and terrifies. Once exploded, it allows the attacker to easily finish off the enemy with a knife-blade.

It's seven in the evening. The man standing on the bridge of the Sirenette, in Milan's center, is carrying two Thévenot bombs on his belt as well as a dagger with a mother-of-pearl handle. Even though no one is looking in his direction, he puffs out his chest and lifts his chin as if he were posing for the benefit of a photographer. Nobody is looking at him, but for half an hour he has been watching the socialist procession on Via San Damiano, a little further on and a little farther down, celebrating the electoral victory. There are thousands on the bank of the *naviglio*, singing, waving flags, exulting. Men, women, children. Coming from Via del

Verziere, they've been streaming by for several minutes and they still haven't all reached *Avanti!* headquarters where the rally will take place.

On the lowered arch bridge, however, the man is alone. He has not covered his face. To get to that spot without being seen from the Arditi headquarters on Via Cerva, he simply had to climb over the wall of Palazzo Visconti and go through the garden. Five minutes in all. Only four cast-iron statues located at the tops of the parapets keep him company. The Sirenette each hold an oar in their hands. Albino Volpi strokes a tin-plated iron cylinder.

The man standing alone, ignored by the world, shakes his head slightly. It's not possible, they're all Italians, yet those socialists are singing the praises of Russia. There are a lot of them, a huge crowd, they could form an army but they aren't marching, they're shuffling about, swarming, plodding along like cattle. Their flags are red, the carnations in their lapels scarlet, but they're disheveled, in disarray, dragged into mixed-up bands. They're disgusting, they have no dignity. They're a mob, not a formation, a troop of degenerates. An orgy of song, wine and grappa, higgledy-piggledy, a mass of red flags waving in the hands of staggering standard-bearers. They are gaunt, unsteady, destitute, physically haggard and consumed, their minds defective, ravenous and greedy, they are beasts of burden. They are animals, not men. A flock of enraged sheep.

And then that song . . . "*Su lottiamo! L'ideale nostro fine sarà . . . L'Internazionale, futura umanità*" . . . (Let's fight! Our ideal will be the goal . . . An International, future humanity) . . . that song has no exuberance, it's solemn but gloomy, low-pitched, earthy, dusty, the dull muttering of the horde. There is nothing Italian about it, those who sing it are a flock, not a people. Yes, the song . . . that song . . . that's the worst thing. The pounding monotony that seems to evoke boundless plains, deserts, foreigners, Siberian frosts, unseasoned beet soups, steppes of endless hunger. Is History this Asiatic herd?

It can't be, and if it is, its course can be altered. He is prone to killing, open to all violence.

Albino Volpi, his eyes still fixed on the crowd, takes the iron cylinder from his belt, removes the safety pin that blocks the spring-loaded striker and extends both arms perpendicularly to his body. He remains in that position for a few moments, wings spread, inhaling the damp evening air, as if he were waiting for the right atmospheric current so he can take flight. Then the equilibrium is shattered, the body tilts, the right hand drops down, the left rises up, the spring stretches, releases, the massive torso becomes a catapult. The bomb soars, unknown to the crowd, describing a perfect arc. The detonation is tremendous. Now no one is singing anymore. Screaming, swearing, the cries of the wounded, entreaties to mama. Now the herd scatters.

The man on the bridge resumes his position as observer, his arms relaxed at his sides. A glance is enough for him to assess the situation: one single man has sent thousands fleeing. It's too dark to count the fallen, but that's not what interests him. It seems to him that humanity can be divided according to the positions it assumes in the face of metal shards. The war veteran assesses candidates who will make history based on their reactions to a bombing. Someone who has been to the front immediately hunkers down in a fetal position, arms folded over his belly. He prudently reduces himself to the smallest animal, essential to protect his tender parts. The others, all the others, run like mad, deluding themselves that they can be saved by an erect position.

Down on Via San Damiano very few hunker down. They are almost all workers and workers didn't go to war with the excuse that they were needed to run the factories. A herd of shirkers. They deserve the mental terror.

Albino Volpi grips a second iron cylinder and spreads his arms again.

The Act of a Fanatic

A socialist procession had stopped on Via S. Damiano, under the windows of *Avanti!*, to cheer a speech by Serrati in praise of socialism. The parade was reassembling and starting out again when, according to the initial account, a stranger from up on the cast-iron bridge threw an object towards the front of the procession, which exploded when it touched the ground; the fragments, from a distance of twenty or thirty yards, tore into the first demonstrators. In the panic that followed, agonized screams rose from the fallen as companions of the injured rushed to help them, while others tried to chase the unknown assailant who was soon lost in darkness . . . The reckless act of a fanatic, who seems to have used a Thévenot petard, stirred general outrage as soon as it became known.

Corriere della Sera, November 18, 1919

MILAN, NOVEMBER 18, 1919

THEY ARREST THEM all on November 18th, 1919. Prefect Pesce's hard line is dictated by Prime Minister Nitti, who that morning telegraphed Milan: "Anyone keeping hand grenades must be considered a criminal a priori."

First to be raided is the headquarters of the Arditi Association on Via Cerva, where numerous SIPE bombs, Thévenot grenades, pistols, daggers, maces and boxes of ammunition are seized. The search ends with the arrests of Captain Ferruccio Vecchi, Piero Bolzon, and Edmondo Mazzucato. Albino Volpi and other veterans suspected of being among the perpetrators of the attack on Via San Damiano manage to escape capture by fleeing over the rooftops.

Then, in the afternoon, following a raid on the fascio headquarters on Via Silvio Pellico 16, and after a delegation of socialists composed of Treves, Turati, Serrati and the mayor, Caldara, went to the prefecture demanding that the Arditi be banned from the city and that the Fasci di Combattimento be dissolved, *Il Popolo d'Italia* gets its turn. The police agents find, hidden in a stove, 13 new revolvers of various calibers, 419 cartridges, and a recently used flare gun. Umberto Pasella, Enzo Ferrari, and Filippo Tommaso Marinetti are arrested. They are all accused of attempts on state security and organizing armed gangs. Benito Mussolini is taken to San Vittore prison. He will occupy cell number 40, where he will remain for only twenty-four hours.

On November 19th, after being subjected to interrogation, he is released following a phone call from Luigi Albertini to Prime Minister Nitti. To persuade the prime minister to free Mussolini, Albertini, senator of the Kingdom and member of the upper bourgeoisie, owner and editor of the *Corriere della Sera*, convinced that fascism's fate is sealed by the electoral disaster, uses an argument typical of liberal thought of which he is one of Italy's leading proponents: "Mussolini is a relic, let's not make him a martyr."

Action-ready nuclei had been in Mussolini's mind and were shortly thereafter a concrete reality: squads of bold, fearless citizens and Arditi, members of the fasci, which the fasci were to dispatch, armed, into piazza demonstrations at the opportune moment . . . In conclusion the existence of a military-type organization has been established, and the existence within the organization of an actual hierarchy of leaders and followers . . . it has been ascertained that the conduct of the rallies, the tenor of the orders, the martial method of reporting were of a military nature, that many of the weapons with which the followers were armed are military, that many of the officers and members of these armed fascist corps were specifically sent here by the Military Command of Fiume. Whatever the thoughts of the leaders and members of the organization, it is therefore certain that an armed force had been formed within Milan's Fasci di Combattimento, not only to oppose the laws of the state, not only bent on usurping police powers, but for the deliberate purpose of committing crimes against individuals.

Report of Public Security Commissioner Giovanni Gasti
to Milan's Public Prosecutor's Office,
November 21, 1919

When Mussolini was in vogue, no one dared touch him: today they arrest him because he appears weaker. We cannot approve such politics, inspired not by respect for the law but by opportunism.

Corriere della Sera, November 19, 1919

A blast of wind has hit fascism, but it won't succeed in uprooting it.

Benito Mussolini,
Il Popolo d'Italia, November 20, 1919

NICOLA BOMBACCI

ROME, DECEMBER 1, 1919
MONTECITORIO

On the day the new parliament of the Kingdom of Italy is ushered in, everyone's head is upturned.

The newly elected socialist deputies are admiring the majestic frieze by Aristide Sartorio that decorates the new hall of parliament. Twenty yards above the semicircular floor are fifty canvases, each over twelve feet wide, using the innovative technique of encaustic, spread out for more than a hundred yards. A second sky of dazzling colors that contains more than two hundred figures, men, women, children and animals, in hues of green, pink, orange and white, in warm, rich tones obtained by squeezing the entire tube in a mixture of oil and wax, illuminated by the natural light of the first sky, the sky of Rome, which pours in from the velarium. A triumph of allegorical images depicting the virtues of young Italy and the salient episodes of the history of its people at its awakening. All two hundred of those giant figures above the pedestals, displaying a predilection for virile nudes and galloping horses, shine radiantly and seem to be surging forward.

Twenty yards below, the legitimate representatives of that glorified people turn their gaze on this spectacular epic, searching for themselves. There are 156 socialist deputies, almost all of whom are sitting in Italy's parliament for the first time; many of them are sons of workers, carters and farm laborers who have never in their lives admired a painted canvas except on a church altar. The sons of those wretched, illiterate subjects will today, for the first time, meet his majesty the king, there to inaugurate the new legislature with the customary crown speech. Awaiting Vittorio Emanuele III is the royal throne, set up in place of the presidential bench, guarded on either side by two cuirassiers with unsheathed swords. For the first time in its history, people are about to meet their sovereign in person, in the flesh, man to man. It is the culminating moment of the epic, the only canvas that is still missing from the admirable frieze painted by Sartorio.

The king's speech is scheduled for 10:30 but the people's representatives, in order not to miss the event, have been flowing into parliament's benches since 9:00 a.m. The socialists, as a bloc, have occupied the first three sections on the left in a still empty hall. They're all wearing a red carnation in the buttonhole of their lapels. The re-elected deputies who in the past had sat in that area complained about finding their seats taken. They could do nothing about it. Even Giovanni Giolitti, the veteran and dominant figure of parliamentary life for the last thirty years, who entered the hall a little before 10:00, had to resign himself to giving up his usual place in the third section on the left. Today, a new history is beginning for the left and it wears a red carnation in its buttonhole. There is no place for Giolitti.

At 10:05, deputy Vittorio Emanuele Orlando, the "premier of victory" over the Austrians, arrives and goes to sit in the fourth section after shaking Giolitti's hand. Shortly thereafter, deputy Bissolati appears in a frock coat. The former president of the chamber crosses the semicircle with a somewhat uncertain step and heads to the committees' bench, immediately welcomed by Montecitorio's elderly parliament members. The leftist sections are already packed, those on the right are slow to fill up; noted in the diplomatic corps' gallery are the duchess of Laurenzana, the marquise Salvago-Raggi, the minister of Romania, the ambassadors of Spain, Poland and Belgium, and many others.

When at 10:28 a royal valet opens the little door on the right, everyone is in place. Approximately 500 representatives of the nation are present before the king. All the senators and all the deputies stand up and cheer, shouting in unison: "Long live the king!" All except the red carnations in the three sections on the left side of the semicircle, who remain seated.

The visual impact is jarring, but parliament's display of affection is thunderous nonetheless and the defection goes unnoticed as yet. Vittorio Emanuele III receives the applause of the deputies and bows several times, touched. Then he takes his place on the throne. Prime Minister Nitti, addressing the assembly, invites the deputies and senators to sit down.

At that point the red carnations stand up. There is total silence. For a few moments everyone is stunned, the cuirassiers tighten their grip on the sabers, then they realize what's happening: the socialists are simply leaving. The people refuse to meet their king. They disavow him.

Nicola Bombacci, his hair disheveled and his beard scruffy, marches at the head of the dissidents. As he passes the throne, he looks directly at the sovereign and shouts: "Long live the socialist republic!" His personal following in the district of Bologna was enormous. Some newspapers call him "the king of preferential votes." With him alone, not counting all the other socialist deputies, more than one hundred thousand Italians leave Montecitorio. The monarch is left giving the crown speech to a half-empty hall.

The scene is memorable, its theatrical effect compelling. The dissident deputies, outside in the Montecitorio piazza, are jubilant, congratulating and embracing one another. Their laughter is genuine, carefree. The dream of a free, just life is coming true. In the tepid winter sunlight of a Roman piazza, they are at this moment the representatives of a people reborn. The euphoria lasts a few seconds. Shortly thereafter, deputies and senators realize with dismay that they have no plan for the rest of the day. The socialists have conquered Italy but they don't know what to do with it.

Because those men don't know what to do, they are beaten. Already that afternoon nationalist gangs start beating them. They hunt them down in the streets of Rome, grab them by their black republican bow-ties and force them to shout "long live the king!" Towards evening the bashings continue with the debut of the royal guards, the newly formed police force for the maintenance of public order. Giacinto Menotti Serrati, the party leader, is forcibly taken to security headquarters and battered.

On the socialist side, as usual, a general strike is called. The first victim is recorded the following day in Piazza Esedra. He is Tiberio Zampa, a worker in *Avanti!*'s print shop, twenty-three years old.

The factories come to a halt again. Milan still sleeps with weapons at hand, in anticipation of the revolution. One breathes an air filled with acrid fury, writes Claudio Treves, a wind of terrorism. Bombacci declares that the revolution is a historical necessity, that parliament is a relic of the past and that it is his duty to strike the final blows that will demolish it. He declares it from his seat in parliament.

At the end of the general strike, there are about ten deaths, in Turin, Milan, Adria, and Modena. To be added to the 110 deaths already caused over the course of 1919 by clashes in the piazzas between socialists and law enforcement. The first year of peace comes to a close with that bottom line.

GABRIELE D'ANNUNZIO

FIUME, DECEMBER 18, 1919

THE COMMANDER IS alone in the operations room. After Lilì de Montresor, a popular singer in the city's cafes, was led out at dawn through a secret door, with 500 liras taken from regulation funds in her purse, D'Annunzio gave the order not to let anyone enter until news arrived.

Watching over his solitude in the vestibule is Tommaso Beltrami, a member of the poet's personal guard organized by Guido Keller with men recruited from the "*Disperata*" company, a unit of undocumented volunteers who spend their days camped in the shipyards, drinking, singing and diving naked from the prows of ships immobilized by the embargo. Beltrami, an ex-Ardito and former syndicalist, is considered by some to be a true irregular troop leader, by others a womanizer, an inveterate gambler, and cocaine addict. Both views, most likely, are true.

Beyond the door guarded by Beltrami, D'Annunzio awaits the results of the popular plebiscite that he has called to decide whether to accept the "modus vivendi," a compromise proposed by the Nitti government. He wears his favorite uniform, that of the "holy march" from the night in Ronchi, the immaculate white uniform with the raised collars of the Novara lancers. In his breast pocket is a silver cannula.

With the "modus vivendi," the Italian government, in exchange for the end of the occupation, pledged to bestow military honors on D'Annunzio's legionnaires and to defend the city with regular troops with a view towards its annexation. The young hotheads of the Commander's personal guard consider it a despicable swindle, the more mature members of his staff see it as an honorable solution. In this case as well, both, most likely, are true.

On November 14th, D'Annunzio left Fiume and set out for Zadar. His entry into the other city disputed by Italy and Yugoslavia was triumphal; the population welcomed him as a hero. There too he spread Giovanni Randaccio's flag out in front of the crowd and everyone knelt before it in the mud. For a moment, it seemed as if the plan to bring the torch of Fiume into the world was not the delirium of a poet intoxicated with himself. The "great Italy" of small Fiume felt once again ready to challenge America. In the command room they resumed planning the march on Rome. "*Marciare non marcire*," March, don't rot, they shouted.

Then, two days later, the results of the country's political elections came from Rome. The socialists had won, national pride took a back seat to bread and wages, the despised Nitti had been confirmed as prime minister. Italy could get by without D'Annunzio's glory but could not survive without America's money, that was the response from the polls.

In Fiume, meanwhile, where six thousand able adult workers out of thirty thousand were unemployed, the population were beginning to feel the effects of a hangover. The Commander had therefore authorized his lieutenants to reopen negotiations with the cesspool in Rome. The proposal for the "modus vivendi" had arrived and he'd left the decision to Fiume's national council. On December 15th, after several meetings, the Council had accepted Nitti's proposal with 46 votes in favor and only 6 against. The epic of the Fiume rebellion was, therefore, about to come to an end. The spirit was dimming.

But as soon as word spread about the decision favorable to compromise, a tumultuous mass of legionnaires and civilians, especially women, began clamoring below the balcony of the palazzo. Shouts of betrayal, calls for insurrection, thousands of voices summoned the Commander to the railing. Again the piazza, again an outcry, an open-air parliament.

* * *

D'Annunzio comes out, very pale, with loose sheets of paper in his hands. He does not orate but, like a schoolboy, reads the text of the "modus vivendi," the compromise proposed by the politicians in Rome. The piazza acclaims each clause of the agreement with a simple "yes" or rejects it with a "no." By the end of the reading the spirit is rekindled. The City Council has already accepted the agreement by a large majority, but here in the piazza the spirit breathes, democracy is direct. D'Annunzio plays to the crowd's frenzy:

"Do you want it?"

The negative reply is unanimous. Annexation, liberty, resistance.

"But resistance means suffering. Do you want it?" They want it.

D'Annunzio calls for a referendum on the 18th. If the people don't think that the arms and the commitment of the legionnaires are necessary to honor the oath, they should say so openly. Then he has Randaccio's flag unfolded and asks the Arditi to sing their battle songs. The piazza explodes in another display of enthusiasm that goes on until late that night. The decision to accept the "modus vivendi" is referred to a popular referendum.

Now, two days after that fervor in the piazza, the Commander waits in solitude for the people's voice to reach him. He must wait until evening. From beyond the door guarded by Beltrami, news of violent episodes has been filtering through since morning. Legionnaires are interfering with free voting. In various precincts they have invaded the polling places, prevented the scrutineers from doing their job, and tampered with the ballots. Nevertheless, before sunset, the result appears assured: the great majority of Fiumani are in favor of the "modus vivendi" proposed by that swine Nitti. D'Annunzio asks to be alone again.

Fiume's voice has become acrimonious, it's changed, the Commander no longer recognizes it. The Roman pestilence has infected its water, the mouth has become bitter, the throat parched. Fiumani, brothers, why these cries, why this anguish? Why are the heroic comrades sad? We have gone from error to error, from violence to violence, from darkness to darkness. We did not come out alive from the rallies without light.

In front of the poet-warrior, the ribbon of white powder stands out against the dark grain of the chestnut wood table. The silver cannula absorbs the light beneath the composed gazes of the solemn portraits of old Magyar rulers. Once the powder is inhaled, the nostrils sting, burn, the capillaries bleed. The increase of dopamine in the cerebral synapses restore the courage of the aviator flying over Vienna.

Sensations increase, awareness grows, sleep, hunger, thirst disappear, euphoria mounts, lust returns. The Commander is again indefatigable.

D'Annunzio summons his personal guard and orders that the referendum underway be annulled. This democracy, after all, is nothing but a big petit bourgeois mistake.

LEANDRO ARPINATI

LODI, DECEMBER 18, 1919

LEANDRO ARPINATI IS released from prison on bail, on the morning of December 18th. He served thirty-six days in jail, in cell no. 22, shared with Arconovaldo Bonaccorsi. They locked him up on November 13th, after the unfortunate evening at the Teatro Gaffurio.

That day, the eve of the elections, about sixty of them had traveled down to Lodi from Milan in three military trucks. The usual band: uniformed army officers, Arditi, Futurists, fascists. Mussolini and Baseggio were supposed to speak there but they'd decided that it was best not to risk it. Three days earlier, in Lodi, in that same theater, socialist militants had prevented the fascist candidate's rally.

As soon as they arrived at the piazza, Arpinati and the fascists acting as escort immediately realized that they would have to fight that evening too in order to be able to speak. The Teatro Gaffurio was blocked and guarded by a crowd of a thousand "reds" determined to prevent that rally as well. The numerical disproportion was about one to ten, but to Arpinati's men, armed to the teeth, that had never seemed like a good argument.

The moment Salimbeni, a local fascist, went up on stage to introduce the speakers, target shooting began from the balcony occupied by the socialists. For a few minutes punches were thrown, objects hurled. In brief, the usual stuff. Then a wooden cornice torn loose from the balcony rained down on the stage from above. So the Arditi had pulled out their revolvers.

None of his Bologna guys had fired at a person. Or, at least, that's what Arpinati thought: when all hell breaks loose, you can't be sure of anything. Bonaccorsi, for example—a hotheaded, former Alpine, just twenty years old, a fighter at the height of his violent years—had been given a nine-month sentence. Bonaccorsi and Arpinati had traveled up together from Bologna but Bonaccorsi would not be going back with him.

In the meantime, he'd had to ask Umberto Pasella, the fasci secretary, for ticket money to return home. At the time of his arrest he had 150 liras in his pocket, now he didn't even have that. While he was in a cell, the Ferrovie had informed him that he had been placed on unpaid leave until his pending judicial matters were settled. He also found himself out of the university because the period for enrollment in the second year of engineering had expired while he was in jail. Moreover the elections that had caused all that pandemonium had ended in disaster. He had nothing left, in short. Not even his hair. To protect himself from lice he'd had to shave it off, like when he was a kid in August 1914; taking part in street clashes on the side of anarchic interventionists, he shaved his hair off then to prevent some socialist from holding his head still while another one punched him in the face.

Now he was out of prison but he'd lost everything. All he had left was that girl, Rina. He'd met her at Ars et Labor, the night school. She worked at the municipality, at the consumer office, and could only study in the evening. His friends had advised him to stay away because she seemed as frigid as a February day on a frozen inland plain. She walked stiffly erect, with measured steps, practically turning up her nose, as if afraid of slipping on a sidewalk flooded by a broken sewer. She was meticulous, focused, constantly questioning the teachers even on the most trivial matters, as if she expected the answer to give her the meaning of life. A real hopeless case.

Yet the haughty beauty of that sad girl had struck Leandro like a slap in the face. It was an absolute beauty, the kind that makes no concessions to the world's pleasures. They had gotten engaged.

It was her Mussolini himself had telegraphed to communicate

the news of the arrest: "Leandro arrested, Lodi matter. Confident will release shortly. Best wishes. Mussolini." It was her the attorney Mario Bergamo had turned to for money for the defense. And it was her again whom the other lawyer, Cesare Sarfatti, had written to, to inform her about developments in the proceedings.

But things were moving slowly and he was sure that she would justifiably drop him. Instead Rina Guidi had taken care of everything. She had come to Milan at the beginning of December, had gone to see Mussolini at the newspaper and Sarfatti in his office, and then she'd also gone to Lodi to visit him in prison. In the visitors' room the sad girl had not even shed a tear. A clear vocation for misery. Leandro would go back to her.

BENITO MUSSOLINI

MILAN, DECEMBER 1919

THERE'S NOBODY LEFT, they've all gone. It is Sunday evening, a winter Sunday in the Po Valley fog.

The only ones left in the editorial office are Nicola Bonservizi and Cesare Rossi—and him, of course, the editor-in-chief, who remains clinging to his desk as if it were a wreck without a mast.

The courtyard at the entrance to *Il Popolo d'Italia*'s quarters has the metaphysical solitude of a site that's been evacuated after an earthquake. Even the Arditi guards have vanished, possibly dozing in the bivouacs set up in the cellar, or maybe they went to visit their mothers. From time to time a cortege of socialists continues to troop through Via Paolo da Cannobio, shouting, but the disarmed fascists no longer seem to be a threat, much less worthy of being threatened. No one comes to see the editor anymore, no one writes to him anymore, and the rooms of the newspaper offices are as bleak as an African desert.

They get by day-to-day. Arnaldo took him aside to talk to him in private. Sales have plummeted, the constant fiscal stopgaps are not enough, the creditors are clamoring, the paper supply needs to be replenished. Under those conditions the newspaper can continue publication for about twenty more days, no longer. He made a show of composure. "OK," he told his brother, "warn me a week in advance so we can divide the chairs among the staff and close up shop." The editorial staff . . . another mortifying barb. On December 5th, Mussolini had to undergo a five-hour interrogation to answer to the charge of unlawfully forming armed gangs. On his return he found a letter of resignation from Arturo Rossato and Giovanni Capodivacca who had been with him since the newspaper was founded. They declared "enormous fatigue" but in reality they wanted to dispute the editorial line. The editor-in-chief told them to go to hell.

After the falling-out, the two dissident editors, despite knowing that there isn't a lira in *Il Popolo d'Italia*'s coffers, lodged an appeal with the arbitration panel of the Lombard journalists' association in order to obtain a settlement. Now he will have to answer that too. Meanwhile, Nitti's delegates continue to offer him lucrative but ludicrous exiles, such as the idea of doing an on-site study of the autonomous republics of southern Russia. There's good business over there, they tell him, winking. Even the postal workers mock him. One of them refused to cash a payment order in his name, pretending not to recognize him. Umberto Pasella confidentially admitted to him that the actual number of Fasci di Combattimento amounted to 37 sections for 800 members.

"Traitor, swine, whoremonger!" The shrill voice of the woman hisses through the deserted courtyard like a mortar shell before it explodes. The emptiness acts like a soundbox.

Here she is, back again! It's Ida Dalser, the madwoman from Trent. This time, however, she has dragged her son, Benito Albino, along with her. The mother clasps the baby close to her body, squeezed between her legs, as parents are advised to do in the presence of ferocious animals so their children won't look like small game to a predator's eyes. But in this savannah of grimy alleys it is she who seems to be the wild animal. Dalser screams as if possessed:

"Exploiter, pig, murderer!"

Benito Mussolini remains riveted to his editor's desk, as his former lover, from the courtyard, in front of his son, his co-workers and a band of Arditi, calls him a gigolo and accuses him of never having repaid the money she lent him when he was a penniless, ambitious climber; she calls him a bigamist, and accuses him of having married her and then dumped her. The courtyard fills with old mistresses of Mussolini's, guttersnipes, petty thieves, prostitutes and pimps. It's Sunday evening: the customers from a nearby wine cellar, already tipsy, rush over in droves. Cesare Rossi and Bonservizi go down to quiet the woman.

"You're in there hiding, huh? Come out here if you dare! Come down and kiss your son. Coward!"

At the sound of that insult, intolerable for any adult male who hopes to maintain the respect of other men, the child's body responds to an urge to escape. His mother grabs him and puts him back in place.

"*Boja de 'n Signur!*" Mussolini swears.

Now the Romagnolo son of Dovia's blacksmith goes racing down the spiral staircase cursing God. He yells at the woman to stop it, once and for all. The allegation of cowardice, as usual, has riled him up; the large crowd, as always, has emboldened him. For some reason, however, Mussolini is gripping a tiny pistol, the type that fits in a purse, a kind of toy revolver. Seeing that little thing in his hand, one might think it was a gift for his bastard son.

Cesare Rossi manages to stop the fasci's founder before he does something stupid. Then he rebukes him sharply. Mussolini, apologetic, mumbles a few incomprehensible words and returns to the office. Two guards on patrol in Bottonuto drag Dalser and poor little Benito Albino away. The woman goes along with them, satisfied. The melodrama is over.

You play it by ear. It never ends, every other day there's a scene, a strike, a fight, for months, for years, what with the dead, the wounded, mothers out of their head, children shattered. But then there's always a small hotel where a man finds comfort, certain late afternoons of shabby squalor that restore the adventurous thrill of life. He discovered one in Piazza Fontana, on the right coming from the Duomo, a stone's throw from the newspaper. He takes the girl Ceccato there, his former secretary, kisses her shamelessly in the street, she chides him, contentedly ("But Benito, it's still daylight and people can see us!"). The owner of the hotel has practically become a friend, an accomplice of those two regulars.

"Would the signora have a room for these poor wayfarers who come from afar and are so weary?"

With the girl, the defeated man recovers his exuberance. In the December dusk, he laughs like a madman, he who rarely laughs, and abandons himself to the euphoria of the disaster ("I don't give a damn, Bianca my love: you alone will be able to tell the world, tomorrow, what Mussolini did with the office of deputy!"). After fucking her with his usual frenzy, he gets carried away reflecting on his isolation, he claims that he has never enjoyed the condition of being rejected so much, that he loves that proud, lousy life, that he has rediscovered a taste for fighting. He even goes so far as to share his political analysis with her: the socialists' success will crush them under the weight of their promises. They promised too much in the electoral campaign, they shouted "long live Lenin!" too many times. Now they have to take action to get on with the revolution. In the cycle of metamorphoses, those who don't act die, and they will not act because they have no revolutionary capacity. They presented themselves in parliament as the new "savages" but they are led by men like Bombacci, a harmless creature who belongs to the species of the perpetually ill who bury the healthy. Just give him, Mussolini, a little time and then, when the socialist tide recedes, he'll show them what it means to be a real savage. And in any case, no one will be able to accuse him of not having squarely faced the triumphant beast of socialism.

Then he falls asleep at her side in the little room in Piazza Fontana. She is in seventh heaven. Gone are the times when he forced her to miscarry at the hands of a backstreet abortionist in a small hotel in Liguria, in an off-season coastal town. The girl is happy now. "I have the smartest man in the world next to me!" she notes in her diary.

With Sarfatti, however, Mussolini gives in to dejection. In front of that mature woman's body, that intellectual who satisfies and challenges him, the man succumbs to the weight of recriminations and fear, the petty spectacle of desertions, escapes, inaction, cowardice. If with Bianca the mercurial braggart boasts, with Margherita the dispirited melancholic confesses. He says he feels like he's been pushed back to where he started, that he hasn't felt so miserable since he was an immigrant sleeping under bridges in Switzerland; he gives in to bouts of discouragement. He proclaims he's on the verge of changing professions. He's been a journalist for too long. He could be a mason—he's very good at it!—or benefit from pilot lessons or, perhaps, even travel the world with his violin or, if he didn't succeed as a roving musician, he could become an actor and playwright. He already has a drama in three acts in mind, *Lamp Without Light*. An impresario made him some offers. Fifteen days at a retreat and he'll write it in one go. But his imaginings always end with the idea of being a novelist. He even has three titles ready: *Vocation*, which takes place on Christmas night in the cell of a young nun; *The Fire Bearers*, a passionate drama; and *The Battle of the Engines*, without a hint of amorous intrigue. In short, someone like him always finds a way to earn a living for himself.

One night, listening to the man she's bet on who is now close to failure, she punishes him. It's an evening when patroness Sarfatti is hosting a salon in her palazzo on Corso Venezia. Everyone is there, Marinetti, the poet Ada Negri, Umberto Notari, Guido da Verona, artists, poets, painters, writers, journalists and entrepreneurs. Most importantly, there is Arturo Toscanini, who has announced that he would like to present a young, extraordinarily talented violinist, a boy just nineteen years old, born in Bohemia, who has come to Milan following a life of wandering. Expectations are high, given that the "maestro" is a notoriously cruel, capricious perfectionist, capable of chasing renowned instrumentalists out of La Scala at the drop of a hat.

That evening, however, Toscanini is in a very good mood, not at all bitter about the electoral defeat. Before taking the stage, he even approaches the chair where Mussolini is sitting, ostracized by everyone, to reassure him that he will pay the pledged contribution of 30,000 liras. Then it's time for Vasa Prihoda, the young prodigy with a mysterious past. The recital is brilliant, the applause thunderous, his future assured. The waiters are already about to serve the liqueurs.

But the hostess taps a silver teaspoon on a crystal glass. When the room falls silent, Margherita Sarfatti reminds everyone that there is a second violinist in the room, then asks Mussolini to play. Everyone knows about their relationship, they know that he's a pedestrian amateur, and they all feign pity for that cruel joke between lovers.

He mumbles something about being indisposed. She insists, standing, while he remains seated. With the venomous politeness of a hostess offended by a vulgar boor, she again asks him to please play something for her.

Two minutes later the boorish *cafone* is out in the street. He is alone. It's cold in Milan in December. Rumor has it that at the end of Corso Buenos Aires, where the city peters out, there is a brothel that offers Chinese whores. From Corso Venezia, walking at a good pace, it must be less than twenty minutes on foot. Benito Mussolini sets out for Piazzale Loreto.

1920

BENITO MUSSOLINI

MILAN, JANUARY 1, 1920

THE SPLENDOR OF a fifth season in the world.

D'Annunzio, speaking to his legionnaires, says that it has been a memorable year, not the year of peace but that of passion. He says that 1919 will be remembered as the year of Fiume, not that of the negotiations of Versailles, where for more than a year the victorious powers of the global war have been dividing up what's left of the world. Versailles signifies decrepitude, infirmity, suspicion, bad faith, barter, it signifies a Europe that is staggering, that is stammering and fearful, and the predatory America of a loony president who has survived a stroke; Fiume signifies youth, beauty, something profoundly new, it is light, life, heroic days and heroic nights, solid faith, songs that dictate the cadence of our steps, it means having behind us all our dead and having before us the future, the legion of those not yet born, more numerous than those killed. The poet therefore chose, against the will of the Fiumani, to remain in Fiume, the place on earth where the soul is freer.

Bravo D'Annunzio. Well done. But the truth is that the Italians did not go along with him. The latest thing is the "reds." The Vate, with all his fine words, is already finished. He is an old man whom fate has ridiculed by turning him into the prince of youth.

Keynes, the economist of the British Treasury who left the Versailles peace conference to denounce it in a book, has the right idea. He claims that the conditions imposed by the Americans, the British and the French represent a Carthaginian peace, that if the

Americans insist on impoverishing Germany with sanctions and war reparations, within two decades there will be another war. The retaliation of the humiliated Germans will be horrific, the atrocity will make the trenches look pale by comparison, and in any case the social order of the old world is over. You can't set back the clock of history, you can't reduce the postwar period to a question of borders and commerce, a civil war cannot be deferred. On this D'Annunzio, the poet agrees with Keynes, the economist: democracy is vulnerable, its wounds profound, the liberal state can be toppled. Fiume has demonstrated it.

We must turn to the East. If the American West rejects us, starves us, humiliates us, we Mediterranean peoples will institute an Eastern policy. We will contest the treaties for peace, for free trade, all the agreements of Anglo-Saxon capitalism. You can't live with a knife always held to your throat. We will find in the East what we lack in the West. Senator Conti, the magnate of the electrical industry, is organizing a Transcaucasian mission. He says that there are huge deposits in Azerbaijan, boundless opportunities on the Azov sea. He has also invited the "dynamic" editor of *Il Popolo d'Italia* to participate. He will go. Nobody said he had to be a journalist forever. Benito Mussolini once again gives in to the attraction of turning his back on his past.

Or he could go even farther East. Fly away with the Commander, thanks to his pilot license, for the Rome-Tokyo raid. A nonstop haul towards the Rising Sun . . . He's always said it: the fascists don't believe in programs, plans, saints, apostles. They don't believe, above all, in contentment, in salvation, in the promised land. We must navigate, always, it is essential. There is no refuge, no haven, no leeward port protected within the circle of primordial needs. Navigate, without setting a course, towards a greater latitude of life. Their future is on the sea. It would be absurd not to take to the water when the sea embraces us on three sides.

Navigate, yes, always, but navigate as you go. What else can you do? People skip over the reports of parliamentary debates altogether. They go straight to the sports pages, focus on the boxing matches. Look at Georges Carpentier, the great French boxer: he's just gone up a category, now he's competing as a heavyweight and people love him, they're bursting with enthusiasm. One of his well-landed punches is all it takes to give millions of Frenchmen the same joyous exhilaration as the victory over the German invaders. That's how it is, it's no use denying it, this postwar period is a tempest, it's a deafening, turbulent sea: nothing but turmoil, chaos, upheaval, weak governments, demagogic preaching, stinging barbs that don't let you sleep.

You can't ignore the reality even if it's sad: at night adult males weep in their beds on the outskirts of the city. They need comforting but they must be baptized with fire, not with water. No more benign preachers, no more theologians, red or black, no more Christianity, neither that of Jesus or Marx! We must oppose all churches, all faiths, all hopes of salvation, oppose all of them. Many or few, it makes no difference: we are all. Against the imposing masses of workers we will continue to launch our professionals at 30 liras a day. Humanity, outside of the individual, does not exist. Aggression has merely shifted from the trenches to the piazzas, the obscure affliction has only experienced a setback; every so often it pauses, but then it begins again, it always recommences, its resumptions are intense. And so we must restart the impervious sound of the factories, we must assist with the recovery, support the national industry, smooth the way for the conversion of the wartime navy into a civilian navy, make do with the materials available after the armistice, settle the enormous volume of debts. I wrote it in my newspaper—"Maritime Italy, let's go!"—and they, the Genoese industrialists, the gods of the national steel industry, the deities of pig iron, promised me: the funds will not be lacking. We will have a new facility, more space, more modern rotary presses.

You have to navigate, navigate as you go. Always keep your eyes fixed on the coast, day and night, summer and winter, eyes narrowed like ruthless chinks in the slow-moving mist of this flat calm sea. Inshore cabotage, countercurrent, along a continuous, inconsequential line of tiny ports, a route of bitter disappointments, sketched in pencil. Navigating is essential. The future is on the sea, shipwreck awaits us.

My dear Commander, it's been a long time since I have written to you, but you must not think that my enthusiasm has cooled. I had a moment of uncertainty when all of Italy . . . was caught up in a web of deceit from which even Fiume was not spared . . . The recent period for me has been a time of great bitterness: two of my editors left me and I could even say betrayed me! I am writing to you now about another matter that is very dear to my heart. I would like to be your journalist of choice among those who have asked to follow you in the Tokyo raid. I am asking you for the high honor and risk of following you to Tokyo. I telegraphed the Air Force and they told me that there are numerous petitioners . . . but that it is up to you to decide. I am not a mere nobody in Italian journalism.

Letter from Benito Mussolini to Gabriele D'Annunzio,
January 10, 1920

The organization of the Transcaucasian Mission, of which I ended up agreeing to become chairman, is now complete . . . Mussolini, who came yesterday for an interview, promised to participate, something that would interest me greatly, offering me the opportunity to spend several months with that dynamic man.

From the diary of Ettore Conti, electrical industry magnate,
January 27, 1920

GABRIELE D'ANNUNZIO

FIUME, MARCH 18, 1920

GABRIELE D'ANNUNZIO RECEIVES a draft of a constitutional charter from Alceste De Ambris on March 18th, 1920. There can be no doubt that this is a revolutionary text, inspired by the most advanced European doctrines of radical socialism and the most evolved libertarian principles. The syndicalist of direct action, called upon by the Commander at the start of the year to be his cabinet head, has come up with a futuristic constitution for Fiume, a democracy founded on the rights of workers and individuals. All people. As the poet leafs through it in private, fingers covered in white silk gloves, the cherry trees are already in bloom outside the palazzo, on the hills of the Karst. The legionnaires pick the first flowering of the new season and stuff the buds into the barrels of rifles and machine guns.

Fiume's spring, however, is a false spring. The "city of life," which has been waiting since September of the previous year for annexation to Italy, has now been in a coma for seven months. It survives attached to the artificial respirator of the government of Rome that, by measuring out its food supplies, turns the flow of oxygen on and off at whim. In January, to sentimentally pressure Italian familism, those under siege were driven to proclaim a "children's crusade": hundreds of Fiume's poor children, starved by the embargo, left the port of Carnaro to be sent to compassionate Italian families. Even Mussolini offered to take one into his home in Milan. In addition, the Commander had even had to prohibit the production and sale of the fabulous pastries that had been the city's pride since the days of the Habsburg Empire. No more buttered sandwiches, no more coffee with whipped cream, no Markenbazar. Food is rationed, the city, for lack of fuel oil, is cold and dark.

The Commander, however, warms himself at the flame of democracy. The Republic of Carnaro, envisioned by De Ambris' Constitution, will recognize the collective sovereignty of all citizens, without distinction of sex, race, language, class and religion. The Constitution will guarantee freedom of the press, speech, thought, religion, even sexual liberty; it will guarantee a life that is worthy, ensuring elementary schooling, physical education, minimum wages, and social assistance for illness, disability, unemployment and old age; above all, and here is the stroke of genius, the Constitution will guarantee that the citizens' lives, besides being worthy, will also be beautiful: "Life," D'Annunzio writes in his own hand, revising De Ambris' text, "that a man renewed by liberty magnificently lives is beautiful and worthy."

For this reason, every workers' association will create its own insignia, its own emblems, its own music, its own songs, its own prayers. The construction workers organization will persuade its employees to adorn even the humblest of homes with some sign of folk art, music will be considered a social institution in the belief that "a great people is not only one which its god creates in his likeness but one that also creates a hymn to its god"; finally and above all, work must cease, after millennia, to be brutal, back-breaking toil, and must become "effort without effort"; work, even the most humble, will aspire to beauty and will beautify the world.

To guarantee all this, De Ambris rightly thought of linking private property to its social utility: the future Carnaro Republic will not permit property to be reserved to a single individual as if it belonged to him, or permit a property owner to leave his land fallow or wrongly dispose of it to the exclusion of any other individual. A noble purpose, no doubt, but with this last clause—the great economist Maffeo Pantaleoni, D'Annunzio's former minister of finance, observes—the magnificent Carnaro Charter is rendered incompatible with every economic and commercial activity of modern capitalism. And so much for that.

D'Annunzio, in fact, keeps the Carnaro Charter to himself. He doesn't reject it, but he guards it protectively, secretly rewriting it each day in his high-flown, oracular language, without changing its substance. He is a poet after all; for someone like him, style is everything. In the afternoon, after lunch, he works at rewriting De Ambris' Constitution, but in the morning, at the first light of dawn, he marches at the head of the troops leading them on martial excursions in the valleys surrounding the city. They assemble in Piazza Roma, in front of the Palazzo del Governo. Each day a different regiment has the privilege of following the Commander. He, in bootlegs and spurs, torso sheathed in the Ardito jacket, always turns up for roll call. Three trumpet blasts, then they set out, marching away, singing, towards the coast or towards the mountain. They all strive to stay close to him as he advances briskly, nimbly. In these springtime dawns the Commander is sprightly, he is a contemporary of his soldiers, he is twenty years old again, like them. The discipline, hierarchy, and cadenced step of the departure are soon forgotten. Before noon they are seen returning in scattered clusters, covered with twigs, garlands of flowers, blooming shrubs. Hardly an army—they look like an untamed garden in motion. Some go off in pairs, holding hands, like the legendary Theban legion.

In the evening they have supper at a trattoria previously known as the Cervo d'Oro (the golden hind), which the poet renamed the Ornitorinco (the duck-billed platypus) after the eccentric Guido Keller stole a stuffed platypus from the natural science museum. There they enjoy a memorable risotto with scampi and the men drink gallons of a local dark, sticky, sweet cherry brandy, it too renamed by the highly imaginative Vate as Morlachian Blood.

After supper they often go to the theater. *La fiaccola sotto il moggio* (The Torch under the Bushel) is playing, an apocalyptic drama written by D'Annunzio in 1905, which portrays the catastrophe of an ancient family composed entirely of flawed, ailing, cursed or corrupt individuals.

The play's author watches the performance from a proscenium box together with his staff officers. The troops, instead, crowd into the balcony and upper circles. But the acting is poor and the troops want to have some fun. When the curtain falls on the second act, a voice erupts, breaking the silence:

"Let's interrupt this boring play and sing our songs!" D'Annunzio himself protests against his own work: the twenty-year-old back from the morning march is in conflict with his old self.

At the Commander's goliardic signal, a chorus immediately rises from the orchestra and balconies intoning *Giovinezza*, then Garibaldi's hymn, then that of Mameli. Now the whole theater is singing, youth, joy, gaiety are everywhere. D'Annunzio sings from his stage box: the poet is happy that he is finally shedding his literature.

Then, however, the simple soldiers call for *'A tazza 'e cafè*. A popular Neapolitan tune, a trifling little song that rings out in cafes and brings to mind a glittering, imaginary life.

The officers exchange embarrassed looks. The troops insist: hadn't they agreed to sing "our songs"? The chorus starts up, without musical accompaniment, raucous, a cappella. Lightly at first, spirited, then fiercely, impetuously, the song rises. In this theater named for Giuseppe Verdi, the triplets of the tarantella, belted out by a thousand baritones drunk on Morlachian Blood and the testosterone their youthful hearts pump into the members under their uniforms, bellow like the guttural roar of a huge enraged beast. The little song swells, frighteningly, brutally, ruthlessly, and its simplistic gaiety buries the pomp of the official songs.

Everyone is making gestures. Even the officers now find it amusing. But D'Annunzio isn't singing anymore. He's turned pale. The people are teaching him their song. He seems to have understood.

Only assiduous producers of common wealth and assiduous creators of common strength are full citizens in the Republic of Carnaro and with it constitute a single functioning entity, a single controlling power . . . each workers association creates its own insignia, its own emblems, its own music, its own songs, its own prayers; it establishes its own ceremonies and rites; it contributes, as liberally as possible, to the corpus of common diversions, feasts and anniversaries, land and sea sports; it venerates its dead, honors its elders, celebrates its heroes . . . every religious faith is allowed and respected, and can erect its temple; but no citizen may invoke his beliefs and his rites to avoid fulfilling the duties prescribed by existing law . . . Life is beautiful and worthy when a man who is made whole again by liberty lives it austerely and magnificently; the whole man is one who each day is able to invent his own virtue, who each day offers his brothers a new gift; work, even the most humble, even the most insignificant, if it is done well, aspires to beauty and beautifies the world . . .

From the Carnaro Charter

MARGHERITA SARFATTI

MILAN, SPRING 1920

SHE IS THE only woman at this table of madmen.

There are evenings when the society queen is pleased to host a salon in her palazzo on Corso Venezia, and for forty-eight hours fawn over beautiful young painters, as delicate as fallen angels; then there are evenings like this one, in which the patrician lady willingly lowers herself at the table of delirious futurists, grim veterans, and hard-hitting journalists, while the ink of Trani's heavy wines flows in a hemorrhagic gush on the checkered tablecloths of popular trattorias. On these nights of convulsive beauty she is the only woman sitting at the table of frenzied men.

At this moment, Filippo Tommaso Marinetti is holding forth, as usual, as if galvanized by an unremitting electric current.

Standing on a chair, he shouts "Down with extravagant toilettes!" as ardently as at other times he has shouted "down with the king!", "down with the past!" or "kill the moonlight!" With the same shrill hysteria of the savior of a humanity threatened by extinction, the founder of futurism harangues an audience of truckers and printers at the end of their shifts—for a moment they raise their heads from their soup plates, amused and bewildered—about the dangers being spread by the ever-growing obsession with female extravagance on every social level, thanks to male imbecility.

"This morbid mania," Marinetti argues, "increasingly forces women into a disguised but inevitable prostitution. Three changes of attire a day is equivalent to putting one's body in a display window, on offer to a market of male buyers. The offer reduces the value of her appeal and mystery. The offer repels the male who despises an easy woman!"

The truckers cheer and drink up; the veterans of the trenches gladly toast to contempt for women; Margherita Sarfatti, the only woman at that table, smiles benevolently at the rowdy uproar, maternal, urbane, well protected by her haute couture evening apparel.

Her self-assurance is absolute. There is not a hint of discomfort in that elegant posture. And, in any case, she is surrounded by "her" artists: Marinetti himself baptized her "the Papess of the futurists." Margherita contributed to the great national Exhibition of Futurist Painters of March 1919 in Milan with a loan of four works that she owned, one of which was a portrait of the collector herself. The males sitting and clamoring at the table of that tavern are mostly artists with whom this inimitable woman has formed a personal alliance. There are the painters Achille Funi and Leonardo Dudreville, the poet Giuseppe Ungaretti, who collaborates with *Il Popolo d'Italia*, all artists who have moved from art to the heady thrill of history, all veterans united by the unspeakable emotion of experiencing war, all alumni of the school of truth that is winter in the trenches.

There is Mario Sironi who paints lifeless urban landscapes in which nature is absent, the atmosphere is charged with menace, and man is prisoner of a hostile world; marginal peripheries unknown to the city's bourgeoisie, worlds that exist only for those condemned to live there, those who are stranded in those shadowy outer fringes, as he is, this impoverished war veteran artist, whom she, patroness Sarfatti, encourages and subsidizes. And then there are the dead. They are also sitting at that table. There is Antonio Sant'Elia, a young, brilliant architect, who died with a cigarette in his mouth while leading his soldiers; there is Umberto Boccioni, the painter of simultaneous visions, of the city rising, the greatest, the most promising of all. Both enlisted and were killed in the "Lombard Battalion of Volunteer Cyclists and Motorists."

First and foremost, beside Margherita at that table is him, her "most devoted savage." He too is silent and smiles indulgently at Marinetti's invectives. The poet thunders, waving his arms about to occupy center stage, but the head of the table is always where he, Benito Mussolini, sits. The autumn elections have mortified him, crushed him, disheartened him, but it is from him—Margherita is convinced of it—that the vigor coming from the street emanates; he, the son of a blacksmith, embodies the "courage from below" announced by Georg Wilhelm Friedrich Hegel, the greatest German philosopher of the previous century. He, Benito Mussolini, no one else, with that clean-shaven face of his, with the intense, dark eyes of a madman, with that vacant gaze, with the virility of the coarse, aggressive body of a cornered animal, will convey to the new century the message that the compromise between the good manners of the old portly socialist leaders and the seething hunger of the malnourished masses is obsolete, that it is now time to burst out like an unexploded grenade, that the old world is done for.

For now Benito Mussolini sits there empty-handed, but he was the first to have understood that he could exploit the rancor resulting from political struggle, the first to have led an army of dissatisfied, demoted failures who spend their days polishing their daggers while he spends them between the editorial office and the street, waiting for things to explode. So that he can ride the shock wave or write about it in his newspaper.

There is no doubt: the patient chain of fathers generating sons was shattered with the war. The mold was broken and only a man like Mussolini will be able to guide the generation to which destiny has granted the right to make history. In any case, society has not afforded her, the only woman sitting at that table, the right to be in politics and, therefore, the only thing she can do, as Anna Kuliscioff did earlier with Andrea Costa and then with Filippo Turati, is place her bet on a man.

And so the grande dame spends her days in the squalid little rooms of the editorial offices of *Il Popolo d'Italia*, then, after closing time, the refined intellectual retires to some small fetid hotel with the crude self-taught man and lets him make love to her. Each time she brings a new book along, she opens his mind, generously bestows her body, educates him on reading the classics and teaches him to wear spats over the worn-out shoes of a scruffy, penniless revolutionary. Machiavelli, the fall of the Roman Empire, white pocket handkerchiefs and a straw hat in summer. Teaching him to use the subjunctive, slipping a flower into the lapel of her man's well-cut black suits, she too prepares to make history. Vicariously.

And besides, he desired her so much, right from the beginning . . . From their first meeting he's shown that he craves the type of full-figured, alluring blonde she embodies . . . And then too, he dedicates amateurish poems to her in which he celebrates the beauty of the sea, of the wind, of his lover, he sends her love letters of ferocious tenderness.

My love, my thoughts, my heart are with you. We spent delicious hours together. If I can, I will come to Tabiano. I love you so much, more than you think. I embrace you tightly, I kiss you with ferocious tenderness. Tonight before you fall asleep, think of your most devoted savage, who is a little weary, a little dispirited, but all yours, through and through. Give me a blood transfusion from your lips. Your Benito

Letter from Benito Mussolini to Margherita Sarfatti,
undated, though between 1919–1922

BENITO MUSSOLINI

MILAN, SPRING 1920

IN THE SPRING of 1920, Angelo Tasca is twenty-eight years old and is one of the most influential young Italian socialists. Scion of a family of Turin's bourgeoisie, he studied at the exclusive Vincenzo Gioberti classical lyceum, then embraced the proletariat's cause; he was a member of the socialist federation, then appointed to the leadership of his city's Labor Board. The previous year, together with Antonio Gramsci, Palmiro Togliatti and Umberto Terracini, he founded the newspaper *L'Ordine Nuovo* (The New Order) which has already established itself as a forge of laborist thought and cradle of the revolutionary movement of works councils. It was Tasca's father-in-law who lent half the capital the young communists needed to found the paper that wanted to expropriate all his wealth.

When Tasca encounters Benito Mussolini in the Galleria Vittorio Emanuele in Milan in the spring of 1920, what surprises him is that Mussolini is bursting with health. On the marble pavement of the covered pedestrian walkway, surrounded by elegant shops and cafes that make it one of the world's shopping centers—a gathering place for the city's bourgeoisie who immediately dubbed it "Milan's living room"—under the Neo-Renaissance style vault that is one of the most celebrated examples of European cast-iron architecture, Tasca sees a man in a black suit walk by who is in peak physical condition. Tasca notes Mussolini's sturdy neck atop a powerful torso, the smooth, self-important face, the arrogant swagger, the barely lit cigarette dangling from the full lips like a shamelessly exposed phallus. In short, Mussolini has the coarse ebullience of a commoner clad in new clothes. For those like Tasca who knew him in 1912, when he was a young revolutionary anarchist with an abject appearance, sagging cheeks, pitiable gauntness, and haunted, feverish eyes, the transformation is disconcerting. Here is a reprobate who has broken all ties with the disheartened down-and-outer of the past and discovered affluence, a man who has lovers, a man who has come to know a taste of life.

And yet, in the days when the encounter takes place, Benito Mussolini is the owner of a newspaper approaching bankruptcy, a hounded womanizer and, above all, a washed-up politician. All the streets he has pounded so far seem to have been dead ends, both the one that was to have led him to win back the proletarian masses, and the one that was to have put him at the head of nationalist avant-gardes. The first is barred by a vindictive wall of hatred, the second is obstructed by the overwhelming presence of Gabriele D'Annunzio. Fascism is on a spur track.

Italy too, however, is shunted off the main track. While Mussolini strolls through the Galleria, often accompanied by Ferruccio Vecchi in his Arditi captain's uniform, the country is submerged by the biggest wave of strikes recorded in its history. The post, telegraph and telephone walkouts started in January, then the railwaymen, who hadn't come out on strike since 1907, took their turn. The agitation, which began as a simple demand for wage adjustments, degenerated into a total paralysis of train traffic, and stations took on the appearance of battlefields, garrisoned by troops in combat deployment. Like a chain reaction, the small and mid-size sectors of workers went on strike: porters, coachmen, clerks and bakers, tram operators, gasmen and even barbers. Day in and day out, Milan looks like a dead city, neither carriages nor automobiles circulate, there's no mail, the city's life is suspended. There are thousands of strikes in the production industry, involving millions of workers, and wholesale prices have increased fivefold.

At Fiat in Turin, at the end of March, a commotion actually broke out over a question of changing the clocks. The Council of

Ministers extended daylight-saving time, formerly adopted during the war. The workers, however, decided that from that moment on they would be the boss of their own time, not Senator Agnelli. The industrialists responded with a lockout. The result was a ten-day general strike that involved 120,000 workers in Turin and the province alone; 60,000 of them occupied the factories to oppose moving the clock hand one hour ahead. Obviously, it is not about clock hands, it is not about "summer" time, but about the supreme hour. The hour of revolution.

Party leaders, however, have again postponed it. Many of them have openly condemned the "clock hand strike." As Mussolini had foreseen, socialism's electoral triumph led the way to internal crisis, accentuating factional divisions: the maximalists don't want participation in power and the reformists don't dare attempt a total power grab. In short, even socialism is on a sidetrack.

Claudio Treves, one of its most influential leaders, acknowledged it in a dramatic address in parliament, immediately baptized the "expiation speech." The revolution, Treves admitted, "is an epoch, not a day." It has the features of a phenomenon of nature: slow erosions, rapid landslides. We are fully in it—he declared—and we will be there for a good number of years. Day by day, episode by episode, hour by hour. We would like to finish it once and for all, but that's not possible. It's not dying that frightens us, it's this non-living that frustrates us.

Meanwhile, Mussolini strolls. He knows Treves well. They fought a duel in 1912, when as a barbaric young man, the rising star of revolutionary socialism, he had stolen the mature, sophisticated, sober intellectual reformist's job as editor-in-chief of *Avanti!* The seconds declared that they had never seen such a fierce duel between party members. The dueling men had to be stopped at the eighth assault. Both sabers, striking with the flat of the blade, were already a couple of useless pieces of twisted scrap metal.

Mussolini strolls. What's new is the fact that the industrialists no longer fight in open order formation. In Milan, not far from the Galleria where he strolls, they convened for a meeting and for the first time founded a national association to defend their interests.

Il Popolo d'Italia's editor, increasingly leaning to the right, always looking for funds for his newspaper, by now ready to break with his disheveled youth as a revolutionary agitator, hailed the birth of the Industrial Confederation. "A breath of vital modernity," he wrote. Mussolini also openly condemned the strikes: workers' rights must be protected but these socialist leaders of theirs want no rules. The choice between the two cultures is simple: the bourgeois world has behind it a centuries-old history of progress and achievements, the proletarian one still has only a chronicle of inexperience and folly. There is no doubt: the reaction of the bourgeoisie will come. It is just a matter of waiting, weapons lowered, and, meanwhile, go strolling in the Galleria.

We left Rome on February 4th, at dusk: none of the members failed to appear at roll call except for Mussolini, who was detained in Italy . . . sorry to say; because I hoped to meet this strange, dynamic man, who isn't easy to decipher from his various appearances . . . One of his newspaper colleagues, Pietro Nenni, who is traveling with us, and who says he knew him well when they weren't on opposite sides of the barricades, sees in him the obscure fascination of a commander, a strong man, who is determined to stand out, to be first, in one way or another; today against the bourgeoisie, tomorrow a ruler; a man therefore who can do a lot of good or a lot of harm, but who will be talked about in any case. It's a real pity that at the last moment he let me down: he would have interested me enormously . . .

From the diary of Ettore Conti, electrical industry magnate,
February, 1920

Today a circular was sent out by the Fasci di Combattimento to about thirty sections in the main cities, calling off current disruptions, and urging them to prepare to react if necessary . . . In the event of danger the fasci are urged to make their forces available to the military authority.

Telephone call from chief of staff Enrico Flores
to Prime Minister Francesco Saverio Nitti,
Milan, April 19, 1920

In recent days, a discharged general went to various localities in the Monza area on behalf of the Fasci di Combattimento, offering industrialists their protection to be provided by squads of Arditi during riots or strikes.

Telegram from Enrico Flores to Francesco Saverio Nitti,
Milan, April 19, 1920

Trying to slow down, to stop this impulse toward disintegration is not reactionary in that it aims to preserve the fundamental values of collective life . . . To the deceitful sellers of smoke, the gutless bourgeois card-carrying members of the Socialist Party, idiots of all kinds, I loudly raise the strong cry: long live reaction!

Benito Mussolini,
"Workers! When You Are Free of
Your Deceitful Leaders,"
Il Popolo d'Italia, April 25, 1920

LEANDRO ARPINATI

BOLOGNA, APRIL 1920

IN BOLOGNA, LEANDRO Arpinati is on his own.

Already at the beginning of the year he sought help in Milan from Umberto Pasella, secretary of the fasci: "A visit from you is absolutely essential. Our fascio is unraveling." The simple prophecy was punctually fulfilled two months later. Pietro Nenni and the other republicans who had founded the Bolognese fascio in April 1919, abandoned it one after the other in 1920. Attorney Mario Bergamo personally communicated the news to the original Milanese fascio: "In Bologna? Since the republicans broke away, the fascio is dead."

The report is correct: there are six remaining Bolognese fascists. They don't even have the money to rent an office. Arpinati has his mail delivered to him at the trattoria on Via Marsala where he takes his meals at lunchtime. Pasella, who knows Emilia Romagna well from his time as a union leader in the Ferrara area before the war, has promised the funds to cover the rent for the first six months, but has not yet sent a lira. Nonetheless Mussolini insists that his friend Leandro assume its management, and also assigned him responsibility for all of eastern Emilia. He suggests following the Milan example. The way to go is to organize civic defense militias against the ongoing strikes. Arpinati asks that they send him a speaker for publicity. He is a man of action, too many words make him uncomfortable.

The truth is that it's all going to the dogs. Since Arpinati finished serving his time for the Lodi events, Bologna is in shambles. There are two chambers of labor in the city competing with each other in revolutionary extremism. Even the socialist mayor Zanardi, who on his own would be a moderate, tries to keep up by inciting people to invade elegant homes, urging tenants to proclaim themselves owners of the apartments. "Callused hands" rule the day. Things get to the point of denying bread to those who don't have a union card, the middle classes are caught between a rock and a hard place, many employers prefer to sell their businesses rather than remain on the verge of disaster like that. There's no way to stem the tide.

Things still aren't that bad in the city. The rural areas are lost. There is no village that is not under the influence of the Socialist Party. Every town has a farmers' union, a *Casa del Popolo*, a co-operative, a cell. The "red" leagues control the situation. They manage to impose working conditions on the landowners that deprive them of practically all property rights on their own land. Landowners who violate the rules imposed by the leagues are subjected to hefty fines that benefit the strikers' coffers. The loathing directed towards tenant farmers and small landowners is particularly intense. Landless farmworkers reserve the most ruthless hatred for these neighbors. The Po Valley, along both banks of the river from its source to its mouth, is the scene of epic struggles for control of the fields.

The battles started, obviously, in Ferrara, a province dominated by "red" leagues. The seasonal farmers, backed by sharecroppers, revolted on February 24th, demanding the renewal of the "*patto colonico*," the collective farm agreement. The call to strike suspended the sowing of the hemp and sugar beet crop on which the entire province relies. Threats, barns set on fire, animals abandoned in the stables. The strikers' struggle was so determined and cohesive that it forced the landowners to admit defeat on all points under discussion. On March 6th, they agreed to wage increases, worker-managed recruitment centers and, most importantly, a compulsory manpower quota obliging landowners to hire five workers for every thirty hectares of arable land in the period from November to April, that is, during the months when there is no work. On March 5th, Ferrara's example was followed in the provinces of Novara, Pavia and in the district of Casale Monferrato. The uprisings lasted forty-seven days. Forty-seven days and forty-seven nights in a state of siege: there too fires, livestock seizures, ambushes, shootings, farmhouses turned into bivouacs for combatants, "red guards" who in Lomellina monitored major roadways and kept an eye out for the presence of scabs. The solidarity between seasonal farmhands and salaried workers was total, their victory crushing. The landowners gave in on April 21st.

Now it's Bologna's turn. The war for the agricultural concordat has just begun and has already left dozens of bodies on the field. The massacre took place in Decima di San Giovanni in Persiceto, a small, insignificant, remote district in the countryside. A rally was held on the collective farm agreement, at which Sigismondo Campagnoli spoke, sent by Bologna's Chamber of Labor. A few references to the agrarian issue immediately followed by the usual invectives against capitalists, priests and carabinieri, and, finally, the usual incitement to the crowd, the usual magic word: revolution.

At that point, after hearing the dreaded word, the brigadier responsible for public order feels obliged to interrupt the rabble-rouser. Another speaker, Pietro Comastri, also from the Bologna Chamber of Labor, goes up to the stage. Comastri promises to inspire cooler heads but, then, within a quarter of an hour he too shifts from the compulsory manpower quota to revolution. The brigadier drags him down from the wooden platform. A test of strength that the foolish officer is unable to enforce: he has twenty men and there are 1,500 furious, fed-up farmhands behind him.

A siphon bottle goes flying, the kind used to add a dash of soda water to improve mediocre wine. For an instant the scene hangs suspended between tragedy and comedy. Everything could still be tossed off with a laugh. But the idiotic sergeant, thinking he was putting them in a safe position, has lined the carabinieri up against the side of the adjacent farmhouse. The soda siphon cracks against the wall and explodes in splinters. A few drops of blood trickle from the deputy inspector's right temple. It is the signal for melee. The speaker is struck, the crowd instinctively rushes towards the oppressors, the carabinieri find themselves with their backs against the wall. An order doesn't even need to be issued. The weapons fire of their own accord. About fifty shots, some from pistols, some from machine guns. Carabinieri Raffaele Barile and Giuseppe Scimmia alone respectively fire seven and ten shots at the unarmed peasants. A massacre. Eight dead and about thirty injured on the ground. It will be said that the soldiers fired in self-defense. But almost all the dead were shot in the back. Campagnoli, the first speaker, was finished off with a bayonet.

From that moment on, as a result of those deaths, the region teeters on the precipice. The Chamber of Labor proclaims a three-day general strike throughout the province. For seventy-two hours, all public and private services are suspended, as workers withdraw their labor. For the bourgeoisie, haute and petite, it is the proverbial straw that breaks the camel's back. Farmers, manufacturers, merchants, professionals, public employees and homeowners decide to organize on their own. On April 8th, at a meeting promoted by the Chamber of Commerce, the Bolognese Association of Social Defense is established. On the 15th, a delegation from the Association presents Prime Minister Nitti with a brief in which it denounces the state's abdication in the face of violent acts by the socialists, and declares itself prepared to replace it in the interest of self-defense.

Leandro Arpinati doesn't know what to do. He is an anarchist railwayman, descended from poor people, the last of six brothers, the son of Sante, a miserable innkeeper of Civitella di Romagna, a remote village in the Apennines, in the narrow valley of the Bidente river. The big landowners who own half of Emilia Romagna, who don't give a damn about Italy, offered him 100,000 liras to defend them against the poor people, his people. On the other hand, those poor people of his, with their strikes and revolutionary delusions, are ruining Italy. Arpinati writes to Milan:

> *Sure, this Bolognese bourgeoisie—and by Bolognese I mean apathetic and vile—hasn't made a move until it felt its own safety and its own wallet were threatened with the last strike, but is that any reason for us not to accept the arms-money so essential to our struggle that this bourgeoisie, albeit out of fear, is now offering us?*

We are prepared above all, and the government should know it, to defend our families and our homes, to protect our right to work and the dignity of our daily routine, by creating, on our own, the means of defense that until now we have ceded to state law, in order to put an end at all costs to the succession of intolerable, ruinous events.

Bolognese Association of Social Defense,
brief to Prime Minister Francesco Saverio Nitti,
Bologna, April 15, 1920

NICOLA BOMBACCI

MILAN, APRIL 19, 1920

When Bombacci arrives in Copenhagen at the end of March 1920, Prince Hamlet's Denmark is still sleeping under a heavy layer of boreal snow. Born in Civitella di Romagna, the same remote village in the Apennines, in the narrow valley of the Bidente river, from which Arpinati comes, Nicolino is unfamiliar with the world. Although he dreams of a planetary embrace in the revolutionary brotherhood of all proletarians on earth, from Mexico City to Vladivostok, the "Lenin of Romagna" has never left Italy's borders, despite being forty years old.

Waiting for him in Copenhagen are Maksim Litvinov, Soviet commissar for foreign affairs, and Leonid Krasin, the "red merchant," plenipotentiary of the commissariat for revolutionary Russia's foreign trade, both lieutenants of the real Lenin. For the "small Lenin" of Romagna, landing on the shores of the Øresund Strait, being able to meet the emissaries of the great Lenin, must be a little like going home, a home that he never knew until he was forty.

The Romagna revolutionary is leading an odd delegation. Officially it is a mission arranged by the National League of "red" cooperatives, promoted by socialist mayor Caldara's city of Milan, but it also has the political endorsement of President Nitti's Italian government that the socialists daily proclaim they want to subvert. The paradox is that Nitti was forced to farm out foreign policy with Russia to the Italian socialists who would like to oust him.

Since December 1919 Bombacci has been working hard to push Italy to reopen diplomatic relations with Lenin's Russia. Bombacci isn't interested in trade talks, he dismisses them as "quartermaster's concerns," but he hopes that this can be a first step towards capitalist Italy's diplomatic recognition of Soviet Russia. Italy after all has always been the "great proletarian," as Pascoli called it, a nation of poor, decent people who cannot fail to recognize the legitimacy of a state founded by their Russian proletarian brothers. Finally, more than anything else, Bombacci is eager to be able to speak, for the first time in person, about the revolution to be accomplished in Italy with the men who have already brought about a revolution in Russia.

Nicolino has devoted himself body and soul to the idea of revolution. At the Socialist Party's national council in Florence on January 11th, he fought hard for the immediate formation throughout the country of "soviets" or councils based on the Russian model. His proposal got 401 votes out of the 440 who voted. A triumph. But the leadership is divided. Even Palmiro Togliatti—a young Turin leader who should have been on his side—spoke ironically about his plan, considering it premature, incomplete, and theoretically unfounded. Even if soviets were formed in Italy, Togliatti ridiculed him sarcastically, they would be a pathetic imitation of the Russian councils, "merely the shadow of a shadow."

But he, the "Christ of the workers," does not capitulate to the vetoes of those communist intellectuals who take pleasure in their isolation and are content to stand alone against everyone else while solely contemplating their strength. The strength of Italian socialism, on the other hand, is enormous: in just fifteen months the number of members has increased tenfold, exceeding 200,000. But it is a strength that must be made to roar, to circulate, that must look around and pull in all possible allies, even D'Annunzio. In the end, however, the socialist leaders steered clear of an alliance with the Vate, expressing reservations and raising petty objections as Togliatti had done to his proposed "soviets." More mockery, more conjecture, more sarcasm. But though Italy's communists quibble, have doubts, and poke fun, the men of Moscow will understand, Bombacci keeps telling himself. The fathers of the revolution, those who really achieved one, can't help but understand.

In Denmark Bombacci first sees Leonid Krasin, the "red merchant." His entire delegation met with him on April 7th in the rooms of a local socialist port cooperative. On the docks of Copenhagen's harbor the ice is melting into grayish slush when Krasin openly declares that his sole mandate is to obtain the Italian state's official recognition of Moscow. Nothing more. For the moment, the Italian proletarian revolution seems to be of no interest to the "red merchants."

Nicolino, then, places all his hopes in the meeting with Litvinov, the man who sits at Lenin's right hand at assemblies of the Soviet Party. The People's Commissar of foreign affairs is a plump man with a ruddy face resembling a cured prosciutto. He welcomes Bombacci with a glass of iced vodka. It's only ten o'clock in the morning and the alcohol, filling the empty stomach of Nicolino's frail, diminutive body, causes him violent spasms. Fighting cramps, he starts talking fervently about the imminent Italian revolution, but as soon as he does Litvinov withers him. In Italy the Socialist Party is strong but the revolutionary faction is weak, he tells him. That said, the man sitting on Lenin's right seasons the analysis with sarcasm, just as Togliatti would have done: Italian socialists would last in power for at most two months. And with irony. "The revolution," Litvinov adds, "has already succeeded in Russia, now the only urgent problem of revolutionary Russia is to resume its political and trade relations with the capitalist states. Nothing more."

A few days later, as soon as he is back from Denmark, Bombacci has to report to the National Socialist Council, meeting in Milan from April 18 to 22. In Italy he is again welcomed with sarcasm and irony. This time around, from the columns of *Il Popolo d'Italia*, it falls to his old friend Benito Mussolini to mock Bombacci for having stopped in Copenhagen, "on the threshold of paradise," for not having felt the curiosity or the sense of obligation to go a little further on, to Moscow.

Speaking at the socialist assembly in Milan on April 20th, Nicolino cannot manage to hide his bitterness. The world, it seems, has disappointed him. The whole first half of his talk projects a wintry melancholy. Then, however, when it comes to once again going on the attack about social democratic cautions, his passion is rekindled. He shouts that the moderates' mistake is that they have not yet understood that the new revolution must be brought about independently of parliament, without parliament, in opposition to parliament . . . that in fact they have already left parliament . . . and moved towards the dictatorship of the proletariat . . . towards the sun of the future . . . that they can walk amid parliament without caring about parliament, just like priests who walk on earth but yearn to go to heaven.

Even if Bombacci has taken the road back this time, paradise remains, after all, his ultimate destination. The masters of sarcasm, however, still wait along the way. The more Nicolino talks and talks of revolution, the more the revolution fades in the shadow of a shadow.

Marx had taught us that revolution is a process of development and transformation of social relations, he had taught us that being in touch with the actuality of these relations, that is, of the economy, the revolution becomes something real and concrete, which the human will itself substantiates: Bombacci is satisfied with form. And revolution . . . for him becomes a word, a shadow: the revolutionary councils he would like to create are the shadow of a shadow.

Palmiro Togliatti, *L'Ordine Nuovo*, March 1920

I really believe that Minister Litvinov has dampened the fervor of "citizen" Bombacci so irreparably that he prefers the road back to this rotten bourgeois Italy to the road that leads to the sublime paradise of the Soviets.

Benito Mussolini, *Il Popolo d'Italia*, April 1920

MILAN, MAY 24, 1920
SECOND NATIONAL CONGRESS OF THE FASCI DI COMBATTIMENTO

THE DEFINITIVE SWING to the right takes place around midnight.

The Congress opened on the morning of May 23 at the Teatro Lirico with the inauguration of the new pennants of the Arditi and fascists. Until the time of delivery, the triangular flags were kept under sheets of pastel-colored tissue paper. Ferruccio Vecchi, receiving the Arditi pennant, swore that the bomb and the dagger would never bend before the hammer and sickle. Mussolini, receiving the pennant of the fasci, vowed that postwar laxity is about to end, that Italy will honor the Arditi again and that Fiume will be Italian. Some care was also taken with the set design: on the stage a swarm of flags, uniformed soldiers in a semicircle, patriotic choirs of little girls beneath the flags. Down in the audience, Filippo Tommaso Marinetti even found the presenters "charming" as they "lustily" recited their memorized speeches. For the first time, some beautiful women attended a political assembly.

The congress itself, however, begins on May 24th. It is the "usual paltry meeting, which conveys the movement's scant vitality," notes Cesare Maria De Vecchi, Turin's fascist monarchist. For weeks Mussolini has been announcing in the columns of *Il Popolo d'Italia* that "the time for revival is near"; Pasella reports exciting numbers but the truth is that there are 600 card-carrying members in Milan,

300 in Cremona thanks to Roberto Farinacci's activism, only 300 in the capital, about a hundred in Bologna, Parma, Pavia and Verona, 40 in Mantua, Oneglia and Caulonia, 20 in Piadena and Recco, and so on. In total, there are 2,375 registered, duly enrolled fascists in all of Italy. This is the militant base that can be counted on.

More than a year has passed since its foundation, but the audience that Mussolini faces in the Teatro Lirico is not much bigger than that of San Sepolcro. Something, however, has changed. The numbers are similar, but the faces are no longer the same. The phalanx of adventurers, misfits and demobilized soldiers holds its position. The veterans' rancor is resolute. But left-wing interventionist unionists have deserted it, republicans like Pietro Nenni broke away in the early months of the year, idealist nationalists like Eno Mecheri left for Fiume in January. The flamboyant manes of aspiring poets, playwrights, and frustrated, unemployed journalists no longer stand out in the audience. In their place, in the Lirico's orchestra, can be seen shopkeepers, civil servants, low-level managers, the respectable, threadbare jackets of the petite bourgeoisie impoverished by runaway inflation. Marinetti and the futurists aren't happy either. A blood transfusion has occurred.

Nevertheless, the first speech of the morning, Mussolini's, is judicious. Since the beginning of the month he has been ranting, making open threats to the socialists. Those people's hatred of him—he writes—is fully understandable. In fact, he will keep the promise he made the night he was expelled from the party: he will be implacable. And now he can sense that the day of his total revenge is not far off.

Yet on the morning of the 24th at the Teatro Lirico, the avenger delivers an opening speech that is one of conciliation. He again claims not to represent a reactionary position, he still distinguishes between the proletariat and the socialist leadership, he reiterates that he wants to move towards the people.

The job of burning bridges is left to Cesare Rossi. For months, Rossi has been preaching the need for them to brutally and resolutely proclaim themselves conservative and reactionary. At the Lirico congress he again declares that he is against taking shots in the dark, he depicts the proletariat as incapable of replacing the bourgeoisie, as a red mob, morally corrupt, selfish, uncultured, soulless, deaf to patriotic values, a flock of deluded fools. Above all, Rossi believes that by now the proletariat is inseparable from the Socialist Party, that it is wed to its cause and for that reason does not deserve any indulgence. We must look to those who do not "work with their hands." The petite bourgeoisie is even more ill-treated than the workers. Fighting a decisive three-man duel is not possible. The fasci must therefore align with the current regime for the moment, even if it's despicable. No anti-monarchical prejudgment but sheer possibilism. Allies are chosen depending on the occasion, the battlefield as well. As long as the fasci were howling at the moon as an anti-party they could well live on air, but now a social base is needed. Coming to terms with the decadent liberal state will govern them from here on out.

Rossi concludes his speech trembling with rage. The extremism of the revolutionary unionist he used to be before the war, when he set fire to barns in the countryside of Parma and Piacenza out of hatred towards the landowners, has never left him. Now, however, that hatred has found a new target: it is turned against the peasants who back then were inciting the revolt. Cesare Rossi returns to his place in the audience amid the applause of most of the onlookers.

The futurists, on the other hand, rise up against the swing to the right. Marinetti is furious. He shouts that the monarchy is a rucksack full of old stuff to be discarded, he rails as usual against the Vatican, he talks about shepherds and flocks, he portrays himself as the intelligent, faithful dog that stands watch when the master is drunk. Then he concludes poetically: "We come from the Karst," he recalls, "we will not go toward reaction."

For supper, Mussolini joins his close supporters at a trattoria in the Bottonuto, behind the theater. They eat greasy food, drink strong, cheap wine. Pasella counts the membership cards sold for 50 centesimi. They need to centralize the organization, retain the Milanese Central Committee's ability to relieve provincial secretaries of their posts, above all they must reserve the right to decide which federations to fund. Giovanni Marinelli, treasurer, plunges into a meticulous description of the revenue accounts. Mussolini is silent; he eats little, unenthusiastically, and drinks even less. He appears to be pursuing a single obsessive thought. Before returning to the theater for the evening session, when Rossi recalls Marinetti's speech, he lashes out against the flamboyant founder of futurism: "Who the hell is this extravagant buffoon who wants to be a politician but who nobody in Italy takes seriously, not even me!?"

Shortly before midnight, before a lethargic audience lulled by the laborious digestion of animal proteins, Mussolini speaks again. The fascists, as the industrialists want, must support the state's liberalistic reduction of the offices of soldier, policeman, judge and revenue collector. Nothing more. They must also foster cooperation between the productive sectors of the proletariat and the bourgeoisie. The bourgeois ship must not be sunk. Instead, they must get on board and take over the engine room. Any institutional prejudgment must therefore be abandoned. The fascists have always tended to favor a republic but if necessary they will also retain the monarchy.

Then the Founder pauses for a few seconds and looks around the room in search of Marinetti. He doesn't see him. So the few who are still awake hear the Romagnolo blasphemer who hasn't even baptized his children state that the Vatican represents four hundred million people throughout the world and that any intelligent political strategy must tap this colossal force. Lenin himself, in Russia, stopped when it came to confronting the authority of the Holy Synod. Religion must be respected.

Barely twenty minutes have gone by and almost nothing remains of the San Sepolcro program. Before midnight, the swing to the right is complete.

The following morning, the work of the second fascist national congress comes to an end. Of the nineteen members of the first central committee only ten were re-elected. Two of these, Marinetti and Carli, will resign the following day. The nine new members come from the provinces and are all right wing.

It is a beautiful spring day in northern Italy. Mussolini and Rossi linger in the doorway. The transition from the dim interior to the light is jarring. The city of Milan appears completely indifferent to the heated discussions that went on in the theater's cavern until a few minutes ago. Employees from the city offices, returning to their desks after the lunch break, sidestep the small knot of idlers lingering outside the entrance to the Lirico, annoyed by them. Nearby, a fruit vendor is restocking his stall. Removing the plums from a wooden crate that arrived from the countryside, he arranges them in a wicker basket and, after rinsing them with a sprayer, polishes them one by one with a soft cloth as if they were brass doorknobs.

Cesare Rossi points him out to Mussolini with a nod of his head. The future belongs to the shopkeepers. Never mind the follies of those futurists . . .

The bourgeois ship must not be sunk, but must be commandeered in order to expel the parasitic elements . . . The issue today is restoration. All large-scale strikes are destined to fail, as in Turin, in France and elsewhere. You can't go beyond a certain limit. The fascists must not change their course of action. After all, one is always reactionary with respect to someone else.

Benito Mussolini, speech at the National Congress of the Fasci di Combattimento, Milan, May 25, 1920

ITALIAN FIUME, JUNE 15, 1920

IT IS THE day of San Vito in Fiume and the whole city is preparing to celebrate. Though in Fiume, these days, it is always San Vito's day and the city is always celebrating.

On June 10th, the government of the despised Francesco Saverio Nitti finally collapsed and in Fiume the event was celebrated. Nitti fell on the political price of bread in a country facing hunger, while in Trieste Arditi units dispatched to reinforce Italian garrisons in Albania rebelled against officials and tore through the city throwing hand grenades. But in Fiume they celebrated anyway. D'Annunzio issued a vehement, jubilant proclamation of insults against Nitti, extolling the "goddess Vendetta."

The nonstop partying, however, is plunging the city into chaos. All the forces of order are leaving Fiume. In May the carabinieri divisions left. At the Cantrida roadblock they were surrounded by the Arditi and a clash with fratricidal fire ensued. A soldier on horseback leveled his musket, was hit in the side by a shot, and slumped to the ground. The horse crossed the barricade without a rider.

In the city as well scuffles break out among the troops, and officers rush to take up arms and secure the volunteers. A military discipline of drunken looters. On the other front, that of revolution, all attempts to reach accord with the socialists, promoted by Bombacci for the common acquisition of power, have failed. As a result D'Annunzio has also been repudiated by them. By this time the Fiume national council is openly hostile to him as well. The Commander is increasingly isolated, cut off from the world. To receive news on what is happening he must wait to read the morning newspapers. But life is a party, Fiume is "the city of life," and poets are ready to redeem the world that repudiates them.

For months Léon Kochnitzky—a young Belgian poet of modest talent but of grand ideals—has been working at the Fiume League, an assembly that brings together representatives of all oppressed peoples to oppose American president Wilson's League of Nations, which D'Annunzio describes as a "conspiracy of thieves and privileged con men." Fiume is isolated from the world but it doesn't matter, because the plan concocted by Kochnitzky with the Commander's enthusiasm extends "to the whole universe." All the oppressed of the earth are to be part of it, all peoples, nations, races. The list that appears in the memos sent to the Commander embraces all nations (and peoples) deprived of liberty, starting with Fiume: Dalmatia, Albania, German Austria, Montenegro, Croatia, unredeemed German lands, Catalonia, Malta, Gibraltar, Ireland, Flanders, and then the Islamic peoples of Morocco, Algeria, Tunisia, Libya, Egypt, Syria, Palestine, Mesopotamia, India, Persia, Afghanistan, and on and on virtually to the antipodes, summoning the Burmese, Koreans, Filipinos, Panamanians and Cubans to the Carnaro as well. Also included among the oppressed races listed by Kochnitzky are the Israelites, the Negroes of America and the Chinese of California. This is the world in D'Annunzio's one-eyed view: a globe sparkling with freedom, dignity and rebellion. The ballroom of a festive spirit. Kochnitzky is inspired; he is twenty-eight years old, and he too is a poet. The Commander has therefore appointed him foreign minister.

These are the idealities. In concrete terms, however, the activity of the Fiume League is reduced to weaving small, obscure Balkan intrigues. Phantomatic leaders of Croatian, Montenegrin, Dalmatian and Albanian rebel armies are knocking at Fiume's doors seeking weapons and money against the Serbs who want to subjugate them to a huge Yugoslavian nation. The physician Ivo Frank, on behalf of Croatian separatists, promises uprisings in the spring. He doesn't need weapons, all he needs is 12 million liras. Immediately. Under these terms he promises sure success. To Kochnitzky this Frank appears to be a key figure in the Balkan powder keg, an important leader. The information from Italian counterespionage is different. In a telegram to General Caviglia, in April, Nitti calls Frank "an opportunist who I believe is playing both sides and acting to restore the Habsburgs." It is with characters such as these that the ambassadors of Fiume command sign secret treaties to redraw the maps of a free world.

On the eve of summer Kochnitzky resigns. In his note to the Commander, he acknowledges that the "Fiume League has been transformed into a Balkan tool." This cannot be the sparkling globe that suits the aims of Gabriele D'Annunzio.

Before leaving for the Flemish lowlands, the young Belgian poet takes part in the party for one last time. On June 15th, Fiume's Patron Saints, San Vito and San Modesto, are celebrated, though the day is more commonly known simply as San Vito's day. This year the ceremony is particularly solemn because the Commander and his entire staff are participating in it, along with a Venetian delegation that brought a marble plaque with the winged Lion of San Marco as a gift. At 11:00 a.m., in Piazza del Municipio, the plaque, which has been set into the wall of the town hall facade, is uncovered. The Lion of San Marco, its clawed paw supporting the evangelist's book, spreads its wings over Fiume and the dream world of Gabriele D'Annunzio. The poet, who has always ideally recalled Fiume's origins in the Serenissima Republic of Venice, is elated. He speaks of a glorious day, etched in the will of "La Dominante." He lists all the cities of Istria and Dalmatia, from Muggia to Pirano, to Parenzo, from Zadar to Sebenico, to Spalato. All of them, for now, have closed the book. All of them are lions. It is the day of their redemption. In the afternoon, there are sports competitions and, in the evening, dancing in the old quarters.

An indelible memory is engraved on Kochnitzky's mind, before he leaves for good. He will not be able to forget that atmosphere of perpetual celebration, the parades, the torchlight processions, the brass bands, the singing, the dancing, the flares, the joyous fireworks, the speeches, the eloquence, the eloquence, the eloquence . . . In the lit square he admires the flags, the grand inscriptions, the flower-decked boats with lanterns, because even the sea plays its part in the celebration, and the dancing . . . there is dancing everywhere: in the piazza, at the crossroads, on the pier; day or night, people are always dancing and singing. And not soft barcaroles, but martial fanfares. People dance and frolic to their rhythm, whirling in a wild bacchanal of soldiers and sailors, women and men. Wherever the eye turns, it sees a choreography of streetlamps, torchlight, stars. Starving, devastated, suffering, Fiume, waving a torch, dances in front of the sea.

As Fiume dances, another young Italian poet, Giovanni Comisso, walks through the partying city. He is on his way to the military hospital to visit a friend. He gets lost and ends up in the venereal diseases department. In that city populated by infantile legionnaires armed and ready to open fire on the world, it is clearly the most crowded ward. Comisso is stunned. The patients' care is assigned to an energetic young woman, a cross between a mother figure and a midwife. With her sleeves rolled up on her plump, pale arms, she treats the terrifying Arditi like capricious little boys. She sternly orders them to strip, makes them lie ten at a time on rough wooden tables, grabs their limp penises as if they were useless protuberances, opens up wounds, removing gobs of filthy cotton, disinfects and flushes them, then closes them back up before massaging those lean, muscular bodies, a perfect leanness inconceivable for people who have known affluence. The men turn over, docile, shy, obliging, and sprawl on their sides, gloomy.

Life is a party. In the impoverished humble houses of the old city, women have removed the images of the saints. Instead small lamps blaze fervently in front of the portrait of Gabriele D'Annunzio. It is the dance of the fervent. In the face of a hostile, craven world, Fiume dances in front of the sea, in front of death. It's not even the end yet: it's almost over, it's the next to the last chance. But it doesn't matter. The Commander keeps his votive lamp lit on the altar of Zarathustra: a man's greatness is to be a bridge, not a goal. And we can love a man in his sunset years.

BENITO MUSSOLINI

SUMMER 1920

THE MAN'S MANGLED corpse lies in Piazzale Loreto. The owners of the bar where he was killed dragged him out onto the sidewalk. The parade of passersby stops in front of the human carcass with a convulsive gasp.

The man's name is Giuseppe Ugolini, he was a carabinieri brigadier and was traveling by tram in a city once again paralyzed by a railway strike, once more under siege. A group of strikers blocked the tram, ordered the passengers to get off and ordered Ugolini to hand over his weapons. The brigadier got out and opened fire, instantly killing a nineteen-year-old worker and an ex-finance guard. The crowd chased him down, mobbed him, and attacked him on the spot. He ended up shot to death: rounds fired point-blank on the already fallen body, in the bar where he had taken refuge. The newspapers report that someone cut off his fingers to steal his wedding band and other rings.

"No previous event in Italian history comes close to the horror at Piazzale Loreto. Even tribes of cannibals don't visit such atrocities on the dead. Those murderers do not stand for progress; they represent a descent into primitive bestiality . . ." In an editorial in *Il Popolo d'Italia*, Mussolini comments with the grave but curt tone of a man who feels real sentiment. In contrast to his usual manner, he seems genuinely shaken. Although he explicitly denies it, one gets the impression that the article's author sees cannibalism on the future's horizon.

The Founder of the fasci seems scared. He even agrees to be followed, at a distance, by two Arditi acting as bodyguards. The tragic saraband of strikes, demonstrations, and street clashes has gone on for weeks, for weeks carabinieri throughout Italy have been firing at workers with the frenzy of obsessed marksmen, the dead and wounded are again counted by the dozens, yesterday's killers are those killed today, the cannibals cannibalized, yet this corpse seems different to Mussolini. For once the histrionic play-actor seems to bridge the gap between the world and his feeling of the world. It's as though the editor of *Il Popolo d'Italia* were writing about his own tortured fate.

In Ancona at the end of June, an entire regiment of Bersaglieri mutinied. They were to be sent to reinforce the Italian military garrison of Valona threatened by Albanian rebels. The city's working population rose up in support of the insubordinate soldiers. The barracks had to be fired on to get them out. The military crisis of the Italian army is disheartening. Mussolini, dejected, writes to D'Annunzio complaining about the "tremendous crisis of disintegration" Italy is experiencing.

There are also moments of elation. This too, apparently, sincere. When on July 17th Francesco Giunta's fascists torch the "Hotel Balkan," headquarters of Trieste's Slovenian national organization, Mussolini is jubilant: "We can say, without being bombastic, that fascism's time has come!"

Giunta is a Tuscan attorney, earlier an interventionist volunteer, a former captain and legionnaire of D'Annunzio, who distinguished himself for having led the assault on a shoe shop during the 1919 riots in Florence against the rising cost of living. After Fiume, Mussolini sent him to take charge of the Giuliani fasci on the Slovenian border. Giunta organized them with military discipline, subdividing them into units assigned to specific territorial garrisons. Trieste responded magnificently. Added to the class enemy in the border zones is the national enemy, to the Bolshevik the foreigner, to the socialist the Slav: Slovenian workers are also communists. The mixture is explosive and perfect for fascism to take root.

The spark occurred during a demonstration called to protest the killing of two Italian soldiers in Croatia. Far from the platform on which Giunta invoked the law of retributive justice ("We must remember and hate"), a boy is knifed in a scuffle between Italians and Slovenians. His name is Giovanni Nini, seventeen years old, from Novara; he's a cook at the trattoria Bonavia. According to some, he simply happened to be passing by. It seems that during the attack, before the blade sliced through his liver, he screamed: "I have no part in this, I have nothing to do with it!" But that doesn't matter. A martyr is a martyr, whatever his opinions might be.

After the stabbing of the Italian patriot, Giunta's fascists quickly leave the piazza marching in disciplined columns, leading many bystanders to see a premeditated plan. Another hour and flames break out in the massive building of the Hotel Balkan, where the representatives of Trieste's Slovenians are besieged and subjected to a barrage of improvised catapults. The following day the headquarters of Trieste's fascio is overrun by a crowd demanding an enrollment card. "The Balkan is our electoral platform," a beaming Giunta announces to all the new members.

Exciting. There is no doubt. That's the way to go. Organize militarily. Cesare Rossi has been saying that to Mussolini for months. On July 18th the Arditi of Via Cerva renewed their oath of personal loyalty to the fasci's founder. A few days later, from Fiume, D'Annunzio issued a proclamation to the Arditi. The poet shouted that daggers and explosives never intimidated him. On the wings of exhilaration—it must be said—Mussolini even resumed his flight lessons. The instructor, Lieutenant Redaelli, sees him arrive in a great hurry, sometimes on a bicycle, still wearing his editor's attire: black suit, bowler hat, gray spats. He is so determined, in such a rush, that when he appears people get out of his way, creating a vacuum. A fearful vacuum.

But then the country sinks into depression again and he with it. The new government decided to abandon the protectorate of Albania, one of the few conquests left to Italy from the Great War, a war paid for at the cost of six hundred thousand deaths. Everything is falling apart. It's all a murky sludge, bourgeoisie and proletariat, government and those who govern. In that dismal land of tribal laws, quartan fevers, typhus and malaria, Italian soldiers—reduced to ghosts, wandering skeletons, eating grasses, drinking from puddles infected by carrion and corpses—had dug roads and marched against Serbian troops. Now the great spectacle of national disintegration is affecting all of us, from the rulers to the masses, driving us to abandon even that worthless overseas possession. Throw away Albania too, throw it all away, spit on ourselves. But peace at all costs will not prevent a new war. It will push us towards it. We must have the courage to set the house on fire in order to be able to save it.

Cesare Rossi swears that on August 2nd he saw Mussolini weep at hearing the news of the withdrawal from Albania. It's an emotional summer. The spirit sinks. You can't ever look beyond the mountain, beyond the sea. There's always some local village that goes berserk and plays at revolution and for a few days becomes the center of national attention while, beyond the borders, the others screw us. We are a buffoon-nation, a vaudeville act. *Canta che ti passa!* as the saying goes, sing a happy tune! Sing "*'A tazza 'e cafè*"! Sing "*Bandiera rossa*" to the socialist red flag! Everything is falling apart. Everything is going to the dogs.

In 1915 he helped write Italy's history into the history of the world, into the world war. He forcefully shook the country awake from her provincial slumber. But this Italy is still the Italy of yesterday, the Italy of always. Forever ready to party. The season of sweet figs is just about ripe again. If you want to play world politics, you have to have shown yourself capable of enduring a national calamity, you have to be cut out for a tragic style. Look at D'Annunzio in Fiume: he isn't afraid of daggers. Here, however, summer always comes too soon and lasts all year.

The worst are the well-to-do bourgeois. They feel finished. They inquire about the date of the revolution to know if they can still count on spending a summer in the country. History is again abandoned and we are reduced to news. The feature editors have already prepared the usual piece on the August holidays.

No event in Italian history comes close to the horror at Piazzale Loreto. Not even tribes of cannibals visit such atrocities on the dead. That lynch mob does not stand for progress, but represents a descent into primitive bestiality . . . Today socialist preaching is committed to hatred and violence; it arouses the masses' most selfish instincts and seeks to develop tomorrow's vehicles of red terror . . . We will continue to be portrayed to the crowds as "assassins," "hired killers," and there will be no possibility of civil truce.

Benito Mussolini, "Crocodiles!",
Il Popolo d'Italia, June 26, 1920

My dear Commander, I haven't written often because the struggle against the widespread divisive brutality absorbs me . . . We have been through two weeks of chaotic, bloody rebellions. Rebellions with no direction or leaders, with no purpose. Italy is going through a terrible crisis of dissolution. The byword is: out! Out of Valona! Out of Tripoli! Out of Dalmatia! It is a phenomenon of spiritual collapse and individual cowardice.

Benito Mussolini, letter to D'Annunzio, June 30, 1920

LEANDRO ARPINATI

PIANURA PADANA, SUMMER 1920

THE PO VALLEY is the largest plain in southern Europe, a very fertile region, with intensive cultivation and very high yield. For centuries in the valley, hard-working peasants have wrung the soil from stagnant waters, from the putrid matter of reed beds, from malaria. With the waters drained, rich lands emerged, and farms sprang up everywhere, along with related industries, roads, and houses inhabited by a burgeoning population. The great river flows along, beneficent and solemn.

In August 1920, the grains lie rotting in fields that have been harvested but not threshed. The decomposition is accelerated by the bowl formation of the plain; the hot, humid air blows in from the subtropical cyclone in north Africa and stagnates. The temperature is almost 104° F in the Po Valley and the grain, not separated from the chaff, encased in the husk, is suffocating. Rising above the rotting grain like the wail of an air-raid siren, and stretching for miles, is the harrowing bellow of unmilked cows. In mortal combat with their masters, the peasants' hatred has made them brutal. They've stimulated milk production by massaging the udders, then nailed the barn door shut. The milk ferments, the bacteria proliferate, the udders become mastitic. The bovines, mouths gaping, their large porous tongues throbbing, launch desperate, high-frequency cries over the great plain. They implore their calves to come and use their mouths, voracious for milk, to relieve their pain.

The unmilked cows are only one instance of the broader peasant leagues' offensive against the landowners. The "red baronies," as they're contemptuously called by Palmiro Togliatti, the communist laborite leader, have decided to fight all-out. In Emilia the socialists control 223 municipalities out of 280. The rural economy and industrial activities are very profitable, but while it's a question of profits for the landowners, for the farmers it's a question of life or death. The farmhand population is able to work an average of 120 days a year, and therefore requires high wages to avoid starving during the idle months. During the spring clashes, the peasant leagues managed to have all hiring of labor go through their placement office. Now they control the entire economic life of the provinces, and manage everything: work shifts, threshing machine operations, seed supplies and crop planting. For the system to function it must be totalitarian, its control of labor complete. If tenant farmers don't respect the proletarian rules of the seasonal farmhands, if some desperate individual accepts a lower wage, if a small breach occurs that enables scabbing, the system collapses. For this reason, those who agree to an unacceptable compromise, reducing the Lebensraum of others, are mercilessly harassed. The baker refuses them bread, people avoid them, they are forced to emigrate. Bounties and fines are imposed on landowners who violate the compulsory labor agreement.

Ferrara is the reddest province in Italy. To emphasize its primacy, red is not enough: they have renamed it "the scarlet province." By mid-May, the first congress of the leagues of proletarian unity recorded 81,000 registered members, comprising agricultural workers, tenants, sharecroppers and small landowners. More than double that of ten years before; the growth is continuous, progressive, impressive. The victory in the spring clashes was overwhelming. First the seasonal farmhands imposed their will on the bosses, then the sharecroppers and tenants. They dictate working conditions, wage levels and even the choice of crops. Landowners are reduced to doing little more than providing capital. The atavistic hatred of masters towards beggars who aspire to a different division of the land is reawakened.

In the other trench, the peasants' expectations are feverish: the revolution promised throughout 1919 cannot be far off. This triumph over the bosses must necessarily be a pre-revolutionary phase. There's no getting away from it. And so, it gets to the point of nailing shut the stables of those who are resistant, setting fire to barns, even mutilating animals and torturing people. In Tamara, near Copparo, an accountant tries to rent his lands to 25 families without an agreement with the leagues. Their fields are burned, the animals killed, the men beaten. Already, by August, only 4 out of the 25 families remained. In Berra, a certain Luigi Bonati buys a small plot of land with the intention of cultivating it personally. The league sentences him to being boycotted for life, forcing him to leave town. In San Bartolomeo in Bosco, a young veteran tries to form a club with nationalist leanings. The father is boycotted until he agrees to throw his son out, his crops left to rot in the fields. Also in Copparo, a tenant farmer named Roncaglia is mortally wounded after he refused to join the strike and abandon the animals entrusted to him. *Mors tua, vita mea*. Power, however, corrupts, it's not satisfied with death, it constantly extends over life as well. In Cona, the league leader even decides on which feast days young people are allowed to dance and has established by law the calendar of puppet shows.

Now the hottest point of the front shifts to the province of Bologna. Peasant uprisings, which began at the end of 1919 over new labor contracts, have gone on for eight months. The conflict becomes dramatic when seasonal farmhands refuse to thresh the crops. Ringing the bells to summon the crowds, they assemble in public streets where the police can't arrest them, and when there are thousands of them, they invade the fields. Men, women and children all storm out en masse to destroy the threshing machine. Up until mid-month, there is still no bloodshed. But it will come . . . it will come.

On August 17th, while those who are able to get away are at the seashore, landowners in Bologna, in the middle of the seething Padana basin, join together for the first time to form a national federation. The General Confederation of Agriculture is born.

Hatred accumulates. Agreements with prefects and police chiefs are made under the table. The ordeal begins.

Leandro Arpinati is missing. At the Central Committee of the fasci of Milan, no one has heard from him. Somewhere along the course of the great river that lends its name to the plain, he must have been sucked into some pond of despair, of revived youthful vitality or of love for his beautiful, frigid Rina.

BENITO MUSSOLINI

MILAN, SEPTEMBER 28, 1920

THE ALFA ROMEO car factory in Portello is an ultra-modern manufacturing plant on the northwestern outskirts of Milan and at the forefront of Europe. Its engineers are preparing the launch of the Alfa Romeo RL model, an innovative sports car with a six-cylinder inline engine, equipped with a two-seat Spider chassis. It will be the first sports model produced after the end of the war, and aims to complete the range by occupying a market segment until now empty. Executives, managers and owners are placing great hopes in the red Torpedo to be produced in series and in multiple versions. However, the workers also nurture great hopes. At the Alfa Romeo Portello factory, on September 1st, they wave their flags, red like the Torpedo but displaying a hammer and sickle.

It all started from there. Always the same events leading up to it: a long, bitter dispute over wage increases. Negotiations broke off in mid-August when attorney Rotigliano, head of the employers' delegation, stood up in the middle of talks with workers' representatives, hiked up his pants and said: "Any discussion is useless. The industrialists are against any concession. Since the war ended, we have continued to give in. Enough is enough. And we're starting with you."

The workers reacted to the breakdown with obstructionism. A form of "white strike" that slows down production rates without abstention from work. On August 30th, despite the fact that Milan's prefect implored him not to do it, Nicola Romeo, a Neapolitan engineer who made money from the war with the help of the much talked about Banca di Sconto, proclaims a lockout in his factory. FIOM, the metalworkers' union, announces its occupation. Within a few hours all of Milan's factories are invaded by workers; the managers, and at times the owners, are held hostage. The following day the industrialists decide on a nationwide lockout. The General Confederation of Labor returns the blow: over 500,000 workers occupy 600 manufacturing plants throughout Italy. The operation is so swift and overwhelming that everyone is taken by surprise. The prefects, completely in the dark, learn about it from the newspapers. From Savigliano to Bagnoli, from Monfalcone to Castellammare del Golfo, from Turin to Bari, the factories in Italy pass into the hands of the workers. Courtyards and sheds are transformed into bivouacs. The red flag flies over Alfa Romeo. Not far from there, Cesare Isotta and Vincenzo Fraschini, founders of the firm of the same name, are sequestered in their offices.

A great fear takes hold of the middle classes. In the Po Valley, the disputes over the agricultural concordat have just concluded with a total victory for the peasants. Now it's time for the factories. Everything points to a civil war. Socialism is coming, they shout in the workshops. "A declaration of war," writes liberal economist Luigi Einaudi in the *Corriere della Sera* regarding the occupation of the factories. The psychological shock eclipses the patriotic joy over the exciting wins at the VII Olympic Games in Antwerp by Ugo Frigerio, winner of two gold medals in race walking, and Nedo Nadi, awarded five gold medals in individual and team foil, in individual and team saber and in team fencing. Abruptly, after the banner headlines, nobody remembers them anymore.

There is no lack of violence. The workers have rigged up armed command centers with guard houses, sentry boxes, sentinels, helmets, rifles. The "red guards" pose in front of the photographer's lens arrayed in double rows, standing or squatting, like in school or football team photos. They hold their rifles leveled. In Genoa, as early as September 2, there was one dead and several wounded. But that was the spark. In Trieste, the populace in the San Giacomo quarter, rebelling during the funeral of a worker murdered by hired killers, tore a royal guard to pieces. It took the Sassari brigade to storm the barricades. But then Trieste is a special case. In Turin, on Sunday afternoon towards midday, industrialist Francesco Debenedetti, an expert hunter and foundry owner, responded to gunshots fired at the Capamianto factory from the attic of his foundry, killing a Belgian shoemaker, Raffaele Vandich, and a certain Tommaso Gatti da Barletta. Nevertheless these are all cases of individual frustration. Everyone is still waiting for the revolution.

These are the days of worker glory, the days when one rises to one's destiny. Production, in fact, has passed into the hands of the workers. Without financing from the banks, supplies of raw materials or the guidance of technicians and engineers, wood-turners, milling-machine operators, pipe makers or simple unskilled workers make the industrial process work on their own. Sturdy, unassuming, rough-edged men discipline themselves rigorously: they prohibit the consumption of alcoholic beverages during factory shifts, they set up surveillance shifts to prevent thefts, and they scrupulously keep watch over the machinery and materials. For thirty memorable days the working class makes up for a lack of money, organization, and technology with a profusion of moral energy, a forward leap towards higher forms of human activity. For four weeks the workers are no longer just strong arms and broken backs, they are no longer living appendages of machines. They are deserving of their revolution.

But, once again, the revolution does not come. Socialist leaders decide, once again, to defer it. Turin's labor leaders fear that by bringing the struggle from inside the factories out into the streets, acting alone, they will be crushed. The disparity, they feel, is enormous. They are armed but the weapons in their possession would not hold up to more than ten minutes of fire. The leaders of the General Confederation of Labor refer the decision back to the directors of the Socialist Party. According to the agreements, the prerogative is theirs. But the party leaders do not exercise it and continue to put off the event. And so Giovanni Giolitti's moment comes.

Eighty years old, sporting a huge grenadier mustache, and five times prime minister with alternating fortunes over three decades, Giolitti is a giant, and not just figuratively, standing over six feet tall at nearly 200 pounds. A patriarch carved in mahogany, one of those men who define not a season but an epoch. He has dominated Italian political life since the end of the preceding century by practicing the art of mediation, of the possible, of compromise, and holding sway over parliamentary events, class privileges, and ministerial bureaucracies. After his firm opposition to Italy's entry into the war in 1915, in the days when the nationalists tried to storm his home, everyone considered him finished as a politician. But in June when Francesco Saverio Nitti definitively fell, with the socialist revolution at the gates and the country starving, the king appointed Giovanni Giolitti to form his fifth government. At the end of this long, arid new season, the bourgeoisie turned to him as a rainmaker.

Long convinced that economic rather than political reasons are behind the strikes, this time too the Piedmontese statesman refuses to suppress them by bloody means as the industrialists demand. To Giovanni Agnelli, who reproaches him for not taking strong action against the workers, Giolitti replies sarcastically: "Very well, Senator, I have an artillery battalion barracked right in Turin. I will deploy it in front of Fiat's gates and I will order it to open fire on your factory."

In this way Giolitti manages to obtain a compromise by which Agnelli, De Benedetti and Pirelli, at the Hotel Bologna in Turin, grant the workers wage increases, regulatory improvements, and even the assurance of worker control and profit sharing. The last two must remain, in Giolitti's intention, a mere promise. In exchange, the proletarians commit to giving the factories back. For the workers it is a significant economic victory and a total political defeat. The revolution traded for a plate of lentils.

Throughout all this turmoil, Mussolini has not moved. He's fretted, he's gesticulated, he's gone this way and that, he's written pros and cons, but he has not moved. Bide your time: sometimes that's all you can do. When the whole world comes crashing down around you, you stay put. He started to sit tight in June when the king appointed Giolitti, his historic enemy from the time of the Libyan war and then of interventionism. Surprising everyone, the editor of *Il Popolo d'Italia*, in a meeting held at the newspaper's headquarters, welcomed the return of Giolitti as the only statesman capable of restoring social equilibrium and reinstating internal order. Afterwards Benito Mussolini continued not to move through all of September. He went everywhere but he didn't move. He flirted with everyone—radical fascists, "red" unionists, workers, Trieste nationalists—but he didn't side with anyone.

In Cremona, with Roberto Farinacci at the assembly of the Lombard Fasci di Combattimento, Mussolini started off the month by hurling threats ("we will shoot point-blank those who attack us"); on September 16th, however, at the Hotel Lombardia on Via Agnello in Milan, he secretly met with Bruno Buozzi, head of the metalworkers' union, reiterating his support for the workers' struggles as long as they did not extend to the political arena ("It doesn't matter to me whether the factories are run by workers or industrialists"). Playing both sides, as usual. Finally, on the 19th, he left for Trieste where, in front of thousands of people, he derided the folly of the home-grown Bolsheviks: "How can anyone think communism might be possible in Italy, the most individualistic country in the world?" It was exhilarating. He hadn't mingled with the people like that since the days of the socialist rallies.

Meanwhile in the factories the siren of expulsion and defeat has sounded. After an entire month of occupation, the decision to clear out is submitted to a referendum among the occupiers. In Milan, 70 percent of the workers approve it. In Turin they give in to the despair of growing, senseless violence. Seizures of owners, shootouts with the police, nighttime ambushes. Workers' funerals. Bloody brawls around the coffins. After the funeral services, a young Fiat employee, a war volunteer opposed to the occupation from the beginning, and a twenty-year-old prison guard are seized by occupiers of the Bevilacqua plant. Subjected to trial by an impromptu popular court that also included three women, they are sentenced to death. The possibility of throwing them into the blast furnaces is ruled out. They've been turned off during the strike. The men's dead bodies will be found three days later, at dawn on September 24th. The time has come for the precipice and recrimination. The evacuation of the factories begins. The working class is drained, exhausted, disillusioned. In a kind of cosmic empathy with that disillusionment, news arrives from the shore of the Vistula that the Red Army's triumphant advance towards the West has been checked by the Poles at the gates of Warsaw. Left on the battlefield is the corpse of the revolution.

Mussolini does not move even now. Glued to his desk, in this morning's editorial he extolled the hypothetical victory of the workers who, as producers, would have won the right to control all economic activity. He emphatically proclaimed that a centuries-old legal relationship of submission would have finally been broken. He added, however, that "when the struggle faces the dilemma either Italy or Russia, the battle will have to be fought to the end and pushed to a decision."

But they are just words. When your enemies are slaughtering one another, the only thing to do is wait. And because the enemies are numerous, you have to be able to wait a long time. You have to give iron enough time to rust away, methane to burn off oxygen, the stomach to digest food. He has become good at waiting: he is revolutionary or conservative depending on the circumstances. He knows it, he's under no illusions about this: he is merely a reactant. You have to give the molecules time to forcefully collide with one another.

Cesare Maria De Vecchi, by now the undisputed leader of the local fascio, reported to him that in Turin, on Corso Moncalieri, on the second day of the occupation, to make the workers clear out, the industrialists even stormed the headquarters of the Combattenti Association with 1,000-lira notes. It's just a matter of waiting. And of being ready. Senator Giovanni Agnelli, the city's boss, returning to Fiat, had to pass under an arch of red flags and hear his workers shout in his ears "long live the Soviets!" Hanging above the desk in his office, he found a portrait of Lenin crowned with a hammer and sickle.

You have to give time some time. The retaliation of those at the helm will explode. For men like Agnelli, even if they have resumed their command post, the factories remain possessed by evil spirits. A massive exorcism will be needed.

There is no industrialist who is not in a state of agitation and rage that makes him conceive of the craziest plans, from that of openly refusing to accept the agreements, to that of sabotaging the results, to that of bringing down the despised government in parliament or in the piazza.

Ottavio Pastore, *Avanti!*,
Turin edition, September 22, 1920

Things are going badly! . . . This control, demanded by workers' organizations for the purpose of managing companies without the need for so-called bosses, would represent a strong setback that would be detrimental to production . . . In any case, the concept must be made quite clear, even to parliamentarians, that as an absolute condition, the industrialists will demand the restoration of the rule of law in the factories and outside, and this before starting any negotiation.

Supporting this requirement is the fact, which has been proven, that thousands of rifles, revolvers and bombs, tons of cheddite and nitroglycerin, were brought into many of the factories. Poor Italy! When I see the red flag flying on the buildings, I feel deeply disheartened. What do these fools hope for? Don't they realize that they are heading for their ruin?

From the diary of Ettore Conti,
electrical industry magnate,
September 8–10, 1920

Anything is preferable to this wretched life, to this shameful agony in which Italy, victorious in the Great War, stammers the language of fear.

Commentary on the occupation of the factories,
Corriere della Sera, September 20, 1920

AMERIGO DÙMINI

MONTESPERTOLI, OCTOBER 11, 1920

THE RED FLAG hangs limply from its pole at the town hall right in the middle of the piazza, alongside the twin clock towers, those too painted red. Its folds are utterly still, as if cast in cement. It's a huge red flag—it must weigh over 10 pounds—it would take a north wind to make it wave. It seems that on election day a crowd of kids, stirred up by the sound of a band playing the workers' anthem, carried it to the first floor of the municipal building. The socialists' victory was crushing. Before tomorrow morning, however, that red rag would be hauled down, even if they had to tear it down in shreds.

On the other hand, they came down from Florence for a reason. Abbatemaggio, who has been there reconnoitering for a week in order to coordinate the mission with the local fascists, says there's nothing to do in town besides drinking Chianti.

When Amerigo Dùmini arrives from Florence with Frullini and two other fascists on the SITA bus that left from Santa Maria Novella, their Neapolitan comrade is already drunk. Gennaro Abbatemaggio is undoubtedly a fine figure of a man, tall, well-built, black mustache, quick to scuffle, cruel enough to break someone's teeth with his bare hands, but he's constantly jabbering in that baritone voice and southern Italian accent of his. Fortunately, it appears that the local folk did not recognize him. They are farmers, they tend to their work in the fields and don't follow the news, apart from *Avanti!*'s sermonizing. Yet before the war there had been much talk about this vile Camorrist who had "squealed" on his buddies.

Gennaro Abbatemaggio. In gangland circles they called him "*'o Cucchiarello*," the coachman, because of the job he did as a front. He had accused six members of a clan in connection with the murder of another Camorrist, a certain Gennaro Cuocolo, and his wife, stabbed in the stomach sixteen times in her bedroom. There was also the story of a ring taken from the victim and found in the stuffing of a mattress. Later the accuser had retracted the accusation and testified against other alleged principals in a new version of the events. He had also accused himself of several thefts. A complete mare's nest. The carabinieri, falsifying evidence, had brought nearly sixty people to court. During the Viterbo trial, *'o Cucchiarello* was kept in a separate, smaller cell, isolated from the cage of the other animals.

During the war, however, Abbatemaggio had redeemed himself: he had fought well on the Grappa, rising to the rank of sergeant in the Arditi. Dùmini had come to know him there, in the trenches. A fierce fighter. It also seems that he had some trouble at home when he returned from the front. They say his wife had betrayed him with one of the carabinieri assigned to protect her from the revenge of the Camorra bosses. So Gennaro had gone up to Florence to reinforce the comrades.

Then again, you take what there is. The Florentine fascio continues to languish. Even here in Montespertoli—a small town at the entrance to the Val di Pesa just twelve miles from Florence—the fascists must number four or five at most out of ten thousand inhabitants. For months those in Milan have been asking them to organize squads for street clashes with the socialists, and Dùmini has tried. He named the platoon "*La disperata*" (the reckless team), and asked Frullini, a house painter by trade, to design a pennant with a skull, a dagger, a labarum and all the rest. But the fascio headquarters on Via Cavour is a single room rented from a tailor, with a table, two chairs, a portrait of Lenin on the floor, used as a spittoon, and up above a sign, also painted by Frullini, with the words *Italian Fascio di Combattimento and Student Vanguard* written on it. That's all. You won't go far that way. What's more, from Milan they continue to refuse him the money to buy guns. Umberto Pasella even sent back the invoice from the Valgiusti Print Shop where the posters had been printed. "Not to set any precedents," he wrote.

Yet there would have been plenty of work to do. On August 10th the munitions depot had exploded in San Gervasio, causing a massacre. Dùmini had personally prepared a flyer against those despicable socialists who once again had not missed a chance to criticize the army. The police chief had prohibited its distribution, however, calling it "monstrous." Then there were the clashes in Santa Maria Novella between protesters and law enforcement resulting in deaths on both sides. Even at the funerals the city had been divided. No one felt the slightest pity for the other side's dead. But the men of "*La disperata*," poorly organized and poorly armed, hadn't been seen around much on that occasion either. In September, then, the occupation of the factories had occurred. The workers, serious and disciplined, ran them beautifully without the bosses. The industrialists and agrarians had felt useless. At that point, finally, they'd found someone to pay for the guns.

And now here they are in the province to take down that cement flag. The decision was made to do this in every Florentine hill town where the socialists become too visible. Night raids, like at the front, on the Grappa.

Here in Montespertoli, however, there are no socialist militants. The piazza is deserted. The red flag hangs limply. Lino Cigheri, the local fascist, invites them to supper at his home. His wife has prepared *ficattola*, a specialty of fried bread stuffed with local cured meats, Sienese cinta salami, capicola, fennel salami.

After supper, they go to the bar. It's the only place open on the town's piazza. The sign reads Caffè Razzolini. Feeling cocky from the wine consumed at supper, the fascists enter in compact formation and instead of saying good evening shout: "Here's to Italy! Here's to Italian Fiume!"

The place is packed, there must be more than fifty people. Not only does nobody respond to the provocation, but not one person turns his head, stops talking or gives any sign of being aware of them. Evidently the "reds" have come to an agreement: if nobody notices them, they don't exist. But any man, even the most worthless one, exists after drinking his fifth glass. And so they order more drinks.

Abbatemaggio, who was also with D'Annunzio, asks for Morlachian Blood, the cherry liqueur that the legionnaires drink in the Fiume mess halls. Old Razzolini, who has been running that tavern for decades, good-naturedly blaspheming the Lord, replies that the only blood he knows is that of Christ. Or they can come back next month when the young wine is ready. That, if they settle for it, is rather sanguine.

The fascists make do with Vin Santo and *cantucci* for dunking. They take a corner table and start singing the Arditi songs. For the villagers, no matter how loud they sing, they still do not exist. Frullini, after the first round, starts retelling his war stories. Drunk, he asks Dùmini to throw in a few anecdotes of the Grappa epic as well. Dùmini, as usual, declines the urging to speak, shaking his head no and staring at the bottom of his glass. At eleven o'clock, after a couple of hours of rowdy singing and being ignored, the tavern keeper finally approaches them. The mere presence of that old man standing beside the table is enough to call them back to reality. But he's just there to ask them to leave. He's closing up, as required by law.

Abbatemaggio starts yapping, making threats, while all the villagers file out through the one door, composed and disciplined, still acting as if the fascists had never boarded the Florence–Montespertoli bus. While the Neapolitan yammers away in his dialect, Cigheri and the other local men show clear signs of embarrassment. They have to live there and they're ashamed. Dùmini orders them all to move out.

Outside, the place is deserted. There is not a soul left in the dark piazza. The villagers have all vanished as if by magic. The eight armed men have again lost their sole reason for existing.

In a fit of irritation, Frullini bangs loudly on the already bolted bar door. He yells to the innkeeper's daughters, who are inside cleaning up, telling them to let them in and threatening to open the door himself with grenades. From the balcony above, the family's other women start screaming: "Help! Help! They're going to kill us." But nobody comes running, as if they didn't represent a serious threat. A straggler hurries by under the arcades. They start kicking him: "Get to bed, tramp!" At the back of the piazza a small group of boys gathers. They scatter them, shooting at the wind. No one else shows his face. They are masters of the piazza. They sent the world to bed. There's nothing left for them to do except go to bed too. They camp out on mattresses thrown on the ground by Cigheri's wife.

The next morning, stultified by their hangovers, the fascists get up late. The others are already lined up on the piazza. They've been there since before dawn waiting for the winos to wake up. Hundreds of men, arrayed in a semicircle in front of the town hall, are ready to defend their right to choose who will govern them, armed with the tools with which they earn their bread: spades, scythes, hoes, pitchforks.

Cigheri's wife, worried about the house and her children, arrives shortly afterwards with the carabinieri. Marshal Cocchi and a squad of soldiers escort the fascists to the adjacent barracks. As they file past, trailing along the walls in their crumpled clothes and long beards, their breath stinking of wine, the whole town, in arms, watches them motionless from the opposite side of the piazza, determined to fight but not saying a word, almost as if no one felt any rancor towards them, any feeling at all, the way animals attack a man.

Dùmini and his men remain in the barracks for hours. They are hoping for reinforcements from Florence—the word must have spread—but support does not come. Instead, Captain Ronchi arrives in an armored car with sixty more carabinieri, a socialist deputy and the provincial councilor Dal Vit. Socialist deputy Pilati cools tempers all around but doesn't mention removing the red flag.

When they cross the piazza again to get in the armored car that will take them back to Florence, Frullini starts singing an Arditi anthem. *Sono Ardito fiero e forte / non mi trema in petto il core /*

sorridendo vo' alla morte / pria di andare al disonor. I am a proud and strong Ardito, my heart does not tremble in my chest, I will go to my death smiling before meeting with dishonor. They sing as they file through a corridor of carabinieri who have come to protect them from peasants armed with scythes. Amerigo Dùmini only murmurs the lines of the refrain. *Giovinezza, giovinezza / primavera di bellezza / della vita e nell'ebbrezza / il tuo canto squilla e va.* Youth, youth, spring of beauty, of life and exhilaration, your song rings out and soars. Before a corporal turns the engine's ignition key, a farmer can distinctly be heard complaining to deputy Pilati: "Was it worth losing a morning's work for a few drunks?!"

Only then does Dùmini speak. A raging howl wells up from his alcohol-inflamed stomach. We'll be back! The promise is lost in the roar of the armored car's diesel engine.

Not even a dozen miles and already the farce becomes epic. When they are in sight of Florence's suburbs, Frullini starts exaggerating the courage with which they all came close to death. It's true: those peasants would have gladly chopped them into little pieces with their hoes and then, with the same tools, smeared their remains on the fields as fertilizer. But the group's leader stops listening. He prefers to wall himself up in silence, tuned into the roar of the engine. It was just another instance of them ending up looking like complete assholes.

Citizens, while everyone mourns the common sorrow, more than a few vile, miserable socialists dare to utter words of cruel derision and bloody sarcasm . . . Citizens, while waiting for justice to do its duty and inexorably punish those responsible, if they exist, show these born criminals no mercy.

Amerigo Dùmini, anti-socialist flyer
drafted after the explosion at the
munitions depot in San Gervasio,
Florence, August 11, 1920

GIACOMO MATTEOTTI

FRATTA POLESINE, OCTOBER 12, 1920

THE COW DIED of anthrax, the disease is infectious, the carcass must not be touched. For this reason, the district veterinarian made large incisions along a good part of the body into which he poured kerosene, then ordered it to be buried, as is done with Christians. Three or four farmers carry out his instructions in the presence of the municipal attendant: they dig a ditch, throw the infected animal's carcass in it, and cover it up. Immediately afterwards, the municipal officer turns on his heels. He leaves without once looking back, as if to say: "I did my job, now you do whatever the hell you want."

The man has just stepped past the edge of the field when about thirty famished peasants armed with shovels, scythes and hatchets come out of the bushes. They advance in line, at a brisk pace, in closed ranks, like a phalanx charging the enemy. The animal is exhumed in no time; some scoop out the last inches of soil with their hands, lying on their stomachs at the edge of the grave. They butcher the cow in groups, their eyes glinting with hunger, fighting each other for a liver, half a thigh. A young man decapitates what's left of the animal with an ax blow. A gaunt old woman starts yelling like a lunatic, leaps at the cow's skull, grabs it by the horns, loads it on her back and dashes away. Two boys chase after her, knock her down and carry off the skull. The old woman, robbed of her trophy, staggers back, drops to her knees on the edge of the pit. Maybe she's praying, maybe she's imploring—from that distance the scene is without a soundtrack—maybe she's about to throw her own bones into the grave now stripped of the bovine's.

Deputy Giacomo Matteotti recalls this childhood memory as he takes the stage where the rally will be held. For a moment he is again the sickly boy to whom his father hands the binoculars on the balcony of the manor house so that the child may learn something about the misery that has made them prosperous. But he has heard the story of the disinterred cow told so many times that he is no longer sure if it's a false memory. He is no longer even positive that the cow had died of anthrax. The only thing certain about that amphibious, pellagrous, malarial land of his is its poverty.

Polesine peasants are among the most wretched in Italy. For centuries they have lived a bestial life, dulled by the pestilential air, always feverish, condemned to die young, raised in sheds crammed with parents, babies, brothers, sisters, grandparents, in a ghastly cohabitation with chickens and pigs contending for their masters' food and oxygen. A debased, infected, undernourished world, where incest is frequent, bodies constantly sapped, diseases always chronic, where the death of a cow is mourned while that of a wife is met with resignation.

Because of this daily apocalypse, this slow-moving, social infarction, deputy Giacomo Matteotti—grandson of Matteo, an iron and copper merchant, and son of Girolamo, a big landowner suspected of lending money at exorbitant interest—is a traitor to his people. His enemies accuse him of being a landowner who crossed over to the proletarians, an agrarian who disowned his class, a "socialist in furs," the son of a usurer who poses as a moralist. His father accuses him of having deserted the field assigned to him by fate.

But who are his people? He made a choice. His people are not his father and his grandfather, they are these squalid peasants, these children blue with cold, these twenty-year-old mothers who look like they are forty. His Polesine is not a land of remorse but of redemption, the swamp scored by 500 waterways, rivers, canals, catchments and ditches, in which thousands of reclamations have been carried out in the last twenty years, where peasant leagues have been established, diseases cured, the rights of poor people affirmed. The Polesine that in last November's elections sent Giacomo Matteotti to parliament along with five other socialist deputies, becoming the reddest province in Italy together with that of Ferrara, the land he chose for himself, abdicating the paternal terrain. The Polesine of the future, in which socialists are now also triumphing in the local elections.

Voting begins in early October with electoral rounds distributed throughout the month. The first results are exciting: the sons of poverty have won in all 25 municipalities counted as of now. There are 38 remaining, including Fratta, Giacomo's birthplace, where Palladio designed his first villa with a pronaos and pediment on the facade, and where Europe's largest Bronze Age necropolis is. Everything leads him to hope that his socialist comrades will win there too and then the party will have total control of the province. It will be the beginning of a new world.

It will take more reclamations, that's for sure. Few things corrupt a people as much as a pattern of hatred. And his peasants love him as much as they hate his father and the other landowners. There is a great deal of violence to be reclaimed: the parish priests have been forced to close the churches, people going to Mass are attacked, squads of communists armed with clubs patrol the polling places, forcing voters to deposit pre-completed ballots in the urns. He himself had to go to the aid of deputy Merlin, a member of the Catholic party and his old secondary school classmate. His own farmers beat him at the entrance to the polls in Lendinara and without Giacomo's intervention they would have left him on the ground.

Merlin himself, after yet another assault by farmers on a small landowner, had accused socialist leaders of sowing hatred, of driving the workers headlong into revolutionary hope, of having obsessed them with Russia, of having captured the masses in a colossal illusion, of having established a regime of terror, of having "turned Polesine into a land of savages," and the Lendinara attack, unfortunately, seems to have proved him right. Merlin maintains that whereas it took courage to be a socialist around here thirty years ago, nowadays it takes courage not to be. He's right about that too.

And yet this destitute crowd waiting to hear word of a redemption from Giacomo Matteotti, socialist deputy and son of merchant, agrarian and usurer Girolamo, this crowd feels hatred because for centuries it has fed on the infected flesh of a dead cow. You have to understand these people, you have to feel sorry for them, be ready to reclaim them the way the land they slave on has been reclaimed.

Matteotti is not a "maximalist," an extremist who stakes everything on the revolution here and now. Matteotti, on the contrary, believes in the gradual liberation of the oppressed class through a protracted, arduous effort of additional sacrifice and struggle further demanded of a suffering humanity. He knows that tomorrow's proletarian revolution will not be a blissful crown of triumph. He reiterated it at the meeting of the reformist socialists group in Reggio Emilia as well, which was held the day before. When he is in Rome, in parliament, Deputy Matteotti always speaks with moderation and good judgment.

But when Giacomo is here, in Polesine, among his peasants who have had a hard life, on his amphibious land, he again becomes the child who watched the quartering of the buried carcass. His people expect Giacomo Matteotti, the redeemed son of the usurer, to say it and he says it:

"Comrades, sell the grain. Sell the grain and buy a revolver."

BENITO MUSSOLINI

MILAN, LATE OCTOBER 1920

"WHEN THE HELL is this pain in the ass going to decide to give up?!"

Arturo Fasciolo, Mussolini's personal secretary, has just told him that Harukichi Shimoi, "D'Annunzio's Jap," has again stopped by the newsroom to remind the editor of his promise to join the Commander in Fiume. The Japanese envoy showed up, as always, with a letter from D'Annunzio which began with the usual greeting: "I send you, my absent, frigid comrade, this brother samurai . . ."

The samurai is a ridiculous little man who walks around in an Ardito uniform with a *wakizashi* hanging from his belt, and speaks Italian with a marked Neapolitan accent. He is a professor of Japanese language and literature at the Oriental Institute of Naples who, at the outbreak of the war, enrolled as a volunteer in the Italian army. He claims that he fought in the assault units, but Albino Volpi insists that he was an ambulance driver.

Shimoi, bewildered by the appointments that have been missed over the previous days, reminded Mussolini that this evening too Umberto Foscanelli, another of D'Annnunzio's close associates, will again expect him on the platform for the midnight train to Trieste. For three nights in a row Foscanelli has awaited him in vain with the tickets for the sleeping car already purchased, and he too still hasn't given up. Only four hours to go.

D'Annunzio wants to march on Rome again. At the end of September he sent another plan for the organization of a revolutionary movement in Italy. The plan envisioned the need to re-establish a "new order" in Italy, to be achieved through the "polarization of all the salubrious energies of the country." The polarizing element was to be, obviously, D'Annunzio himself. Fiume's intervention in Italy had to be done, obviously, on the basis of the Fiume Constitution. Fiume—the Commander insisted on believing—would redeem Italy.

Mussolini sent back the insurrectional draft modified at the places where it conferred all powers to D'Annunzio. In the new plan, revised by the Founder of fascism, the organization of the volunteer forces was assigned to the Central Committee of the Fasci di Combattimento. D'Annunzio had agreed. But Mussolini—secretly informed by foreign minister Sforza—knew that Giolitti was amassing troops on the borders of Fiume to take military action against D'Annunzio, while at the same time negotiating with Yugoslavia a diplomatic agreement between sovereign states. So Mussolini had dictated a second condition to D'Annunzio: a coup d'état, a march on Rome by fascists and legionnaires, could only be risked in the event of an eventual unfair settlement of the Adriatic contention with Yugoslavia (that is, only in case Giolitti's secret negotiation were to fail). D'Annunzio, who unlike Mussolini was unaware of the negotiations underway, had agreed to this as well. By now he was in. On October 5th he even deigned to obtain a fasci card.

The only condition that D'Annunzio did not agree to was to postpone the insurrection to the spring of 1921. He wanted to act immediately. He was again elated after Guglielmo Marconi, the brilliant inventor of the "wireless telegraph," had gone to Fiume. Sent by Giolitti to persuade him to surrender, Marconi had instead allowed the poet to broadcast one of his magnificent, incomprehensible and useless orations to the world from the radio station installed on his yacht *Elettra*. Then, before leaving, Marconi had seized the opportunity to ask for a divorce from his wife, which was permitted by Fiume's libertarian legislation and prohibited by Italian law.

For Benito Mussolini, however, divorcing D'Annunzio would have been much more difficult. Many fascists still dreamed of the

Commander's admirable feats, and for this reason Mussolini too continued to proclaim from the columns of the newspaper that he would defend Fiume at the cost of his life. In truth, however, he had no intention of getting drawn back into the blind alley of defeat. D'Annunzio's rarefied air was certainly intoxicating but the cannons that Giolitti was positioning around Fiume offered much more concrete prospects here on earth. The fascists' time was coming: the battle, here and now, was finally about to engage.

Until a few months ago the fascists were despised by everyone. They'd been accused of being outlaws, hired killers, corrupt assassins, but many of those who scorned them yesterday were now beginning to tremble. Many of those uneasy consciences were now anxious. At the October 10 meeting, Mussolini had managed to convince the fasci national council not to participate in the local administrative elections. The ballot box wasn't for them. All the liberal and conservative parties were finally coalescing into a national bloc against the socialists, all the bourgeois press supported the bloc without further distinction, but the fasci would still be left out. Circumstances had shown that they had to assert themselves through shootings, fires, destruction. Let the others grow old in the voting booth. To each his own. Fascism wasn't an assembly of politicians but an order of fighters. So on the evening of October 16, its founder had met with Lusignoli, the prefect of Milan who reported to Rome, and had assured him that the fasci would oppose by whatever means necessary Italy's ruin at the hands of the Bolsheviks. He had stressed "by whatever means." Lusignoli, satisfied, had telegraphed Giolitti.

The situation had become clear two days earlier, on October 14th. The socialists had organized demonstrations throughout Italy in support of Soviet Russia and the fascists had definitively lined up to defend the reviled liberal state against the assault of the "reds." In Trieste the fasci had set fire to the offices of *Il lavoratore* without encountering any resistance from the platoon of militarized police stationed in defense of the newspaper; in San Giovanni Rotondo the carabinieri had opened fire on socialists confronted by fascists in front of the town hall (11 dead and 40 wounded); in

Bologna Malatesta's anarchists had attacked the barracks of the royal guards on Via Cartoleria (5 dead and 15 wounded); in Milan anarchists had set off two bombs at the Hotel Cavour. By the following night, the entire insurrectionary anarchist movement had been virtually obliterated by a wave of arrests. All this within twenty-four hours. Approximately twenty dead and seventy injured from sunrise to sunset, from Trieste to Puglia. It was undoubtedly a period of rich, promising, prodigious development.

In the following hours, as the results of the electoral rounds decreed the socialists' victory, news of the formation of new fasci came from the reddest provinces. Arpinati had seen to Bologna, in Ferrara they had established one on October 10th, in Rovigo in the midst of the electoral campaign with the support of the agrarians. From everywhere they wrote to the Central Committee in Milan asking for weapons or money to purchase them. The founders were new faces, exponents of the middle classes, yet, from another angle, they were still the same people: rancorous, diverse, fearful, anti-socialist. The children of war, discontented with everything.

In a word, the situation is finally propitious. Then too in a few days Bianca Ceccato, his "little girl" lover, will give birth to his son. The child will be a bastard, of course, but he certainly can't ignore him.

Benito Mussolini has no time now for D'Annunzio's quixotic nonsense. The midnight train for Trieste will leave without him this time as well.

Had visit from Mussolini, who declared fascists and nationalists firmly determined to oppose by any means, even violent, acts of extreme parties who are leading Italy to ruin . . . He declares he and his followers ready to observe law and order if government authorizes law enforcement intervention, otherwise no excess would be spared.

Telegram from the Prefect of Milan to Giovanni Giolitti,
October 17, 1920

Power, law, right . . . it will be solely our power, our law, our right against that of those who have been parasites since man formed a civil consortium . . . We do not want to debate with our enemies; we want to bring them down.

From the local elections platform
of Mantua's socialists

IF THERE MUST BE CIVIL WAR, WELL THEN SO BE IT!

Il Fascio, newspaper of the Milan fasci,
full-page headline, October 16, 1920

FERRARA, NOVEMBER 3, 1920

THE FIRST STONE of Ferrara's Estense Castle was laid on September 29th, 1385, the feast day of Saint Michael, protector of gates and fortresses. The citadel was commissioned by Marquis Niccolò II d'Este following a violent popular uprising that broke out in May of that same year.

In the two centuries that followed, Ferrara's castle became one of the greatest architectural, artistic and urban masterpieces of the European Renaissance. Its halls hosted one of the most splendid Renaissance courts and made Ferrara, a remote village isolated in the marshes, one of the foremost capitals of the world. In his studio, the magnificent alabaster *camerino*, Alfonso I d'Este, husband of Lucrezia Borgia, created one of history's first art collections.

Four centuries later, on November 3rd, 1920, the red flag flies on Saint Paul's Tower, built on the southwest corner of the Estense Castle, right in the center of Ferrara. Conspicuous on the massive wall in front of the ducal chapel and the orange tree garden is a hastily dashed off graffiti in phosphorescent fuchsia-colored paint. The scrawl reads "long live socialism!"

The local elections marked yet another victory for the socialists. In the Ferrara countryside, the workers' party alone obtained 10,185 votes against 2,921 of all the other parties combined. The party of the proletarian revolution took 54 municipalities out of 54. Its control over the province is now complete.

Within the walls of the castle, after having held the first meeting of the council in the Games Salon where the Este received their excellent guests under a magnificent vault decorated with athletic and mythological scenes, the leaders of the farmers leagues and the Chamber of Labor have prepared a banquet in the Government Room. They do not conceal their spiteful satisfaction: the lord and masters did it, so can we. They eat, drink and sing under a coffered wooden ceiling with lacunars of various shapes. On the plates is a succulent, popular specialty, *salama da sugo*, a pork sausage prepared by grinding various parts of the pig—neck, cheek, tongue, liver—and seasoned with salt, pepper and nutmeg. In the glasses, wine that goes down easily in the afternoon. To lend a proletarian touch, they put the castle's doorkeeper at the head of the table. His name is Ghelandi and, according to the prefect's reports, he is a violent man. Enthroned in the seat of honor, in the place that belonged to the Renaissance prince, the door attendant, after several glasses of Lambrusco, incites his fellow diners: "Do what I do, I always go to the head of the demonstrators' columns, even if it means beating up anyone who tries to stop me."

Right after the local elections, Eugenio De Carlo, prefect of Ferrara, writes to Rome. The situation appears incendiary to him. Five carabinieri were beaten to a pulp in Fossana, numerous voters were led to the polling stations with their hands raised above their heads, the proletarian militants feel they are immune, administrative abuses multiply. Socialist councilmen even go so far as to vote for financial coverage of their propagandistic and electoral expenses with public funds. The Socialist Party of Ferrara was represented at the elections by a platform based on the agenda of Giuseppe Gugino, its secretary, who openly declares that he is participating in the electoral battle for the sole purpose of getting his hands on state machinery to start the revolution. The leaders of the Chamber of Labor have no doubt that the revolution is on its way. Deputy Ercole Bucco, a tiny little man with round accountant's glasses, a propagandist in the Ferrara and Mantua areas and now secretary of Bologna's Chamber of Labor, systematically boycotts any agreement, even if advantageous for the peasants, raising the stakes in order to make it fail. On Via Emilia, Bucco bets on disaster to bring about the revolution.

Meanwhile in Baku, in September, the Congress of the Peoples of the East has promoted communism in Asia. Russian comrades have conquered Kazakhstan, toppled the Emirate of Bukhara, and are marching on Samarkand. Baku, located on the western shore of the Caspian Sea, in Azerbaijan, Central Asia, vanished in the legends of Marco Polo and its silk road, but revolutionary intoxication is also mounting in Ferrara, in the Po Valley, along the banks of the Po. Intoxication mounts, the red stain spreads, blood is not far off. They are poised on the razor's edge: "A moment's hesitation and the province will be lost for many years, perhaps forever," the prefect warns.

At this point, a dark note slips into the prefect's reports, almost like that of a martyr revealing his own destiny. From his offices on the east side, he notes that the moats around the Estense Castle are still full of water. It wouldn't be the first time in Ferrara's history that unwelcome cohabiters have drowned in them.

Then, however, in the west, the Red Army is surprisingly defeated at the gates of Warsaw. In the same days, in the fields around Ferrara, a sudden hailstorm reduces the beet harvest by one third over the previous year. Besides that, since July the price of hemp has fallen sharply. Sometimes a bad harvest is all it takes . . .

The provincial socialist conference resolves that the party should participate in the electoral battle for the conquest of both the municipalities and the province, for the sole purpose of seizing and paralyzing all powers, all bourgeois state machinery, in order to make the revolution and the establishment of a proletarian dictatorship all the more unswerving and effortless.

Socialist Provincial Conference of Ferrara,
September 18, 1920,
Gugino agenda

We need a man in Italy who with decisive resolve will say "enough!" to this mad dash to suicide. A man who does not have the nagging daily preoccupation of maintaining parliamentary stability [. . .]. A man who is able to face reality, who will not stand for half measures [. . .] Gangrene cannot be cured with hot compresses. Does such a man exist? Let this man come forward and he will have a unanimous national consensus behind him.

Gazzetta ferrarese (conservative newspaper),
October 20, 1920, editor's note

LEANDRO ARPINATI

BOLOGNA, NOVEMBER 4, 1920

IN THE END he jumped right in. In September, after the summer's devastation, he returned to the city and jumped right in. He's been doing the same thing since he was a boy: recklessly jumping right into a brawl. On this occasion too it had all started with a brawl. Quite simply, when it came to fighting, men followed him the way wolves tag along behind the pack leader.

Under Bologna's arcades, come September, he found unfamiliar faces. They were no longer the same people as before the summer. Demobilized officers who couldn't find a job, civil servants who could barely manage to eat, swarms of brokers, shopkeepers, tenant farmers, contractors who detest socialist consumer and labor cooperatives and the municipalization of businesses, students and young unemployed graduates incensed at senile politicians, former revolutionary unionists abandoned by the masses, eighteen-year-olds angry because the war ended before they too could join the fight, unprecedented flocks of teenagers, brought up on sensational films. In short, a whole crowd of heroes who had been forgotten. It was as if they had stayed holed up at home for months, for years even, and then, with the arrival of autumn, driven by the announcement of winter, they all poured into the streets with a knife between their teeth, lectured by veterans who preach in cafes as if they were on the battlefield.

Arpinati had never been to war but, as soon as he dived in, they followed him. And never mind that he of all people, an anarchist railway worker, son of commoners and in all respects a member of the working class, found himself serving the interests of agrarians and industrialists, people he despised. The taste for brawling would set that right too.

It took courage but they jumped right in. Bologna sits, dazed, in the center of a vast agricultural region that is entirely "red." In October, the longest battle in union history over agricultural agreements was concluded. Ten months of strikes and unrest. The disastrous defeat of the agrarians and the triumph of the peasants. It took guts to challenge the wrath of the masses. There was an initial phase to reconnoiter. Arpinati sent his patrols to walk the streets, usually abandoned to the workers' movement, with orders to sing *Giovinezza*. They came back without ever finding any adversaries. So he convinced himself that the socialists would never bring about a revolution. Just then, however, the agrarians got scared and realized that they were not able to defend themselves. They looked around to find a strategy for fighting back. That was when they found him.

Arpinati and his followers got busy on September 20th in front of the Salaborsa library. Their baptism by fire took place with a throng of socialists who were celebrating the fiftieth anniversary of Italian Unification at the monument to Garibaldi, on Via Indipendenza. There were numerous injuries, one man later died. Enrollments in the fascio immediately surged. On October 10th they re-established the fascio on Via Marsala. Arpinati wrote to Milan full of enthusiasm. Then there were fierce arguments with those who refused to take money from the agrarians. He cut them short: this is no time for debates, you have to jump right in. From Milan they agreed with him. Mussolini, through Cesare Rossi, invested him with full powers. Carte blanche, keep on fighting, no holds barred. Four days later, Malatesta's anarchists, incited by Ercole Bucco, secretary of the Chamber of Labor, attacked the barracks on Via Cartoleria. In addition to an assailant, a brigadier from the royal guards and a deputy police inspector remained on the ground. The fascists couldn't have asked for anything better. On October 16th, fascist squads led the funeral procession. They are at a point of divergence.

Until then, there was general talk of civic defense, of anti-Bolshevism; now they are going on the attack. First, as always, came the war of symbols. Arpinati personally led an attempt to plant a tricolor flag on the municipal building. The assault was repelled. So then open confrontation was sought. They fired at the socialist party's newsstand right beside the town hall. A farmer who had come to the city for the market was shot dead. Within a week, the fascio had over a thousand members. Events surpassed all expectations. Groups of young people follow them, the mass of *squadristi* swells. Everyone looks to Arpinati as the spokesman for their rancors.

Now it's November 4, the second anniversary of Italy's victory in the Great War, and the time has come to escalate the level of the conflict. Last year this glorious date was not celebrated because that coward Nitti, fearing explosions of violence in the heated climate of the moment, had prohibited it. But now the war of symbols has started again and the time has come for violence to explode. Arpinati got into the Palazzo d'Accursio and displayed the tricolor flag. Police officers, disobeying orders, let him do it. Then he got bolder and, together with a group of uniformed officers, climbed to the top of the Palazzo del Podestà's tower to ring the "*campanone*," the "big bell." There too they let him do it. And so, at the end of the assembly at the Teatro Comunale, the patriotic procession parades through the streets in a riotous blaze of flags fluttering in the wind and the sound of ringing bells.

Along the way, people stand there gawking, hands in their pockets, most with their hats on their heads. It's been too long a time since the country has had a parade and they no longer know how to behave. The fascists teach them how with "take off your hat, salute the flag," and an open-handed slap. When that isn't enough, cattle prods, brought along for any eventuality, are also put to use. Meanwhile, in the piazza, tram cars are stopped and decked with flags, and any tram drivers who object are beaten, as the police stand by watching. The tram operators—all socialists—abandon the service as a sign of protest. The fascists, who remain masters of the field, then start driving around the city in a crazy carousel of tricolor tram cars, racing all through the streets until night falls. They stop only when the prefect has the aerial electricity turned off.

By now the piazza is deserted, apart from the fascists, but no one in the city is sleeping. A different kind of electricity rises from the land, which must not be wasted. It is at that point that a retired lieutenant, a veteran of the Grappa, says "let's go flush them out," and all of Arpinati's boys unite as one and head towards Via Massimo D'Azeglio.

The Chamber of Labor is a small fortress. All of Bologna knows that the previous night about a hundred "red guards" arrived from Imola, a stronghold of the communist faction, and barricaded themselves inside with rifles and pistols, under the command of deputy Francesco Quarantini. They are said to have a machine gun too. The war of symbols is reignited.

As soon as the fascists show up, the royal guard scatters, as if by magic. In the time it takes to assemble on Via D'Azeglio, the shooting starts. There are shots fired from outside at the building, and from inside the building at them. Being out in the open, a fascist drops, wounded; they have to fall back. They crouch in the doorways. There doesn't appear to be any way of getting in, there's nothing left to do but go home beaten, but then a platoon of carabinieri arrives with leveled rifles. Welcoming them at the door is Ercole Bucco, the maximalist secretary of the Chamber of Labor who has been preaching revolution for years, every blessed day, since he indoctrinated the peasants in the countryside of Cento. Bucco is terrified—you can tell even from a distance—and greets the carabinieri with evident relief, inviting them to come in. It is already rumored that, after hearing the first gunshots, it was he who called the police command center to send the carabinieri to come and rescue them.

After a few minutes the door opens again and the "red guards" come out in single file, chained together a dozen at a time, escorted by the carabinieri. Also led away in handcuffs is the deputy who commanded them. The carabinieri arrest Bucco too, the revolutionary who for protection called upon the guardians of the very authority that day after day he promised to overthrow. As they take him out to the street, a captain charges him for possession of dozens of rifles wrapped in a sack, and pounds and pounds of explosives seized in fruit crates.

Bucco, flustered, now surrounded by carabinieri and fascists, is then heard defending himself. He declares he's innocent, swears that the weapons were brought into the house without his knowledge, that they were brought there by people who were strangers "to his wife." He whines and wails, reiterating that "his wife," hearing the first shots, opened the door of the apartment where they live, next door to the Chamber of Labor, and strangers carried in the weapons. But the two of them knew nothing about it, they were in the dark about everything. The agitator who until yesterday promised revolution each and every day now lies shamelessly, accuses his comrades, and drags his wife into it. He's heard repeating "my wife . . . my wife." He's finished. With an unintentionally merciful gesture, the carabinieri drag him off to the barracks, rescuing him from the ridiculous scene.

The door of the Chamber of Labor, unguarded and unprotected, remains wide open. As in the tales told by old peasant women of the Po Valley, if you leave the door open at night, the damned spirits of the unburied dead will enter. The fascists, undisturbed, invited by Bucco's cowardice, turn to looting. It is just past midnight. The tower's bell tolls the symbolic death of revolutionary socialism in Bologna.

BENITO MUSSOLINI

MILAN, NOVEMBER 15, 1920

THE TREATY OF Rapallo between Italy and Yugoslavia to resolve the Adriatic question was announced unexpectedly on November 12th. Italy's eastern borders were shifted to Monte Nevoso, leaving Trieste safe. However, Italy has relinquished Dalmatia. Only Zadar was assigned to it, without a surrounding inland area and without the adjacent islands. By so doing Zadar remains an Italian rock in a Croatian sea. In the spirit of diplomatic compromise, Fiume was accorded full independence, but Sussak, the eastern coastal suburb that includes Port Baross, went to Croatia. The "holocaust city," the "city of life," for now is neither Italian nor Croatian, and what's more it is cut off from maritime trade with the East. The news is a bomb. A ton of TNT exploded on D'Annunzio's dreams.

Nevertheless, on the same day, from the columns of *Il Popolo d'Italia*, Mussolini declared he was "frankly satisfied." Regarding Fiume he drew a distinction, but he also stated that the solution was the best of those previously proposed. On the subject of Dalmatia he grumbled about deferring the possibility of a revision: peoples' rights, he wrote, do not lapse. Overall, however, he openly, soundly approved the compromise reached by Giolitti. The article is a heavy blow. Dealt directly to the Fiume fascists' jugular.

In Fiume, even card-holding fascists take part in the bonfire in Piazza Dante, burning the bundle of copies of *Il Popolo d'Italia* containing the offending article. They send a bitter telegram to the newspaper. The word "betrayal" begins to be thrown around openly. That word again.

To exorcize it, he, Benito Mussolini, the eternal traitor, the chorister of war, was forced to appeal to peace. To peace and greatness. To regain them—he wrote the following day in his newspaper—we must raise our eyes to the horizon. We must not fix our gaze on the Adriatic, which is only a modest gulf of a great sea, the Mediterranean, in which the possibilities of Italian expansion are very bright.

Benito Mussolini may have appealed to peace from the columns of his newspaper but, as always, he is preparing for war. The line of the front runs from the Po Valley, from Milan, to Cremona, Bologna, and Ferrara, not beneath the slopes of Monte Nevoso, on the border between Italy and Yugoslavia. The socialists, triumphant at the polls, begin accruing defeats in the piazzas, they pull back, they buckle, the routed army must be pursued. To do so, the ranks must be opened to all reactionary forces, to the bourgeoisie that actually believed the fairy tale of revolution. Until now they have had to fight as one against a hundred, but after the retreat everyone will find courage. Let D'Annunzio remain fixed on the idea of the Adriatic, let him hang himself on it, if he wants. Mussolini, through prefect Lusignoli, sent the message loud and clear to Giolitti: if necessary, the prime minister has the all-clear to move to repress the Fiume legionnaires. The fascists of Milan will not move a finger.

His old friend Pietro Nenni was in Fiume in September for the promulgation of the Carnaro Charter on the first anniversary of the march on the city. Back in Milan, Nenni reported on biblical excesses, farcical debauchery. He says that one day D'Annunzio mimics medieval feudal lords, and the next day poses as a Renaissance prince. The police send accounts in which Fiume is described as the "Eldorado of all vices," the "land of plenty." Meanwhile, the squalor is such that district hospitals report cases of bubonic plague. Nenni also did an imitation of the Vate communing with the people from the balcony of the government building. Tomfoolery, all tomfoolery. Enough blank checks issued to poets.

With Giolitti you enter the big league and the big league requires eclecticism. You can't remain hypnotized by two rocks in the Adriatic. Playing big-time is for presbyopics, and he, since he was a boy, has always been long-sighted. In him, a lesser focus corresponds to a greater capacity for overall vision. A superior power of vision that carries with it the consequence of not being able to distinguish the trifling minutiae, having to lose sight of insignificant details. Undoubtedly a serious deficiency, in times when the insignificant is the only thing that matters. But Benito Mussolini doesn't care. His sight gets blurry when he has to look at the tiny scribbles that populate the lower regions of the universe, but the big letters in block print up above, those he sees as sharply as few others can. It's time to play in the big league.

The Central Committee of the Fasci di Combattimento on November 15th is a meeting of presbyopics. For this reason, the atmosphere is quite tense. At the headquarters on Via Monte di Pietà, the two sides can already be distinguished by the arrangement around the table. Cesare Rossi, Massimo Rocca and Umberto Pasella are on his side. On the other side are Cesare De Vecchi, Piero Belli, Pietro Marsich and all the other undeterred Fiumani. There is also a delegation of Dalmatians who are standing, lined up against the wall, like a tragic chorus.

The Founder speaks first. He reiterates the reasons already explained in his newspaper columns. The Treaty of Rapallo is overall satisfactory, with regard to the new borders of Venezia Giulia and also to Fiume. Certainly it is not so with respect to Dalmatia. Yet we must accept it as a fait accompli, with a show of national discipline. The country is very tired, the socialists are lying in wait, ready to take advantage of a crisis to raise their heads again, people don't even know exactly where Dalmatia is. He proposes an agenda that reflects these positions. D'Annunzio's sedition was a spectacular initiative but it became gangrenous, and gangrene must be severed.

The internal opposition's reaction hits him with unprecedented force. Pietro Marsich, the most fervent D'Annunziano among the fascist leaders, openly attacks him. He is the head of the Venetian fasci, an attorney, a man of great erudition and the utmost integrity, an idealist and an asshole. He speaks like a patriot of the Risorgimento. He shouts that the "base Rapallo negotiators" can go ahead and apply the "nefarious agreement" but this does not mean that the Fiume movement is over. The "bold revolution" begun in 1915 against "the old, cynical, soft and faint-hearted Italy, deservedly represented by Giovanni Giolitti," will continue.

It's not hard to shut Marsich up. Just agree with him. The problem begins when the Dalmatians speak. They are Italian, they have been Italian since the time of the Roman Empire, and the treaty sentences them to the Croatian yoke. Emotion spreads through the room and emotion among adult males is always dangerous.

So Mussolini intervenes a second time. Let the Dalmatians clearly state what they represent. Everyone in that hall is their supporter but there is a need for clarity. What do they want? Annexation as far as the Bay of Kotor? An Italian-Yugoslav republic? Full autonomy? The discussion continues, still on a surge of emotion. He intervenes a third time. He understands that the Dalmatians feel they are simply followers of D'Annunzio but they are not, they are responsible to take action! If tomorrow D'Annunzio were to get the notion of annexing all of Dalmatia, they couldn't very well follow him. Let the Dalmatians clearly state what they want. The discussion goes on with the same tenor as before. He intervenes a fourth time. They must understand that the question is not only an emotional one: the fate of the nation is at stake. If they go on that way, he will keep his agenda pure and simple.

Two hours later, Benito Mussolini backpedals. He withdraws his agenda and accepts another agreed-upon one. It is a compromise, as always. He applauds the new borders, objects strongly to Dalmatia and reiterates that Fiume must be Italian. The crisis within fascism is averted. Not even Cesare Rossi understands it. Even Cesarino is stunned by this about-face. He stood at Mussolini's side throughout the diatribe and now he won't agree to the reversal. The agenda is approved with his negative vote.

That same evening the fasci's founder wrote to D'Annunzio: "My dear Commander, my long silence has not dimmed my voice nor diminished my dedication . . . we must define our objectives in order to move, stir and steer the national conscience. Namely: All of Dalmatia from Zadar to Kotor? Or focus our efforts instead to save at least that of the London Treaty? Give me your thoughts on this topic. As for how and when, I have faith in you." A masterpiece of hypocrisy. But, after all, is it really so grave to be called a traitor again?

D'Annunzio doesn't answer him. No other letter from the Commander comes to Milan after that. In the days that follow, many abandon the poet, especially those among the high-ranking military: Admiral Millo, grenadier commander Carlo Reina, Luigi Rizzo, the heroic "Sinker" of the *Santo Stefano*, and general Ceccherini, who in insurrectional fantasies was to have led the Bersaglieri in an assault on Rome's parliament. The Commander, left to his fate, falls silent. It will be the Vate who speaks, in a talk at the Teatro Verdi on November 20th, on the occasion of a concert held in Fiume by Toscanini: "Here we are alone again, alone against the world, with our solitary courage," he will say.

Italy needs peace in order to recover, to rebuild itself, to set out on the course of its inevitable greatness. Only a madman or a criminal can think of triggering new wars that are not imposed by some sudden aggression.

Benito Mussolini,
Il Popolo d'Italia, November 13, 1920

LEANDRO ARPINATI

BOLOGNA, NOVEMBER 23, 1920

"WOMEN AND CHILDREN should stay home on Sunday. If they want to be deserving of the country, let them display the Tricolor from their windows. On the streets of Bologna, on Sunday, there must be only fascists and Bolsheviks. It will be the test. The big test on behalf of Italy."

Arpinati had it spelled out in black and white. He and his men went around personally putting up the ultimatum on every street in the city. He'd had to duplicate the posters at home with a cyclostyle because the police chief had denied the approval to print them.

The anticipation of the clash is fervent, unanimous, equally shared by both sides. Having reached this point, there will be fighting: that is the only point on which the enemies agree. On November 12th in Cremona, Farinacci's fascists warned the socialist city councilors: "If tomorrow, after taking over the town hall, the socialists were to think about taking over the piazza, they should know that there are people willing to kill and to die." Two days later in Modena, where the socialists took 59 municipalities out of 68, the provincial council president, opening the assembly, announces in a kind of distant rejoinder: "We do not want to debate with our enemies; we want to bring them down." The battle's front line now runs along the entire Po Valley.

In Bologna, the Socialist Union met on the evening of November 16. Overcoming numerous internal divisions, it decided to gear up to repel fascist violence with violence. The socialists' victory in the elections was clear, the voters' mandate is unequivocal, the police forces cannot be called upon because the state is "the executive committee of the bourgeoisie." We'll defend ourselves against the fascists on our own, it was resolved. To emphasize the victory, a huge popular demonstration was ordered for the council's inauguration ceremony at Palazzo d'Accursio. They decided to hold it on Sunday, November 21, to enable the working-class crowds to participate. Armed security duty was assigned to the "red guards." In response, on the evening of the 17th, the approximately 400 members of the Bologna fascio met on Via Marsala. They too determined to be ready and vigilant.

On both sides there is exhilaration, there's a rough and ready euphoria in the air, bizarre explosions of vitality. The long wait now seems over.

The clash appears inevitable, the skirmish is announced, premeditated, even negotiated. On November 18th, in parliament, for the first time socialist deputy Niccolai denounced the spread of fascist violence; while *Avanti!* underscored the government's collusion, the *Corriere della Sera*'s response spoke openly of the "welcome reaction of public opinion" to socialists' abuses. In Bologna, the prefect and police chief are fully aware that the only thing needed to ignite the fire is the spark. Rumors are circulating about the crates of bombs that the socialists are said to be storing in Palazzo d'Accursio for the council's swearing-in ceremony, anonymous letters are sent, symbols are discussed. Police chief Poli personally went to the fascist headquarters on Via Marsala to negotiate the rules of engagement. After lengthy secret parleys on both sides, an agreement worthy of an imperial protocol was reached: the fascists will not attack as long as the "*campanone*" is not rung and providing the red flag is not displayed except at the end of the session when the newly elected mayor will look out over the piazza to thank the voters. Only then can it be tolerated as a party flag. Meanwhile, the police chief urged the prefect to send 1,200 more troops and 800 carabinieri to reinforce the 400 royal guards already available. On the morning of November 21, according to reports by prefect Visconti, 900 infantrymen, 200 cavalry, 800 carabinieri and 600 royal guards converge on the streets of the historic center. Bologna is a city in a state of siege.

Palazzo d'Accursio has always been the seat of Bologna's civic power, be it senatorial or municipal. It is a crenellated building, next to the basilica of San Petronio, overlooking Piazza Maggiore. Around 2:00 p.m. processions of socialist delegates begin streaming in. They number a couple of thousand, no more, in accordance with an agreement made with the police. The piazza is barricaded, all the entrances from Via Rizzoli and Via Indipendenza are closed off. A cordon of carabinieri secures it on all sides.

It seems, however, that a number of fascists have managed to get in before the closure. There are perhaps a dozen of them, gathered under the canopy of the Restaurant Grande Italia, in the piazza jammed with thousands of socialists crowding around the Neptune fountain. Inside the Palazzo, they are preparing for the start of the inaugural session. In the courtyard about fifty royal guards are keeping an eye on the entrance, while "red guards" armed with rifles and grenades appear on the balconies. Every last person is under fire. You can hear a pin drop.

At 2:30, however, despite the prefect's precautions and despite the agreement with the police chief, a red flag is flown from the Torre degli Asinelli.

The fascists, Arpinati leading them, leave the headquarters on Via Marsala en masse and march towards the piazza in squads. A handful manages to slip in from Via Ugo Bassi through an opening made to let the cavalry pass through. There are probably no more than fifteen of them. They sing their anthems standing at the edge of the socialist crowd.

At 3:00 p.m., inside the building, the Council session begins. The inaugural address of the new mayor goes smoothly. His name is Enio Gnudi; a railway worker and a communist, he pays the usual tribute to the Russian revolution. Half an hour later, while the fascist group increases its clamor, Gnudi, fired up, leans out over the balcony of the Red Room to greet the crowd, surrounded by the red flags of the socialist associations. For him it is a day of celebration and he is looking at his own ruin. He frees some doves from a cage and they circle as a flock over socialists and fascists alike, without distinction. The birds too have little red flags tied to their tails. A shot rings out from the Restaurant Grande Italia.

At the catastrophic signal, a group of 26 Ferrarese fascists break through the security cordon with clubs. From the Grande Italia they are still firing, the shooting is returned from the balconies of the building, and more shots are fired from the Neptune fountain. The crowd is caught under the crossfire. Terrified, they scatter in all directions. Most of them swarm towards the building's courtyard. Pandemonium ensues.

The socialist farmers and workers are sweating, trembling, they're scared they're going to die, they feel numbness, asphyxia, tingling in the limbs, tightness in the chest, faintness, shortness of breath, they're afraid they're losing their minds, their hearts beat more and more rapidly, their blood pressure rises then falls, they feel flushed, chilled, nauseated, they are afraid they won't be able to recover, they feel that the worst is yet to come. A sensation of irreality takes over.

From the balconies the "red guards," seeing their comrades seeking safety in the courtyard, mistake them for fascists rushing to attack the building. They launch five grenades. The corpses of their comrades pile up on the threshold.

As a socialist concludes his speech in the council chamber, which is packed with members of the public, local police, "red guards," and duty officials, the echoes of the detonations rise up from the piazza. The fallen bodies are visible through the windows. The socialist councilors, unaware of what actually happened, leap to their feet in the majority benches, flanked by on call firemen. "Murderers! You're killing our comrades," they shout to the few minority councilors. Nationalist attorney Aldo Oviglio throws his revolver on the table: "I'm not killing anyone."

It's a world of armed men today inside Palazzo d'Accursio. On the other side of the chamber, one of those men—an anonymous socialist militant—stands up, levels his gun at the unarmed gentlemen who at the moment appear to be responsible for a bloodbath that was largely caused by his own comrades, and fires.

He will never be identified by the police or handed over by party leaders. Attorney Giulio Giordani, minority councilor of the nationalist party, former soldier, silver medalist, missing a leg, dies instantly. In life he wasn't even a fascist but he will become so, dead. Attorney Biagi slumps to the floor, slightly wounded. Attorney Cesare Colliva drags himself on all fours, bleeding, towards the exit.

It is said that Leandro Arpinati was seen inciting the fascists to attack, clinging to the statue of Neptune. Others swear that they saw him dash into the courtyard of the building, gun in hand. Rumors, hearsay, legends. What is certain is that there are 10 dead and 50 wounded. The credibility of the socialist military organization is destroyed, the party's reputation as well. The democratically elected municipal council, overcome by the arrests and scandal, resigns en masse. Bologna will be governed by a commissioner appointed by the prefect. A new season has begun.

Whose fault is it? Who but the Socialist Party aspires to civil war in Italy? Who but the Socialist Party creates and fosters this atmosphere of savage battle? A battle necessarily finds its fighters, on the other side as well . . .

Corriere della Sera, November 23, 1920

It is time for everyone to decide to disarm and demobilize their hearts, to not only lay down their material weapons, but to disarm and demobilize their hearts . . . Hands in the air, everyone!

Filippo Turati, socialist leader,
speech to the chamber, November 24, 1920

Against the brutal vileness of the "reds" lying in wait in Palazzo d'Accursio . . . an eye for an eye, a tooth for a tooth . . . Out with the barbarians!

L'Avvenire d'Italia, a Catholic newspaper,
November 24, 1920

BENITO MUSSOLINI

TRIESTE, EARLY DECEMBER 1920

"When a unit is besieged in a city without provisions it has only one way to avoid being crushed: to go out and face the battle in an open arena."

Alceste De Ambris thrusts his head forward, bringing his musketeer's goatee close to his interlocutor.

The founder of the Italian Trade Union and that of the fasci have known each other for years. They were side by side at the time of interventionism; De Ambris helped draft the first Fascist Manifesto. Mussolini has admired the revolutionary unionist since 1908, when Alceste led the first major agrarian strike in Italian history, in Parma. The king had had to send the Lancers of Montebello to clear the indomitable Chamber of Labor out of the proletarian village of Oltretorrente. De Ambris that day had forced his way into the pantheon of revolutionary socialism.

Now, twelve years later, Gabriele D'Annunzio has sent Alceste De Ambris to make one last attempt to move the fascists to defend the Fiume legionnaires. At dawn on December 1st, on Giolitti's orders, two armor-plated battleships, eight torpedo destroyers and two tugs were deployed in front of the port of Fiume. The siege has begun. The city is under fire. De Ambris leans closer.

"Is Mussolini a friend?"

The question hangs in the air between the two old comrades. Mussolini opens the yellow leather satchel that he always carries with him, takes out a handkerchief and blows his nose:

"This cold won't go away. I'm always running around with it, that's why it's hanging on so long."

"Is Mussolini a friend?" De Ambris presses him.

"Of course I'm a friend! I even reiterated in the newspaper yesterday that I would be the first to urge the Italians to rise up as one against the government if it dared order the army to open fire on the legionnaires."

"And are you willing to put your men under D'Annunzio's command?"

The third man in the room, the young Umberto Foscanelli, charged with taking notes, looks up from his pad, waiting for the answer. It was established that the minutes of the meeting would be sent to both the fasci central committee and to Commander D'Annunzio.

Mussolini snaps: "You must convince D'Annunzio to accept the Treaty of Rapallo. There is only one way to negate it: rebellion from within against the government that signed it. But rebellion from within is unthinkable because 99 percent of the Italian people have accepted the fait accompli with a deep sigh of relief. They are all abandoning you."

The list of desertions is long. The economist Maffeo Pantaleoni wrote to D'Annunzio imploring him to desist. Even Admiral Millo, who guarded Zadar with regular troops, reiterated his loyalty to the king and broke with D'Annunzio. General Ceccherini and Colonel Siani left, complaining about the intolerable lack of discipline among the legionnaires. The Commander's reply to their regretful farewell letter was that he could not cede absolute power: "It is necessary that I retain this prerogative. It is the only joy in so much boredom."

De Ambris persists. Insurrection is not impossible: from Fiume they can march on Rome. He rattles off the details of an exit strategy. This list too is long. In Fiume there are various naval units: the cruiser *Mirabello*, the destroyers *Abba*, *Bronzetti*, and *Nullo*, and the fully manned MAS flotilla. It is true that the *Dante* and other ships of the royal navy keep watch offshore, but trips to Zadar with some of these vessels have already been made; from Zadar to

Ancona then the distance is not excessive. Fiume troops would be set ashore in Ancona, where a regiment of Bersaglieri already rebelled in July over being sent to Valona. It's a matter of making arrangements with the fascists in the Marches. Captain Giulietti's seamen are still friends . . .

"And what about the socialists of northern Italy?! And red Bologna!?" Mussolini explodes. Until that moment he's been listening, dabbing his nose with the handkerchief, then suddenly his eyes fly open; rolling them impatiently, as he usually does when he wants to galvanize, he keeps at it: "After the massacre in Palazzo d'Accursio, by now it's all-out war. What, don't you people read the newspapers in Fiume!?"

De Ambris does not seem bothered by the outburst. He goes on with the presentation of his meticulous planning. Those from Parma are all with them, he assures him. We need to let the working masses know that the D'Annunzians bring the Statute of the Regency of Carnaro, its legislation that protects work above all; we must make it clear that theirs will be a revolution specifically for the people; we must remedy the fact that the Carnaro Charter has not been divulged . . . that its innovative spirit has not been adequately made known . . . even *Il Popolo d'Italia* is somewhat to blame for this . . .

Mussolini gives the impression that he is no longer listening. He now replies in monosyllables, detached, evasive, constantly blowing his nose, he hints at the various difficulties—but they are only distracted hints—at the Yugoslav troops pressing along the border, at the scarcity of provisions, at a winter without coal.

The meeting ends on the rigors of the season, the dampness, colds. Foscanelli is asked to tear up the pages on which he had recorded the minutes. It is the only point on which Mussolini and De Ambris agree. The torn sheets end up in the stove.

Italians of Trieste, Italians of all of Istria, Italians of all of Venezia Giulia, from the Timavo to the Carnaro, the crime is about to be committed, blood is about to be shed. Those doomed to die bid their farewell to you. Those doomed to die bid their farewell to the homeland, near and far. They dedicate their sacrifice to the future . . . The One-eyed Man of victory is about to be brought down by the Hypermetropic traitor. This was so written; and this is tremendous. Behold, brothers! If my throat is slit I will nonetheless find the strength to spit out my blood and hurl my cry. Plug up your ears with some unyielding mud. Long live Italy!

Gabriele D'Annunzio,
proclamation against the Treaty of Rapallo,
Fiume, November 28, 1920

BENITO MUSSOLINI

MILAN, DECEMBER 20, 1920

THE CAR THAT parks on Via Lovanio is a Bianchi S3 Torpedo, the evolution of the one used by Italian Army staff officers during the Great War to observe military maneuvers. An elegant vehicle (four seats plus folding ones), worthy of a commendatore, but with the tangentially spoked wheels that flirt with the world of sports cars.

The Duce is driving it himself. On the passenger side an elegant lady is expected to exit, and Margherita Sarfatti does not disappoint expectations. She is wearing a skirt flared at the hemline and form-fitting at the waist, woven in jersey, a stretchy, shiny fabric that clings to the hips, in the Paris fashion. Via Lovanio is a street no less elegant, not far from the Brera Academy, just behind Via Solferino where the great newspaper of the bourgeoisie, the *Corriere della Sera*, is located.

In a few days, the editorial offices of *Il Popolo d'Italia* will also relocate here. The print shop has already moved, the presses are in action. It is a whole other Milan compared to the Bottonuto's alleyways reeking of piss. In the rank cubicle on Via Paolo da Cannobio, Mussolini's typewriter has already been packed up, together with the stagy revolvers and the Arditi flag.

Today even the editor sports an unusually distinctive appearance. Black suit, bowler hat, shirt with starched collar, silk tie, white handkerchief in the breast pocket. Contrary to his customary practice, he has been to the barber's to get a shave. His first sitting for posed photographs required it. As soon as she steps out of the car, the woman who first dressed him and then got him here takes his arm, satisfied.

Michele Bianchi, the managing editor, Manlio Morgagni, who now handles advertising sales, and Mussolini's brother Arnaldo, who replaced him as administrator, are already there waiting for the editor-in-chief. The brief inspection soon leads to the room that will house the management. It is at least three times as big as the cubicle on Via Cannobio, luminous, furnished with a mahogany desk, shelving, file cabinets, paintings chosen by Sarfatti, the newspaper's art critic, and an armchair to read in.

"An armchair!? What the hell is an armchair doing in my office!?" Mussolini curses, widening his eyes and rolling them upward at the familiar piece of furniture as if he'd spotted an avowed enemy. "An armchair for me!? Get rid of it, or I'll hurl it out the window. An armchair and slippers are a man's ruin!" Margherita smiles, the decorator shows no sign of being bothered, the performance for his lover's benefit has gone well.

The tour continues in the adjoining room, a vast space that is still unfinished, completely bare, with no roof and no brickwork over the concrete. It will be used as a training studio. The editor will be able to take his usual fencing lessons without having to take too much time away from the newspaper. In his bourgeois clothing, with the bowler hat on his head, in that empty, unfurnished room, Benito Mussolini strikes a *sabreur*'s pose, parry in tierce, arm extended. Violence is increasingly on the agenda.

The escalation exploded after the Bologna massacre. The progression was exponential, its guiding principle unequivocal and obvious, as if driven by an instinct of the species. Immediately after the bloodbath, while the bodies of the dead and wounded still littered the piazza, the fascists were already assembled, moving through the city's streets singing their anthems. Their ascent had begun the very next day—thousands of new members in just a few days—and the fascists had no intention of disarming. Arpinati had publicly declared it: until the period of violence ceased in the countryside, until the state agencies were back in control of the situation, the Bolognese fascio would continue to remain with weapons at the ready.

Mussolini had immediately sent Cesare Rossi and Celso Morisi from Milan to coordinate the formation of the squads. The fascist paramilitary units, long dreamed of in vain by the Founder, were now sprouting by spontaneous generation from the blood shed in Piazza Maggiore, in Bologna. Rossi had told him that on November 23rd, during the funeral procession for Giordani, the fascists had actually marched in formation between the parted crowd, carrying the city flag. The socialists were absent. They hadn't even found the courage to proclaim a general strike in protest against the fascist assault. Total political annihilation. That same day the council members had resigned their posts; by that evening interim administration had been assigned to a prefect, and the prefectural commissioner had taken office the following day. Then the red witch hunt had begun.

On the 28th Arpinati, accompanied by a fascist squad, had left for Monte Paderno to warn the head of the league and had brought back the red flag. They burned it on Via Indipendenza. On December 4th at the Teatro Comunale, at an assembly of all the anti-Bolshevist associations, the fascists had been met with cries of "out with the barbarians!" On December 7th, they had sacked the Chamber of Labor at Castel San Pietro, on the 9th, there had been a clash in Monzuno, on the 18th, they had attacked and beaten socialist deputies Bentini and Niccolai at the entrance to the tribunal, and on the 19th, deputy Misiano, the deserter, had his turn. And so they had arrived at today, December 20, only five days before Christmas.

Just this morning, Arpinati, elected secretary of Bologna's fascio by popular acclaim, announced by telegram that he was leaving on an expedition to Ferrara in support of a demonstration by local fascists to commemorate attorney Giordani on the thirtieth day following his assassination at the Palazzo d'Accursio. From Ferrara they had actually requested 3,000 flags to ensure the event's success. They had even pledged to pay for them in advance.

A wave of enthusiasm, in fact, and a chorus of approval greeted the actions of the fascist squads everywhere. Victory had been total, the push had turned things around, the red spell had been broken. And not just in Bologna. Triumphal violence spread down Via Emilia with the speed of contagion: in the Rovigo area, supported by the landowners, the fasci were rife along the Cavarzere-Cona-Correzzola-Bovolenta axis, at Adria the squads had driven out farm laborers who had occupied the vast estate of Oca, in Modena they had attacked the municipal councilmen, in Carpi the Chamber of Labor; from there actions had seeped into Reggio and Mantua; in Bra, in the Cuneo area, fascists led by De Vecchi had beaten the "red guards," even pursuing them into the offices of the town hall. It was an avalanche effect; rushing from self-defense to counterattack, fascism flourished unstoppably in every province of Italy. An air of battle hovered over the countryside.

Mussolini himself had proclaimed it from the columns of his newspaper: soon they would be invincible, their supreme, finest hour was approaching. Spirits up! Let's turn fear into hatred and rail against the enemy. Let's make all our lives into a battering ram!

The socialists, poor devils, had instead shouted "hands in the air"! Filippo Turati had raised his prophet's beard to the benches of parliament and given a very noble speech. He had denounced the acquiescence of the authorities, he had mourned the involuntary slaughter of his socialist comrades, he had defended institutions and statutory liberties. Turati had made it clear that his intent was not to recriminate but to take steps for tomorrow. It was necessary to put a stop to the excesses on all sides, by eliminating the causes. It was time, he had concluded, that everyone decided to disarm and demobilize their hearts. To seal it, he had also elegantly dropped a cultured and ironic literary quotation.

The hall of Montecitorio had listened in absolute silence, moved. The enlightened press had applauded admiringly: the old socialist guru had managed to pull off the miracle of restoring a socialist conscience to the deputies of his group and a liberal conscience to the democratic delegates.

Reading the transcript of Turati's speech, Mussolini had shaken his head, amused. There was nothing you could do: those people just didn't understand brutality. A beautiful speech—of course—but the sphere of violence was not for the socialists. Sure, the leagues threw their weight around in the countryside; the chambers of labor in the cities oppressed enemies of the revolution with fines, boycotts, and extortion; socialist peasants had even set fire to some barns, mutilated a few cows, beaten some tenant farmers to a pulp, shot some policeman or agrarian in self-defense; they had even, in rare cases, gone so far as to savagely deface corpses or rape girls on their way back from Mass; they had even bludgeoned a few fascists, but in the end these were always eruptions of ancestral anger, a back that's whipped that in a burst of desperation straightens up and seizes the whip, the sharecropper who after centuries of abuse, on a night with a full moon and some grappa, slits the throat of the sleeping bailiff who had raped his daughter, then sets fire to the barn and hangs himself. Socialist violence was an unquestionable reality but it all came down to that impulse. The socialist leaders blabbered about planning the revolution through an army of armed militants when in truth there was no plan. He knew those people well, he had for decades. When it came to violence, they were and would remain outsiders.

The bare training studio suddenly fills up. A messenger has come running from Via Cannobio: all hell has broken loose in Ferrara.

Mussolini rouses himself from his meditations on his sword fantasies. He asks for more details, which the messenger provides.

There were violent clashes on the sidelines of a rally convened by Ferrara's socialist mayor. Shots were fired from a procession of nurses on its way to the rally, waving the red flag, towards a counter-demonstration led by about fifty Bolognese fascists headed by Arpinati. It is not clear who fired first, but it seems that the Bolsheviks also opened fire from the battlements of Estense Castle, where the police recovered several grenades. The "reds'" attack on the blackshirts was, in short, planned. It seems at least three fascists remained on the ground.

"Arpinati?"

"Arpinati is alive."

Neck muscles contract, nerves tighten, bodies turn on their heels. The tour of the new offices on Via Lovanio is over.

Mussolini gets back in the Torpedo; Michele Bianchi is now by his side, where Sarfatti was sitting before. Waiting for them is Lusignoli, the prefect of Milan, their liaison with the prime minister in Rome. He wants reassurances as to the fascists' conduct with regard to D'Annunzio. Mussolini has for some time been promising him that there in Milan they will not make a move, but for days, in *Il Popolo d'Italia*, the editor has surprisingly expressed harsh criticism of Giolitti, who is threatening to clear out Fiume with cannon fire. Prefect Lusignoli wants reassurances and he will get them: the promise to Giolitti will be kept, the journalistic polemic is merely smoke in the eyes of the fascists loyal to D'Annunzio.

After the stop at the prefecture, they immediately leave again in the Torpedo S3. Off again, fast, full throttle. You always have to play on multiple tables, fight on various fronts, remain in perpetual motion. Now he has to give a speech at the Automobile Club hall where the first anniversary of the "National Legionnaires' Association of Fiume and Dalmatia" is being celebrated. President Elisa Rizzoli and Countess Carla Visconti of Modrone Erba, sponsor of the association's emblem, will be present. They too will not be denied satisfaction.

On the 20th of this month, a large rally will be held here in Ferrara, in a theater, to commemorate the thirtieth day following the death of attorney Giulio Giordani of Bologna. It is our intention, on that occasion, to give a full demonstration of our forces in the city and the province. We need two or three thousand flags right away, so that we can distribute them to all of our fascists and supporters. We will then immediately send you payment to cover the cost. We repeat, the utmost speed is required in sending said flags, since they are indispensable if we are to show everyone, especially our adversaries, the strength and number of the forces available to Ferrara's fascio.

Letter sent to the Central Committee
by the fascio of Ferrara,
December 8, 1920

ITALO BALBO

FERRARA, DECEMBER 22, 1920

At the parliamentary elections of November 1919, the Socialist Party, in the province of Ferrara, obtained 43,000 votes: three out of four of Ferrara's electorate voted for revolution. The following year again, in the local administrative elections of November 1920, the bloc of anti-revolutionary parties received fewer than 7,000 votes throughout the province. Yet only a month later, on December 22nd, in Ferrara 14,000 people attend the funeral of the three fascists killed in clashes with the socialists in front of the Estense Castle. The balance of strength is being reversed, the confirmation of powers must be substantiated day by day.

Despite the fact that the clash was undoubtedly caused by the aggression of the Bolognese fascist squads led by Arpinati, the grenades found in the Estense Castle, brought in by the socialists in preparation for defense, enabled the aggressors to shift responsibility for it. An alarmed telegram was sent to Giolitti from Ferrara, signed by all the bourgeois associations for civil self-defense: "Even here from the towers of Estense Castle, seat of socialist provincial government charged with public administration, citizens are premeditatedly and treacherously murdered. We call for Bologna's parliamentary investigation to be immediately extended to this province as well. Respectfully."

The government in Rome identified the prefect as scapegoat, and he was quickly removed from office. A reward of 20,000 liras was offered to anyone who could provide a clue as to the "names of the murderers." Those responsible for what the bourgeois and fascist press describe as a "cold-blooded, premeditated massacre" are hunted down. Socialist mayor Temistocle Bogianckino, Zirardini and the other leaders of the Chamber of Labor are no longer able to go out on the street without being insulted and threatened. The proletarian front retreats: *La scintilla*, the local socialist daily, has suspended publication. Their dead are disregarded. The death of Giovanni Mirella, a socialist militant nurse who fell in the clashes, is even attributed to the Popular Party.

The fallen fascists, on the other hand, are honored as "martyrs" for liberty. They are Natalino Magnani, a nineteen-year-old member of the Bologna fascio, Giorgio Pagnoni, a farmworker from Gaibana, and Franco Gozzi, a Bersaglieri lieutenant on leave and a pioneer of fascism in the province. At the funeral ceremony the speakers emphasize their courage. It is recalled that Gozzi, in the entire province of Ferrara, had managed to form only five fascist circles. Whereas in the same province, during the same year, 1920, as many as 192 barn fires set by the "reds" had been counted. The bravery of the men who faced thousands, while numbering only a few dozen, is exalted. Praise be given to these unseen men who "were the first to break the ice of indifference of our friends and the ironclad arrogance of our enemies. But let us not weave garlands of our regret. The dead march alongside the living."

The funeral ceremony unfolds solemnly, memorably, a stately ritual, yet its purpose is not to bury the dead. On the contrary, everything about it, the homily, the *mea culpa*, the Our Father, the parted crowd, must serve to leave them unburied. Do not throw earth upon their graves. The dead should not be commemorated: they should be vindicated.

Once the funeral procession has passed, the fascists, about a thousand strong, assembled as squads, return to the streets of the city center in column formation, singing their anthems. The entire bourgeoisie, grande and petite, line up to make way for them, hailing them. Merchants, industrialists, tradesmen, shopkeepers, small landowners, tenant farmers, sharecroppers, clerks, professionals, artisans. The sleepy city center of Ferrara, deserted by the working class, wakes up. The parasitic capital of the vast agricultural empire breaks out of its petit bourgeois lethargy. In two days it will be Christmas, but this year the traditional *cappon magro* will have a different flavor.

Anonymous among the thousands, a captain of the Alpine troops also attends the funeral of the fascist "martyrs." He is a young man of twenty-four, tall, thin, strong, the son of a respectable provincial elementary schoolteacher. He attended the prestigious Ariosto secondary school in Ferrara but was expelled for poor performance and misconduct. From the time he was a boy, his passion has always been politics. A fervent republican, and follower of Mazzini and Foscolo, at sixteen he'd already run away from home to join Garibaldi's grandson who was organizing an expedition to support the freedom of the Albanian people. His father had had to send some friends to bring him back.

Later on, when the boy, now a man, finally left to go to war, he distinguished himself by leading an assault battalion in the final offensive on Mount Grappa. After capturing the enemy trench, he was saved only by pretending to be dead for a whole day. He received a silver and two bronze medals. Discharged in May 1920, like other reserve officers, he was assigned to Pinzano al Tagliamento, a town in central Friuli, in the role of prefectural commissioner. There he fell in love with Emanuela Florio—and she with him—a girl of Dalmatian origin, daughter of one of the richest families in Friuli. The father, Count Florio, was opposed to the union with a destitute down-and-outer. But the valiant captain of the Alpini has no intention of giving up. Instead, he is planning to go back to her, on the banks of the Tagliamento. On December 22nd, he is only passing through Ferrara, having returned to his native city just long enough to spend the Christmas holidays there. It is only by chance that he attends the funeral on December 22nd. He has long, unruly hair falling over his forehead and a thick black goatee hanging from his chin. His name is Italo Balbo.

The loss that has struck us strengthens our muscle and our faith. And our Dead will not be deprived of the most just vengeance. United now and always, united in blood, in sorrow and in Victory: We shall win!

A. Del Fante, founder of the fascio of Ferrara,
letter to the fascio of Milan, December 22, 1921

BENITO MUSSOLINI

MILAN, DECEMBER 24, 1920

"HERE THEY ARE preparing to commit the crime. Are you ready with your men to invade the prefectures, to assault the police headquarters?"

The appeal conveyed by those under siege in the letter that reached Milan from Fiume is dramatic. For two days Milan has been shrouded in fog. These are the coldest days of the year. Rime settles in particles on the roofs of cars parked along the curbs. When Mussolini enters the fascio headquarters on Christmas Eve, D'Annunzio's letter is in the inside pocket of his jacket.

The desperate letter from D'Annunzio had been delivered to him personally that morning by Captain Balisti. The Fiume command officer had traveled all night. Knowing that before long the city would be cut off from communications with Italy, on the evening of December 23, on the last departing steamer, the Commander sent several of his trusted men to the city's supporters. At any moment Giolitti will order a coup de main on Fiume. Handwritten by D'Annunzio himself, the despairing letter asks the fascists to keep their promise to rise up in the event of a "fratricidal" attack. After reading it in private, Mussolini snapped to D'Annunzio's emissary:

"That poet of yours is a great man. But he's crazy. We already have the police on our backs. They'll arrest us in the blink of an eye."

The situation in Fiume is on the brink of the precipice, the outcome of the Milan meeting appears uncertain, the wives and children of the fascist leaders are expecting them home for Christmas Eve dinner.

In the upper Adriatic these are days of ultimatums and constant deferments. Already at the beginning of December, General Caviglia, at the head of the contingent sent from Rome to enforce the Treaty of Rapallo, ordered D'Annunzio to free the towns of Veglia and Arbe, occupied in contempt of the treaty. On December 20th a new ultimatum from Caviglia reached D'Annunzio, giving him forty-eight hours to bring his legionnaires back within the borders of the state of Fiume recognized by the treaty. Simultaneously Caviglia effectively ordered a blockade by land and sea of the Fiume territory.

D'Annunzio responded to the ultimatums with proclamations. He issued three within twenty-four hours. With the first, on December 23rd, he appealed to the Italian navy's sailors who were besieging their Italian "heroic brothers" of Fiume: "The country today trusts that each of you will do his duty by disobeying." In the second, briefer one, he surrendered to melancholy. Fiume has been sold out. Everyone has only one duty today: to resist. And, if necessary, die. In the third proclamation, again addressed "to the brothers who are besieging their brothers," the poet played the desperate card of appealing to the mothers. If Caviglia's soldiers were to spill the blood of their countrymen deployed in defense of Fiume's *italianità*, their mothers—the one-eyed seer assured them, scrutinizing the crystal ball of emotional blackmail—would disown them. "I did not give birth to you, my son."

Mussolini in Milan has also been busy writing in the last few days. In various articles he urged Giolitti to officially recognize the government of the D'Annunzian Regency, protested strongly against the blockade imposed on the city and, above all, railed against rumors of an imminent military action against the legionnaires. From the columns of his newspaper, the editor of *Il Popolo d'Italia* shouted that ordering Italian soldiers to attack Italian legionnaires would be an ineradicable crime, called the blockade a "barbaric coercion," and threatened terrible consequences.

Nevertheless, he stated that he was still confident that blood would not be spilled.

Mussolini reiterated his certainty today as well in an article, already sent to the printer, which will appear tomorrow in the Christmas edition. At the same time, playing at two tables as he usually did, the Founder of the fasci continued to reassure Giolitti. In his talks with prefect Lusignoli he made it clear that he disagreed with the poet's disastrous conduct. The prefect, in turn, reassured the head of government: "It's tactics, what Mussolini is doing, it's just tactics." The fasci will not make a move. The way is clear.

The secret meeting of the central committee on December 24th goes smoothly. Expressions of common sense make the rounds, conventional formulas such as "healthy realism," "civic spirit," "more moderate advice" are repeated. Given the conciliatory climate, Mussolini goes so far as to confide to his collaborators that the question of Fiume is of secondary importance. Fascism must not be seen as intransigent in foreign policy. Its future lies elsewhere. In internal politics.

Only the Trieste fascists offer some resistance. But in Milan it is Christmas Eve, in the streets the fog thickens in an icy coating that drapes the spires of the Duomo in an opaque mantle, and by now a majority of those in Milan consider the Commander to be an insane megalomaniac. The capon broth is already simmering on the fire. The last desperate letter from D'Annunzio remains in the inside pocket of Mussolini's jacket.

When Italian regular troops launch the attack on Fiume at five o'clock in the afternoon, the secret meeting of the fasci central committee is already over and its members are hurrying home to join their families in celebrating the Blessed Birth of our Lord Jesus Christ.

I had a talk with Mussolini who strongly disagrees with D'Annunzio's conduct. At my question as to why in his newspaper he supports recognition of the Fiume Regency, he replied that such recognition, even excluding annexation, would put an end to the current dispute. However, he cannot support the opposing view because he would be considered a traitor by his followers.

Telegram from Alfredo Lusignoli, prefect of Milan,
to Giovanni Giolitti, December 20, 1920

Advance immediately all along the front line, overcoming anyone who tries to prevent our soldiers from obeying. Enter Fiume as quickly as possible. The salvation and honor of the nation requires it. The action is to be continued until the city is occupied.

Order of the Italian government
to General Enrico Caviglia,
December 24, 1920

GABRIELE D'ANNUNZIO

FIUME, CHRISTMAS 1920

THE COMMANDER IS no longer himself. Since the assault began, he's been staring at a distant point, as if bewitched by an African mirage. When news of the offensive reaches the command room around 6:00 p.m. on December 24th, it takes Major Vagliasindi, a Legionnaire Inspector, an hour to obtain D'Annunzio's order to fire on the attackers. Meanwhile, the first garrisons of legionnaires to advance near Cantrida have already been surrounded and captured by regular troops of the Italian royal army.

For weeks, D'Annunzio has proclaimed himself ready to die for the cause. Only five thousand legionnaires remain to defend Fiume, and death, not hope, appears to be his last goddess. Now that the death so often invoked has actually arrived, however, brought by strong Alpine and carabinieri units that attack different parts of the front from Val Scurigna to the sea, the Commander seems bewildered rather than unwilling. So is this the end, this column of men with that funny black feather stuck in the red band of their felt hats?

The attack by the regular troops, launched despite the legionnaires—commanded not to engage in combat—having had to retreat to the last line of resistance around the city, was lightning fast. The pathetic signs appealing to brotherhood among Italians—"Brothers, if you want to avoid a grave disaster, do not go beyond this limit"—were ignored. Yet, after finally receiving D'Annunzio's order to open fire, the legionnaires succeed in reinforcing the breaks in the defensive line and even manage to counterattack. The effect of the surprise action is neutralized. Before nightfall, the line of resistance around Fiume is reconstituted.

Having learned that the attack was repelled, General Ferrario, Army Corps commander, orders the massive use of all artillery for the resumption of the action on Christmas Day. However, hoping for repentance from the D'Annunzians, General Caviglia, head of operations, imposes a truce until dawn of the 26th. In the twenty-four-hour hiatus between living and dying, the poet finds inspiration again. He gives his aide a proclamation to be issued on Trieste and Venice: "The crime has been committed. Fiume's soil has been bloodied with fraternal blood . . . In the night we are transporting our wounded and our dead on stretchers. We resist desperately, one against ten, one against twenty. No one will pass if not over our bodies . . . And will Italy, disgraced forever in the eyes of the world, not raise a cry? Will it not lend a hand?"

But Italy is at the table for Christmas dinner and the only cry it raises is that of ritual toasting. Only in Trieste is there an uprising in support of Fiume. It is quickly suppressed, partly due to the public's scant participation.

At 6:50 a.m. on December 26th, the regular troops resume the attack. The action, supported by artillery fire, focuses on the central sector. It fails again. The legionnaires flex but hold the line, then counterattack by capturing a cannon and taking prisoners. By midday it is clear that entering the city will require a massacre.

At noon, General Caviglia orders Admiral Simonetti, commander of the battleship *Andrea Doria* off the port of Fiume, to open fire against the city's military targets.

D'Annunzio, after drafting the proclamation, appears absent again, apathetic and distant, distracted by his mysterious mental vacancy. Alone in the command room, he wanders out onto the balcony from which he has spoken to the world for more than a year and is lost in contemplation of the horizon. The *Andrea Doria*'s gunner, just 800 yards offshore, clearly distinguishes him in the telescope's sighting. Moments after the poet goes back inside and closes the balcony's French door, two 152-gram grenades explode against the building's facade. One of the bombs hits the mark, striking the architrave of the study window. D'Annunzio is jolted in his chair and lurches forward, the blast violently slams his head onto the desk, flakes of masonry debris rain down from the ceiling, slightly wounding the back of his neck. Three officers rush into the study and carry him out bodily. On the floor of the entrance hall a machine-gunner is writhing around with a cavity in his back carved out by a grenade fragment. Rescuers decide it's pointless to waste time with the dying man.

The blast puts an end to any illusions, on both sides of the front. D'Annunzio wakes up. The cannon strike catapults him out of his depressive lethargy and into vengeful rage. In retaliation against despicable Italy, he orders that the battleship *Dante Alighieri*, stuck in the port of Fiume, be torpedoed. The order is not executed.

Meanwhile, word has spread that the poet is supposedly dead. He is alive however and, having reached that point, intends to remain so. His anger again spurs him to take pen in hand. He dashes off the second proclamation since the attack began. "O cowards of Italy, I am still alive and implacable." The Vate rails against a people unable to stand up for justice and even incapable of feeling ashamed. He who offered his life gladly a hundred times, is now no longer willing to do so. He openly declares that until the day before he was prepared to sacrifice himself, but is no longer ready to do so.

One might say that for the first and last time in his long, flamboyant existence, Gabriele D'Annunzio is stirred by a sense of the ridiculous: after all, even with all goodwill, how does a man sacrifice himself for a people that can't tear itself away from the Christmas orgy for a moment, not even while the government is murdering its heroes with ruthless determination?! No heroic death makes sense for the Italians, always quick to pull out a knife to butcher one another in tavern brawls, but incapable of moving a finger for Italy, that geographical and political abstraction you can't even have a chat with, a couple of laughs, a drink, that empty word you can't invite to dinner.

During the next forty-eight hours the bombing of the city, though not heavy, continues. One dead and several wounded are counted among the civilian population. On the morning of December 28, General Ferrario refuses to negotiate terms for the legionnaires' surrender and threatens to intensify the bombing. Citizen representatives implore D'Annunzio to surrender. The Commander gives up his powers: "I am today, as I was on the night in Ronchi, the Leader of the legions. I retain nothing but my courage . . . I cannot impose ruin and absolute death on this heroic city . . . I hand over to the Mayor and the People of Fiume the powers that were conferred on me on September 12th." Throughout the entire week of fighting, the poet-warrior hardly ever left his study, he has not once joined his legionnaires on the firing line. A shadow on the wall.

At 4:30 p.m. on December 31st in Abbazia an agreement is signed for the legionnaires' total demobilization from the city. In the hours that follow, as midnight approaches, Gabriele D'Annunzio sees the future. Soon this year of grief and horror will move on. Soon the new year will begin. It is already ours. It belongs to us.

A death's head crowned with laurel appears. The skull grips a dagger between its bared teeth and from its deep eye sockets stares out at the unknown. Tonight the dead and the living have the same appearance and make the same salute.

To whom the unknown?

To us!

BENITO MUSSOLINI

MILAN, DECEMBER 31, 1920

CHRISTMAS SHOULD BE abolished. All that time off, all those hours spent at the table, all that food, sniveling kids, wives chattering away, bellies bulging . . . That's how a man loses his vigor, he softens like soaked cod. A man ages a year for every ten days he spends with his family during the Christmas holidays. If it were up to him to decide, he would have no qualms about suppressing them.

For Christmas dinner, the Mussolini family sat at the table for over three hours. Ten people gobbled down a tray of baked pasta that would have fed a regiment. Rachele, in addition to the panettone that he had bought at Cova, even decided to try her hand at a cake "artistically" dusted with powdered sugar using a cutout cardboard stencil, as suggested by a women's magazine. Then he also had to listen to little Edda's Christmas nursery rhyme and the prayer of thanks to our Lord Jesus Christ recited by her brother Arnaldo.

But on Saint Silvester's Day, December 31, 1920, Benito Mussolini spends the afternoon in peace, at the home of Bianca Ceccato, his young lover, in the vicinity of the Duomo. After their bastard son was born at the end of October, he got her a small flat on Via Pietro Verri 1, for which he paid six months' rent in advance, equal to 1,200 liras. The girl lives there with her mother and little Glauco. They named him that, after the Homeric hero Glaucus, who together with Sarpedon storms the wall erected by the Achaeans in defense of their ships.

Glauco has his father's dark eyes and hair, even if his name suggests "light-blue" and even though the birth record at the registry lists only the mother, Bianca: "Glauco Ceccato, father unknown." In any case, the girl brims with joy when Benito goes to see them: she takes off his shoes, settles him comfortably in an armchair, doesn't ask him a thing.

This afternoon, moreover, he has shown up with pastries and spumante to toast the new year. She flatters him, coaxing him to play some violin for them. She says nothing can soothe little Glauco like the violin played by his father. And he gladly plays. It is no longer the time to divide himself between home and brothel, between wife and whores. He will be thirty-eight years old in the coming year: he's getting to be too old for that. On the other hand, even a serious family man has the right—and perhaps even the duty—not to renounce life's pleasures.

And then too, he deserves a little relaxation: these last days have been difficult ones, as always. On December 27th, the fascist Executive Commission insisted on issuing a statement vehemently condemning the government's military action against Fiume. The motion was unanimously approved with only his vote against it. But the following day, for the readers of the newspaper, he published a fiery article in defense of D'Annunzio. He called it "The Crime!" complete with exclamation mark. Fiume, in any case, is water under the bridge. The Italians looked the other way so they wouldn't have to see. And D'Annunzio, for that matter, could not continue his performance in front of an empty theater.

The fasci theater, by contrast, is now filling up with surprising speed. For the first time, Umberto Pasella is no longer forced to lie about enrollment numbers. After the bloody events in Bologna and Ferrara, memberships jumped from 1,065 cards sold in the two-month period of October–November to 10,860 sold just in December. By now there are 88 sections throughout Italy for 20,000 members. In Bologna alone, they've already reached 2,500 members, whereas at the beginning of November they were only a few dozen. Furthermore, entire trade union groups are abandoning the socialist Chamber of Labor. In a few weeks, municipal and provincial employees, customs officials, tenured professors, as well as local police, teachers, and charity workers, all tore up their General Confederation of Labor card to get a fascist one. Every time a fascist squad burns a red flag in the piazza, hundreds of petite bourgeoisie get in line at the fascio offices. It's a domino effect, fascism is spreading with the speed of an epidemic. They are all new people, unfamiliar people, people he wouldn't even have had coffee with a year ago, a host of clerks and shopkeepers who, before the war, were indifferent to politics, neither right nor left, nor center either, neither red nor black, people who always and forever move in the gray zone. But now they are no longer watching indifferently. Oh, yes . . . the audience is changing.

Sometimes, as in Ferrara, a bad harvest is enough to spread panic. Such a wonderful thing, panic, the midwife of History! Cesare Rossi is constantly saying that this can actually be a miraculous trade for them: hatred in exchange for fear. The new fascists are all people who until yesterday trembled in fear of the socialist revolution, people who lived in fear, ate fear, drank fear, lay down in bed with fear. Men who whimpered in their sleep like babies and when a wife asked "What's wrong, dear?", sniffled and said "Nothing, it's nothing, go to sleep." Now at the beggars' stock exchange they are trading the heavy metal of fear for the hard currency of mortal hatred.

Petit bourgeois haters: their army will be formed of those people. The middle classes downgraded due to big capital's war speculation, the petty officers who cannot accept losing a command to return to the mediocrity of everyday life, the pen-pushers who more than anything else feel offended by the farmer's daughter's new shoes, the sharecroppers who bought a piece of land after Caporetto and are now ready to kill to keep it, all good people gripped by panic, seized by fear. All people shaken to their innermost core by an irresistible desire to submit to a strong man and, at the same time, to hold sway over the defenseless. They are ready to kiss the shoes of any new master as long as they too are given someone to trample on.

Baby Glauco is sleeping, the sound of the violin has quieted him. Via Pietro Verri is nearly deserted, except for a streetcar running along on its way to Montenapoleone. The lull before the storm: in a few hours fireworks will be set off on the balconies of the tenements, the celebration will get underway, a brand new year will begin.

The Founder looks at his reflection in the panes of the old arched windows and doesn't recognize himself. The spread of the movement that he founded less than two years ago is mirrored back to him cloaked in the solemnity of someone else's thought, someone else's life.

Who are these people really? Where were they holed up until yesterday? He can't have been the one who gave rise to these crowds of onlookers who are suddenly all wielding clubs. Nor was it the war. To be honest, not even war can be the father of all things. The virus that is rampant along Via Emilia, infecting thousands of postal workers ready to set fire to the chambers of labor, must have been pre-incubated in peacetime. It can't be otherwise. They were not reborn in the war, the war only returned them to themselves, made them become what they already were. Fascism, perhaps, is not the host of this virus that is spreading, but its parasitic guest.

Events must just be precipitated. That's all. It may be that the new year will call on him to arbitrate the match. At this rate, it won't be the communists who bring about the revolution, it will be the owners of two rooms and a kitchen in an outlying apartment house.

1921

NICOLA BOMBACCI

LIVORNO, JANUARY 16–17, 1921

GIACOMO MATTEOTTI

FERRARA, JANUARY 18–22,1921

IN LIVORNO—A TOURIST destination popular for its prized bathing establishments and thermal spas—the XVII Congress of the Italian Socialist Party opens at 2:00 p.m. on January 15th, 1921, with a moving recollection by Interim President Giovanni Bacci of the Spartacist insurrection of 1919. Right after him, Secretary Francesco Frola reads, in Italian translation, an address to the delegates from the Executive Committee of the Communist International: a very harsh attack by Moscow on reformist comrades and on those who still persist in not expelling them from the party. It is at that precise moment, right after lunch, that the tragedy of the Italian proletariat begins.

Nicola Bombacci listens to those inaugural, already definitive words from the left's upper-tier boxes in the Teatro Goldoni, where the delegates of the 58,000 electors of the communist fraction are grouped. The seating of the congress attendees tangibly reflects the division between the warring factions: the communists in the tiers on the left, the orchestra seats occupied by "centrist" delegates who are 100,000-strong, and in the tiers on the right the reformists, who account for 15,000 votes. The work has just begun and yet there is a bleak feeling in the theater that the game is already over.

At the previous July's congress the Communist International had made its choice, articulated in 21 peremptory theses like nails driven into the coffin of proletarian unity: in order to remain in the International, the Italians had to change the name of the party and renounce as counterrevolutionaries all the comrades-in-arms who believe in socialism but not in revolution. The problem is that in Italy, after the unsuccessful occupation of the factories, Bombacci and his followers are now the only ones who believe in it. A clear majority of secretary Serrati's "maximalists" no longer even believe in it, though they still preach it in words. They no longer believe in it despite the fact that, out there, Italian socialism is still widespread. In the November elections, the party achieved a resounding success, winning a majority in 2,162 municipalities; it numbers 156 parliamentarians, has 216,000 party members divided among 4,300 sections—tripled in two years—and *Avanti!* exceeds a circulation of 300,000 copies daily. Out there, the Italian proletariat is still ready for a heroic effort, but in here, in the Teatro Goldoni in Livorno, discord is raring to go, in here it's gang warfare.

Christo Kabakciev, delegate of the International, spoke on the morning of the 16th. After adjusting his bow-tie and thick round glasses, the Bulgarian communist thundered his final ultimatum: there is no more time to waste, the situation is revolutionary, anyone who impedes it by siding with the lukewarm reformists is a traitor. Consequently the Comintern of Moscow will expel those who vote for the maximalists' unitary motion. Bombacci and the communists applauded him while sarcastic shouts exploded from all the other sectors of the theater: "Major excommunication! Long live the Pope! Long live the Papachieff! We're not slaves, we don't want papal legates!" In short, an equestrian circus. With three rings.

Throughout the day of the 17th, the controversy continued in a turbulent climate between reformists and revolutionaries, unitarians and secessionists, intransigents on the right and on the left, politicians and unionists; then, towards evening, Vincenzo Vacirca took the floor; a Sicilian trade unionist who at age sixteen organized the

Ragusa peasant league, he has previously escaped attacks on his life several times, both in Italy and in the United States. Vacirca passionately pleads the cause of the southern farm laborer, finding everyone in agreement, then, however, when the assembly is already becoming distracted by the mirage of supper, he attacks Moscow's directives in the name of freedom of thought and unity of action. For the enemy of Sicily's large landed estates, communism and socialism are one and the same. The blame for the reaction that is sweeping the workers' and peasants' movement is, if anything, due to the windbags who hollowly preach violence, thereby evoking bourgeois repression, the blame is that of the "penknife revolutionaries."

A breath of reality unexpectedly blown into the prison of ideological formulas. In the Teatro Goldoni, all of a sudden, there is silence. Vacirca's expression is ambiguous but the reference is clear, direct, the mockery personal: in an interview given the previous October regarding the violence, Nicola Bombacci, the "Christ of the workers," a gentle, sincere man, stated that he couldn't "even use a penknife."

So that his derision of Bombacci will sting even more, Vacirca takes a small knife out of his jacket pocket, and with an air of defiance and ridicule slowly releases the blade folded into the handle. For an instant the divisions are unified: everyone in the room turns to the left's boxes where the "Lenin of Romagna" sits behind his flowing chestnut-colored beard.

Nicola Bombacci, as if stirred by the powerful current of shame that courses through the hall, gets to his feet. He is quivering with rage but doesn't know what to do.

"Take this, show him what you're capable of." Behind Bombacci, the voice of Umberto Terracini, a communist leader favorable to Moscow's theses, hisses in his ear. Lower down, out of sight, his hands hold out a revolver.

Nicola Bombacci has never held a weapon in his life. He grabs it, leans over the balcony and points it at Vacirca, now paralyzed on the speakers' platform, his arm still outstretched in the mocking, accusatory gesture.

"This is not a penknife, now you'll see!"

Bombacci is hysterical over the insult, his strangled cry resounds in the theater. The delegates around the stage hastily duck under their seats. However, the plump, rosy, delicate hand holding the weapon wavers under the weight of the hefty revolver.

The firearm is lowered. Bombacci slumps in the shadows of the tier box. The tragedy ends in farce.

Factional hatreds, slavery to formulas, ideological blindnesses, hammering away on formal questions of pure logic, the eternal circle of personal rivalries, deafness to the world's clamor, to the promises of dawn.

All this grinds away in the wheels of the train that clatters along the Po Valley, on its way towards the sea and its outlet. The destination is not far, the steam whistle swallows up the miles along with centuries of thought, criticism, discussion, sacrifice, striving; along with the millennial struggles of exploited workers of all races, ages, languages, latitudes, religions of all stripes; with the hopes of nameless comrades, of a fraternal and unknown humanity; with the definitive construction of history. His temples throbbing, Nicola Bombacci's feminine hands succumb under the unbearable weight of a revolver pointed at his comrades.

Giacomo Matteotti had to leave the congress in a hurry, he had to leave Livorno when it was still night, on the regional train to Florence. Then he took the Florence-Bologna local and again a regional to Ferrara. He even had to forgo speaking to the congress in order to rush to the capital of the district where he was elected to assume leadership of the Chamber of Labor. Its secretary, following the incidents of December 20, had been arrested along with the mayor. For two days, in Livorno, in the frenzied auditorium of the Teatro Goldoni, Matteotti had listened to dozens of talks by warring men who had come from all over Italy and half of Europe to spend hours debating the question of socialist unity, the dogmas of Marxist orthodoxy, and Moscow's theses. About the fascists and what their squads are doing in Emilia and Romagna, not a single word.

The train enters the station at exactly 12:00 p.m. A small delegation of comrades welcome Deputy Matteotti and bring him to

Corso della Giovecca, to the office of Attorney Baraldi for a preliminary planning meeting.

Not even an hour later, the first disturbances can be heard from the street. Within a few minutes, the news has spread and there are already thousands of demonstrators, their number boosted by students coming from the schools. A horde of club-wielding fascists await the socialist deputy who has arrived from Livorno.

Matteotti refuses to avail himself of a car and goes on foot to the Chamber of Labor, surrounded by a police patrol to protect him from the crowd's violence. The walk progresses in a via crucis on a minor scale. Spitting, lobbing vegetables, punching the back of his neck and his ears. The carabinieri who arrive as reinforcement close ranks, encircle the victim, and disband the demonstrators, who scatter and then regroup. A club blow penetrates the cordon and strikes Matteotti on the temple. He replies several times, shouting to the attackers: "Troublemakers! Villains!"

And this is only the beginning. The next day a socialist baker, Ettore Borghetti, is killed by a pistol shot while leaving a meeting at the Chamber of Labor. In Ferrara, a city governed by an overwhelming majority of socialists, Giacomo Matteotti can't step foot in the street without an escort. On the morning of January 22, he presses the city's prefect, Samuele Pugliese, to remove his police guard. His comrades armed with clubs will be enough to protect him, he insists. In the morning papers, he's just read the news: in Livorno the maximalists refused to expel the reformists and so the communists split from the maximalists.

The day before, while Giacomo Matteotti was being hounded by the fascists in the streets of Ferrara, at the Teatro Goldoni in Livorno communist leader Amadeo Bordiga had gone up to the rostrum of the conference and with his usual cold, contemptuous tone, his customary battle style, ordered the delegates of the communist faction to leave the auditorium.

The communists, according to the news reports, walked out intoning the *Internazionale*, agreeing to meet at a second theater, the Teatro San Marco, a few hundred yards away, where they founded the Italian Communist Party. On the uneven flooring of the orchestra, in front of tattered curtains hung across the stage, under wide rifts in the drenched roof from which torrents of icy rain poured in, there were neither seats nor benches on which the founders could sit. Having certified their party cards with the hammer and sickle, they remained on their feet for hours, standing in the rain.

From Ferrara, Giacomo Matteotti writes to his wife Velia: “It was my duty to firmly assume the post in defense of Ferrara; and it was of immense help against all the bullying.” His wife, close to giving birth to their second child, and reminding him of his responsibilities as a father versus those of a hero, replies: “It is difficult for me to believe that having reached this point you are not permitted any act of weakness, even if it were to cost you your life. Certainly all the rest must be forgotten.”

We feel we are heirs of the teaching that came from men at whose side we took our first steps and who today are no longer with us. We, if we must leave, will carry with us the honor of your past, o comrades!

Amadeo Bordiga, leader of the secessionist communist faction,
at the XVII congress of the Italian Socialist Party,
Livorno, January 19, 1921

We were—it must be said—swept away by events, we were, reluctantly, a part of the general dissolution of Italian society . . . we had one consolation, to which we clung tenaciously, that no one would be spared, that we could claim to have systematically predicted the cataclysm.

Antonio Gramsci,
co-founder of the Italian Communist Party,
with regard to the Livorno secession,
L'Ordine Nuovo, 1924

It was in Livorno that the tragedy of the Italian proletariat began.

Pietro Nenni, PSI (Italian Socialist Party) activist,
earlier founded Bologna's Fasci di Combattimento, in 1919,
Storia di quattro anni, 1926

ITALO BALBO

FERRARA, JANUARY 23, 1921

THE LIQUEUR IS viscous, high proof, its color dark, the color of congealed blood, the turbid red of a clot, of sexual blood or of diseased, nasty blood, the kind you have to worry about if you find it in your stool. The taste, however, is very sweet. It comes from the cherries, the pits and pulp left to steep for months in the brandy. Because of its sugary pleasure, cherry brandy appeals to women: it is the perfect drink when you want to tumble them onto their backs. But it is also enjoyed by the men of the fascist squad "Celibano." The name was given to them by Arturo Breviglieri, a former machine-gunner in the assault units, a member of Ferrara's Fasci di Combattimento since its founding, employed by Bignardi & Co. It seems that cherry brandy was never missing at the tables in Fiume, and that D'Annunzio himself, owing to its blood-red darkness, had come up with the sobriquet Morlachian Blood to evoke the fearsome nomad warriors of the Latin populations who for centuries survived barbarian invasions in the shadowy valleys of the Dinaric Alps. Be that as it may, these particular warriors drinking cherry brandy at the Caffè Mozzi on Corso Roma in Ferrara, in front of the loggia of the Estense Castle, owe their name to the brandy that gives them courage to fight. "Celibano" is, in fact, a dialectical distortion of "cherry brandy," their favorite liqueur.

The punitive expedition leaving Ferrara on January 23rd, headed for the rural outskirts and surrounding towns, is the first to be formulated with military methods. The men who assemble number in the dozens, and they are all well armed and organized to strike numerous targets simultaneously. To destroy the peasant leagues of San Martino, Aguscello, Cona, Fossanova San Biagio, Denore and Fossanova San Marco, they are relying on the resolve of premeditated violence, on the element of surprise and on trucks provided by the Agrarian Association. This is why there must be a sizeable force. The "reds" are likely waiting for them and the suppression must not leave any room for uncertainty in the clash.

Gathering on the square of the bus station outside the city walls are men who are worlds apart: there is the violence personified of the sturdy, bull-neck Ardito in a uniform decorated with ribbons; the Latin professor who is a fervent enthusiast of legionary aesthetics; and a fragile son of privilege like Barbato Gattelli, scion of a family of landowners and veteran of the Great War, who started an industrial concern in the automotive sector. The Ferrara squadristi ready to hammer the countryside on January 23rd, 1921, are numerous. Numerous, but not all of them are there.

Olao Gaggioli is not there. On December 17th he resigned as secretary of the city's fascio in protest against Mussolini's break with D'Annunzio and the interference of the agrarians. His defection is difficult to swallow because Gaggioli founded the fascio of Ferrara, because before that he was in Piazza San Sepolcro on March 23rd, 1919, because he was an Arditi lieutenant decorated with four medals of valor, because he'd been a legionnaire at Fiume, because he had led the Ferrara squad during the assault on Palazzo d'Accursio, because he also clashed with the socialists in the Castello Estense massacre, and because he is a man of gigantic proportions and immense strength. At the end of December his brother Luigi, like him opposed to playing the bosses' game, even wrote a letter to the Central Committee of Milan in which he openly denounced the fact that the fascio of Ferrara was financed by the Agrarian Association and that it was becoming the "guardian of the grande bourgeoisie."

To understand what was happening, and to maintain control over the province, Mussolini sends an inspector. His name is Marinoni and he is to concede that the many new sections that arose in the province within a month after the slaughter at Castello Estense are "devoid of any political and ideological" content and have the sole purpose of opposing the socialists. Of course the agrarians are elated and provide material support. The leading figures sign up as supporting members and register their children as squad members. Since December 20, they have already poured 20,000 liras into the fasci coffers. Everyone is rushing in: big and small landowners, sharecroppers, shopkeepers, tenants.

From Milan, in the columns of the newspaper, to prevent rural fascism from appearing to be a vassal to the interests of the large landowners, Mussolini launched the slogan "the land to those who work it," with a plan to give uncultivated land, subdivided into small plots, to settlers who personally farm it. A "land office" run by the fascists was to administer the transactions. The local fascio's new organ, *Il Balilla*, which publishes its first issue on January 23rd, also disassociates itself from the agrarians, making clear that Ferrarese fascism was born "in the piazza" and not "in the salons of the rich." Appointed as its editor at Milan's bidding, is Italo Balbo, the young Mazzinian ex-lieutenant of the Alpine troops, attached to the assault units; a fervent patriot and avid anti-Bolshevist, he too is a war hero and he too is demobilized, in search of a destiny and a job.

Murky, intriguing stories are already circulating about this Italo Balbo, who popped up out of nowhere. It is said that in Trentino he seduced the daughter of a Count Florio, that in Florence he earned a degree in social sciences by physically threatening his professor, that he came to fascism by chance and for personal gain. It seems that during the funeral of the December 20 martyrs he was playing poker in the back of a cafe; watching from the doorway and seeing the squads march by in formation, he is said to have asked: "Who pays those guys?" It is rumored that when he was invited to join the fascio, his first response was: "*Sass ciapa a far el fascista?*"—"Do you get paid to be a fascist?" It is alleged that he accepted the invitation on three conditions: a monthly salary of 1,500 liras, appointment as political secretary, and the guarantee of a job as inspector of the Banca Mutua, the mutual bank owned by Vico Mantovani, president of the Agrarian Association.

But none of this matters now because the trucks have started up. Now words turn to weapons, nothing else matters.

Balbo sits next to Breviglieri and the other men of the "Celibano" squad in a war surplus caisson headed for Denore, a village on the right bank of the Po di Volano. Now all the squadristi, whatever their motivations, their experiences, their travails, whatever the condition of their birth and the trade by which they earned a living until yesterday, are just a pack of armed men squatting in a caisson where you can't either sit or lie down, under a milky sky that hangs oppressively over an archaic countryside. Before them, dumb gray oxen slowly plow the fields in a crystalline silence, their impassive gaze and huge hearts completely unaware of the story of those men who have come to shatter that stillness. Above them, herons in colonies of ten, who nest not far from there among the shrubby willows of the lake basins near the estuary, follow the plodding labor in the fields. They bring a brackish echo of sodden meadows and swashes, dunes and sandbanks formed by the progressive deposit of sediments and the receding sea. Higher up, a hawk wheels slowly, tracing smooth circles against the pale flat sky.

Some of the men interpret it as an auspicious sign. A bottle of second-rate sparkling wine is passed around. Why this killing, this dying? Fear grips the fascio: they must surely have been seen setting out, someone may have spread the word. Everyone knows that three days ago, in Fossanova, the socialists shot and wounded a tenant farmer who was leaving the rectory where a political meeting had been held. Today it might be one of them, one of the brothers in arms crouched on their heels in that caisson like a caravan of gypsies. The quiet of the fields weaves a web of constant menace around them. They expect an ambush behind every hedgerow, at every low-lying tract between the bank and the flood plain. The cold metal of the gun, secretly fingered in their pockets, consoles them.

At the Stellata crossroads the trucks separate. Two squads head towards Cona and Fossanova, the others towards Aguscello and Denore. At the entrance to Aguscello, a carful of local agrarians welcomes the fascists and escorts them through the town's few streets. Resistance from the socialists is half-hearted. Someone fires at them with a quail hunting rifle. The pellets barely pierce the thick jackets. The peasant league's quarters are easily invaded, the windows shattered, the furniture dragged out and smashed in the piazza. The carabinieri arrest the socialists who defended themselves with a shotgun.

The aggressors, exalted, climb back into the trucks. Now they're singing, the wine flows in rivers down the liberated gullet. When they reach Denore, agrarian Giuseppe Gozzi leads them to the peasant league's headquarters. Here, however, the socialists are numerous, barricaded, ready to defend themselves.

Italo Balbo jumps off the truck, brandishing a mace used by the Hungarians on Mount San Michele in the Isonzo Karst to bash their wounded enemies' skulls. Here, though, the violence is heated, personal, direct, immediate, without the interminable waiting of duty in the trenches, here men are not wiped out like tens of thousands of germs by the thermal apocalypse of heavy artillery. Here there are only self-assured bodies, irrigated with hot blood and strong wine, who leap into the fray as though into the fracas of an orgy. The clash is furious, the peasants don't give up, a fascist pulls out his revolver and seriously wounds two of them. Balbo, Breviglieri and Chiozzi also report slight casualties.

On the way back the fascio of armed men also wreaks havoc on the headquarters of the defenseless league of San Biagio. Now hatred has free rein. Now the men in the caissons lurching at every pothole are no longer Arditi, Latin professors and landowners' sons, now the blood that was spilled has coalesced them, no one is alone anymore, divisions or factions no longer exist, social equality is the gift resulting from the elemental experience of killing together.

Now, in the trucks, they are stirred by the memory of a venture already ancient, though completed just half an hour earlier; they are joking, singing at the top of their lungs: the fascio of men exposed to the risk of lethal aggression has every right to express its feelings, its appetites. Now the squadristi of the "Celibano" and Balbo's men have all earned the same round of Morlachian Blood that awaits at the Caffè Mozzi, the same hearty meal of spicy hot *salama da sugo*, and the well-deserved lecherous spree at Rina's brothel on Vicolo Arnaldo da Gaggiano.

Before that, however, the oxen in the fields along the right bank of the Po di Volano respond to the exploits of those men with their dumb, uncompromising bovine gaze, the same with which they had discounted them a few hours earlier.

The immediate revocation of licenses to carry arms in your provinces is ordered. Please see to it immediately . . . Pursuant to the law of December 26, 1920, persons found in possession of arms will be arrested and remanded in custody to the Judicial Authority.

Circular issued by Prime Minister Giovanni Giolitti to the prefects of the provinces of Bologna, Modena and Ferrara, January 25, 1921

Doing my best . . . but won't deny difficulties over agrarian class resentment against order to revoke arms which they say leaves those residing in rural lands far from towns and carabinieri stations with no defense.

Telegram from the Prefect of Ferrara, Samuele Pugliese to the Ministry of the Interior, February 5, 1921

Although the central committee, promoter and motivator of the movement, was based in Milan, the real cradle of fascism was Emilia, which had been the scene of the most bitter economic clashes. Bologna, Ferrara, Modena and Reggio were the provinces most troubled by fascist disturbances: then the same disturbances became widespread in several neighboring provinces in Piedmont, Lombardy, Veneto . . . They are raids carried out by armed fascists in trucks, aimed at punishing (via incursions, the destruction of associations, leagues and cooperatives, seizures of individuals, intimidation and violence, especially against opposition leaders) real or alleged offensive and unjust acts committed by socialist, communist or populist adversaries; and they are the latter's vendettas against the former: they are clashes that almost always end in numerous injuries and deaths.

From the report of the Inspector General of Public Security
Giacomo Vigliani, June 1921

MARGHERITA SARFATTI

MILAN, JANUARY 30, 1921

THE HALL OF the Institute for the Blind on Via Vivaio is packed with men and women who have come to commemorate a young man. Today they are mourning and honoring Roberto Sarfatti, who was born in Venice on May 10th, 1900, and died on the Col d'Echele on January 28th, 1918, at age seventeen, with a bullet hole in his forehead.

In the first rows, dozens of the institute's guests sit beside the mother, the father and the hero's sister. Only the newly blind—most of them from the war—seek dialogue in the darkness, their heads swaying in rhythm to the speakers' voices. The others, those who have never known the world's light, sit motionless, as if besides being blind, they were also deaf to the anguish of the living for the dead. Behind them, hundreds of young militants from the Milan Fasci di Combattimento, which organized the commemoration, await Benito Mussolini's speech. After the events of Palazzo d'Accursio and after the start of the raids that have been pounding the Po Valley countryside, memberships have risen like a flood, in Milan as well.

The speakers follow one another on the stage of the hall of honor. Many have already spoken—Buzzi, Panzini, Siciliani—the poet Ada Negri spoke. A lapidary, perfect farewell composed by Gabriele D'Annunzio before the *Natale di sangue* was even read, yet everyone is waiting for Mussolini. He parries:

"Today I will not be up to my task. My oratory is burdened by twenty years of petty battles. The celebration of heroes should be reserved for poets, for the select spirits who live above the daily, furious fray in which we so-called 'political' men are immersed up to our necks."

After this preamble, Mussolini recalls the fifteen-year-old who, in 1915, the same age as the century, already burned with the desire to fight. He recalls the sixteen-year-old who, under a false name, spent a month in the barracks in Bologna thanks to a spurious document procured for him by Filippo Corridoni. At the mention of Corridoni, standard-bearer and martyr of interventionism, the crowd jumps to its feet and clamorously applauds. The speaker continues, reading passages from the letters of the seventeen-year-old who, having finally enlisted after the defeat at Caporetto, was eager to leave for the front: "Whoever is able to defend Italy must do so at once, without waiting. This is more than a battle, it is a confrontation between two races: barbaric Teutons and Cimbrians against the Latin peoples. It is incumbent upon Rome to stand up to the confrontation and it will stand up to it." The crowd again applauds the hero.

His mother, on the other hand, in the front row, remembers a very gentle boy who, while waiting to go to war, kept twisting his hands nervously, cracking the knuckles of his knotted fingers in a chilling way. It had been a starry night, and both of them, mother and son, had been so despairing! With eyes full of tears they'd read the tragic news bulletins about the enemy's implacable, unstoppable advance. Women wept as trains of endless refugees from the Veneto passed. Both mother and son could feel their hearts being trampled by the tread of those boots, Turks, Germans and Bulgarians invading their country. But the mark left was not the same: "I'm not doing it for Italy, I'm doing it for myself, for my duty, for my conscience," the son had protested.

Now Mussolini also indulges in a personal memory. He recalls January 1918, when the boy, already promoted to corporal for his distinguished service, had returned home on special leave and had gone to see him at the newspaper office. He had asked about the troops' morale, and the boy had reassured him that morale was high, very high. "We want to win, we must win and we will win," were his parting words.

The audience applauds again, but the mother remembers the two men studying one another as if to drink in the other's soul, the proud lie of the son and the uncaring satisfaction of the other. She remembers a grim, frantic, incoherent boy, a boy she no longer recognized and the words that she had in vain said to him: "It is no longer a romantic time to win or die: you have to live; it is essential."

The following Monday, at ten in the morning, on the Asiago plateau, Roberto had led his Alpine troops to the assault on the Col d'Echele. He'd seized an enemy machine gun and then, as though possessed, had rushed to attack the last stronghold on the summit. A bullet had exploded in his face.

"Among the first to reach the trench, he threw himself into the enemy ditch . . . exceptional demonstration of valor and sublime military virtues . . . He again launched into the attack of a tunnel . . ." Benito Mussolini reads the documentation for the proposed gold medal. Those blinded in war crane their necks in search of light, those blind from birth are resigned, no one speaks in that poignant hush. Benito Mussolini is exalting Roberto Sarfatti as fascism's first martyr.

By now three years have passed. Roberto is dead. And sleeps, alone, in a small lonely cemetery, far away. And the mother has only one way to keep vigil over her son's grave: those violent army veterans in their gray-green uniforms, those men in black shirts who bring death to farmers' houses are now her family. Margherita Sarfatti was a socialist, devoted to the cause of those peasants, long opposed to intervention in the war, but then life is always a personal matter and, if it isn't that, it's nothing.

Since the day of the funeral, Benito Mussolini has bowed to her maternal grief and asked if he could share some of her pain. Only he—not Cesare, her husband, who since that day has been lost in a fog of remorse; not her old socialist comrades who continue to scorn the combatants—only he has shown that he is able to understand it. Giving herself to Mussolini, she keeps the lamp lit on

Roberto's grave. Only fascism can give meaning to your child's death.

And so the mother lingers until late in the evening in the cramped office of that newspaper, deserting the salons of the building on Corso Venezia, to stay a little longer with her son, and afterwards the woman will give herself, naked, shamelessly, to the erotic fury of that man, in the squalid little rooms of sad hotels, so as not to abandon her Roberto. The wife will betray her husband—her husband and everything else—so that the mother can remain faithful to her son.

My dear Roberto, I want to write the new date of the new year, for the first time, on the letter that will bring you the expression of my love and ardent affection. Happy New Year! My blessed big little son, you are such a great part of my happiness, your well-being, your health, your contentment, all these are essential integral elements, necessary for my well-being and I can only say a prayer from deep in my heart, every hour and every moment: May God bless you! Today I received three of your postcards and one yesterday, thank you my dearest darling for your dear words and for the effort that you are making to send us word of you regularly and diligently.

Margherita Sarfatti, letter to her son Roberto,
January 1, 1918

GIACOMO MATTEOTTI

ROME, JANUARY 31, 1921
PARLIAMENT OF THE KINGDOM OF ITALY

THE CHAMBER OF Montecitorio is semi-deserted. Most of the deputies have not yet returned from their lunch break. They are probably lingering in the *buvette* or sprawled in an armchair in their office, dozing.

When the parliamentary session of January 31, 1921, takes up the motions on internal politics following the report on the scandal of supply depots in Libya, there are no more than 70 deputies present in the room and almost all are sitting in the benches of the left. Of those 56 members the first to speak is Giacomo Matteotti. As soon as the president of the assembly, De Nicola—a Neapolitan attorney from the liberal sector elected on the Democratic Party list—gives him the floor, the young Venetian deputy heatedly lashes into the empty hall. The elderly men sagged over the government benches are immediately roused from their postprandial slump. An unprecedented note rings out under Aristide Sartorio's frieze: for the first time the denunciation of fascist violence is openly on the Italian parliament's agenda.

"We are a party that does not aspire to a simple succession of ministries, which instead wants to achieve a grandiose social transformation; and therefore necessarily anticipates violence. We know that, by affecting an infinite number of interests, we will provoke more or less violent reactions, and we have no regrets. Therefore we do not complain about fascist violence."

Matteotti allows a deliberately studied rhetorical pause, lets the word "violence," associated with fascism, hover in mid-air under the glass dome that encloses the immense space of the Montecitorio hemicycle. Then he tightens his lips and, catching his breath, spits his challenge right at the government benches:

"We will not whine about the crimes nor will we relate them. We have no need to beg the government for any service, we ask for nothing, neither of the government nor of anyone."

Now everyone's attention is glued to the thin upper lip of that young son of landowners devoted to the cause of indigents. After pride, Fratta Polesine's deputy moves on to intellectual honesty: "We are a party of the masses and we do not deny any error by the masses. We are indeed ready to acknowledge that sometimes the theorization of revolutionary violence, which aims to suppress the bourgeois state, may have led some of our militants into the error of episodic acts of violence."

"What gall!" Deputy D'Ayala's shout, coming from the benches of the liberals, is quickly stifled by the socialists' protests. Matteotti resumes.

"But today in Italy there is an organization of armed gangs, whose members, leaders, and headquarters are publicly recognized and known, who openly declare that their aim is to carry out acts of violence, retaliation, threats, and torching, and who execute those acts as soon as workers commit an act—or are claimed to have done so—against the bosses or the bourgeois class. It is a perfect organization of private justice. This is incontrovertible."

As Giacomo Matteotti reels off his indictment of the Italian agrarian bourgeoisie, of which he is a son, rather than of the fascists, from whom he is forced to go around escorted, the chamber slowly begins to fill up with men roused from their slow reptilian digestion by that spectacular invective. Matteotti lets fly at them. He points a finger at the vile, affluent bourgeoisie who finance the squads' violence rather than against the violence itself.

"Whereas the hypocrisy of not openly supporting fascism persists in the great majority of the country's capitalist society, we recognize its courage to expose itself."

"Long live the faaasciii!!!"

The shrill cry, practically strangled by a hysterical falsetto, is hurled at the socialist speaker from the benches of the right. The individual who shouted is Valentino Coda, a war veteran, elected among the monarchist nationalists.

Matteotti reflects it towards the prime minister. He shouts in turn that the agrarians are willing to let the country perish in order to save their pocketbooks, then he points a trembling finger of disdain right at patriarch Giolitti:

"Which of you takes responsibility for fascism?!" The socialists applaud, greeting their champion with jubilation. He, however, has not finished.

"The government claims to be outside and above the classes, guardian of public order . . . We instead contend that Honorable Giolitti's government is complicit in all these violent events!"

"Even you don't believe that!"

Giolitti is on his feet, still physically threatening at his six-foot-plus height despite his eighty years of age and fifty years of parliamentary compromises.

"No, Honorable Giolitti, at this moment parliamentary skill is perfectly useless."

Matteotti continues, in no way intimidated by the old leader who could be his great-grandfather:

"This game of yours, at which you are very accomplished, is worth nothing now. The question is much simpler. We ask nothing of you. First of all, we do not trust a servant like you who would always be untrustworthy. We ask for nothing. The rumor that we asked Honorable Giolitti for protection is a journalistic falsehood. We are not begging you for anything!"

Giolitti sits back down. Matteotti has disavowed him. He disclaimed his institutional role as guarantor of rights and freedom, he severed the tie that could still have bound socialism to the state. We ask for nothing, we beg for nothing. The nothing repeated by the socialist deputy in his speech echoes through the chamber like the final word.

The young socialist champion's talk continues with its Marxist analysis: this is the moment—Matteotti proclaims—when the bourgeois class, which possesses wealth, an army, courts, and police, steps outside the law and arms itself against the proletariat to preserve its own privilege. A democratic state resting on the principle of "the law is equal for everybody" is a joke. "The seeds of violence will bear fruit; yes, they will yield . . . they will yield generously . . ."

By the time Giacomo Matteotti returns to his seat, the air in the chamber has become unbreathable. The word "violence," like a gas leak, again pervades it. The door is closed.

After him, it is deputy Sarrocchi's turn, and the motion of the liberals is presented. Meanwhile the room has filled up again. At least 250 deputies are now seated there, fully rested thanks to their afternoon doze; they listen to Sarrocchi heap blame on the socialists for the violent situation that is shaking the Po Valley. The liberal deputy rattles off the usual litany of boycotts, extortions, protection money, unrestrained acts, occupation of factories.

"Some of those boycotted," he says in a paroxysm of patheticism, "without a roof anymore, without the possibility of earning a living, after going around from town to town, even had to emigrate."

"That was the wandering Jew!" The socialists laugh loudly at Matteotti's gibe. The others protest. Sarrocchi continues.

"Do you want to know the total amount of damage caused by the red leagues over these past years? Eleven million!"

"That's still not much!" shouts Deputy Belloni, a communist. Shouting, protests.

"Irresponsible idiot!" someone yells.

Though the session goes on for quite a while longer, it was essentially over some time ago.

One can therefore, with a serene conscience, describe the speech by Deputy Matteotti as partisan and contrived. The socialist speaker did not present us with a complete picture of the situation in Emilia; he has not bothered to look for its remote, deeply rooted causes . . . The Socialist Party and the organizations under it now fear that, due to the unexpected fascist reaction, they will suddenly lose the fruits that the tenacious work of twenty years promised would be abundant in the political and economic arenas. Faced with the action of its adversaries, socialism is forced to take a defensive stance in parliament and in the country, and accordingly tries to make us forget its past acts of violence . . . We must now wait for Deputy Giolitti to disclose in broad terms the plan by which he intends to inspire his political action, which meanwhile may benefit from an element that was lacking to his predecessors: the spontaneous reaction of public opinion against the socialists' excessive power.

Unsigned editorial,
Corriere della Sera, February 1, 1921

BENITO MUSSOLINI

MILAN, END OF FEBRUARY 1921

VIOLENCE, ALWAYS VIOLENCE, purely violence, all they talk about is violence . . . As if there was anything to say about violence! Do they think they can reduce fascism, politics and the century to a bloodstain on the pavement?

They are accused of bringing violence into the political struggle. He said it loud and clear: the fascists are violent whenever they need to be. Period. There's nothing more to add. They smash, destroy, and set fires whenever they are forced to do so. That's it. It seems like a satisfactory formula to him.

Even the conclusion of the parliamentary debate on the Bologna massacre seems to have proved him right. Despite the denunciation of that Matteotti, who hopelessly looked to fascism as an excuse for the socialists' revolutionary ineffectiveness, the Montecitorio chamber on February 3rd reconfirmed its complete trust in Giolitti. Which means that the notion of opposing violence with violence has won acceptance, that the moderates view the fascists as a pathogen that is virulent but essential to the higher cause of survival of the social organism. A type of vaccine against socialism injected under the skin.

So a young fascist, Mario Ruini, is killed on the night of January 22 in Modena, ambushed by three anarchists? And the following day, during his funeral, in the clashes between blackshirts, communists and royal guards, two more fascists are killed and Leandro Arpinati is wounded in the leg? Well then, the same evening, the

Chamber of Labor on Via del Carmine is torched in retaliation, and then, the day after that, Arpinati himself also sets fire to the Chamber of Labor in Bologna, the headquarters of the Socialist Union and the newspaper *La squilla*. That's how violence, politics' idiot brother, works. It's no use embroidering elaborate theories on it. If you do that you lose sight of the general picture, and the general picture is complex.

After the secession, the socialist crisis is irreparable. The fifteen thousand delegates of Livorno no longer represent anyone but need to move quickly to reap the benefits. As soon as the moderate democrats realize it, they will breathe a sigh of relief and easily think that they no longer need the fascists. It is quite probable that Giolitti, the old rainmaker, will take advantage of the socialists' weakness to dissolve the chambers, call new elections and deepen the rift in the red wall by bringing Filippo Turati and his moderate reformists into the government. It's essential to move quickly, climb on board, travel light and jettison the ballast.

The violence must go on just long enough to make those old bourgeois fools understand that they can't do without the violent bullies. But those unruly maniacs who kill for sport in the countryside must also be kept in check. On this point Cesarino Rossi is right: they need to make a clean sweep, do some drastic weeding, too many people have shown up in the fascist ranks with the flood of success. Get rid of them! With no hesitation, ditch the ballast. Then they also have to worry about maintaining the continuing ties with the left. Those votes will also be needed in the upcoming elections. That's why a slogan is already waiting: "Land to those who work it, land to those who make it produce." Eliminating the centuries-old hunger of the rural masses should do it. And then there's the Commander. D'Annunzio has now retired to Cargnacco, on Lake Garda, in a lavish villa, embalmed in comforts and luxuries, where he swears he wishes to devote himself to the sole occupation he has ever known: himself. His friends describe him as weary, suddenly aged, disillusioned, half-blind, and beaten, nevertheless it's essential to come to some agreement with him to prevent him from becoming an obstruction. His princely desire for isolation must be accommodated, he must be helped to become the interior decorator he has always been, to bury himself alive in his pyramid on the lake's shore, along with his faithful, his goldsmiths, his laurels, his cannons, his horses, his old and new mistresses, his obsessions, and his beloved dogs. Just a few months of lacustrine agony will be enough and the Commander will become the dog of his nothingness.

It is a matter of finding Italy a place in the world, finding Italians a place in history, not about finding a human being a place in the cosmos. Foreign policy cannot depend on the deliriums of a D'Annunzio. At the meeting in Trieste on February 7th, held at the Politeama Rossetti, Mussolini made it clear to those who accused him of abandoning Fiume: violence is brief but political art is long, the scenario vast, complicated, diverse, the times uncertain. It takes a broad assessment of the world situation, not just improvised marches on Ronchi, not just impromptu bursts of violence. It's always the same old question. With history it's like the theater: there are cantankerous audiences who, having paid for a ticket, demand a grand finale at all costs. But revolution is not a rabbit that you pull out of a hat!

At the international level the overall situation is even more complex. Europe is finding it hard to regain its equilibrium, there are sharp differences between the United States and Japan, the axis of civilization is shifting from London to New York and from the Atlantic to the Pacific. The great enigma remains Russia. In a Europe that is struggling to recover its balance, there is no doubt that tomorrow's history will be mainly written in the Russian and Germanic arenas. The dilemma that awaits Italy is this: either share with Germany or Russia the responsibility of directing the life of the old continent or become a big international "bordello." A nation of waiters and whores where wealthy Slavs, Germanics, Orientals and Americans come on vacation to indulge their vices.

He, Founder of the Fasci di Combattimento, tries to fly above it all, but now the petty tabloid press latches onto him again and drags him down: the secretary announces that Mr. Cucciati is waiting in the newsroom to see the editor. What a pain: the petitioner's daughter married a hothead, a certain Bruno Curti, an inconsequential leader of the Milanese squads, heir to a bronze industrialist, who shot someone somewhere in a scuffle and is now rotting in jail. In short, the usual rigmarole about violence again. But this time too he won't be able to stay out of it: Giacomo Cucciati is an old comrade from the socialist days, one of those scions of wealthy landowners who became obsessed with the cause of beggars, just like Giacomo Matteotti. Let him come in.

Mussolini decides to receive the postulant sitting down. It's a proven technique to discourage pains in the ass like that. Him seated, them standing up, the meeting ends quickly.

Something unexpected happens, however: along with Giacomo Cucciati, a waft of perfume, chiffon and lace drifts into the editor's office. Cucciati has brought his daughter with him, the little bride of the violent idiot. Mussolini stands up.

The exchange of pleasantries between the old comrades is brief. The editor's attention is plainly magnetized by the young woman. The girl has big dark eyes, high cheekbones, a strong chin, a cascade of raven black hair falling over her shoulders, broad hips, and full breasts. She is a woman made to arouse men and this man is aroused. The Founder stares at her, wide-eyed, as if posing for a photograph to be handed down to posterity. The father lets go of her arm, takes a step aside, doesn't interfere.

It is the father-in-law who relates the sad case of his son-in-law. Mussolini, chin up, appears to be interested.

Bruno Curti is rotting in jail on a murder charge.

Where?

Here in Milan, in San Vittore.

OK.

He was a member of a Fasci di Combattimento.

One of ours.

His squad taught a lesson to a professor, a certain Gadda. A Bolshevik.

Well-deserved.

Gadda later died as a result of his injuries.

It's the war . . .

He was shot. The investigators are uncompromising.

We can try it but it's not easy. They're on our backs about this violence business . . .

Giacomo Cucciati does not reply to Mussolini's last, worried sigh and observation. The father now remains silent and turns to his daughter. She too takes a deep breath, lowers her eyes shyly and says only one thing.

We got married so young. I'm only twenty-two . . .

Angela Cucciati Curti, sitting quietly beside her father, wipes away a tear with a tiny organza hanky and looks up modestly. Benito Mussolini stares at her as if it were a trickle of sperm running out of the corner of her mouth.

Giacomo Cucciati is a man of the world and can see that his plan has worked. He therefore excuses himself with a trivial excuse.

As soon as Cucciati has left the room, the editor of *Il Popolo d'Italia*, the Founder of the Fasci di Combattimento, the Duce of the Arditi squads, the fearsome revolutionary, immediately violates the intimacy barrier: he approaches the girl, and whispers in her ear.

We are accused of bringing violence to political life. We are violent whenever it is necessary to be so . . . Ours must be mass violence, always inspired by criteria and ideal principles . . . When we come across clerics and red priests, we, who are opposed to all churches, while respecting decorously professed religions, will burst into this vile flock of sheep and make a clean sweep of them.

Benito Mussolini, "To the fascists of Lombardy,"
Il Popolo d'Italia, February 22, 1921

The daily papers are full of episodes of violence in the struggle between fascists and socialists . . . Now, in view of the continuation of the struggle, we must set the "agenda" for the exercise of our violence, so that it may remain typically fascist . . . First of all we must declare again that for the fascists violence is not a whim or an intentional objective. It is not art for art's sake. It is a surgical necessity. A painful necessity. Secondly, fascist violence cannot be a violence aimed at "provocation" . . . Finally, fascist violence must be chivalrous. Absolutely . . . Lines are not crossed with impunity. Violence, for us, is an exception, not a method, or a system. Violence, for us, does not have the quality of personal revenge, but the quality of national defense.

Benito Mussolini, "Concerning Violence,"
Il Popolo d'Italia, February 25, 1921

POLESINE COUNTRYSIDE
END OF FEBRUARY, 1921, NIGHT

THE FARMHOUSE SLEEPS. It sleeps in the silence and darkness that mark the chill winters of the Po Valley. It is the middle of the night, the light of day as yet remote, equidistant. It is the meridian hour of oblivion, the hour that does not flow, the hour of the wolf. Every creature is asleep, in the house and outside, for dozens of miles in all directions. Babies and old people are sleeping, women and men are sleeping, fathers, mothers, children are sleeping, animals in the stable, dogs in their kennels and hundreds of wild species are sleeping, including mammals, reptiles, amphibians and fish that winter in the marshlands of the delta.

The truck took off from Ferrara. The men sitting in the open caisson—about half a dozen of them—had had a big meal in a trattoria, laughed, gambled, then waited for it to be time, guzzling liquor in the usual tavern. The truck, a war surplus remainder, proceeds slowly on full tires, lost in foggy meanders through the drainage canals of amphibious lands, on low-lying expanses largely below sea level. Its full tires worsen the subsidence, the slow sinking of this continental strip, bearing down on detrital layers thousands of yards thick within the soil's crust.

When it comes within sight of the farmhouse, the truck slows down even further, moving nearly at a crawl. Someone suggests turning off the headlights but there is no moon, the sky is dark and they would lose their way. Attracted by the glow of the headlights, all the lowly creatures that live close to the ground come creeping out of their burrows. Mice, moles, brown lizards and green lizards, geckos, snakes, worms, grubs, toads and centipedes edge close to the approaching car on their bellies. Among the first to be drawn to the artificial day of the headlights and collide with them are moths of all shapes and sizes.

The small globular body of a spadefoot toad meets the wheel. It tries in vain to tunnel into the soil with its spurs. The insignificant pliant mass receives the crushing weight on its brownish olive-mottled back, the gelatinous sphere is flattened to the extreme, then releases the sound of a rush of air combined with a gush of fluids. The tire regains full contact with the ground as the truck roars into the front yard of the farmhouse.

The squadristi surround the house and call out the name of their prey. The name echoes for thousands of yards in the silence of the paralyzed countryside. They are all armed with muskets from the Great War, both Italian and Austrian. All except a tall man wearing a black leather raincoat, his face hidden by a pair of big motorcycle goggles. He wields a large wooden truncheon with an iron-reinforced head. It's he who shouts into the night.

The league leader, who heard the truck coming and spotted the glow of the headlights in the dark, flees into the fields from a back door. He is already gone, already safe, when the man in the black trench coat breaks down the front door of the house with his truncheon. The devastation is methodical, simple, unopposed. Caught up in their simplistic euphoria, the wreckers even fire a few revolver shots at the cupboard where the day-old bread is kept. The man running away, hearing the terrified screams of his wife and daughters in the distance, comes back. He spreads his arms towards the squadristi in the farmyard:

"You want me? Here I am."

They put him up against the wall. They make his elderly parents, his wife and children come down to witness the execution of their son, husband and father, and line up in front of the victim in a caricature of a firing squad. The two little girls—maybe seven and nine years old—don't scream, don't cry, rendered speechless by their father's imminent death and by the apocalypse of their world.

The squadristi level their weapons. At the command of the man with the motorcycle goggles they open fire. But the league leader is still standing: they had staged a fake execution.

At that moment the wife bursts into relieved sobs and dissolves into uncontrollable weeping. Her husband steps away from the wall and makes a cautious move towards her. Only the older child understands. She holds out a small hand, palm open, facing up and out, and cries out, a scream that will be with her for her entire life:

"No, Daddy, run, run!"

The man with the goggles twirls the truncheon over his head and brings it down on the league leader's skull. Knocked to the ground, his face covered in blood, the father drags himself towards his daughters, stammers incoherent words, and crawls on his belly between the legs of the squadristi who beat him with their clubs.

It appears to be over. The head of the murderous gang, however, motions to his men to stop the massacre. Then he walks slowly to the man on the ground, steps over him with his right leg, and straddles him; he leans over his knees in an odd position, an awkward, inelegant pose, crouched on his heels, almost as if driven by a sudden urge to defecate. Instead he draws a revolver from his trench coat pocket and shoots the dying man in the back. The body jerks. Now it's over.

On the way back, piled into the truck bed, the murderers sing. Their song is lost to the east in the early light rising over the world from the delta floodplains, as it did on the first day of creation. After this night, life will never be the same in the Polesine countryside. Terror spreads everywhere, subtly, steadily, in a veil of frost.

We didn't give a damn about a day in jail / we didn't give a damn about base death / to prepare these strong men / who now don't give a damn about dying. / The world knows that the black shirt / is worn to kill and to die . . .

Song of the Ferrara squadristi

AMERIGO DÙMINI

FLORENCE, FEBRUARY 27–MARCH 1, 1921

THE WORD IS passed from mouth to mouth, from corner to corner: the assembly is at 3:00 p.m. at the headquarters on Via Ottaviani. The "reds" set off a bomb at the corner of Palazzo Antinori. All fascists in arms.

The detonation was heard throughout the city center as loudly as the noon cannon. But it wasn't the cannon. It was the usual godless "Bolsheviks," without country or family, the usual backstabbers, the bullies who tortured fallen enemies, the perennial cowards. Some said they saw a fluttering black republican tie, others spoke of red carnations, still others claim it must have been the anarchists, but it makes no difference. The Liberal Party, supported by nationalists and fascists, was inaugurating the pennant of a student group, people were streaming from the Masses at San Marco and at the Duomo, heading towards the pastry shops, the leader of the patriotic procession had just reached San Gaetano when the bomb exploded between his legs. Those are the facts.

No one sees the bomb thrower, the terrorist. The carabinieri begin shooting wildly, randomly; the ground—littered with shells—looks like a battlefield. The Misericordia carry off on a stretcher a soldier with cranial matter flowing out of his skull and a young comrade torn apart. They both die before reaching the hospital. The wounded, some gravely, are numbered by the dozens. The death count can only rise.

The city is in the grip of convulsion and terror. People along the ambulance route are shouted at to take off their hats in respect for the victims. At the Loggia del Bigallo, a guy with a red carnation in his buttonhole angrily waves the newspaper. A carabiniere escorting his fallen colleague, clinging to the car's running board and crying with rage, points the musket he holds with one arm, like a pistol, and shoots him on the spot. One shot. The same ambulance picks up his body as well.

At the fascio headquarters on Via Ottaviani there must be barely a hundred. It's Sunday and, as always on weekends, at least five squads are out conducting raids on the surrounding towns. The fascists left in the city crowd into the meeting room. There are the usual ones: Chiostri, Moroni, Manganiello, Annibale Foscari, the Venetian "young count," delicate and pale as a ghost, the enormous Capanni, disheveled as always. The nasal drone of the madman Pirro Nenciolini rises above the buzz; bald and bent, he gesticulates and swears to himself as if possessed: "Goddammit! Jesus Christ! In the name of God! . . ." In a corner Bruno Frullini, grim, loads his revolver.

They are waiting for the Marquis Dino Perrone Compagni to speak. In recent months in Florence the fascio had split in two: on the one hand those with connections to the palazzi of the aristocrats, on the other those like Dùmini, barely supported by elderly parents, or Umberto Banchelli, obsessed with his tics and rancors, or Tullio Tamburini, with a criminal record for theft. Desperate wretches, ready for anything. But after the beatings in Pisa, the blaze at the socialist newspaper, the uproar at the provincial Council over the "reds" displaying the tricolor, they nevertheless find themselves unified. The payback has been the same for everyone. The hatred identical.

Now to heal the split they have pulled this marquis out of a hat. He is getting on in years—he must be over forty—he talks too much, and he still lives in his mother's house. She, the marquise, seems to have once owned an estate in Greve, but it was all frittered away in gambling debts. During the war the young nobleman evaded military action in the orderly offices, and later, in peacetime, was demoted from cavalry officer to simple soldier because of the gambling. Dùmini and Banchelli mockingly call him the "Conte di Culagna" and even true patricians have always looked down on him. But the Florentine notables weren't too picky. He played their game and they feathered his nest.

Perrone Compagni finally speaks. He stresses each syllable as if dictating a telegram:

"An eye for an eye, a tooth for a tooth! Before tonight the Bolshevik leaders will have paid for this last infamy!" A roar of response. Perrone Compagni continues: "We must act before the police and the carabinieri. We are the ones who must enforce public order and carry out the actions of justice." As he speaks, he unbuttons his jacket to display the revolver that he keeps tucked in his belt.

They argue a little, they rant about the action plan, they split up into five squads. Some politicians come to implore them not to burn down Florence while seeking revenge. No one pays any attention to them. The fascists are hell-bent on retaliation.

Dùmini sets up his team's general headquarters at Café Gambrinus. At his side are the inevitable Banchelli and Luigi Pontecchi, known as "Gigi," fifty years old, a former professional cyclist, an oddball who is blind in one eye and ruthless with a club. All afternoon the squads go about ordering the shops to close for mourning, instructing that flags be displayed at half-mast, and clearing out the restaurants with some back-handed blows. Occasionally they stop someone, inspect his documents as if they were policemen. If someone protests, they beat him up. But the streets empty on their own as far as the eye can see. Armored cars move along the boulevards, military floodlights illuminate Piazzale Michelangelo, police machine guns in battle array guard the Arno's bridges leading to the working-class sections, the "red" districts. A nightmarish air hangs heavily over everything throughout the city. No one knows where to go looking for revenge.

Then someone gets an idea. The squad, about thirty men, marches militarily, three by three, down the middle of the street. Some are wearing helmets, others the black fez with the tassel, many are wearing army uniforms. On Via dei Ginori they encounter a funeral procession. The men move aside, the commander orders the military salute, each man snaps his head around. The passersby, terrified, see that all the squadristi are holding a revolver: they hold it barrel up, resting against the right shoulder.

The squad continues along Via Taddea, arriving at number 2 of the cobbled side street just before 6:00 p.m. It's sundown, a cold, dry gusty wind is blowing, the door of the railway workers' union is open. There is no one guarding it. Most of the squad's men stay behind to stand watch over the street, only Italo Capanni and two others go up.

They move cautiously. The door on the first floor is also ajar. Nobody. No one in the corridor leading to the offices either. Maybe the "reds" are holed up in the Oltrarno districts. Silence. Dim shadows. But a sliver of light filters through the door of an office. They push it open. The man they are looking for is there, sitting at his desk, with a cigarette in his mouth. Florence is in a state of siege and he, Spartaco Lavagnini, secretary of the railway workers' union, editor of the newspaper *Azione comunista*, the man from whom all the Bolsheviks of Tuscany expect the revolution, sits at his workplace, head bent over a sheet of paper, pen in hand. He is writing; untiring, unarmed, disciplined to duty, he is correcting drafts as if fate could depend on some careless slip-up, some typo.

When Spartaco Lavagnini looks up from the page, the murderer who has come to kill him is standing in front of him, three feet away. He points the revolver at the center of Lavagnini's forehead. He is an excellent marksman, a longtime hunter, he claims the first shot on the defenseless game for himself.

Yet the shot misses the mark. Lavagnini is wounded superficially, under the nose. His head drops, and he bumps into the table as he falls to the floor, but he's not dead yet. The second shot strikes him on the ground, from the left, at point-blank range, and scores a bull's-eye right in the center of the ear. Additional shots, aimed at the big target, pelt him behind the armpit after he is undoubtedly already a corpse. By now the victim lies motionless.

Then the murderer is seized by a kind of diabolical second thought. As if wanting to restore a cosmic order that his own cruelty had violated a few moments before, he grabs the victim's disfigured body by the hair, sits him back in the same chair on which he had surprised him at work, takes the cigarette out of the corner of his mouth—which he'd never stopped smoking during the entire time it took for the execution—and jams it between the dead man's broken teeth like a wedge. The murderer's saliva mixes with the blood in his victim's mouth.

That night the city splits. When the tragic dawn breaks, Florence wakes up divided in two along the rift drawn by the Palazzo Antinori bomb and Spartaco Lavagnini's murder.

During the hours of darkness, the same artisan skill that built the city over the centuries, erecting drystone walls and fortifying itself with paving stones, separates the left bank of the Arno from the rest. The masses, fearing an attack, have barricaded themselves in the working-class districts and in the outskirts, from San Frediano to Scandicci. On the other bank, fearing an uprising from the people, the army has been deployed.

Four 65 mm cannons in Piazza Vittorio command the streets, police in battle array block the bridges. Repression is imminent. No one, not even the police, ventures into the districts at night. No one sleeps, across the Arno. Spartaco Lavagnini is mourned, no one is under any illusions, and questions are raised. Who threw that bomb? Who could have had an interest in endangering fifty years of workers' gains? Some say that when a bomb explodes in the crowd, no matter who armed it, no matter who was mowed down by it, the ultimate victim is always the proletarian left.

In the city, life has been shut down since morning. The railwaymen, as soon as news of Lavagnini's murder made its way around, halted trains at the Rifredi, Campo di Marte and San Donnino stations. Immediately afterwards, by their side, the tram conductors got on board, followed by the electricians and then, little by little, by almost all sectors of proletarian workers. There's no water, gas or electricity, no trains or trams, the shops are closed.

The fascists don't appear on the streets until around noon. They spend the night at the Via Ottaviani headquarters fighting off sleep with rum punch. After lunch, they emerge in columns to attack San Frediano but they are forced to cross the river by the San Niccolò bridge farther away and come back up the steep inclines and the Viale dei Colli. There are few of them, and when they venture into a *borgo* the people defend themselves with the determination of those who know that if they don't win now they will never win again.

In Piazza Tasso, Dùmini and his men find themselves surrounded by a hail of projectiles of all kinds: roof tiles, fragments of plaster and masonry, porcelain washbasins. Even a stone sink hails down on them. The women, inciting their men, shriek like lunatics. Shots are fired from the windows. One of the assailants lies on the ground, wheezing. A trickle of dark blood drips from his gray uniform, staining the sidewalk. The Arditi are forced to take cover in a doorway. The army's cannons remain on the right bank of the river. The assailants manage to get to safety only when an armored police vehicle arrives to rescue them.

After the failed raid, the police request the army's intervention. Orders are given for the 84th and 69th infantry units, flanked by the Bersaglieri, to enter the Oltrarno from the Santa Trinita and Carraia bridges. The "reds'" barricades are forced open with armored cars but the proletarians do not give up. The units have to attack house by house and flush out the nuclei of resistance one at a time. The fascists now infiltrate the wards in the wake of the army and police. They go from one act of vendetta to another, as the Misericordia's sirens shriek throughout the city, and rumors of atrocities mount.

At the bridge spanning the Arno, guarded by a crowd of fierce communists, an improvident young man on a bicycle wearing gloves and knee boots—all things unknown to the workers—was killed and thrown into the Arno when he insisted on passing. It is said that the fascist had clung to the parapet of the bridge and that the communists had crushed his hands to make him fall. His body was fished out by dragging the riverbed with hooks. There were several contusions on his face but no sign of wounds on his hands.

A second night of darkness descends over Florence. In Borgo

Ognissanti, at the Vespucci hospital, and under the arcades of Santa Maria Nuova, an anxious crowd stands watch, awaiting news of wounded relatives and friends.

On the morning of March 1, the battle is renewed. At Ponte a Ema, where women and children were sent to safety in the hills, the defense is broken only by 75 mm field guns. At Santa Croce the fighting goes on for five hours. Finally, towards evening, the troops return to the city celebrating triumphantly. The Bersaglieri, in their red fezzes with blue tassels, sing Mameli's anthem; they brandish red flags taken from the communist enemy and a large portrait of Lenin. When they reach Via Martelli, the cannons and their carriages are strewn with mimosa flowers.

Everywhere, using the police and army as shields, the fascists have devastated the headquarters of the enemy's associations. Now law enforcement no longer threatens them with jail, on the contrary, the Army Corps supplied them with 120 muskets and three crates of SIPE bombs loaded on a 15 Ter truck.

At the end of the day, in the Chamber of Labor hall on Via Tintori, squadrista Pirro Nenciolini, after having cursed God nonstop for the last fifty-six hours, sets fire to a pile of benches, registers and red flags. As everyone clears outs, some jeer at him:

"Hey, Pirro, watch out or you'll burn your new shoes."

"Leave me alone, leave me to it, today I want to burn these too, Goddammit."

Pirro Nenciolini, the compulsive curser, the broken record stuck on perpetual rage, the rabid dog shunned by his own comrades, remains alone in the room with the pyre. He warms his hands at the blaze and he's happy.

Citizens, the champions of a "New Humanity" and of a "New Order," the corrupt crusaders of peace at all costs . . . have hatched and perpetrated another barbaric crime . . . emerging from their squalid burrows . . . they have killed our sons and our young brothers, guilty only of being pure and innocent.

Florentine fascists' wall poster
after the attack on Palazzo Antinori,
February 28, 1921

While we all feel the deepest sympathy for Gino Mugnai who died with the sun before him in the intensity of the conflict that claimed him as unwitting victim, the gruesome death of Spartaco Lavagnini breaks our hearts as brothers . . . He died while quietly seeing to his duties as secretary . . . victim of his freely professed ideas . . . he died in his innocent activity, smoking a cigarette, as he went to open the door to his killers . . . Let stations and maintenance yards be deserted until they repose forever in the eternal peace of the sepulcher.

Florentine socialist railway workers' wall poster,
February 28, 1921

The revolt of the Florentine proletariat was comprehensive, proud in its enthusiasm and impetus. Those who write its history must say how for two days the people were masters of their homes and wards and defended them, weapons in hand. They must exalt the sang-froid of the workers who stood up to machine guns and cannons with their paltry weapons . . . We salute the leaders and followers who have fallen, but we loudly affirm that we are all ready to attack and to fall, to die and to kill, in turn. Better, a hundred times better, to leave fifty dead on a city's pavement than to tolerate violence and offense without reacting.

Palmiro Togliatti, "The Example of Florence,"
L'Ordine Nuovo, March 2, 1921

We were not able to achieve anything. After the capitalists' war, we too waged our war, but our war is a war of ineffectual weaklings. Today we have a counterrevolution without having had a revolution.

Rinaldo Rigola, socialist reformist leader,
from the rostrum of the congress of the CGdL,
March 1, 1921

Never has order been so troubled in Italy as it has since the fascists took on the job of restoring it.

Luigi Salvatorelli, "Class and Nation,"
La Stampa, February 22, 1921

BENITO MUSSOLINI

MILAN, MARCH 5, 1921

"BENITO MUSSOLINI, EDITOR of *Il Popolo d'Italia*, had an airplane accident yesterday afternoon at the Arcore airfield while training, under the guidance of pilot Cesare Redaelli, to obtain his pilot's license. The aircraft was seen to suddenly veer out of control and plummet from an altitude of approximately 130 feet . . ."

A pinecone in the engine's cooling pipe. Sometimes a banal accident can be enough to divert the course of history. And it all ends in a twisted metal wreck at the edge of a cabbage field in Arcore, the shithole of the world.

With the coming of spring, Benito had finally managed to resume his flying lessons. On the night of March 2, however, Rachele had had a bad premonition, like Julius Caesar's wife. But he was determined to become the first European politician to travel by plane, piloting the aircraft himself, and would not let himself be held back by the superstitions of an ignorant peasant woman. He had therefore left his fur-trimmed flight jacket home to appease his wife and had gone to Arcore by bicycle.

At the second take-off, after a turn around the countryside, the engine speed had begun dropping. There had been no time for an impromptu landing: the plane, now lacking thrust, had gone into a spin and plunged from 130 feet up. Redaelli, apart from a few scratches, had emerged unscathed. He, on the other hand, had suffered a slight head injury and a substantial contusion to his left knee. He'd had himself treated at the Porta Venezia clinic. When he got home, Rachele had burst into hysterics. "It serves you right!" she'd shouted.

The good thing is that the *Corriere della Sera* is now writing about him, even for just a trivial accident. They're giving him the same amount of space they'd given to covering the foundation of the fasci two years earlier. No matter how you look at it, the new, dominant reality of Italian politics is fascism. They're heading towards the elections and this time they will be in the game. Better yet, they will be the ones dealing the cards. He said it clearly in the newspaper the day before the accident: parliament is aging ten years every day. Time for a new state of affairs, new men, a new chamber.

No, they will not nail them to the cross of violence. He never tires of repeating it, like someone who wants to convince himself first of all: violence is a cross they bear in a spirit of sacrifice, nothing more. From Tuscany news of savage events arrives daily. On the first of March, in Empoli, the Bolshevik masses, fearing a punitive fascist incursion, ambushed some navy stokers sent to Florence to run the trains halted by the strike of other Bolshevik railway workers. Nine dead and dozens injured. It seems the terrified peasants tore those poor sailors to pieces like savage beasts.

Everything that's happening is sad from a human point of view but is an inevitable historical necessity. He continually repeats this as well in his articles in *Il Popolo d'Italia*. Through this crisis the world will regain its equilibrium, and the fascists are determined not to give an inch: after every socialist crime, the retaliation will hit hard, inexorably. It goes on. Nonstop. They were not the ones who started this civil war but they will finish it. It's about making violence increasingly smarter, about inventing a surgical violence.

He's written and rewritten it in his newspaper: violence is not art for art's sake. It is a harsh necessity.

But how can you write when you're lying in bed with a bandaged head and a blood clot in your knee joint? The night before his fever rose to over 104. Dr. Binda had to give him five stitches in his head and draw blood from his leg. It's the same leg and the same knee that were injured in 1917 by the mortar explosion. Back then too the wounds would not heal, he'd had problems walking and experienced a loss of sensation in the limbs. Binda says it may be the infected blood. *Tabes dorsalis*. Tertiary syphilis. The doctor administers gold salts.

Meanwhile, Edda is crying in the kitchen after being smacked, and Vittorio and Bruno are squabbling over a rocking horse. No man can survive seven consecutive days at home with the family.

Rachele announces he has a visitor. She looks angry, almost livid. These days there have been all sorts of nuisances, well-wishers, not counting the soldiers singing *Giovinezza* below the window.

Appearing in the doorway of their bedroom—there, in his home, with his wife standing behind her—is Margherita Sarfatti. She is impeccable as always: elegant and refined. She addresses him formally. She's brought gifts for the children. He tries to sit up in the bed he shares with Rachele.

The woman, obviously, could not resist. In recent times they've been inseparable, at the newspaper and outside the office. They even keep a kind of joint logbook, in which he renamed his lover "*Vela*," his sail, somewhat in the manner of D'Annunzio.

Now that she's there, however, "Vela" struggles to smooth out a wrinkle of disgust at the corners of her mouth. Discovering the prosaic nature of plebeian marriages, plebeian dwellings, and plebeian lives always has this effect on the upper class. But the society lady composes herself. She talks about European politics. She reports that she has learned of a very flattering assessment from the great Georges Sorel, the theoretician of the myth of violence. It seems that Sorel told a friend of his: "Mussolini is no less extraordinary a man than Lenin. He invented something that is not in my books: the union of the national and the social."

He, the extraordinary man, lying in his matrimonial bed, feels the blood pounding in his knee.

When Sarfatti leaves, Rachele explodes: "Some people really have a lot of gall! The least you should have done is thrown her out the window!"

Her husband tunes her out and turns his back to her. He tells his wife she's got some crazy ideas in her head.

Everything that's happening is sad, considered from a human point of view, but it is inevitable. It is through this internal crisis that the nation will regain its equilibrium. The fascists are firmly determined not to give an inch: they will make their violence increasingly intelligent, but they will not abandon it until the white flag of surrender is raised, and with sincerity, from the adversary's camp. The fascists stand in closed ranks, ready for all events . . .

Benito Mussolini,
Il Popolo d'Italia, March 1, 1921

If the socialists truly disarm, the fascists will disarm in turn. We repeat that we do not have a taste for violence, that violence for us is an exception, not the rule: we have accepted this kind of civil war as a terrible necessity . . .

Benito Mussolini,
Il Popolo d'Italia, March 5, 1921

GIACOMO MATTEOTTI

MARCH 10–12, 1921

On the afternoon of March 10, 1921, Giacomo Matteotti takes the floor in the Italian parliament chamber to denounce fascist violence for the second time.

Before he can speak, the chamber, under the presidency of De Nicola, and as proposed by Deputy Guglielmi, expresses unanimous condolences for the assassination of the Spanish prime minister that occurred two days earlier at the hands of revolutionary anarchists. The Italian socialists join in deploring individual attacks on human life but, speaking through Deputy Vella, have a qualification recorded in the minutes: they hope that Spain will adopt a policy of freedom towards workers. Whatever Matteotti is about to say, it will therefore fall into the seething Tartarus of the European civil war, an apparently bottomless abyss.

Before his speech, it is Interior Undersecretary Corradini's turn. He replies to Matteotti's preceding denunciation tracing the violence back to the battle over the renewal of the agricultural concordat, recognizing that the agrarians have been "immoderate" but assuring that the government is doing all that's necessary to suppress the fascist raids. Chamber president De Nicola then yields the floor to the socialist deputy, allowing him to declare himself satisfied.

But Giacomo Matteotti does not declare himself at all satisfied:

> In the middle of the night, while decent men are asleep in their homes, fascist trucks show up in the villages, in the countryside, in hamlets composed of a few hundred inhabitants; naturally they arrive accompanied by the leaders of the local Agrarian Association, as usual led by them, since otherwise it would not be possible for them to find the league leader's house or the small shabby job center in the dark, in the middle of desolate rural lands.
>
> They appear in front of a house and give the order to surround the place. There are twenty, a hundred of them armed with rifles and revolvers. They shout to the league leader and demand that he come out. If he does not come out, he's told that they will burn his house, his wife, his children. The man comes down. If he opens the door, they grab him, tie him up, shove him in the truck, put him through the most unspeakable tortures, pretending they're going to kill him, to drown him, then they abandon him in the middle of the fields, naked, tied to a tree!
>
> If the league leader is a man with guts and rather than open the door resorts to weapons to defend himself, then he's immediately killed in the middle of the night, a hundred against one. That's the method used in the Polesine.

The chamber listens in silence. For once, there's no clamoring, no protests can be heard, no applause, no jeering. It seems that a patch of Polesine night has projected its darkness onto the hill of Montecitorio.

Matteotti then begins reading his list. Meticulous, precise, pedantic. His oratory, compared to the preceding denunciation, has taken a more down-to-earth turn, aimed at facts, the minute details of lives quotidianly absorbed in the shadow of things closest to them. As if now only the names of villages, roads, and people deserved the dignity of being mentioned.

In Salara, an unfortunate night worker hears a knock at his door. Who is it? he asks. Friends! they answer him. He opens the door a crack and through the opening twenty rifle shots lay him out, a corpse. At Pettorazza, the league leader hears someone knocking at his house at night, always at night . . . At Pincara, a small village in the middle of the countryside, a truck arrives at midnight in front of the employment bureau, a miserable shack, a tiny room . . . In Adria they go at midnight to the house of the socialist section's secretary, they seize him, tie him up, take him to the Adige, submerge him and leave him bound to a telegraph pole . . . In Loreo . . . in Ariano . . . in Lendinara . . . And the story goes on like that; but nobody intervenes, nobody is exposed, nobody knows who the guilty parties are. Night after night, day after day, there are acts of destruction and murderers who commit them. By now people in the ill-fated Polesine valley know that when someone knocks at the door of the house at night, saying they are the police, it's a death sentence.

At this point in Matteotti's denunciation, murmuring starts up in the chamber of Montecitorio, remarks from the benches on the right. Once the government's responsibilities were touched on, the spell of unanimous silence was broken. Matteotti raises his voice:

"This is assault, by an organization of thugs. It is no longer a political struggle; it is barbarism; it is medieval."

The speaker continues with his somber litany, amid acclamation from the left and outcries from the right. The president, impatient, urges him several times to conclude.

The rejoinder does not come from a fascist, from a right-wing extremist, or from one of Matteotti's enemies, but from Deputy Umberto Merlin, a member of the Catholic party founded by Don Sturzo, the only one to have been elected in the Rovigo-Ferrara district. He is the same age as Matteotti and was his classmate at the Celio secondary school in Rovigo. In 1919 Matteotti saved him from being beaten by his socialist peasants by bodily coming between them.

"Matteotti must acknowledge," Merlin says, "that even before the socialists mourned their dead, the fascists wept for their own."

The Catholic deputy's affirmation appalls the socialists. Merlin cites a young man knifed in Gavello and another stabbed in Badia by socialists, to which the outbreak of homicidal fury in the Polesine can be traced. Then he goes on to plead the cause of the Catholics: "Whereas thirty years ago in my province it took heroism to proclaim oneself a socialist, today the parties have reversed and it takes courage for all those humble workers to join our organizations and, in a completely red province, reaffirm their faith, the faith of their fathers." Finally he turns to the benches where his old schoolmate sits: "I say loyally and peaceably to the socialists; do you want this state of shameful, intolerable events, unworthy of a civilized country, to cease? To do this, to bring about peace, we must do more than condemn the violence of others, while making every excuse for our own violence, even when we disapprove of it."

The chamber applauds. Matteotti's second denunciation of fascist violence is drowned in the cauldron of the European civil war.

Two days later, on March 12th, Giacomo Matteotti is in Castelguglielmo, in the province of Rovigo, for a political meeting, accompanied by the mayor of Pincara. Hundreds of fascists who have converged there from all over the province await him. As always, many squadristi came from nearby Ferrara.

The socialist deputy is dragged to the office of the Agrarian Association. Perhaps he is unarmed, perhaps a revolver is seized from him. In any case, the squadristi order Matteotti to sign declarations of abjuration. He refuses. The fascists then set fire to the headquarters of the peasant league and load him onto a truck.

They drive him around the countryside, subjecting him to abuse, insults, death threats. Afterwards, at night, they abandon him near Lendinara.

The abduction lasted several hours. Giacomo Matteotti has become one of the victims in his stories. Rumor has it that the mistreatment even went as far as sodomy.

Ferrara is the Italian city that has the highest percentage of brothels. It seems that the record number is due to the presence of five barracks. The "houses of ill-repute," in compliance with the Crispi decree that issued the first regulation on the matter, are divided into three categories: first, second and third. The law sets the rates, which range from 10 liras for deluxe houses to 4 liras for plebeian ones. Almost all of them are found among the quiet streets of Via Croce Bianca, Via Sacca, Via Colomba and, in particular, Via delle Volte, the axis along which "linear" Ferrara developed. The clients of the brothels, walking through the area, enjoy the sight of fourteenth- and fifteenth-century palazzi, as well as the charm of the eponymous arches.

In accordance with an unwritten rule, politics remains outside of the bordellos. A free zone. Yet for days and weeks, in all the brothels of Ferrara, there's been talk of nothing but the torturing of the socialist deputy. The flippant witticisms germinate in an atmosphere polluted by the bluster of the squadristi, frequent, regular customers. Even the penniless students who linger in the downstairs parlor, unable to afford a visit to a girl's room, even they have learned to joke with the madam about the alleged bludgeoning and sodomization of Deputy Matteotti. The boys, snickering, ask which guests practice "the Matteotti," about the legality of the "Matteotti," about how much a "Matteotti" costs.

Meanwhile Giacomo Matteotti is banished from his land. During the seizure in Castelguglielmo, the fascists were clear: if he wanted to live, he had to leave the province and not return.

And so his life as a stray dog begins. He moves about incognito; wherever he goes he is in danger, he is a man with a price on his head, condemned to execution. No one, not even the postman, must know the whereabouts of his temporary residence. He spends a month in Venice to be closer to his family, but then he's recognized and has to flee from there too. He writes letters to his wife Velia with no return address:

> *It will take years to start over and in the meantime we will go back to how it was thirty years ago. I don't mind so much for myself—I can always make a new life in hundreds of different ways—as I do for our entire movement, created with such effort, and for those poor people, who even if they went too far, had finally liberated themselves from conditions of servitude.*

Then he reassures her:

> *Meanwhile don't worry, because I assure you I will exercise the maximum prudence. It is no longer the time for a courageous act that earlier could have been useful; today that too would be perfectly useless, and harmful not only to the one who performs it but to others as well.*

LEANDRO ARPINATI

FERRARA, MARCH 18, 1921

It's all a precarious seesaw, in and out of jail.

Leandro Arpinati is arrested again on March 12th, as soon as he gets off the train from Bologna. In Milan he is supposed to meet with Mussolini, who is waiting for him to assemble the big fascist rally scheduled for the beginning of April in Emilia; but Mussolini will wait in vain because "our friend Arpinati" doesn't even have time to set foot in the city. They stop him at the head of the platform, put him, handcuffed, back on a train to Romagna, and transport him to Ferrara's judicial prison on Via Piangipane. It's the fifth time in eighteen months that Leandro Arpinati has ended up in jail.

The first time he was detained, in November 1919, it was for the bloody events at the Teatro Gaffurio in Lodi during the first fascist electoral campaign, and he was in there for forty-six days. The second time they arrested him was about a year later, in Bologna, in September 1920, following the killing of militant socialist Guido Tibaldi during clashes with nationalist civil defense troops; they released him almost immediately, however, after just three days, because despite being present, he had not taken part in the shooting. He then returned to prison in Bologna a third time on December 18th for the beating of socialist deputies Bentini and Niccolai, who had already been threatened several times in the preceding days and who were attacked upon leaving the court where they insisted on defending the Bolsheviks. But by then the tune had already changed: the decisive battle at Palazzo d'Accursio had already taken place, the shifting wind was already filling the fascio's black sail, and he'd ended up in a cell because he had voluntarily appeared at the police station to boldly accuse himself of the punitive raid along with three other comrades. The police chief had been forced to arrest him, but had merely charged him with contempt and threatening members of parliament, dropping the charge of assault. With the new year came a fourth arrest. And finally this fifth arrest in Milan. This time they accused him of having procured the trucks for a raid to Pieve di Cento during which a worker was "unfortunately" killed, even though he had not participated.

That's how it goes, it can't be avoided, it's a real civil war. He stated it very clearly in *L'Assalto*. Socialists and fascists are inveterate enemies, bound in a mortal struggle. An air of hatred whirling around their heads as though essential to their very reason for being.

There's been much discussion in the fascio about whether they are playing the agrarians' game too much, whether the squads are becoming a tool of the reactionaries, but when it comes to debating at meetings and ticking off theories, he loses his patience. During the assembly on January 3rd, the left wing of the fascio, backed by the Fiume legionnaires, lashed out against the right, accusing it of having become a slave to the "old Italy." It only came to an end thanks to the mediation of Dino Grandi, who also took over as editor of *L'Assalto*.

Arpinati, though secretary, kept out of it and was unable to influence the members' votes. When it comes to clashes in the piazza, however, he's the one other men follow, including Grandi. He is the idol of the squads, it's him they acclaim as their "duce." For him, fascism is intemperance, it is youth's unbridled tread on the ancient stones of Piazza Maggiore, it is an organization of free, violent spirits who are rousing a country of apathetic slaves. He doesn't understand the rural countryside, but the city, Bologna, the city is all his.

On weekends, Arpinati and his boys travel to the towns in the province. They attack the *Case del popolo*, the union headquarters, the "red" town halls, they put an end to the boycotts, beat people up, destroy things, seize the enemy's flags and then burn them in Piazza Maggiore at public bonfires that spark excitement. Sometimes, as in Paderno, it's not even necessary to fight: threats are enough to make the *capilega*, league leaders, humiliate themselves and hand over the flags.

At other times it's a tough fight. In addition to injuries sustained in the brawls, Arpinati has already been shot twice. The first time in Ferrara in December, and the second in Modena on January 24th during the funeral of fascist Mario Ruini, killed three days earlier. And to think they'd gone there as if it were a cheerful outing, the way you go to a party! They'd even brought their wives and girlfriends from Bologna. He had been accompanied by Rina and her sister. Two comrades had died, twenty-two and nineteen years old, and he himself had been wounded by a pistol shot to the ankle. During the night, in retaliation, they set fire to the chambers of labor, first in Modena and then in Bologna. The police had not made a move.

Now Giolitti has gotten it into his head to disarm the fascists. He sent Cesare Mori to Bologna, a new prefect who has already distinguished himself for the harsh repression of banditry in Sicily and of D'Annunzian unrest in Rome. Mori's first measure was to prohibit the circulation of trucks in the provinces from Saturday afternoon to Sunday night, the hours when they set off on the raids. So to carry out the foray to Pieve di Cento, for which Arpinati was arrested again, they had to park the trucks at farmsteads and assemble the men out in the fields.

Mori won't stop them that way. Those withered old politicians so lacking in humors won't crush their fervor, not with travel bans. Of course, every now and then something goes wrong. In Pieve a poor woman, a worker—it seems her name was Angelina—was shot right in the face by mistake, while she was closing the shutters.

But Arpinati wasn't at Pieve di Cento and the Bolognese fascio's reaction to its leader's arrest was vehement. In addition, many supporting parties expressed their solidarity with Leandro Arpinati, the man who stopped the Bolsheviks in Bologna. The Confederation of Trade and Industry even threatened a lockout of shops in solidarity against his arrest.

Arpinati is released from prison for the fifth time on March 17th, at night. *Il resto del Carlino*, the city's leading newspaper, reports that on his return to Bologna, a "tide of people" welcomed him as a hero and escorted him to Piazza Nettuno. The police account speaks of a cortege of approximately three thousand people. These days things move quickly: a person is jailed today and released in triumph tomorrow.

BENITO MUSSOLINI

MILAN, MARCH 23–27, 1921

IT'S 11:00 P.M., almost time for the good hard-working bourgeois of Milan to go to bed. This year Easter falls early, the last Sunday in March, but tomorrow is only Thursday, they still have to go to work.

In her palazzo on Corso Venezia, after a light dinner, Margherita Sarfatti is sipping a tisane of wild fennel, hibiscus and valerian in the company of some friends. Fennel is said to aid digestion, valerian sleep; no one recalls the beneficial properties of hibiscus anymore.

Suddenly the Chinese porcelain cup trembles on the saucer, then the fine-grained vitreous china cracks. A roar follows the blast by a fraction of a second: the panes of the large French windows overlooking the boulevard reverberate, the building seems like it's about to be knocked off its foundations.

They all rush to the windows but it's deserted out there, everything is silent. Another two minutes and the street is jammed with crowds running away. They are fleeing from Porta Venezia, headed towards the center.

Every so often someone turns around, still running, and points behind him, into the void, towards the horror from which he's bolting. No one screams, however, there's not a sound: whatever its cause, the horror is mute. A multitude of voiceless, demented specters surges through the Milan night.

* * *

The performance at the Kursaal Diana had started very late due to the firing of a member of the orchestra who was later reinstated thanks to his colleagues' protest. The fifteenth and final reprise of Franz Lehár's *The Blue Mazurka* was being performed.

The bourgeois public adores the operetta, its simple, improbable plots, its taste for parody, its lavish stage sets, its lively music, its immediate enjoyability and, above all, it adores the almost maniacal omnipresence of the dances, choreographed for ten, twelve, sometimes sixteen dancers, which recall the carefree joy of sentimental stories set in late-century polite society. "My friend, put on your splendid finery, look your best, the night for making merry has come . . ." Ladies and gentlemen, here for you are the pleasures of life before the world war.

The masses too, however, delightedly flock to the recital hall of the recreational and cultural complex that is the Kursaal Diana. This evening, moreover, the mazurka—a much-loved favorite of the poor—was on stage, that triple meter whirling dance of Polish peasants, so similar to Viennese waltzes, but with a more moderate rhythm, and much sharper movements, accentuated by heel-clicking, that unrestrained, graceful dance to be performed as couples arranged in a circle: the magic circle of ancient, primitive dances, a symbol of the union and strength of small, courageous communities of men and women who at the edge of a dark forest dance in a tiny pool of light surrounded by infinite shadows.

The bomb seems to have exploded at the end of the first act.

It must have been placed near the performers' entrance, on the Via Mascagni side, because the street is buried under debris there, and the stage strewn with the orchestra members' mutilated corpses can be seen through the skeletal window frames. The royal guard patrols are clearing the way to Via Melzo.

In front of the entrance, partially closed by the lowered shutters, a small squad of Bersaglieri sent from police headquarters prepares to stand guard, lining up to form a semicircle. The blaring of the firefighters' sirens echoes throughout the district, while a team of about thirty men extinguishes the flames with a hose. Each time the stretcher-bearers re-emerge from the rubble with a stretcher, the crowd that has flowed into the street from Corso Buenos Aires accompanies the appearance of the disfigured body with a shocked cry.

The nearby clinic of Porta Venezia is already full of dead bodies or victims seriously injured. Others are sent on ambulances to more distant emergency care centers, while many are treated in homes opened to the tragedy by neighborhood residents. At the entrance of what's left of the theater, relatives who were spared howl in pain like wolves in the Milan night, and reporters meticulously record the mutilation of the bodies for the morning papers: lying on the ground just past the last level, near tier box no. 8, is a piece of a skull covered with a woman's long hair; in box no. 10, amid plaster debris, shards of glass and bone fragments, is an elegant female arm still covered by the sleeve of a silk blouse; between box no. 13 and the stagebox is the bare trunk of a little girl's body.

Anarchists. There is no doubt this is their work. Errico Malatesta, their old historical leader, in prison in Milan, has been staging a hunger strike for days to protest his unwarranted arrest and for days small-caliber bombs have been exploding more or less everywhere. Some of the survivors say they saw an anarchist throw the bomb at the stage. It is almost certainly nonsense but, just as certainly, this is their work.

Benito Mussolini is familiar with anarchists. He also knows the Kursaal Diana very well: he's gone there several times to meet with police chief Giovanni Gasti who lives in an apartment above the Hotel Diana Majestic, adjacent to the theater. It is him the terrorists likely wanted to strike.

A group of fascists summoned by the explosion catch sight of the Duce in the crowd. They huddle around him, voicing immediate intentions of retaliation. They outdo one another in vengeful audacity: the offices of *Avanti!*, the labor union headquarters, the offices of *Umanità nova*, the anarchist paper published by Malatesta. The targets are always the same, hatred almost always lacks imagination.

Mussolini doesn't discourage them, but he doesn't incite them either. Let them go off to retaliate, he stays behind to contemplate the scene of the tragedy. Alone, anonymous, blended in the crowd. He puts his hat on his head. This bombing-disaster changes everything, marking the end of an era in Italy's political life. This providential bomb marks a new beginning.

The fascists are young, they have no history—he wrote that in *Il Popolo d'Italia* just that morning—or maybe they have too much history. Yet there are days when anniversaries bring a shiver of cosmic conspiracy. As if a bloody, idiotic god chose destiny's dates on the century's calendar with perfect cruelty: it was exactly two years ago, on this same day, that he founded the fasci. At that time they were only a few, now they are many. But this carnage is the past, the carnage of the future belongs to them.

Fascism is not a religion, it is a training ground, it is not a party, it is a movement, it is not a program, it is a passion. Fascism is the new force. Now it's a matter of looking deep into the abyss, of emphasizing the right quality of light in the optical spectrum of violence. One thing must appear patently evident to the eye looking into the weapon's sights and Benito Mussolini, the Founder, writes it loud and clear in his newspaper: the fascists beat, shoot, burn, but they do not put bombs in theaters. Fascists fight the socialists on the open battlefield, but they would never harm the operetta's audience, decent, defenseless people indulging in an evening of diversion with *The Blue Mazurka*, fascists are warriors, not terrorists. The massacre is the dark violence of others, of anarchists, of communists. Fascist violence is light, its wavelength vibrates in the range of yellow, orange, red, not in the blind spot of black, its phenomenal war is the antithesis of terrorism. What's more: the fascist war is *the* war against terrorism.

The article for the following day is already written. And the one for the day after that, as well. Starting tomorrow, he will step forward to govern the nation.

The funeral procession takes place on Easter Monday. Five days have passed since the massacre—for five days and five nights the corpses have remained in the morgues—because agreement could not be reached even in the face of mass killing.

The socialist junta of Milan had immediately offered to arrange for the funerals at the city's expense, but the delegations of numerous citizen associations were opposed to the socialists' participation, considering them to be supporters of the terrorists. Right away, in fact, the investigations, as expected, identified those responsible as militant anarchists of the extreme left. Furthermore, in Turin and Milan the communist faction did not sharply condemn the massacre. Therefore, after lengthy negotiations, the Gordian knot was resolved by Rome: through the prefect, the government called for state funerals. Only the Italian tricolor will fly, draped in mourning. No other flag.

There are twenty dead, eighty wounded, at least thirty of them seriously. At the Cimitero Monumentale, from the altar of the Famedio chapel, fifteen priests from the Santissima Trinità bless the corpses amid the whispers of devout worshippers. Then the clergy descends among the coffins and the funeral procession proceeds to the cathedral, led by a platoon of mounted carabinieri and by the 3rd Savoy cavalry, lance flags flying in the wind. The first coffer to exit the crypt is that of Leontina Rossi, a five-year-old girl, the small coffin adorned with white ribbons.

Immediately behind the coffins stands a dense column of 2,000 fascists. Criss-crossed by garlands of flowers, divided into platoons, they march at a cadenced pace. As vowed, they have avenged the dead in their own way, attacking the headquarters of *Avanti!* and that of the anarchists' newspaper. This is the first time that Milan, a working-class city, a "red" city, is witnessing a parade of blackshirts on its own streets. Everything suggests that it will not be the last. The fascist cortege goes by, observed with respect. No one protests.

In the preceding days Mussolini insisted on having his squadristi trained by Major Attilio Teruzzi, newly returned from military campaigns in Cyrenaica. They drilled on the steps on Via Monte di Pietà, in front of fasci headquarters. Rowdy, used to going around in packs, it wasn't easy to make them go down that set of steps in closed-ranks formation. Now, however, as they advance on Piazza del Duomo, they march in a column. Benito Mussolini marches at the head of the squads, in a black shirt, his face somber, his head high. No one remembers that ten years earlier he had extolled the anarchists who threw bombs at the audience at the Teatro Colón in Buenos Aires.

In the churchyard of the cathedral, Archbishop Ratti, lined up with the clergy in solemn vestments, grants the bodies absolution and benediction. Behind him, from the open doors, the Christian temple is resplendent with mercy and with song. In front of him, on the steps, at the head of the squads, Mussolini confronts him, jawbone thrust forward. He is obviously on foot, but Margherita Sarfatti, blending with the crowd, has the impression that the Duce of fascism is on horseback, like an equestrian statue.

One is horrified at the thought of the monsters that the shadows of big cities harbor. One cannot imagine the heart of a man who decides to murder other men, not people guilty of different opinions, but complete strangers who are in a theater to earn a living or to seek a modest respite from their daily work, and who are suddenly swept into an atrocious death, torn to pieces, mangled . . . The theories and deductions of leaders who awaken in dark hearts ideas that are capable of such perversions do not have a right to dwell in any place where life has meaning and civilization even a tenuous ray of light.

Luigi Albertini,
Corriere della Sera, March 24, 1921

Today all the newspapers are outraged over the horrible events of the Teatro Diana tragedy. Not a word about the horrible acts of armed attacks against the peasants in Bologna, in Ferrara, in the Polesine, in Lomellina. Italy no longer knows what justice is.

L'Ordine Nuovo,
communist newspaper founded by Antonio Gramsci,
Turin, March 24, 1921

Let them hold funerals for the victims. We will not take part in a demonstration that has a deviously anti-proletarian nature.

Manifesto of the Milan section of the Italian Communist Party

---

We must immediately protest in order to avoid a gross distortion of the truth . . . specifically, they are trying to frame the barbaric attack in the context of the clash between fascism and socialism . . . It must quickly be said that there is no relationship between the two things . . . The Diana massacre is an eruption of terrorism.

Benito Mussolini,
Il Popolo d'Italia, March 25, 1921

BENITO MUSSOLINI

BOLOGNA-FERRARA, APRIL 3–4, 1921

"IN THIS MANY-HUED reflection we grasp what is life."

It is decided: he will tamper with Goethe to describe to the readers of *Il Popolo d'Italia* the vision of colorful pennants that welcomed him to Bologna. Benito Mussolini has never experienced such a moment in his first thirty-seven years of life, not even when he was the idol of the young socialist revolutionaries: outside the station, waiting for him amidst a forest of pennants and flags organized by Leandro Arpinati, is a crowd of 10,000 fascists.

An apotheosis: the squadristi in columns, divided into four battalions, plus a battalion of cyclists, motorcycle patrols, the Avanguardia Giovanile Fascista (student youth organization), the women's group and the fasci music bands. Almost all in uniform, the fascist black shirt or the army's gray-green, only he and Arpinati in civilian clothes, he in a beige trench coat over a black wool sweater because he is still recovering from the plane crash, Arpinati in a shirt and flannel slacks. They look like kings who stand out from their throng of subjects by exhibiting the elegance of exclusive boutiques.

Parading to the sound of the brass band's military marches, the cortege makes its way through the entire city, then passes Palazzo d'Accursio, the same day the prefect has announced the dissolution of the city's socialist administration following the investigation into the November 21 massacre.

Afterward, in front of San Petronio, the youth squads troop past the open car in which the Duce of fascism, standing on the driver's seat, reviews and commends them with the Roman salute: arm outstretched, hand open, palm turned down, fingers aligned. Bells ring out from the tower of the Podestà. A genuine imperial triumph. Such a collapse of "red" power would have been unimaginable in Bologna only a year earlier.

Bologna acclaims Mussolini as a condottiere but the city is not his. Bologna is Arpinati's, it's Dino Grandi's, it belongs to other "leaders" whom Mussolini doesn't even know. The triumphant welcome shown to the guest is also a display of power. The guest did not generate that power, he simply came to seduce it. Before tomorrow night, with his big, hairy body, he will have to have deceived her, possessed her. In Bologna, the great mother, the queen bee, he is not the father of fascism, he is only her drone.

Emilia Romagna is the preeminent force of the movement at the moment: Bologna has 5,130 members, Ferrara 7,000, Milan only 6,000. The pennants of 117 Emilian fasci parade past the drone, standing upright in the car, while in Lombardy they haven't reached 100. It is an uncurbed force: the squadristi's violence in the countryside doesn't submit to constraints, the thugs only respond to the men who lead them in the assaults; and the administrators of the local fasci refuse to turn over the substantial funds received from the agrarians to the Central Committee of Milan.

Then too, Bologna now has Dino Grandi, a rising star, the thinking head of the group, a man who, within a few months, went from the liberals, to the republicans, to the fascists, who only became a card-carrying member after Palazzo d'Accursio, and who confided to a journalist friend that he dreaded "being considered only a fascist and nothing more." But he has always been a radical, an interventionist, a captain of the Alpini, decorated for valor, with a degree in law earned before being dismissed from the army; he had quickly become editor of *L'Assalto* and was immediately appointed to the board of directors. It's he who is the political mind of Bolognese fascism: he professes a mixture of revolutionary romanticism, nationalist syndicalism, and a derivative D'Annunzianism. He associates fascism and Fiumanism, preaches about wanting to redeem the peasant masses from socialism by distributing land to them on behalf of the nation, and meanwhile he takes money from the agrarians. A confused but keen head, a reptilian brain. They will have to reckon with him.

And it won't be easy because Mussolini has come to Bologna to have two bitter pills swallowed: the moderation of violence and an electoral alliance with Giolitti. He must persuade these savage men who idolize D'Annunzio to ally with the man who fired cannons at him, he must persuade them that in order to purge the syphilis of a parliament full of old imbeciles, they must join forces with the most worn-out whores of the Roman brothel, above all he must persuade them to contain the orgasms they get from bashing the communists. He must persuade the youth that to defend purity one must go to bed with the old harlot.

The decisive meeting takes place in the Teatro Comunale, the same location where not even two years earlier Italian socialists, seized by exaltation, had embraced the Bolshevik revolutionary program.

The morning begins in the best of ways: the leader from Milan is preceded by the announcement that on April 5th, after months of frostiness, he will meet D'Annunzio in Gardone, and the D'Annunzian Dino Grandi hails him with a genuine paean:

> I salute in Benito Mussolini the first fascist of Italy, the sole man, the iron man who never bends, who constantly stood alone among all, alone against the world, amid contempt and apathy and the apparent denial of history, to fight—a general without an army—the most tragic and unfair battle. Today he returns among us in this purified old Bologna, from which he departed, chased out by the socialists, a bunch of second-rate actors without a country. Today he returns as Duce, triumphant.

Here's a stage and, when there's a stage, the stage is his. As always the fundamentals of the theater—stage, curtain, rigging, audience, orchestra—rouse Benito Mussolini. Grandi's introductory tribute allows him to start with where it all begins: with himself. An abrupt, choppy style, sentences broken into fragments made up of a single clause, each prefaced by the raised flag of a reiterated "I": when the war ended, I felt that my task was not finished; when we were defeated in the 1919 election, I, proud of my 4,000 votes, said that the battle would continue; I, only at times, I who claim paternity for this creature of mine so brimming with life, I sometimes feel that the movement has indeed overflowed the modest banks I had assigned to it.

Then, addressing the issues of violence and the elections, comes the most difficult part. Here two different languages must be spoken at the same time: "We must move forward preceded by a column of fire," the Duce proclaims to his warriors. Shortly afterwards, however, the politician speaks: "But I tell you right now that we must hold the line on fascism's necessary violence, a distinctly refined style or, if you prefer, a distinctly surgical one." Now it's time to turn to the elections. The tribune then becomes a poet. Mussolini speaks of "an old Chamber and, worse than old, rotten and corrupt"; of a "worn-out semi-tragedy of used and abused men and, worse still, feeble"; he speaks of elections that will sweep away the old men of the old Italy. To make them swallow the alliance with Giolitti, the oldest and most feeble of all, he veers from "I" to the plural "you" and plays the ace of D'Annunzio: "Don't you feel that the helm is passing by spontaneous transition from Giovanni Giolitti, the old neutralist of 1915, to Gabriele D'Annunzio, who is a new man!?" Prolonged applause, shouts of "viva D'Annunzio!" Mission accomplished: Bologna has been seduced.

At the end of the speech, with everyone on their feet and a lengthy ovation, the fascists again parade past their "Duce" who came from Milan. In the evening, the demonstration goes on by the light of torches, lanterns and tricolored lamps.

The following day, in Ferrara, things go even better, if that's possible. Here to receive Mussolini, instead of Arpinati, there is Italo Balbo, and instead of 10,000 there are 20,000 fascists to acclaim him. Here there is no need to even persuade them to accept the electoral compromise: behind the scenes, Ferrara's fascists ask

Mussolini for the honor of being able to nominate him in their province together with the large landowners. At the Ferrara station, the man whom everyone is beginning to call the "Duce" of fascism has arrived accompanied by two men who, not even ten years earlier, had headed the incendiary local socialist Chamber of Labor—Umberto Pasella and Michele Bianchi—and who now line up alongside Vico Mantovani, the reactionary head of the Agrarian Association against whom the peasants rioted before the war.

But now, through systematic violence and the promise to redistribute the land, Italo Balbo has reshuffled the cards around here. The socialist peasant leagues are even starting to go over to the fascist unions en masse. The first was that of San Bartolomeo in Bosco.

Rather than being proud of his triumph, Balbo seems amused. With his curly hair, scandalously long and teased in back to make it even fuller, holding the club for which he is famous, he strolls lazily, lanky and grinning, beside Mussolini, bald and glowering, who struts stiffly. If some blundering admirer gets in their way, however, Balbo immediately clears a path with a couple of angry cudgel blows. Then, amiably, still in a good mood, he continues on, not turning to look at the individual who was clubbed.

"*Me ne frego*, I don't give a damn." Balbo really seems to be the embodiment of D'Annunzio's motto, now adopted by the fascists. He truly gives the impression that other people's lives don't matter to him, and that, all in all, he doesn't care about his own either.

The stage is set up on the lawn of the Palazzina Marfisa, beside the residence built in the sixteenth century by Francesco d'Este for his daughter. Seventy socialist flags taken from the enemy fly behind the stage. Below the stage, a huge crowd. On the stage, before taking the floor, Mussolini has a moment of consternation:

"Are all these your people?" he whispers to Balbo. The Romagnol club-wielder smiles. Yes, they're all his people.

At night, after the banquets, they leave by car with Dino Grandi and head towards Gardone where D'Annunzio awaits them. Balbo, as usual, has had a lot to drink. The curly head lolls right and left, then ends up on the Duce's shoulder. The Duce, patient, puts up with it.

The assembly today in Bologna celebrates a year of fascist battles. It is the consecration of a victory. It lays the groundwork for other battles and other victories. Fascism is rampant because it carries within it the seeds of life, not those of dissolution. It is a movement that cannot fail before reaching its goal. And it will not fail.

"In this many-hued reflection we grasp what is life," old Goethe says before the awe-inspiring sight of a rainbow between the mountain and the sea . . .

Benito Mussolini,
Il Popolo d'Italia, April 3, 1921

They slandered us, they refused to understand us and, as much as we may deplore violence, in order to shove our ideas into those resistant heads, we had to ram them in with bludgeons.

From the speech by Benito Mussolini
at the Teatro Comunale in Bologna,
April 3, 1921

My dear Balbo, once again a fervent thank you . . . I experienced hours of unspeakable emotion. I will hold onto the grateful memory for the rest of my life.

Benito Mussolini,
private letter to Italo Balbo, April 6, 1921

BENITO MUSSOLINI

APRIL 23–MAY 1921

"THE PARTY TICKET is not open to discussion. We vote."

Even the final hurdle has been cleared. From the columns of the *Corriere della Sera*, Senator Luigi Albertini, owner and publisher of the liberal bourgeoisie's newspaper, urges readers to hold their noses in the face of the malodorous alliance between liberals and fascists. In those words Benito Mussolini finally reads the leap fascism has made from the bloody mud of the trenches to the hall of parliament.

Until two days before, the same Albertini had tenaciously vetoed the fascists' being part of the "national blocs," the union of all the traditional anti-Bolshevist parties with which Giolitti intends to strengthen his power. Now that Albertini has also yielded, only *La Stampa* of Turin, owned and published by Frassati, another liberal senator, is left to argue that liberals cannot, without committing suicide as a party, morally be mixed up with those who exalt violence. But Frassati no longer matters, now.

What indeed matters is that on April 7th, on the very day of the dissolution of the chambers, upon returning from the Bologna and Ferrara rallies, and from the deferential visit to D'Annunzio, the central committee of the fasci, including Dino Grandi, voted to join Giolitti's "blocs," and that the following evening the Milanese fascio assembly confirmed it. What matters is compromise. The editor of *Il Popolo d'Italia* wrote it clearly: life, for those who don't want to spend it in the usual ivory tower, requires certain contacts, certain transitions and, let's say the terrible word, certain compromises. There are pages of compromise in the lives of all great men and they are not pages of shame: they are pages of wisdom. Compromise is what matters, the rest is *allegria di naufragi*, tenacity.

Giolitti has a plan of his own: to curb fascist lawlessness, considered a passing phenomenon, by tethering it to the constitutional arch. Mussolini has a counterplan: to stir up disorder to show that only he can remedy it. Unleash the squadristi with one hand and then rein them in with the other. To do this, however, two battles must be waged on two different fronts, in which allies and enemies trade places. It takes a hypnotic spell that enables you to do and undo, to affirm an idea and its opposite, to consciously convince yourself of the truthfulness of something while unconsciously knowing it is false; above all you must be able to forget and forget that you have forgotten. In short, it requires the ability to doublethink. That way you are always in sync with the prevailing attitude.

The squadristi, it goes without saying, don't play his game. They are violently anti-parliamentary. They know they have set themselves apart from parliament and now they don't give a damn about having ten or fifty fascist deputies. They're right: fascism originated entirely as an anti-parliamentary movement. But the Duce reassures them: nothing has changed, the march continues unabated, with the same goal. Only now they will go to parliament to preach against parliament.

Mussolini's problems, however, do not end there. There are D'Annunzio's legionnaires to think about, who are anti-Giolitti. How will he get out of it? Easy: the fascists will ally with Giolitti but claim that his blocs are anti-Giolittian—as Mussolini himself wrote on April 26th. Furthermore, a few days after the vote the Duce will declare that Giolitti cannot insist on governing forever because he is old, and even outdated. Doublethinking, it always takes doublethinking.

With Giolitti at the top, moderate voters, in turn masters at doublethinking, are simultaneously reassured and horrified by fascist violence. You can't blame them, after all: on April 13th those blackshirted savages from the Pisan hills shot Carlo Cammeo, an activist in the teachers' union, in an elementary schoolyard, under the eyes of the little girls who, lined up two by two in their white smocks and pink ribbons, trusting and orderly, followed behind their teacher. A few days later, in the Arezzo area, Florentine squadristi, in retaliation for the killing of three comrades during a punitive raid, killed nine defenseless people after improvising a court in Foiano's town square: they made the communist peasants get on their knees, they interrogated them, then they shot them point-blank. Faced with this unprecedented savagery, Giolitti's moderates are abandoning him.

So here a second move is needed. Mussolini knows that public opinion, appalled, cannot be allowed to identify fascist violence with that of the "reds." Therefore, the "Scottish shower" tactic is called for. Turn up the heat with one hand and chill things down with the other: while the Founder of the fasci exalts the violent reprisals against socialist barbarism, the editor of *Il Popolo d'Italia* takes a stand against violence. Fascist violence, he writes on April 27th, is "chivalrous"; fascism has "a sense of bounds," namely, to make maximalist socialism toe the line, it has given Italy back "the notion of what is wisdom and the notion of what is folly." And the doublethinking goes on.

That's the beauty of violence, you see: it's poison and, at the same time, an antidote. In it, evil and its remedy are the same substance administered in different doses. After all, isn't it true that Pasteur vaccinated us against rabies by injecting spinal marrow from infected rabbits?

During the election campaign, Mussolini is seen very infrequently in the piazza. He holds a rally in Milan on May 3rd, just to mark the date by returning to the place where it all began. In Piazza Belgioioso, he has the satisfaction of speaking from the balcony of the private palace of the prince who two years earlier hadn't even wanted to receive him.

Then he holds a second rally in Verona and a third in Mortara. No others. He stops in Lomellina because, together with Tuscany, the province of Ferrara and that of Cremona, where Farinacci rules, it is the area in which the squads are widespread. Its leader is Cesare Forni, son of one of the richest tenant farmers in the region, a dissolute cocaine addict in his youth, later an artillery captain with seven medals for valor during the war. Tall, heavyset, blond, with perennial bags under his eyes, he is generous and choleric; over the Saturday and Sunday of the second weekend in April, Forni personally led the raids to wreak havoc on the Mutual Aid Society of Bigli and the socialist headquarters in Garlasco, Lomello, Tromello, San Giorgio, Valle Lomellina and Ottobiano. All destroyed in forty-eight hours.

Mussolini, however, seems more interested in another local legend about the anti-Bolshevist crusade: the Countess Giulia. Born into a poor family, blonde, well-endowed, with the full breasts of a healthy plebeian, Giulia Mattavelli married Count Cesare Carminati Brambilla, pale, lanky, eccentric, afflicted by a constant rictus at the corner of his mouth, a globetrotter and idler, apathetic and perverse, a cavalry officer and now a landowner. Together the two, having hired several armed men, terrorize the peasants of their fiefdom. On the towers of their manor—where Milanese squadristi sought by the police often hide out—they also mounted powerful spotlights that slash across the countryside at night. It seems that the countess personally takes part in the raids, mounted on her horse. It also seems that Giulia, Amazon warrior woman and whore, willingly gives herself as a reward to the most useful or the most violent men. It seems that the count, a soured, bored, cunning man, lets her do it, or uses her for his career.

Mussolini arrives in Mortara on Sunday, May 8, accompanied by his brother Arnaldo and Michele Bianchi, exactly one week from election day. It's not his first visit to the town of Pavia: he was there once before, in the spring of 1914, as editor of *Avanti!*, to inaugurate the Casa del Popolo now destroyed by his squadristi.

The Duce of fascism galvanizes the town hall piazza, teeming with blackshirts. He says he is moved by that reception. After leaving the stage, he expresses his intention to return to Milan immediately following the banquet in his honor. The celebrations culminate with the presentation of a medal. Conferring it is the

Countess Brambilla. Then and there, Benito Mussolini decides to stay for the night-long "Italian Tricolor Veglione," as well. They dance. Then the two leave the party for the Albergo dei Tre Re, room number 5.

The following day word has it in Mortara that the maid found the room a wreck. Traces of sex everywhere. It seems that there was even a bloodstain.

The party ticket is not open to discussion, we vote. Even though, glancing through the list of names, the critical spirit, awakening likes and dislikes, dissociates itself. But the bloc is intended to join forces . . . The list, as such, is a "position" from which we must fight the common socialist enemy.

"The Candidates of the Bloc," *Corriere della Sera*, April 23, 1921

Liberals cannot, without completely committing suicide as a party, be morally mixed up with those [like the fascists] who affirm, exalt and practice violence as a principle of life and social struggle.

"To the Liberals," *La Stampa*, April 29, 1921

We are not part of the mob of irritated spinsters and virgins who are always afraid of losing their virginity (privilege) (while, deep inside, they crave it!); we fascists are not part of those who have a constant fear of being contaminated, of being cheapened, of tarnishing, even if only a touch, their splendid, onanistic *isolation*.

Benito Mussolini, speech at the Milan fascio assembly to justify the alliance with the liberals, April 8, 1921

Here Italy's good name is at stake and therefore no weakness can be tolerated. What is happening in Bolzano is unworthy of a civilized country . . . Suppression is required to set an example. All those who took part in the heinous action must be arrested.

Giovanni Giolitti, ally of the fascists,
telegram to the chief commissioner of Bolzano
after a raid by fascist squads,
April 27, 1921

ITALO BALBO

APRIL–MAY 1921

In the photographs that begin to immortalize fascist actions in the spring of 1921, Italo Balbo is the only one who is laughing. Mussolini always displays his already famous scowling, wide-eyed, magnetic look, the other leaders assume serious martial poses, while Italo Balbo shows his teeth. And it's not always a wicked grin. Sometimes it is a young, benign smile, head slightly thrown back, as in the shot depicting Ferrara's squads posing in front of the Basilica of San Marco during an expedition to Venice to storm the workers' district of Castello, their clubs more or less hidden under the bourgeois overcoats. The atmosphere in which these cruel excursionists gravitate is tempestuous, compelling, maybe even deadly but, all in all, carefree: *Venice, spring 1921—As if there were no tomorrow*: this could be the caption of the souvenir photo taken among the pigeons in Piazza San Marco. Before nightfall someone will die a violent death along Salizada San Francesco, nevertheless you almost feel like joining the outing.

This carefree ferocity cannot be deduced from Balbo's legend. Whether spontaneous or deliberately nurtured, what remains is Balbo's penchant for joking around, the pranks of an inveterate naughty boy. When prefect Mori forbids the use of walking sticks, the Ferrarese squadristi resort to dried cod gripped by the tail as cudgels, delighted to spread salt on the wounds. Balbo, in any case, urges them to use their clubs "with flair." Which means bashing both sides of the mouth, both mandibular joints, in order to fracture the jaws. In mid-April, the men of the "Celibano" squad even take the train to go and destroy the league of Voltana, near Ravenna. While everything burns, the engineer waits for them. When the roof collapses, they get back in the compartment and give the signal to leave. The train arrives in Ferrara only half an hour late.

It is a carefree yet systematic and disciplined ferocity, however. The actions always adopt a military tactic that bases the superiority of firepower on force concentration and movement. Their planning is scientific, rigorous, lethal. The outcome of the clash is left neither to chance, to the courage of the combatants, or to the whim of the divinities of battle. From this point on they almost never run the risk of defeat. The spring countryside, from a strategic angle, deploys a war of advancement. The schedule of its progress is laid out in forced marches.

On April 8th, as soon as the chambers are dissolved, the employment bureau in Jolanda is set on fire and the administration is forced to resign. Two days later, when squadrista Arturo Breviglieri is killed during a raid in Pontelagoscuro, his comrades militarily occupy the town, set fire to the Chamber of Labor and force the socialists to kiss the corpse's hands. On April 11th, Balbo's men attack Granzette's Chamber of Labor in the Polesine and kill the treasurer Luigi Masin at home, in front of his family. On the 14th, about a hundred squadristi hold Ferrara under siege for two days, storming the Casa del Popolo and the railwaymen's association. On the 15th, in Roncodigà, during a rally of league members who switched over to the fascist union, Umberto Donati proposes a return to the Chamber of Labor. He is killed on the spot. And it goes on like that, demolishing the leagues of Bondeno, Gaibanella, Ostellato and still others. In a few months, 9 chambers of labor, a cooperative and 19 peasant leagues are obliterated in Ferrara. The Rovigo Chamber of Labor, in which Matteotti was shaped, its material possessions already destroyed several times, permanently ceases to exist. It is dissolved.

The socialist collapse is vertical. *La scintilla*, Ferrara's socialist newspaper proclaims, "Do you gentlemen of the fascio and of the Agraria think that your triumphs achieved by virtue of such methods will have a reliable stability? It is childishly naive to believe that such a vast political edifice can collapse in an instant under the blow of a club or the threat of a revolver." Yet that is what happens. The juveniles are incessant.

In many places the peasant masses now tear up the red flags and go over to the fascist unions; the many who nonetheless resist, in desperation, invite still more shootings and destruction; their animals are killed and their vines uprooted. Matteotti continues to fight, preaching evangelical docility:

"Stay in your homes; do not react to provocations. Even silence, even cowardice is sometimes heroic."

All the other leaders of the peasant movement are stunned to witness the speed and extent of the collapse. A sort of psychic paralysis turns them to stone, a cry of panic chills the countryside, humiliating surrenders are too copious to count.

The socialists hand over their flags without a fight, they agree to trample them in public ceremonies, they openly capitulate. In Codrea, for example, they vote to resist, but then the scores of squadristi present at the proletarian meeting beat up the secretary in front of the assembly. The peasants join the fascio right then and there.

Communist leader Angelo Tasca, who with Gramsci and Togliatti in Livorno recently decided to split from the Socialist Party and who personally witnessed some of these devastating acts, tries to explain the unexplainable. The fascists—he writes—are almost all former Arditi or ex-soldiers, led by officers; they are frequently transferred, as at the front, and can live anywhere. Workers, on the other hand, are bound to their land, where they have achieved admirable gains over the course of lengthy struggles. This situation leaves the enemy with all the advantage: that of the offensive over the defensive, that of a war of movement over a war of position, that of unpunished lawlessness over scrupulous legality, that of easy destruction over laborious construction, that of those who have nothing to lose over those who have everything to lose.

The Case del popolo (community centres) are the result of three generations of sacrifices, the workers love these social centres and instinctively hesitate to use them as if they were a simple instrument of war. When flames devour them, their hearts are torn, fraught with despair, while the assailants, breezy, lighthearted, insolent, laugh. In the struggle between the truck and the Casa del Popolo, the former will always win. The industrious anthill will always be at the mercy of the legion.

And yet, there is something mysterious about this sudden collapse. The 63 municipalities in the province of Rovigo, all in the hands of the socialists, are occupied one after the other without it ever occurring to them to join forces in order to oppose the aggressor. The Socialist Party, which had total control of the province, loses it in just one winter. Shrouded in this mystery, they go to vote on May 15th.

Balbo laughs. They say that one of the tricks he's mastered is the castor oil routine. You seize a diehard socialist, ram a funnel down his throat, and force him to drink a quart of laxative. Then you tie him to the hood of a car and drive him through town while he farts and toots and shits himself. A low-cost scheme, with no bloodshed, no threat of arrests. Impossible not to laugh.

Then too, the tragicomic has other advantages. It prevents the victim from becoming a martyr because disgrace discourages sympathy: you can't devote a cult to a man who shits himself.

Finally, ridicule has great educational value. And as a bonus, it lasts a long time, it shapes the character. Shit, more so than blood, extends its shadow over the future of a nation. The idea of revenge, if soiled with excrement, is handed down for decades, from generation to generation. For the purgative's shame, witnessed or experienced, to be wiped clean, requires nothing short of an apocalypse.

It is essential that we see to the regular, military formation of our forces as soon as possible. So everyone should get to work, sparing no effort. By next September Ferrara's fascist regiments' ranks must be in magnificent order. Only with a disciplined army will we achieve decisive victory . . . The most appropriate individuals to command the action squads are former officers, particularly from the Arditi and the infantry . . . Gunners must be familiar with Austrian machine guns and with Fiat, Lewis and S. Etienne machine guns and automatic pistols . . .

Federation of Ferrarese fasci, confidential circular n. 508,
sent by Italo Balbo to all political secretaries,
July 1921

Stay in your homes; do not react to provocations. Even silence, even cowardice is sometimes heroic.

Appeal of Giacomo Matteotti to Po Valley peasants,
in *Critica Sociale*, no. 7, 1921

BENITO MUSSOLINI

MILAN, MAY 16, 1921

VENUS, THE "TERRESTRIAL" planet, our twin planet, so similar to Earth in size and mass, the brightest celestial body in the night sky apart from the Moon, can only be seen shining for a few hours, and only after sunset or before dawn when the fierce solar brilliance—which gives it light while at the same time denying it, keeping it on the short chain of its own strict orbit—grows faint. This is what normally happens. Today, however, the whitish yellow of the evening star has begun to shine very brightly on the horizon to the west, at least two hours before vesper.

The diurnal luminescence of Venus is a rare phenomenon, almost as infrequent as a solar eclipse. As several editors explained to the notoriously superstitious editor of *Il Popolo d'Italia*, observing it from his office on Via Lovanio, the ecliptic on the horizon is the primary factor for Venus' visibility. It seems that in the northern hemisphere the inclination is greatest at sunset during the spring equinox. But spring has long since arrived, and more so than in science, he believes in destiny. He therefore stood at the window of his new office for at least an hour, contemplating the star glimmering in a cloudless sky still illuminated by a low sun. Venus, the evening star, has been known since ancient times as the "morning star." It is a sign of good luck. There is no doubt. Benito Mussolini's horoscope is auspicious.

The data coming from the Ministry of the Interior is incontrovertible. The socialists are losing, but less badly than expected: they remain the leading party with 25 percent of the votes, and most of what they are losing is being gained by the communists, at 3 percent, or the republicans, climbing to 2 percent. The populists hold on at 20 percent and the parties of the national bloc are expanding, but less than Giolitti had hoped: democrats, liberals, nationalists and their minor allies, when all the votes are added up, will barely reach 47 percent. There can therefore be no doubt. The winners of these May 1921 elections are the fascists.

After negotiating with Giolitti's emissaries to the point of exhaustion, slogging away for a month like a flunky, Cesarino Rossi had managed to get eighty fascist candidates on the national lists. At least forty of these will go to parliament, elected almost everywhere at the top of the electoral ticket. They are still few, they are nothing compared to the hundreds of socialists or liberals, but in many cases they are young men under thirty, commanders of squads armed to the teeth, something totally new, a literally disruptive force, marking the complete failure of Giolitti's old tricks.

The election campaign ended, as it had begun, in a whirlwind of violence, with the blood of new victims and the blaze of fires. On election day alone there were deadly clashes in Biella, Novara, Vigevano, Mantua, Crema, Padua, Lecce, Foggia, and Syracuse: 29 dead and 104 wounded in one day. Nevertheless, and because of this, votes poured in from tens of thousands of new sympathizers seduced by that blood, by the cohesive phalanxes of new small landowners willing to shed it, and the urns purified and redeemed it.

Giolitti, the old fox, the rainmaker, the old whore, wanted to tame them and instead he legalized them; he wanted to use them to precipitate the collapse of socialists crushed by their clubs in order to strengthen his own government; instead he will have an ungovernable parliament split into incompatible parties, into groups torn apart internally by hostile, voracious factions. In short, the same old shit, deeper and deeper, more and more shit.

The crisis of democracy is now entering its most acute phase, parliamentary decline is irreversible, a fixed star, low on the horizon of the equinox sky. In its twilight, the young, small, robust Fascist

Party will begin its parliamentary life with the XXVI legislature, the last of the decline, preparing to fight alone for the XXVII assembly that will be the first fascist legislature.

And then there is his personal triumph. Benito Mussolini was at the top of the list in Milan with 197,000 votes, and in Bologna with 173,000 votes. Third among the top ten elected at the national level!

The success is such that, upon receiving the news, in a very rare surge of conjugal fervor, the winner even embraced his wife Rachele, then pinned her to the kitchen door and, looking into her eyes as he never does, forewarned her with emotion: "Rachele, remember that this will be one of the best periods of our lives." The woman, frightened by the prophecy of an unfamiliar joy, not knowing how to accept it into her plebeian home, lowered her eyes to the ocher and black particle floor.

Now, however, left alone, Benito Mussolini moves away from the window, leaves the evening star to its sunset, and paces around the room, filling it with his euphoria. The ghosts to be dispelled are many: the puppet of his corpse drowned in the canal by the miserable 4,000 votes of 1919, the traitor driven out like a rabid dog by his comrades in 1914, the angry emigrant who slept under bridges in Switzerland in 1908, the schoolteacher who walked a mile from town, barefoot on the railway tracks, with his shoes slung over his shoulder so as not to wear out the soles; reverberating in the very rare diurnal luminescence of Venus there is even the specter of the child who, many years ago in the Romagna countryside, on a clear sunny morning—the grapevines yellow and the vats ready for harvest—hears the bell tolling in the September air for his dead grandmother.

"Deputy" Mussolini. His hour is approaching, the hour for all of them, the hour for revenge. He won with the money of the agrarians who starved his childhood, under the aegis of Giolitti, alongside the enemies of his people, of his youth. Yet he won.

For a moment he regards his new elegant office with mistrust, with rancor. But Sarfatti's voice is quick to whisper in his ear: "We must be men, youth sows, manhood reaps."

By now, in any case, he is going on forty, he is almost bald, before long he won't have a hair on his head anymore, sowing has its time, a short time. We must reap, we must conclude, we must win. And then go back and win again because the world has no mercy for winners.

Deputy Mussolini no longer holds back his insolent joy. He has become the man he despised as a boy.

BENITO MUSSOLINI

ROME, JUNE 21, 1921
PARLIAMENT OF ITALY

DEPUTY MUSSOLINI TOOK a seat on the last bench on the right, where no one before him had dared sit. Isolated from all the others, way up there—solitary because he is always waiting to be ambushed and vice versa—to those looking at him from below and from the benches of the left he looks like a vulture hunched on his aerie. Today the carrion-feeding bird, its head featherless, will have to give his first parliamentary speech.

He willingly claimed the lofty perch spurned by all. After a brief, awkward moment of irritation when he first entered the Montecitorio chamber and, with almost infantile astonishment, realized that the benches of the left, where he had instinctively headed, were all occupied by the contempt of his former socialist friends and those of the right by the arrogance of his despised new Giolitti friends, he relished climbing up to the extreme bastions.

He doesn't like parliament, however. He confided to a journalist that to him the chamber seems "gray in things and people." When they speak, they do the opposite of what normality would require: they speak from the bottom up, whereas it should be the reverse. The incorrect vertical organization causes everything to deteriorate into useless chatter. Then too the corridors . . . all those whispers of lost steps, all those colleagues who address him informally, who treat him with saccharine familiarity, even touch him—claps on the shoulder, prolonged handshakes—all those disgusting bourgeois who by day line up, panting and breathless, to follow fascism, and in the evening, in their living rooms, report to the horrified and excited ladies that they have met the fascists, those savage cannibals, those exotic animals that Giolitti, the old explorer of the parliamentary jungles, promised to tame in his circus.

But Benito Mussolini is determined to remain an unknown beast. In Rome, in the first weeks of his term, he's made very few personal acquaintances. No friends. You can't have friends and he doesn't want any. That's why he appointed Alessandro Chiavolini as his personal secretary: Chiavolini the traitor, his only editor who refused to sign the letter of solidarity in the darkest moments, after the disastrous electoral defeat of 1919, when the editor-in-chief of *Il Popolo d'Italia* was put on trial by the jury of Lombard journalists. No, no friendships, only submission. The traitor Chiavolini offers more guarantees than a false friend.

"I do not mind, honorable colleagues, starting my speech from the benches of the extreme right, where, in the days when the trafficking of the triumphant socialist beast had a very brisk trade, no one dared sit anymore. I immediately declare to you that in my speech I will support reactionary propositions. Mine will be an antidemocratic and anti-socialist speech." A show of approval from the right. "And, when I say anti-socialist, I mean anti-Giolittian." General hilarity.

The deputies are not surprised by the jab that Mussolini has made right off the bat at Giolitti, his chief electoral ally. For that matter, the Founder of the fasci, in a bombshell interview in *Il Giornale d'Italia* the day after the elections, had already denounced the alliance with Giolitti, frustrating any hope of the old schemer being able to use him for his parliamentary games. It had immediately been clear that the fascists would promptly bring the methods of their fight into Montecitorio's chamber and would have no regard for anyone, much less for Giolitti whose plan to tame him had failed. From now on they'd be playing with a new deck of cards. Mussolini spurned the kitty and staked on the bank. In liberal and industrial political circles, influential and experienced men were kicking themselves.

Mussolini devotes the initial thirty minutes of his first parliamentary speech to a harsh indictment against Giolitti's foreign policy. In a crescendo of nationalistic fury, he accuses him of acquiescence, of forsaking the greatness for which Italy is destined. He reproaches Giolitti's failure to safeguard the Italian presence, *italianità*, on the eastern borders, the sacrifice of Montenegro's independence. Nothing escapes this orbital view of the world, not even a reference to the issue of troublesome interreligious coexistence in Palestine. Giolitti is already disposed of, his government has just been born and yet—as everyone now knows—it has only a few days to live.

Then the speaker descends into the hall, so that his voice can be heard better, and moves on to a second panorama, with a shorter range. He examines, one after the other, all the parliamentary forces sitting in the hemicycle. First, the communists. Communism is a doctrine that arises in times of poverty and despair, a neospiritualistic philosophy that, like oysters, is great on the palate but then hard to digest. Mussolini ridicules them, mocks them but then paternalistically draws them into a theatrical sense of guilt: "I know the communists. I know them because some of them are my children . . . in a spiritual sense, mind you." General hilarity, both from the right and from the left. When it comes to the socialists, the stick and carrot tactic is accentuated. First Mussolini nails them to their responsibilities, then he makes a distinction—between the labor movement and the political party, between party leaders and union representatives—and lastly he makes promises: "Listen carefully to what I tell you. When you introduce a bill for an eight-hour working day, we fascists will vote for it." Finally, it's the populists' turn, those who represent the Catholic masses. He tosses them a carrot too: "The Latin and imperial tradition of Rome is represented today by Catholicism . . . You can't be in Rome without a universal idea and the only universal idea that exists today in Rome is that which radiates from the Vatican."

In short, stick and carrot for everyone. In the end, above all, and as usual, violence. Here too, first the threat, then the promise. If the socialists persist on that terrain, they will be beaten on that terrain. Accept it: the world is moving to the right, not to the left, the history of capitalism is just beginning. If they disarm conceptually, the fascists will disarm as well. Violence is not a sport. The sad chapter of the civil war can come to an end. We are human and nothing that is human is foreign to us. That's all I have to say.

The applause from the right is vigorous and persistent, the congratulations numerous, the comments extensive.

Now that he has made it to parliament, however, the Founder of the fasci must clean up at home. His child has bastard origins, she was born from the crucible of violence, from the contractions of a promiscuous affair. The bourgeoisie is beginning to tire: while at first it used the fascists as a defense against violence, it will soon repudiate them as a new form of violence. The electoral success must be made to bear fruit, and Italy is a country where revolutions never follow revolutionary methods.

Fascism, between capitalism and communism, must be the broker separating two litigants. The one that benefits. It must remain nimble to allow for all kinds of about-faces, alliances, maneuvers, twists and somersaults. Fascism is not one of the two great warring classes, it is the intermediary stratum, the profound travail of a psychological crisis of insecurity on the part of the petit bourgeois who is enraged because he fears he is losing everything, while not yet having enough, the greengrocer who feels caught between the anvil of big capital and the hammer of communism, who no longer knows what his place in the world is, and doubting that he has one, even goes so far as to doubt his own existence. A new all-inclusive party of the world's middle masses is needed, set within a reassuring parliamentary perspective. The petite bourgeoisie needs solace, the country needs peace, they must be given to them both.

The throne has been empty for too long, violence never comes without its dark shadow, the sword must be placed back in its sheath. Politicians, not soldiers, will be at the helm of fascism, and the head table is where I will sit. Now we must call back the silent barking of the dogs of war.

AMERIGO DÙMINI

SARZANA, JULY 21, 1921

IT SEEMS THIS is how it went.

It was one o'clock in the morning and Amerigo Dùmini was leaning against a seaside cabana with Banchelli, the "Mago," at the beach of Avenza on the Massa Carrara coast, smoking in silence. There was a nearly full moon high in the western sky, the medieval tower on the mouth of the river illuminated in the luminous night, and in the background, towards the east, the crown of the Apuan Alps encircling the horizon. The rally was going well. About five hundred fascists were assembling on the sandy shore, having arrived by train, bus or makeshift transports from Pisa, Florence, Viareggio, Prato, Pescia and other nearby villages. A fair number were beginning to gather but not as many as they had hoped. At least half of the arrivals, moreover, were sixteen- or eighteen-year-old boys, who'd jumped into the adventure alongside the adults; they took everything literally, cursing the communists under their breath, and, even at that time of night, intoned their songs in the shadow of the pennants with the fervor of those destined to die.

Two of Renato Ricci's men came to let them know that, according to some rumors, the entire countryside around Sarzana was on the alert: the peasants were being equipped with revolvers, hunting rifles, and rudimentary bombs prepared by anarchist miners of the Apuan Alps, tough men who all their lives and for nameless generations had been used to shattering marble with dynamite.

In Sarzana they had been on the brink of war for months and

on edge for days. They had been at loggerheads with the fascists forever. Each time the peasants saw a suspicious face, word went around and armed men poured into the streets. Renato Ricci, the fascist leader of the area, a man who had subdued almost the entire Carrara region by running around terrorizing people, wearing his brigand's fez, had ended up in jail in Sarzana in yet another failed attempt to storm the "reds'" stronghold. The carabinieri had arrested him along with his wayward squadristi, surrounding him on the dry bed of the Magra among the willows on the banks. So they had to go and free him. That was why Dùmini's Florentine squadristi were spending the night on the beach of Avenza. It was time to do away with those people once and for all.

There was no plan of operations, everything proceeded ad hoc, many of the squadristi didn't even know each other. They set off along the sea illuminated by the full moon. Sluggish, sleepy, in single file, straggling as much as ten yards apart like a bunch of drunks; once they left the coast, they relied on the railroad, clambering up the path that runs along the escarpment, then following the tracks. A night train, seeing them in the way, slowed down and stopped before setting off again. One tired fool, who must have hoped to get a ride, shot at it.

Announced by that reckless gunshot, the avengers in black shirts reached the Sarzana station at 5:30 a.m., half an hour past the summer sunrise. The sun was already high above the marble quarries of the westernmost Alps, but the hostile city still seemed deserted, silent, surprised as it slept. Dùmini called muster, then ordered the caretaker to open the gate leading to the square. Facing the fascists who had come to wipe out the enemy's stronghold was a beautiful avenue lined with plane trees, named after Garibaldi, the hero of two worlds.

At the end of the avenue, however, a platoon of carabinieri was deployed in a single line. There couldn't have been more than fifteen of them and their machine guns had been left unguarded in the back of the parked vans. Fifteen against five hundred. And besides, the carabinieri had always been friends, the squadristi's accomplices on punitive raids. "Viva the carabinieri, viva the army, viva Italy!" the fascists shouted, as always.

At this point—it was now six in the morning—they encountered the second surprise of the day. Dùmini, who had come forward to talk terms, smiling politely, was confronted by two carabinieri, one in civilian clothes and one in uniform. Both decidedly hostile. The captain of the troops even held a leather whip in his gloved right hand.

Dùmini, coming straight to the point, dictated his conditions for the release of Renato Ricci and for retaliation against the communists. They were rejected as unacceptable.

"To us!" The fascists began advancing, disorderly, reckless, assured of victory and invincibility. The fifteen carabinieri were ordered to assume the position, knee on the ground, ready to use their bayonets and fire their weapons. Then, as always happens when rifles are leveled, a shot was fired. A carabiniere fell, and the barrage from his cohorts mowed down the front row of the bunched-up fascists. A burst of firing on both sides followed.

Career soldiers know that after the first furious volley between two groups of armed men there is always a mysterious moment of hesitation, sometimes due to running out of cartridges at the same time, sometimes to a sacred reluctance when faced with the epiphany of blood. At that instant the fascist leaders and Captain Jurgens of the royal carabinieri managed to stop the fire. They resumed parleying.

But by then the screams of the wounded were slashing the veil of dawn, bodies soaked the square's stones with hemorrhagic fluids, and the fascists, shocked by the unexpected resistance, were leaping over hedges, ditches and walls; they fled, scattering through the countryside by the hundreds. Captain Jurgens' hopeless shouts followed them, practically begging them to come back.

That's when the third surprise of that turbulent day occurred: crouched among the brambles, the "reds" were waiting for them. Bands of peasants armed with pitchforks, hatchets and throat-slitters rounded up the runaway band of avengers who had come to set fire to their houses and who were now running away, terrified. They dragged them behind a thresher, a barn or a hedge and slaughtered them with their cutters, the way you slaughter a pig. Some corpses were left in the sun, others hanged from trees.

Then the firing stopped. Reinforcement troops—royal guards who had come running at the sound of the first shots—scoured the countryside in search of the dead. What was left of the fascist column had taken refuge inside the station building. Many of the boys were weeping, huddled under the benches, crying for help.

Dùmini, meanwhile, had obtained Ricci's release from prison. The surviving squadristi who were supposed to storm Sarzana were escorted to a special train that would take them back to where they had come from. Some of their companions' bodies would lie there for days, mangled, food for the animals living in caves in the woods scattered along the slopes of the nearby mountains.

"We have built our fortunes on catafalques. We must now be careful that such good fortune does not fall to our adversaries."

The Duce of fascism whispers it to Cesare Rossi before entering the hall where he convened the national council as soon as word of the Sarzana massacre reached Rome. It is the night of July 21, a sultry night. Rather than being appalled by the reports of death, Mussolini seems more upset by what his superstitious inclination interprets as the ominous omen of another death, less certain but more terrible. "Fascism cannot die" are his words before addressing the assembly.

His plan to save fascism from the lethal consequences of its own violence is, at the same time, simple and delirious: to make peace with the socialists. The name of the plan is the "pacification pact." The provincial squadristi have boycotted him since the beginning of July. On the 12th, in Milan, the fascist national council, led by Farinacci and Grandi, had defied Mussolini, voting against any possibility of pacification. Meanwhile, 1,500 squadristi have militarily occupied Treviso, setting fire to the headquarters of Catholics, populists and republicans.

But now the situation has changed. Giolitti has fallen. He was succeeded by Ivanoe Bonomi, the socialist reformist whom Mussolini himself had expelled from the party in 1912, and Bonomi, despite his socialist origins, managed to bring the Catholics of the Populist Party into his government. If Bonomi were able to bring other moderate socialists on board as well, they would together form a united front against the fascists and it would be the end for them. The isolation must be broken. If they don't want to commit suicide, they must go back to being principled, they must stop the work of "extermination." Otherwise Bonomi, having liquidated the maximalist socialists with fascist violence, and allied with the moderates, would soon deal him a knockout punch.

Sarzana demonstrated that the police already bowed to a new byword. And it also demonstrated something else: if 500 men were routed by 15 carabinieri, it meant that the ferocity of the squads, accustomed to raging against unarmed, disorganized enemies with the complicity of the authorities, would vanish at the first shot fired by a trained army.

"A noose of hatred is tightening around fascism. We must break it. Italy's piazzas must not turn into festive slaughterhouses. The country needs peace. We must distinguish between our youthful fanatics fired by anti-socialist hatred, insofar as socialism denies the nation's sacred values, and the paymasters of the various Agrarias whose only aim is to suppress the workers' leagues and union gains. The nation came to us when our movement was announced as the sunset of a tyranny; the nation would repudiate us if we assumed the aspect of a new tyranny."

The members of the central committee listen in silence to Mussolini's directives to implement a precipitous backtracking: the cessation of all individual violence, the prohibition of any punitive raids, an examination of the members' criminal records, the removal of newly enrolled fascists from positions of command, investigation into those responsible for harmful actions.

Faced with these proposals, an argument erupts. It lasts until dawn, especially bitter on the part of the provincial leaders—Farinacci, Tamburini, Forni, Perrone Compagni, Balbo, Grandi—who are determined to oppose any pacification with the "reds."

At the end of the meeting, the Duce takes Cesare Rossi aside and orders him to start negotiations with the socialists.

"There will be no schisms. We are an army, not a swarm. And I command this army . . ."

Today, after many contradictions, Mussolini threatens to destroy fascism if fascism does not correct itself.

It is a utopian dream. Fascism will destroy its duce, and this man who has betrayed the socialists, the revolutionary interventionists, the Fiumani and the fascists of the first hour, will throw himself at another party or group with the same indifference, tenaciously starting a new contrary campaign, opposite to what he has done so far.

Will he find other deluded dreamers to follow him, or will the good sense of the Italian people end up triumphing, crying out "enough!"?

Ugo Dalbi, revolutionary unionist,
Sindacato Operaio, July 30, 1921

ITALO BALBO

GARDONE, AUGUST 18, 1921

GABRIELE D'ANNUNZIO HAS noticeably gained weight. Despite having dedicated a veritable rhetorical cult to a trim figure, and despite being completely abstemious, eighteen months of self-exile on Lake Garda have produced a drinker's belly under his sternum—taut, swollen, bulging—which no jacket can conceal. It is hard to look away from the Commander's abdomen, especially for those who, like Balbo, extremely thin, meet him for the first time after having venerated him from afar for years. He and Dino Grandi left Bologna for Gardone on the night of August 16, right after the meeting of the Po Valley fasci who had decided to rebel against the "pacification pact" put forth by Mussolini. They have come to offer the warrior poet the post of fascism's leader.

The Vate, photophobic, receives them on the morning of the 17th in the semi-darkness of heavy draperies and diffused lighting in his villa, a setting asphyxiated by tens of thousands of objects and books arranged in a precise, inscrutable play of symbolic references, as in a mausoleum consecrated to the memory of a living mummy. D'Annunzio speaks at length to the two exuberant twenty-year-olds about the new, definitive edition of *Notturno* that he is working on: his poetic meditation on death composed in 1916 during the months of his temporary blindness caused by a dramatic crash landing while flying to Trieste, which killed his friend and pilot, Giuseppe Garassini Garbarino. During the dissertation, he refers to himself as the "one-eyed seer," then stops speaking and listens to their proposal in silence. After that he offers them some exquisite hazelnut chocolates from a polychrome crystal vase, then asks for one night to reflect. As he says goodbye to them, he explains that, as always, before any decision, he will have to consult the stars.

The two ambassadors of fascist dissidence spend the night in a dreary lakeside pensione. Each of them passes the time as best he can. Grandi writes letters to the conspirators, Balbo goes after the maids.

The "pacification pact" that is supposed to decree the end of the conflict between "reds" and "blacks" had been signed on the evening of August 3 in the office of Chamber president Enrico De Nicola by a delegation of representatives of fascist and socialist parliamentary groups and by Baldesi, Galli and Caporali for the General Confederation of Labor. The first signature on the list was that of Benito Mussolini. In accordance with the pact, the two parties undertook to immediately cease all types of violence and to prosecute offenders. It seems that, after the signing, the socialist leaders refused to shake hands with the Founder of the fasci. While that may only be malicious gossip, the rejection by provincial fascist leaders is, in fact, a resounding certainty.

The fascists of Tuscany, Veneto and Emilia, convened at an assembly, denounced the pact sooner than forty-eight hours after the signing. Mussolini responded scornfully, labeling them "*rases*," the name for barbaric Ethiopian war chiefs. In an article in *Il Popolo d'Italia* he addressed them as a father who must not "spare the rod" to correct his wayward son. He lamented them as ignorant peasants, bound to petty parochialisms, incapable of emerging from their environments, of seeing and even of believing "the existence of a more vast, complex and formidable world."

Grandi replied to the Duce on August 6th, inaugurating open dissension with an article in which he asserted that the "father" was not Mussolini but D'Annunzio, and that, if anything, genuine fascism was born in Bologna, with the Palazzo d'Accursio massacre, not in Milan. Then it was Balbo's turn to attack the Duce, without being diplomatic about it. The struggle between fascism and socialism—Balbo wrote—will only be resolved with the eradication of one of the two. That's the reality, all the rest is "infantile fantasies, womanish sentimentality."

Mussolini, backed by Cesare Rossi, replied that Emilia's fascism, slave to the agrarians, was no longer fascism. He threatened to drive them out or even to leave himself.

Mussolini's plan, as always, was astute and, as always, was spoken with forked tongue. If it were to succeed, the image of a "respectable" fascism would prevail and he, welcomed with open arms by the liberals, would earn a ministry. If it failed, he would still be credited as the only reasonable fascist in that gang of savage rases in the provinces. In short, Mussolini had everything to gain from those shams.

Whereas they have everything to lose. Pacification, for people like Balbo and Grandi, means a certain, swift end, being sentenced to a limbo of obscurity, with no action, no history for lack of light and no light for lack of history. And they are willing to give their life, but not to throw it away.

And so they'd come to the Bologna assembly on August 16th, where six hundred fasci of Emilia Romagna renounced the Duce, proclaiming that, as long as that state of affairs lasted, they would not lay down their weapons of violence. Then they went to offer the Vate the leadership of the movement.

D'Annunzio's response, however, is long in coming. Balbo and Grandi are left to rot for almost two days in that lakeside limbo of moribund pensioners clinging to their last breath with bridge games and spa treatments. On August 18th, late in the morning, after respecting the poet's rest until nearly noon, the two pilgrims return to the villa of Cargnacco. D'Annunzio does not receive them. He sends his servant to say that they must wait a little longer still: the night was murky, Diana herself did not appear, perhaps "the stars are not propitious."

Balbo and Grandi, scorned and furious, can only go back to where they came from or, maybe, head for Milan. But in town, meanwhile, the paperboys are shouting the news of the day: Mussolini has resigned from the fascio central committee.

"The game is now over. Those who lost must leave. And I am stepping down from the top ranks. I remain, and hope I can remain, a simple follower of the Milanese fascio," the Duce of fascism wrote today in *Il Popolo d'Italia*.

Local fascists are decidedly opposed to pacification, which they consider ruinous to the development of their agricultural program. Socialists, on the other hand, while willingly agreeing to the idea of pacification, do not have much faith . . . Communists and anarchists are against it. Populists look favorably upon it, but do not demonstrate that concretely. Liberals and radicals remain out of it. The press, cowed by the fasci, doesn't dare pronounce itself.

Telegram from prefect Cesare Mori
of Bologna to the ministry,
July 12, 1921

Dissent, discomfort and sometimes repugnance for certain acts that offend all our sentiments as free men—for example, my friends, have you ever stopped to think about what's sacred about those people's houses with all their possessions and attachments that our followers in some areas of the Po Valley have no qualms about burning simply because they are inhabited by adversaries?

Cesare Rossi, letter of resignation
as deputy secretary of the fasci,
August 21, 1921

If it is necessary to wield powerful hammers, to hasten the ruin of this fascism, I will adapt to the disagreeable necessity. Fascism is no longer liberation but tyranny; no longer the nation's protector but the defender of the private interests of the most opaque, deaf, despicable castes that exist in Italy; a fascism that assumes these features may still be fascism, but it is no longer that for which in the grim years—with our numbers few—we faced the anger and gunfire of the masses, it is no longer the fascism that was conceived by me.

Benito Mussolini, "The Cradle and the Remains,"
Il Popolo d'Italia, August 7, 1921

He who has betrayed, will betray.

Anti-Mussolini graffiti that
appeared on the walls of Bologna,
August 1921

BENITO MUSSOLINI

MILAN, SEPTEMBER 28, 1921

THE ACE THE rases have up their sleeve is their narrow-minded vision, an unparalleled advantage when it comes to living one's life. Old local grudges, Sunday trysts, a diamond ring for the mistress, a sports car parked in front of the tavern. The petty bosses in the provinces get by on restricted news, they gauge eras by the tape measure of the present and so all of life becomes chronic, reduced to a long-term incurable disease. As a journalist by trade, he is well aware that news always consists of crime or gossip: amours and car accidents, tawdry tales of infidelity or random stabbings. Everything is polarized to the extremes, it all ends up with a woman on her back or a back that's broken. That's all there is, the world reported by the columnist is always merely a "news brief."

For example, look at the revolting spectacle of these merchants, shopkeepers, landowners, retail profiteers, this ineffectual old bourgeoisie that would sell their mothers to avoid giving up their privileges, watch them join the fascists, display the flags and shout "Long live the king, viva Italy" in the same nasal voice with which they shouted "Viva the Republic!" during the days of "red week." Look at this inert, leaden, opaque mass, these men without loyalties and ideals, ready for any and all betrayals, watch them prevail.

But when it comes to the lives of commoners it's a different story. When Benito Mussolini, son of a humble blacksmith of Dovia, resolves to live and recount every day of his life as if it were already part of History, then the panorama expands to include the world, the horizon explodes, and the dancer can no longer be distinguished from the dance.

On August 27th, the fasci national council in Florence rejected his resignation. The rases remain opposed to pacification but no one, not even Grandi, who puts on airs as a philosopher, would in the end dream of taking Mussolini's place on the national scene.

The only ones who suffered from it were Cesarino Rossi, dismissed from the central committee because he had remained loyal to Mussolini in Milan, and Leandro Arpinati, removed from Bologna as secretary because he had remained faithful in the province. At the moment, nothing can be done for them, but a lot can be done to take control of the movement again. What good is a leader if he only commands himself?

Throughout Italy Mussolini has been proclaimed irreplaceable and, at this point, the time has come for him to collect on this forced solidarity with the petty provincial bosses. But the rhetoric of a return to the origins doesn't work, a sprint forward is needed. A contempt for traditional political parties has been the polestar guiding the fascist movement since its origins, but to rule the country now a real party is needed. To govern the ungovernable, to harness the chaos, requires a party, a political body that restricts squad violence, an ecumenical doctrine that embraces the heretics of all the other doctrines, a party of anti-parties. The Fascist National Party. The life or death of fascism will be decided on this.

He proposed the transformation of the fascist movement into a party on September 7th at the parliamentary group's discussion. The proposal passed with a few "no" votes but it must now be approved by the national council, and then a congress will be required. It must be called quickly and it will all be decided there. Some of the rases, like Marsich in Venice, have already raised a cry at the betrayal of the original spirit, and in Bologna Dino Grandi and his followers, party or no party, have decided to vote against the pacification pact in any case. But these are mere skirmishes. The real threat to the idea of a party comes not from nostalgics like Marsich but from the army, and not from the king of Italy's gray-green army but from that of the black-shirted squadristi.

The rases did everything they possibly could to sink the pacification pact. And they succeeded. On September 12th, to mark the sixth centenary of Dante's death and the second anniversary of the Fiume occupation, Balbo and Grandi were able to assemble three thousand squadristi and have them march in columns, in military formation, on the road from Romagna to Ravenna. For the first time Balbo even managed to make everyone wear the black shirt as a uniform. Such a thing had never been seen before, a display of frightening force, the birth of an actual fascist army. Now the real dilemma is no longer between movement or party, the real dilemma is: form a party or create an army? The Gordian knot as usual must be cut: better a party but one that is capable of converting itself into an army, immediately transforming its members into soldiers ready to fight in the arena of violence. A convertible party, a party-militia. Something like that, certainly, has never been heard of either, but these are new, uncertain times, tomorrow is mysterious and unforeseeable.

Meanwhile he, the Duce, back to being a follower again, prepares. He prepares himself for the leap in the dark by raising the stakes. He establishes a Commission for Transformation, a school of political philosophy. A rather big word, undoubtedly, but to tame the murderers of the Sunday chronicles it is necessary to drag them to the assault on History. And, then, from the summit of the cliff, they must look at the nation's moral and political—Mediterranean and global—greatness. Several philosophical questions must now be answered: what is fascism's place vis-à-vis the state? Vis-à-vis the regime? Vis-à-vis capitalism? Vis-à-vis syndicalism, socialism, Catholicism, vis-à-vis the Church and its God? What is fascism's place in the cosmos?

Don't just stop at hating the porter whose head you bashed because he's a socialist, raise your eyes, look at History happening, look at the appalling famine raging in Russia, millions of people reduced to starvation; look at the uprisings against British rule promoted by that Gandhi. India's independence, he predicted in one of his articles, "is no longer a question of possibility; it's a matter of time."

After the rupture with the rases, Benito Mussolini reappears before the fascist masses in Modena, on September 28th, on the occasion of the funerals of no less than eight fascists.

What happened was this: two days earlier, several squadristi, in a fit of exuberance, raised their truncheons against a captain of the royal guards and the latter mowed them down like ripened wheat.

Now in Piazza Sant'Agostino, packed with soldiers, under a clear September sky with hundreds of pennants crowning the coffins, the Duce of fascism speaks to History as a statesman: "For these young men who have fallen, for the others who survive, Italy is neither the bourgeoisie nor the proletariat: nor is Italy the individual who governs or malgoverns the nation while hardly ever understanding its soul: Italy is a race, a history, a pride, a passion, Italy is a greatness of the past."

Fascism will lose all of its miserable glamour and all of its strength as soon as it ceases to be violent . . . Fascism will empty like an inverted wine-skin and will return to being the tiny minority movement it was in early 1919, but with the added memory of its violent acts, which is definitely not likely to open doors for it in the future. I could be wrong; but that is how things stand, as I see them.

Luigi Fabbri, militant anarchist,
La contro-rivoluzione preventiva,
Bologna, 1921

A drama has been imposed by the origins and by the course of the fascist crisis: either a party is formed or an army is created . . . In my opinion, the problem must be resolved in these terms: we must establish a party so solidly organized and disciplined, that it can, when necessary, be transformed into an army capable of fighting in the arena of violence . . . This topic should be placed on the agenda of the Rome congress.

Benito Mussolini, "Towards the Future,"
Il Popolo d'Italia, August 23, 1921

In September 1921, I made the first grandiose experiment: the mobilization of 3,000 men, the march on Ravenna. For the first time the squads of the two provinces—Ferrara and Bologna, with representatives from Reggio—were divided into two columns of 1,500 men, each column divided into companies and platoons.

Each captain with his ranks. Making its first big appearance as a military uniform on this occasion was the black shirt, which was ordinarily worn by workers in Romagna and which became the uniform of the soldier of the revolution.

Italo Balbo, *Diario*, 1922

BENITO MUSSOLINI

LIVORNO, OCTOBER 27, 1921

THE SPECTACLE IS truly bizarre. Two small male specters, surrounded by nothingness and about to return there very soon, have shut themselves up on the ground floor of a country house to evade the police; they have set up a makeshift piste with sand and resin and are now flexing their knees, no longer young, ten paces apart, waiting in that ridiculous stance, point-in-line and baricenter low, for the referee to call "*allez!*" so they can rush at one another, thrusting the opponent back into non-existence.

The duel that he is about to fight against Francesco Ciccotti Scozzese is Benito Mussolini's third one. The last one was fought in March 1915 in a villa at the Bicocca, outside Milan, against Claudio Treves, at the time his comrade in the Socialist Party and his predecessor as editor-in-chief of *Avanti!* Francesco Ciccotti is also a socialist deputy, he too a former comrade, but unlike Treves, of whom Mussolini has always been a rival, Ciccotti is an old friend of his. In 1912 Ciccotti, having moved to Romagna to replace Mussolini as editor of *La lotta di classe* (Mussolini had been jailed following the riots against the war in Libya), had enthusiastically supported his rise to the leadership of the party. Later, at the outbreak of the war, he had remained neutral, but even then he had never attacked the traitor who had blatantly crossed over to the interventionist front.

Yet Mussolini had sought out this duel against his old friend with the fury of practiced hatred. Ciccotti had already avoided the challenge of other fascist swordsmen, but Deputy Mussolini forced him into sending seconds with an article of vicious insults ("Franceschiello Scozzese is the most despicable being among those who pollute Italian public life"); he even presented his first and only Parliamentary Question against the Bonomi government's mobilization of the Italian police specifically to prevent the duel between the two parliamentarians. Not satisfied, despite being under surveillance, on the morning of October 28, followed by law enforcement vehicles, the duelist braved a blizzard on the Abetone pass, insane automotive maneuvers and twenty-four hours of travel to be able to attack his old friend.

Although he boasts of being an ace behind the steering wheel, Mussolini had himself driven by a demoniacal driver in order to escape the surveillance tail. Aldo Finzi, son of a wealthy industrial miller of Badia Polesine, a town not far from that of Matteotti, had been awarded a gold medal during the war as the aviator of the 87th squadron who flew over Vienna with D'Annunzio; the previous September he had debuted the racing car of a new Italian industry, the "500 Normale" of Genoa's Moto Guzzi, at the Italian Motorcycling Road Racing Championship. His love for speed is matched only by his contempt for the impoverished paupers who work his father's estates. It seems that Finzi achieves the culmination of both his great passions when, at a curve in the road, finding the way blocked by a flock of sheep, he steps on the gas, slaughtering the animals on which the peasants' survival hangs by a thin thread. With Finzi at the wheel, the car patrols in pursuit end up colliding with a hay wagon somewhere around Piacenza.

When they reach Livorno, the place designated for the duel, however, Mussolini and Finzi are informed that Ciccotti is under guard at the Palace Hotel. Most likely, knowing that he was being sought by the police, Ciccotti went down to that hotel in the center to identify himself, with the intention of once again dodging the duel. Actually, instead of being a coward, Francesco Ciccotti Scozzese has a heart condition.

To flush him out, Mussolini—for the one and only time in the series of duels—sends his driver, Aldo Finzi, to the Palace Hotel to pick up the man he's challenged. The deputy pursued with such determination is guilty of having used the columns of his newspaper, *Il Paese*, to accuse the fascist squads of being a criminal association. An offense shared, for that matter, with the Italian socialist press as a whole. But now Italian socialism has committed suicide and the affront cannot be forgiven. Had the socialists been victorious, they would not have forgiven him a thing, and Mussolini knows it. Franceschiello Ciccotti, therefore, cannot be pardoned. The drowning dog needs to be beaten.

Socialism is undoubtedly drowning. Only two weeks ago, socialist leaders, having passed up every revolutionary opportunity in the previous two years, again voted down any theoretical parliamentary collaboration with the Bonomi government on antifascist grounds. Their expulsion from the Communist International had already been decided in Moscow and in Italy as many as 100,000 militants failed to renew their membership after the insane split in Livorno: their isolation, now that they have rejected the responsibility of governing the country with their old comrade Bonomi, is therefore complete. From the columns of his newspaper Mussolini sighed with relief and exulted: "We, therefore, declare ourselves particularly satisfied. Fascism now has a playing field of vast possibilities before it."

At the moment, in a basement of Villa Perti, on the outskirts of Livorno, on an improvised piste made of sand and resin, Benito Mussolini has only Francesco Ciccotti Scozzese before him. And he smells and wants his blood. In order to prevent lethal consequences, Dr. Ambrogio Binda, his personal physician, disinfecting the swords, has concealed a pumice stone in an alcohol-soaked cloth hoping to dull the blades; Benito Mussolini angrily orders him to stop.

As soon as the referee gives the starting signal, the challenger lunges at his opponent. Ciccotti, suffering from a cardiac condition, falls back, breathing hard, retreating beyond the assigned limit.

The call to halt is almost immediate. Already at the first thrust, the socialist deputy's inferiority is obvious. On the second charge Ciccotti begins to wheeze. His heart doesn't pump enough blood and, if it does, it does so only at the cost of abnormal ventricular pressure. At the fourth and fifth assaults, the tip of Mussolini's sword pricks the body. First above the elbow, then about four inches below the armpit. The duel is suspended. Ciccotti is bleeding. Mussolini, furious, is adamant about continuing.

The subsequent rounds are brief, punctuated by the wounded man's rattles. Ciccotti is pale, out of breath, bathed in sweat, he has no more strength. Mussolini insults him, calls him a quivering weakling, insists on carrying on. Ninth, tenth, eleventh rounds. The palpitations increase. The doctors appeal to the seconds to stop the slaughter. Mussolini protests, rails. Twelfth, thirteenth, fourteenth assaults. Ciccotti is drained, in his atrial recesses the thrombotic risk skyrockets, the arterial hypertension mounts, fibrillation starts. The defeated man is taken to a bed in a room of the villa, he is given injections of strophanthin and camphor oil.

The winner, down in the basement, won't declare he's satisfied this time either. Pinned to a chair, impatience gnawing at him, arms folded and sword raised, his eyes fixed on the hilt, Mussolini is champing at the bit, foaming with rage; he rails that he's disgusted by the outcome of that miserable duel, he shouts that it must be resumed immediately, or else that same evening, or at most the next day, or, better yet, that it be concluded with pistols. The winner insists on taking revenge on the corpse of a cardiopath in retaliation for the millions of tongues that for years—he rants, beating his chest—have shouted "traitor" at him.

Dr. Binda, faced with that hysterical performance, looks to his medical expertise for some grounds to calm his patient's homicidal fury. So he takes Mussolini's pulse.

To his great surprise, the pulsation is regular, the values are normal, even low, no more than sixty beats per minute. The rate of a resting adult male, the heart of a man who, after a night's sleep, has just awakened. Dr. Binda can't help but smile beneath his French mustache.

ROME, NOVEMBER 7–9, 1921
TEATRO AUGUSTEO,
NATIONAL CONGRESS OF THE FASCI DI COMBATTIMENTO

THE HOUR HAS come for fascists who are unknown. Fascism must become depersonalized, the responsibilities must fall on the masses, removed from the shoulders of a single man. He is therefore ready to take a step back. Mussolini repeats it before making his entrance into the packed hall of the Auditorium Augusteo, his journalists faithfully record it and will report it in his personal propaganda organ: I am ready to step back. Tomorrow. Today, however, the theater of Rome, built on the spot where the mausoleum of Octavian Augustus, Rome's first emperor, once stood, and the site of jousts, hunts and bullfights over the centuries, seems to have returned to the ancient skirmishes.

In the hall of the Augusteo, the black sea of fascists hailing from all over Italy, wearing the spiked boots of an occupying force, has split into factions clustered in groups around their leaders. The "exterminating" divisions of the Po Valley, of Tuscany, of Umbria, of Veneto and of Apulia, which have rejected the peace proposed by the Founder, seem to hold the majority. Standing out above them all is Florence's "Disperata," one of the most infamous squads, radiant in its new uniform: a red lily on the chest, two flames at the shirt collar and, in particular, a white skull on a black field—the latter recalling the labels found on tincture of iodine bottles:

"Warning, do not ingest, lethal." The men of Tullio Tamburini, leader of the "Disperata," nicknamed "the great *bastonatore*" (basher), guard the entrance, check cards and hurl shouts of contempt at passersby: "*Me ne frego!* I don't give a damn is our motto, I don't give a damn about dying, I don't give a damn about Giolitti, and the sun of the future, the dark black banner tightening around us, I don't give a damn about the police chief, the prefect and even the king!"

Beyond the doorway there's squawking, whistling, clamoring, people chanting war songs. Yelling, pandemonium, excitement. The squabbling is intense, the applause heated, the whistling deafening. The atmosphere is electric, tense, full of the hysterical violence that attends a showdown. The presidential desks have been arranged in the orchestral pit, surrounded by the rases who are preparing to do battle.

The state of siege, however, is not just inside the theater. The fascist assembly feels besieged in turn. The first street clashes had already occurred with the arrival of the special trains: the Romans' reception was hostile almost everywhere, the squadristi from the provinces say they are appalled by the big city's frosty welcome. For them, Rome is the loathsome parliamentary capital of all the nation's vices, the prime target of fascist revolt, a filthy, listless, indolent, spineless city, which they tramp through at a measured pace—smelling the stink of rot, of ministerial apathy, of southern degeneracy, of widespread corruption—eyed contemptuously from head to toe by the eternal Capitoline plebs in an opaque, convex mirror, as if they, the cleansers of that fetid ruin, and not the Romans, were the barbarous rabble come to invade the sacred Basilica.

It is in this climate that Mussolini goes up to the rostrum. As he enters the theater, the applause is contained, whereas Dino Grandi, the leader of the dissidents, received an ovation. During the morning's work, anyone, from Pasella to De Vecchi, who proposed shelving the discussion on the pacification pact to calm people's nerves was greeted by booing. For hours, the assembly remained divided between supporters of Mussolini or Grandi.

But then the ras of Bologna took the floor and began by declaring that those opposing hecklers inspired him with a profound sense of sadness and melancholy.

The squadristi who erupt, cry out, seethe, don't know it, but the day before the two contenders had a secret meeting: Mussolini traded the pacification pact for the establishment of a Fascist Party. The agreement with Grandi is practically a done deal and peace with the socialists is buried. All that remains to be determined is how to constitute the party. The squadristi, therefore, shout themselves hoarse as though they were protagonists though they are mere walk-ons in a previously written play.

After Grandi has prepared the scene for him, Mussolini is also welcomed by a unanimous ovation. He lets it go on for a few seconds, hands on his hips, lips pursed, chin thrust forward as if to catch the scent of the coming times in the roar of applause. In the currents of the theater erected over the first emperor's tomb, the Duce of fascism sniffs out the dying animal and joins with the winner.

When he begins to speak, Benito Mussolini appears perfectly composed. Smiling, jovial, he sways on his legs, nods his head to what he himself has said and gestures little. Only from time to time does he free his arms and whirl them over his head, the words pouring out in torrents, then the furor subsides and the speaker, still nodding to himself, puts his hands back in his pockets.

The matter is simple: if the congress does not want to come to a vote on the pacification pact, he will not insist, but if on the other hand it must, he will engage the battle on all fronts. Either they vote or they don't vote but, if they vote, they must be relied on. Down to the last man. As usual, the speaker is at his best dealing out blandishments and threats. Then he jokes: he is a unitarian but he is not a Turati. Laughter, applause, shouts of "bravo!" He is unitarian as long as unity is possible. He refers the decision of whether to vote on the pact back to the congress. Let them decide. In his opinion, there are other vital questions facing fascism: the program and the foundation of a party.

An instant of stunned silence.

And here, with his usual acrobatic agility, Mussolini has overturned the prediction. The pacification pact that divided the assembly is already behind them, sacrificed. There is no longer any bone of contention, gone. All the squadristi have to do is agree to the party and, by magic, harmony will be restored among the comrades-in-arms.

At the end of the speech, Mussolini receives a second ovation. He hit the mark.

Grandi takes the floor again only to reiterate that the purpose of the congress is to unite all fascists in a solid bloc, then the young Romagnolo leaves the stage. At that instant the fascist crowd instinctively leaps to its feet in an interminable ovation, as if released from the oppressive weight of internal conflict and free to anticipate the imminent joys of violence turned outwards, against "others," rather than against themselves. Like the ocean that returns to the river, the incessant applause seems to propel Dino Grandi back to the source and he knows it. He makes his way through a small group of colleagues and heads towards Mussolini, already standing at the presidential desk. He throws his arms around his neck.

The congress attendees' enthusiasm then quiets down: everyone is standing, in the galleries, in the orchestra, in the tiers. The kiss between the fellow comrades is infectious, everyone lines up to hug and kiss Mussolini. A huge man hoists him up to the presidency table. His name is Italo Capanni, he is the man who shot Spartaco Lavagnini in the face, point-blank and in cold blood, in Florence, then stuck his cigarette between his victim's shattered teeth. The Fascist National Party is born.

The following day, after the spectacular reconciliation, Mussolini takes the floor again. The new party needs a program for the future and he provides it. He speaks for three hours, off the cuff, reeling off the new fascist creed in a picturesque speech.

His vision is panoramic, leaving nothing out, his will is pantocratic, ready to reshape the world. First comes a roundup of recent history, covering the usual points and the other parties. Fascism is the synthesis of everything. We will absorb liberals and liberalism because by the use of violence we have buried all previous methods. Then, looking to the future, he introduces new themes. Fascism will complete the nationalization of Italians. Fascism will ensure that within our borders there are no longer Venetians, Romagnans, Tuscans, Sicilians and Sardinians but Italians, only Italians. Beyond the borders, however, fascism hearkens to the imperial myth. There can be no national greatness if the nation itself is not driven by the idea of empire. Then too, the Roman Church, with its universal, millennial magisterium, falls within the apologia of empire. Enough foolish anticlericalisms. As for the state, the question is simple: we are the state. The economy? Liberalism in the most classic sense of the word. Then a clarification on the "conquest of the masses," a theme dear to Grandi and the trade unionists. They say: we must conquer the masses. There are also those who say: history is made by single individuals, by heroes. The truth lies in the middle. What would the masses do if they didn't have their interpreter? We are not anti-proletarian, we want to serve the masses, educate them, but when they're wrong, flog them. Finally, the problem of ethnicity remains to be dealt with. If Italy were to be full of sick people and lunatics, greatness would be an illusion. The fascists, therefore, have to see to the health of the bloodline because ethnicity is the material with which we intend to construct history.

Having summarized the whole century in three hours—parties, nation, church, empire, state, the masses, ethnicity—the Founder of fascism is left with the final point of the program for the future. The final point of the program for the future is him, Mussolini himself. He admits that he has made mistakes because of his awful temper. But they will not be repeated: "In the new organization I want to disappear, because you must recover from my sins and walk on your own two feet. Only in this way, by facing up to responsibilities and problems, are great battles won."

When, towards evening, Mussolini finally falls silent after three hours of unprecedented speaking, wild enthusiasm erupts in the Teatro di Augusto. Shouting, singing, cries of *eja*, *alalà*, endless applause. The Duce is kissed, embraced, strewn with flowers. The session is adjourned, the excitement pours into the street, the fascists, in formation, march towards the Altar of the Fatherland.

Five days before, on November 4th, on the anniversary of the victory over the Austrians, after traveling across the entire country on a special train with cheering crowds extending the length of the peninsula, the body of the Unknown Soldier was buried in the most solemn ceremony ever celebrated in unified Italy. It was the first time that the body of an unrecognizable fallen soldier was chosen by lot to represent them all, the first time that people prayed on the grave of their deceased loved ones as though before the altar of an unknown deity. Only this marble coffin for an unknown corpse can be a fitting altar for the cult of a war in which the act of killing has become a mechanical operation and death a collective, impersonal, indifferent experience.

While the squadristi from the North, having escaped the command of the political leaders, provoke brawls in the narrow streets of Rome's popular districts, the founders of the National Fascist Party, Mussolini at its head, gathered in prayer in the exact center of the eternal, alien and adverse city, remain kneeling for more than half an hour on the marble of this unnamed soldier. There must be no remaining doubts about it, politics is becoming a religion.

In me two Mussolinis contend, one who does not love the masses, the individualist, the other utterly disciplined. Though I may have fired harsh words, they were not directed against fascist militias, but against those who intended to make fascism subservient to private interests, whereas fascism must watch over the nation. I prefer the work of the surgeon who sinks the gleaming blade into gangrenous flesh rather than the homeopathic method that drags its feet over what to do. In the new organization I want to disappear, because you must recover from my sins and walk on your own two feet.

Domination is the instinctive need of every individual who tries to make his way in life, and when people no longer feel its sting they are no longer living flesh.

Benito Mussolini, speech at the
Third National Congress of the Fasci,
November 8, 1921

GIACOMO MATTEOTTI

ROME, DECEMBER 2, 1921
CHAMBER OF DEPUTIES

FASCISM IS NO longer a passing phenomenon, fascism will endure.

When for the third time Giacomo Matteotti takes the floor on December 2nd to denounce fascist terror in the Polesine to the Italian parliament, the promises of Deputy Mussolini, pronounced the day before, still echo through the hall of Montecitorio. The fascists retracted the pacification pact on November 14th after their assaults were repelled by the proletariat in the streets of Rome, allowing Mussolini, however, to rattle off the list of his fallen men to the parliamentarians.

Matteotti begins by declaring that he would have preferred to forgo speaking but that he cannot exempt himself from voicing the cry of pain coming from his region. The tone of his opening is more even-tempered compared to his previous denunciations, a melancholy note softens it. Since the summer his opposition to fascism has changed course, oriented by a new star of intransigence, more amenable, less incandescent, a star of redemption but also a mature, realistic star.

In the days of the signing of the pacification pact Matteotti worked to put together an antifascist bloc that would unite socialists and populists, then committed himself to the proposition of a socialist collaboration with the Bonomi government in defense of democratic institutions. At his party's conference on October 15th he implored his comrades to abandon dogmas and stop dawdling, begging them to open up "to the vast world of workers that is out there waiting for action."

Now, in Montecitorio's chamber, for the first time Giacomo Matteotti finds himself denouncing fascist violence in the presence of the fascists themselves, elected in April thanks to Giolitti. Despite the new reasonableness of his words, and regardless of the bitter twist to his mouth as he utters them, his rigorous punctiliousness requires him to nail the misrepresentations to the facts. The pact, for the squadristi from the provinces, has always been just "a scrap of paper." Large-scale punitive raids have ceased, it's true, not in observance of the pact, however, but because the assailants had met with resistance. Minor forays, those against villages, peasants' houses, have never stopped, the squads openly claim responsibility for them in their combat bulletins, the gangs go armed with clubs, wearing the uniform of death, with revolvers, muskets, grenades, gasoline, and, as always, they remain unpunished. There have been fascists killed, granted, but they died attacking people's homes. Socialists, instead, have died defending them. Power is in the hands of terrorist associations, criminal organizations, and professional killers.

Hearing those words, the disturbances, shouting, and clamoring that have interrupted the socialist deputy's speech since the beginning break out in open protest. Cesare De Vecchi jumps onto the bench yelling that he will not tolerate those insults. The president adjourns the session.

When the session resumes ten minutes later, at 5:00 p.m., Matteotti again tries a moderate approach. But the words "felons," "murderers," "criminals" continue to pour out, and so the interruptions, the shouting, the brawling begin anew. In the end, the passion for justice again gives way to melancholy:

"For many long months I even urged my comrades to endure all the violence, not to react. I even, I must confess, exalted cowardice, because even cowardice can be an act of heroism. But after long months of sacrifice, of waiting, of forbearance, I now feel, Deputy Bonomi, and honorable colleagues of the chamber, that it is no longer possible to continue on like this, and that we must decide to change our stance." The change imposed on men of goodwill by fascist violence is, according to Matteotti, drastic, radical, tragic. It sadly requires them to bid farewell to what they have believed in, to what they have been and hoped to become. It requires the conviction that humanism and revolution, civilization and deliverance are not compatible. Politics, the polestar of redemption for generations of socialists, is today dishonored. Either one adapts, or one succumbs.

The following day, a man who is already a legend at only thirty years of age, rises from the benches of the right to reply to Matteotti. Aldo Finzi—the demonic driver of Mussolini's car in the duel with Ciccotti—is Polesano like Matteotti; he lives in Fratta, less than ten miles from Badia. And like Matteotti he is the son of a rich landowner. Unlike the socialist deputy, however, he has not repudiated his class. Extravagant, bold, and talented, a pioneer of motor racing, he is a war veteran who has been decorated several times for valor. Most notably, Finzi flew to Vienna with D'Annunzio. On August 9th, 1918, while Matteotti was interned in Sicily because of his neutralist propaganda, Finzi took the controls of one of the ten single-seaters that took off from Padua at six in the morning, flew to the Austrian capital, and flooded it with propaganda leaflets dropped from the sky, thereby becoming a luminary. In other words, Matteotti and Finzi could be brothers who grew up in the same house, only one chose to venture out into the world through the front door, the other from the one reserved for servants.

Finzi's rhetorical assault on Matteotti is head-on, symmetrical, specular. It was the socialists' dissemination of hatred, the venom of their demagogic irresponsibility that brought violence to the Polesine. The argument is well known, almost a given by now, but coming from that twin voice, it has the effect of completely upending the analysis, of returning the accusation: "It's not fascism's fault that it arose in our towns, rather than somewhere else; it was you yourselves, you apostles of human brotherhood, who by establishing a regime of terror, forced all decent people, even the most peaceable, to rise up in the end, because our situation left us with the tragic choice: either defend ourselves or die."

The parliamentary archives do not record a reply by Matteotti to Aldo Finzi. That same day, however, Giacomo writes to his wife, with pride and a hint of coquetry, referring to himself in the third person: "A big battle yesterday. Just imagine, they had got it into their heads to silence Gian—with everything else that he must already swallow—about the poor, tormented people of the Polesine. But they had to hear me out until the end, relentlessly. They looked like they'd been bitten by vipers. But those people feel neither remorse nor any kind sentiment."

Ten days later, the reply from Velia, now forced to raise even their second-born child, Matteo, on her own, in hiding, living apart from a hunted father, shows no trace of the adrenaline-induced euphoria that can be read in her husband's words: "When I think of these years that are said to be the best ones, passing by without a glimmer of light, I just keep thinking that a woman's life is pretty bleak, and any remote desire vanishes like a vain promise."

Yesterday Deputy Mussolini ridiculed socialist indecision. Yes, this is the tragedy of our soul, having to repudiate the principle through which we came to socialism. We are painfully ascertaining that it is no longer possible to unite our aspiration for civilization and for the redemption of the proletariat. There is no longer any possibility of life on that terrain. We cannot ask our poor peasants to give their whole lives, drop by drop.

Giacomo Matteotti, parliamentary speech,
December 2, 1921

BENITO MUSSOLINI

DECEMBER 28, 1921

I AM BLINDFOLDED. *I lie supine in bed, my torso immobile, head thrown back, a little lower than my feet. The room is devoid of light. I write in the dark, I trace my signs in the night, which lies solid against both thighs, like a board nailed in place. I am learning a new art.*

The cultural world is in a state of excitement over the publication of *Notturno*, Gabriele D'Annunzio's new book. The Vate wrote it in 1916 while lying in bed immobilized and temporarily blinded in an accident: a plane crash that occurred during one of his astounding war exploits. He penned it in darkness, word by word, on ten thousand scrolls, each sentence a scroll. The cultural realm wonders if this violently visionary prose of a temporarily blind man—a prose that is yet, in its own way, spare and arid as a bone, as a walnut kernel, like the arid death it faces—can be considered a minor masterpiece by our greatest poet, or in turn an accident. But there's one good thing about the cultural realm: like the Vate about whom it wonders, it is blind to the ways of the world which liberally returns the favor.

In addition to the new edition of *Notturno* from Milanese publisher Treves, autographed by the poet, Mussolini is given a second text to reflect on at the end of this year. It is a plan for the military organization of the fascist squads drawn up by General Asclepio Gandolfo, commissioned by the newly born national party leadership. Gandolfo designed the army of fascist militias on the model of the Roman legion, subdividing them into two formations:

Principes and *Triarii*. Each squad will be composed of 20 to 50 men, four squads will form a centuria, four centuriae a cohort, and three to nine cohorts, a legion. A legion, commanded by consuls, will have the Roman eagle as its insignia and its standard-bearers will carry the *fasces lictoriae* surmounted by the star of Italy. Everyone will wear the same uniform but each legion, with prior authorization, will be free to adopt small badges and their own emblems. All ranks will be elective because in the regional context the squads will enjoy maximum autonomy. Fascism, in fact, is still, for the moment, a heterogeneous aggregation of militants who elect their own leaders, not soldiers subjected to orders. The political leader and the military commander will therefore coincide in the same person. General Asclepio emphasizes the difficulty of reconciling the electivity of ranks with the hierarchical principle, but the guiding principle—on this they all agree—is a three-pointed star: militarization, discipline, hierarchy. Politics—on this too there can be no doubt—is a civil war against one's adversaries portrayed as enemies of the nation. Fascists and socialists alike, each and every one of them, have all done this since the end of the Great War, except that socialism limits itself to protest rallies and a war of symbols while fascism goes beyond that. For the fascists, evidently, the war has never ended.

. . . a mysterious breath raises reliefs of human and animal forms from the blinding expanse. Before me is a rigid wall of red-hot rock, carved into men and monsters. The difficulty is not in the first line, but in the second, and in those that follow.

Even Prime Minister Bonomi has finally realized that this is the prediction. Poor man, since the summer he has been floundering in the convulsions of the liberal state: the plans to harness the squads are worthless, the carabinieri convert to fascism, the Disciplinary Council absolves them, the judiciary is impotent. On December 15th, Bonomi had tried again with a prefectorial circular that equated truncheons with weapons requiring a license, and that included fascist paramilitary groups among formations considered illegal. He was frustrated within forty-eight hours thanks to orders issued by Michele Bianchi, the newly elected secretary general of the PNF (the National Fascist Party), which affirmed that party sections and combat squads form an inseparable unit. The directive was brazenly published in *Il Popolo d'Italia*.

Faced with the secretary of a party that has deputies in parliament claiming to have formed an armed militia, a state worthy of the name would have had them all arrested. Immediately. But that state no longer exists. Bonomi, in fact, merely sent out a second circular to the prefects on December 21st, in which he complained that many of his orders concerning public order had not yet been complied with. In particular, the one prohibiting ordinary citizens to routinely wield spiked clubs and maces during the Sunday promenade along the avenues.

My eyelids are unprotected, completely exposed. The tremendous heat burns under my brow, inescapable. Yellow turns to red, the plain is transfigured. Everything becomes bristly and jagged.

Michele Bianchi is the right man for Fascist Party secretary. Calabrian, from a bourgeois family, Bianchi was first a socialist, a revolutionary unionist, an anti-militarist, an anticlerical and an anti-imperialist unionist, then, like Mussolini, overnight, he went over to interventionism with the same ardor, in the belief that the world war would lead to proletarian revolution. Whatever position he adopted in life, Michelino always held to it with relentless fanaticism, the same with which he smokes one cigarette after another. Physically inconsequential, politically acute, he can't stand uniforms; he wears the black shirt over civilian clothes and knows that he is mocked for his funereal appearance. Blood-streaked sputum, a constant slight temperature, night sweats, weight loss: the diagnosis is obvious. Tubercular, Michelino Bianchi carries death on his back. He is only thirty-two but does not have much time left to live. Everyone knows it, anyone who sees him can tell, even a stranger at the end of the corridor who might hear the demise announced in his persistent fits of dry coughing. It is this destiny of a glaring, imminent death that makes him the perfect secretary for the National Fascist Party. No personal ambition for power, just a fanatical dedication to the revolution. And the unappealable authority that only the wheezing of pulmonary necrosis can confer.

Everything is dark. I am at the bottom of a hypogeum. I am in a coffin of painted wood, narrow and fitted to my body like a sheath. . . . as if an embalmer had indeed practiced his art on me. My comrade is dead, buried, released. I am alive, but precisely situated in my darkness, like him in his.

In short, the new year begins under the best auspices. The Founder of the fasci said so plainly at the end of his parliamentary speech on December 1st: dictatorship is a high-stakes card, which is played only once. And, just as plainly, he wrote it in his newspaper: dictatorship involves terrible risks but there is no guarantee that a period of greater freedom, greater democracy may come. The suffragettes have perhaps had their day. From a government of the many, of all, it is probable that there will be a return to a government of a few or only one. In terms of the economy, the experiment of a government of the many or all has already failed. In Russia they have gone back to factory dictators. Socialism, however, made the mistake of guaranteeing people a minimum of happiness: a carafe of wine, a chicken, cinema and a woman. But happiness does not exist in life. Fascism will not make the same gross error of promising it.

In any case, politics cannot put off following the economy. The masses are already longing for a dictator.

Glory kneels and kisses the dust. We go out. We chew the fog. The city is full of ghosts. Men walk soundlessly, wrapped in mist. Vapor rises from the canals. Some drunken singing, some shouting, some sort of row. I have sunk my lips into the fullness of death. My grief has sated itself in the coffin as in a feeding trough. I could not stand any other form of nourishment. I tremble before the first line I am about to trace in the shadows.

I am sending you *Il Popolo d'Italia* with an article by Mussolini, who announces the need for a dictatorship, or rather a dictator—who of course is himself—in order to save Italy.

Letter from Anna Kuliscioff to Filippo Turati,
November 24, 1921

1922

BENITO MUSSOLINI, PIETRO NENNI

CANNES, JANUARY 8, 1922

THE DAY IS dying on the band of the horizon. Shadow overtakes the pinewoods, touches the sumptuous villas on the coast, and submerges the port, swallowing up the city. Hotels and cinemas light up, the winter air is gentle, mild. The tender night descends on Cannes.

It was Aristide Briand, the French prime minister, who insisted on the elegant opulence of the Côte d'Azur for the conference that is to launch the economic and diplomatic reconstruction of a Europe devastated by the apocalypse of the war. Lloyd George, the English premier, is staying in Villa Valletta, Briand came down to the Carlton Hotel, the army of photographers and film cameramen has been stationed in front of the nautical club, and on the Promenade de la Croisette politics is being discussed in all languages of the world. For the first time since the end of the war, a German delegation is also expected. The Germans, the vanquished aggressors, have asked for a moratorium on reparation payments; while the British are favorable, the French are opposed. Briand fights valiantly for reconciliation among the great European nations, but journalists report the latest news from Paris. It is bad news. Briand, back in Paris, encounters a vote of no confidence. Nationalists' revolvers lurk in the shadow of the trees. The palms are feral, the arguments heated. Only late at night does the ferment calm down.

The moon now reigns in a sky glittering with stars. The sea is gleaming. The waves break gently on the port's breakwater. The two men who can be seen walking along the Croisette are from across the border, from Italy, a country where not a week goes by without some bloody event having to be recorded. They are arguing animatedly but they are *compaesani*, from the same town, once friends and it was impossible to avoid one another. Pietro Nenni and Benito Mussolini are now enemies, though they once shared a cell during the struggle against the imperialist war; their wives became friends in the prison visiting rooms, Pietro held little Edda, his friend's daughter, in his arms, Benito hired him as managing editor at his newspaper and had him at his side until 1919. In April of that year Nenni founded the first Fasci di Combattimento in Bologna and cheered the devastation of *Avanti!* Two years later, however, in March 1921, he rushed to the defense of that same newspaper during the second fascist attack. That day, he went from being a republican fascist sympathizer to being a socialist, and he is now in Cannes as a correspondent for the newspaper whose destruction he had once cheered.

The fascist movement, meanwhile, born anti-party, anticlerical, socialist, revolutionary, and republican, has transformed into a conservative, monarchical party, armed with its own army, allied with the ruling class that the two old comrades fought together as boys.

As they stroll along gesturing under the palm trees, the nocturnal amblers are talking face to face for perhaps the last time and from opposing sides.

It is only the second time that Mussolini has traveled out of the country. The previous time he did so as an emigrant in search of a living in Switzerland. This time he also allowed himself a stop in Paris, to be stirred by the memory of youthful revolutionary fantasies, and to break the routine of day-to-day brutalities. Arriving in Cannes, before going to interview Briand, he played at the casino, lost, then, to hide the frayed seams on his shoes, bought a pair of white spats.

"The civil war was a tragic necessity. I take responsibility for it. We had to stop the Bolshevik threat, restore authority, save the nation."

Mussolini's peremptory voice, strident, metallic, is the only disturbance in the quiet night. The hour is late, it begs for silence, but Nenni presses him:

"For the bourgeois classes whose tool you have become, the workers' right to organize to defend their gains is called Bolshevism."

"I am not unaware of any of this. I am not their tool. When the time came, I proclaimed that it was necessary to break the bloody circle of violence."

"That's when you were abandoned."

"When I talked about peace, they laughed in my face; I had to accept war."

The ghost of the pacification pact hovers over the Croisette like the aborted soul of a stillborn child. The squadristi opposed it from the beginning, the communists attacked the socialists for having agreed to it, the socialists only signed it out of tactical necessity. Both old friends know that in those days the squadristi were singing: "*Botte, botte, botte sempre botte / se con noi non marcerà / anche a Mussolini botte in quantità*," "Thump, thump, thump, if he won't march with us, Mussolini too will take his lumps"; they know that the walls of Bologna had been plastered with posters reading "Once a traitor, always a traitor," that to stay in the saddle the general had to follow the temper of the troops.

Nevertheless, Pietro Nenni does not let up on his old comrade: "It's your individualism that leads you astray. I don't know what you will become but I'm sure that everything you do will be branded by the red-hot iron of willful license. Because you lack any feeling for justice."

The waves on the port's breakwater are now the only sound intruding upon the night's silence. But Nenni hasn't finished. In the heat of the altercation between the two Romagnoli, dialect mixes with the language. For two years politics has been a *rissa*, a brawl. Why? Do the fascists have a program? Do they aspire to something higher than the brutal desire to assert themselves?

"The pacification you offer my comrades would be their end. Then too, you forget too many things. You forget that you were the head of the Socialist Party, you forget that the socialists whom the fascists now attack became so in former times in response to your appeal, you forget the dead . . ."

By now the voices are weary, almost pained, the bench is besieged by the sea crashing against the breakwater's rocks. The wakeful night becomes an outdoor pulpit for a melancholy meditation on the past.

Mussolini is silent, reflecting. Nenni is wrong to attribute everything to his cynical individualism. Individualism is relentless, it's everywhere, individualism is modernity itself. It's not in the least a personal inclination on the part of Benito Mussolini. Since the individual has been enthroned at the center of everything, everyone is free to create his own ideology, to design his own style of being, to toy with ideas according to what's expedient. The romantic cult of personal feelings, spontaneity, heart palpitations, freedom to love oneself, has generated all this. Cynicism came along with the whole package, complimentary. Now when even the lowliest, somewhat bored moron yawns it seems like it takes over the world.

Benito Mussolini fears and scorns his squadristi, and the feelings are in large part reciprocated, but by now the circle of hatred is tightening all around. Perhaps, if he could, he would go back. But it's too late. The base life of a class intoxicated with revenge must be obeyed. A vague presentiment of triumph drifts on the night breeze.

"I know the dead weigh heavily on the conscience. I know it better than anyone. I often think of the past as a foreign land." The fascist's voice is grim, morbid. His tone solemn and conclusive. Dawn breaks on the horizon. The breeze carries away the echo of the last words.

"But in life there is no place for sentimentality. Your friends need to understand that. I am ready for war as well as for peace."

"You've lost the chance to choose."

"In that case, it will be war."

There is nothing left to say now. What do the delusions of two niggling men on a night on the Riviera matter in this immense tragedy? All modern life is the planning of necessary massacres. If anyone were to rise up in defense of life he would be crushed in the name of life itself. The industrial civilization, like war, feeds on carrion. Blood on the battlefield and blood on the streets: blood behind the scenes and blood in the workplace.

Besides, cynicism lies in actions, not in appearances. Take French women . . . all dissolute whores. He saw them cream in the brothels of Paris. French women love Negroes. Because instead of a sturdy, strapping dick, they have a very, very long one and women seem to crave that more. Yeah, they're crazy about Negroes, those French women. All of them.

Benito Mussolini makes his way back along the Croisette alone, his strong jaw hunched into his broad shoulders, like a boxer ready to take the punch, head bent over the white spats of an upstart pauper.

AMERIGO DÙMINI

PRATO, JANUARY 17, 1922

FEDERICO GUGLIELMO FLORIO couldn't ride a horse but he loved to walk through the streets of the center with a riding crop. Everyone in Prato remembers him: a cigarette in his mouth, old hat pulled down over his forehead and, in his right hand, the whip. He had a taste for lashing the wool mill workers across the face. Their blood spattered onto the leather-covered handle. To re-educate them, he said, to curb the arrogance of the wool workers who were victorious in the 1919 strikes. In reality, he enjoyed it the way a slave driver enjoys whipping his slaves. And everyone remembers that too.

But now Federico Guglielmo Florio lies in a mahogany coffin, shot point-blank in the belly by a worker who didn't want to have his face whipped. Now bells toll, factories are shut down, tricolors fly at half-mast in front of closed shops, now citywide mourning is proclaimed, the Chamber of Labor has been burned down, its secretary wounded, the town hall invaded. Now Florio has been elevated to the rank of fascist martyr, his role as squadrista now entirely exonerated.

The procession has set out. Mass was celebrated in the cathedral by Monsignor Vittori himself, the bishop of Prato and Pistoia. He spoke of a trinity of light born of blood, of veins emptying to form the new baptismal font, he invoked a community that binds the dead to the living, the generations that were to those that will follow, the bitter duty of yesterday to the even more bitter one of tomorrow.

Tens of thousands of people throng the streets. The start was abrupt, sharp as the burst of a firecracker, stark as a trumpet blast. Legions of fascists stood at attention. At the second shot, pennants were unfurled in the wind, the fascists saluted and the band performed the anthem. At the third shot, everyone stood at rest again. Then they started marching towards the cemetery.

Along the way, the crowd, docile and primitive, kneels on the ground in the mud as though moved by the passage of the coffin. Everything is in slow motion, sorrow expands time disproportionately. The top authorities of the National Fascist Party parade by one after the other, from secretary Michele Bianchi to Dino Perrone Compagni, from Achille Starace to Pietro Marsich. Mussolini sent a salutation, he will write an obituary in *Il Popolo d'Italia*. The Florentine squads follow in full formation, the "Disperata" in the forefront.

Since the founding congress they've done nothing but argue about whether the party should be led by the bosses from the provinces or those from the capital, the rases or the deputies, the fighters or the politicians. The usual useless chatter. Here the leaders are all squadristi, here there is no distinction between politicians and fighters, here adversaries are despised, the dead are avenged, and tolerance is scorned, here the mentality is extremist, the conquest of power is a requisite consequence, here politics is militancy, life brutal, and death sacred, here there are only men united by the experience of a life of struggle. The art of human assembly has its songs, guttural, and its myths: war, the nation, youth. During the march to the cemetery the crowd kneels, time expands, sorrow is sublimated. The time has come for the myth to prepare to become history.

When they reach the churchyard, the fascist groups line up in close formation under the cemetery's arcades. It is almost night. Deep silence. At the center the catafalque, at the sides four enormous candelabra. The funereal light of the torches transforms the living into a legion of ghosts. The evening breeze drifts down from above like a signal arranged for the burial hour. Darkness falls, the watch begins. The sentry stands guard over the gate. For this night and for all the nights to come.

Michele Bianchi reads Mussolini's farewell address: "There are names that are symbolic. Noms de guerre and rallying signs. Snatched by death, they burst into immortality." Then Bianchi kneels before the martyr's mother. The woman is pale, tense, her blank stare seems to be fixed on the pavement, on the bloodstain that had been her son. Around her, the whole world is saturated with symbols, all the dead rise from their graves to repopulate the houses of the living, everything is over and has not yet begun.

Singing is heard from the squads. It is joyful, exuberant, practically brazen. It exalts youth, it replicates the anxiety of a declining, deceased world. Yet it is a callous song, full of pain, the priest doesn't understand it, the mother who has seen her son die seems to shake her head slightly.

At the end, the hymn rises to a strange tonality, the profound note of a trumpet awakening the sleepers. Then it plunges back into silence, faces crumple, hardened and withered, suddenly aged. The fascists stare at the catafalque as if any minute they might see the resurrection of a Christ armed with a riding crop.

"Where is comrade Federico Guglielmo Florio?!"

The squad leader's voice suddenly slashes the night in a demented shout. He is asking about the dead man, who everyone knows is imprisoned in the coffin. Maybe he's gone crazy, maybe he drank.

Florio's mother starts, terrified, stifles a sob. The undertaker's knuckles turn white as he grips the spade like a club, the priest crosses himself three times.

"Present, sir!" The voices of a thousand surviving soldiers rise from their chests in unison. "Comrade Federico Florio, present!"

The cry fades in the night. The pennants, purified, bow down. The ritual is over, having taught how to both bury the dead and leave them unburied.

GIACOMO MATTEOTTI

JANUARY–FEBRUARY 1922

For Giacomo Matteotti and his wife Velia Titta, distance is like the wind. It puts out small fires and lights big ones. In the winter of 1922, however, the fires are those ignited by a malicious hand to the ancestral home, to the house that had belonged to the forefathers, the one in which the children should have been raised in peace. After they have been dragged out of bed by squadristi in the middle of the night, naked and trembling before a decision too great for anyone, the fire suddenly forces them to ask themselves: "What will we do when everything burns?"

Giacomo and Velia met in July 1912, when she was twenty-two and he was twenty-seven. From that day on they never stopped writing to one another. A dense, torrential correspondence, full of letters mostly dominated by sad passions: introspection, commiseration, pining. Giacomo's first letter to her is sent in August of that year, Velia's first reply comes in September. For a whole year they will decorously use the formal form of address. A slow-release love.

Velia is the younger sister of baritone Ruffo Titta, one of the most celebrated opera singers of the time; born into a wealthy family, she was educated in Catholic schools that marked her soul with a contemplative, profound faith, to the point that she considered taking the vows to put the walls of a convent between her and the world. As an alternative to a definitive repudiation of the world, the nun manqué wrote and published novels as a girl.

The two young epistolary lovers marry in Rome, on the Campidoglio, at 4:00 p.m. on January 8th, 1916, and from that moment on they are forever separating.

Giacomo, a dangerous socialist agitator, is immediately sent into exile in Sicily for three years, the most serene period of his life, as he tells it. But even when the war ends and he returns to set up house with his wife, the wind of distance starts to blow again. Elected to parliament in the sweeping socialist ascent of 1919, Deputy Matteotti throws himself heart and soul into parliamentary affairs. Then the persecutions and banishments begin, the solitude of a hunted animal. They have a very strong love, a desperate need of the other but, in fact, separate lives, pledged to an essential distance. Even when they could be together, Giacomo and Velia prefer to write to each other from afar, she in Fratta Polesine, he in Rome, she in Varazze, he in Milan. Ten years of melancholy letters: my dearest Velia, my dearest Giacomo, I love you in suffering, as one should love.

On January 7th, 1922, on the eve of their wedding anniversary, the sixth one, Giacomo Matteotti writes to Velia from Verona: "A number of years have passed and we have found them sown with more pain than joy. When we thought we would find tranquility after a period of time, we sometimes found only a new upheaval . . . Yet, despite everything, hope and love do not diminish." But then a shadow—always the same eternal shadow—is cast over the myth of hope, over the other now and forever, their love, and Giacomo adds: "Perhaps for you it is not this way."

The following week he is in Vicenza. Denied the disavowal or confirmation on which his life depends, he openly implores her: "Tell me that you love me despite this terrible life that never enables us to take pleasure in one another."

In the ensuing letters, in mid-February, the outside world again prevails over intimate feelings, and the husband cedes the pen to the public figure. The indefatigable champion who has replaced the man in love updates Velia Titta on the political situation. The Bonomi government has fallen. The hope on which it was born, the pacification pact that was to soothe the civil war, faded months ago. Already in November it was understood that its attempts to disarm the fascists would fail, and that Mussolini was keeping it artificially alive until February for reasons of his own convenience. Paradoxically then it was the socialists who sank it. Unwilling to join a governing coalition with the capitalist parties, they preferred to once again denounce the state's impotence towards the criminals rather than strengthen it at the price of compromising. The result is that everyone is now convinced that the matter cannot be resolved by treating fascism as a mere police problem. On the contrary, the fascists must be brought into the government. In the meantime—Matteotti informs his wife—the longest parliamentary crisis in Italian history is dragging on, and, on top of that, a split between reformists and maximalists is taking place within the Socialist Party. Another schism.

Velia's reply throws out a life preserver. It is the reply of a shipwreck survivor desperately clinging to a raft, who will not accept the folly of a man willing to drown in life in order to save himself in history. To her the disputes between reformists and maximalists are meaningless: "With certain idiotic, arrogant people, you get nowhere." The following week she piles it on thicker, shifting the focus of her bitterness to her husband: "I am convinced (between us it can be said) that you really don't hear my anger . . . I would almost say that in some cases you are behaving just like a little boy . . . if you can, a few days' rest will do you good." Giacomo protests, vehemently, crestfallen, just as a disappointed child would do: "How quick you are to condemn. You even go so far as to feel resentful. I never thought it possible for a person who loves someone to feel bitter about what the other person does . . . Undeniably you are very distant; and not just when I am away." Again that shadow . . .

Velia's response to her husband is exasperatedly harsh, echoing his enemies' accusations of extremism: "Even ideals shouldn't be taken this far . . . Since you've been embroiled I've known only bitterness, disappointment, and dark times because of you . . . Any light must therefore be within you, because I have never seen it outside." And so the shadow expands to swallow up the world.

I imagine that all of you were disappointed by Bonomi . . . he has always been the socialist who makes do, but he is the most absolute antithesis of a statesman. As an intelligent thinker, as an individual walking the middle path, as an honest man who says what he thinks, as a man without personal vanity or partisan interests, Bonomi is all that, and you can't ask any more of him . . . but he relied solely on moral and spiritual means to treat the insane psychology of fascism and communism.

Filippo Turati, letter to Anna Kuliscioff,
December 1921

A government determined to suppress fascist violence should have been willing to go up against a civil war, because the fascists are strong, bold, bursting with appetites. All in all it is a terrible situation, day by day the country is getting closer to the precipice.

Anna Kuliscioff, letter to Filippo Turati,
8 February 1922

BENITO MUSSOLINI

MILAN, FEBRUARY 25, 1922

IN THE EARLY months of the year, Deputy Mussolini devotes himself more often than usual to fashionable society life. He often attends performances at La Scala and the Teatro Manzoni, giving himself the air of a spectator au courant and causing a stir among the regulars, who are horrified by his tuxedo worn over canary yellow shoes. He acts as best man at his comrades' weddings, and is even seen at the San Siro racetrack complete with binoculars, black bowler and the ever-present white spats, a permanent part of his wardrobe after the return from France. In any case, Milanese industrialists have begun financing him again, depositing funds directly into the coffers of the central management, moreover, unlike the agrarians who contribute to the provincial fasci. Achille Ratti, the reactionary archbishop of Milan who the year before blessed the fascist pennants in the Duomo, ascended to the papal throne just as Mussolini ascended to the Quirinale, summoned by the king for consultations following the latest government crisis. The great world, in short, is holding out its hand. Why not grab it? Why just bite it?

On February 25th Mussolini agrees to attend a banquet in his honor following the inauguration of the pennant of a local fascist group dedicated to him. Surrounded by the enthusiasm of young militants, he drinks a glass of Barbera, dances a lively mazurka with a shapely supporter and radiates confidence. The government crisis has finally ended and the mustache of Luigi Facta has put him in a good mood. Facta, an innocuous, drab, foolish provincial lawyer whom the king has appointed prime minister, is an honest, upright, candid man; his only political ambition is not to displease his patron Giolitti and his one personal pride is a grotesque handlebar mustache to whose care he devotes the first half hour of the morning after having gone to bed no later than 10:00 p.m. without fail.

February's ministerial crisis was devastating for the country. It took the king nearly a month to find someone willing to assume the responsibility of government. A dark crisis, with no glimmers of light at the end of the tunnel, a perpetual twilight situation. The last straw leading to the crisis was the bankruptcy of the Banca di Sconto, whose owners, the Perrone brothers, industrialists who had gotten rich on war profits, had misappropriated savers' deposits to finance their facilities, thereby ruining thousands of small account holders. From that moment on, complete chaos had erupted in parliament.

In a nominalistic delirium of suicidal actions, the two groups that supported Bonomi's liberal majority—Liberal Democracy and Social Democracy—had merged into a third—the Democratic Group—for the purpose of overthrowing their prime minister. Left to support Bonomi were Don Sturzo's populists, they too divided between the "white" leagues of the left, fascism's enemies, and conservatives close to the Vatican who, for its part, strongly opposed Sturzo, founder of the Catholic party. As for Don Sturzo, when the crisis broke out, he had refused to support a new appointment for Giolitti, his historic adversary and the only man capable of controlling fascism. Thus, while even the socialists, who would have benefited most from an antifascist coalition, were about to break up into three sections, one of their deputies, the reformist Celli, by proposing a motion that called for strengthening public order, had unintentionally brought about Bonomi's fall. As thwarted vetoes, personal rivalries, and factional hatreds threw the last shovelful of earth on the coffin of parliamentary life, Mussolini, with a masterly stroke, had nimbly avoided isolation and the formation of an antifascist government by supporting socialist Celli's agenda, put forth against him. The king and Don Sturzo, who had always been personally opposed to Giolitti, had done the rest, barring the way for the influential statesman's return and naming his shadow in Facta.

The state is now on its way to complete collapse, Mussolini can clearly see it. All that's left for him to do is breathe a sigh of relief, dance with a beautiful woman and enjoy a few glasses of Barbera.

Facta's mustache is all well and good, but what worries him is the table of violent thugs, the one back there in the darkest corner of the social club, the table where they're drinking from flasks. The squadristi sitting at that table don't even know the names of the ministers of the new government that Facta's mustache is so proud of having formed in Rome. It's always the same problem with those people: for them power is eating, drinking, fucking and breaking heads. Always armed with a knife, the implement of eternal brawling, nymphomaniacs of violence, drunk on their urges, bent on achieving immediate pleasure, they act compulsively, always, incapable of experiencing the anticipation, the restrained force, the ascending intensity of true battle. With them no respectability, no elevation is possible. Those people drag you down.

Now Cesarino Rossi is also sitting at their table. After being ousted by order of the rases in August during the conflict surrounding the pacification pact, he returned to the ranks on February 2nd as secretary of the Milanese fascio and aligned himself with *rassismo*. The experienced political leader, the manipulator of congresses and assemblies, the astute mediator, is reborn as head of the Lombard squads. Now Rossi has his back protected by Amerigo Dùmini, the Florentine thug who took refuge in Milan, who boasts of the murders he committed and was the architect of the Sarzana disaster. Rossi no longer takes one step without Dùmini behind him. And Dùmini, of course, immediately bonded with Albino Volpi, who is also seated at the corner table at the back of the dance hall.

On the other hand, he still can't do without these people. And so last November, hundreds of people in a Milan courtroom heard Deputy Mussolini give false testimony to clear Albino Volpi of the charge of shooting and killing Giuseppe Inversetti, an old worker who was playing cards at Spartacus, the socialist club on Foro Bonaparte. And again he, Deputy Mussolini, thanks to his ties with the police, had two forged documents sent to Dùmini, who was holed up under Cesare Rossi's wing.

In short, it's impossible to get away from the violent thugs, his back is always to the wall no matter what. He has to avoid looking at the table at the back of the room, hoping that the back of the room doesn't lead back to him. Besides, the dance floor is full of beautiful girls. Look over there.

The world picture is also positive. You just have to turn your gaze on the distant, broad horizon. At the beginning of the year Benito Mussolini founded a journal of political thought, entitled *Gerarchia*, and appointed Sarfatti as its editor-in-chief. Forget the squalid slums, stuff for high-minded thinkers, for more refined readers! He inaugurated it with an article entitled "Which Way is the World Headed?" He himself provided the answer: the world is moving to the right. Democratic inebriation ended in a hangover. When the party was over, you woke up in the morning with a bloody shirt, a severe headache and your face in the toilet bowl, vomiting your guts. Spirits are weary, people look back longingly on strength. In the long run, there will be no difference between respectability and extermination. It is a matter of hunkering down, once again, and waiting for the worst.

The current regime is unraveling. All that remains is a collection of decrepit statesmen who communicate their paralysis to parliament and to government bodies. The prefects no longer have a compass. What a circus! We fascists pay no attention to it. It's extraordinary how my squadristi don't even know the names of the resigning ministers or those in office.

Italo Balbo, *Diario*, February 25, 1922

People are anxiously seeking institutions, ideas, men that represent firm points in life, that are safe havens . . . Left-wing regimes such as those established throughout Europe between 1848 and 1900—based on universal suffrage and social legislation—gave what they could . . . The century of democracy dies in 1919–1920 . . . The process of restoration of the right is already visible in concrete manifestations. The orgy of unruliness has ceased, enthusiasm for social and democratic myths is over. Life returns to the individual. A classic recovery is underway.

Benito Mussolini,
"Which Way is the World Headed?",
Gerarchia, February 25, 1922

ITALO BALBO

FERRARA, MAY 12–14, 1922

In his region Italo Balbo has the situation under control. Over the course of 1921, 80 percent of the socialist and Catholic organizations of northern Italy, beleaguered by the squads' raids, were dissolved and put under the administration of the prefects. In many cases it was the socialist mayors themselves, terrorized, who resigned. In the province of Ferrara, the rural masses collectively migrated from the red leagues to the fascist unions. In some cases, league leaders even stooped to the humiliation of publicly trampling on their flags. Hundreds of thousands of socialist farm laborers became fascists within a year. A Eucharistic miracle of transubstantiation from red to black.

The new year also began in the best possible way. On January 6th, in Oneglia, Balbo secretly met with General Gandolfo and Perrone Compagni, the ras of Tuscany, to start off the national organization of the fascist militia. On April 11th, during the Minister of Agriculture's visit to Ferrara, having never lost his taste for pranks, Balbo upped the ante by personally toying with Cesare Mori, prefect of Bologna, the last, most loathed, adamant representative of the state who is imposing compliance with the law. As the minister gathered with bankers, bureaucrats and sacristans, the ras of Ferrara, with the usual smirk on his face, approached Mori, threatening that with just one whistle from him thousands of fascists would surround and seize the minister. Mori had to promise the release of Gino Baroncini, one of the leaders of the Bolognese squadristi, arrested during a punitive raid.

On April 25th, Balbo is in Milan with Mussolini to illustrate his plan. The situation is this: for the squads spring is the season for big assaults, but for the farm laborers of Ferrara it is the season of hunger. During the winter, thanks to the accord that obliges landowners to hire six farmhands for every thirty hectares, the laborers find work, but between April and May they remain idle. The numbers are biblical: fifty thousand, seventy thousand unemployed pellagrins. In the past the state provided for it with ten, fifteen million public works. Now that the countryside is in the hands of the fascists, however, the government of Rome, influenced by socialist deputies, wants to make the farmers pay for their conversion to fascism by starving them. Balbo's idea is explosive: occupy Ferrara with a mass mobilization that would force the government to give in and you demonstrate the fascists' ability to provide bread for their followers. In addition, the plan would have the advantage of securing work for farm laborers at the expense of the state without affecting the interests of the agrarians who finance the fasci. When he completes his exposition, Balbo, as always, grins.

Mussolini listens to him in silence. In the diabolic smile of that tall, lean, strong young man he sees the past and he sees the future. Fascism, student and heir to the socialist lesson: the masses no longer relegated to the margins of history but summoned to the political scene. Performance mixed with violence, mass theater, the city of socialism transformed into a stage for the recitation of a transfer of power to fascism with the peasants playing themselves. It's an insane plan.

The Duce authorizes it. The terms, however, are clear: if it succeeds, the merit goes to fascism, if it fails it's Balbo's problem.

The implementation of the plan starts at once the following day. Balbo circulates a top secret memo to all the provincial bosses ordering them to be ready to mobilize. Everything must succeed to perfection, the orders are peremptory, detailed, abstemious: beatings are utterly prohibited, even for the worst enemies, the use of alcohol is absolutely prohibited, even in limited quantities, and visits to brothels are also prohibited.

The mobilization starts at midnight on May 11th. From the most remote farmhouses of the Ferrarese countryside, organized by the fasci leaders, thousands of impoverished bands start marching towards the city in the silence of the night, on foot, by bicycle, in wagons, on barges pulled by horses or by men on the canal banks of the Po of Goro or of Volano.

Ferrara wakes up the next morning occupied by an army of indigents: fifty thousand farm laborers, emaciated by hunger, covered by a coating of grime, blankets thrown over their shoulders, with only slices of polenta and cheese in their haversacks, their thirst quenched by hoses, controlled by fascist detachments, parade in a column along the Corso della Giovecca under the wide-eyed stares of the bourgeois.

The countryside has swarmed into the city, the city is invaded and paralyzed. Balbo had the telephone lines cut, requisitioned school buildings for billeting, and ordered the closure of all shops and businesses. The mobilization, considered impossible, has succeeded beyond all expectations. Thousands of miserable wretches camp in the streets, lying on straw pallets, the castle is surrounded by a starving militia, the prefect, terrified, asks to talk with the commander of the invading army. When Balbo shows up at the drawbridge, he is accompanied by the shouts of thousands of famished, toothless mouths.

Wearing his usual white vest with a gold chain spanning his round, soft, heaving paunch, Prefect Bladier is given Balbo's ultimatum: the police must be recalled to the barracks, the fascists will ensure public order, the peasants will not demobilize until the government guarantees the concession of public works.

Forty-eight hours go by, two days and two nights of hemming and hawing, negotiations, meetings and encampments, the municipal kiln produces 45,000 pounds of bread. Then, at dawn on May 14th, the news arrives: Minister Riccio has agreed to everything, the state has capitulated, victory is complete. Balbo gives the order to demobilize. Ferrara is now his.

From Milan, Mussolini exults but is astounded at the sudden change of allegiance on the part of those farm laborers who until yesterday were socialists and today are fascists. He senses the greatness of the hour, yet within him some hidden fiber of anxious presentiment shudders at how quickly people's loyalty can be reversed. Ephemeral or enduring? Appearance or substance? A passing wave or something that will last?

Dear friend, you will have realized from today's federal manifesto how crucial a demonstration of strength by us against the government is, in order to obtain the vital public works that can alleviate unemployment in the Province . . . You must therefore be fully prepared, so as not to be caught off guard by a possible order to move that I might send you at any moment . . . A demonstration will take place in Ferrara that must be the most formidable of Ferrarese fascism and that will mark the measure of our power . . . Upon receiving the order, you must be in Ferrara, at a time that will be indicated to you, with all your fascists and with as many union workers as you can assemble . . . Trusting in your spirit of discipline, in your loyalty, I tell you in addition that I have never sent a more resolute order than this. Fraternal greetings.

Italo Balbo, confidential circular
to the fasci of the province,
April 27, 1922

The agrarians, who in general would appear to be the true financiers of the fasci, and in particular of the recent strike, must consider themselves the unwitting creators of unemployment, due to the selfishness that led them to neglect the rational cultivation of land and consequently a more extensive use of labor; having failed to honor the commitment to give land to the peasants, they have now joined the fascist unions to pressure the government and its representatives and force them to make up for their negligence with public funds.

Report of Prefect Gennaro Bladier,
removed following the occupation of Ferrara,
May 19, 1922

BENITO MUSSOLINI

MILAN, MAY 13, 1922

"AGRARIAN SLAVERY."

The accusation is ignominious. What makes it intolerable is the fact that it comes from D'Annunzio, the Vate, the poet, the man of grand deeds and grand ideals, the warrior of pure, selfless glory. In recent weeks D'Annunzio has been emerging from the silence he has observed until today in his gilded self-exile at Gardone, only to look down with disgust at the fascist sewer and brand it with the mark of infamy: agrarian slavery. An irate, calculating semi-divinity, always lying in wait from the zenith of his Olympus, always ready to reprove the petty men muddling along down below, their arms up to their elbows in shit and blood: out of the way, from here on I'll see to things.

The man who seems to have put that malicious, brilliant phrase in D'Annunzio's mouth now faces Benito Mussolini's sword. His name is Mario Missiroli. He is the prince of Italian journalism, a liberal from the right, a Freemason, and he edits *Il Secolo* after having edited *Il resto del Carlino*, a Bologna daily from which he was forced out, ostracized by the local squadristi.

Missiroli had never held a sword in his life and yet, when Mussolini publicly insulted him by calling him the "most out-and-out coward," he immediately reacted by sending his seconds with a challenging notice in which he imposed very harsh conditions. Then he trained every day with the famous swordsman Giuseppe Mangiarotti, and showed up punctually at the Corso Sempione velodrome accompanied by Francesco Perrotti, a docile managing editor at his newspaper. It is 6:00 p.m. on May 13th and this refined intellectual, completely inexperienced in dueling, awaits the assault bravely, wearing a magnificent silk shirt open over the chest. Insufferable.

Everyone knows that Missiroli is right. The peasants in the Emilia countryside, left on their own by the destruction of the socialist leagues, surrender due to hunger. The agrarians are conducting a merciless war of revenge that nullifies decades of social reforms. Fascist organizations deal directly with the landowners, abolishing the rural concordats, one after the other, or, when that's not possible, discontinuing the collective nature of the contracts. In this way, the individual farmer is left to face the boss's vengeful cruelty by himself. When the peasants still find the strength to protest, the strikes are crushed by scabs, even more desperate, who pour in from other provinces like swarms of locusts, escorted by armed squadristi.

Forced to put up with the dominant role of fascism in the provinces, Mussolini attempted to provide a theoretical justification in his newspaper, distinguishing between agrarians—large conservative landowners—and rural ones—small revolutionary landowners. Fascism is rural, not agrarian, he wrote. But it didn't help. Now, the accusation of slavery is standing in front of him, wearing a magnificent silk shirt brazenly open on his chest.

Yet the Founder does everything possible to civilize fascism. At the beginning of March he traveled to Germany to broaden his horizons. He saw the Germans wearing the mask of a republic and of pacifism with his own eyes. Under the mask, Germany too is turning to the right again. He had to hurry back to Italy, however, because of opposition from Pietro Marsich, the D'Annunzian ras of Venice, who questioned his leadership, relaunching the accusation of parliamentary betrayal of the movement's original ideals. This was followed by a fratricidal saber duel with Major Baseggio, a Sansepolcrista, mastermind of Arditismo, founder of the mythical, iniquitous "Death Squad," and a supporter of Marsich.

Then, on March 26th, after the bout with Baseggio, Mussolini managed to have twenty thousand young fascists in black shirts parade through Milan, the capital of Italian socialism, in close ranks, without incident. They were so handsome, virile, composed and respectable that the ladies in Piazza del Duomo applauded them after checking their makeup. Immediately afterwards, however, the barbaric squadristi in the provinces went on the rampage again, to drag him into the pits. That's how it is: he's a solitary man, he doesn't have and can't afford to have friends.

At the national council on April 4th Mussolini spoke plainly. The aura of approval that surrounded fascism in 1921 is on the wane. The affirmation of the movement in the rural provinces is occurring at a time when the bourgeoisie feels that the justification for the squads is fading. The socialists no longer scare them. The Milanese industrialists extend a token of thanks with one hand while with the other they are ready to hand the insolent servant his marching orders. They're even talking about starting to do business with Soviet Russia again. In other words, there's the danger of finding themselves sealed off. The beatings must stop. Defensive violence is sacrosanct, but those who enter houses, who lurk behind a hedge, are not fascists. The idea of insurrection cannot be excluded, but at the moment it is unrealistic. Fascism must be fully a part of national life, the moribund electoral game must be accepted. Participation in the government cannot be ruled out: parliament must be held in contempt, agreed, but it must be used to advantage.

Dino Grandi supported him, everyone voted for his motion, but even that is of no use. The Fascist Party continues to increase the volume of its members but, apart from the right, none of the other parties represented in parliament wants them in the government. The socialists hate them, the populists fear them, the democrats and moderate liberals look down on them. There were some backroom parleys with Facta. There is talk of no more than three undersecretaries. The usual, miserable plate of paltry scraps. Insufferable. Fascism has no friends, and doesn't want any.

When Mussolini lunges at Missiroli his face is livid with rage. At the first thrust the sword tip breaks. The weapon must be replaced. Gripping the reserve sword, Mussolini lunges at the challenger again. Missiroli remains calm, parries the blows. The attacker is fuming with rage, exposing himself at every assault, exerting savage blows with the flat of the blade, as if instead of wielding a sword he were clutching a saber.

Perrotti, the nonviolent editor-in-chief of *Il Secolo*, whom Missiroli dragged along as a second, keeps fervently repeating to Dr. Binda, the duel's physician: "You have to stop them, you have to end it!"

At the third assault Missiroli is wounded. The wound is considered slight, and the duelists are brought back to the piste. Mussolini, furious, lunges once again into an attack. Perrotti now screams openly: "We have to stop it, we have to stop it, we'll have a dead man on our hands!" At the seventh attack the tip of Mussolini's sword penetrates deeply into the venous fascia of his opponent's right forearm. Missiroli's inadequacy is now plain. The duel is over. Neither of the two contenders declares himself satisfied.

While Dr. Binda treats his bleeding arm, Missiroli is as calm as ever. His improbable second, shaken by a hysterical tremor, politely approaches the doctor and whispers in his ear. He tells him about his little daughter's mysterious illness, and begs him to go and examine her. They have taken her to the seashore, to Salsomaggiore, hoping that the wholesome air would help her get well. She is his only daughter, a delightful little creature, he can't stand the idea of her having to suffer, the world is a place governed by evil.

Ambrogio Binda, Mussolini's personal physician, grants Perrotti's plea and leaves for Salsomaggiore the following day. The following week, Francesco Perrotti, Mario Missiroli's second at the duel at the Corso Sempione velodrome, decides to take his own life.

I cannot complain about how business is doing at my company nor at others, mainly in the electrical industry, in which I have an interest . . . The resumption of economic relations with the USSR will enable the expansion of Italy's activities until the establishment of our companies in Russia . . . I believe that Italy did well to take the initiative of this trade treaty. For us the communist danger is in decline. The combatants' organizational structure and the affirmations of fascism have created a climate of resistance to the spread of Bolshevist theories.

From the diary of Ettore Conti,
electrical industry magnate,
April–May 1922

The march as such, however, was a grand success, impressive, orderly. About 20,000–30,000 people took part; who could estimate the number? All those young men, 17 to 25 years old, strapping, vigorous, handsome boys in military formation—if you didn't know what vile ends their actions are bent on, they'd give a magnificent impression of beauty and strength.

Anna Kuliscioff, letter to Filippo Turati
regarding the fascist parade of
March 26, 1922, in Milan

The dueling gentlemen will be provided with a glove and footwear. It is forbidden to use foulards to bind one's wrist and straps to secure the weapon to the wrist. Pants can be held up by a belt to a maximum height of four centimeters. The match will take place bare-chested. The use of suspenders is prohibited.

From the preliminary agreements
to the Missiroli–Mussolini duel,
May 13, 1922

LEANDRO ARPINATI

BOLOGNA, MAY 28–JUNE 2, 1922

"You have to take back your position." Mussolini, writing from Rome, personally ordered him on February 19th, and he resumed his post as head of the Bolognese fascists. Rina, now his wife, was disconsolate.

Leandro had married her in a civil ceremony on June 8th, 1921, shortly before being forced out. His anarchic nature had always instinctively stood him in opposition to the Ferrarese model—squadrist subjugation of the rural masses in the fascist unions—and for that reason the assembly, on June 20th, had elected Gino Baroncini as secretary of the provincial federation in his place.

During the clash with the rases over the pacification pact, Arpinati, although opposed, had remained loyal to Mussolini. He had not attended the meeting of dissidents and he had not participated in Balbo's march on Ravenna either. His faction had emerged defeated from the subsequent assembly of the Bologna fasci, and he hadn't been a delegate at the party's founding congress either. They had even slandered him with the accusation of arbitrary use of the association's funds. Ousted from everything.

"Somehow we'll get through it," Leandro had promised his wife, and went back to continue his studies. He re-enrolled at the university, requesting a transfer to the Agricultural College. With Arpinati, Rina Guidi had enjoyed a rare moment of pure happiness, glimpsing on the horizon the mirage of a simple, industrious, peaceful life.

Then, in February, Benito Mussolini had called her husband back to the firing line.

The enemy is no longer the socialists now, it is the state and, in Bologna, the state is called Cesare Mori. As often happens with inveterate enemies, Mori, although he is the only Italian prefect who is harshly fighting the squadristi, is perhaps also the only one whom the squadristi would instinctively choose as their leader. Raised in a Pavia orphanage, he has Mussolini's square jaw, and was a police commissioner in Trapani in the early 1900s; Mori fought the mafia with unrelenting, violent methods, surviving numerous assassination attempts. Upon returning to Sicily in 1915, and establishing special squads, he eradicated banditry using those same methods, even going so far as to personally kill two bandits and having as many as 300 of them arrested in a single day.

Now, sent by Bonomi with full powers over the regional coordination of public order, Mori in Bologna hasn't changed. With three simple moves he put the fascist organization on the ropes: by preventing the driving of vans on weekends he restrained the squadristi's raids; by mandating government employment offices, he took control of the rural masses out of the hands of the fascist unions; by prohibiting the immigration of seasonal labor, he is stamping out the practice of hiring scabs. The fascists' fierce polemic against the state's ineptitude requires that Cesare Mori, who embodies its efficiency, be brought down.

Balbo showed the way by occupying Ferrara. They must march. March, no longer just to impose their will on the state, but to openly oppose it. Marching is a tactic but it is also a discipline. They must stir up the piazza and hurl it like a stone at prefect Mori's windows.

Leandro Arpinati turns to Italo Balbo. When Michele Bianchi, the party's national secretary, orders the mobilization of all of Bologna's squads on May 28th, Balbo prepares to descend on the city with his squadristi from Ferrara. Since the 29th, thousands have arrived from Codigoro, from Portuense, from Copparo, and are assigned thirty-hour shifts. The residents of Bologna are amazed at the sight of thousands of men who spend four nights under the arcades on strawboard pallets.

But the march, once again, espouses violence. Along the way the fascists, as usual, systematically devastate all the socialist and communist headquarters, together with those of the Chamber of Labor and the agricultural cooperatives. What's new, however, is that they now beat socialist deputies and police commissioners without distinction. When Mori stations cordons of carabinieri, royal guards and plainclothes agents around Palazzo d'Accursio, the fascists crash through them by pretending to force the center, then breaking through with a diversionary maneuver on the opposite side. When the squadrons on horseback advance, the fascists stand firm waving white handkerchiefs or setting off firecrackers. The horses shy, rear up and unseat their riders. Arpinati, despite having to tolerate Balbo and Grandi's actions in his own city, leads a squad in an attack on the prison of San Giovanni in Monte to free 60 detained fascists.

The state surrenders. On May 29th, a citizens committee of Bologna's bourgeoisie sends a telegram to the Ministry of the Interior requesting the removal of Mori. On the 30th, Giacomo Vigliani, public security director, is sent from Rome to conduct an inquiry. The senator of the Kingdom accuses Mori of excessive zeal. Much of the national press supports the fascist insurrection against him. The cavalry officers, having been called back to more arduous duties, do not hide their sympathies with the insurgents.

Besieged for three days in his office in the prefecture, the mayor telegraphs Rome continuously to receive orders. His telegrams obtain vague, elusive answers. Rising up from the piazza, meanwhile, is the singing from the bivouacs: *Mori, Mori tu devi morire . . .* "Mori, Mori you must die / with the dagger we have sharpened / Mori you must be killed."

If anyone were to open fire it would trigger a massacre. That order, however, does not come. Instead, the confrontation is defused with a prank. The Balbo method requires that the march be conducted with "youthful gaiety." And so Giacomo Vigliani, senator of the Kingdom, the investigator sent by the government, informs

Rome that the squadristi have been lining up, taking turns, and with perfect discipline, one after the other, for hours, have been pulling their dicks out of their pants and peeing on the prefect's building. The circle of ridicule tightens around the Italian state and around Cesare Mori who embodies it.

After five days of Bologna's occupation, having received assurances regarding Mori's transfer, Mussolini on June 2nd promulgates the demobilization order. "This example," the conclusion reads, "will be epoch-making in Italian history. Should it be necessary to repeat the demonstration, I make a formal commitment to come with you to lead it. But it will then have a broader extent and more far-reaching objectives." After Ferrara, after Bologna, they start thinking about Rome. Everything out in the open, Balbo's march set an example.

In those same hours Arpinati, the first of those not elected in May 1921, learns that, due to the withdrawal of fascist candidates unable to meet the minimum age requirement, he will be going to parliament.

Deputy Arpinati packs his bags, kisses Rina and he too leaves for Rome. Italo Balbo, commenting on the occupation of Bologna, notes on the June 5 page of his diary: "Dress rehearsal for the revolution."

Those people still haven't understood that bandits and the mafia are two different things. We have struck down the former who, unquestionably, represent the most conspicuous aspect of the Sicilian criminality, but not the most dangerous. We will deal the truly fatal blow to the mafia when we are allowed to rake up not only those found among the prickly pears, but in the corridors of prefectures, police headquarters, grand palazzi, and, why not, a few ministries.

Statement by Cesare Mori to one of his collaborators after the newspapers had carried the headline "Mortal Blow to the Mafia," Sicily 1917

A wave of antifascist reaction . . . has struck. Commissioner Mori, that would-be Oriental viceroy, Nitti's filthy police hound . . . continues his dismal displays in redeemed Emilia with a tragic crescendo. Persecutions, housebreakings, arrests follow in succession, statutory freedoms are abolished.

Statement of the Modenese Federation of the PNF, February 1922

Prefect Mori called the colonel in his office for every little thing, sometimes even at night.

From the report of the inspector general of public security, Paolo Di Tarsia, on the fascist occupation of Bologna, July 15, 1922

He is no longer anything, this man who with the inept, pedantic arrogance of a policeman held the special office of Po Valley viceroy.

"That Dog Mori,"
L'Assalto, organ of the fascio of Bologna,
July 1, 1922

BENITO MUSSOLINI

JULY 19, 1922

"DEPUTY MIGLIOLI AND Deputy Garibotti are deprived of hearth and home forever."

In the end, it was that buffoon Roberto Farinacci, the ras of Cremona, who brought down the Facta government. A man capable of banishing both the socialist and Catholic deputies from their lands with a single proclamation, failing to use the subjunctive. And yet he was the one to actually shove aside the prime minister, appointed by the king only four months earlier: it was the work of this character straight out of Italian folklore, this son of a Molise policeman immigrated to Cremona, this fiery interventionist who did not intervene, this patriotic railwayman whom opponents nicknamed "*tettoia*" (station canopy) because, after invoking intervention, he spent the war under the platform roofs of a provincial railway station, this founder of the newspaper *Cremona Nuova* who trips over grammar, this squad leader who never fights in person, this fanatical, mediocre pipsqueak of a murderously violent man.

With the start of fine weather, Farinacci's squadristi in the province of Cremona went on a rampage in a widespread campaign of devastation against all the peasant leagues and town councils, both "red" and "white," socialist and Catholic: thirty-five municipal administrations resigning within two months for "inability to withstand the situation." On June 16th, the blackshirts occupied the prefecture and set fire to the home of Deputy Miglioli, the Catholic deputy who for years had led the "white" peasant leagues threatening to make the agrarians end up "like Judas," hung upside down "from the trees of our lands." On July 5th, on a suffocatingly hot summer day, Farinacci sneaked into the town hall alone—the custodian was sleeping in the cool shade of the entrance hall—and from the mayor's private office, on paper whose letterhead bore the municipality's seal, notified the prefect that he had appointed himself mayor of Cremona. Ten days later he returned with thousands of squadristi to besiege the city: three days and three nights of devastation, killings, administrative impotence. Two more days and the government fell.

Now fascism has everyone against it again. During the parliamentary debate, Deputy Treves openly called Facta's ministers "eunuchs"; Turati, evoking a return to the Dark Ages, reinforced it: "If we do not hasten to take remedial action, we are verging on the collapse of a civilization," he shouted, his voice consumed by an anger now close to desperation. And this time the liberal newspapers supported the socialist protest: the *Corriere della Sera* finally deplored the blackmail of fascist violence; in Turin's *La Stampa* Luigi Salvatorelli held the ministers of the right responsible for their abetting inaction: either defend the state or not a minute more in power.

Benito Mussolini, as usual, carries his cross soaked in the blood of others. During the days of violence, from the columns of *Il Popolo d'Italia*, he cheered the war of conquest: "They still and always will call us bandits, felons, savages, slave drivers, brigands, traitors," he wrote. "We don't give a damn. Go ahead, you people, print your useless, offensive words. We respond by crushing you politically and syndically."

Behind the scenes of propaganda, however, he was the one who ordered Farinacci to demobilize from Cremona. After a first refusal, he had to physically threaten him. On July 18th he also took pains, through the prefect of Milan, to reassure the state of his intent to contain the squadristi in order to enter government through legal channels. Since June Mussolini has been knocking on every door in order to end the fascists' isolation. He tried sweet-talking the king, Nitti's old liberals, even the odious Don Sturzo and the socialist reformists. His attempts failed.

So Deputy Mussolini took the floor in parliament on July 19th, renewed his usual threat, and spoke openly about his tribulation, his dilemma between a party of rule or a party of insurrection.

Then the fascist Leader played his old surprise hand again by voting against Facta along with the Catholics and socialists who'd lost faith in him precisely because of his inability to defend them from his squadristi's attacks. But it was just one more clever sidestep to avoid being buried under the rubble of yet another collapse. Nothing more.

The truth is that there's tribulation, yes, but there's no dilemma. The fascists don't give a damn about anything or anybody; the fascists claim to be authentic representatives of a sound, virile, strong nation against the melancholy puppets operating in the theater of Montecitorio, but the truth is that, if the Italian parliament is pathetic—and on this there is no doubt—Italy is no better. No use kidding oneself, the dissolution makes no distinctions, there is no deviation, no margin, no gap. Mussolini's strategy is the same as always: he waits, and waits, and waits . . . because you have to wait until the corpse comes through the door. But the dead body is already out the door, liberal democracy's cadaver has been laid out among the sofa's dust and mites for so long that it is no longer noticed. No, there is no dilemma, violence has no windows. Mussolini's tactic is always the same: apply sparingly, dilute, dilate, and then treat from positions of strength. And as a result they are condemned to continually watch the horizon from the top of incinerated trees to spot the flames of the next fire. The only real difference between the Duce and his squadristi is that for him violence is simply a sharp tool while for the violent it is a bloody craving for light, a thirst, an appetite, for him brawling is a mere fact of life, for them the armed squads' impact is mythic. There's no match.

While in Rome, on July 22nd, Mussolini in his white spats climbed the stairs of the Quirinale to be consulted by the king of Italy, in Trecate, a godforsaken hole in the province of Novara, De Vecchi's squadristi were demolishing the Chamber of Labor with trucks chained to the supporting columns; they completed the job by setting off dynamite charges. The following day there were turbulent scenes in Magenta, not far away.

Now it's July 26, 1922, and in his office on Via Lovanio, in Milan, Benito Mussolini is waiting and trembling. Filippo Turati, the old patriarch of Italian socialism, has, for the first time, agreed to go up those same stairs to confer with the king. The communists say that he has prostituted himself, but the Catholics for once seem willing to accept the socialists in the government and the socialists are willing to take part. And so the union of Marxism and Christianity, the two churches, the two religions of the twentieth century, is announced. It is also said that the king wrote to Giolitti, who is enjoying the thermal waters in Vichy. In either case, whether the socialists enter their first government, or whether Giolitti is called back to form his sixth, for the fascists it would be over.

He, meanwhile—always, still—goes on talking to everyone, nationalists, liberals, democrats, populists, even the socialists. Then all he can do is wait, pacing back and forth in his office on Via Lovanio. However, he must be very careful not to step on the black chips of the floor's ornamental fret pattern border. Superstition is the only religious faith geared to this despicable world, the fear of a lesser, unknown, bizarre and vindictive god.

Fascism is now close to resolving its internal tribulation: whether to be a legitimate party, that is, a governing party, or whether it will instead be an insurrectional party . . . In any case, no government can last in Italy if it plans to use machine guns against fascism . . . If by chance a government of violent antifascist reaction were to emerge from this crisis . . . we will respond to that reaction by rising up . . . I hope that fascism can be a part of the state through a groundwork of legal conquest. But there is also the other eventuality, which I must, in all conscience, point out, so that each of you in tomorrow's crisis . . . may take into consideration these statements of mine, which I commend to your meditation and to your conscience. That is all I have to say.

Benito Mussolini, parliamentary speech,
July 26, 1922

ITALO BALBO

RAVENNA, JULY 27–30, 1922

While in Rome Benito Mussolini talks with everyone to bring the fascists to government or to avoid an antifascist government, in Ferrara Italo Balbo receives a letter from Ravenna: "The situation is very grave. They bludgeoned Balestrazzi to death. General shooting. Seven dead. The city is in the hands of the subversives. Come quickly."

The letter was sent to him by a twenty-year-old who, in 1917, at age fifteen, falsified his date of birth to enlist as a volunteer in the Arditi. He is strong, athletic, always in the front line in clashes with the socialists. In Fiume, where he was terrorizing with the "uskoks," the pirate band assigned to plunder merchant ships to resupply the besieged city, D'Annunzio himself renamed him "Green-Eyed Jim." His name is Ettore Muti.

The situation is plain, always the usual story: during a conflict between fascist and socialist unions over the transport of threshed wheat, a fascist carter sustained cudgel blows that staved in his skull. Upon receiving the letter, Balbo issues the order for all Romagna squads to march on Ravenna and sets off.

That's how Balbo is, for him it's all about marches, tents, songs, camps and smiles, he's always smiling. For him going to the right or to the left simply means acting, moving, maneuvering, marching, bivouacking. Today the game is played in Ravenna, outside parliament.

While Balbo deals with the socialist and republican leaders of the

Labor Alliance in the city, the militants are fighting in the province. In Cesenatico Leandro Arpinati was the victim of an assassination attempt. He was shot in town, in the piazza, as he was driving a car headed to Ravenna. He was unharmed but his companion, Clearco Montanari, one of the founders of the Bolognese fascio, was killed instantly. The attack on the Provincial Confederation of Socialist Cooperatives, to avenge Montanari, is launched during the night.

The old building, a bastion of the red leagues, is completely destroyed. Like blood coughed up on a tubercular's handkerchief, the building's blaze spits out its flames in the dark. Ravenna does not have an aqueduct, the copious material accumulated over the years through the efforts of thousands of farmers burns on for hours, uncontested. The conflagration seems inextinguishable. Like primitives in caves, mesmerized by the fire, men stand and watch.

Then the circle parts, broken by the arrival of an elderly man who is in despair. He pleads with the firefighters to step in, wrings his hands, tears his hair, wants to rush into the flames. His name is Nullo Baldini, and he is the founder of the cooperative; a moderate socialist deputy, he has dedicated his whole life to the farmworkers of Romagna. He is witnessing the pyre of the dreams and toil of a lifetime.

Baldini is sixty years old. In the eyes of Ettore Muti and the other twenty-year-old squadristi, he is an old man. No one lays a hand on him. In his diary Balbo notes: "We must give the opponents a sense of terror." In the moments when that inconsolable old man, unharmed, faces his shattered life, terror hangs over everyone.

Then the march resumes, with its singing, its boisterous laughter, its bivouacs. From Rome Michele Bianchi telegraphs Balbo on behalf of the party to immediately stop the violence. Mussolini is negotiating to enter the government and they, with their acts of bravado, are making it impossible. But in the outskirts and rural areas there are already nine dead, and people are trembling with fear, alone on the immense plain. Rome is far away. Here they must decide on another angle of attack, here the sense of terror is the sense of fighting.

Ignoring Michele Bianchi's reprimand, Balbo goes to the police commissioner and threatens to burn all the houses of Ravenna's socialists if within half an hour he does not get a column of trucks supplied with gas to transport the fascists. The police chief provides them. Balbo gets in the car that leads the column and they leave.

The crusade begins at eleven o'clock on the morning of July 29, just as Filippo Turati, for the first time in the history of the Socialist Party, climbs the stairs of the Quirinale to meet with the king, and ends at the same time the following day. Twenty-four hours of constant movement, during which nobody has a moment's rest or touches any food. Twenty-four hours of carnage.

The fascists tramp through Rimini, Santarcangelo, Savignano, Cesena, Bertinoro, through all the towns and countryside of the provinces of Forlì and Ravenna. Their passage is marked by a pillar of fire. The entire plain of Romagna, as far as the hills, burns.

They return to Ravenna at dawn. When the news reaches Rome, all negotiations cease. Even Turati's attempt has gone up in smoke: the socialists have again proclaimed a general strike.

I take my place . . . in a car that leads the long column of trucks and we set off. This march, which began at eleven o'clock yesterday morning, the 29th, ended this morning, the 30th. Almost 24 hours of being constantly on the move, during which no one had a moment's rest or touched any food. We passed through Rimini, Santarcangelo, Savignano, Cesena, Bertinoro, through all the towns and countryside of the provinces of Forlì and Ravenna, destroying and burning all the red houses, and the headquarters of socialist and communist organizations. It was a night of terror. Our passage was marked by tall columns of fire and smoke.

Italo Balbo, *Diario*, July 30, 1922

AMERIGO DÙMINI

MILAN, AUGUST 3, 1922

IN FRONT OF La Scala, the most famous opera house in the world—where in 1783 the joyful notes of *The Barber of Seville* celebrated the pleasures of life before the revolution for the last time; where on an afternoon in 1846 during the dress rehearsal for *Nabucco* the employees were moved to tears listening to that incomparable chorus evoking the springtime of the people; where in 1907 the hopeless anguish of *Madama Butterfly* said goodbye forever to the world of the romantic century—a truck has gone crazy and plows into the crowd. On the side of the murderous truck is a sign in black paint that reads: "Terror!"

Standing on the caisson, the sleeves of his black shirt rolled up to reveal his muscular arms, a powerful man grips the sides to command the assault. The son of one of the richest landowners in Lomellina, thirty-two years old, ash-blond, heavy serous bags under feverish eyes, Cesare Forni spent his youth amid cocaine, brothels and poolrooms in Turin, then, like many men of his generation, he found that war gave meaning to a life that hadn't had any. An artillery captain, he was decorated for valor eight times on the battlefield. After returning to his father's house, he sowed terror in his lands, leading the fascist squads in the systematic destruction of all the peasant leagues in the surrounding area and then throughout all of southern Lombardy. After clubbing farmers by the hundreds, he forcibly assigned them to fascist unions, demanding their total subordination to the party. His men worship him. He brought 700 of them to Milan from Mortara to crush the subversives' strike in their stronghold. Now the truck on which Cesare Forni stands like a madman drives at full throttle into Palazzo Marino, which houses the municipal council of the city that gave birth to Italian socialism. Right opposite La Scala.

The fascists have been trying all day to seize Palazzo Marino, but the commander of the Milan division has concentrated hundreds of royal guards in its defense. The squadristi, holed up under the theater's arcades, have been facing soldiers on horseback since morning. Someone, climbing up the window grating on a side street, even managed to get inside, waving the tricolor from the balcony of the council chamber, but was immediately arrested. Now, however, the driver of the truck, urged on by Forni, steps on the gas in front of the police cordons.

The cops scamper out of the way just in time, the nose of the truck crashes into the ornate, Art Nouveau style wrought-iron railing. The crunch of twisting metal mixes with the frenzied whinnying of the horses. While the police are left deafened by the clangor, carloads of fascists storm into the piazza, preventing the platoon of mounted guards from maneuvering. At the same time, three columns of fascists emerge from Via Verdi, Via Manzoni and Via Santa Margherita. With shouts of "to us!", they overwhelm the military and invade the building. For an instant everything stops: the world crystallizes in a senseless roar, a shout of utter rebellion against reality, an irrepressible urgency to overturn it.

Cesare Rossi is out of his mind with joy. He has been waiting for this moment for forty-eight hours, since workers throughout Italy proclaimed a general strike to protest Balbo's "column of fire," but it seems he's been waiting for it all his life. Since dawn, he's had Amerigo Dùmini with him, ordering him to stick to him like a shadow, to watch his back, and he began issuing orders to the squads arriving from all over Lombardy. Mussolini is missing, he's supposed to be in Rome but he can't be found, word has it that he's lusting after a new conquest, he took her on a romantic trip to the Castelli. Arnaldo, his brother, tries calling the switchboards of all the hotels between Ariccia and Frascati every half hour. The Duce has fled the coop.

What happened was this: as soon as news of Balbo's "column of fire" got out, the Labor Alliance made a last attempt at resistance by proclaiming a general strike starting at midnight on July 31st. They renamed it a "legalitarian strike": all the workers' and peasants' organizations of Italy ready to fight as a solid bloc to defend political liberties and those of unions. One of those battles that don't allow a rematch, where the player stakes everything on the last card, prepared to blow his brains out afterwards should he lose.

The announcement of the strike was mistakenly disclosed in advance by a newspaper staffer in Genoa, throwing the plans into turmoil. The king, who was still negotiating the socialists' support for a government of the left, summoned Facta and tearfully implored him to form a new cabinet without the socialists. By five in the afternoon Facta had already set up a ministry identical to the previous one. You can't say no to a king's tears.

On the first of August, at the start of the unrest, Michele Bianchi, no less excited than Cesare Rossi at that not-to-be-missed opportunity offered by the socialists' folly, issued the fascists' ultimatum: "We give the state forty-eight hours to prove its authority in regard to all of its employees and those who threaten the existence of the nation. Once this deadline has passed, fascism will claim full liberty to act and will replace the state that will once again have given proof of its impotence." Mussolini, from the columns of his newspaper, was exultant: "We ask only this: to have free rein to fight, to live, to suffer, to win; better yet: to triumph. And we will triumph."

Now, as he paces around the mayor of Milan's offices invaded by squadristi, Cesare Rossi is indeed triumphant. He keeps turning to his bodyguard and repeating that those poor demented socialist leaders, proclaiming yet another general strike, have resurrected the only ghost that could still justify Balbo's violence: the specter of a Bolshevik revolution. An irrational fear in exchange for an irrational hope. "Can you imagine," Rossi continues beaming at his bodyguard, "now the outlaws aren't our men who have been setting fires and killing for months, but the ones who are striking out of respect for the law!"

When the ultimatum expired, fascist armed action was triggered throughout Italy, an unrestrained, unpunished counterattack, again supported by the fears of the bourgeoisie and the liberals. Starting things off in Milan was Aldo Finzi, who at eight o'clock in the morning personally drove tram number 3 out of the depot on Via Leoncavallo. The squadristi at the windows pointed their muskets and machine guns at the crowd of strikers.

In the rooms of Palazzo Marino, among the exhilarated fascists, rumor has it that some of them have gone to summon D'Annunzio. The Vate, by chance, is at the Hotel Cavour, on Via Manzoni, a ten-minute walk away. His presence has nothing to do with the strike and its suppression. D'Annunzio is in Milan to negotiate one of his usual fabulous advances with his publisher. But it seems that the Commander wouldn't even receive the fascist messengers. The attorney Colseschi, who is accompanying him, asked them not to persist in trying to involve the poet's name in a violent act that he disapproves of with every ounce of his being.

Finzi and Rossi consult with one another. After the accusation of "agrarian slavery," Mussolini despises D'Annunzio more than ever. But Mussolini isn't there, he's in Ariccia, or in Frascati, or maybe in Albano, to fuck and guzzle sparkling wine. Rossi orders his men to spread the word that Gabriele D'Annunzio is about to arrive at Palazzo Marino and rushes to the Hotel Cavour with Aldo Finzi.

The Commander can't refuse to receive Aldo Finzi, who had flown over Vienna with him, but he's recalcitrant, even irritated by this invitation which he obviously considers offensive. Finzi opens the windows of the room overlooking Via Manzoni. The crowd, wild at the announcement of his arrival, shouts the poet's name as in the days of Fiume.

"It is not we who invoke you, Commander, it is the people of Milan."

Gabriele D'Annunzio is not a man who can resist that kind of flattery.

"Let's go."

Down in the street, the car is waiting.

At Piazza della Scala, Cesare Rossi has had the Fiume flag hung alongside the black pennants on the municipal building. When D'Annunzio sees it, he is moved and goes up to the balcony. Overwhelmed by the crowd's enthusiasm, for once the Vate doesn't know what to say and improvises:

"Citizens of Milan, rather, men of Milan, as a captain of demanding times would say, this is the first time since the exploits in Ronchi that I find myself again speaking from a balcony . . . at this balcony that for too long was deprived of the tricolor, deprived of that divine communion that Italy's emblem has with the sky of Italy . . ."

His renowned eloquence remains vague, he gets lost in affected metaphors, in literary preciousness, the crowd's adrenal delirium drowns it. But it doesn't matter, by this time words don't count. The poet's diminutive, tense, portly body straining towards La Scala is impressed on the day like a seal on wax. The man of letters even attempts a humanistic appeal to brotherhood:

"Here it may seem that I am speaking fighting words whereas I am only speaking brotherly words . . . Never like today, while wounds are still bleeding, never like today have words of compassion held so much power. I invoke the great fire of compassion, not an inert compassion, not weakness, but virile compassion, that which marks just limits . . ."

This appeal doesn't count either. At the very moment when Italy's Vate is invoking the fire of compassion and brotherhood among all workers, a few streets away, on Via San Damiano, Forni and Farinacci's squadristi are preparing to burn down *Avanti!*'s premises for the third time. One of them will be electrocuted on the wire mesh fencing set up as a defense, a second will be blown up by a bomb, and then the flames will rise from the paper archives. Now there are no more obstacles to obstruct the way, a broader retaliation can be planned.

Two weeks ago fascism did not enjoy great favor with the public. Its raids and the methods used to carry them out seemed extreme given the diminished obstinacy and weaker resistance on the part of the adversaries . . . Today Italy is much more favorably disposed towards the fascists. It's no use dissembling . . . The general strike was the mirror in which the nation once again saw reflected the Bolshevik face of the dismal years following victory.

"Reality,"
Corriere della Sera, August 6, 1922

BENITO MUSSOLINI

MILAN, AUGUST 13, 1922

FROM ROME HE returned to Milan by plane, the warm August air slapping his stubbly face at the controls of a Macchi M.18 seaplane, the summer version with open cockpit, Isotta Fraschini Asso engine, 150 horsepower, 621-mile range, and a maximum speed of 116 mph. After all, he made a promise to Sarfatti and he intends to keep his promise: he will be the first European head of state to travel by plane, piloting it himself.

Italy seen from up here is beautiful; the whistling of the air swallowed up by the roar of the engine accompanies him like a melody of subdued, mysterious oboes alternating with the sudden frenzy of the strings. As he flies over, the aviator goggles clouding his gaze, the hills and slopes seem like the solemn, still body of a beaten adversary. It makes a man feel alive.

Socialism is now on the ground. It will not rise again. The punishment inflicted by the fascist squads was implacable; it did not stop even when the defeated Labor Alliance called off the "legalitarian strike" on August 4th. Indeed, at that point it raged pitilessly against the battered enemy for days and days: hundreds of cooperatives, associations, and chambers of labor were destroyed throughout the country, while socialist administrations resigned. He flew over Italy on August 12th, and the smoke from the fires could still be seen in Tuscany, in Emilia, in the lower Po Valley. A real coup de grâce.

Just that morning, before taking the controls, Mussolini read an article in *La Giustizia* in which Turati himself wrote a report of the defeat: "We must have the courage to admit it: the general strike was our Caporetto. We emerge from this attempt soundly defeated. We played our last card and left Milan and Genoa at stake, which appeared to be the unassailable points of our resistance. In all the main centers the fascist volley delivers the same destructive violence. We must have the courage to acknowledge it: the fascists are today masters of the court. If they wanted to, they could continue dealing out formidable blows."

Italy is indeed a glorious country: forty-eight hours of beating and clubbing succeeded where a century of struggles had failed: the socialists are shattered. Look at those men down there, those newspapers, those socialist organizations that until yesterday vitalized the plains, the coasts, the ridges of this magnificent country. Look at them now . . . not a move, not a cry, they don't even dare breathe.

Turati is right, once again, but he goes too far with his pessimism. Now there is no longer any need to strike the socialists, now there are only two forces left: the fascists and the liberal state and it will be a duel to the death. Wait a period of time before taking your only shot. That's the rule that must be followed. As always, for that matter.

But it won't be easy, it never is. In Milan the squadristi were exultant about the overwhelming success of the initiative taken in his absence. When the Duce gave Bianchi a dressing-down for having ordered the mobilization without his approval, Michelino reiterated his absolute loyalty to him but was bold enough to assert that he would not follow him in his palace maneuvers "to enter a weak government," that they were ready for a leap towards the conquest of real power. Cesare Rossi, when he called him on the phone on August 5th, even advised him not to return at that point just to bury the three fascists who'd died in the assault on *Avanti!* And then Rossi, Bianchi, Finzi and the others, gripped by enthusiasm, all started ranting about a coup that made no sense, in which they enlisted just about everybody without discrimination. They even went as a delegation to announce it to the *Corriere della Sera*, where Albertini's brother showed them to the door.

In Rome meanwhile, on August 9th in parliament, during the debate on the vote of confidence in Facta, while a communist deputy was attacking them harshly, Leandro Arpinati got up from his seat and, without a word, calmly headed towards the communist deputy's bench. Parliament's clerks managed to stop him when he already had his hand on his weapon.

That's not good. Even Mussolini, swept along by events, claimed responsibility as usual for the squadristi's repression of the legalitarian strike, but he will not follow them into a leap in the dark. The fascist militia must be organized militarily but only a demented lunatic could rely on pure and simple military action. The army to date has never really opened fire on the squadristi and, when it has, as in Sarzana, there was no match. Even the socialist sheep were able to stop the squadristi when they organized. As happened in Parma, on August 6th, with the defense mounted by the Arditi del Popolo in the workers' district of Oltretorrente. There Balbo with 4,000 blackshirts wasn't even able to get past the river.

And then there's the Mezzogiorno, that splinter of the Dark Ages embedded in the nation's flesh, still a vassal of old local notables like Nitti. Except for Puglia, and to some degree Naples, fascism has not yet set foot in the country's south. The majority of the rases from Emilia, Tuscany and Lombardy have never been south of Rome. A complete terra incognita.

And then there's D'Annunzio, still him, always him. After the speech from the balcony of Palazzo Marino, he reacted angrily to Rossi's press releases that counted him among the fascist ranks, and publicly dissociated himself. But mixing with the crowds also made him cocky. The depressive cyclothymia of the cocaine addict seems to be giving way to a new blaze of political passion.

In short, the control stick must be maneuvered gently otherwise the plane will plummet. Through tireless confidential negotiations, he, masterfully piloting, was able to arrange an unthinkable secret meeting with D'Annunzio and Nitti, the two old archenemies, to plan for a three-way government that would hold it all together, North and South, legality and illegality, revolution and the restoration of state authority, palace and piazza, shit and blood, arcane ministerial secrets and the prodigious miracles of the race. The meeting is scheduled for August 19, in Tuscany, at the villa of Camillo Romano Avezzana, Italy's former ambassador to Washington. The only problem is that, obviously, D'Annunzio will want to command.

At the conference of fascist leaders held in Milan on August 13th, nobody knows any of this apart from Bianchi and Rossi. Present at the meeting are the party leadership, the central committee, the parliamentary group and the Confederation of Corporations; all the fascist bosses are there, many participating for the first time in such a summit, Caradonna from Puglia and Aurelio Padovani from Naples have even come, yet they are all in the dark about the secret plan to enter the government with D'Annunzio and Nitti. The meeting is held in the fascio premises on Via San Marco, behind closed doors, in a simple, bare hall.

The report on the general situation is given by party secretary Bianchi who, chain-smoking one cigarette after the other, lays out the dilemma: "We are faced with enormous responsibilities: huge masses of workers come to us . . . fascism must assert itself . . . either it will become the life blood that nourishes the state, or it will replace the state." The dilemma is between insurrection and seizing power lawfully through new elections. Aside from Bianchi, Farinacci and Balbo, nobody is really considering insurrection. Dino Grandi, followed by many others, declares himself openly opposed. But Bianchi is right about one thing: they are at a critical point, the point of no return. Preaching in vain about a socialist revolution has shown that: from here on out, either power or collapse. Vilfredo Pareto, the great theoretician, wrote as much in a message sent to Mussolini from Geneva: "Either now or never."

During the lunch break, Bianchi and Mussolini approach Balbo, who has insisted on a centralized organization of the combat squads, and drawing him aside, assign him leadership of the militia at the national level. Balbo smiles, accepts. The decision is made to support him with two generals to maintain the army's conduct. The choice falls on De Vecchi, the ras of Turin, and Emilio De

Bono, a prematurely aged, retired general, who for years has been seeking political acceptance in every party throughout parliament.

Work resumes in the afternoon and only the few members of the party leadership participate. Mussolini personally leads the discussion. Four agenda items are put to a vote: militarization of the squads under a supreme command composed of Balbo, De Vecchi and De Bono; a request to parliament for new elections; fascism's penetration of regions as yet immune; a confused resolution of intransigence towards eventual electoral alliances, which no one understands.

Evening has fallen. The committee is ready to wind up for the day when the phone call arrives: D'Annunzio is at death's door. The Commander fell from the window of his villa. The head injury is severe, the loss of blood considerable.

The news generates enormous dismay, which is destined to increase when the cause of the fall is reported: it seems that the poet was molesting Jolanda, a minor, and the younger sister of celebrated pianist Luisa Baccara, his resident lover, while Luisa sat at the piano entertaining them both. It is not clear which of the two women was the one to push him out, the furious lover or the molested younger sister. Or perhaps the poet's flight is due solely to the typical inability to judge the risk associated with the white dust. In any case, Italy's history is at a turning point.

Benito Mussolini is once again excited as he is only when flying his airplane. This time, however, he gets behind the wheel of his sports car. He takes young Balbo with him and drives him around Milan. He floors the accelerator in the summer twilight, the car careens a little on the paved city streets and sometimes slides on the tram tracks. But it doesn't matter. The Duce of fascism happily regales his young friend with talk of the nation's cultural destiny. Various newspapers, even some on the right, reporting on the daily violence between "reds" and "blacks," clamor about dark times, about decline. Imbecilic Jonahs. They don't get it. Even the *Divine Comedy*, the greatest poem in the Italian language, was the epic of our eternal civil war. If the Guelphs and the Ghibellines hadn't been at each other's throats for a century, Dante wouldn't have been inspired to compose his work.

Hearing his Duce in a good mood for once, Balbo then jokes about poets, about their inspiration, about their flights and their falls from a balcony. Spirits are high! It's a beautiful summer evening, the sports car streaks along Milan's porphyry paving stones and life is great.

Before setting off on their little excursion, the driver, smiling craftily, dictated a press release from the fascist party leadership. It says that the march on Rome is a "rumor without any foundation."

Now it is once again necessary for anyone who preserves a crumb of governmental good sense to counter the fascist dilemma—either elections or violence, so openly enunciated—with the legalistic prerequisite . . . It must be considered inadmissible in accordance with the legal forms of our constitutional regime for a party to appeal to the verdict of the polls in order to affirm its strength, and at the same time openly threaten revolt, armed sedition, and a coup d'état. The confusion on which the game is being played is meant to make people believe that fascism is forced to pose this dilemma between legality and revolution for its own salvation; but this is precisely opposite to the truth. Fascism is not facing any crucial crossroad, because no one is threatening it and no one disputes its place in the sun: it is up to it, and to it alone, to choose between the ballot and insurrection.

La Stampa,
Turin, August 15, 1922

Fascism has won its pitched battle, soundly beating its opponents and routing them . . . it is the authorities' intention, when the uproar has calmed down, to proceed to the seizure of weapons. Give strict orders in this regard, so that weapons and ammunition may be put in safe custody without delay.

Michele Bianchi,
confidential circular to the fascist provincial federations,
to be read and destroyed, August 7, 1922

There is a military plan for fascism, expertly formulated by generals and officials who direct the action squads . . . At this point there is a pause, but a pause of a few days, if not a few hours. The fascist army is preparing for its final round, to conquer the capital . . . The capital is the goal.

Avanti!,
Rome edition, August 6, 1922

The rumor being circulated that the fascists are aiming at Rome to attempt a coup d'état is devoid of any foundation.

Il Popolo d'Italia, April 8, 1922

GIACOMO MATTEOTTI

OCTOBER 10, 1922

"I BELIEVE THAT I will resign as deputy before long because it is all useless action and wasted effort. You are against the other parties; and yet your party does nothing that it should do. So what's the use?"

Discouragement begins to descend on Giacomo Matteotti already in the spring of 1922. These few lines of May 20 to his wife testify to it. Day by day the world appears more and more in ruins, yet the man now seems to have nothing left to counter the world's devastation, not even himself. Faced with Velia's reproaches, protest, the last god of desperate hours, disappears from his letters. The question is no longer "what to do" but "what's the use?" The dilemma of lost battles.

Two days later, on May 22nd, the occasion of his thirty-seventh birthday, it seems that for Giacomo it is already time to take stock: "Today I am thirty-seven years old; really thirty-seven . . . Everything is the same as it used to be; but thirty-seven is certain, and I have a great fear of time passing so swiftly; above all, indeed almost solely, of everything that has taken and takes me from you, your love, your person, your affection. I think that it is perhaps the only thing I am irreparably losing."

At the beginning of the summer, while the last, decisive fascist offensive is unleashed, Matteotti retreats towards a more intimate conversation in his letters to his wife, his loving words focus on conjugal love as a complicity of two souls in and against the world;

his life as a public figure, dedicated to the struggle, is privatized: "Yes, I think of you. You have been my great and true and only love. My thoughts of you have occupied entire hours of each day. You have fully filled my heart for years on end."

A nod to the political situation, a single mention, emerges from his *de profundis*, on June 29th: "Here we are out at sea . . . there is no one outside of our party who senses the full tragedy of the current situation." Isolation, solitude, a desert, a shipwreck, politics is reduced to this for Italian socialists in the summer of 1922.

On June 1st, at the request of CGL, the Labor Confederation, the socialist parliamentary group had voted for the Zirardini agenda, which bound the deputies to seek an accord with the government for the restoration of public liberties and the re-establishment of law. But the maximalist leaders of the party had rejected it, accusing the reformist wing of collusion with the bourgeoisie. As that was happening, 221 administrations of the left fell in the province of Novara alone between the end of July and the beginning of August. As Pietro Nenni had noted, the leaders of the proletariat performed like Church doctors who, while their world is in ruins, debate the literal interpretation of the sacred texts. Meanwhile, the proletariat was left to itself, without help or protection.

The toxic fallout of factional aversions had settled by the time Turati climbed the stairs of the Quirinale on July 29th to meet with the king. Radical socialism as whole had condemned the event as a real betrayal. The communists had even mocked "Turati's corpse." The following day, the general strike had delivered the coup de grâce to what was left of the socialist movement. The people who would not give in, railway workers seized at home, under armed threat, and forced to go back to work while their houses were burned, workers who had gone on strike a hundred times and, despite everything, still responded to the call, presented an admirable, moving sight to Giacomo Matteotti's eyes, the display of an act of faith with no tomorrow.

At the end of August, defeated on all fronts, Matteotti dares to at least hope for a little peace. Summer, as we know, stirs these hopes. He and Velia have chosen Varazze, on the western coast, for its exceptionally mild climate. Protected from the tramontana winds by Mount Beigua to the north during winter nights, on summer afternoons the coastal town is cooled by the lively breezes of the Ligurian Sea. But here too Giacomo Matteotti is recognized and on August 29th he is forced to leave, escorted to the train station by police officers and squadristi from the local fascio.

The laceration is consummated on October 3rd in Rome, during the sessions of the XIX congress of the Italian Socialist Party, another melancholy, agonizing assembly. The main thing to avoid is another split. Divided, the revolutionaries will not be able to bring about a revolution, nor the reformists collaboration. Yet they split, a suicidal split but at this point inevitable: two extremisms of the same desperation can be read in the motions of the right and left. Party Secretary Giacinto Menotti Serrati's proposal to expel the reformists carries by a handful of votes. Filippo Turati and Giacomo Matteotti are ousted from the Socialist Party to which they have dedicated their lives. After the amputation, the congress resolves to join the Communist International and to send a new delegation to Moscow. The discussion ends, bitterly, on who should be part of it.

Those expelled—Turati, Matteotti, Claudio Treves, Giuseppe Saragat, Sandro Pertini—establish a third party of the Italian left that they christen the Unitary Socialist Party—who knows whether out of a taste for paradox or prompted by habitual, insurmountable desperation. The young, energetic, indomitable Giacomo Matteotti is elected secretary. Now they are free of the "maximalist" ravings about a revolution that is always heralded and never attempted. They are free but they no longer know what to do with their freedom.

Giacomo Matteotti, apparently persuaded by the common sense of his wife, who for years has been pleading with him to withdraw, writes to her on October 10th: "I want to protect the children and you, and myself as well. Extreme sacrifices are pointless, they are of no help . . . Meanwhile, to drown completely, I have also accepted the post of party secretary. But not for long, I hope."

The political discussion you had with the monarch, the start of your collaboration with the monarchy and with the bourgeoisie, marks the end of your relations with us as a party. We do not question your good faith—which is not in doubt—we assert that you yourselves, with your own hands, shattered that unity which, until yesterday, you wanted to make us believe you were firm, unwavering advocates of.

Avanti!, addressed directly
to Filippo Turati and his associates,
July 30, 1922

Turati went to the king. The socialist movement is crumbling. It is one less corpse to drag along to the future.

Palmiro Togliatti,
L'Ordine Nuovo, July 30, 1922

The Labor Alliance, which unifies the proletariat, must live, it must be strengthened for the further development of the proletarian defense movement. The more furious the enemy's efforts to drive victory away, the closer it is.

Manifesto of the Socialist Party leadership,
August 8, 1922

BENITO MUSSOLINI

MILAN, OCTOBER 16, 1922

"AT THE FIRST shot fired fascism will totally collapse."

General Badoglio supposedly said this at a meeting in Rome in the presence of bankers, journalists and even General Diaz. Spoken in a parlor in Rome, a pestilential city by definition, the words loom over the men meeting in secret in Milan, at the original fascio's headquarters on Via San Marco 16, like a pistol pointed at the temple. Among them are four army generals and all of them know that Badoglio is right. The only one who doesn't know it seems to be Italo Balbo. On October 6th, summoned to Milan by the Duce, Balbo assured him that the militarization of the squads is proceeding promptly. The men in the provinces are said to be ready for any event.

At the end of their talk, contrary to his custom, Mussolini amiably invited Balbo to lunch at Campari. Conversation between the two at the cafe was cordial, the atmosphere relaxed. Yet Mussolini must know that Balbo's thugs are not soldiers, that the boldness of a brawl is different from the courage of battle; the savage aggression towards defenseless men and combustible property for the purpose of terrorizing a hostile village is a spectacular action, but it is not war. To use trucks against bicycles, an offensive against stasis, the frenzied assault of motorized squads against placid democratic trust at socialist mass demonstrations is exhilarating, but it is not war. The new regulations of the National Security Militia, drafted by De Bono and De Vecchi in mid-September, imposed military discipline on the squadristi, provided for hierarchy and military ranks, and did away with elective commanders, but despite the names and adjectives, the truth is that a real fascist military force does not exist. The Paduan squads have only a few thousand rifles and no one is training the squadristi to use them.

At the first shot fired by the regular army, fascism will fold. They all know it. Yet four experienced generals and four multi-decorated veterans meet one autumn afternoon in Milan to decide on an armed insurrection against the state.

The meeting is called for October 16, 3:00 p.m., in the small parlor of the fascio's directorate on Via San Marco. The invitations were issued four days earlier by Mussolini, with orders not to miss it. Besides Michele Bianchi who is already there, the invitees are the commanders of the Balbo militia, De Bono, De Vecchi, Ulisse Igliori, leader of the Roman squads and recipient of a gold medal in the Great War, and two new figures, Generals Fara and Ceccherini, both with a brilliant career behind them. The building is guarded by a double row of royal guards outside and by squadristi inside.

Before starting, a diplomatic clash must be ironed out: De Bono, unaware of their having been summoned, flares up at the presence of Fara and Ceccherini. Warned of the controversy, Mussolini shrugs: the newcomers are distinguished soldiers. Ceccherini led the Bersaglieri in the second battle of the Isonzo, Fara captured the Bainsizza plateau and saved Italy's honor in Libya at Sciara Sciatt. Outside of military circles, nobody knows De Bono. Things settle down, and the meeting begins. Balbo, who on all occasions is the youngest, takes the minutes.

The Duce of fascism takes the floor and explains why they are there. They are there because a state that can no longer defend itself has no right to exist. If there were a real government in Italy, the royal guards would enter that door this very moment, break up the meeting, occupy their headquarters and arrest them all. An armed organization complete with officers and regulations is not conceivable in a state that has its army and its police. Except that in Italy the state does not exist. It is useless, the fascists must necessarily come to power, otherwise the history of Italy becomes a joke.

The syllogism is elementary: Italy is a nation but it lacks a state. Fascism, therefore, will give it a state. Mussolini said it clearly at the fascist convention in Udine on September 20th: "Our program is simple, we want to govern Italy."

Prime Minister Luigi Facta, concealed behind his big handlebar mustache, persists in deluding himself, trusting in fascist participation in his third ministry. But Facta is the man who on September 24th, at Pinerolo, to celebrate the thirtieth anniversary of his parliamentary life with his constituents, attended a banquet based on vol-au-vent and *vitel tonné* with 3,200 dinner guests including 71 senators and 117 deputies. A first-class funeral.

The ministerial mummies persist in considering the march on Rome a metaphor, but the march is already underway, in history, because Rome is infected and it is necessary to march to purge the wound, to take it out of the hands of inept politicians. The militia is ready, reformed by the violence of an army at war, the prophecy of violence is coming true, there is a violence that liberates and one that shackles, the masses are sheep, the century of democracy is over, the liberal state is a mask, fascism is young, strong, virile Italy, the clash is inevitable, the time is propitious, this is the hour of attack, the prophecy is now. When the bell tolls, we will march as one man.

Listening to the Duce's fighting song, Balbo's eyes blaze with an instinctive desire for action, while Bianchi reduces yet another cigarette to ashes. De Vecchi, pale, asks to speak:

"Duce, no one more than me despises the contaminated, putrid, senile, contemptible Italietta, a nation of castrated pacifists, but here the fundamental point of the question is being ignored. Without a military structure that is capable of handling the fascist forces, the plan is doomed to failure."

Mussolini and Bianchi exchange a complicit look, then both, as one, turn their eyes to the objector. De Vecchi goes on:

"The militia is not yet prepared and it will take some time for it to be able to act as a coordinated force."

Mussolini, livid, shuts him up. De Vecchi is asking for time precisely because there is no time, the attack must be launched within a few days.

"It's absurd, unless you want disaster rather than success." De Vecchi tries one last time, then lowers his demands to put it off by just one month and asks what the others think.

Italo Balbo says he's worried: "The maneuvers of the old parliamentary parties are becoming more pressing. Fascism is likely to be ensnared, albeit unwittingly, by the intrigue that they are cooking up to damage it with the ruse of the elections. If we don't attempt the coup immediately, by spring it will be too late: by the first warmth of Rome, liberals and socialists will come together."

Michele Bianchi intervenes, supporting Balbo, and adds political reasons for immediate action. De Bono and Ceccherini, instead, consulted by Bianchi, cautiously back De Vecchi's proposal favoring deferment. General Fara says he doesn't see the need for immediate action, that he hasn't gotten to know the men and commanders yet. He's in favor of delaying.

Finally, Mussolini takes the floor again. His tone has softened, he's over his sullenness at feeling ambushed:

"The revolutionary act of marching on Rome must take place immediately or it will never happen. The negotiations that I am conducting with Facta are just a diversion. The time is ripe and the government is rotten. The specter of Giolitti is slowly advancing and you know that with Giolitti in power it's best to think of something else." He pauses, looks at them all to weigh the effect of his words on them, then resumes: "I understand that some of Facta's collaborators are considering a resounding reconciliation between Giolitti and D'Annunzio. I met with D'Annunzio last week in Gardone and we came to an agreement. He's with us for now. But the embrace with Giolitti planned by Facta must take place on the Altar of the Fatherland, in the presence of the wounded and former soldiers, on November 4th, the anniversary of the victory. You don't need a prophetic mind to see that such a gesture, as theatrical as you like, but undeniably significant, would give Giolitti renewed strength. We must act before this happens."

The decision is made: violent action. The designation of the exact day is deferred until after the big conference planned for October 24 in Naples. All that remains, therefore, is to consider the modes of action. The moment the military assault begins, all political hierarchies must vanish. A quadrumvirate will be set up, consisting of Bianchi, Balbo, De Bono and De Vecchi. The military command will take over with full powers. Monterotondo, Tivoli and Santa Marinella, a night's march from Rome, will be the sites for the massing of the troops. Perugia will be the headquarters of the quadrumvirate and Foligno that of the Reserves.

Mussolini takes a piece of paper out of his pocket. To the astonishment of those present, he reads the proclamation to be sent to the fascists at the start of the insurrection. He's kept it in his pocket, ready, for days:

"Fascists! Italians! The hour of the decisive battle has struck . . ."

Among the many bare or empty rooms at the offices on Via San Marco, Cesare Rossi's is the only one lavishly and stylishly furnished. As soon as the meeting ended, Italo Balbo, before leaving with the others, even teased him about the pretentiousness of that high-class boiserie. Now Mussolini, scowling, is pacing back and forth in that elegant setting. Then he stops in front of Rossi's desk.

"If Giolitti returns to power we're fucked."

He spells it out—"f-u-c-k, fucked"—his voice strident, the notes rising shrilly on a wave of anguish.

"Remember that in Fiume, on a similar occasion, he had D'Annunzio shelled. We have to move fast. Those people didn't get it . . . But I put my foot down. Preparations must be completed by the end of this month."

The voice falls silent, the feet resume their pacing in that 200-square-foot space. Rossi knows that the Duce will continue his line of thinking before long and offers the support of his silence. To the heir apparent, familiarity with his leader suggests the true picture of the situation:

"Fascism is overreaching everywhere; now it's trying to give itself the appearance of a military organization. Antifascism is no longer capable of putting up any decisive resistance, other than keeping an eye on a few isolated areas and some men. The Carabinieri and the royal guards, especially in the provinces, are evidently with us. The army's cadres will support us because they feel that we're the Italy that has come out of the trenches; at the very least they will remain passive. The Facta government will not fire on us. The monarchists are reassured by my speech in Udine, and I will be even more explicit in Naples. The parliamentary ranks, after all their failed maneuvering, will only think of fixing things between us. They're nothing but a bunch of decadent suicides . . . Industrialists, bourgeois, landowners, they all want to bring us into the government. Even liberals like Albertini now claim that this is the priority, whatever the cost. Even Luigi Einaudi in the *Corriere* shows he likes us . . ."

Mussolini stops again, puts his hands in his pockets, as if the obstacles to the march to power prevented him from even pacing in Cesare Rossi's office.

"The dark aspects of the situation are: Parma, where the communists keep the city armed, D'Annunzio, the king, and the fascists' undisciplined behavior. It would be maddening if they were bottled up in the middle of the Po Valley in a decisive action. D'Annunzio always exerts a certain appeal, among our people as well, even after he fell from the balcony, but he is ineffectual. He wrote *Alcyone*, and I will certainly never write something like that, but as a politician he's worth nothing. He is the man of great strides . . . but then, once he's gone the distance, nothing remains of his passage but a shadow . . . It will not be difficult to bring him around, even if he is surrounded by many of our enemies . . ."

Again the pacing stops.

"No, the ones who worry me most of all are the fascists. As human material, for a large-scale action, they are shoddy goods. Personal feuds, local oligarchies, small jurisdictional satrapies . . . We must rein them in . . . As for the sovereign, he is certainly an enigmatic figure, but there are levers surrounding the throne that we will operate . . ."

The allusion to the queen mother and the duke of Aosta, notorious supporters of the fasci, remains suspended in the dusk that seeps into the room. Together with the unmentionable allusion to Freemasonry. Mussolini puts his hands back in his pockets, and shakes his head again.

"The buttons on the gaiters are missing . . . Do you see, Cesare!? If this favorable moment passes, it's over for us. And De Vecchi, De Bono and those other operettist generals of ours tell us that the uniforms aren't ready! As if they were organizing a parade of honor instead of marching on Rome . . ."

In the office of the Milanese fasci's secretary it's gotten dark. The days are beginning to get shorter. In northern Italy in mid-October night comes early.

Cesare Rossi finally gets up from his desk to turn on an art deco lamp. At this point, his stubborn silence and penetrating gaze draw the outline of an embarrassing question on the wall, casting a shadow of sarcasm on the martial proclamations. The expression "march on Rome," swallowed up in that silence, becomes meaningless.

Benito Mussolini catches Rossi's eye and smiles. The understanding between the two men is seamless.

War is too serious a thing to be left to the generals. Those men lack duplicity, they don't think that way, they don't distinguish between war and psychological warfare, between the threat of violence and violence itself. Instead you have to act "as if," it's all a matter of thinking "as if" . . . Proclaim, mobilize, arm, even kill each other a bit and then . . . then pretend to march by really marching. Or vice versa, your choice. In any case it's all about fanfare, clamor, anthems, a few bloodstains, it's about a fiction that requires an excess of reality to be believed as true. In the end, every great act is, at best, a symbol. At worst, best not to even talk about it.

"Now or never," the great Pareto even wrote to him in a telegram from Geneva. But then the distinguished scholar also added: "Italians love big words and small deeds."

Fascism is a revolution, agreed, but we must avoid putting everything at stake. Some firm point must be left, the impression that everything is collapsing must absolutely be avoided. Otherwise the waves of enthusiasm of the first phase will be followed by the waves of panic of the second. A temperate barbarism. There . . . that's what's needed to seize power: a temperate barbarism.

The clash is between an Italy of faint-hearted politicians and a sound, strong, vigorous Italy, which is preparing to give the final blow to all the incompetents, to all the mediocre hacks, to all the corrupt dregs of Italian society . . . In short, we want Italy to become fascist.

Benito Mussolini,
Cremona rally, September 24, 1922

By now the liberal state is a mask behind which there is no face . . . The stupidity of the liberal state lies in granting liberty to all, even to those who use that liberty to topple it. We will not grant that freedom . . . What separates us from democracy isn't quibbling over elections. People want to vote? So vote! Let's all vote until we're bored out of our minds! Nobody wants to suppress universal suffrage. But we will have a policy of reaction and severity . . . We divide Italians into three categories: "indifferent" Italians who will stay home and wait; "sympathizers" who will circulate; and finally "enemies," and these will not circulate.

Benito Mussolini,
speech at the district Amatore Sciesa club,
Milan, October 4, 1922

That sly fox Giolitti is paving the way for the defeat of fascism. I believe that if the fascists let themselves be tamed they are finished . . . The masses that are now abandoning the socialists will abandon the fascists as well because they won't be able to enable them to reach for the stars. It is therefore essential to bring about the revolution before being abandoned, otherwise the party's over.

Letter from Maffeo Pantaleoni
to Vilfredo Pareto,
October 17, 1922

The fleeting moment that the socialists failed to seize is now in the hands of fascism; we men of action will not let it slip away and we will march.

Benito Mussolini,
to the men of the Sauro and Carnaro action squads,
Milan, early October 1922

NICOLA BOMBACCI

MOSCOW, LATE OCTOBER 1922

DEMOCRACY HAS VERY poor style. Bad literature. Trotsky is right.

The liberal newspapers dealing with the fascist assault are there to prove it: they stammer, take sides, then retract, a pedantic, convoluted, timorous prose. The prose of late democracy, devoid of ideas, of will, that looks around fearfully, adding one caveat after another in its writings, translating from English, a language not its own, which in turn echoes ancient Greek, a foreign past. Italy doesn't know what democracy is. Russia doesn't know either but there, at least, to compensate for ignorance, they gave the world communism.

At the end of October Nicola Bombacci leaves for Moscow, where the IV congress of the Communist International awaits him. He leaves along with a delegation of the Italian Communist Party, which split from the Socialist Party in January 1921, in Livorno, and which in turn split into two wings: a right, minority wing, headed by Angelo Tasca, in favor of meeting with the socialists after they expelled Turati's reformists at the beginning of the month, and a left, majority wing, led by Secretary Bordiga, opposed to a "unified front." The Russian Bolsheviks are pushing for merger, so that they can oppose fascism with a solid bloc of the entire proletariat, but Bordiga is resistant. From his point of view democracy is already fascism, the capitalist counterrevolution has already won, what difference could it make if the fascists seized power? With

Bordiga, Trotsky persists in emphasizing the distinctive features of Italian fascism, owing to the unprecedented mobilization of the petite bourgeoisie against the proletariat, but Bordiga remains deaf. For those like him, democracy and fascism, no matter what Trotsky says, remain one and the same.

Bombacci, always aligned with Moscow, is for re-establishing a "unified front." At the Rome congress in February he fought openly against abstractionism, the purism of the Bordiga faction, concerned only with avoiding any contamination with the socialists. The result was ostracism by his own comrades, isolation, mistrust, and ultimately his expulsion from the party's central committee. He wrote a poignant letter to Grigori Zinoviev, lamenting his "political assassination."

When the delegation of Italian communists—after being defeated by the fascists, splitting from the socialists, then splitting internally—arrives in Russia at the end of October, communism in Russia is at the height of its triumph. Leon Trotsky, the one Bordiga turns a deaf ear to, who before the revolution was a man of letters nicknamed "Pen," had risen from his desk and in a few months organized the Red Army, the largest popular army in history. Millions of armed workers and peasants, a new conception of the war of movement on a planetary scale, at the head of which, in four years of bloody civil war, he crushed all the enemies of the revolution on two continents and dozens of fronts. The communists of the East, routed by internal and external enemies, are now on the verge of founding the Union of Soviet Socialist Republics and inaugurating a new era in world history. The communists of the West, on the other hand, experiencing one defeat after another, are retreating on every front. Within the Comintern, the international organization made up of all the communist parties in the world, the absolute hegemony of the Russian comrades looms ahead. As for the others, Bordiga in the lead, wherever they will have to hide out, all they can do is support the Russians' conquest as best they can from the depths of their own defeat.

Nicola Bombacci, well advised judging from the faint hint of melancholy that clouds the blue irises of his porcelain-doll eyes, is aware of his subordination in Moscow. He's proclaimed it to comrades gathered at assemblies since Livorno: "We will go ahead, behind the light of the Russian revolution, even if full of terror, even if full of grief." Then, during the following year, he fought in parliament for the Italian state to reopen trade with Russia and recognize its legitimate government. In this battle, he found himself supported by strange fellow travelers, industrial magnates like Ettore Conti. Business and communism lined up side by side. The mocking destiny of the defeated must bend to these ironies of history as well.

In Moscow, photographs of the glorious Russian revolution have already rightly entered the central archive of time. They are proudly displayed in executive offices and conference rooms. *July 1917: troops loyal to the provisional government fire on the crowd on Via Sadovaja. September 1917: groups of Bolshevik workers, rifles leveled, patrol the streets of Petersburg from the back of a truck. October 1917: sailors on board the* Aurora *battle cruiser prepare for combat.*

By far the most beautiful photo is dated October 25, 1917: *red guards run towards the entrance of the Winter Palace.* The photo of the proletarian assault on the main residence of the tsar of all the Russian republics and a symbol of his power, was taken from above, maybe by a photographer who climbed on top of a lamppost. It depicts a horde of dark figures against the white surface of the snow-covered square, rushing at a stone wall; it too dark, which blocks the horizon of the future behind it. The inimical rampart seems like an insurmountable barrier, a peremptory denial in the icy chill of an endless winter, mute and deaf, yet none of those tiny figures rushing to assault it has both feet on the ground. They're all running, racing at breakneck speed, forming an almost perfect pyramid, faithful to the mathematical laws of Renaissance perspective, as if a Masaccio or a Piero della Francesca had painted their triumphal struggle. In the eyes of Nicola Bombacci and the other Italian delegates, at this end of October 1922, the communist revolution cannot yet appear as remorse on the part of the victors—it will take several years for that—but there is certainly the regret of the defeated.

Antonio Gramsci, the most brilliant mind of the PCI, the Communist Party of Italy, and a member of the delegation along with Bombacci, is in very poor health. In order to participate in the Moscow congress, he returned from the sanatorium a few days ago, after a six-month stay which only served to prevent his illness from worsening. Gramsci is suffering from chronic fatigue, amnesia, and insomnia.

Unfortunately, Lenin, the greatest man of the century, is also ill. When he receives his Italian comrades, he has already had a stroke, but he welcomes them smiling, addressing Bordiga and Camilla Ravera in Italian, reminiscent of his youth as an exile in Capri. Bordiga expresses everyone's apprehension for his health.

"I'm fine," he responds readily, "but I have to obey the tyrannical prescriptions of the doctors. So I won't fall ill again . . ." Then, leaving his short future uncertain, he asks about events in Italy.

Bordiga brings up the question of relations with the Socialist Party, but Lenin quashes it. He has no time for these diatribes. He wants to know what's happening with the fascists in Italy.

Bordiga, obedient, relates the facts, repeating analyses and opinions already expressed. Suddenly the great man interrupts him and asks what the workers and peasants think of those events. Bordiga, head of the Italian communists, is left speechless, like a student caught unprepared by a question he didn't expect.

In Italy, meanwhile—in the very hours when tens of thousands of blackshirts in Naples' Piazza del Plebiscito are shouting "To Rome! To Rome!"—the top leaders of the Socialist Party in Milan, agreeing not to take them seriously and to consider the threat unrealistic, reassured by the absolute certainty that nothing significant is happening, board the train to Moscow.

Assuming the state possesses a minimum of capacity to withstand a violent takeover by fascism—if only for traditionalist reasons—we have never believed and we do not believe in the march on Rome.

"A Conflict That Will Not Happen,"
anonymous editorial, *Avanti!*, October 15–16, 1922

ON THE MARCH

OCTOBER 24–31, 1922

NAPLES, OCTOBER 24, 1922
TEATRO SAN CARLO, 10:00 A.M.

THE APPEARANCE OF Benito Mussolini at 10:00 a.m. on October 24th, 1922, on the gigantic stage of the Teatro San Carlo in Naples, the queen of the Mediterranean, the world capital of ready enthusiasms and incurable disillusionments, sets off a new kind of euphoria. It is an emotion similar to that aroused by the speeches of D'Annunzio, but purified of his lugubrious vein. Now the charismatic leader no longer demands sacrifices from the jubilant crowd, he promises orgasms.

Stunned and awed by the visible manifestation of the century's foremost innovation—the masses as the protagonist of history—the journalists write of a "magical, almost religious demonstration," a "magnificent sight," about it being impossible for the reader to "form a precise idea of the vibrant emotion." In short, you have to have experienced the dazzling moment to know how the seven thousand Neapolitans felt, crowded for two hours in a theater with little more than a thousand seats, when Benito Mussolini, surrounded by 500 pennants and announced by a trumpet blast, finally appeared on stage. He is welcomed by the police prefect, the mayor, the entire council and a group of southern deputies, as the band plays *Giovinezza*. Everyone is on their feet, singing in unison at the top of their lungs, moved.

The Duce, aware that the Neapolitans are a cheerful people, starts off with a few jokes. Then he delivers a frank but measured speech to the city's bourgeoisie crammed into the royal theater. Fascism, no use hiding it, is an armed party because in the end it is force that is decisive. This is why they have assembled, vigorously organized and firmly disciplined their legions. Fascism, clearly stated, wants to become the state. Parliament is a plaything, but fascism will not take away the people's plaything. Let them keep it, amuse themselves with it, our goal is different: our myth is the nation, its greatness.

At this point, the speaker takes the plunge. The republican ideal is definitively shelved. The rules of the game are these: the king is not an issue unless he decides to make himself an issue by opposing the fascists. The army is absolutely revered. But, even with the king and the army, the time has come. We are at the point where the arrow must be released from the bow, or the bow string, too taut, will snap. We fascists do not intend to enter power by the back door. We will not give up the formidable ideals of our origins for a miserable plate of ministerial scraps.

The crowd of seven thousand people cheers wildly, jubilant. Every one of them, without exception. The liberals don't understand a thing. In a second-tier box, sunk in a baroque armchair upholstered in crimson velvet, Benedetto Croce also applauds heartily. The Neapolitan philosopher is probably the nation's loftiest intellectual authority, leader of that liberal thought explicitly trampled by fascism. He is fifty-four years old, and has been a senator for twelve; he was minister of public education in Giolitti's last government, he abhors the socialists whose revolution he views as the revolt of the ignorant against the cultured, and he despises the crude, self-taught man that is Mussolini, the beggar of ideas. And yet Don Benedetto applauds.

Sitting beside Croce, Giustino Fortunato, an expert on Italy's South, shudders: "There's too much violence in these people."

Croce, quoting the philosopher, reassures him with a condescending smile: "But Don Giustino, have you forgotten what Marx says? Violence is the midwife of history."

On the way out of the gallery, literary scholar Luigi Russo, a pupil of Croce, finds the nerve to overcome his veneration for the master: "Will you explain to me, Professor, why so much applause? To me Mussolini seemed like a histrionic actor."

The great philosopher, affable and pedantic, with the air of a man of the world who has seen it all, gives the intemperate young man a lesson in the school of eternal cynicism: "Of course, Luigi. But you know as well as I do that politics is theater. Politicians are play-actors. That Mussolini is a good histrionic."

Moreover, the stage on which Mussolini receives the final applause of an interminable ovation still displays the stage set for *Madama Butterfly*, performed the night before. It all fits, it all ties together: exoticism, chinoiserie, the supremacy of the West, brilliant dramatic synthesis.

PIAZZA SAN FERDINANDO, 4:30 P.M.

THE SHOW OF strength succeeded to perfection. No less than twenty thousand fascists—some go so far as to estimate forty thousand—descended on Naples, unchallenged, from all over Italy, traveling on special trains made available by the railways of the state they declare they want to seize.

The squads were assembled and organized at the Arenaccia sports field, in accordance with directives issued by order sheet (*foglio d'ordini*) no. 1 of the militia. Despite the alert that for days had worried the prefect and the government, the parade proceeds martially but peacefully through the streets of the city, with the exception of a few isolated incidents. The men are armed, weapons on display, there is even a squadron on horseback from Apulia. The military attaché of the British embassy in Italy admires its bearing and militaristic equipage. All the same, Luigi Facta in Rome breathes a sigh of relief. The chamber president, liberal attorney Enrico De Nicola, even congratulates Mussolini. The dreaded insurrection has not happened.

At 4:30 p.m. the Duce, surrounded by fascism's entire high

command, after having won over the bourgeoisie that morning at the Teatro San Carlo, reviews the troops from a stage erected in Piazza San Ferdinando. The swarm of blackshirts spills over into the adjacent Piazza del Plebiscito. As the comrades applaud and cheer, Mussolini is silent. In the distance, beyond the rise known as the "pallonetto" of the Santa Lucia district, the gulf's waters reflect the last light of day.

Then Italo Balbo steps down from the platform, finds his Emilian comrades in the crowd and gives the order. Towards the stage, and up towards the hill, a wave of incitement rises and swells in the squalid alleyways: "Roma! Roma!"

The squadristi beat time in the late afternoon, chanting the two syllables nonstop. Then Mussolini speaks:

"Blackshirts of Naples and all over Italy, today without striking a blow we have captured the vibrant soul of Naples, the ardent soul of the entire South of Italy. The demonstration is an end in itself and must not turn into a battle, but I tell you with all the solemnity called for by this moment: either they will give us the government or we will seize it, descending on Rome! By now it's a matter of days and maybe hours."

The brief address ends with an invitation to the crowd to acclaim the army under the military command's windows. Rising from the piazza are shouts of "Viva fascism! Long live the army! Viva Italy! Long live the king!"

On stage, Cesare De Vecchi, a fervent monarchist, leans over to Mussolini's ear:

"You shout it too: Long live the king!"

Mussolini doesn't answer.

De Vecchi presses him: "Shout it, long live the king!"

Mussolini continues to ignore him. De Vecchi grabs him by the arm and insists for the third time. As the crowd turns its back to swarm below the command building, the old republican who still exists somewhere in Benito Mussolini rubs a hand over his face and squeezes his cheekbones in his usual weary gesture before pulling free of De Vecchi's grip.

"Stop. They're shouting, that's enough. It's more than enough . . ."

NAPLES, OCTOBER 24, 1922
HÔTEL DU VÉSUVE, MUSSOLINI'S ROOM, NIGHT

The caldera of Vesuvius extends through miles of extinguished pumice stone to the south and east. Its dark silhouette, scoured by the pounding rain, dominates the gulf like a deeper smudge of black. Under the volcano, the city of Naples sleeps, prone, unconscious, doomed to dissolution. She sobs in her sleep, unaware of herself and the reasons why she is crying.

"Come in." Benito Mussolini sits by the window, mesmerized by the storm out at sea.

"To us!"

De Vecchi, De Bono, Balbo and the party's deputy secretaries Teruzzi, Bastianini and Starace salute, arms outstretched. They're all wearing black shirts, military uniforms and medals on their chests. Cesare De Vecchi conceals his prominent belly under a wide, black silk cummerbund and perfectly ironed gray-green trousers. Balbo leaves footprints on the Persian carpets with his muddy boots. The only one who does not extend his arm in the Roman salute and who is sporting baggy, frayed civilian clothes is Michele Bianchi. In his black jacket that hangs loosely due to his sickly gauntness, he looks like an undertaker come to officiate at the others' funeral.

"To us, to us . . . take a seat. You, Balbo, take notes."

"I have no paper, Duce."

"Write on the telegram forms, there on the table. This meeting is confidential. Never mind formalities. Let's get to it."

They sit down. Only Bianchi remains standing, facing Mussolini's armchair, where it's possible to meet his gaze, unseen by the others.

Mussolini explains the plan. The political hierarchies of the Fascist Party will transfer powers to the quadrumvirate at midnight between October 26 and 27. From that moment on, everyone, including him, will have to obey the orders issued by the quadrumvirs from their headquarters in Perugia. The military strategy is the one conceived in Milan on October 16th and finalized at the secret meeting in Bordighera two days later. Italy has been divided into twelve zones, each of which is assigned to an inspector general. The most important one, which includes Piedmont, Liguria and Lombardy, has been assigned to Cesare Forni, the ras of Lomellina who led the assault on Milan's town hall. On the appointed day, the zone inspectors will issue the mobilization order and fascist forces will occupy key points in the provinces. The actual march will start from three locations near Rome: Santa Marinella, Mentana and Tivoli, where squadristi from all over Italy will assemble on the night of October 27. The goal is the conquest of power with a ministry that has at least six fascists in the most important dicasteries.

"Comrades, these are the two horns of the dilemma: whether to mobilize immediately or whether, prior to mobilizing, strike in situ, occupying public buildings in the key cities. My view is that occupation and mobilization must be simultaneous. Opinions to the contrary?" Mussolini's tone is peremptory, an order masquerading as an idle question.

Emilio De Bono, as if talking cost him an immense effort, says he agrees. A career general, consumed by the ambition to become a minister of war in one way or another, he'd wept in public in a Rome office two weeks earlier when he was forced to choose between two alternatives: resigning from the army or from the Fascist Party.

After him, Bianchi also says he's in favor. It seems quite clear to him that they are play-acting in that room—the Duce has already decided everything—and he goes along with the performance. A simple nod of the head is sufficient for him, as in a pantomime for children that requires nothing more demanding. Even Balbo agrees. He merely expresses concern about Parma, the one city that resisted the attack by his army of squadristi.

The only one to object, as usual, is De Vecchi. Whining that the military plan is not in place, that the weaponry is insufficient. But then he says he is confident that there will be no collision with the armed forces. They just have to confront the sovereign with a parliamentary crisis, De Vecchi adds, then he'll "see to the rest."

Balbo has stopped writing. He stares at De Vecchi defiantly.

Discernable in the words of the reluctant quadrumvir is the agitation of a man with his back to the wall. The transfer of powers to the military command in Perugia at the outbreak of the insurrection—prearranged by Mussolini with his customary cunning—would dump all responsibility on their heads. Everyone understands this. But De Vecchi with his vague, ambiguous words—"I'll see to the rest"—is in fact asking for authorization to conduct separate negotiations with Rome's politicians and the court before the ultimatum expires. And everyone understands that too.

The melancholy certainty of prophetic moments founders in the look that passes between Mussolini and Bianchi: you will always find a traitor, a coward.

Deeming his monarchical schemes irrelevant, Mussolini in any case authorizes De Vecchi to negotiate whatever he wants. Then he takes out the quadrumvirs' proclamation agreed to in Milan. He reads it aloud. Finally, he says goodnight to the comrades and goodbye to Rome. The following day, while the cover-up conference goes on in Naples, he will return to Milan.

Now it's all decided. The plan is laid out in the "Five Phases of the Revolution": 1) mobilization and occupation of public buildings; 2) convergence of blackshirts in the vicinity of Rome; 3) ultimatum to the Facta government for the surrender of powers; 4) entry into Rome and seizure of the ministries at all costs; 5) in the event of defeat, retreat towards central Italy, establishment of a fascist government and swift assembly of blackshirts in the Po Valley.

It's an infantile plan. Even a military ignoramus would see that. The last two points, in particular, even make you smile. Rain continues to fall on the sleeping city at the foot of the volcano.

I wish to extend my personal, cordial greetings to you and to all the colleagues present in Naples.

Telegram from Enrico De Nicola,
president of the chamber,
to Mussolini, at 10:30 a.m.

Fascist demonstration orderly. Nothing to report . . . Then Mussolini gave a brief talk in which he said . . . that if the government is not given to the fascists, fascism will take it by force.

Telegram from Angelo Pesce, prefect of Naples,
to Prime Minister Luigi Facta, 7:30 p.m.

Fascist assembly Naples proceeded peacefully: two small incidents caused by panic were of no importance . . . I believe plan to march on Rome now faded.

Telegram from Luigi Facta to the king,
who is vacationing in San Rossore, 9:40 p.m.

We'd like to think that the Naples speech is more a sign of impatience than of resolution.

Corriere della Sera, October 25, 1922

Play-actors . . . a parade of puppets.

L'Ordine Nuovo,
communist newspaper, October 25, 1922

We must grab the miserable ruling political class by the throat.

Benito Mussolini,
Piazza San Ferdinando, Naples, October 24, 1922

ROME, OCTOBER 25, 1922
PLATFORM AT TERMINI STATION, 7:30 P.M.

"I'M EXPECTING SOMEONE."

A few minutes ago, when the express train from Naples came to a stop under the platform roof that was being hammered by the rain, those laconic words were all Mussolini uttered in the red-velvet-covered compartment as he fastened the ever-present white spats. Neither of the two men traveling with him—Cesare Rossi and Alessandro Chiavolini, his personal secretary—would be surprised if the Duce availed himself of a woman in the half-hour stop before the train continues on to Milan. That animal need, they know, strikes him even at the most serious moments. Indeed, especially at those times.

The station appears quiet, the alarm sounded in the morning has ceased, the special trains on which the fascists returning from Naples are traveling have been diverted to the Orte line, and the idle carabinieri are crowded around the buffet windows. Huddled together in small groups, they're warming their hands with the sour breath of empty stomachs, like oxen on the night in Bethlehem.

It's not a woman. A group of distinguished gentlemen, led by a bespectacled man in a bowler hat, approaches the train. Mussolini steps out. The man with the glasses draws him aside and frantically begins filling him in. He waves his hands about, he's in a hurry, time is short. They're making a deal, it's obvious. They're buying and selling something.

He's been dealing with everybody, for days, for weeks, under the table, nonstop. No one knows it better than Cesare Rossi. He's dealing with Antonio Salandra, the would-be liberal, reactionary as a Prussian baron, the contemptuous, vile Apulian landowner who still counts his estate properties in souls, the honorary fascist more to the right than the fascists themselves, the former prime minister who dragged Italy into war against the nation's will and carries millions of dead and wounded on his conscience. To sweet-talk him, Mussolini had stopped at his home in Rome on the way to Naples. He promised him a new presidency in exchange for five dicasteries and asked for nothing for himself. He's dealing with Nitti, the southern notable, the great, irreplaceable expert on financial matters, the most insulted man in Europe, whom Mussolini privately calls "the swine" because he granted amnesty to the deserters of the Great War, and whom D'Annunzio dubbed "*Cagoja*," vile coward, when he opposed the liberation of Fiume. He's dealing with Facta, with his French gendarme's mustache, the mustache of a provincial notary, of a camp quartermaster, the mustache of an inadequate, weary man, faithful as a retriever to his master Giolitti, tempted by the crepuscular joys of retirement yet conflicted by the desire not to make a poor showing in History, seduced by the vanity of one last tilt in the joust. Most of all he's dealing with Giolitti, the old octogenarian statesman, the only one with whom he is seriously dealing, the only one still capable of restoring the state's authority, of imposing a shady ministerial compromise on Mussolini. Rossi is dealing with him himself, through Milan's prefect Lusignoli. But Giolitti is in Cavour, in Piedmont, his own terrain, where the pharmacist tips his hat when he passes by, where his eighty years are celebrated.

They are dealing with everyone, taking advantage of parliamentary short-sightedness, playing hide-and-seek, betting at more than one table, wagering all the stakes, relying on vetoes that cancel each other out, rekindling factional hatreds—Sturzo's veto of Giolitti, the rivalry between these two and Nitti—tempting the vanities of each, and each one takes the lure. In the end, everyone is promised the same thing: the presidency of a coalition government, the support of the reformed fascists in exchange for four or five ministries. And everyone is fed the same bum deal. The primary goal, Mussolini's "secret plan," remains, in fact, the same: to stall for time, to bring the political crisis to a point of no return, the point where any alternative solution to a fascist government is no longer possible, then, and only then, to press Facta to resign, threatening insurrection and seizing power without firing a shot. The third phase of the revolution that becomes the first.

And it is, in fact, all a question of timing: they must avoid moving "too soon," which would still allow others to form an emergency government that would exclude the fascists, or "too late," which would expose their military bluff. If Facta steps down when the fascists are already at the gates of Rome, no one will have the authority to order a bloodbath and then the squads' weight can tip the scale. "There is only one person who can shoot down the fascists, and that's me." Mussolini repeats this to everyone in his secret negotiations, and promises one and all that he will discharge the squads the minute after entering government. There is only one man who can save the country from the chaos of squad violence. It is the same man who must first trigger it.

A flurry of clasps and handshakes breaks out on the station platform. Mussolini says goodbye and extends his hand palm down in the fascist salute, as the station master urges him into the compartment, worried that the problematic traveler might remain in Rome to cause trouble. The train departs again.

"That was Raoul Palermi, Grand Master of the Scottish Rite of Freemasonry. He assured me that officers of the royal guard, those of Rome's garrison, and General Cittadini, the king's first aide-de-camp, will help us in our move. Maybe even the Duke of the Sea, Grand Admiral Thaon de Revel. All people from the Freemasons of Piazza del Gesù."

The Duce communicates this to Cesare Rossi almost immediately, with the millenary arches of the Roman aqueduct still in sight, in the gruff tone of those times when he can't contain his excitement.

Now they have to hope that the vacation season persists. Hope that Giolitti doesn't rouse himself too soon from the torpors of the Piedmontese autumn, that the king doesn't return too soon from the hunts at San Rossore to decree a state of siege, and that D'Annunzio, or what's left of him, doesn't shake off the lethargy of his perversions and attempt a last venture. D'Annunzio . . . always D'Annunzio . . . still D'Annunzio. Who knows whether the Vate's vanity may have taken the bait thrown at him . . .

The express train departing at 8:00 p.m. heads northwards. Away from Naples, away from Rome, away from Perugia, away from the comedies of epochal orations, of government or combatants. Away, towards Milan! That's where the game will be played. Negotiate, threaten, deceive. The piston that transmits motion to the connecting rods, and from these to the drive wheels, seems to recite the words like a forsaken rosary. Negotiate, deceive, threaten. Negotiate with everybody, betray everybody.

GARDONE, OCTOBER 25, 1922
VILLA DI CARGNACCO

It's still raining, his nose is running, his head aches, the dampness has congested his respiratory tract. Getting old, putting on weight, catching cold every time the season changes, feeling nauseated at the subterfuges and cowardice of the men whom you once liked to scorn, there, that's the reward you get for surviving.

They've been harassing him for days, everyone wants a pound of Gabriele D'Annunzio's flaccid flesh, whose prolapse not even a white double-breasted Prince of Wales jacket of the finest sartorial cut is now able to hide.

The first to insist on a meeting, he must acknowledge, was Mussolini. The Vate had to respond categorically that he was unable to receive him. Then it was Facta's turn. On October 21st, in a letter which attempted to imitate his style, the prime minister invited him to celebrate the anniversary of the victory in Rome with great fanfare at the tomb of the Unknown Soldier: "My dearest friend, what will take place in Rome on November 4th will be grand. To say the word peace to Italy, having it burst forth once again from those who have given Italy everything, everything, everything, is the greatest act that can be done in these times . . . Meanwhile the nation eagerly drinks the fresh, cool water that springs up at the call: never as in this moment did it thirst for peace. Farewell, until November 4." Pathetic. Truly pathetic.

In the past the adulatory imitations of his "inimitable" style had flattered Gabriele D'Annunzio, but now, as he grows older, he sees them as a sign of ill omen. Pathetic and inauspicious. That poor man Facta who dreamed of his Piedmont from the depths of the "Roman cloaca" had staked everything on D'Annunzio's participation in the celebrations of the anniversary of the victory, that is, he had based his entire defense system on an aged poet who, surrounded by thousands of maimed and crippled war veterans, was supposed to rescue Italy from disaster. The poet, seized by a scruple of sobriety, had accepted the prime minister's offer in telegraphic style: "Thank you for your fond words stop. All my strength recovered stop. Will meet again in Rome. I am thirsty for the water of Trevi stop."

But the proposals to the Vate were not over. Shortly afterwards he'd been offered a government with Nitti and Vittorio Emanuele Orlando. Then Mussolini had made another attempt, sending Aldo Finzi, his companion on the flight over Vienna. He'd had to receive him but he had also dictated strict conditions: no attack on workers' organizations, not a cent from industrialists and agrarians. Two days later, on October 24th, that nagging bully who called himself Duce had sent his personal secretary Tom Antongini, an aspiring poet and handsome young man, lanky and wholesome, to propose that he flank him in "his" march on Rome. A mocking proposal for the man who had conceived of a march on Rome since the days of Fiume. Yes, they had really taken everything from him: the anthems, the mottos, the salutes. All they discarded were the ideas and the ideals. The poet-warrior was furious, ready to jump back into the fray if only for the pleasure of spoiling Mussolini's plans.

But then it began to rain, his nose started running, his throat became sore. The poet had therefore sent for the doctor, gone to bed, and written to his friend Aldo Rossini: "I am still practically aphonic, as in the sky over Trent at 17 degrees below zero! By the doctor's frank, strict orders, I must remain silent. And I feel deeply sorry for myself. You know that I had planned to come to Rome but I can't promise anything. If I get better I will come." When Dr. Duse arrived at the villa towards evening, he enjoined him:

“The horde of petitioners has left me on my last legs. Prescribe solitude for me.”

Dr. Duse had done as ordered, informing the newspapers of a medical prescription of absolute rest drafted in perfect D’Annunzian style.

Less than twenty-four hours later, however, on the afternoon of October 25th, Gabriele D’Annunzio leaps out of bed and instructs Duse to notify the newspapers of a sudden improvement in his health—those newspapers which that morning, along with the brief mention of D’Annunzio’s illness, dedicated entire pages to Mussolini’s triumph in Naples.

The recovered poet now dons his Prince of Wales jacket and settles into his knick-knack crammed study. He is about to receive a visit from Alfredo Lusignoli, the prefect of Milan, a key man in the current frenzied negotiations. Maybe it’s even stopped raining.

Lusignoli speaks of the many D’Annunzian fascists who would like to see him in the nation’s government, of the many industrialists and bankers who would like Giolitti back in government, then, just like that, he proposes that Gabriele D’Annunzio enter into an accord with Mussolini and . . . with Giolitti!

Turned to marble in his foppish posturing, D’Annunzio stares for a few moments at the insolent imbecile who is nonchalantly suggesting an alliance with the man who had fired cannons at him in Fiume.

Then the poet gets up and opens the window that looks onto the garden. It’s still raining. He closes it again. He dismisses Lusignoli with a limp handshake and a laconic: “We will do what we can.”

As soon as Lusignoli gets into the car, the poet dictates a telegram to his fiduciary in Rome: “I am more ill than before. Punished by transgressions. Impossible to receive anyone. I’m giving it all up, irrevocably. Any attempt will be in vain. D’Annunzio.”

Finally, in his own hand, Gabriele D’Annunzio pens a notice to be affixed to the villa’s door like a scroll and goes back to bed.

Meanwhile, evening has fallen. The alabasters, the crystals, the gaily colored porcelains gleam in the shadows, drinking in the faint glow of a rainy sunset over Lake Garda. In that faltering light, the proclamation to the world, with which the weary poet hopes to be able to stop the march of history at the entrance to his villa, can barely be read:

"What do I have in common with the man with the naval cannon who tried to kill my indomitable idea in Fiume? I am saddened *usque ad mortem*. In Rome I see nothing but cloacae."

MILAN, FORO BONAPARTE, OCTOBER 26, 1922
MUSSOLINI'S HOME, MORNING

THE MAN OF the house, leaning forward, lowers his head over the soup bowl, like a predator sinking its mouth into a prey's intestines. All his concentration seems focused on not staining the stiff collar of his starched shirt. His wife, still in her dressing gown, watches her husband, who has just arrived from Rome, sip his milk and coffee.

Benito and Rachele don't talk to each other. They know from experience that, as always between husband and wife, no words would be worth the risk of breaking the silence. If he were to confide to her his aspirations to become prime minister, Rachele would respond with a peasant proverb: "*Chi lascia la via vecchia per la nuova, male si trova*," whoever leaves the old path for a new one finds himself worse off. If he then told her that it was an honorary appointment, without pay, she would insult him: "Some job, being prime minister! Becoming an errand boy for all Italians—what's more, for free! Some honor!" The undue misery he's swallowed with that woman advises Benito Mussolini to keep quiet.

Welcoming him on his return from Naples an hour earlier, Rachele informed him that she had gotten rid of the hand grenades that he kept hidden in the house. Too dangerous with the imminent risk of searches. Her sister Pina, a tubercular at the last stage, transported them to Castello Sforzesco, one at a time, hiding them in her bosom, and threw them into the moat.

He then asked her if she still had the gun she'd demanded in order to defend herself from infatuated rivals. Yes, that's still hidden under the mattress on the sofa where little Vittorio sleeps.

The phone rings. It's Michele Bianchi from Rome. Through a hail of static, he informs him of the situation. Despite official denials, rumors about their imminent mobilization are circulating in the corridors. The Council of Ministers has been convened for that afternoon, they say that Facta is about to resign. Bianchi met with him the night before, as soon as he returned from Naples, pushing him to stall with the promise of fascist participation in his eventual new government. He also told him that they would be willing to settle for only four ministries. The king, fortunately, is still vacationing in San Rossore. Unfortunately, however, as Bianchi had foreseen, De Vecchi has practically parted company with them. He might not even go to Perugia. He's negotiating with the monarchist right for a Salandra government. They say that in view of this goal, Minister Riccio, close to the fascists but Salandra's man, could bring Facta down, having him tender his resignation that same afternoon. At De Vecchi's side is Dino Grandi, whom De Vecchi appointed the quadrumvirate's chief of staff.

Mussolini, however, does not seem alarmed by this news.

"Never mind them. They can't do any damage. Keep an eye on them."

"Lusignoli went to Gardone."

"Has D'Annunzio made any decision?"

"No word yet."

"Keep reassuring Facta. Let him think he's our man. Drag it out as long as possible with him. But keep in mind, Michelino, there's no going back."

After hanging up the receiver, the husband orders his wife not to leave the house for the next forty-eight hours. She is to stand by the phone and scrupulously make note of all the calls. There are momentous events on the way. He will sleep at the newspaper.

Benito Mussolini strolls along unhurriedly. The walk to Via Lovanio is peaceful. Via Brera, Via Solferino, Via Statuto are as they always are. People are working, artists are hanging around the academy, his dreary whores, worn out by the night, are still sleeping their morning slumber on Via Fiori Chiari. When heard from Milan, the clamor of Naples and Rome's rumors sound like the incoherent ranting of a drunk.

MILAN, VIA LOVANIO, OCTOBER 26, 1922
OFFICES OF *IL POPOLO D'ITALIA*,
AFTERNOON–EVENING

THE TELEGRAM RELAYING D'Annunzio's abdication was obviously intercepted by the prefecture of Brescia, which at 8:45 p.m. on October 25th informed the Ministry of the Interior in Rome. The situation accelerates.

Once D'Annunzio, the linchpin of his defensive strategy, is out of the picture, Facta can no longer wait. The reopening of the chamber, scheduled for November 7, is too far off. The situation is accelerating and it's accelerating too rapidly. It is now a race against time. Furthermore, from the prefecture of Milan, Lusignoli informed the government that he has confirmed that the fascists are preparing a coup de main for the night of October 27. Just this morning, evidently hoping to still be able to seal the Giolitti–Mussolini accord and, perhaps, to also join the new government, the prefect of Milan informed Rome of this, setting out three suggestions on how to confront the fascist assault: overpower them with numbers, suppress them with weapons, or even ignore them.

Discarding the absurd third suggestion of their colleague from Milan, at 12:10 a.m. Interior Minister Paolino Taddei, via a coded telegram from Rome, ordered all the prefects of the Kingdom to meet any possible fascist insurrectional attempt with armed resistance. Taddei himself has arranged for the immediate arrest of fascist leaders, beginning with Mussolini, at the first sign of sedition. The telegram that would put an end to the march before it begins is on Lusignoli's desk.

All this Mussolini, on Via Lovanio, cannot yet know. To be forearmed, however, he had a barricade set up along the gate, manned by soldiers with muskets. The barricade was constructed with rolls of rotary press paper from the newspaper's print shop, already disintegrating in the incessant rain. Then for his own protection he resorted to the apotropaic powers of language: the newspaper's offices were dubbed the "small fortress." In the absence of more tangible armaments, he resorted, in short, to incantation. The thaumaturgical word was pronounced, in an apocalyptic tone, that very afternoon during an editorial meeting in which shifts were doubled and maximum print runs prepared: "Starting this evening we must all consider ourselves mobilized," the editor-in-chief proclaimed. "We will have to provide for armed defense of the building and the equipment. Revolutionary action is about to begin and everyone must stay at his post. This is a small fortress, our fortress, and we must defend it at all costs."

Meanwhile, however, the Duce of fascism uses a completely different tone with the outside world, the conciliatory, self-satisfied tone of one who until yesterday courted the world and is now courted by it. All of a sudden, it's others who want to negotiate with him, and he does not deny anyone a compassionate lie. He continues to assure Lusignoli that he prefers the combination with Giolitti; to Costanzo Ciano, leaving for Rome, he specified fascist readiness for an agreement with Salandra upon the assignment of five ministerial portfolios; he even received Nitti's ambassadors, holding out the possibility of a re-appointment, now impossible, for the former prime minister.

Protected from machine guns by a soaked paper barricade, Mussolini speaks the language of wisdom and measure. He speaks this same language to the "captains" as well, when, on the late afternoon of October 26, after years of differences and disdain, they finally decide to climb the stairs of the "fortress," poorly illuminated by the reddish glow of light bulbs. A delegation of key Milanese and Lombard industrialists, led by Alberto Pirelli, making their way through the rain in the narrow passageway between the reels of sodden paper, visited him towards evening and paid their respects. They discussed the chief concerns of the moment, in relation to the direction of the exchange rate, the performance of government bonds, and the country's credit abroad. They all admired how the leader of the revolutionary insurgence underway, the barbarous proclaimer of violent threats, was able to discuss those problems with great reflection and a keen sense of their importance. As soon as they left the "fortress," the Lombard industrialists ordered the Banking Association to deposit two million liras into the account of Giovanni Marinelli, administrator of the Fascist National Party.

Shortly thereafter, the news arrives from Rome that Facta has not resigned. The Council of Ministers decided on an intermediate resolution: the ministers remitted their portfolios to the prime minister who, perhaps, is still deluding himself that he can make room in his government for the fascists. A sigh of relief is breathed in the fortress on Via Lovanio. For now the march is safe.

Outside it is still raining; it rains on the rolls of paper, now practically reduced to mush. The mass of newsprint turned to pulp by the rain is reminiscent of the corpses of fellow soldiers decomposing in the trenches of the Great War.

But maybe it won't be necessary to get to that point. In the country of meridian heat, even under a torrential rain, an intermediate solution remains the best course. For now Minister Taddei's telegram with the order to arrest the leaders of the fascist insurgency languishes on the desk of the prefect who still hopes to become a minister. We'll wait to see how events develop.

Unexpected reports suggest possible fascist attempt. Government will take forceful measures. Mussolini sent word yesterday willing to enter ministry even giving up requested portfolios provided ministry led by me. Not to sever, I replied to delegate this was something to examine together.

Telegram from Luigi Facta to Vittorio Emanuele III,
October 26, 1922, 12:00 noon

Various reports coming in re insurrection attempts supposedly planned by Fascist Party to be implemented immediately seizing government offices in certain cities. When such attempts seem imminent, resist with arms, all other steps taken.

Telegram from Minister Paolino Taddei to the prefects,
October 26, 1922, 12:10 p.m.

Confidential to staff stop—Signs of imminent insurrectionary movement reported from various parts intended to seize state powers by violent means stop—I have certainty no military element will be able to join such movement breaking essential sworn military duties . . . Your Eminences must have your subordinate Commands ready to assume powers to maintain public order stop

Telegram from the minister of war
to the military commanders,
October 26, 1922, 5:00 p.m.

Italy asks its children to desist from the fighting that is destroying it: Italy asks, for its prosperity and for its greatness, that an exacerbation that produces only pain and ruin be truncated without delay.

It is not possible to refuse to accept this appeal.

Minutes of the Council of Ministers,
October 26, 1922, 7:30 p.m.

The only possible solution to the crisis consists of entrusting the succession of the Facta ministry to Deputy Mussolini. The party that brought about the crisis is the Fascist Party; it is therefore the head of that party who must be called upon to form the new ministry. We are in an extraparliamentary crisis. It is no longer the chamber that appoints, but the Nation. Who represents the Nation at this time? It's us, the fascists . . . It is the others who refuse to recognize the reality of the situation. We are already here in Rome.

Michele Bianchi, secretary of the PNF,
statement to journalists, Rome, around midnight

This specter of the elections is more than enough to blind the eyes of old parliamentarians, who are already working to invoke our alliance. With this lure we will do what we want with them. We were born yesterday, but we are smarter than them.

Italo Balbo, *Diario*, 1922

MILAN, VIA LOVANIO, OCTOBER 27, 1922
OFFICES OF *IL POPOLO D'ITALIA*,
2:40 A.M.

THE RINGING OF the telephone shatters the insistent rotation of the presses and the relentless pelting of the rain. A voice answers irritatedly from the "fortress" that is being assailed by an Atlantic trough driven by western winds sweeping over the continent; it is that of Cesare Rossi.

Milan—"So what's up?"

At the other end of the line is Michele Bianchi from the Viminale in Rome, asking the switchboard operator to get Benito Mussolini on the line. Although telephone conversations are severely disturbed by the succession of storms streaming across the peninsula, Bianchi can't be unaware that an employee of the Ministry of the Interior, left hand pressed to his headset and right hand ready to scribble shorthand, is intercepting him.

Rome—"The ministers placed their portfolios at the disposal of the prime minister and Facta will decide today . . . You understand . . ."

Echoing in the pause, amid the pouring rain, is Michele Bianchi's concern that an agreement between Mussolini and Giolitti in Milan could abort the march. Bianchi, with tubercular death filling his lungs, is the most fervent supporter of the venture at all costs. Two hours earlier, on his own initiative, to precipitate a deadlock over the seizure of power, the quadrumvir called a press conference in which he declared that the only possible solution to the crisis was to entrust the nation to Benito Mussolini.

Rome—"How do you assess the situation in Milan?"

Milan—"Excellent."

Rome—"Then we remain in agreement with what was said in Naples?"

Milan—"Yes . . . but . . . there's something new."

Rome—"What is it?"

Milan—"How can I tell you over the phone? Briefly, there's some arrangement in sight."

Rome—"Uh-oh!"

Milan—"But look . . . I'm telling you that I predict this 'arrangement,' which for that matter would only be for a few days, will be rejected by both parties . . ."

Rome—"But what kind of an 'arrangement' would it be . . ."

Milan—"Utilitarian."

Rome—"I get it, partly to make the water rise a little higher."

Milan—"Right . . . I mean . . . look, Finzi is here too, he wants to talk to you."

Rome—"Here I am, put him on."

Aldo Finzi takes over from Cesare Rossi. It's 2:45 a.m. He alludes to the resignation of the Facta government.

Milan—"Is the transition certain for tomorrow?"

Rome—"I believe so."

Milan—"All right, good."

Rome—"As for us, we must not retreat one step."

Milan—"Absolutely."

Rome—"It seems to me that our course is marked out."

Milan—"Firmly."

Rome—"What you say is very comforting. Onward!"

Milan—"Goodnight, Michelino."

MILAN, VIA LOVANIO, OCTOBER 27, 1922
OFFICES OF *IL POPOLO D'ITALIA*,
3:00 A.M.

IN THE "FORTRESS" the phone rings again. Only fifteen minutes have passed since the last call. It's Michele Bianchi calling again. Evidently, given Cesare Rossi's reticence, Finzi's assurances were not enough for him.

Again the call is to the editorial offices of *Il Popolo d'Italia*, again it comes from the Viminale, and is being tapped. This time, however, the editor-in-chief himself answers.

Bianchi—"Benito . . ."

Mussolini—"What is it, Michelino?"

Bianchi—"My friends and I wanted to know what arrangements you've made."

An interval of silence. Mussolini is baffled.

Mussolini—"Arrangements I've made?"

Bianchi—"Yeah. What's new?"

Mussolini—"What's new is this: Lusignoli went to see Giolitti in Cavour and says that he can get four key portfolios and four sub-portfolios from him."

Bianchi—"What would those portfolios be?"

Mussolini—"Navy, treasury, agriculture, and colonies. Then there'd be the war ministry that would be given to a friend of ours, and in addition there would be the four undersecretaries."

Bianchi—"And then?"

Mussolini—"Then he had them call me from Cavour to say that he'll be back this morning at nine."

Bianchi—"Benito . . ."

The appeal to his friend's name has the inflection of a plea.

Mussolini—"What is it?"

Bianchi—"Benito, will you listen to me? Will you hear my firm, unwavering resolve?"

Mussolini—"Yes . . . Sure . . ."

Bianchi—"Tell him: NO."

Silence.

Mussolini—"Of course . . . naturally, the machine is now assembled and nothing can stop it."

Most likely the stenographer is sweating as he transcribes the words that will be reported to the interior minister, from him to Facta and, through the prime minister, to the king.

Bianchi—"What is about to happen is as fateful as destiny itself . . . The time is past to discuss portfolios."

Mussolini—"Naturally . . ."

Bianchi—"So we are still agreed. Can I also communicate this in your name?"

Mussolini—"Wait first . . . Let's hear what Lusignoli says . . . we'll talk again tomorrow."

Bianchi—"All right."

Mussolini—"That way I'll keep you up to date on the whole operation. I'll also give you a run-down on what Lusignoli tells me."

Bianchi—"Good . . . good . . ."

Mussolini—"Goodnight."

Bianchi—"Goodnight, Benito."

MILAN, VIA LOVANIO, OCTOBER 27, 1922
OFFICES OF *IL POPOLO D'ITALIA*, AFTERNOON

COSTANZO CIANO ARRIVED on the first morning train. On Via Lovanio he found men showing signs of just a few hours of sleep, most of them stolen on mattresses tossed on the ground.

The hero of Buccari, exhausted from shuttling between Rome and Milan, seemed even more tired than those proofreaders camped out on the floor like assault troops. The reckless torpedo boat raider, who now amasses wealth by running Giovanni Agnelli's shipping company, sank his huge body into the armchair in front of Mussolini's desk and immediately began to fill him in on Roman maneuvers. He reported on the talks he had with Salandra, on the visit to Giolitti on behalf of Vittorio Emanuele Orlando, on the rumors about the imminent government crisis and the king's expected return to Rome. Finally, Ciano delivered a letter in which Facta was still insisting that the Duce come down to Rome to negotiate personally with him.

As he took notes on scraps of paper, tabloid margins, and telegraph forms, his usual practice, Mussolini knew that sitting before him was one of the members, along with De Vecchi and Dino Grandi, of the small fascist conspiracy still working to avert the march on Rome at all costs. He let him talk, just as he had let them do what they wanted earlier. Every subterfuge of theirs, every whisper in the corridors of Montecitorio regarding the "wind of folly that would rage over the fascists stirred up by Michele Bianchi," and the "bloodbath" that the insane hotheads would provoke at the gates of Rome if they weren't stopped, plays into the hands of the fascists, since it evokes the specter that they are striving to exorcize. The only reality behind an exorcism, Mussolini knows, is fear of the devil and fear itself. And fear, this too Mussolini knows, is their only sharp weapon. The march, until yesterday a blob of shapeless clay, and now vitalized thanks to the conspirators' whispers, has become a monster that lives and breathes on its own. The sight of thousands of men in black, risen up out of darkness, armed and marching on the capital to seize power, is one of those ancient prophecies that need only be pronounced to come true.

Shortly before Ciano's arrival, in order to gain another six or twelve hours, Mussolini sent Rossi to Lusignoli to announce that he would soon be coming to conclude the negotiation with Giolitti.

The phone call from Antonio Salandra, however, arrives at *Il Popolo d'Italia* at 10:25 a.m., when Ciano is still sitting in front of the director. The two rivals for the conquest of power size each other up, both bluffing, like two poker sharks.

Salandra—"The ministry has resigned, placing portfolios at the disposal of the president."

Mussolini—"And has Facta actually handed his resignation to the king?"

Salandra—"That I really don't know."

Mussolini—"Ah! And . . . is there a chance that the president may resolve the crisis?"

Salandra—"Who knows . . .? It will depend on what happens."

For a moment the play-acting stops. Mussolini's eyes meet those of Ciano and Cesare Rossi who are listening. The next stroke requires a different tone of voice.

Mussolini—"But if . . . if you yourself were to be designated to form the new ministry, would you accept the job?"

Salandra—"Well . . . I can't say now. Come to Rome instead!"

Mussolini—"I can't. It's not possible for me to shuttle back and forth between Milan and Rome."

Salandra—"At this time you need to be in Rome because no one, neither I nor anyone else, has a chance of resolving the crisis without you. Have you seen Ciano?"

Mussolini winks at the big man sitting across his desk.

Mussolini—"Yes, he's here in my office and that's exactly why I wanted to hear from you."

Salandra—"Well then, Ciano can tell you what was done yesterday. If I have any more news, I'll let you know."

The conversation ends on that note of impatience. A round in which both boxers have only tested themselves, taking care not to reveal anything, disclaiming what they know and claiming what they cannot know. But unlike his adversary, Mussolini, bobbing and weaving through those conversations, is getting ready for the uppercut to the jaw.

Having said goodbye to Ciano with an emotional embrace and a vague "see you at the Quirinale!", Mussolini spends the rest of the day on Via Lovanio biding his time. By now the "march" is on a downhill course. A few more hours and, at midnight, if no one arrests them that afternoon, squadristi will storm the prefectures in provincial capitals throughout Italy. Those few hours will be the final ones in which he will say yes to everyone. Yes to a Salandra ministry through Ciano, yes to Giolitti through Lusignoli and so on. Everyone is now begging Mussolini to go down to Rome to offer him three, four, five portfolios. The other candidates in power, having agreed to deal only with him for the same post, have lost the chance of spinning the wheel in his absence. They are old ex-presidents at the end of their careers hoping for a final appointment, traditional politicians who can only offer one more ministry, men of the last century, who have outlived themselves.

After saying his final "yeses," Mussolini calls Cesare Rossi to his office and reads him the list of ministers of his government. Rossi grins: this madman has decided that he will be prime minister!

But the madman has not yet exhausted his surprises. He picks up the telephone receiver and asks the secretary to reserve him a box at the Teatro Manzoni. Tonight they are performing Ferenc Molnár's *The Swan*, a play that is being much talked about. He will go to see it with Signora Sarfatti.

"Tonight I'm going to the theater!"

He announces it to one and all, in a voice loud enough that everyone will hear. It's time to be sought after, it's time to disappear. It's time to teach those old petty politicians of the last century that in the politics of annihilation inaugurated with the twentieth century there is no "yes," there is only a single, gigantic, bloody NO.

All that remains to be seen is whether the king's army will open fire on the blackshirts. In that case, however, the slaughter of fascist comrades will fall on the quadrumvirs mired in Perugia. At the stroke of midnight, when the curtain is lowered on Molnár's *The Swan*, they will be left holding the bag.

PERUGIA, OCTOBER 27, 1922
HOTEL BRUFANI, HEADQUARTERS OF THE QUADRUMVIRATE, EVENING

MICHELINO BIANCHI AND Emilio De Bono have been poring over the maps for hours. Both emaciated and wraithlike, sweaty and bewildered, one in civvies and the other in uniform, they look like they're wearing the hand-me-down clothes of an older brother. They are studying the maps because the territory they're supposed to control is completely unfamiliar to them.

The small Umbrian city is, in fact, totally unsuitable to function as an operations command site: cut off from main railway lines, the regional ones being few, circuitous and bogged down in mud, with telephone and telegraph communications practically non-existent. From Perugia no one knows anything about the rest of the world. Just imagine how anyone could coordinate an invasion! After hours of inactivity, one of them proposed moving the command to Orte, a railway hub near Monterotondo, Santa Marinella and Tivoli, places designated for the concentration of troops that the quadrumvirs are supposed to direct but whom they are out of touch with in Perugia. They had to give up the idea because it wasn't possible to reach Mussolini, who is still in Milan, for permission. The phone is silent. The headquarters of the march on Rome is cut off. The quadrumvirs are completely in the dark.

The fascist command of Perugia is made up of several local centuries and the squads "Satana," "Toti," "Fiume," "Grifo," and "Disperatissima." The name of the latter, meaning "Extremely Desperate," seems to everyone the most appropriate given the situation.

At the stroke of midnight, squadristi from nearby towns who overrun the city then clamber up the steep slopes of the surrounding hills with their bare hands, armed only with hunting rifles, clubs, billhooks and knives normally used to slaughter hogs, are to occupy post offices, telegraph centers, and other public bureaus, as well as the city's gates and road junctions guarded by the army in battle gear, armed with dozens of heavy machine guns. On those same hills, artillery reserves commanded by experienced officers keep their guns aimed at the Hotel Brufani.

Down below, in the sights of the guns that have it covered, the hotel's windows appear to be reinforced with bags of sand and soil. The doorman has been sent away, and the entrance is guarded by fascists with bayonets fixed to their muzzles. Two machine guns, one on either side, try in vain to give a threatening appearance.

On the same piazza, in front of the Brufani, just a few dozen yards away, the prefecture that the fascists are supposed to attack is defended by a triple cordon of royal guards and carabinieri lined up under the building's colonnade. On the rooftops are dozens of machine guns. For the moment, the local command's troops are consigned to the barracks, but at the first shot fired the fascists would be besieged. There is no doubt that if the army were to open fire, the fascist command would be overcome in no time.

At 8:00 p.m. the news arrives. It seems that the Tuscan squadristi and those of Farinacci in Cremona have acted earlier than planned and are making a mess of everything. In Florence the men of Tullio Tamburini, the militia's consul—ever more proud of being nicknamed "the great *bastonatore*"—arrested several officials and laid siege to the prefecture where a banquet was being held in honor of none other than General Armando Diaz, the "Duke of Victory" of the Great War.

"Imbeciles!"

It's the last word that Bianchi and De Bono hear Italo Balbo mutter before he gets in his car to speed to Florence on the muddy roads, in the dark, in the pouring rain. A fascist offense against General Diaz would mean having the entire army against them. It would be carnage. Not to mention that the "Duke of Victory" has the Ministry of Defence in his pocket in an eventual Mussolini government.

To live up to his reputation, though he's infuriated and concerned about the news from Cremona and Florence, Balbo issues orders: with the car already waiting for him outside the hotel, he instructs the squadristi guarding the entrance to laugh heartily at the royal guards deployed in front of the prefecture building every two hours, at regular intervals, starting that moment.

Cesare Maria De Vecchi, still busily conspiring in Rome to avert the march, hasn't even arrived in Perugia yet. Once Balbo leaves, what's left of the quadrumvirate, waiting for zero hour, kill time as best they can. Emilio De Bono, a gaunt skeleton of a general in a starched black shirt, returns to his map. Michele Bianchi, shaken by his tuberculotic wheezing, slumps into a chair, the inevitable riding crop abandoned between his legs.

CREMONA, OCTOBER 27, 1922
PREFECTURE PALAZZO, EVENING

DARKNESS WAS THE starting signal. At 6:00 p.m. the electric lighting, sabotaged by a squadrista, suddenly went out in all the rooms of the Lombard town's prefecture and the adjacent streets. At that signal, in darkness, about seventy squadristi, on the orders of Roberto Farinacci, invaded the building. Carabinieri and royal guards, serving in a province that had yielded to the fascists for years, complicitous though taken aback, let them enter without putting up any resistance. At the same time, other squads occupied telegraph and telephone offices. A surprise attack, lightning fast, but carried out several hours earlier than the established time without assessing the consequences. An act of impatience, of an internal lack of discipline, evidently prompted by the desire to stand out, a gesture of pure arrogant incompetence. Typical of Farinacci.

The prefect, after an initial moment of confusion, able to think again, alerted the garrison command and, once military reinforcements arrived, arrested the fascists. The forty captured squadristi, locked up in a single room, whining like children disappointed by adults' failure to keep their promises, protest with the state authorities who are normally complicit. To persuade the prefect to release them, the prisoners assure him that at that very moment a mobilization is underway throughout Italy, arranged by their supreme Duce with top state officials. The prefect has no word of it. He only knows of a fire started by several of their comrades in San Giovanni in Croce, a small village outside Cremona.

A few hours later, a second fascist contingent attempts another assault. A few squadristi ram a speeding car into the cordons of soldiers closely stationed around the prefecture, others try to climb up to the windows using rope ladders. Two bugle calls ring out. Then the boom of musketry. In tight formation, rifles aimed at the attackers, the soldiers of the town command advance up Corso Vittorio Emanuele.

Farinacci, incredulous, rushes at his men: "Stop, don't shoot! They must surely be firing blanks . . ."

ROME, OCTOBER 27, 1922
HOTEL LONDRA, 10:00 P.M.

MILAN—"UP THERE they want to conclude. And from the news I received as soon as I arrived, I saw that here too they think it's advisable to conclude. I'll call you in half an hour."

Rome—"Thank you."

Luigi Facta's day had begun with a promise. Returning from a meeting with Giolitti in Cavour ("up there"), waiting to receive Mussolini ("here"), Lusignoli had promised him a phone call within half an hour. The rest of the day, however, had been spent in a distressing, futile wait.

At 8:05 p.m., however, Vittorio Emanuele III had finally arrived. Waiting for the sovereign at the station, in addition to Facta, were the prefect, the director general of public security and the police chief of Rome. When he stepped off the train, the king shook hands with the prime minister and with him withdrew into the station's special room set aside for royalty. Vittorio Emanuele said he was tired, disappointed, and disconsolate, and threatened to abdicate and retire to the country with his wife and son.

Then, however, with a surge of pride, the sovereign declared that Rome must be defended at all costs. If the fascists showed up armed at the gates of the capital, the simple transfer of powers to the military authority would not be enough. The words "state of siege" were then pronounced for the first time. That proclamation alone would be enough to crush the march.

"Maintain public order." The peremptory injunction resounded in the royal room of Termini station as though to dismiss Facta. The king added nothing more. Leaving the station, he retired to Villa Savoia.

Around 9:00 p.m. the long-awaited phone call from Lusignoli finally arrived. Mussolini had gone to the theater, the negotiation had failed.

Luigi Facta, at that point, had to ask for a second meeting with the sovereign. He went to Villa Savoia and capitulated. Had the prime minister resigned even just twenty-four hours earlier, it would have enabled the country to have a government capable of confronting the fascist aggression, to do so now would leave it without a government to confront the threat. Facta resigned right then.

Back at the Viminale, Facta granted staff permission to go to bed. "We have resigned," he said, "there is a crisis. See you tomorrow morning." The director general of public security said he agreed. "Besides," he added, "the fascists won't arrive in Rome before 7:00 in the morning in any case." Reassured, Facta then announced:

"I'm going to sleep too."

This night too, as he has habitually done for at least thirty years without exception, Luigi Facta of Pinerolo goes to bed before 10:00 p.m.

It has been a rough day. In his single room at the Hotel Londra, the elderly gentleman doesn't even have enough energy to turn down the covers. Stretching out on the bedspread, he throws his coat over himself, still damp with rain, and falls asleep.

Efrem Ferraris, his young chief of staff, on the other hand, returns to the Ministry of the Interior and begins his vigil at arms.

For hours, dumbstruck, in the dark of night, he watches the blinking of the telephones that link the prefectures to the ministry. For hours, in the silence of the grand halls of the Viminale, Ferraris listens to the clacking of the teleprinters and notes down the names of the occupied prefectures, the invaded telegraph offices, the military garrisons that consorted with the fascists, the requisitioned trains that are on their way to the capital, loaded with weapons. The grand spectacle of the disintegration of a state goes on until dawn.

MILAN, OCTOBER 27, 1922
BOXES AT THE TEATRO MANZONI,
SHORTLY AFTER 10:00 P.M.

LUIGI FREDDI IS a promising young man. One of the early squadristi, chief editor at *Il Popolo d'Italia*, he demonstrates a particular talent for propaganda. One of his articles that appeared in *Il Fascio* aroused a certain interest. In it he wrote that "the punch is the synthesis of theory."

Now, however, Freddi hesitates. When he appeared at the Teatro Manzoni, signaling that he had urgent news, Mussolini motioned him to wait. He and Signora Sarfatti lean over the balustrade, hand in hand, captivated by the second act of Ferenc Molnár's *The Swan*.

But at the intermission, as soon as he hears what happened in Cremona, Mussolini rushes to the newspaper. The messenger is a guy they call "Volpevecchia," sly old fox. Bristly beard, rawhide leather jacket, aviator goggles lowered around his neck, he is waiting for them beside a black motorcycle whose broken headlight is caked with mud. Volpevecchia seems to embody the inevitability of destiny. You look at him and his Moto Guzzi, dagger on his belt, revolver tucked in his pants, and you wonder what else a petty thug like that could have done in life if he hadn't climbed on those two wheels. Obviously, things had to go that way. In Cremona it's a massacre.

The soldiers had fired point-blank on Farinacci's squadristi who were trying to climb up to the windows of the prefecture using ropes. Volpevecchia had arrived in Cremona from Perugia when the bodies were still warm. Hearing that the action had started earlier than expected, Balbo had sent him with the order to call it off. Farinacci, instead, gave him a note written in his own hand to be delivered to the Duce: "Here we die. No calling off."

Back in his office, Mussolini receives a call from Balbo in Florence. He informs him of the mess that Tamburini's incompetent bunglers were making. Fortunately, he managed to stop them in time and pay his respects to General Diaz.

After hanging up the phone, Mussolini asks to have the quadrumvirs' proclamation, written by him the previous week, brought to him. The document can't be delivered. Alessandro Chiavolini, to whom it was entrusted, placed it in a safe deposit box at the post office, which is now under police guard.

As soon as the text of the proclamation is produced, its author, having learned that Facta has resigned, modifies a few words. As if he were a Christ Pantocrator who need only say "light" for there to be light, the director of *Il Popolo d'Italia*, from his office on Via Lovanio in Milan, in the name of the four ill-fated unfortunates scattered throughout the four corners of Italy on this rainy night, writes: "The Secret Quadrumvirate of Action declares the current government fallen, the chamber dissolved and the senate adjourned. The army is consigned to the barracks. It must not take part in the battle." Mussolini knows very well, and the news from Cremona proves it, that if the army were to participate, there would be no battle.

As he spends this night waiting to find out if the king of Italy, that damned dwarf who despises him for his plebeian origins, will proclaim a state of siege, putting an end to his march, his final endeavors are two acts of devotion to the propitiatory powers that the lesser deities of the word sometimes grant men, to keep reality at a distance, despite the facts.

First of all, ever the journalist, he dictates to his staff the headline of what could be the last edition of his newspaper, omitting mention of the Cremona slaughterhouse: "Italy's history at a decisive turning point—Fascist mobilization already completed in Tuscany—All Siena barracks occupied by fascists—Gray-greens fraternize with blackshirts." Then the fascist censor summons Cesare Rossi and orders him to go around to Milan's editorial offices together with Aldo Finzi to enforce a friendly press.

"This is it," Mussolini concludes, dismissing his adviser with an almost resigned expression.

Cesare Rossi, in order to lend credibility to his rounds to intimidate the newspaper editors, takes with him the Tuscan squadrista who enjoys introducing himself to strangers by boasting about his crimes.

"Pleased to meet you, Amerigo Dùmini, nine murders."

ROME, OCTOBER 28, 1922
MINISTRIES OF DEFENCE AND OF THE INTERIOR, NIGHT

SHORTLY AFTER ONE o'clock in the morning, in his bed at the Hotel Londra, Prime Minister Facta is still lying in the same position his exhausted body landed in three hours earlier. When he goes to wake him up, his young chief of staff Efrem Ferraris sees only an aged man in that prostrate body huddled under the cover of his own damp coat. Less than an hour later, the haggard cadaver is at the Ministry of Defence.

The meeting that takes place there at 2:00 a.m. is dramatic. Interior Minister Taddei expresses to General Pugliese, commander of the Rome division, his sorrowful surprise at the fact that the armed forces were not able to prevent the fascist takeover of numerous prefectures. Pugliese, outraged and fuming, heaps the responsibility on the inaction of the political class. The general has prepared the defense of the capital for some time and has been asking for written orders to implement it for two days. Minister Paolino Taddei assures him that he will now have them.

When the meeting ends, Facta goes to Villa Savoia to see the king. Twenty minutes later, after their talk, he turns to Amedeo Paoletti, his personal secretary:

"Order the driver to bring me back to the Viminale. I have to prepare the state of siege that the king will sign tomorrow morning."

Returning to the offices of the Ministry of the Interior, the old Piedmontese gentleman even manages to draw on a bit of heroism:

"If the fascists want to come, they will have to carry me out of here in pieces," he hisses in his dialect.

The Council of Ministers is convened for 5:30. On the agenda, the state of siege. This exceptional legal provision which, faced with a serious threat to the sovereignty of the state, suspends constitutional guarantees and transmits all powers to the military authority, has not been adopted since 1898. The text of that earlier proclamation is therefore sent for. It is retraced, softening the most violent and inappropriate tones. The result is a manifesto that is grave but moderate, firm, concise and dignified. With that, Luigi Facta at nine in the morning will again go to Vittorio Emanuele III. All that's needed is the king's signature to ensure that the fascists' march ends up not in Rome but in jail, or at the graveyard.

Shortly after 6:00 a.m. Facta transmits to General Pugliese the written orders for the defense of Rome that the commander has been awaiting for days; half an hour later the telegram with the arrest order for those responsible for the sedition is sent to the prefects; at 7:50 a.m. the telegram informing the military authorities of the initiation of the "state of siege" is drafted; at 8:30 a.m. the manifesto is posted in the streets of Rome.

Giovanni Amendola, minister of the colonies who was beaten by the fascists on Christmas Eve, founder of the Italian Democratic Party and of the liberal newspaper *Il Mondo*, whose headquarters in Naples was burned down by the squadristi on October 24th, finally has a momentous moment of rare exhilaration:

"The fascists shall not pass: we have decided to order a state of siege and tomorrow these derelicts will be put in their place," the sincere democrat rejoices at the resolution of the decree.

The Council of Ministers unanimously resolves to propose to the king the proclamation of the state of siege.

From the minutes of the Council of Ministers,
October 28, 6:00 a.m.

The government upon unanimous resolution of Council of Ministers orders you to maintain public order . . . using any and all means, at any cost, and with the immediate arrest without exception of leaders and promoters of the insurrectionary movement against the powers of state.

Telegram from the prime minister's office
to prefects and military commanders of the Kingdom,
October 28, 1922, 7:10 a.m.

No. 23859—Council of ministers authorized proclamation state of siege in all Kingdom provinces from noon today. Relative decree will be issued right away. Meanwhile immediately use all exceptional means for maintaining public order and safety of property and persons.

Telegram from the prime minister's office
to prefects and military commanders of the Kingdom,
October 28, 1922, 7:50 a.m.

No one has ever dared march against Rome, mother of civilization, to suppress the idea of freedom that she personifies. It is up to you to defend her to the last drop of blood and be worthy of her History.

Orders of the day from General Emanuele Pugliese
to the officers and soldiers of the garrison of Rome,
dawn of October 22, 1922

SANTA MARINELLA, MONTEROTONDO, TIVOLI, OCTOBER 28, 1922, 8:30 A.M.

WHILE THE PROCLAMATION of the state of siege that is supposed to crush the insurrection is being posted in the streets of Rome, in the Lazio countryside the uprising has already failed.

The division to defend the capital, under the command of a determined General Pugliese, amounts to 28,000 men in all, including soldiers, carabinieri, finance guards and royal guards, equipped with 60 machine guns, 26 cannons, and 15 armored cars.

Compared to this imposing defensive bastion at the time the action is to begin, the three fascist columns that have reached the concentration areas number perhaps 10,000 men in all. The men are on foot, thirsty, hungry, rain-soaked, dejected, and inadequately armed. Many have only pistols, daggers and farm utensils on their belts, in their hands they wield short bats, clubs, and leather straps. Most of them are without weapons altogether. Those holding a military rifle don't have cartridges. The centuria leaders order the younger ones to hand over the few rifles to the sharpshooters, the veterans of the Great War, so that they can align in formation at the front and sides of the columns. The torrential rain hammers them mercilessly: it pelts down sideways, stinging them in the face, it drips under their capes, splashes into the puddles raising a muddy spatter. The disruption of the railway lines at Orte and Civitavecchia, ordered by Rome's command, requires the fascists to continue on foot. They scatter through the woods and fields.

The young revolutionaries, after marching all night from all over Italy to go to the assault on History, camp like uncivilized primitives in sheds or caves, or seek shelter from the rain under the elms. Damp or wet haystacks serve them as pallets, soaked socks are replaced with newspaper. Rations are scarce—a few sacks of potatoes, rice cakes. The forlorn vagrants, arriving in the towns, rush to the fountains but find them without potable water. Sore, limping, unprepared, they keep going. Some take off their riding boots and, carrying them, swinging, on their backs, continue barefoot. Around them everything is deserted. When they spot a house under construction, the men are fooled. They take refuge there by the hundreds, and the water pours in torrentially. Nevertheless, many sleep soundly, impervious to it all. Others doze, comatose.

It's not the battle but their provisioning that occupies the entire horizon of the men's existence: they beg for bread, they contrive abattoirs where animals are slaughtered by makeshift butchers. They are "derelicts," tens of thousands of young men who have come from all over the country to bring about the revolution, but no one orders them to either retreat or attack. As in the three years spent in the trenches, they are caught in this new no man's land between Orte and Tivoli, and there—forgotten, drenched, trapped, with their viciousness, with their craving for looting, with their ideals—they are left to rot in the rain in this dead end of history.

MILAN, VIA LOVANIO, OCTOBER 26, 1922
OFFICES OF *IL POPOLO D'ITALIA*,
AROUND 8:00 A.M.

THE GALLERIA IS blocked by the royal guards, three machine guns are aimed at Piazza della Scala from the Commercial Bank building, the trams that cross Via Manzoni have been diverted. Seemingly uninvolved in events until yesterday, this morning all of Milan has the impression that the state of siege is already underway. There's no doubt about it, the battle promises to be unequal: the squadristi have lined up chevaux-de-frise in front of the fascio headquarters on Via San Marco, but along the rain-swollen canal, at the intersections of Via Solferino, Via San Marco and Via Brera, the king's soldiers are setting up heavy machine guns on trestles.

Having spent the night at home, Mussolini has been at the newspaper for two hours already when Enzo Galbiati, a former bricklayer then head of the Brianza squads, now in command of defending the "fortress," announces that three armored cars from Via Moscova and a battalion of royal guards from Via Solferino are on their way to occupy the newspaper headquarters. Most likely they are coming to carry out the order to arrest the sedition leaders.

The first to parley is Cesare Rossi. He proposes a modus vivendi to avoid bloodshed. The Arditi and the fascists who are out in the streets flaunting muskets and grenades in front of what remains of the barricade of paper rolls dissolved by the rain, will withdraw inside the building and the police forces will stop at the corner of Via Moscova.

The royal guard major, however, isn't budging. He has orders and he will execute them.

While the mustached major prepares to stamp the word "end" on the march, Benito Mussolini himself shows up at the crossroads of events. The major won't be tamed, and has threatening words for the Duce as well.

Mussolini, who until a short time ago continued to promise the interior ministry to prefect Lusignoli, turns to the police commissioner, his subordinate, who is standing beside the major:

"Gentlemen, I advise you to reflect on the nature of our movement. There is nothing that you won't approve of." Then he bluffs: "In any case your resistance would be useless: all of Italy, Rome included, has fallen into our hands. Ask about it."

Words—words yet again—prevail over reality, keeping it at bay. Small causes, big effects. Commissioner Perna nods his agreement, the major falters. Bloodshed is deferred.

Luigi Federzoni's phone call arrives an hour later, while Facta is meeting with the king for the signing of the state of siege decree. Federzoni—close to the king, leader of the nationalist movement whose blue shirts are lined up in defense of Rome yet sympathetic with the fascists ready to attack her—is playing a double or triple game. Mussolini doesn't want to talk to him. He tells Aldo Finzi to answer and Cesare Rossi to listen in on a second headset. The voice from Rome is fraught with the sense of imminent catastrophe.

Federzoni—"I spoke with General De Bono in Perugia, who, since he cannot communicate with Milan, urged doing everything possible to see that Mussolini comes to Rome as soon as possible. The situation here is paralyzed by the fact that the king cannot confer with any of the fascist leaders. De Vecchi is in Perugia, they say, but as of half an hour ago he had not yet arrived. Here there is no one, and we run the risk, tell Mussolini right away, that as the situation worsens the king may leave."

Finzi—"I'll tell Mussolini right away."

Federzoni—"De Bono asked me to please let Mussolini know that as commander general he wants Mussolini to come to Rome immediately."

Finzi—"I understand. One thing though. Milan's orders for military authority must be a little different. We can't distance ourselves from the fascio and start shooting."

There's shouting now from Rome.

Federzoni—"Let's not lose our heads! In order for the king not to make any decisions that would aggravate the situation immeasurably, he must be able to act without delay under conditions of ostensible freedom, that is, giving the appearance that there is no, in short, . . . external . . . pressure. On the other hand, he stated that he did not want to be responsible for any bloodshed; in that case he would leave. There is a state of siege throughout Italy, so the military authority is also acting on its own . . ."

"Bloodshed" . . . "state of siege" . . . Benito Mussolini enters the phone box.

Finzi—"Here's Mussolini. I'll let him talk to you."

Federzoni—"Let me say that it was I who initiated this conversation. I spoke with De Bono who reminded me of the terms of the situation: there's a conflict; and if this situation continues, if that thing happens . . . the king will abandon the throne. Here there is absolutely no one who can represent the fascio. De Vecchi hasn't arrived in Perugia. De Bono asks me to please let you know all this and asks that you come to Rome immediately."

Mussolini—"I can't come to Rome because the action in Milan is underway. You have to talk to them there, you know who, the supreme command. I will accept any solutions that the supreme command decides to adopt . . ."

Federzoni, exasperated, stressing the Emilian dialect that associates him with the Duce, interrupts him.

Federzoni—"How can the command in Perugia let you know, if they can't even communicate with Milan!?"

Mussolini—"It's up to you to keep me informed, you have to communicate with Perugia. Make sure the movement is serious throughout Italy."

Federzoni—"Now it's a matter of not destroying our foothold; otherwise it's all over."

Mussolini—"Get in contact immediately and say that Mussolini defers to whatever the commanders decide."

Federzoni—"Listen, don't move from *Il Popolo d'Italia*."

Mussolini—"I won't move. But make sure that the crisis goes to the right, you hear me, to the right . . ."

Federzoni—"What do you mean?"

Mussolini—"A government of fascists."

The enormity triggers a moment of silence. Then the double-dealer recovers.

Federzoni—"Sure, we're in agreement, there's no doubt. But we must avoid an armistice situation. By tomorrow night I personally will make sure you get what you want."

Mussolini hangs up the receiver. He leaves the booth, Cesare Rossi follows him. Benito Mussolini chuckles.

"I told you so. They want to make me go down to Rome. An expected maneuver."

It continues to rain on a Milan in a state of siege. At the end of Via Lovanio, on the corner of Via Moscova, at the spot where the platoon of royal guards is barring access, the water streams down the dark barrels of the machine guns.

The full burden of the incipient carnage was again dumped on the shoulders of the four walk-on actors who, isolated from the world, scrutinize the horizon of events from a hotel room in Perugia.

PERUGIA, OCTOBER 28, 1922
HOTEL BRUFANI, SUPREME COMMAND
OF THE MARCH ON ROME,
SAME TIME (AROUND 8:00 A.M.)

PUDDLES OF WINE and champagne reflect what's left of the dawn. The sour smell of vomit is added to the acrid whiff of ashes given off by the hundreds of butts drowned in dregs of grappa or stuck in leftover pieces of bread and salami and slices of cake.

Cesare Maria De Vecchi, having just stepped out of his Blue Lancia with Dino Grandi, his hands pressed to his kidneys after an eight-hour journey through the mud, feels his stomach turn. Four squadristi lie snoring on the floor in the command room, amid the stink of heavy breaths and nocturnal revelry. De Vecchi wakes them up, kicking them. It looks as if there will be a brawl. The topographic operations map dangles from the wall, held by a single tack. This is the fascist revolution.

De Bono is cadaverous, Bianchi is rattled by tuberculotic wheezing. Both have very little news of the outside world. De Vecchi informs them of what's happening in Rome, about what he saw on the way to Perugia: scores of haggard fascists, plagued by rain and cold, marching south, staggering and unarmed, wraiths of a battle that will not be fought.

At Balbo's arrival, the quadrumvirs, still as statues lamenting the dead Christ, come to life again. His hair disheveled—impossible to tell whether he's still intoxicated or only exhilarated Balbo tears into De Vecchi with scorn and contempt. He accuses him of being a petty politico, he boasts about the occupation of Perugia's prefecture seized in his absence.

"Bravo, bravo! And the division command? Did you occupy that too? And the command of the Alpine brigade that pointed guns at you? And the troops, did you disarm them?" Rage makes Cesare Maria De Vecchi's gums bleed.

Shortly afterwards, around 10:00 a.m., news comes from the telegraph office that a state of siege has been proclaimed and an order issued to arrest the leaders of the insurrection. Bianchi tries desperately to communicate with Milan and then with Rome. He fails with both. Total darkness.

A fascist on a bicycle stops in front of the Hotel Brufani. There is a phone call from Rome at police headquarters. They want to talk with quadrumvir De Vecchi. Unless it's a joke, they're calling on behalf of the king.

It's not a joke. Vittorio Emanuele III's aide-de-camp, Cittadini, asks that De Vecchi return to Rome immediately. The sovereign wants to confer with a high-ranking representative of the fascist movement and Mussolini will not move from Milan. De Vecchi ventures to ask if there are any new developments. There are.

Before leaving again in the car of a braggart who promises to get him to Rome in four hours—"I drive à la Mussolini," the man boasts—De Vecchi meets with an old associate, General Cornaro, commander of the Alpine Brigade, based in Perugia.

Cornaro criticizes him for the folly of that mise-en-scène but between colleagues the reproach is benevolent. De Vecchi asks for patience, indulgence, tolerance, soldier to soldier.

None of those, Cornaro replies, can be granted. Since that night there has been a state of siege, the orders are precise. De Vecchi then assures him that they will change; he reveals that he's been summoned to Rome by the king. He implores the general to avoid any fighting. Cornaro responds pleasantly:

"Fighting? There won't be any. The city is cut off, no one will come to your rescue, the machine guns are positioned."

Then the general takes the fascist by the arm, points to the roofs of the buildings, the hills above the piazza and, almost in a whisper, adds:

"You wouldn't want to do me the disfavor of thinking that I don't know how to position the artillery, would you?"

Cesare Maria De Vecchi reports his conversation with General

Cornaro to the other quadrumvirs. Balbo, as usual, swears, hissing insults and threats, and muttering under his breath.

"You go ahead and kiss ass. . . . go on, have your revolution by phone . . . I'm going to resist, and if I have to die it will be only after I've fired the last cartridge."

While De Vecchi gets in the car alongside the impromptu chauffeur who "drives à la Mussolini," Balbo's voice, tensed to hysterical frequencies, shrieks after him.

"The revolution has begun . . . I will shoot . . . I'll fight."

MILAN, VIA LOVANIO, OCTOBER 28, 1922
OFFICES OF *IL POPOLO D'ITALIA*

no. 23871—Attention: the orders in today's telegram no. 23859 re state of siege must not be carried out.

THE TELEGRAM FROM the prime minister's office to the interior and war ministers is sent at 12:05 p.m. At 12:30 the Ministry of War communicates the order to suspend the state of siege to the division command. Shortly afterwards, the Stefani press agency reports the news: the king, contrary to all the preliminaries and all the commitments, has not signed the decree. The state of siege is revoked.

No use asking why. The reasons are numerous or none at all. The sphinx of history sits mute, immovable, on what has been, what will be, what could have been and what instead will never be.

Benito Mussolini learns the news in his office on Via Lovanio, while receiving a visit from Alfredo Rocco, leader of the nationalists and a distinguished jurist. Rocco has come personally from Rome to persuade him to support a Salandra government. Mussolini gives Rocco a list of ministers. The only ministry possible. His. By now, he declares, it's too late for any solution that does not include him.

Alfredo Rocco, roused by a sudden intuition that grasps the reality after only a forgivable moment's delay, forgets Salandra, rushes towards the Duce and embraces him excitedly:

"You're absolutely right, you for sure will bring Italy good luck."

The Founder of fascism has won, Mussolini knows it. Now that the threat of the state of siege is over, only that of the fascist squads gathering at the gates of Rome remains. He spends the rest of the day in the usual activities of a victor.

The new master of general destinies draws up lists of undersecretaries, promises ministries, consults by telephone with the editor of the *Corriere della Sera*, prepares a special edition of his newspaper in which he announces his triumph, says "no" with a simple jerk of his finger to all phone calls coming from De Vecchi and other Roman fascists complicit with his rivals. Then he also refuses the official invitation of the king's aide-de-camp to go down to the capital for talks. He will go down right away, what's more on a personally piloted plane, but only to receive the commission to form his government.

At 5:00 p.m. Mussolini grants an interview to a journalist from *L'Ambrosiano*: "They persist in fooling themselves that the solution can be found in Rome and they don't see that it is in Milan that they should look for it. By now there is only one solution: the Mussolini solution." At 6:00 p.m., when a platoon of royal guards marches back to Via Lovanio by mistake, the Founder, certain that they will not fire, grabs a musket from the cabinet and rushes out into the street to confront them in person. At 7:00 p.m., for the second time in two days, he receives a delegation of industrialists: Giuseppe De Capitani D'Arzago, Giovanni Pirelli, Antonio Benni, Silvio Crespi, Ettore Conti, who by this time have learned the way. At 8:00 p.m., having knotted his tie over the stiff collar of his good shirt, he goes to the theater again, this time, however, not with Margherita Sarfatti, his longtime lover, but with Rachele Guidi Mussolini, his legitimate spouse. Around midnight, finally, he agrees to take yet another call from Rome to a phone that has been ringing unanswered for hours. De Vecchi, Ciano and Grandi make one last attempt for a Salandra government. The new master has no hesitation:

"It wasn't worth mobilizing the fascist army, creating a revolution, having men die, to witness the resurrection of Don Antonio Salandra! I do not accept."

In Rome as in Milan the sharp thwack of the receiver being slammed down can be heard.

PERUGIA, OCTOBER 28, 1922
HOTEL BRUFANI

At the Hotel Brufani the news arrives just as the royal guards are about to reoccupy the Post Office building: the state of siege is revoked. Michele Bianchi and Emilio De Bono, overcoming their mutual physical revulsion, embrace one another like passionate lovers.

Out there on the street, however, they still don't know. And just a few yards from the entrance to the hotel, at that very moment, the troops led by General Cornaro march down Via Mazzini ready to attack the public building guarded by the "Disperatissima" squad's blackshirts with only a couple of machine guns. Bugles blow, weapons are aimed, the fascist leaders, pale, deliberate between the two firing lines.

At that moment, Emilio De Bono, with the rheumy eyes of a man prematurely aged, places his skeletal body between the two formations ready to fire. "The state of siege has been revoked," De Bono cries practically in falsetto. "The king has summoned Mussolini to Rome, his appointment is imminent." General Cornaro stands down for the second time.

A few hours later, De Bono goes to pay a visit to General Petracchi, in command of the piazza in Perugia. The officers and troops salute him militarily, then secretly laugh at him behind his back. Petracchi, who until a few hours earlier, scornful, infuriated, belligerent, hadn't even wanted to receive his former colleague, threatening to let the cannons talk, has now immediately converted to the fascist cause; he justifies himself and apologizes, trying to seek favor with the new masters. As De Bono is leaving, after reassuring him, General Petracchi launches a final appeal:

"The radio, please, the radio, let me get it working again."

At the Brufani there is already a flurry of people coming and going; comrades, those simply curious, petitioners. Cameras also arrive. Bianchi, De Bono and Balbo let themselves be immortalized at the fateful moment, all leaning a little forward. They feel the weight of the absurd when the drama suddenly turns into a comedy with a happy ending.

TIVOLI, MONTEROTONDO, SANTA MARINELLA, OCTOBER 28, 1922

THE BIVOUACS ARE crowded, new arrivals contend with the old unfortunates for a spot around the fires, reduced to ash by the rain. The 3,000 men of the Sienese legion turned up after lunch; 500 from Ancona and 300 Sabines in the afternoon; the 2,000 troops of the first Florentine legion, 2,000 of the Arezzo legion and the Valdarno cohort, and the 3,000 of the second Florentine legion arrive in the evening.

They get there and they all collapse, consumed by a feverish wait. There is no potable water, no food provisions, no money. Worst of all, there are no orders. All they know is that Balbo rode by on his motorcycle to command them not to move so as not to compromise the political production. Then nothing more, for hours, for days. No action, no communication, no news, no order sheets, other than the one that imposes all the prohibitions: do not leave your billeting for any reason, do not cause any damage, do not fire guns, do not steal the farmers' chickens.

The march gets mired in the mud; the legionnaires, forgotten in the rain, reduced to stealing chickens, wander through the camps, worn out by absurd watch patrols, shivering from fevers caused by the downpours and the anguish of living without a purpose, deprived of any answers.

The column encamped near Tivoli is commanded by Giuseppe Bottai, a young would-be poet, son of a wine merchant, who volunteered as an officer of the Arditi in the Great War, a futurist first, and later a leader of Rome's squadristi. Bottai has situated his command in a small hotel perched on the rocks in the Tivoli woods from where the tops of Villa d'Este's cypress trees can be seen.

Bottai, along with those men who came from all over Italy to march on the Caesars' capital, remains there for days, waiting for a signal, entranced by the hypnotic roar of the cascades. Rome is a hazy blur on the horizon, a distant image out there towards the east, beneath a leaden sky slashed by lightning.

If this situation is not stopped soon, we will be facing bigger problems. Mussolini is determined to come to Rome if they give him the appointment . . . If he had the answer quickly he would even come by plane; but the essential thing is that they make a decision . . . In the end, I believe that once he's come to Rome to form the ministry, he can be influenced to put together a better cabinet than the one he already announced yesterday evening.

Luigi Albertini,
editor-in-chief of the *Corriere della Sera*,
on the phone with Salandra's
former chief of staff,
October 28, 1922

The situation is this: most of northern Italy is fully under the control of the fascists. All of central Italy . . . is occupied by the "Black Shirts" . . . The political authority—somewhat surprised and quite dismayed—was unable to stand up to the movement . . . The government must be decidedly fascist . . . Let that be clear to everyone . . . Any other solution is to be rejected . . . The obliviousness of certain politicians of Rome oscillates between absurdity and fatality. Let them decide! Fascism wants power and it will have it.

Editorial by Benito Mussolini,
Il Popolo d'Italia,
October 29, 1922

Each consul will personally see to the formation of legionary patrols, which must, under the personal responsibility of the patrol leaders, ensure that no damage of any kind is done to property, that no chickens are stolen.

Order sheet no. 4 of the fascist
command of Santa Marinella,
October 28, 1922

BENITO MUSSOLINI

ROME, OCTOBER 31, 1922
HOTEL LONDRA, THE PRIME MINISTER'S ROOM, EVENING

IT SMELLS LIKE feet.

He has slipped off his spats, untied his shoelaces, and loosened his belt; in his shirtsleeves, he sinks into the armchair. Cigarette dangling between his lips à la française, he stretches his legs out on the chair in front of him.

"We have to admit that the splits among the others helped us considerably . . . Hah! All those government aspirants: Bonomi, De Nicola, Orlando, Giolitti, De Nava, Fera, Meda, Nitti . . . all saints of a parliament in its death throes, it was like a desperate roll call. And how about that poor devil Facta, starting a ministerial crisis right after our assembly in Naples?!"

Cesare Rossi, along with a few other close associates—because the Duce persists in not wanting any friends—listens as Mussolini, now relaxed, coolly and bluntly recalls the victorious campaign for the benefit of those present. But Rossi knows that even at this moment of triumph, especially at this moment, he is talking to himself first of all.

"And then too, the antifascists' passivity . . . Sure, OK, after the legalitarian strike that idea was full of holes . . . But, after all, even a little general strike of any kind would have put a spoke in our wheel and left us very *entravés*."

Bustling about all day, and still bustling, outside the parlor made available to the new prime minister by the Hotel Londra's management, are arrogant squadristi, neo-ministers, undersecretaries, active and retired generals, men and women from Rome's demimonde, *brasseurs d'affaires*, all in pursuit of a viaticum, a promotion, a prebend, all having descended on Via Ludovisi with the keen scent of birds of prey. Now, however, the querulous clamor of those people does not reach the luxury bivouac where the wayfarer, barefoot and with his belt undone, turns to look back at the road he's traveled.

"Of course, if Giolitti had been in government, maybe things wouldn't have gone so smoothly . . . In our regions there would have been fierce resistance, but we wouldn't really have made it. When a state wants to defend itself, it can always defend itself, and then the state wins. The truth is that the state in Italy no longer existed . . ."

The soliloquy to his audience goes on—mild, soothed by victory, almost a cradlesong, a lullaby—as meanwhile it has finally stopped raining and Rome's autumn rewards men's labors with a pleasurable night before winter comes. The victors thank the god of autumn and enjoy it, knowing that winter will come, it is already on its way.

The oration of the final hours begins. Someone slides the liquor cart along the marble floor.

Benito Mussolini had demanded a written telegram from the king's aide-de-camp who, after Salandra's resignation two days ago, on October 29th, summoned him to Rome to assign him the charge of forming the government. "If I get the telegram, I'll leave right away, even by airplane." The telegram had arrived, but he had not left, not even by train. The special train prearranged by Lusignoli for 3:00 p.m. had awaited him in vain. First he'd wanted to wrap up the special edition of his newspaper announcing his triumph.

Only after allowing himself a brief moment of emotion with his brother Arnaldo ("Ah, if only papa were alive!"), and finalizing the front page, had he gotten on the no. 17 express, departing from Central station at 8:30 p.m., with an expected arrival in Rome at 9:30 a.m. the following day. His farewell to the crowd was brisk.

The new prime minister had demanded that the departure be on time ("From now on, everything must run perfectly"). The anthem of the Milanese fascists—"*giovinezza, giovinezza* . . ."—was left behind in the distance as the last carriages glided through the darkness.

Unfortunately, the train reached its destination more than an hour late. The blackshirts, planting themselves in the middle of the tracks, had in fact blocked it in Fiorenzuola, then in Sarzana, then in Civitavecchia, and the Duce had had to get out to review them ("Victory is ours, we must not waste it. Italy is ours and we will lead it back to its ancient greatness").

From the window of the sleeping car, throughout the night until dawn of the following day, Benito Mussolini had watched Italy glide past at his feet. Finally, upon his arrival at 10:50 a.m., six airplanes even took off from Centocelle airfield to salute him in the skies of Rome.

At 11:05 a.m. on October 30th, 1922, when he climbed the stairs of the Quirinale to receive from the king of Italy the charge of governing the nation, Benito Mussolini—of plebeian origin, a gypsy in politics, self-taught at power, just thirty-nine years old—would be the youngest prime minister of his country, and the youngest ruler in the world at the time of his ascent; with no experience in government or public administration, having entered the Chamber of Deputies only sixteen months earlier, he was wearing a black shirt, the uniform of an armed party unprecedented in history. With all that, the blacksmith's son—the son of the century—had climbed the stairs of power. At that moment, the new century had begun and, at the same time, ended in his wake.

The following day it had been necessary to let the squadristi enter the city. He could not do otherwise. The king himself, now that Benito Mussolini had achieved what he wanted, had asked him to send them back, to safeguard the capital. But he'd replied that if they weren't given the satisfaction of marching, he would not answer for their reactions: those poor bastards had been left to rot outdoors in the rain for three days and three nights, though they had already reached the gates of Rome before he arrived on the train the morning of the 30th. Even then, Giuseppe Bottai, who pleaded for permission to march on the city at the head of his column of derelicts, had been refused. But on October 31st, once the fascist government was formed, it would not have been possible to send the squadristi back home without granting them an apocryphal, paltry triumph. Some of them, in the provinces, had persisted in dying even after Mussolini in Milan had already received the telegram from the king's aide-de-camp. As Rachele was already packing the Duce's bags, eight of those foolish, generous young men in black shirts, led by Leandro Arpinati in Bologna, after liberating dozens of comrades held in the prison of San Giovanni in Monte, had gotten themselves killed attacking the barracks of complicit carabinieri and ammunition depots that were now utterly useless. Eight posthumous corpses.

And besides, an aura of heroism and violence was needed. In this new century, it served to consecrate the power of its favorite son. A military insurrection would have failed, unquestionably, but the performance had become reality and the knife had to remain pointed at the throat.

And so, on the morning of October 31, as the government was being sworn in at the Quirinale, they had all been assembled at Villa Borghese. The cortege set off at 1:00 p.m. along the Lungotevere, where their Duce reviewed tens of thousands of muddy, famished fascists, dressed every which way, wearing daggers on their belts and twirling clubs. They were then herded together in Piazza del Popolo, with maximum order and discipline enforced; any violent action for which they had been mobilized was prohibited, the prime minister, guarantor of lawfulness, now being Mussolini himself. After that they'd been made to march in a column down Corso Umberto to the Altar of the Fatherland and, from there, past the windows of the Quirinale.

The king, on the balcony, closely flanked by General Diaz and Admiral Thaon de Revel, had greeted them briefly. The Duce appeared for just a few minutes at the window of the Council. The parade went on for six hours.

After racking up additional miles through the streets of the capital, acclaimed by the cowardly Romans who, no longer fearful, waved enthusiastically along the streets, the fascist squadristi—overcome by exhaustion that set in following the nervous tension, kicked out like dogs from church, the flesh and blood protagonists of a phantom story—found themselves on the train before they knew it, bitterly swallowing the gastric juices of their victory.

Some, certainly, even there, had disobeyed orders. After years of weekend clubbings and punitive raids, driven by violence, groups of unruly fascists had ravaged Nitti's small villa, wrecked the office of Deputy Bombacci, and repeatedly beaten Argo Secondari over the head, leaving the leader of the Arditi del Popolo collapsed on the ground with a terminal brain concussion. Others, more daring, or more reckless, had tried to bring the battle to the enemy's camp, penetrating, armed, into the working-class districts of Borgo Pio, San Lorenzo, Prenestina, and Nomentana, from which they'd been driven out the year before. They'd been forced out this time as well.

Mussolini himself, hearing of the incidents, had rushed to Termini station to make sure that his last, diehard squadristi were forcibly loaded onto the trains. Rome had to be cleared out, Italy normalized. Tomorrow is a new day.

Now, in his room at the Hotel Londra, the Duce of fascism sprawls in the armchair, stretches his legs out in front of him and, getting ready to go to bed, pleasantly lulled by the intimate malodorous whiff issuing from his bare feet, lets his voice drop an octave and repeats to his few acolytes what he has already said that afternoon to an editor of the *Corriere della Sera*:

"Tell the truth, we pulled off the only revolution of its kind in the world. In which epoch of history, in which nation has a revolution like this ever taken place? While public services continued functioning, while business carried on, employees in the offices, workers in the factories, farmers in the fields, while the trains kept running regularly. All in all we had 30 deaths, including 10 in Mantua, 8 in Bologna, and 4 in Rome. Apart from Parma, apart from San Lorenzo, and a few other isolated cases, Italy stood by and watched. It's a new style revolution!"

No one objects, no one counters. The new initiates are taught the rudiments of the art of docility.

What will tomorrow bring? No one can say, not even anyone in that room. They are intoxicated by what they've accomplished: they have come to power, now they want to keep it. The Roman autumn night is dulcet.

Respecting the darkness with silence, one drifts softly towards the twilight of consciousness that leads to sleep. There will be plenty of time in the future to assess what has been irreparably lost by allowing that man sprawled in an armchair to forcibly seize power over the world after traveling down in a sleeping car.

Here we are witnessing a fine young revolution. No danger, plenty of color and enthusiasm. We are having a terrific time.

Richard Washburn Child, US ambassador to Italy,
October 31, 1922

We acknowledge that there has been a peaceful resolution of events . . . Unfortunately, however, the absence of tragedy, at certain moments in the life of a people, can signify a lack of moral gravitas.

La Stampa, November 1, 1922

A wound has been opened in our national life . . . for four years Italians have become accustomed to viewing violence as a way to advance or an opportunity for solutions, and to consider a party all the stronger the more threatening it is . . . this is demonstrated by the acquiescent indifference with which the population at large has witnessed the fascist insurrection, the degrading collapse of every state authority and the humiliation of all state powers, without exception.

Luigi Albertini,
Corriere della Sera, November 2, 1922

I share your pain for the way things went these days; I feel the damage that has been done and is being done to freedom, a wound that will not soon be healed. But I wonder if you don't feel somewhat responsible for all this, for not having raised your voice in time against the illegality, the abuses, the brutalities that were being committed. You made apologies for the fascists' clubs and sharp teeth too many times, to be able to complain today about what, in short, is nothing but their logical conclusion.

Giuseppe Prezzolini, letter to Luigi Albertini,
November 3, 1922

The semi-socialist system under which the country had suffered in the past has finally disappeared . . . of course, there was a revolution, but it was a typically Italian revolution, a plate of spaghetti, and the way in which the change took place shouldn't arouse too much apprehension simply because it was completely unconstitutional.

Monsignor Francesco Borgongini Duca,
Secretary of the Sacred Congregation
for Special Ecclesiastical Affairs,
November 6, 1922

There has been talk of a fascist revolution. The pronouncement is pompous, resounding. The facts are perhaps more modest. The abdication of state powers had reached such a point that by then the fascists had only to reach out a hand to grasp the ripe fruit of their efforts . . . Fascism wasn't all a bluff, but there was a lot of bluffing, and faced with the machine guns that would have rung out, the fervor of the blackshirts would have been greatly mitigated.

Pietro Nenni,
Avanti!, November 14, 1922

BENITO MUSSOLINI

ROME, NOVEMBER 16, 1922
CHAMBER OF DEPUTIES, 3:00 P.M.

THE CHAMBER IS jam-packed. The hall of the Italian parliament has a "fantastical aspect" that—as *L'illustrazione italiana* notes—not even the oldest reporters can recall in thirty years of attendance. The galleries of senators, diplomats, and ex-deputies are overflowing with elegant gentlemen and ladies in furs, the public galleries are literally teeming with onlookers, the side corridors crammed with commoners who have flocked to meet the new government. The spectacle of the crowd is festive, even stirring, but all cameras are focused on the presidential desk.

At 3:00 p.m. on the dot, not a second late, preceded by Enrico De Nicola, chamber president, and followed by all the ministers of his government, the honorable Deputy Mussolini enters escorted by General Diaz, minister of war and "Duke of Victory" over the Austrians. All the deputies, except the representatives of the left, rise to applaud him. The public galleries join in the ovation. Italy, no matter how you look at it, is enjoying a honeymoon with this man who enters the parliament with a triumphal step, lifted so high above the ground that, even while walking, he gives the impression of riding in on a horse.

Just fifteen days have passed since the so-called "march on Rome." The national and international press has written about it copiously—"a beautiful, joyful revolution of strong young men," "a bloodless revolution," "a momentous test, the dawn of a new era," "something typically Italian, a plate of spaghetti," a "farce." Just fifteen days have passed, in Rome alone during those fifteen days there were 19 dead and 20 seriously injured, yet the march on Rome is about to be forgotten.

No one seems to want to remember the agonizing days for the multitudes of black-shirted men marching on the world, all attention is focused on this single man who rolls his eyes threateningly, eyes that even to his contemptuous adversaries appear to gleam "like beacons in the night." The expectations around him are enormous. It is expected that this nocturnal animal who emerged from the shadows himself will put an end to darkness.

The first to see a promise of peace in the Duce of fascism are, paradoxically, the liberals. Benedetto Croce continues to applaud, Giolitti hopes that Mussolini will pull the country out "from the ditch where it ended up putrefying," Nitti promises "no opposition," Salvemini urges him to sweep away these "old mummies and dregs" of the rotting political class, even Amendola, whose newspaper the squadristi set fire to, expects the Duce to restore lawfulness. Included in his government, in addition to fascists, are populists, nationalists, democrats, and liberals. Giovanni Gentile, the philosopher renowned throughout Europe, accepted the Ministry of Public Education, General Armando Diaz and Admiral Paolo Thaon de Revel, victorious in the Great War, accepted those of War and the Navy. Italy is fed up with the usual games, hallway whispers, useless sighs, bloodless and inconclusive palace conspiracies, people are sick and tired of being represented only in parliament's failings. The Italians are, in short, disgusted with themselves. Almost everyone, even some of his victims, wish the emergent man long life and an "iron constitution" so that he may drain the infected wound. An illness that must cure itself.

Benito Mussolini doesn't seem intent on disappointing them. After the long applause for General Diaz and for the king of Italy, he stands up and, in the chamber's perfect silence, articulating the syllables as he usually does, begins with sarcasm:

"Gentlemen! What I perform today in this hall is an act of formal deference to you, for which I ask no explicit recognition."

A lengthy pause, allowed to draw out so that the Montecitorio mummies may have time to appreciate the insult: the prime minister has just declared to the deputies of his parliament that he deigns to address them only out of respect for the formalities. Then, immediately afterwards, he resumes his talk, appealing to the people against them.

"Now it so happens that the Italian people, in their best judgment, have passed over a ministry and given themselves a government on the outside, above and contrary to any appointment by the parliament . . . I affirm that the revolution is fully legitimate. I am here to defend and empower the revolution of the blackshirts to the maximum degree."

Hearing that unexpected reference to the "revolution," thunderous applause breaks out in the galleries occupied by the squadristi. Their Duce has just evoked the march on Rome that everyone was ready to forget. The march has suddenly invaded the parliament, you can almost hear the cleated boots pounding on the travertine corridors, the march—"my dear gentlemen"—will not be forgotten. Don't look back, look ahead. The journey has just begun.

Meanwhile, on the benches of the democrats and liberals, uneasy glances begin to look up towards the galleries where the squadristi are clamoring. Mussolini recalls their attention:

"I could have made a clean sweep and I refused to. I imposed limits on myself."

A sense of relief drifts over the hall. Many of the deputies who a moment ago were eying the squadristi fearfully, now heartened, nod their approval: their Leader declares that he does not want to be intemperate. That's good. The relief and gratitude of the mouse spared by the cat.

Benito Mussolini, however, unexpectedly pulls the whip out from under the ministerial bench:

"With 300,000 young men fully armed, determined to do anything and almost mystically ready for my order, I could have punished all those who maligned me and tried to drag fascism through the mud. I could have turned this deaf, gray hall into a bivouac for maniples of squadristi."

A crack of the whip, squarely in the face. The insult to the parliament echoes in the chamber of parliament itself: this deaf, gray hall! Now it is clear that the democratic institution survives through the merciful concession of the man called upon to govern it, to respect it, and it is he himself who declares it. The thought of punishment—spared though perhaps only deferred—becomes, for the dishonored deputies, the punishment itself. A quick blow of the whip. Almost all of them, feeling they've deserved it, take it without even trying to dodge it, neither defending themselves nor reacting.

While the squadristi cheer enthusiastically in the galleries, the impression sparked by Mussolini's insult is, for all the non-fascists, painful and profound. Yet only Francesco Saverio Nitti, outraged, leaves the hall in silence, only Modigliani and Matteotti jump to their feet at the socialists' benches. Only a single cry—"viva parliament!"—rises in the humiliated parliament. It's as though the rest of them, almost all of them, feel they deserved the humiliation. Their silence is an act of supine contrition. When Mussolini starts talking again, he's speaking to an assembly of guilty parties:

"I could have barred the doors to parliament and formed a government of fascists only. I could have but, at least at this initial time, I chose not to."

Again that mournful sense of relief, again those resigned nods of approval among the benches. The lawful representatives of democratic liberties are accepting the fact that they be granted to them from above, purely arbitrarily, and on condition that they no longer make use of them. What remains of the democratic institution adjusts to living life as debtors. Evidently, none, or almost none, of its representatives feels worthy of representing liberty, entitled to defend it.

After subjugating the assembly, the prime minister can now proceed to touch upon the major themes of international politics—the triple entente, relations with Turkey, with Russia, with other countries—but for the deputies of Montecitorio, who are distractedly listening to their pulses to make sure they are still alive, his speech is over.

At the tail end, before concluding, having come to the topic of state authority, an instant after having trampled on it, the leader of the fascists promises to restore and defend that power even against the unlawfulness of the fascists themselves. Applause from all sides, from Facta, mutual congratulations, even from the socialists. Mussolini, joining his forefinger and thumb in a ring raised to his forehead, has resumed playing cat and mouse, but the mouse, clawed, now barely twitching with a quiver of life, looks up at the predator and even seems to smile at him, almost an apologetic smile.

Then comes a final crack of the whip, preceded as always by a title that, with familiar contempt, replaces the proper "honorable deputies," or the respectful "colleagues" or "fellow citizens" with the generic "gentlemen":

"Gentlemen, I have no wish to govern against the chamber . . . as long as it is possible for me to do so . . . but the chamber must recognize its peculiar position which makes it possible to dissolve it in two days as well as in two years."

And, with this ultimatum, the XXVI legislature is buried. The most intelligent doubt that there can be another. It will survive, two days or two years, paying off its death on credit.

So that there may be no remaining doubt about who is in command, Benito Mussolini also asks the chamber for the delegation of "full powers." Again no one rebels.

During the session's break, a group of parliamentarians presses Giovanni Giolitti to protest in defense of the chamber's dignity. "I see no reason to," is the old statesman's reply, "this chamber has the government it deserves."

He will not be proven wrong. The Chamber of Deputies, despite the fact that the Fascist Party accounts for only 35 of its members, passes a solid vote of confidence in the Mussolini government that has shown no confidence in it. The vote passes with 306 in favor versus 116 opposed and 7 abstentions. It also grants full powers. Even the indignant critics like Deputy Gasparotto or Deputy Albertini vote in favor. An adamantine will to capitulate.

After the speech by the head of government, this assembly no longer has any reason to exist.

Deputy Luigi Gasparotto,
address to the chamber,
November 16, 1922

Mussolini gave the impression of being in command of the situation, and though the parliamentary institution has found many defenders today, the actual chamber found none, not even among its members.

Camille Barrère,
French ambassador to Rome,
November 18, 1922

The whipping the other day at the chamber, De Vecchi's insults to the populists, the fanciful ambition of making a proud gesture before dying on the part of some of the more prominent parliamentarians . . . everything settled down before the vote, and the 306 who voted for the ministry were all quickly tamed by the more parliamentary tone of the tamer . . . of rabbits . . . And what happens now? . . . the deputies, like beaten dogs, will return to their districts in the hope that in the spring elections they can return as squadristi in the national blocs.

Anna Kuliscioff, letter to Filippo Turati,
November 18, 1922

Dear Emilia, I only just finished my daily letter yet I feel the need to write again to urge prudence, prudence, prudence. I read the report from today's chamber and my heart sank. I can imagine how you will feel tomorrow. But a love of liberty is not shown by compromising oneself in idle chatter. This is a time to remain silent. The time to talk will come and we must stand fast for that.

Gaetano De Sanctis, letter to his wife,
November 17, 1922

GIACOMO MATTEOTTI

ROME, NOVEMBER 18, 1922
CHAMBER OF DEPUTIES

GIACOMO MATTEOTTI DOES not remain silent. There are men, albeit rare, for whom speaking and standing firm are one and the same.

A political vote of confidence in the government having been accorded by the chamber, Matteotti takes the floor two days later, in the debate on the extension of the provisional budget for fiscal year 1922–1923. After the capitulation of the preceding days, many speakers who signed up to speak forgo it. He does not. He still has permission to speak and speak he does.

The secretary of the Unitary Socialist Party declares at once that his talk, carefully prepared, meticulous, even pedantic, will focus exclusively on technical issues. And one cannot believe that he lacks the lucidity, like many of his liberal colleagues, to understand what is happening. His first words mercilessly crucify the distortion of the present, nailing it to the cross of the looming dictatorship:

"Honorable colleagues, on behalf of the group I must make a few brief statements on the provisional budget presented by the government. There is no need to repeat here the political remarks that were made yesterday. We will limit ourselves to strictly technical observations, as though we were in a regime of democracy and not of dictatorship."

Matteotti's awareness of the dictatorial threat is absolute, even extreme: he senses that the request for a provisional budget foreshadows the threat of the chamber's dissolution, its "immediate jugulation," which demands a second "vote of approval and contrition" from the humiliated parliamentarians after that of the previous day, and yet, on the edge of the precipice, Matteotti talks at length, point by point, on matters of detail, on the minutiae of budgets: equalization of taxes, circulation of floating debts, treasury forecasts on railway deficit. With the scrupulous precision of a pathologist who distinguishes a disease by small signs, Matteotti reads the degeneration of the democratic fabric in the minute misrepresentations found in the budgets of Mussolini's economic ministries, with the doggedness of an implacable enemy he disputes even the slightest miscalculation, with the oppressive pessimism that arouses relentless hatred he predicts that, after the numerous revolutionary proclamations, the fascists too, like the old political figures who preceded them, will resort to issuing the usual treasury bonds.

"To hell with the stargazer!" shouts an anonymous voice that rises from the benches of the right against this persistent prophet of doom.

But there is nothing that aspires to be remembered in this speech by Matteotti given right after the historic one by Mussolini. It almost seems as though the antifascist has given up memorable words and left them to his enemy. To find a word that still stings the flesh, that's still able to leave even a small claw-mark on the earth's crust, public oratory must be abandoned. As the shadow of dictatorship spreads over the world, life, we all know, withdraws into the private sphere.

And so it is in the letters that the young, combative secretary of the Unitary Socialist Party addresses to the old patriarch Filippo Turati, his most illustrious supporter, that what remains of his fighting spirit must be sought—letters in which Matteotti vows that he will not retreat one step, in which he bemoans his colleagues giving in to the enticements of the new powers that be, in which his fierce moralism rips into the declining morality of a party that he defines as a "brothel," in which faced with the extraordinary power of seduction exercised by Benito Mussolini he formulates a precise diagnosis: "We are neither dishonest enough, nor ingenuous enough to comply with it."

Even more telling, it is in Giacomo Matteotti's letters to his wife that the truthful account of these tormented days may be found. If we take a step back, we discover, in fact, that just at the beginning of October, when his persecutors were threatening to descend on Rome, this man—who has been constantly used to living away from his loved ones, long accustomed to leading a semi-clandestine life without a permanent residence, living in hotel rooms and makeshift shelters—was looking for a house in the capital. Faced with extreme danger, it seemed that he could no longer live away from his wife and children. And he looked for a house in Rome, as if the poet were right to say that there where the greatest danger grows, salvation also grows. On October 10th he wrote:

> *I want to protect the children, you and myself as well. Extreme sacrifices are pointless, they are of no help. Even if I had a house here in Rome I wouldn't give the address to anyone.*

Then, however, twenty days later, at the end of the month, when the fascists had already marched on the capital, Matteotti, who once again saw with lucidity how the farce did not exclude tragedy but, on the contrary, mingled with it, just when the feverish search for a house in Rome seemed finally over, there he is, in his letters to Velia, questioning the advisability of his intention to construct a domestic refuge in the eye of the cyclone, doubting himself:

> *It appears that the tragedy-farce is over . . . Just tonight the trains are departing again and if I could I would come to see you first, to counsel one another. Given the disturbances, which I had so long foreseen, the idea of not having you here in any danger was once again confirmed. I had even thought of taking you all out of the country.*

The only one who never doubts is Velia. Unquestionably sinking, basing her utterances on the basalt of an impregnable melancholy—

melancholy is her rock, her only certainty—Velia Matteotti writes her husband beautiful, loving words:

> *Your life too is miserable, and worst of all without any affectionate domesticity, without any material comfort, ever. You've reached the age you are living like that, and up till now not even I could give you those things. But presently it will end, we will be united forever, even if matters were to cause you to be away, and we will have a bed of our own, a lamp of our own, a nice warm corner where we can spend a restful hour together and be able to talk quietly, do you remember?*

BENITO MUSSOLINI

ROME, DECEMBER 31, 1922
OFFICE OF THE PRIME MINISTER

THERE THEY ARE, all lined up, not a one missing. Great economists, great philosophers, victorious generals of the world war. All the members of his government have filed by to wish their prime minister a happy new year—the young, formidable statesman whom the American press salutes as "the most interesting and powerful man in Italy." Everyone is now thrilled to pay homage to the endeavor. The fascist coup occurred and the sky did not fall.

On November 24th the parliament, humiliated by his inaugural speech, granted Benito Mussolini full powers for civil service reform and the reorganization of finances. But his personal affirmation goes beyond national borders: the previous week the rising star had personally participated in the Lausanne Peace Conference, meeting French president Poincaré and British foreign minister Curzon for the first time on an equal footing; Mussolini had even demanded that they be the ones to come to see him at Territet—a small town on the outskirts of Lausanne—and had extracted a promise to reopen discussions on colonial mandates in the Middle East. A great success, the first step to enable Italy to return to being a great power. That is the goal. He now proclaims it to his obsequious ministers who listen to him, standing, while he sits, arrogantly, at his desk:

"The historical task that awaits us is this: to make this nation a state, that is, a moral idea that embodies and expresses itself in a system of well-defined hierarchies whose members, from the highest to the lowest, take pride in doing their duty, a unitary state, the sole depository of the entire history, of the entire future, of the entire strength of the Italian nation."

The ministers nod their agreement, the undersecretaries applaud, the fascist revolution has just begun.

An immense undertaking awaits the Duce of fascism, an epic of re-foundation that will take years, decades. Only those who are soft in the head, the authors of various plans for universal happiness, believe in miracles and rapid transformations. But he is not just passing through, he has come to stay, and to govern. The first ones he will whip into shape, thanks to his full powers, will be Rome's civil servants who don't want to give up their afternoon siesta. They defend that hour of sleep fiercely, clinging to it tooth and nail, claiming it as the centuries-old right of a torpid, languid people to whom nothing that can't be undone ever happens. But they too must and will obey him, he will transform them into a clockwork mechanism. To shake up the Italians, he is ready to battle enemies, friends and even himself.

Of course, to do that he does not intend, for the moment, to step outside the laws, or disregard the constitution. Mussolini said it clearly in parliament: the revolution has just begun but we cannot upend everything and slap together a new world; he does not intend to "capsize the universe." A few stable points, fundamental in peoples' lives, must be respected. The afternoon siesta, however, will not be one of them.

It will take time, no rushing, they have to let him do his work. He's organized all his affairs to be able to devote himself to Italy, he even left Rachele and the children in Milan to avoid any family interferences. Then as prime minister he wrote to the prefect of Trent to have that madwoman Dalser who keeps harassing him confined in an asylum. And he arranged a small, well-furnished flat for Angela Curti, the woman who came to him in March 1921 to obtain her husband's release and immediately became his habitual lover—the sweet Angela who on October 19th, a few days before the march on Rome, gave him another illegitimate daughter. But this time he did things right: he suggested the name of Elena—another Homeric name—for her daughter and had her moved to Rome in an elegant apartment in Parioli.

He himself is satisfied with little. He lives in a hotel room at the Grand Hotel, where his only attendant is a certain Cirillo Tambara, a cross between a waiter, chauffeur and bodyguard who even cooks him minestrone with pork rinds, his favorite dish. For the rest, a monastic life, military discipline. At 6:00 a.m. the Duce is already up, at seven already on his way, at eight already in his office at Palazzo Chigi, where he starts making phone calls to check that all forty thousand employees of Rome's bureaucracy are at their posts. He will reform those civil servants even if he has to shoot them; he will rouse that monstrous pachyderm, perpetually befuddled by sluggish digestion, dozing in the eternal siesta of a sultry afternoon that never fades to dusk.

And besides that he has to cage the other beast, the one ready to spring, the ferocious one. After the seizure of power the squadristi stepped up to settle the final scores. In Milan they blatantly occupied the benches during administrative consultations, in Brescia they went so far as to club priests in the rectories, and then there were the events in Turin . . . Barely a month after the vote of confidence for his government . . . Turin . . . a slaughterhouse. Even Francesco Giunta, one of his most violent squadristi, whom he sent to Piedmont to look into it, tells of unprecedented savagery, of a horde of thugs, of an entire city in the grip of murderous gangs.

In Turin it seems this is what happened.

During the night between December 17 and 18, near the Barriera Di Nizza tram station, a communist tram driver killed two fascists during a street clash. It appears it was a personal matter that started it, something to do with a woman. Piero Brandimarte, the leader of the local squadristi and a brute, immediately assembled 3,000 blackshirts from all over the region. "Our dead are not mourned, they are avenged" is his slogan. To honor it, Brandimarte's squadristi, from 1:00 p.m. on December 18th until the afternoon of

December 20, went on a rampage, two days and two nights of raids, seizures, fires, destruction, flagrant assassinations, and swift executions, two days and two nights of unrestrained violence, colossal blunders, mistaken identities, innocent victims. An innkeeper dragged into the back of his tavern and slain with two revolver shots to his skull, his liver split open with punctures and stab wounds; fathers murdered while having dinner with the family; young workers dragged into the street and bludgeoned to death; the streets of the city center awash with blood; bodies found in ditches and gullies and in the wooded areas on the hills, corpses carried back by the swollen river. Unspeakable atrocities, unimaginable barbarities, widespread suffering. And to top it all off, a fire at the Chamber of Labor, the third in a row, and Brandimarte's squadristi, as ecstatic as hounds at the scent of blood, hoot and sing and dance against the reddish background of the flames.

The Duce immediately repudiated them. Prime Minister Benito Mussolini called the massacre "a discredit to the human race," and threatened punishment to make an example of them. However, on December 23rd, three days later, he proclaimed a general amnesty for politically motivated blood crimes committed for "national ends." On December 28th, with Christmas over, he issued the first decree to the Council of Ministers for the creation of a Voluntary Militia for National Security. Which is to say that, in order to avert more of their transgressions, Brandimarte's killers had to become a state institution, a kind of national guard, the foundation of the armed nation. That's how the Duce intends to cauterize the wound.

The paradox does not escape him, nor does the absurdity. But you have to be realistic: when a group comes to power it has the obligation to fortify itself, to defend itself against everyone else, and besides, the country is tired. Italy has just started breathing again for having narrowly escaped after the agonizing wait for the march on Rome. Now the time of disorder, of reckless strikes, of skull bashing must end. At any cost, even at the cost of promoting criminals to gendarmes. Moreover, it wouldn't be the first time. Fascism in power must relieve Italy of the burden of its own threat. Italy wants to rest, it must be bathed in calm.

Acquiescence spreads, engulfs the peninsula. Many newspapers haven't even commented on the Turin massacres, because everything casts shadows, everything casts suspicion. Now it's all over, now people must finally be able to sleep, now they *must* sleep, because he's there now, the new man, to watch over them. Close your eyes, think sweet dreams, dreams of greatness, of Mediterranean power, dream of tomorrow too, because tomorrow awaits us and we are moving towards it, because the new year is beginning in his name, in the name of Benito Mussolini, the master of exhaustion.

1923

BENITO MUSSOLINI

ROME, JANUARY 1923

IN ALL LIKELIHOOD, these months will be the happiest of his life. He keeps telling Rachele that in his phone calls from Rome. He calls her once a day, every day, without fail (the family is important, even if it's far away, especially if it's far away): "Rachele, the happiest time of our lives." Then he hangs up the receiver and launches into his work as though catapulted. To Rome's ministerial functionaries he seems like a man possessed, gripped by extreme euphoria, astonished and nearly incredulous over the fact of his spectacular rise. To the small crowd that congregates in the lobby of the Grand Hotel, where he has moved, just to see him pass by, the Duce of fascism already appears surrounded by an aura of legend.

It happens all the time now, wherever he goes: as soon as he's recognized, his body crossing a space attracts people with the force of a sexual urge. If Mussolini simply tries to walk the distance between the office and the Grand Hotel, the crowd in Piazza Colonna immediately recognizes him, presses round him, wants to touch him, adoring, excited, orgasmic over this new politician who comes from the streets, from the masses, who lives by direct, personal contact with them, this flashy, crude outsider, this blacksmith's son who will sweep away the old petty politicians unfamiliar to the people, hiding behind the secrets of their intrigues and palace maneuvers. Wherever he goes, the crowd out there, in the piazza, surrounds him, embraces him.

Ecce homo. The new man, the man of youth versus the "antediluvians," of rebirth following decline, of vigor versus degeneration. Behold the arbiter of chaos, the initiator of an era, the obstetrician of history, that difficult birth. By comparison, the tired politicos of old Italy, who still bustle about babbling stale parliamentary formulas when they show some meager sign of life, give the impression of larvae crawling out of prehistoric cemeteries.

Behold the virile man, the man of strength, physical strength—there is no other kind—the man of violence who will placate it, the man of ferocity who will tame it, the man of confrontation who will put an end to it because soon there will no longer be two fronts but only one, the man who will restore safety to the poor souls who until yesterday were caught in the middle, the man who created a desert and called it peace, behold the lion tamer, the man who enters the cage while the audience holds its breath and, with a crack of his whip, makes the beasts open their jaws wide and then close them, on command, at his order, because they are *his* lions.

Behold the child of destiny, preceded by signs, prophecies, and premonitory events, the brilliant despot capable of subjugating the masses and restoring order, the stirring victor so long awaited by a people dispirited by the effects of an interminable, inconclusive, tedious drama, in which one thing leads to another but nothing is ever fateful.

He knows it, he cannot be unaware of it, his adversaries, the latest ones, keep telling him again and again: the country is weary, torn apart, dejected, it dreams of repose, it dreams of a dreamless sleep, a dream of ease. The country is tired and, for this very reason, he is indefatigable. He has moved his offices to Palazzo Chigi, home of the Ministry of the Interior, and settled into the so-called Galleria Deti, where his desk is surmounted by a vault decorated with stuccoes and frescoed with biblical scenes and heraldic symbols. He arrives there at eight in the morning without fail, has them bring him a pencil with a sharpened point and a basket of fruit, and dives into work, keeping at it into the evening, into the night, for ten, twelve, eighteen hours every day.

Destiny's man eats and drinks little, he's also had to reduce his consumption of coffee, but he pours all his appetites into an irrepressible reformative dynamism. There is a huge backlog of work, the boat is leaking like a sieve, the laxity of the civil servants is shameful. And so he carries the whole load on his shoulders, he doesn't delegate—he doesn't trust anyone; he reads all the newspapers himself, even those that aren't worth reading—almost all of them; he produces a storm of decrees that rain down on Italy, starting with the simplification of the bureaucracy; he receives hundreds of visitors each day, who anxiously await him in the anteroom, adjusting their ties and checking their shoe tips as though primping for a romantic tryst. Then at the end of the day, he carefully rearranges all his papers, even the useless ones, the superfluous ones, puts them back in his yellow leather briefcase, which has been with him for years, and returns to the hotel. The next morning he wakes up at dawn, practices on the fencing piste, and since he is also learning to ride a horse, he takes riding lessons from Camillo Ridolfi, his sword master, galloping half an hour through the tree-lined avenues of Villa Borghese on a bay stallion called "*Ululato*" (howl).

The only pleasure that the lion tamer allows himself, in addition to power, is women. That indulgence he couldn't do without. And besides, why deny himself? The nature of the two pleasures is identical, his erotic energy is uncontainable, his strange bachelor life permits him to give free rein to it without restraint.

Margherita Sarfatti purposely comes down from Milan, to the Continental Hotel, and he, evading surveillance through a back door on Via Cernaia, joins her there. Rome's law enforcement commissioner and the police chief go through anxious nights while the two lovers make love, jointly prepare his speeches on the nation's future, and draft the article on the "second phase of the revolution" that the new man has promised the editor of *Gerarchia*.

Together the lovers write that the first phase, in its violent, convulsive beauty, is completed, that it is irrevocable and unalterable, that there is no going back. Now it's a matter of normalizing, of leaving everything unchanged for the moment, of reconciling the old with the new, proceeding to one compromise after another, advancing slowly but inexorably. Their enemies should not delude themselves: the fascist state will not tolerate them; it will oppose and destroy them. This is its central hallmark. And the fascist state cannot remain subject to parliament for long—a parliament that must be humiliated daily, publicly scorned—because by now fascism represents Italy. Whoever stands apart from fascism is either an enemy or a dead man. Not one day will go by without a clear line being drawn.

Then, at dawn, having vaticinated, threatened and copulated, he can allow himself the ultimate pleasure, perhaps the most priceless, that of solitude in the city that he has conquered.

Benito Mussolini raises his collar, lights a cigarette, shoves his hands in his pockets and, alone, without a bodyguard, sated, walks down a deserted Via Goito.

The era of the Giolittis, of the Nittis, of the Bonomis, of the Salandras, of the Orlandos and the minor deities of the parliamentary Olympus is over. Between October and November, there was a gigantic purge: of men, of procedures, of doctrines . . . There is no doubt that the second phase of our revolution will be extraordinarily difficult and extraordinarily vital. The second phase will decide the fate of the revolution . . . the fascist revolution will not demolish the delicate, complex machine that is the administration of a great state entirely or all at once; it will proceed by degrees, a bit at a time . . .

Benito Mussolini, "Second Phase,"
Gerarchia, January 31, 1923

MARGHERITA SARFATTI

JANUARY 1923

My dear Benito, my adored darling.
It is the morning of January 1, 1923. I want to write this date for the first time on a letter addressed to you, as a consecration and a dedicatory epistle.

Benito: My Adored Darling.

I am, I will be, always and forever entirely and ever more yours. Yours.

THESE ARE THE idyllic days. The lovers' apotheosis has exploded to conquer the world. Since, however, pain is eloquent but joy mute, even Margherita Sarfatti, the genteel *salonnière*, the highly cultured lady, has had to resort to the mawkish clichés of a smitten servant girl. Adoration and reiteration. Reiteration and adoration. That is the way, the only way, earthly love challenges eternity.

True to this line of pathetic, obtuse and sublime intrepidness of lovers, before the first day of the year is over, Margherita Sarfatti again takes up the Hotel Continentale's stationery and pens a second letter to the illustrious guest at the Grand Hotel in Rome.

The early hours of 1923.

My beloved, my adored darling!
I want to begin the year by writing your name on a piece of paper: Benito, my love, my lover, my adored darling! I am, I

proclaim myself, I glory in being, passionately, wholly, devotedly, hopelessly yours: now, for all of 1923 and, if you want, my beloved, since you love me as I love you, forever. Yours.

Again that solemn commitment, that protest against time in the fixed match that pits us against eternity: "I will love you, forever, forever . . ."

Then the woman, madly in love, promises her man to live obscured in the shadow of his light, implores him to allow her to remain at his side, silent, secondary, merely to afford him a little peace and quiet, some affection, the certainty of an infinite love, to be nothing more than the safe harbor in which the "great glorious ship," having navigated all the oceans, comes to repose.

Faithful to this impossible promise, for the first few days of the year Margherita waits for Benito a long time in her room at the Hotel Continentale but, when summoned by desire or need, she is willing to use the Grand Hotel's back stairs reserved for servants. For her man, the woman in love will climb even those shabby stairs.

These are the idyllic days but they are also days of pride. She writes it to him, loud and clear, she proclaims it as she proclaims her love.

I too am part of your militia: openly and behind closed doors. And I pledged myself to you, I reconfirmed my oath, as your friend, your woman, your spouse; I pledged myself to you, master and spouse, leader and lover. With the absolute fidelity and devotion of a partisan, of an Italian, of a citizen, of a mother, and of a lover . . . I am proud of you, but for what you are, not for what you appear to be. I am so proud of you that it borders on fanaticism and even madness, but for your intrinsic value, not for the crowd's fetishism of you.

Although she is the only one who intimately knows the true face—tormented, angry, often uncertain—of that public man who to the world always poses as a granitic despot, the woman in love, the conscript of eternal love, does not hesitate to blend in among the crowd, one of a thousand, to admire from afar her lover's "square-jawed bust of an ancient Roman." That's how far the luxuriant, precocious, brazen flourishing of this passion, long nourished by a secret lymph, goes. Yet, as any reader of romance novels knows, every rose has its thorn.

Margherita offers herself wholly to Benito fully naked, she prostrates herself in the submissive, supine pose that is proper to a creature in the presence of the divinity. And yet, in her admiration for that "square-jawed ancient Roman bust" that rises dominantly over the crowd, the pride of creation is expressed. It was she who refined the rough-hewn peasant, who dressed the provincial bumpkin, who educated the autodidact, who introduced the blacksmith's son to high society, it was she who encouraged the wavering vacillator when it came to casting the die, who made her country estate in Brianza available to him so that he could flee to Switzerland if the gamble of the assault on history failed, it was she who held his hand in his box at La Scala the night when it was all or nothing, she who lent her car to the man on foot so he could go catch the train that would take him to Rome. And she did all this for her man with her last flare of youth.

Next April Margherita Sarfatti will turn forty-three. It is easy to predict that soon, during one of the many, endless waits in the room at the Hotel Continentale, catching a glimpse of her own reflection in a vanity mirror, she will see only the sagging face of an aging woman.

BENITO MUSSOLINI

ROME, JANUARY 12, 1923
GRAND HOTEL, APARTMENTS OF PRIME MINISTER MUSSOLINI
FIRST MEETING OF THE GRAND COUNCIL OF FASCISM

THE SITTING ROOM on the second floor, which is entirely occupied by the apartments of the honorable Mussolini, is an absolute ferment of old grievances.

He wanted to do things in grand style for this first meeting of fascism's top party leaders. The newly founded advisory assembly is still an informal body, it's still part of the petty chronicle of party life; it meets in his private apartments, yet its originator wanted to lend it historic significance with a name taken from the doges' glorious "Serenissima" Republic of Venice. Mussolini christened this small, nocturnal conclave—illegitimate, semi-clandestine and hastily summoned—the Grand Council of Fascism. At the last minute he even sent for a photographer with a studio on Corso Vittorio Emanuele—an ex-socialist like him—to immortalize the event with magnesium flashes.

And yet, despite his efforts, the rases of fascism, who should be his most grateful and trusted collaborators, have turned the parlor they are sitting in, gathered around the curved legs of small empire-style tables, into an absolute turmoil of old rancors.

Look at them, dissatisfied, embittered, quarrelsome. They are the main drag on Mussolini's speed, the millstone around the neck of the second phase of this revolution. And they're all fascists. The photograph of their disgruntlement is printed on a glass plate coated with silver bromide. A toxic cloud of disappointed ambitions, revolutionary frustrations, confirmed biases, a fetid miasma of familiar rivalries, local constituencies, tribal vendettas, village squabbles, a suffocating spray of factions, dissidences, extremisms. Participants of the Grand Council include secretaries, deputy secretaries and members of the party's leadership, ministers, undersecretaries and prominent fascist figures, public security directors, railway officials, secretaries of union corporations, managers of cooperatives, and political advisers. For the most part they are mediocre, greedy, petty men, raised to their rank by the updraught stirred up in Italy's sky by the Mussolini cyclone and appointed directly by him, the supreme Leader, yet, instead of gratitude, the beveled glass mirrors of the Grand Hotel reflect devious, scowling, gloomy looks of discontent.

The fascist leaders had started complaining the day after the march. For his coalition government, Mussolini had appointed only three fascist ministers, in addition to the ministries reserved for himself. And so, already at ten o'clock in the morning on October 31st, Bianchi and Marinelli, political secretary and administrative secretary of the triumphant party, had gone to the Hotel Savoia to present the Duce with their resignations in protest against the failure to appoint De Bono minister of war. Already at that time, twenty-four hours after the revolution, they spoke of his "betrayal." To placate them, De Bono had to be put in charge of the police. Then it was Costanzo Ciano's turn to protest the failure to appoint him minister of the navy. And so he was named commissioner for the merchant navy. And then Alfredo Rocco, overlooked at first, after the usual protests, was appointed undersecretary of the Treasury, and had to put up with being subservient to Minister De Stefani who had been his student in criminal law at the University of Padua. And so it went, through an endless queue of posthumous reparations, inexhaustible envies, undisciplined soldiers in solitary flight.

But even dismal passions find their leaders. The day after the march Roberto Farinacci became the promoter of fascist discontent just as he had been its enthusiastic leader up until the day before. Excluded from any top-level assignment, he refused a secondary role and entrenched himself in his provincial fiefdom of Cremona to organize the internal dissenters. As self-appointed guardian of original purity, vestal of intransigence, he started spewing accusations of betrayal from his local newspaper, *Cremona Nuova*, against any negotiation, along with warnings not to disarm against "the enemies of yesterday who are the enemies of today," not to pollute fascism with "impure contacts," and calls to root out any dissenter as one would an infesting parasite.

That night, at the first meeting of the Grand Council of Fascism convened in the private apartments of the prime minister, the provincial Farinacci sits there in a back-row chair, lurking behind his mustache, ready to sabotage any plan for normalization, any order for demobilization. Because that's exactly what Mussolini wants to impose on his party leaders—Farinacci knows it, everyone in this parlor adjoining his private apartments knows it.

The plan to be sabotaged is called the Voluntary Militia for National Security. It was announced to the fascist leaders in mid-December and approved by the Council of Ministers on the 28th of that month. For three weeks now the decree has been lying on the desk of the king who is still hesitant to sign it. If he did, he would be christening the birth of a second armed force—parallel, partisan, factious—alongside the national army. Through the militia, a body of armed volunteers incorporated into the military through regular recruitment but bound by oath solely to the prime minister, Mussolini aims to normalize fascist violence by legalizing it, but also wants to demobilize the provincial squads by regimenting them in his new personal army. With one fell swoop, he would appropriate legitimate violence, which in the modern age belongs only to the state, and would put a tight rein on that of the squads.

As usual, his maneuver is Janus-faced. The squadristi, after raising him to power, and then being sent back to their home towns where they refuse to disarm, are becoming a critical problem. They must therefore be taken away from the local leaders who could use them against him. On the other hand, he must continue using them to keep parliament and the monarchy under his thumb. The veiled threat of civil war remains the chief guarantee of his power.

"The fascist revolution can last an entire generation."

The announcement with which the Leader inaugurates the meeting jolts those men in their chairs who had believed and hoped that they had already victoriously concluded their struggle and were getting ready to simply enjoy its fruits. For a moment the staggering suggestion of an entire life of violence scatters the clouds of discontent. De Bono takes the floor and presents the plan for the Voluntary Militia for National Security.

Its objectives will be to defend the fascist revolution and to maintain public order. That duty will no longer fall on the army, and the royal guard who performed it in recent years will be disbanded. Recruitment will be nominally voluntary but restricted solely to members of fascist military formations. All the squads will be dissolved and any squadristi who want to remain fascists will have to join the militia. The high-level officers will come from the army, supported by some consuls, promoted to the rank of colonel. The oath will be to Italy and, above all, to its prime minister, Benito Mussolini. Obedience must be "blind, prompt, respectful and absolute."

After the presentation, before opening the discussion to those assembled there, Mussolini speaks again briefly. Widening his eyes and looking around, he plants his gaze on Farinacci, half hidden to his scrutiny:

"I'm speaking to the gentlemen in the second row of seats. I warn you: Italy tolerates one Mussolini at most, but not several dozen."

Cesare Rossi approves the nationalization of the militia without hesitation. All the "moderate" fascists approve it. Massimo Rocca—ex-anarchist, interventionist, top byline of *Il Popolo d'Italia*, national leader of the Fascist Party, and principal advocate of "normalization" in contrast to the continuation of squadrist violence—also approves it, though claiming to have to choose the lesser evil.

But discontent is already rising again in the parlor. Farinacci, personally addressed, for now only declares that the squads are much more effective than the militia at holding the country to obedience. Then he adds, slyly: "Especially in case of danger." His remark sparks a protest. Attilio Teruzzi—a highly decorated officer, deputy secretary of the party—passionately advocates for "the need to maintain the revolutionary spirit"; Francesco Giunta complains that it is useless to remain in the party if the party is to serve only the Duce's pals; Balbo, who though named to oversee the militia along with De Bono and De Vecchi, for the sheer polemical relish of countering the Leader displays the privilege of addressing him informally and asks him:

"Tell me, Benito, was the revolution done for you, or for all of us?"

At Balbo's question, the session breaks up. Michele Bianchi, with a few pragmatic words, adjourns it until the following day.

Purging and intransigence must be our weapons to preserve fascism as we created it, defended it, strengthened it . . . And we will remain vigilant in defending these supreme interests against everyone and everything. Before exploiting fascism, before offending the memory of our dead, they will have to have the courage to trample on our bodies. And that will not be easy.

Roberto Farinacci,
"We must defend ourselves and purge,"
Cremona Nuova, February 17, 1923

Siam fascisti assaltatori / allegri e pieni di gioventù / perché mutarci in assessori / o Benito, o Patria, o Gesù? We are fascist aggressors / cheerful and alive with youth / why make us into councilmen / O Benito, O Fatherland, O Jesus?

Il lamento dell'intransigente
(The lament of the intransigent),
fascist chant, 1923

For some time now, faced with criticism from friends and adversaries, that is, of the fascist revolution having given Italy only one man, albeit an extraordinary one, and very few collaborators worthy of him; for a long time I've wondered whether the Fascist Party represents a necessary political support for Benito Mussolini, or if instead it lives parasitically on his back.

Massimo Rocca,
member of the national leadership of the PNF,
Critica Fascista, 1923

With the exception of three or four names, I can no longer have any esteem for the new national leadership . . . weak, deceitful and corrupt: this opinion of mine is shared by many and it is spreading.

Giuseppe Bottai, co-founder of the Rome fascio,
squad leader, column commander in the march on Rome,
private letter to Mussolini, January 13, 1923

MARGHERITA SARFATTI

MILAN, MARCH 26, 1923
PESARO GALLERIA D'ARTE

"I FEEL PART OF the same generation as these artists. I took another path; but I am also an artist who works with a certain medium and pursues certain resolute ideals . . ."

Benito Mussolini wears a well-cut grisaille suit—no black shirt—and, contrary to his usual practice, does not speak off the cuff but reads his brief remarks from a typewritten sheet. Listening to him, inside the art deco salon of Lino Pesaro's gallery, are not only critics, collectors and artists, but everyone in Milan who matters: powers that be, politicians, industrialists and journalists.

Outside, on the launching pad of Via Manzoni's flagstones, the "roaring twenties" are ready to take off. With the war behind them, industrial development accelerates, money circulates, commerce prevails. And technology dominates—automobiles, radios, phonographs—new gods are invented, myths are lived on the cinema screen, the trend is towards progress, modernity, and everyone in the Kingdom is invited to participate; thanks to gramophones, everyone can listen to the music, they can all dance to the syncopated rhythm of the explosive jazz age. Women burst out, impertinent, brazen; suffragettes, tomboys, they bare their shoulders, demand the right to vote. Meanwhile, by the millions, the masses discover leisure time, hobbies, extravagance and pleasures reserved in the past to a dozen or so princes and marquises; composers write rhapsodies inspired by metallic clanking, by the rhythmic clatter of trains; crowds of Sunday bathers flock to Lake Michigan, and in the Hollywood hills Rudolph Valentino, an Italian immigrant born in Castellaneta di Taranto, wearing the garments of the White Sheikh, magnetizes the world with the "killer gaze" of a myopic unfit for military duty. It all takes place under another gaze, the blank gaze of two gigantic blue eyes whose supreme indifference from a huge billboard up above propitiates the reawakening of a resurrected world.

Of course, all this takes place overseas, in America, but even here in Milan the century roars. In Lombardy, a stretch of roadway intended to facilitate car traffic between the capital and the tourist areas of lakes Como and Varese has just been inaugurated and some say it's the first "motorway" in the world, expressly designed for fastmoving metallic cars driven by indefatigable combustion engines, not for wagons drawn by sluggish animals. There are even those who say that patriotism will not be what saves Europe: the Americans will save it, to make it a huge mass consumption market for their industry's new products.

All this is happening out there and in here, in Lino Pesaro's art gallery, where the voice of Benito Mussolini celebrates the new century, the Italian century: "The twentieth century is an important period because it marks the time when most of the Italian population entered political life. You cannot make a great nation with an insignificant people. You cannot govern by ignoring art and artists; art is an essential manifestation of the human spirit. And in a country like Italy, a government that took no interest in art and artists would be deficient."

Mussolini, as usual, articulates the words syllable by syllable: "De-fi-cient." "Art-ists." People in Lino Pesaro's gallery are astonished. A head of state who attributed such importance to art was unheard of, nor was it even conceivable that Benito Mussolini—the formidable savage who had subjugated Italy with a newspaper and an army of squadristi, the new stern face of power that everyone is courting—would come in person to inaugurate the exhibit of seven painters whom the small crowd of politicians and industrialists barely know. Most of all, it seems incredible that Italy's "strong man" is doing so by reading someone else's words from a typewritten sheet of paper handed to him by a woman. This above all is astonishing: it is his stentorian, steely voice that resounds in the elegant rooms but it is she who is speaking. Benito Mussolini is Margherita Sarfatti's ventriloquist.

Today it is she who triumphs. She brought together seven of her artist friends—Funi, Sironi, Bucci, Dudreville, Oppi, Malerba and Marussig—and decreed the birth of a new movement. It wasn't even possible to come up with a coherent name for it. Thus, the exhibit is simply entitled "Seven Painters of the Twentieth Century." But she is very clear about the fact that this inauguration will mark a new beginning, a new Renaissance, the end of Futurist chaos, the art of a "modern classicism" that reflects the hierarchy and order Benito Mussolini has restored to the world. A new art for the new fascist era. Above all, she is very clear about the fact that the high priestess of this new fascist art will be Margherita Sarfatti. For this reason, when the Duce's talk ends, applauded briefly, it is she who, with an elegant but imperious wave, orders the waiters in white gloves to serve the aperitifs.

Light sparkles through the frosted glass of lamps resting on heavy stelai of ornate cast iron, yet the shadow of power spreads over Lino Pesaro's gallery. On November 3rd, after the march on Rome, several of the artists exhibited this evening signed a warm, fawning, congratulatory note to Mussolini. Yet not everyone is of the same mind. Anselmo Bucci and Leonardo Dudreville were horrified when Sarfatti announced the Duce of fascism's participation in the inauguration and now, as champagne is uncorked on Via Manzoni, the two dissenters blatantly toast with vermouth at the Caffè Cova, not far away.

The most toxic shadow, however, is a different one, that of disaffection. Three months of Benito in Rome were enough for Margherita to feel betrayed. The earlier letters of joyful adoration are already a memory. She still writes to him, a constant stream of letters, but now they are words of heartache, indignation and recrimination, words with no replies, letters to no one. The career woman complains of ingratitude, demands appointments for herself and for her husband Cesare, the independent woman protests the capricious tyrant's despotic scenes of jealousy, the woman in love pines away waiting vainly in deserted rooms:

> *Dear friend, I am physically and morally shattered. You know why. I can't take it anymore, I can't, no more, no more. This is goodbye! I'm leaving, going away, leaving immediately. Oh, how I wish I had already left. Goodbye. Everything went bad, everything, even the phone call that was supposed to be next to last. All that matters is this bitter fierce sadness I feel inside.*

As almost always happens, in this case too the grand passionate affair soon deteriorates into the back-page news of pathetic lovers. An endless trickle of farewells, absurd, ignoble, degrading scenes, impulsive contrition, fits of sacrifice, tender presentiments: "My love, you are infinitely good. When I forced myself to be gay tonight, I saw that you looked at me with eyes that were full of sadness and pity. Thank you, my love, for that sadness and that pity."

She vacillates. Sometimes she proclaims she is ready to sacrifice herself, willing to leave the whole world outside "to mark time and pry," content to be able to hold her beloved in her arms even for just a few hours, to "appease her hunger of him a little," and he of her, her "great savage wolf." At other times she rears up and demands independence, respect, dignity, the right to share power, his over politics, hers over art.

And then she asks him again to permit her to travel to Tunisia with her son Amedeo—another piece in the mosaic of her mission as a free woman and voracious intellectual—a trip barely concealed behind the banal pretext of looking into the problems facing the schools, hospitals, and real estate market in overseas territories. He—a possessive, jealous, despotic lover—has always denied her permission. But the trickle continues, in the end they both have regrets, they both cry, even he cries—incredible to say—and then he, in the end, leaves her alone in her deserted rooms to see to the history of art because he has a lot more than that to do: he has the history of the world to attend to.

And so, when spring comes, the "great savage wolf" finally grants his lover permission to leave for Africa, and Margherita leaves.

Our applause for the young head of state . . . the Man who will rightly assess the influence of our dominant Art on the World.

A tribute to Benito Mussolini
from poets, novelists and painters,
Il Popolo d'Italia, November 3, 1922
Carrà, Funi, Marinetti, Sironi (among others)

Show me tenderness because it is mine. Other than that, I ask only that you not interfere in my external life to diminish it, restrict it, smother it, with a series of absurd prohibitions and requirements, spiteful acts, temper tantrums and scenes . . . You have your grand destiny; and your colossal mission . . . I have my unassuming life, and my unassuming work, modest, but which to me are sacred and dear. I ask you to respect them, I do not think it is asking too much . . .

It could have been such a beautiful day! Alone, in a corner by the fire, absolute love was ours, and absolute intimacy. Instead you poured out every venom for me! Violence, insults, insinuations . . . Afterwards you were repentant and crying and confused . . . your tears with mine, you made your grand, sublime gestures of which only you are capable . . .

Margherita Sarfatti,
letter to Benito Mussolini, 1923

BENITO MUSSOLINI

ROME, APRIL 17–23, 1923

COUNT SANTUCCI'S PALAZZO in Rome has two entrances. Entering from the one on Via del Gesù is an atheist, materialist and anticlerical who a few years earlier publicly challenged God by giving Him two minutes to strike him dead as proof of His existence; arriving from the entrance on Piazza della Pigna is Cardinal Gasparri, a man who has served God all his life, each day betraying his celestial city for the terrestrial one. The two enter separately and separately leave Palazzo Guglielmi, silently and hurriedly slipping through deserted halls and stairways.

The conversation between Benito Mussolini—up until now a compulsive blasphemer, rabid anticlerical and free love advocate—and the Vatican state secretary takes place in private. The palazzo's host, Catholic Senator Santucci, president of the Bank of Rome, isn't even present. No one must know and no one will know what is said in there, it must and it will remain confidential. What is certain is that the meeting lasts a long time. And that upon leaving, the secretary of state of the Holy See, walking out into Piazza della Pigna, says he is satisfied with his conversation with the Duce of fascism.

The secret negotiations with top-level Vatican officials for reconciliation with the Church, begun months ago by the prime minister, are the ace up his sleeve in the confrontation that pits him against the Popular Party, the political party of Italian Catholics. Corresponding to the hush-hush level are the manifest government actions that grant one concession after the other to the Vatican, disguised as technical measures: equalization of school taxes, restoration of the crucifix in classrooms, obligatory religious instruction, the ecclesiastical authorities' ability to choose teachers, and, most important of all, exemption from the special tax on the seminaries' assets. Mussolini is ready to grant this and more to the Pope just to be rid of Don Sturzo, the founder of the Catholic party, towards whom he feels an entrenched dislike that borders on physical repulsion.

"It's time to quit having priests who are politicians," Mussolini often repeats privately to Cesare Rossi. Then he adds comments that his closest collaborator, always at his side—now in the delicate role of head of the prime minister's press office—could never communicate to the public: "Don Sturzo, that misshapen politicking priest who never celebrates Mass and goes around manipulating petty politics."

Mussolini despises Sturzo to the point that, after the march on Rome, despite having included the populists in his coalition government, he refused to receive Sturzo, their party's founder. He shouted at Rossi, who insisted on giving him an audience, with an outburst of his youthful anticlericalism: "It's absolutely out of the question that I will receive that man. I admitted some ministers into my government whom I consider suitable and qualified but I have no intention of becoming a puppet in their hands. As for Don Sturzo, I consider him ruinous to the functioning of any government. Enough of this *éminence grise*! Priests belong in church. They should not drag their soutanes into ministerial antechambers!"

But apart from the personal antipathy between two inflexible human types, the falling-out is political. The founding of a party of Catholics by Sturzo, son of the great Sicilian landed aristocracy, which occurred in 1919, was the most important historical event since the time of the Unification of Italy, along with the foundation of the Fasci di Combattimento that same year by Benito Mussolini, son of a socialist blacksmith from a village in Romagna. Up till then, the Pope had forbidden Catholics to vote in elections and to take part in political life. From that moment on, their party, with its 110 deputies, evenly elected throughout the country, became the needle that tipped the balance of parliament's scales. The Catholic deputies are indispensable to the formation of all governmental coalitions, and they provoke and resolve crises; in the spring of 1922, at Don Sturzo's bidding, they blocked the way for Giolitti's return, smoothing the way for the fascists. Now, however, the Sicilian priest, after indirectly aiding them before the march on Rome, and openly supporting their government afterwards, is the fascists' sole real adversary standing in the way of a complete conquest of power.

The Catholic party too is split internally, however. The right wing, close to the Vatican hierarchy, is for full cooperation with Mussolini and participates in his government with ministers and undersecretaries. The left, a representation of the "white" peasant leagues constantly targeted by the squadristi, is radically opposed to it. The center, headed by Don Sturzo and his young secretary Alcide De Gasperi, is for collaboration contingent on acceptance of the Catholics' moral principles and full autonomy from the fascists.

The decisive assembly of the Popular Party opens in Turin on April 12th. At stake is not only the unity of the populists but also the unity of Italian Catholics. Don Sturzo, despite never revealing himself openly, prevails. The platform adopted by majority vote on April 15th marks a clear victory for him: the populists' collaboration in Mussolini's government is conditional on respecting their autonomy, parliament's integrity and constitutional freedoms, and, above all, on the preservation of an electoral law based on proportional representation.

That is the real issue: electoral reform. Mussolini can keep parliament under his thumb with the threat of violence and that of dissolving it, but he counts only 36 fascist deputies in that congress. In order for his power to become stable and absolute, new elections are needed along with an electoral law that will give him a rock-solid majority, and total control over his troublesome allies and over dissident fascists as well. Thus, since February, there's been talk of nothing else: electoral reform.

The Grand Council of Fascism assigned an internal commission to study various proposals. Notable liberals of the south and fascist rases in the provinces would like a uninominal single-member district system to guarantee themselves the vote of their local constituencies. Farinacci has openly come out in favor of it. Mussolini on the other hand wants a majority system based on national lists, with a premium for the relative majority party. Giacomo Acerbo, undersecretary to the prime minister, is studying a law that would assign two-thirds of parliament's seats to the party that gets more than 25 percent of the assenting votes, almost certainly the Fascist Party. This law would hand its Leader, Benito Mussolini, the parliament and the nation. Its moral effects would be shattering, devastating: any opposition, external or internal, would be thwarted, any demand for autonomy by allies stifled. Anyone hoping to return to parliament would have to agree to being a candidate on the national fascist lists and Mussolini, from his hotel room on the second floor of Rome's Grand Hotel, would be able to nominate the two-thirds however he pleased with a simple pen stroke that would decide the candidates' standing in the lists. For the Duce, passage of this law would be the crowning achievement of his personal success, a veritable seizure of power, it would in short be a wonder of wonders.

Unfortunately, however, there is Don Sturzo who wants the proportional law instead. And, unfortunately, his 110 deputies can impose it. The Catholic party's congress, which concluded on April 15th in Turin, spoke clearly.

On April 17th, Mussolini summons Stefano Cavazzoni, the Popular Party's remaining minister after Tangorra's death, together with the Catholic undersecretaries. They are all on the party's right, and wound up defeated at the Turin congress where Don Sturzo won. The prime minister reads them a declaration in which he thanks them for their "loyal and willing" collaboration and gives them back "the utmost freedom of action and movement." In other words, the Duce is getting rid of them.

Cavazzoni has no choice but to make the portfolios available again. He signs a blank letter of resignation: "Mr. President, the leaders of the Popular Party fully understand the need to collaborate with the government."

"I don't doubt that, Cavazzoni, but I need a more explicit clarification of your position." Mussolini's tone is now conciliatory. In exchange for reconfirming the Catholic ministers and undersecretaries, the Duce asks for a vote in his favor from the parliamentary populist group, called for April 20. Cavazzoni promises it.

"Good. Then after the vote I will make my decisions." The meeting ends.

On April 20th Cavazzoni keeps his promise. *Il Popolo d'Italia* triumphantly announces the vote of the parliamentary populist group: "Complete and loyal collaboration with the fascist government."

But Sturzo, although betrayed by his ministers, does not give up: the conditions he dictated for supporting the government remain unchanged. Three more days go by and Mussolini surprises everyone. Cesare Rossi is the first to be astounded when the Duce asks him to communicate that, despite their act of submission, the prime minister has accepted the "resignation" of Cavazzoni and the undersecretaries of the Popular Party. Parliament begins to tremble again.

Faced with Sturzo's resistance, Mussolini has decided: he will return to a confrontational approach, he will go back to the use of force. He stated it loud and clear in the March *Gerarchia*: in this new century, of which he is the son, force and consensus are one and the same. Liberty is a means, not an end. As a means it must be controlled. It takes force to control it.

So Benito Mussolini once again switches masks. The moderate conciliator, who after the march on Rome preached "normalization" to his rebellious rases, again gives way to the bellicose first honorary corporal of the militia. Enough dancing around, the titan is back on stage now, who, within a month's time, at La Scala, welcomed by Toscanini, revels in unanimous applause from the orchestra, boxes and gallery; the avant-gardist who at the Pesaro Gallery in Milan inaugurates the exhibit "Novecento," twentieth century, curated by Margherita Sarfatti to show the world the art of the new century; the secular pontifex who with powerful pickaxes launches the construction of the motorway from Milan to the Lakes; the patriot who addresses Italians in North America while signing the agreement to lay telegraph cables across the ocean between the mother country and the new continent.

Compared to all this, liberty is decidedly overrated. Enough of priests in politics.

Liberty is a Nordic divinity, worshiped by the Anglo-Saxons . . . Fascism knows no idols, it does not worship fetishes: it has already stepped over and, if necessary, it will again imperturbably step over the more or less decomposed body of the Goddess Liberty . . . Liberty, today, is no longer the chaste, austere virgin for whom the generations of the first half of the last century fought and died. For the intrepid, restless, fierce youths who face the crepuscular morning of the new history, there are other words that exert a much greater attraction, and they are: order, hierarchy, discipline.

Benito Mussolini, "Force and Consensus,"
Gerarchia, March 1923

ITALO BALBO, AMERIGO DÙMINI

ROME, MAY 29, 1923

When Italo Balbo, as commander general of the Voluntary Militia for National Security, travels nonstop throughout all the provinces of Italy, even the most remote, to organize reluctant or unruly squadristi, he wears the uniform that he himself invented—black shirt, military pants, Ardito jacket with black flames, fez; and when both friends and foes begin to call him "the generalissimo," whether out of hatred or with admiration, he lets them do so. After all, the other two commanders general have been absent—De Bono sucked into the role of police chief, De Vecchi stymied in the role of undersecretary of the treasury and war pensions—while he, at age twenty-seven, earns a monthly salary of 3,000 liras, equal to that of an army corps general; even better, he commands an army of 150,000 men. That is more than enough to rekindle his fervor after February's discontent, even if the new role of normalizer secures Balbo the rancor of many squadristi for whom he was an idol when it came to wielding a club. The problem, if anything, is just that those 150,000 men are not soldiers and the militia is not an army.

There is no standard dress, no barracks, no transport, there aren't even any muskets, and the 30 million allocated for extraordinary expenses has nearly all been spent on uniforms. Above all, there is a lack of precision, competence and initiative, a lack of discipline. He said it loud and clear at the Teatro Lirico in Milan in April:

enough talk about which course to follow, all the fascists have to do is "stride and act." But for years he was the first to teach those men to answer "I don't give a damn," to exult in rebellion, he taught them life as gang warfare. Hard to call them to order now that even the leaders are sinking their teeth into one another as in a dog fight.

On April 25th, in Rome, on a grassy field outside of Porta del Popolo, two prominent figures of fascism such as Francesco Giunta—now risen to secretary of the Grand Council—and Cesare Forni, the ras of Lomellina, even fought with sabers over a matter of personal rivalries, women, territorial control, and betrayed ideals, all jumbled up. After the duel, in protest against the corruption of Rome's fascists, Captain Forni, a legend among the squads, his labial artery severed, resigned as commander of the militia of the first zone, the largest and most important one covering the entire industrial triangle. It's the same story everywhere: unbridled appetites, clashes, discords, individual passions, unacknowledgeable objectives. Now that the Bolsheviks have been swept out—between December and February De Bono had all the Communist Party leaders arrested—Italy is split into fascist feuds in conflict with one another.

Now it's Alfredo Misuri's turn. Balbo has known him since Misuri was a squad leader in Umbria after having founded the Perugia Fasci di Combattimento in January 1921. But in 1922, before the march, Misuri switched over to the nationalists over rivalry with Bastianini, the other leader of Perugia's squads. Now, however, the nationalists have joined the PNF and Misuri found himself a fascist, like it or not. Four days after the merger of fascists and nationalists, the party's executive council expelled him for past dissidence. Having remained personally devoted to Mussolini, the unwilling prodigal son informed him beforehand that he would be giving a speech in the chamber on "fascist opposition." The Duce warned him against it, threatening to have him arrested. Misuri replied by appealing to constitutional liberties: "Tell the prime minister that the statute stands between me and him."

On the morning of May 29, the chamber is packed with deputies and the public. They are all there to listen to Alfredo Misuri's criticisms. It is in fact the first time that a fascist is expected to give an opposition speech. Handed around among the benches is the day's edition of the *Cremona Nuova*, in which Roberto Farinacci openly suggests the need for a new campaign of squadrist violence, so that the revolution may be completed and all dissension crushed. This time "definitively." The article is entitled "Second Wave."

In the chamber's absolute silence, as if agreeing with the ras of Cremona notwithstanding his personal loyalty to Mussolini, and offering himself as the first target, Alfredo Misuri—his forehead marked by a high receding hairline, his face perfectly shaved, his polished speech that of a zoology professor—begins with bowed head: fascism is degenerating—Misuri shouts—half a million members have overwhelmed the sound nucleus, the latter-day "simoniacs" are polluting public administration. The state must be distinct from the party, the militia must be incorporated into the ranks of the army, the democratic function of parliament must be restored, the government's base must be extended to other national parties.

Misuri's speech makes an enormous impression. Many deputies hasten to congratulate him. Almost as if Mussolini weren't sitting there watching them behind the prime minister's desk, a number of fascists, undersecretary of agriculture Corgini and five other deputies, congratulate him as well.

Cesare Rossi, leaving the press box, openly threatens the dissident: "Tonight you'll see!"

The Duce is livid. In the corridors of Montecitorio, surrounded by his inner circle, he shakes his head, crosses his arms over his chest, then lowers them and plants them on his hips: "Intolerable . . . it's intolerable. The party can't allow such talk. He must be punished. Immediately. Mercilessly."

"I'll take care of it." Balbo bounds forward like a tightly wound spring. "Arconovaldo Bonaccorsi is in Rome. I'll get him on it."

Amerigo Dùmini is in the back seat, along with two of Bonaccorsi's Bolognese squadristi, on the curbside. They found the Lancia K in one of the courtyards of the Palazzo del Viminale, planned to become the headquarters of the prime minister and still under construction. When, late in the evening, Professor Misuri finally left parliament, they followed him step by step through the streets around Montecitorio, with the engine at a slow crawl. Then they parked in a pool of shadow between the streetlamps on Via Due Macelli.

The car is spacious but Arconovaldo Bonaccorsi, tall, heavyset, spills over, filling the space of the passenger seat. He runs his tongue over his upper lip, permanently disfigured by a scar, and from across the street, studies the exit from the "*vespasiano*" on Vicolo dello Sdrucciolo. The Roman spring stinks of piss from the public urinal.

Bonaccorsi lights a cigarette. With the window lowered, he takes a drag with his right hand. His left hand grips a cudgel thick as a wagon wheel hub, tucked between his thighs. He grips it naturally: the Bolognese squadrista has done this all his life since the days of the "red biennium" when, as a twenty-year-old, he served in the army units assigned to maintain public order during street clashes with the socialists. Having gone through the riots, the professional thug has been a fascist since San Sepolcro; he was arrested for the first time back in November 1919 when, having gone to Milan for the elections along with Arpinati, "Bonaccorsi the iron man," as he likes to be called, took part in the shooting at the Teatro Gaffurio in Lodi. Ten months in jail. Since then he's never quit: dozens of arrests for offenses, assaults, political violence, dozens of releases, dozens of injuries, including the permanent one on his mouth that makes him look like an aberrant child born with a cleft lip, as if violence had already marked him in the maternal womb, the cartilaginous tissue not fusing properly, as a sign of destiny.

When Alfredo Misuri emerges from the urinal, Dùmini doesn't even have time to get out of the car before Bonaccorsi is in the street. Now he's holding the club in his right hand; he doesn't hide it, he doesn't brandish it, he wields it with absolute nonchalance, as if it were a mere extension of his arm. Misuri, who is still fumbling with the fly of his pants, doesn't see him coming.

The crack on the skull echoes in the narrow alleyway. Just one blow, and the bludgeoned man is on the ground. The three Bolognese squadristi are on top of him, clubbing him and kicking him savagely. Misuri shields himself as best he can, inadequately, with his arms. Then Bonaccorsi bends down and, pressing his bogus cleft lip to a forearm, bites off a strip of skin still smelling of piss.

A patrol of carabinieri comes running over. Dùmini draws out a knife and aimlessly waves it about. Then, yammering about wanting to kill all the enemies of fascism, he disappears into a nearby bar, the Caffè Cilario. Bonaccorsi doesn't let the carabinieri intimidate him: "You can't arrest me," he yells, "I'm your superior, I'm a senior officer of the militia." Deputy Misuri remains on the ground, lying in a pool of blood.

The following day, May 30, voting on the provisional budget, his colleagues in parliament, as if nothing had happened, confirm their confidence in the government with 238 votes in favor and 83 against.

GIACOMO MATTEOTTI

SIENA, JULY 2, 1923

THE PALIO IS not folklore exhumed for the curious or for tourists, the Palio is the life of the Sienese people over time.

Since 1644 these twelve Maremma horses, with their sturdy hooves and low barycenter—working animals, accustomed to rocks and brush, enduring the hard work along with the peasants—mounted bareback by a jockey who is light as a feather, have been confronting the sharp curve of San Martino to make three feverish laps around Piazza del Campo in barely three minutes, less than a minute per round. And for three centuries the city of Siena, divided into seventeen *contrade*, or city wards, has been getting fired up over this wild, three-minute race amid a frenzied blaze of people that, with a few moments of jubilation, makes up for entire lives of tepid submission, broken backs and nameless generations.

Some socialists impugn the Palio. It's true, for example, that Modigliani, a courageous party member, in a meeting with the miners of Siena, criticized the spectacular brutality of this breakneck race that often injures the horses, but Giacomo Matteotti nevertheless brought his wife, in a very rare moment of diversion, to witness that marvelous manifestation of popular ardor fused with animal fury. For the occasion, Velia pulled out of the closet one of those sober, elegant dresses that she is never able to wear alongside her husband. Now she can cling to his arm under the cross-ribbed vaults of the Loggia della Mercanzia, behind Piazza del Campo, and hidden in the crowd with him, watch the historical procession staged by the seventeen *contrade*.

No, Modigliani is wrong. The elite bourgeoisie, the captains of industry, the magnates, the agrarians may enjoy the brutal spectacle sheltered by a parasol, in the exclusive stands mounted around the piazza, or from the balconies of the surrounding buildings, but the Palio belongs to the people crammed into the center of the piazza, dazed by the sun directly overhead, keyed up enough to start brawling, hemmed in by the horses thundering around them in that tumultuous bedlam. Yes, the star of the Palio is the people! True, here too the upper crust stand on top and the people down below but, if you look carefully, you realize that in the Palio, as in history, the elite gentlemen are merely spectators of people's lives, and that—however much they may dominate, determine, and even end them—it's the people who suffer and foam with sweat on the earthen tuff there in the middle of the Campo.

And today like never before the people are Giacomo Matteotti's element. The anonymous crowd enfolds him, conceals him, protects him. The guest of honor on whom the Sienese authorities lavish the utmost reverence is philosopher Giovanni Gentile, minister of public education, whose school reform, focused entirely on extolling the humanities, was recently approved; vaunted by Benito Mussolini as a great success of his government, Gentile is highly praised even by Benedetto Croce. It seems that those in Rome want to downgrade Siena's university and the minister's opinion—on an official visit to the second Tuscan city—will be decisive in avoiding the demotion. The fascist leaders' full attentions are, therefore, turned to Giovanni Gentile, and Giacomo Matteotti can sink happily into the amniotic womb of his people.

For months his intransigence has also been souring his life within his party. Many, especially union members, are inclined to collaborate with the fascists, in the hope that Mussolini's socialist past and his course of normalization might result in some benefits to workers. Then too, for many decades now those "palace" socialists have been used to parliamentary compromises. They don't realize that the march on Rome marked the beginning of dictatorship, not the end of conflicts. Matteotti never tires of repeating that those comrades either have no ears to hear or they don't want to see. We always make the mistake of expecting catastrophe in the future, then one morning we wake up with a suffocating weight on our chest, we look back and we discover that the end is behind us, the minor apocalypse has already happened and we didn't even notice it. The "second wave," now openly invoked by Farinacci, is already submerging them.

To prove it, Matteotti has been hard at work for months, with his usual dogged meticulousness, on an exhaustive effort to expose every act of fascist violence. He records them one by one in the pages of a book that he intends to publish at the end of the year with the title *Un anno di dominazione fascista* (A Year of Fascist Domination). To date, he has already recorded and documented 42 killings, 1,112 clubbings, beatings, and injuries, 184 destructions of buildings and homes, and 24 newspaper fires. With each new entry, however, the author of the denunciation is increasingly insulated. The circle of solitude tightens around him, even within the party of which he is secretary, as the list of violent acts gradually grows longer. Even Turati urges him to abandon the book project, accusing him of "preconceived hostility" towards their more moderate colleagues. In order to keep his position, the young isolated secretary can only continue to threaten to resign. At times we get the impression that the only way he can convince the lukewarm fence-sitters of their delusion is by inciting fascist reprisals against himself.

The only other way to save this increasingly lost Italy is to go abroad. With the start of the first year of fascist domination, Giacomo Matteotti began increasing his travels outside of the country to forge alliances with French, Belgian, German and English comrades. In February he was in Lille at the French Socialists Congress, the following month in Paris, then he went to Berlin to meet with the German Social Democrats. But this course was also blocked. After the trip to Germany, Mussolini had his passport revoked.

Now, under the Loggia della Mercanzia, Siena is preparing for the big event. The procession with the banners of the *contrade* and the hundreds of people in medieval costume is tapering off. Soon the ropes will be tightened and the horses will begin entering the piazza to be ready for the "start." Giacomo and Velia Matteotti, arm in arm, happily join the stream of reveling people.

Someone, however, yells out his name. Shouts it the way you shout wolf, the way you shout thief. The name of an outlaw.

The men who recognized him aren't even wearing black shirts, just the bright colors of a *contrada*. The eagle, the crested porcupine, the goose, the wave, the panther, the tortoise. They're on top of him in any case. Velia clings to her husband's arm, he shields her with his body. No one pays any attention, scuffles among *contrada* supporters happen all the time.

This time, however, there's a woman in the fray, a refined lady. It's odd, a few people notice and stop. This is a disgrace, even for the factious belligerence of *contrada* rivalries: you don't lay a finger on a woman.

A police car makes its way through the crowd. Amid the general confusion, the police rescue the distinguished couple so that the race can begin. While Giacomo and Velia Matteotti are escorted to the station, expelled, banished from the festive city, the clamorous roar of Piazza del Campo rises towards the clays and vineyards of Siena's hills baking and fermenting under the July sun.

In the evening, Giacomo Matteotti takes up his book again, adding a bead to the rosary of fascist domination. On the date of July 2 he writes: "Siena—Deputy Matteotti, appearing with his family, is attacked by fascists and forced to leave the city. The police look on, helpless."

That's it, no other detail is provided, no comment offered.

We merely point out that these people [the socialists] are so profoundly ignorant that they do not yet understand what world they're living in. The truth is that such individuals have been left in circulation temporarily, the fascist revolution will collar them sooner or later and then civil death will be followed by physical demise as well. And so be it.

Article on Giacomo Matteotti's expulsion from the Palio,
La scure, organ of the Fascist Federation of Siena,
July 3, 1923

ROME, JULY 15, 1923
ITALIAN PARLIAMENT, CHAMBER OF DEPUTIES

HERE THEY ARE awaiting the fascist "second wave." The tension of waiting is such that it nearly becomes an invocation, a mute prayer to the deaf god of history: let it come, if it really must come, this "second wave," and sweep us away with it. Waiting for it most of all are those who were spared, the ones who survived the first wave.

The chamber of Montecitorio is packed, both the benches and the public galleries. The reform of the electoral law—which would hand parliament to the fascists—is being discussed and the liberal, democratic, socialist and populist deputies are called upon to put up one last barrier. The parliamentary commission has surprisingly approved Acerbo's proposed bill which provides for the allocation of two-thirds of the seats to the list that receives a relative majority and, if the chamber does not vote it down now, the next elections could be the last.

Outside the chamber, for weeks now, Fascist Party leaders have been threatening, more or less explicitly, a second wave of violence in the event of defeat. Inside the chamber ears are trained close to the ground to pick up the sound of the earth's muffled vibes, eyes are raised to the galleries where squadristi in black shirts fiddle with their daggers beside ladies in their summer frocks. The unremitting nervous tension is leading most people to exhaustion. It's true that life is meaningless without a small apocalypse on the horizon, but it's also true that one cannot live by seeing omens of the end in each day's morning coffee.

The ones mainly called upon to erect the barrier are the deputies of the Popular Party. It's known that Giolitti's liberal followers have already decided to accept the monstrous electoral system proposed by Acerbo, holding the usual hope that it will tame fascism and that many socialist reformists would even be willing to collaborate, justifying their actions with the standard argument of worker protection. The populists, on the other hand, are at the crossroads of their political history: on July 10th, Don Luigi Sturzo, whom Monsignor Pucci, on behalf of the Holy See, publicly urged "not to create problems," was forced to resign. Mussolini had demanded the end of Sturzo's political career and the Vatican, subjected to constant threats of reprisals against Catholic institutions and associations, even against the churches, granted it to him. With its founder banished, the survival of the Catholic party is now in the hands of its deputies. Without their votes, battling the opposition is useless, and now the only battle that can be fought is this: to vote against the bill. There's no other way. Every single vote could decide victory or defeat, determine which point of the shoreline the wave's crest will crash on and where the undertow will begin.

Following the majority report, when it was the opposition's turn, Filippo Turati took the floor to personally nail the Christian deputies to their small cross:

"Today you are called upon to mark your destiny with your own hands. Today you will decide—today or never—whether you will be a new force, or whether you are content to remain a pawn skillfully playing and being played on this miserable parliamentary chessboard. Will you be our allies of a not too distant tomorrow, or will we be left to take this inheritance as well on our modest shoulders? This is the dilemma of Italian politics today. Think about it!"

From the benches of the center, the Catholics listen to the socialist leader's appeal in utter silence. Their tension is spasmodic. Rising from the fascist right to break the strain is the baritone voice of Cesare Maria De Vecchi. The jibe is directed at Turati, at his small, bulging, porcine eyes, his low forehead, his prophet's beard:

"You're too ugly to be a siren!"

General hilarity, commotion on the left, remarks from the center.

Then, finally, it's his turn. Deputy Benito Mussolini, prime minister, approaches the speakers' rostrum accompanied by the reverberation of the wave. The Montecitorio chamber is transformed into the conical, mother-of-pearl spiral of a conch shell. If you hold it to your ear, you can hear the sea.

Mussolini, however, smiles. He begins with a witty remark. He announces that he will inform the hall of important foreign policy issues in an upcoming session unless "the chamber wishes to indulge its whim of dying prematurely today." Laughter, animated murmurs, prolonged comments. Then his voice, usually sharp, metallic, softens into emotional tones. The Duce declares himself serene, composed, he recalls the glorious history of the Risorgimento, touches all the chords of persuasion. Fascism is not against elections, it is not against parliament, it simply wants the elections to bridge the gap between parliament and the country. Fascism is shedding its skin: "It's amazing how a squad leader who becomes a councilman or a mayor changes. He realizes that you can't attack the municipalities' budgets, you have to learn about them." Murmurs of assent, applause from the center, silence elsewhere. The speaker flies high, soaring to the Olympic peaks of philosophical wisdom: "Does liberty exist? It is fundamentally a philosophical-moral category. There are *liberties*. Liberty has never existed." Then he too makes a conciliatory appeal to the opposition, to the populists, to the socialists: "You know that I would be happy to have direct representatives of organized workers in my government tomorrow." Finally, Mussolini addresses the ultimate appeal, that of responsibility towards a nation that needs a solid government, needs an end to the period of anxiety. An appeal to conscience:

"I tell you: don't leave the country once again with the impression that parliament is aloof from the soul of the nation . . . Because this is the time when parliament and the country can reconcile . . . listen to the solemn, private counsel of your consciences."

Mussolini's last words are greeted with thunderous applause. They applaud on the right but also from the benches of the left. The ovation goes on at length. The public in the galleries joins in. Down in the hemicycle, Giolitti makes his way through the deputies who have come to congratulate the prime minister and shakes his hand repeatedly.

The second wave has not broken. Quite the opposite: the sea is a flat blue slate, barely rippled by a light breeze, a pleasant bright summer day shines on Italy: Benito Mussolini, surprisingly, wore his most conciliatory, urbane mask, that of the even-tempered statesman. On the benches of the center, occupied by the deputies of the Popular Party, it is disorienting.

At 8:10 p.m. the president of the chamber, De Nicola, reopens the session. The hall is packed, the benches are all occupied, from the extreme left to the extreme right. The president points out that the government asks for a vote on the agenda. Either they approve the legal principles of electoral reform and move on to discuss the individual articles, or there will be a ministerial crisis.

Alcide De Gasperi, secretary of the Popular Party after Don Sturzo's resignation, takes the floor. The hall becomes silent, attentive.

"Honorable colleagues, I ask that the agenda be divided into two parts. A separate vote for the first part, 'the chamber reaffirms its confidence in the government,' and for the second, 'approves the principles of electoral reform.'"

Frenzied shouting from the fascist benches, animated commentaries in all the other sections. De Gasperi has just announced that the Catholics will put up a fight. They are solidly aligned to resist: they are willing to reaffirm their confidence in Mussolini but not to approve his electoral law. They want to modify the articles. The threshold to be declared a majority must be raised to 40 percent.

It is 9:00 p.m. After six hours in session, the heat in the chamber is stifling. In the galleries there is a constant flurry of folding fans and handkerchiefs. On the benches, the deputies fan themselves with sheets of paper.

Then, however, Deputy Cavazzoni, a former minister who

resigned from the Mussolini government, asks to speak for the populists:

"I take the floor on behalf of myself and a group of friends . . ." Parliament erupts with raucous laughter. Cavazzoni's reference to a "group of friends" is enough to set off general hilarity among all the benches. The preamble is all it takes for Cavazzoni and his friends' intentions to appear clear to everyone. The somber, bitter laughter of the left has the baritonal grimness of a collapsing dam.

Cavazzoni prevails over the uproar: "I have always remained obedient to party discipline but there are times . . ."

Laughter, mixed with murmurs, drowns him out again, while from the benches of the center, around him, many colleagues of his party are already protesting and waving their arms about.

". . . There are times when we must not betray the commitments already made to this government. I believe it is right, fair, and honorable, to vote for passage of the articles of the bill along with confidence in the government."

Clamors, heated comments, protests from the center. The unity of the Popular Party has been shattered. After Cavazzoni, the "collaborationist" socialists also take the floor. They announce their opposing vote but they want to clarify that it does not imply "the opposition of the trade unions they represent," which are by nature apolitical. From them too, in other words, more petty distinctions, appeals to circumstances, compromises. The wall of opposition is crumbling.

Confidence in the government gets 307 votes, with 140 opposed and 7 abstentions. The move to discuss the articles of the Acerbo law, which paves the way to its approval, is voted for by 235 deputies, with 139 opposed and 77 abstentions. It passes with the determining support of the secessionist Catholics.

Everyone's eyes are focused on the now almost completely bald pate of the winner. Emilio Lussu, a deputy of the left who has just shouted his resignation in protest, watches him leave the hall laughing like a child. Though at the end of the month, in a few days, he will turn forty, Benito Mussolini remains the youngest prime minister in world history.

Giolitti's complicity in the attack on the nation's democratic constitution is a black mark on the statesman's historical merit. His actions are more than a culpable weakness, a lapse of conscience, they are true political suicide.

Zino Zini, writer and philosopher,
diary 1914–1926
(on the approval of the Acerbo law),
July 1923

At the time of the vote 30 or 40 of ours were missing, which means that *we were the ones who handed fascism the victory*! [underscored in the text]

Filippo Turati,
letter to Anna Kuliscioff,
July 20, 1923

Somewhat like Caporetto.

Commentary on the rout of the populists
in the voting on the Acerbo law,
Civiltà Cattolica, July 24, 1923

I am not, gentlemen, a despot who stays locked up in a castle. I walk among the people without concerns of any kind and I listen to them. Well, the Italian people, thus far, have not asked me for liberty. The other day, in Messina, the crowd of people that surrounded my car did not say "give us liberty," they said "take us out of these hovels." The day after that, the towns of Basilicata asked for water.

Benito Mussolini,
parliamentary speech, July 15, 1923

ITALO BALBO

FERRARA, AUGUST 24, 1923

Don Giovanni Minzoni, a native of Ravenna, was the archpriest of Argenta. During the war he had volunteered to go to the front as a military chaplain. He had received a silver medal.

After returning to his villagers, he had opposed fascism from the beginning. After the populists exited the Mussolini government, Catholic bankers and agrarians of the Ferrara region, having abandoned their party, had begun to stream into that of the fascists. In Ferrara all the Popular Party leaders had torn up their party card. In the southern part of the province, Don Minzoni remained the only one who wanted to educate young Catholics to something beyond fascist ideology and to organize workers outside the fascist unions. Many socialist peasants followed him as well. By his actions, Argenta's parish priest had irritated both the ecclesiastical hierarchies and the "red" unionists. Yet he had continued tenaciously on his path. In July, during an assembly of Young Explorers organized by the priest at the parish church, he had nearly come to blows with Ladislao Rocca, the leader of the local fascio.

On Thursday, August 23, Don Giovanni Minzoni was returning to the rectory accompanied by one of his young pupils. They were walking by the Recreational Center, in a dark, narrow street; it must have been around 10:00 p.m. In the screening room they were showing the usual film.

From around the corner, two men came out of the shadows. A single blow with a club, delivered forcefully, struck the priest on the back of the neck. Don Minzoni staggered for a moment, then collapsed. With his skull literally crushed, he struggled: he managed to get to his knees and crawled a few steps closer to his residence, before collapsing again. Permanently. They'd carried him home and laid him on the bed in his small room. The doctor said there was nothing he could do; the carabinieri lieutenant had not been able to question him. The antifascist priest could no longer speak, he seemed to be murmuring incomprehensible Latin phrases under his breath. Two sisters of Charity prayed and wept, bent over the dying man on either side. He died just after midnight.

A trickle of dark, thick blood comes from Tommaso Beltrami's right nostril as he reports the incident to Italo Balbo, who has rushed there from Rome. The bleeding is slow, very slow, somewhere between clotting and oozing, so imperceptible that Beltrami doesn't seem to notice it. D'Annunzio's former lieutenant in Fiume, whom Balbo appointed secretary of the Fascist Federation of Ferrara, speaks frenziedly, convulsively, gripped by incomprehensible bursts of euphoria. Subjected to interrogation by Balbo, Beltrami repeatedly turns to look over his shoulder wild-eyed, his dilated pupils suffering from hallucination.

Italo Balbo motions him to shut up and ponders the threat that this killing casts over his Ferrara fiefdom. It has not been easy for "generalissimo" Balbo, in recent months, to reaffirm his absolute power. In the December administrative elections, following the march on Rome, the socialists hadn't even run, and the fascists, unchallenged, had triumphed in every town in the province. He had strengthened the alliance with the agrarians by overhauling the municipal taxes to their advantage after having placed friends, relatives and even dissidents in key roles in public administration and in the party. Everything seemed tuned to perfection by subtle scores orchestrated by his absolute power.

Then, however, spring had arrived and, with spring, unemployment for the seasonal farmhands. The peasants' hunger had fed that of the fascist dissidents. The first to walk out was Brombin, the founder of the city's fascio, stating that he did not want to "be a slave to the fascist Masonic clique." After him, an avalanche. First

Beltrami had resigned in protest against the agrarians throwing their weight around and shaking down the peasants, then his friend Caretti had also tossed in the towel so as not to find himself "serving the plutocratic bourgeois class profiting from the blood of hundreds and hundreds of our brothers." A real messianic expectation of revolt had spread in Ferrara. After the clubbing of Alfredo Misuri, a graffito appeared on some of the city's walls:

"Viva Misuri, D to Mussolini, D to his hitman Balbo."

The dissident's hand had not considered it necessary to spell out the full word: in those parts, the initial was enough to invoke the enemy's death.

Faced with internal revolt, Balbo had applied the rule he himself had established. Busy teaching the militia's discipline to the national squads, he had kept himself ostensibly apart. He had sent Dino Grandi as commissioner for the city's fascio and ordered a senior officer of Perugia's militia to send six trusted men to Ferrara: just small fish, but merciless—jaw breakers—that was the mandate. It had been executed. The six Perugian squadristi had tracked down Ferrara's fascist dissidents, one by one, even in the brothels of Via Croce Bianca, traditionally considered by fascists to be inviolable places of asylum. With the absolute complicity of the police, blood had mingled with sperm. By the end of June all dissent had disappeared. The dissidents had been scattered. Beltrami had been restored to command.

Now it is he who reports the killing of Don Minzoni to Balbo and it is to him that Balbo dictates a statement for the press, dissociating themselves from the murderers, two ordinary squadrists, two junkyard dogs:

"We express our condemnation of the lowlifes whom we hope will soon be brought to justice, degenerates who have nothing in common with us, though they hide in our ranks."

Beltrami stops writing, he hesitates. Finally he notices the blood trickling from his coke-head nostrils and wipes it on the sleeve of his jacket. Balbo motions for him to say something.

"The idea was Forti's. Maran is also involved. I myself helped the two escape from the house where he had hidden them."

Augusto Maran is the secretary of Argenta's fascio, Raoul Forti is a consul in the militia and a personal friend of Balbo. For an instant, the "generalissimo" sees himself in Beltrami's dilated pupils. Then he shakes his head:

"Let's hush this thing up."

BENITO MUSSOLINI

END OF AUGUST 1923

LEVANTO, A SMALL town on the Ligurian coast overlooking the sea at the mouth of a valley covered with olive groves, pine trees, and vines, is part of their family lexicon, memories of a life together. They went on outings there when they were still dirt poor and Rachele insists that Edda was conceived there. Now the wife has rented a small villa surrounded by vineyards and her husband has managed to carve a weekend away from his duties as prime minister. In the morning, as soon as he wakes up, he likes to leave the house already wearing his bathing suit, bare-chested, and head quickly to the sea with tourists crowding on either side of him as he goes by. He likes to expose his now famous body to the comments of the German, Slavic, and Hungarian women. The bodyguards who form the presidential escort have to deal with it: his power emanates from the multitudes, and his chest, his bare thighs, his back muscles have to constantly be in the scorching zone of contact with the crowd.

He realized it at the beginning of the summer as he went around Italy, offering up his body to the sea of people everywhere, as no prime minister before him had ever done. In Bologna at Arpinati's, then in Romagna for a return to the paternal home, then in Messina for a sudden eruption of Etna, then in "squadrist Florence" and, finally, even in Rome, speaking for the first time from the balcony of Piazza Venezia to an assembly of former combatants. Everywhere he went, engulfed by his people, he tried out dialogues with the crowd stolen from D'Annunzio from the time when he was master of Fiume. "Must liberty continue to mutilate the victory?" "No!" "Must liberty continue to sabotage the nation?" "No!" "Tell me, Tuscan blackshirts, if it's necessary to start over, will we?" "Yes!" "To whom does Italy belong?" "To us!"

Not even in Levanto—back with his wife and children for forty-eight hours—is he ever really with his family. Now more than ever, his person belongs, by right, to the history of the century, not to back-page domestic news. Only to Edda, who at age twelve is on her way to becoming a woman, does he devote a little of his time. She has always been his darling and he has always kept her with him whenever he could, ever since she was a child and he taught her to play the violin and took her to the newspaper office on Via Paolo da Cannobio, in the miserable alleys of Bottonuto, remaining there till the early dawn hours. Then, after trading night for day, father and daughter would take a carriage in the piazza and go home to sleep until late. Never a slap for Edda, never any punishment.

Now it is she who plays the violin for him, but she has never stopped waiting for his return. When he arrived in Levanto by train on August 26th, the train station was heavily damaged by a surreal plane crash. A young pilot, descending to a very low altitude as a salute to his girlfriend, had plunged into the station building. Edda, who was waiting for her father to arrive, had persisted in thinking that the accident had injured him. Not even his appearance, unharmed and in the flesh, had managed to completely convince her that the tragedy had not been intended for her. Evidently, in the eyes of that stubborn little girl, the Duce's body did not have the last word.

His daughter is not the only one who isn't easily persuaded. July was a month of triumphs: Don Sturzo ousted, the populists in disarray, the parliament subjugated, the electoral law approved, the international press comparing him to Alexander the Great, and yet his men obstruct him. He says it all the time to Sarfatti when they meet at the Hotel Continentale: he wants to turn his attention to Europe, to Italy's position in Europe and in the world, and the squadristi, on the other hand, expect him to get worked up over dissension among the fascists of Tradate. Italy is bottled up in the Adriatic, a basin good for washing your face; compared to matters of world politics, which now play out on two oceans, even the Mediterranean seems small, but Benito Mussolini can't deal with the bigger issues because there was a brawl in Roccacannuccia or because they killed a priest in Argenta and all of Italy is talking about nothing else.

At the conclusion of these outbursts, Sarfatti hears him repeat the usual refrain: he must do away with the troublesome, reckless, violent hotheads, with thugs who live only for beating people up, driven by an innate turbulence, the frenzy of those urgently needing to empty their bowels or their bladder. The dueling carnival must end—he even had it written in *Il Popolo d'Italia*—but those people don't want to hear it.

And so, as always, this year too his summer persecution has returned. From the middle to the end of July, he had to preside over no less than fourteen meetings of the Grand Council, all dealing with dissensions within the party. He had to examine one by one, province by province, the various conflicts of power, of competence, of personal rivalry, in the unions, in the federations, in the cooperatives; above all, he had to overcome the resistance of the squadristi led by Farinacci to the establishment of the militia. Now the ras of Cremona, whose speeches and articles are full of bloopers, has protested the requirement that officers undergo examinations to have their ranking confirmed. In a vehement editorial of August 16, he declared that such fanciful aspirations would end up "bastardizing" the fascist squads, purging them of the most valiant fighters. The Duce silenced him by replying that he would gladly free himself of that dead weight, that he would gratefully give a hundred or two hundred thousand fascists of that kind to anyone who wants them.

Even that wasn't the end of it. There's nothing he can do: no matter how hard the Duce of fascism strives for elevation, the fascists drag him down. He would like to unleash his horde on the future, to relaunch the Latin, imperial tradition of Rome, he'd like to turn his band of pirates loose to reconquer the Mediterranean, but they, instead, keep him weighed down. And it's not only the troublemakers who sandbag him; there are also the crafty ones. In those interminable party meetings it's a free-for-all of reciprocal accusations of duplicity, all a gang of frauds.

Names are mentioned, the details of the misdeed are denounced but then he stops listening to them: men are nothing, only crowd scenes count. Individual cases don't interest him, they bore him. He has an incomparable nose to pick up the moods of a people but he doesn't understand individuals: he sees them as though watching a movie. Yet the scavenger hunt has begun and for profiteers every triumph, like every catastrophe, is just another good opportunity. Sarfatti is right: that's how revolutions die, at the crossroads between money or blood.

At the very end of summer, luck, as always, comes to his aid. It is August 28 and he has just returned to Rome when the news arrives: in a remote godforsaken town somewhere on the Greek-Albanian border, a delegation of Italian officers on a mission for the Allied powers was slaughtered for unknown reasons by a gang of Balkan brigands. And as luck would have it, foreign secretary Salvatore Contarini—a highly experienced diplomat and proponent of a policy of alliance with Great Britain and the other major powers—is still on vacation. Here, finally, is the chance to play the cards of Italian nationalism in the Eastern Mediterranean, to break free of English subjection for once. Benito Mussolini has been waiting for the occasion for years and will not let it slip away.

Before Contarini can return to Rome with his recommendations for caution and moderation, Mussolini has a telegraph sent to Athens. He demands outrageous reparations from the Greek government: the most extensive apologies, a solemn funeral ceremony, honors to the Italian flag, an investigation conducted by Italian inspectors, capital punishment for the guilty parties, and compensation of 50 million liras. The Greek government, which declares that it is not involved, clearly cannot agree to the demands, and appeals to the League of Nations, counting on Great Britain's protection. Benito Mussolini responds by sending a naval squadron to occupy the Greek island of Corfu. If he does not get satisfaction by August 29, when the ultimatum expires, he will order the landing to begin by bombing the Old Venetian Fortress. What he is doing is unheard of: a member nation of the League of Nations is openly violating its statute. It's the first time that has happened since the end of the Great War.

Enthusiasm soars back up. Fascism finally takes off again thanks to the audacity of its Duce, no longer weighed down by the petty ambitions of his hangers-on. An offshore wind is finally blowing, from Italy to the Balkans, the Middle East, and the African continent. Forty Italian ships, seven thousand armed troops with ammunition and gear are marshaled off the coasts of Epirus. During the hours of vigil, the entire nation, in the sweltering, tormented sleep of a late August Mediterranean summer, once more begins to breathe as one. That night Benito Mussolini does not sleep, he stays awake to watch and wait, his ear pricked to the telegraph that, hour by hour, transmits the navy's radiograms.

The old parties have been discredited; the Fascist Party is nearly just as discredited; Deputy Mussolini enjoys enormous popularity. The disappearance of Mussolini would have the same consequences in Italy that the disappearance of Alexander the Great had in the Greek world.

L'Êre Nouvelle,
Paris, July 1923

Italy wants the great nations of the world to treat her as a sister, not as a housemaid.

Benito Mussolini,
statement to the press, November 3, 1922

AMERIGO DÙMINI

TRIESTE, SEPTEMBER 3, 1923

SINCE THE ITALIAN navy landed in Corfu, not a day goes by without the prime minister's press office chanting the cerulean glory of this Mare Nostrum. For Amerigo Dùmini, on the other hand, the Mediterranean, this closed sea, as ancient as gangrene, is only a cemetery of encrusted bivalves on corroded hulls, wreckage sunk in brackish water, lost vessels, bituminous discharge, an oily stain widening over the nautical maps of an eternal inshore cabotage with no landfall. When the sun is high on the horizon, its azure dazzles viperously. He looks at it and reads a chronicle of military history, nothing more: conflicts, shipwrecks, and wars, his, that of the Duce, those of the squinting legionnaires hunkered on the Balkan cliffs, even earlier those of the Venetian merchants on the spice route, and so on, until the weapons war.

War surplus is a colossal business. Dùmini realized it right away. Tons of firearms, bullets, medical products, vessels, fabrics, vehicles, clothing, fuels, combustibles, sold by the state at bargain prices and then resold by traffickers at market prices with huge profits. Entire aborted epics of war materials sold at auction for Homeric speculations.

The mechanism of the fraud is simple: the law establishes that the myriad associations of former combatants, those wounded and disabled in war, anarchistic and unemployed workers—on whose wretched condition ringing patriotic appeals are made each day—must be given preference in the auctions; nevertheless the better lots—through dummy fronts or phantom groups with bellicose names—always end up in the same companies owned by big speculators. Unscrupulous businessmen like Filippo Filippelli, a Calabrian attorney, former personal secretary of Arnaldo Mussolini and now editor-in-chief of the pro-fascist daily *Corriere Italiano*, or Carlo Bazzi, a shady operator from Milan, cousin of quadrumvirate and police chief Emilio De Bono, prosper in the shadow of the "Italian Association of Tubercular Trench-fighters." And so, materials declared surplus in the evening become reusable the next morning and once again invade the world to equip spectral armies.

Indeed the march on Rome was financed in large part thanks to the business of surplus goods but then everyone jumped in: starting with De Bono who, as police chief, should be on the lookout for fraud, then Aldo Finzi who exploits his role as deputy interior minister, up to Cesare Rossi. And Dùmini also got into it, under the protection of Rossi, who, having settled into the prime minister's building as press office chief, wanted Dùmini beside him to attend to the "dirty operations," which in the jargon of the new fascist power do not refer to misappropriation of public funds but to beating up dissidents in the shadow of the state. Amerigo didn't need to be asked twice. By January he had already planted himself at a desk in Rossi's office, where with his good hand, the same hand that wields a club, he types letters all day, delivers messages, and issues orders and reprimands to undersecretaries of state. Then, at lunchtime, together with the group's other *camerati*, he goes with Rossi to dine on sliced Chianina beef at Brecche's.

At first the "dirty operations" proceeded unsystematically. When an opposition deputy or a dissident fascist had to be taught a lesson—as in the case of Professor Misuri—Balbo, Giunta, De Vecchi, Finzi, Marinelli or Rossi assigned the job to the first club-wielder who was at hand. When summer came, however, things began to change. Rossi now wants to centralize the "minor tasks" and has charged Dùmini with forming a squad of men they can absolutely rely on. He also started paying him a monthly salary on the prime minister's books: 1,500 liras per month to cover expenses. He provided him with a false ID and a fake passport issued by the

Directorate-General of Public Security: "Bianchi Gino, son of Emilio and Franceschi Fanny, born in Florence on January 3rd, 1895, resident in Rome, status journalist." It was Dùmini himself who asked to be able to live his fictitious life as a journalist. He has always liked to write, since the time in Florence when, solely on his own, he edited and wrote his aggressive paper, the *Sassaiola Fiorentina*.

But this "minor" assignment is the easy part of the job. Living tissue is not very demanding: if you strike it with a blunt instrument, it suffers, if you stab it with a sharp point, it bleeds. The difficulties come with inert matter: rusty rifles, ferrous wrecks, fossil fuels. He's tried for months to make them pay off. It started with the recovery of an Italian merchant ship sunk during the war along the coasts of Libya, at Derna, Brega, Bomba and south of Benghazi. To study all aspects of the business in depth, he went to Cyrenaica in person. Days and days of scouring the sandy bottoms of a shallow, unvarying, barren coast, trapped by watery graveyards, deserts and depressions. In the end, nothing came of it. Then, still posing as Gino Bianchi, a wounded ex-Ardito, and once more thanks to the backing of Rossi who from the Viminale pressured the Ministry of Agriculture, he tried again with a batch of fuel oils found at Rome's river port. After all it was still war surplus, just like he was.

But Giuriati, minister of the liberated lands, commissioned by Mussolini himself to investigate the scandals regarding the surpluses, got in the way. Giuriati, a fervent nationalist, D'Annunzio's former chief of staff in Fiume, and a scrupulously upright idealist, recommended reporting Dùmini and his associates to the judicial authorities for that stock awarded at a quarter of its set value and, as a result, once again everything fell through. The director of the petroleum office canceled the contract.

In March, however, the wind finally turned in the right direction and Dùmini obtained an option from the war ministry, with an expiration date of June 16, on a gigantic consignment of Austro-Hungarian surpluses: 35,000 Mauser rifles, 630,000 Mannlicher rifles and 20 million cartridges. Enough to load up a whole ship, enough to be fixed for life. Million-dollar guarantees for the penniless veteran had been provided by Alessandro Rossini, a managing director of the Adriatic Bank of Trieste, who often financed the fascists in the trafficking of materials to then be sold abroad, especially in the Balkans.

Dùmini, however, having been awarded the consignment, had decided to go it alone. He tried Greece first, but the cargo ship had been sent away from the port of Piraeus. Then, between spring and summer, "Gino Bianchi" started his tourist visits to Belgrade, the city at the confluence of the Sava and the Danube, and to all the tragic regions of Europe where war is as endemic as hunger is in certain African regions, and from where he never failed to send affectionate postcards to Cesarino Rossi in Italy. The only problem was that Yugoslavia, due to the dispute over Fiume, was still among the countries that were enemies of Italy. But in order to get around the proscription of arming the enemy, he had relied on a fictitious company of Marseilles.

Looking good, therefore, everything just fine. Then, however, Francesco Giunta—the ras of Venezia Giulia's fascists, who in Rome had become party secretary—heading a rival profiteering group, had denounced the "traffic in arms with an enemy country" from the columns of his newspaper, *Il popolo di Trieste*, and had personally informed Mussolini. Amerigo Dùmini, aka Gino Bianchi, had been stopped by the Yugoslavs in Pola. As soon as he set foot in Trieste they had arrested him on the orders of De Bono, he too in Giunta's cartel. Gino Bianchi had spent the August holiday locked up in the Coroneo, the penitentiary built by the Austrians just before the Great War.

Nothing, there wasn't a thing you could do: Austrians, Italians, blacks, reds, it made no difference for the small fish that gasp for breath in the shoals of that great bituminous sea. It was always perpetual guerrilla warfare, always the never-ending work of disposing of war surpluses from previous battles.

But though Gino Bianchi had ended up in jail, his alias, Amerigo Dùmini, was not discouraged. From the upper tier of the prison, you could still glimpse that same viperous azure of the same derelict Mediterranean down below, beyond the Portorosso canal; from there he had telegraphed Cesare Rossi, Michele Bianchi, and Arturo Fasciolo, the Duce's personal secretary. To each of them the same threat: he would not let himself be crucified for them, he would not act as a shield for anyone.

They had released him after two days, with many apologies, and moved him to the Grand Hotel. Even from there, the same sea.

In the following days, Arnaldo Mussolini had personally taken up the defense of "our friend Dùmini" in *Il Popolo d'Italia*, the Duce had ordered the invasion of Corfu, the splendor of glory had again shone along the waterline of the battleships, the Mediterranean had once again become a different sea, and he, despite spending the mid-August holiday in jail, had been ready to forget.

Now, however, Francesco Giunta relentlessly persists in his persecution. At the beginning of September, he presents a second parliamentary question regarding arms trafficking with enemy countries and Gino Bianchi must again take up his pen. He drafts a detailed report on the Yugoslav affair portrayed as a secret mission with patriotic objectives, and sends it to the party's leadership. It is accompanied, however, by a personal letter from Amerigo Dùmini to Cesare Rossi that brazenly skates over suggestions of threat and blackmail:

"Being forced to justify my activity abroad is distressing for me, but I am willing to consider what happened an accident. If, however, this account of mine, which is only meant to be documentary, were to become defensive, I would find myself in the regrettable position of having to reveal the acts of individuals within the interior ministry."

Amerigo Dùmini was deported from Yugoslavia for having had fascist propaganda pamphlets translated into Slavic . . . Dùmini's arrest and the accusations made against him were the result of a misunderstanding . . . Dùmini had given ample clarifications . . . documenting the groundless nature of the accusations, as his prompt release by police authorities attests to.

Communiqué of the prime minister's office,
Rome, August 19, 1923

Our friend Dùmini, a valiant former soldier of long-standing, proven patriotism, is the victim of an atrocious injustice over alleged arms smuggling.

Arnaldo Mussolini,
Il Popolo d'Italia, August 21, 1923

ITALO BALBO

EARLY OCTOBER 1923

THE MASSES ARE a flock of sheep, the century of democracy is over, the masses have no tomorrow.

The Duce's tenets are clear. Individuals, left to themselves, cling together in a jellylike clump of elementary instincts and primordial impulses, a bloody gelatin moved by an abulic, disjointed, incoherent dynamism. In short, they are simple matter. Therefore, "His Holiness the Mass" must be toppled from the democratic altars. Democracy has a predominantly political conception of life. Fascism is something entirely different. Its conception is militaristic. Hierarchies of a military order must be "rigidly constituted." Military discipline comprises political discipline. Its enlisted ranks are, first and foremost, soldiers. The party card is equivalent to a dog tag retrieved on the corpses of soldiers in the trenches.

The Duce's precepts are clear and Italo Balbo, the "generalissimo" of the militia, even before sharing them, is determined to put them into practice. The main obstacle, however, is represented by the individuals themselves, the "material" that, as the Duce sees it, is to be molded: it's substandard. The exams for confirmation to the rank of consul in the militia, which Balbo—the very one who managed to wrangle a law degree by threatening to beat up his thesis supervisor—is subjecting the squad leaders to with his usual determination, are proving it beyond any possible doubt: the human material is really substandard stuff. As long as it's a matter of general knowledge, it's still OK, but when it comes to military and professional disciplines, the results are bleak. Balbo wrote to Mussolini about it: "The officers have shown that they have little or poor knowledge of everything pertaining to the military disciplines. And they have shown even greater incompetence in executing a tactical exercise in the field." Yet nearly all of them have fought in a war, many of them in assault units. They don't seem like the same people. On the other hand, it's not surprising, since nearly all of them show that they are also unaware of the regulations of the very organization that they are supposed to command. If things proceed at this rate, the "generalissimo" will be forced to propose the introduction of army officers into the cadres of the fascist militia.

While the Duce tries to impose his will on the world, the world obeys chaos. Farinacci has openly aligned with chaos. Despite the penalty that provides for expulsion from the ranks for those who will not undergo the exams, the ras of Cremona has refused, certain that nobody will tear the stripes off his epaulets. During the summer he also engaged in a confrontation with Mussolini in a bout of telegrams over the assignment of some command posts to his acolytes in the legions of Tripolitania. They managed not to have the conflict leaked to the press but Mussolini had to telegraph Cremona's prefect in secret ordering the rebellious ras' arrest for insubordination if he did not withdraw his resignation. Only then did Farinacci telegraph Rome. The threat of resignation was withdrawn. "With undiminished affection and unwavering loyalty."

Despite the efforts of Balbo and Mussolini, discord spreads. In Rome Bottai's squads clash in the streets with those of Calza Bini, and in Piacenza there was even armed hostility between the fascist factions of Amidei and those of Tedeschi. Then at the end of September the "revisionist" controversy broke out in the party's rearguard. In *Critica Fascista*, the journal founded with Giuseppe Bottai, Massimo Rocca published an explosive article in favor of "normalization." According to Rocca, fascism should "convert Italy" after raping her, the squadrists should come together with yesterday's enemies, the Fascist Party should make its peace with Mussolini's Italy. By way of response, the party chiefs, Farinacci leading them, expelled the "revisionist." But their victory only lasted a few hours. Mussolini demanded the resignations of the entire executive council that had decided on the expulsion. He got them.

Despite all this, the Duce's directives remain clear. And Italo Balbo is determined to put them into practice. And so, "generalissimo" Balbo, with the same meticulous ferocity with which he bashed heads in the Romagna countryside, continues to administer exams to the men who bashed heads alongside him, as if they were recalcitrant schoolboys. He makes no allowances for anyone: themes on the rules of the militia, general oral quizzes, exams on military tactics. And he also keeps writing merciless assessments alongside the column listing their poor grades.

In the florilegium of the future ruling class you can find all kinds. Together with the knowledge and skills of men such as Rocco, Turati, and Gaggioli, there is the ignorant brutality of Carlo Scorza, a former lieutenant of the Arditi and head of Lucca's squadristi: "His development of the theme was somewhat convoluted and based on few concepts. He has shown complete deficiency in knowledge of the most basic tactical matters. The practical exercise in the field confirmed the judgment made on the oral exam." Grade 43/80. Failed. There is the juvenile recklessness of Enzo Galbiati, head of Brianza's squads, he too an ex-Ardito, and a former Fiume legionnaire: "The reports sent by the Milanese fascio are absolutely damaging: they declare him insincere and irresponsible enough that his willfulness and lack of tact made relations between the militia and the region's political authority untenable." Grade 47/80. Must retake the exam. There is the violent neurosis of Bernardo Barbiellini Amidei, count, landowner, war volunteer, decorated for valor, ras of Piacenza, and personal friend of Balbo who, alongside his name, notes for Mussolini: "He is an honest young man, not lacking in intelligence: but he has a neurasthenic temperament, I would say almost epileptoid. He is not a normal individual, and does not have the prudent criteria to judiciously pilot the ship's helm."

Then there is Farinacci, the indescribable, indomitable, ludicrous Farinacci, yet he of all people—the very quintessence of a club-wielding fascist, adamant in preaching a "second wave" of bludgeonings—finds admirers even among the last surviving socialists, like the boy from Turin, that Piero Gobetti, sickly, feeble literati, bound to life by a faint filament of lament; such individuals would definitely be submerged by that wave, and yet—whether because they have a taste for paradox, or because of the intellectual's invincible attitude of always displaying a superior detachment from common sense, or because of a premonition of death—they praise Roberto Farinacci from the columns of their journals. Yes, there is Farinacci but he is a special case, he eludes judgment. Perhaps the future will judge him, though certainly without any jurisdiction.

Per threat of collective resignations, I urge deputy Farinacci and company to reflect on advisability and gravity of gesture they propose stop. Current militia policy exclusively up to me, my role stop I declare my aim to free the militia not from fascism but from the party that is a vast pitiful panorama of idiotic interminable squabbles, object of laughter and daily scorn by all adversaries stop

Benito Mussolini,
telegram to the prefect of Cremona,
September 17, 1923

The followers of Farinacci defend personal positions that are illegitimate, but won with sacrifice and strength . . . We must respect in this ignorance and in this barbarism a sense of dignity and a test of sacrifice . . . The real profiteers are the ones who enjoy salaries in Rome while fabricating theories. The real exploiters are the intellectuals; not these hale and hearty illiterates who write ungrammatical articles, but are able to grip a sword and wield a club. If fascism can be of some use to Italy, it is a fascism of the truncheon.

Piero Gobetti, "Eulogy for Farinacci,"
La rivoluzione liberale, October 9, 1923

BENITO MUSSOLINI

MILAN, OCTOBER 28, 1923
FIRST ANNIVERSARY OF THE MARCH ON ROME

THE ASSEMBLAGE FOR the first anniversary of the march on Rome begins at 08:00 a.m. along the avenues of the park: army battalions, militia centuriae, civic and patriotic associations. The Duce appears on his horse, wearing the uniform of an honorary corporal of the militia: fez, black shirt, Arditi jacket with flames on the lapel, dagger on his belt. Thousands of men with gold medals on their chests welcome him with an exultant ovation. He salutes them with outstretched arm, palm of the black-gloved hand turned down, his eyes focused straight in front of him, gazing into infinity.

There is really nothing on the earth's surface that can't be captured in its purest form mounted on the back of a battle-ready beast of war. Viewed from up there, Milan has never seemed so beautiful. At the end of the rigorous perspective of the avenues, the already snow-capped peaks of the Alps can even be glimpsed. Only a year has passed since he left Milan in a wagon-lit to conquer Rome. Now the entire program can be summed up in a single verb: endure, endure, endure. Just one year . . . and now he's already commemorating it on horseback. Time is a bitch.

After the troop review, the commemorative ceremony continues in Piazza Belgioioso. Another temporal crevasse, another one of those rendezvous with one's own history that can't be missed. Only four years earlier, in this small elegant piazza opposite Alessandro Manzoni's house, Benito Mussolini, in fact, held his first fascist rally. A few hundred at that time, thousands today. Back then, the caisson of a truck, now the balcony of a princely palazzo. Piazza Belgioioso. He goes back there as often as he can. A kind of urban sundial, a time-tracking device based on the position of the sun. He is the sun. Preceded by three trumpet blasts, he speaks:

"Glorious, indomitable and invincible blackshirts, fate has once again granted me the opportunity to speak in this piazza that is by now sacred to the history of fascism. Here just a few hundred faithful gathered, men who had the courage to challenge the beast that triumphed in those dark times, bastard times, times that will never again return . . ." A riot of jubilant applause greets the bastard times that will never return.

We were small maniples, today we are legions. At that time we were very few, today we are a boundless multitude. Certainly, there is something mysterious in this revival of our passion, something religious in this army of volunteers that asks for nothing and is ready for anything. It's spring, the resurrection of the race, it's a people who become a nation, it's a nation that becomes a state, which pursues the course of its expansion in the world.

The speaker's joy spreads through the piazza, the surge of his words washes over the soldiers, the current of excitement flows back in a long ovation of applause. Then the ovation is repeated. So he decides to engage in dialogue with them, he says he is sure that their responses will be on key and formidable.

"Blackshirts, I ask you, if tomorrow the sacrifices were greater than today, would you be willing to endure them?" A huge "yes!" confirms it.

"If tomorrow I were to ask you for what could be called the sublime proof of discipline, would you give me that proof?" Shouts of enthusiasm.

If tomorrow I were to tell you that we must resume the march and drive it all the way to other directions, would you march? If tomorrow I were to sound the alarm, the signal of heroic days, those in which the destiny of a people is decided, would you respond? The crowd responds: the fascist choir scales the peaks of the highest range of frequencies. At that moment, it does indeed seem that the "bastard times" will never return.

Then time is restored and for a moment casts its shadow on the speaker. He speaks of their adversaries, of the philosophers of history, of those "melancholy masturbators of history who never understand history."

"They said we were short-lived, that we didn't have a creed, that the fascist government would barely last six weeks. It's been twelve months. Do you think it will last twelve years?"

The piazza again erupts in a thunderous ovation. For a moment, however, the speaker falters, as if he's stopped himself. His voice breaks off.

Giuseppe Bottai, standing beside him on the balcony, observes Mussolini perform a rapid internal calculation. In twelve years he will be only fifty-two. The number must seem modest to him. With the staccato volley of practically coalesced syllables characteristic of his oratorical frenzies, the Duce corrects himself:

"Twelve years times five!" The piazza acclaims him.

We will endure because we have not eliminated volition from history, we will endure because we will systematically disband our enemies, we will endure because we have the will to endure.

After the banquet given in honor of Mussolini at the Grande Italia restaurant, the rest of the day is spent on a commemorative tour of the recent past, living history, wounds still open and bleeding. To the rhythm of *Giovinezza*, the cortege proceeds up Via San Marco, seat of the original fascio, skirts the local fascist clubs, goes as far as Via Paolo da Cannobio, and stops in front of the miserable rooms that were the offices of *Il Popolo d'Italia*. Everywhere you look, ribbons, garlands, brass bands, generals, councilmen, mothers and sisters of martyrs. The mayor, on behalf of the municipal council, announces that a stretch of road that extends from Via Gamboloita to Rogoredo will be dedicated to Benito Mussolini.

Fascist Milan celebrates the first year of fascist rule in a rush, with the same frenzy with which its Duce lived it, piling up reforms upon reforms, multiplying the decrees willed by him, forcing the limits of a single season. Mussolini boasts about the numbers resulting from the effort: in just one year the Council of Ministers met sixty times to deal with 2,482 matters and approve 1,658 decrees. Everything is going Mussolini's way: the Acerbo reform bill that will hand parliament over to him at the next elections will become state law in a few days, the risky international controversy triggered by the occupation of Corfu was settled at the end of September with Italy's prestige restored and 50 million compensation for damages, and relations with the Vatican have once again become cordial after half a century of animosity.

Even the oppositions have been tamed. The socialists—apart from Giacomo Matteotti's obstinacy—virtually don't dare breathe anymore, internal dissidence was quashed at the Grand Council of October 12 with a move that sacrificed Massimo Rocca's "revisionists" in order to sideline Farinacci's "intransigents": now the new regulation provides that the directorate be proposed by the federal secretaries but that the final choice lies with the Duce who appoints from above. Finally, the free press was harnessed that summer with a series of censorian decrees that allow the police to break into newspaper offices the same way they do for illegal gambling parlors and houses of prostitution.

Despite this, the liberal philosophers who should blast him actually greet the first year of Mussolini's rule favorably, led by Benedetto Croce who, just yesterday, in an interview given to the newspapers, reminded his followers of the "duty to accept and acknowledge good from wherever it has come, to prepare for the future." Even the great Italian artists celebrate Mussolini. Luigi Pirandello, the brilliant playwright who with his *Six Characters in Search of an Author*, highly regarded by the Duce, revealed that every man is only his own mask, came up to Palazzo Chigi before leaving for America to pay his respects to the Leader. He was echoed from America by Luigi Barzini, the admired journalist, who sent a telegram rejoicing over Mussolini's "magnificent ascent."

In the next few hours the king and the royal family will also publicly encounter Benito Mussolini, the blacksmith's son, at a reception at Palazzo Venezia, which the entire Capitoline aristocracy is expected to attend. Then Spain's sovereigns will have their turn, on an official visit to Rome accompanied by Primo De Rivera, the general who seized power with a military takeover, and who openly declares being inspired by the example of Italian fascism. Liberal philosophers, royal families, generals who incite coups, no one is lacking. Everyone willingly joins the chorus of jubilation.

In this atmosphere of enthusiasm, on October 28th, 1923, the cortege celebrating the march on Rome, cheered by hundreds of wounded and disabled veterans, by mothers and widows of the fallen, arrives at Corso Venezia 69 to inaugurate the new headquarters of the fasci of Milan.

At the end of the brief inaugural speech, a messenger from *Il Popolo d'Italia*—with the permission of Cesare Rossi who closely shadows the Duce—approaches Mussolini. He informs him that in Filettole, a rural town in the province of Pisa, near the Trionfo club, the body of a socialist peasant, a certain Pietro Pardi, was found with a bullet wound to the temple. A few hours earlier, in a bar in Vecchiano, Sandro Carosi, the region's squad leader, had insisted on celebrating the anniversary of the march in his own way, by shooting the heads off a few customers. Like William Tell, he'd said. Pardi had refused. Carosi—a psychopath arrested for a variety of crimes and always released because he was protected by Filippo Morghen, the ras of Pisa—had gone after him.

Mussolini looks like he's been bitten by a tarantula. The news of the idiotic killing has undoubtedly ruined the party for him. Furious, the Duce begins spinning around in all directions, giving orders for police measures, for press coverage, for purges in the local fascio. Then, retreating to a small room, Benito Mussolini sprawls in a chair. Evening begins to fall over the neoclassical elegance of Corso Venezia. In that autumnal dusk the first glorious year of fascist history seems to lapse into the sensationalism of a tabloid.

Cesare Rossi, the only one authorized to approach him in those moments of withdrawal, brings him two photographs to sign with his dedication. They are intended for Emma Gramatica, the great actress, who also performed Pirandello, and the celebrated singer Luisa Tetrazzini, both admirers of Mussolini.

Faced with his own photographic effigy, the Duce rouses himself. Rossi watches him as—with a square-tipped fountain pen, D'Annunzio's favorite kind—he writes polished words in honor of the two excellent devotees. Then he sees him add an indecipherable abbreviation below the signature: "Year II—E.F."

"What are you writing there, Benito?"

"Year two, Fascist Era. We must start moving forward in time."

I have always had great admiration for him, and in fact I believe I am among the few capable of understanding the beauty of this continuous creation of reality that Mussolini is achieving: an Italian and fascist reality that is not conditioned by the reality of others. Mussolini knows, as few do, that reality lies only in the power of a man to construct it, and that it is created only by the energy of the spirit.

Luigi Pirandello,
interview in *La tribuna di Roma*,
October 23, 1923

In life it is necessary to endure; after a time we will understand each other better.

Benito Mussolini,
interview with the foreign press,
November 1, 1923

NICOLA BOMBACCI

NOVEMBER 30, 1923

TODAY THE CHAMBER is unusually crowded. When Deputy De Nicola opens the session, 250 deputies can be counted in the various sections, an unusually high number for a parliament that is almost always nearly deserted. Seated at the government bench are also various undersecretaries. Under discussion is the conversion into law of a 1921 decree between the Kingdom of Italy and the Russian Socialist Federative Soviet Republic. In the same semicircular hall, from the amphitheater-like seats sloping gently downward, beneath the glass and iron velarium magnificently adorned with the organic forms, curved lines and floral predilections characteristic of Art Nouveau—the embellishments of a style still fresh at the end of the promising last century and already irremediably passé at the start of this new one—in that hall, communism and fascism, the two titans of the era, confront one another.

After the customary announcements, the prime minister, Deputy Mussolini, enters the chamber accompanied by Deputy Acerbo and takes his seat at his desk. The session begins.

The first talks are pragmatic. As announced, Deputy Ayala, on behalf of the Popular Party, declares that he is in favor of ratifying the decree to foster the development of trade agreements between fascist Italy and Soviet Russia. Costantino Lazzari, on behalf of the socialist maximalists, engages in the usual polemical skirmish with Francesco Giunta—Fascist Party secretary who boasts of bringing the squadristic style into parliamentary debates—contrasting the arguments of communism with those of capitalism. The same old story.

Then, however, Nicola Bombacci takes the floor. He's Moscow's man, everyone knows it. The leaders of the victorious Russian Soviet revolution have always favored him over all the players in the failed Soviet revolution in Italy. But Nicolino Bombacci is also Benito Mussolini's friend and everyone knows that too. When they were both schoolteachers in remote villages of Romagna, little more than boys, they shared the bread of science together as well as that of hunger. It is spitefully rumored that in the recent wave of arrests of communist leaders, he was spared by orders from his old friend Benito.

The certain fact remains that—if you adopt a short-focus lens, if you tighten the frame to a close-up shot of the faces,—the titanic forces of the century, locked in mortal combat, reveal people, not historical figures, and those people have a childhood, an adolescence, often shared, small idiosyncrasies, manias, sometimes determinant, small vanities—the shaved skull of a condottiere, the flowing beard of a prophet—small expressive signs at the corners of the mouth, or a furrowed forehead, and it is those minutiae, those empathies or antipathies, those silly memories of drinking at the tavern, that trace people's course, in life as in history. An epoch's implacable animosity is as mute as a bloodthirsty Babylonian deity. Men, however, talk to one another.

And so, Nicola Bombacci, Lenin's Italian fiduciary and Benito Mussolini's friend, takes the floor amidst the ironic laughter of the extreme right. For years Bombacci has been working to stipulate trade agreements between Italy and Russia that would lead to Italy's recognition of the Soviet state.

The communist leader immediately declares that he will not address the politics of the two nations but will focus on the economic issues that tend to unite them: "The governments before the fascist one have done nothing in this regard . . ."

Already at this point Mussolini interrupts him: "Good thing you recognize it!"

Bombacci: "It's the truth."

Giunta: "So then, long live fascism!" (Hilarity; clamoring from the communists)

Bombacci resumes, urging the government to negotiate with Russia in an atmosphere of cordiality. He addresses Mussolini personally, his old friend who, thanks to a vagary of history, has become a bitter enemy, reminding him of his commitment not to put political biases above other considerations.

Bombacci: "You say you want to rebuild not only Italy but also Europe . . ."

Mussolini: "I'm satisfied with Italy!" (General hilarity) "Besides, I've signed dozens of commercial treaties."

Bombacci: "Do so with Russia as well."

Mussolini: "It takes two."

Bombacci: "Let's hope so. Furthermore, another reason to conclude a treaty with Russia is to confront the efforts at trade penetration enacted by the French and the British to seize Russian markets and cut Italy off. I protested . . ."

(Ironic shouts from the right: Bravo!)

Bombacci: "Even the Americans are dealing behind closed doors to get the oil monopoly. Italy must therefore protest loudly . . ."

Giunta: "Bravo! We have a party card ready for you."

Bombacci: "Any Italian citizen who wants to do his duty doesn't need a card in his pocket. Italian industrialists who wanted to do business in Russia would be readily welcomed. I pray, though this word is not used by us communists (hilarity), that the Italian government through Deputy Mussolini will enact a treaty, in part so that the two revolutions, the fascist and the Russian, may yet end in an alliance between the two peoples . . ."

Here Bombacci's speech falters, overwhelmed by the gravity of the words just spoken and those about to follow them. The speaker falls silent for a few moments and looks up at the velarium looming over him as if he sensed the wing of a premonition flutter over him. Then he goes on:

Bombacci: "Russia is on a revolutionary plane: if you, as you say, have a revolutionary mentality, there should be no difficulties with a definitive alliance between the two countries." (Spirited laughter from the right and from the center, clamoring from the left.)

Men talk to one another, but ideologies don't. The Babylonian deities do not countenance ironic subtleties, impassioned magnanimity. The "Bombacci affair," provoked by the words of the communist deputy, explodes the following day in fact. *Avanti!* denounces him. For the socialist newspaper, drawing a parallel between the Russian revolution and that parody of a revolution put on by fascism is inadmissible. The monolithic contempt for fascism is a stance of dignity and unity that must not be deviated from. Even Antonio Gramsci publicly deplores Bombacci's "cordiality" that would stoop so far as "to adulate the fascist revolution and Mussolini's delusions of grandeur."

On December 5th it's the party's turn. Its executive committee calls on Deputy Bombacci to resign as a deputy of parliament. Some members of the parliamentary panel defend him: they see no reason to accuse him of unworthiness. The working-class base that has venerated him for years doesn't understand it either: Bombacci spoke for Russia, for Lenin, why does the party want to drive him out?

The "Christ of the workers" does not resign. His resistance and good faith, however, prove useless. The Communist Party of Italy enjoins Nicola Bombacci, the "Lenin of Romagna," to resign his post as deputy in the very days when news comes from Moscow that Vladimir Il'ic Ulianov, the real Lenin, following another stroke, confined to a wheelchair, has ceased all communication with the world. His body's paralysis is now complete. All that remains is to prepare for his death.

1924

BENITO MUSSOLINI

ROME, JANUARY 28, 1924
PALAZZO VENEZIA,
ASSEMBLY OF FASCIST LEADERS

THE CHAMBER WAS dissolved on January 25th. Elections have been called for April 6. The inauguration of the XXVII legislature is scheduled for May 24. More so than a vote for or against the fascist regime, the upcoming elections promise to be a plebiscite for or against him. A year after the march on Rome, fascism has weakened, but he, Benito Mussolini, has become stronger. He towers.

The party leader appears before the Grand Council of the fascist leadership at the Sala del Concistoro in Palazzo Venezia, the first of a lengthy series of assemblies, on the evening of January 28, 1924; he is the same statesman who, just the day before, a few streets away in Palazzo Chigi, was able to sign an accord with Yugoslavia granting Fiume to Italy, healing a wound that had been bleeding since 1919. From Belgrade, King Alexander of Yugoslavia hailed the epochal pact, praising its creator: "Only a man of Mussolini's brilliance and strength could have succeeded in such an arduous undertaking." And so the dispute that for years had kept the global wounds of the Great War open is now mended; he, Benito Mussolini, mended it with a skillful diplomatic move, not with the fanciful exploit of a poetic dreamer. And with that he also threw another shovelful of earth on the monumental tomb that his longtime rival Gabriele D'Annunzio is building, still alive, on the shores of Lake Garda.

In some respects, despite the hyperbolic successes and praise, this Mussolini, at the start of 1924, is still a modest man. He shaves himself, badly, every other day; the doorkeepers at Palazzo Chigi, seeing the poor devil with no one to iron his trousers, often wearing rumpled clothes, feel sorry for him. He lives on Via Rasella, not in a palace, not in a patrician villa, but in an apartment in Palazzo Tittoni, owned by Baron Fassini who offered him paid lodging while also maintaining the right to cohabit with the head of government. Only a single personal maid sees to him, a certain Cesira Carocci, born in Gubbio, who also cooks him frugal meals that the boarder eats at home, often alone, and hurriedly; in addition, according to backstairs gossip, she acts as a procuress for sexual frenzies that are hastily swallowed as well, with his pants tangled around his ankles. Cesira looks after him but doesn't show him any undue deference, in fact she complains to the only policeman standing guard on the landing about a lion cub that the Duce received as a gift from the owner of an equestrian circus, and which he insists on keeping in a cage in the living room.

And yet, if you look at it from another angle, Benito Mussolini is the conqueror who, if he goes to London on a state visit, is greeted at Victoria station by a delirious crowd, he's the thinker whom Giuseppe Ungaretti now asks to write the preface for his poetic masterpiece *Il porto sepolto* (The Buried Port), he's the charismatic leader whom industrialists, longtime politicians, bishops and soldiers anxiously wait hours for, to meet in the anteroom of his office in the Hall of Victories. Even a crocodilian combatant like Albino Volpi, despite being an old acquaintance, accords him a reverential awe: arriving at the session with a pair of new shoes, realizing that the soles are squeaking and fearful of irritating the Duce, the ex "Caiman of Piave" asks the attendant for a glass of water and wets the soles with a dampened handkerchief. From this standpoint, at the start of 1924 Mussolini's face is already the totem that sculptor Adolfo Wildt is portraying in a colossal bronze-cast bust mounted on a marble column, imbued with the tragic, disturbing aura of a modern idol.

It is this ill-shaved idol who appears before the Grand Council of Fascism assembled at Palazzo Venezia to set the course for the next electoral battle. Mussolini takes the floor after Minister Giovanni Giuriati, who spoke on behalf of the government, and after Enrico Corradini, who spoke on behalf of the party.

To begin with, he announces that he will not make any more election speeches: he considers them the "most mortifying of his life." Though elections must be held, they bring out the worst in everyone, and should therefore be discounted. Then, having quickly dismissed the democratic fetish of electoral sanctity, Benito Mussolini devotes himself to debunking two other fairytales. The first is that of original purity, constantly invoked by the "intransigent" squadristi led by Farinacci: "It must be said without purisms and without euphemisms that the mania for purism and 1919-ism based on the old guards, for fascism of the first hour or of the twenty-fourth, is simply ridiculous."

In the rear, there are murmurs of discontent from the Farinacci wing, but the speaker is already dismantling the second fable, that of the "good dictator" who nevertheless is said to be surrounded by "bad advisers," to whose mysterious influence he is supposedly subject. Here the tone becomes mocking: "All this, beyond being fantasy, is idiotic. My decisions mature, often at night, in the solitude of my mind. Those who are said to be the tyrant's five councilors are five or six people who come to me each morning to inform me of everything that is happening in Italy, and who, above all, share with me the salty bread of direct responsibility of the fascist government." The Duce thanks them and expresses his friendship for them. He does not name them but everyone knows who the recipients of his intimate gratitude are: Francesco Giunta, Emilio De Bono, and, most of all, Cesare Rossi, Aldo Finzi, and Giovanni Marinelli.

Having dispelled the malicious fairytales of his internal adversaries, he moves on to strategy for the next political elections: fascism will not ally with any party. However, he agrees to include men of all parties in his lists or, even, of no party, provided they are useful to the nation. The strategy is clear: to drain the other parties and siphon them into the fascist one. To do this, it is necessary to terminate once and for all the random violence of the fanatical squadristi, to put an end to the hotheads, the extremists, those destined for certain death. Fascism will triumph in the elections by following "the legalitarian way." But they must also put an end to the opposition's grumbling about trampled liberties: "The fascist revolution is not garlanded with the sacrifices of human victims; it has not to date created special courts; there has been no rat-tat-tat of firing squads; it has not exercised terror; it has not promulgated any exceptional laws."

At the end, the tone becomes solemn, the concepts elevated: "Fascism, as a doctrine of national potentiality, as a doctrine of strength, beauty, discipline, and sense of responsibility, is now a beacon that shines in Rome and to which all the peoples of the world look. When it comes to the nation and to fascism we are ready to kill, we are ready to die."

The last words are spoken with passion. All those present, as if electrified, rise to their feet and applaud. The applause goes on in surges, for several minutes.

While the courtiers flock around the "good tyrant" in the hope that he will include them in those "electoral lists open to anyone," Cesare Rossi withdraws together with the other "bad advisers."

Despite the public proclamations concerning the "legalitarian way," on January 10th, Rossi, Giunta, Marinelli and De Bono gathered at Mussolini's place, in the house run by Cesira Carocci on Via Rasella, and there, after playing with the lion cub awhile, they decided to establish a secret unit directly under their supervision to strike at the enemies of fascism. The Duce considers it indispensable: in this phase of transition, in which the laws still reflect traces of the liberal spirit, it can't be done by legal means. The gap must be closed.

During the meeting, Mussolini also expressed his admiration for the ruthless energy with which Lenin, in the nascent phase of the communist state, had not hesitated to authorize the Cheka, the Russian secret police, to use terror methods. Toadyism therefore immediately suggested to the advisers that they christen the clandestine organization the "Fascist Cheka." At the end of the meeting, the Duce, satisfied, sniffed his hands: "I smell of lion!" he exclaimed.

The name of Amerigo Dùmini was proposed to lead the "Fascist Cheka." The Duce gladly welcomed him. In recent months, the Florentine squadrist had carried out several secret missions in France to eliminate dangerous exiled antifascists.

Lenin died on January 21st and they will have to procure a railway pass for Dùmini.

Dear Mr. President, Amerigo Dùmini, *to carry out my mandates or those of Finzi or others*, is very often forced to travel by train. This need will increase from now on, especially during the electoral period just beginning. It is necessary that you, perhaps by telephone, ask Torre or Chiarini to provide him with a permanent railway pass beginning February 1: all this for obvious reasons of economy. Regards, Rossi.

Cesare Rossi, letter to Mussolini,
January 23, 1924 (italics in the original)

CESARE ROSSI

ROME, FEBRUARY 1924

SINCE HE WAS put in charge of the committee assigned to compile the electoral lists, Cesare Rossi hasn't had a moment's peace. The hopeful aspirants give him no respite. He found one postulant at midnight, curled up on the steps in front of his door on Via dell'Arancio: a former deputy from the province of Catanzaro, whom the housekeeper had unsuccessfully tried to send away. "The commander has to pass this way," the man with a thirst for re-election told her, unmovable. Another went to track him down even on Via Frattina, in the office of Dr. Visconti, a well-known chiropodist, and read him letters of recommendation from high-ranking prelates and princes of royal blood while the doctor filed an ingrown nail on his big toe.

The committee is composed of Mussolini's usual trusted men: Michele Bianchi, Aldo Finzi, Francesco Giunta, and Giacomo Acerbo. The newspapers have renamed it the "pentarchy," but the real leader is him, Rossi. On February 1st, he took an office at the Viminale, in the big room adjacent to the central corridor of the prime minister's offices, and from there—consulting with prefects and mayors of provincial capitals, buried in hundreds of telegrams piled on the desk, pursued by thousands of self-nominated candidates who knock at all the parties' doors at the same time—he must draw up the "long list" of 350 names, divided into 16 districts, which, according to Mussolini's plan, are to form the first parliament with a fascist majority.

In public the Duce continues to make a show of disdain for the race to a parliamentary seat: "We have entered the period of the so-called electoral battle. Please! Don't get too worked up over these paper games. All this is old official Italy, the ancien régime. Nothing more ridiculous than thinking of a Mussolini laboriously compiling electoral lists!" And in private the people's condottiere continues to be irritated over the frantic rush of aspiring parliamentarians that distracts him from treaties with Yugoslavia and from pondering Lenin's death.

Nevertheless, the tactical master gave Cesare Rossi precise instructions for compiling the lists. First: if the men of the old parties want to enter the fascist "long list," they must be cut off from the herd. They have to go in one at a time, head bowed, defenseless. Being forced to renounce their membership in their original party, their re-election will be tantamount to surrender. Their seat in Montecitorio will mean political insignificance. The end of traditional parties, the depoliticization of parliamentary life, a single great "party of the nation," the fascist one. The second instruction: whatever party those sifted out came from, their destination must have only one end. Submission to the Leader, total subjection to his will and, perhaps, to his caprice. The system of appointments must, therefore, rain down from above. In short: only single individuals, not parties, and all of them appointed by a single man, the only one who counts.

Having received the directives, Cesare Rossi has to contend with a carnival of aspirants, a madhouse of at least three thousand supplicants who pour into Rome, trailed by impressive retinues of backers and solicitors; they crowd into the ministry building, undeterred, and camp there for hours and days, forcing the officer on duty to clear out the crowds of deputies with the old police cry used for strikers in the piazzas: "Move along, people, move along . . ."

The squads' rases, who have always publicly scorned the "parliamentary medal of honor," compete in a race that is no less bitter than that of southern notables who have always made it a way of life.

The internal struggle within the National Fascist Party (PNF) grows fierce. In Turin the fascist left supports Gioda, Ponti and Torre, while De Vecchi's right opposes them. Each day the prefect is forced to quell the squabbling. In Ferrara, Olao Gaggioli, recently won back to orthodoxy, demands of Balbo that other dissidents also be included in the list; in Piacenza at least three different fascist factions are competing for candidacy. Lombardy, in general, is a disaster, a flurry of dissenters and expulsions.

On a political level, however, Mussolini's strategy is bearing fruit. It's not only the conquest of a majority that is at stake, but a vast transformative effort to corrupt what little remains of the ideals of the Risorgimento: an opus of moral demolition. This is the goal that Mussolini sets himself by driving the major liberal leaders, with all their talk about constitutionality and democracy, to enter the "long list" and thereby become indebted to the fascists for their re-election. Giolitti, courted for some time, though supporting the fascist "long list," insists on forming his own "parallel" list, but almost all the others have accepted the absorption. By mid-February, among the most notable names of the old political world, Cesare Rossi can count on Salandra, prime minister at the time of intervention in the Great War, on Orlando, prime minister of the victory, on De Nicola, president of the chamber, and on another hundred or so liberals, social democrats, independent democrats of the left and populist dissidents, willing to renounce their heralded ideals in exchange for a seat. Even Senator Agnelli, owner of Fiat, haggles with Rossi to exclude some fascist unionists from the Turin electoral district who limit his overwhelming power over the workforce in his car factories.

Everything, in short, seems to be going right. The field of the left raises no concern: more than ever possessed by a suicidal demon. Wavering between abstention and participation, the socialist movement is divided into three factions: unitarians, maximalists, and communists. As if these divisions weren't enough, on the eve of the filing of the lists, a fourth dissident group was announced: the third internationalists. Among these there is also Giuseppe Di Vittorio, the trade unionist revered by all the farmers and workers of Apulia. The upshot: while the Duce's political genius forces almost everyone to enter a single fascist list, the opposition will present no less than 21 lists. Not even the most kindred line-ups have been able to form a bloc among themselves. Moral: too many oppositions, no opposition.

Only Matteotti is left to rattle on with his accusations. He has just published his libelous pamphlet entitled *A Year of Fascist Domination*. The usual useless ejaculation. A voice in the transformist desert.

What worries the Duce is fascist dissidence. In particular that of Cesare Forni, the war hero, the ras of Lomellina, the captain who led the squadrist assault on the city of Milan, the head of the Lombardy-Piedmont section during the march on Rome. Forni threatens to introduce an autonomous list in the electoral district of Mortara, where he is as revered by Lombard squadristi as Di Vittorio is by Apulia's farmworkers. The reasons for the dissent are always the same: accusations of a "betrayed revolution," directed against the profiteering of Rome's fascists, an appeal to the purity of the origins. In Forni's case there is also a personal enmity with Francesco Giunta, with whom he fought a duel, and even a bedroom rivalry for the favors of that whore, the so-called Countess Mattavelli.

Amerigo Dùmini, sent by Rossi to look into the Lombard situation, relayed an alarming report. So Rossi then summoned Forni to Rome in an attempt to make him see reason. In exchange for the withdrawal of his candidacy, he was offered the generous post of supervisor of the colonial troops in Somalia. Captain Forni, imposing his personal legend, and the considerable heft of his 6 feet 4 inches, 242 pounds, refused the offer. For Mussolini, a real thorn in his side.

"Whoever is not with us is against us."

This and only this is what the Duce keeps repeating to Cesare Rossi in the rare moments when he deigns to cast a contemptuous, irate glance at the mush that is being stirred up in the lowly electoral kitchen.

Fascism's situation in Milan, and in some parts of Lombardy, requires vigorous and immediate measures . . . The Forni-Sala wing together with Silva's could—if the secessionist movement were to spread—result in a pincer movement on a not inconsiderable part of provincial and Milanese fascism, and more seriously on squadristic power in particular.

Report by Amerigo Dùmini
to the Ministry of the Interior,
end of February 1924

Forni's electoral stance creates an irreparable break between him and our party. I consider Forni an enemy of my government.

Benito Mussolini, telegram to Umberto Ricci,
newly appointed prefect of Pavia

Go ahead, go after me, Mr. President. I will not bow down until you have had my life taken. We are fighting a holy battle, not against you, nor against your government, but against the degeneration of the party.

Cesare Forni, open letter to Benito Mussolini,
Corriere della Sera, March 2, 1924

You are ordered to consider Caesar Forni and Raimondo Sala as the most formidable enemies of fascism. As a result of this, and together with instructions issued by the head of government to the prefects of the provinces, life must be made impossible for the aforementioned gentlemen . . .

Telegraphic circular sent by the National Fascist Party
to the provincial federations of Lombardy and Piedmont,
March 11, 1924

AMERIGO DÙMINI

MILAN, MARCH 12, 1924
CENTRAL STATION

"WHAT'S DÙMINI DOING, *jacking off?!"*

The atrium of Milan's railway station is teeming with people of assorted ages, genders and circumstances crowding around the exit turnstiles, but regardless of how they earn their living, they all move forward with a light, quick step: unlike Amerigo Dùmini, none of them have the weight of the Duce's furious disappointment to carry.

"What's Dùmini doing, jacking off?!"

Sales reps, businessmen in gray tailcoats, soldiers on leave in their gray-green uniforms, two priests in black tunics, a mother with children, probably returning from a visit to the grandparents. They all seem a little breathless but, all in all, happy. No irate deity has sentenced them to the legend of blood. At an overall, passing glance, humanity appears to be a pointlessly frenzied and moderately content species. So it seems observed from the top of a staircase in a railway atrium during weekday rush hour, when, standing apart, searching for the face of a single individual in the streams of people, you ask yourself: "Where am I in that flow?"

Amerigo Dùmini is stationed at the edge of the scene. He is alone with his malediction—*"What's Dùmini doing, jacking off?!"*—smoking one cigarette after another. Waiting beside a newspaper stand, he smokes unfiltered cigarettes with dark tobacco.

Those angry words from a Mussolini infuriated by Forni's dissidence were reported to him on the phone by Cesare Rossi, urgently summoned on March 9th by the Duce, who complained of being surrounded by dickheads, of having to always do everything himself, of having the misfortune of "being the point man all the time."

Amerigo lights yet another cigarette on the crushed embers of the previous one. Losing the Duce's favor would be a disaster. After his secret missions in France to hunt down antifascists, Mussolini had personally congratulated him. The secretarial staff at the fasci's foreign office had a silver cigarette case made for him—the one he's now using—with a dedication from the Duce: "To Dùmini, the Iron-hearted." Then Mussolini also sent him an autographed photo that Dùmini immediately published on the front page of his provincial newspaper, the *Sassaiola Fiorentina*. As if that weren't enough, at the beginning of February Mussolini even received him at home, on Via Rasella, and appointed him to oversee the "Fascist Cheka." Giovanni Marinelli, the party's treasurer, who was present at the meeting, proposed that he be provided with a cover by having him hired as a traveling sales supervisor for the *Corriere Italiano*, directed by Filippelli, a shady operator working for the Mussolini family who got rich thanks to war surpluses. A monthly salary of 2,500 liras. Besides that there's the newspaper's car at his disposal, the room at the Hotel Dragoni, the rent of 400 liras a month for the apartment on Via Cavour, the payments, the tips, the bonuses to be shared at will among his trusted men, the reserved table at a trattoria, at da Bracche or Al Buco. All at the party's expense.

Unthinkable to lose all that, out of the question. Those who have known him for years say that, in recent times, his personality has even changed. Now they describe "il Dùmini" as exuberant, lively, a jovial, easy-going type, quick with words and instinctively scornful.

When Rossi tracked him down in Perugia the day before, where he had holed up with a woman, and ordered him to rush to Milan to coordinate the operation, he phoned that madman Pirro Nenciolini in Florence, his buddy on punitive raids in the old days, and procured a small group of trusted comrades; then he hopped on the first train. Waiting for him in Milan he found Asvero Gravelli, who reported directly to Francesco Giunta, party secretary. Gravelli handed him 5,000 liras, recorded in Rossi's payroll ledger with the notation "for special political assignment." From Rome they also mobilized the Milanese Arditi of Via Cerva to carry out the job, those of Albino Volpi, the "raw meat squad." That way the mission would be more assured, though involving the Florentine squadristi was essential: Rossi worried, in fact, that if left to themselves the young guys of the Lombard fasci would not be able to perform the task. For them it would mean having to age thirty years in one afternoon. It would be like trampling their youth.

Travelers continue to crowd around the exit. The staircase is congested. At that hour, three different trains arrive at practically the same time. Nenciolini and Volpi's club-wielders are stationed at the foot of the stairs, in front of the turnstiles, where people exit into the piazza overhung by the station canopy. Between the two groups there must be more than twenty of them. Clubs and iron rods. Their man still hasn't appeared but they can't miss him. He's an unmistakable man.

He's the sort of person you would always want with you, never against you, but he asked for it. At the elections he presented his own dissident list: the national fasci. Mussolini has tried everything: he offered him a command in Africa, he threatened him, he ordered the prefects to sequester his newspapers, to arrest his friends, to disband the party sections in his territories, but no dice, he didn't bend. Then he went too far. In a meeting in Biella, in a piazza packed with thousands of people, thousands of fascists, he pointed a finger at the party's brass: "I know by first and last name individuals in sad financial straits who in 1920 and 1921 were begging me for a few liras to be able to eat. And today they live in Rome in elegant apartments, paid for with the money of the Italian people." And the fascists applauded him. Even Vittorio Sella, founder of the city fascio, after taking the floor for a rebuttal, instead of countering praised him.

Here he comes. Cesare Forni stands at least a head taller than the hundreds of featureless, oblivious and moderately happy passengers. Impossible not to notice his still blond hair and heavy eyelids in that flow of simple passersby. Hard to imagine violence in the midst of that crowd of priests, accountants and businessmen.

Will they confront him openly? Will Volpi, Nenciolini or one of the other Arditi afford Captain Forni, with his nine medals of valor from the Great War, the honors of war?

They assault him from behind. They immediately club him over the head, the first blows striking the back of his neck. A savage, unquestionable, desire to kill. A swarm of flesh flies pupated by larvae deposited in food scraps, in the carrion of dead animals. Scattered by the centrifugal force of violence, the crowd around Forni melts away.

Left alone in the circle of attackers, the besieged man seems even bigger. Huge, unarmed, he fights. Kicking and punching, bare-handed. With his hands already fractured by the blows, he wrests an iron-plated rod away and strikes out blindly with it. A man who was with him joins in. Some of the attackers are bleeding, they back away, the circle breaks. Drawn back in by that moment of touch and go, some of the passersby reverse their flight and draw near.

Then the whirlwind of blows resumes, the circle closes again, dozens of wooden clubs smack against skull bone, fracture humeri, scaphoids, metacarpals. Cesare Forni, his face masked with blood, staggers, leans against a wall, collapses. They continue to beat him even when he is on the ground. The crowd shouts "Enough! that's enough!" When everyone leaves him, all that's left of Cesare Forni is a pile of rags in the immense empty space of a railway atrium, a tiny, random bloodstain in the infinite universe.

In an article he writes on March 15th—originally entitled "He Who Betrays, Perishes"—Benito Mussolini claims fascism's right to punish its traitors. It's easy for him to argue that fascist violence is insignificant compared to the ferocity with which the Bolsheviks exterminate dissidents: just the day before in Russia, with Lenin dead, Stalin publicly attacked the theories of Trotsky, the main architect of the revolution. And besides, Forni isn't even dead.

And so the following week, to thank him for the treaty granting

Fiume to Italy, Vittorio Emanuele III awards Benito Mussolini the collar of the Supreme Order of the Most Holy Annunciation, the highest honor of the House of Savoy. Now the son of Predappio's blacksmith is formally a cousin to the king.

As brother it is with anguished heart that I denounce attempted assassination organized and implemented today Milan station and on family behalf ask Your Excellency to ensure that authors and organizers of vile act, easily identifiable, are brought to justice, for good name of fascism and Italy.

Roberto Forni, telegram to Benito Mussolini,
March 12, 1924
(made public in the *Corriere della Sera*)

Bolshevism physically suppressed the Menshevik dissidents. Nor did a better fate await the socialist revolutionary dissidents . . . With what shameless brazenness do these filthy reptiles of Italian subversivism dare raise loud lamentations if some traitor of fascism is more or less resoundingly punished? We are still a long way from the systems of Russia.

Benito Mussolini,
Il Popolo d'Italia, March 15, 1924

One must be either for or against. Either fascism or antifascism. Whoever is not with us is against us.

Benito Mussolini, speech commemorating
the foundation of the Fasci di Combattimento,
given at the Teatro Costanzi, Rome, March 24, 1924

GIACOMO MATTEOTTI

ROME, APRIL 1, 1924

DESPONDENCY ENTICES THEM with the lure of abstention. Abstention or defeat? This has been the dilemma of what remains of socialist oppositions since the election rallies began in January. Abstain en masse, this is the tempting demon of their desert.

Avoid the event. Don't sit at the cardsharp's table. Oppose the world's rigged game with a preemptive, absolute refusal.

At first even Giacomo Matteotti favored this position. Anticipating an electoral battle dominated by clubbings, it seemed to him that the table had to be overturned. Fearing the foul defeat of the fascists' dirty game, virtue suggested that he sidestep it, avoid playing, fight a battle of detachment, giving the present up for lost. In the end, under that sky of violence, where not even its azure grants any respite, even the elections were just a chapter. All you had to do, and all you could do, was hold your position, strengthen it for a distant future, say "no" to the present even if there was no sign of a different future on the horizon.

In the early months of the year, Matteotti operated on this strategy. For a moment it seemed that his desperate hope could bring all the antifascist forces together in a united show of mass abstention. In February an accord with the democrats of Giovanni Amendola, who'd been beaten by the squadristi at the end of December, seemed close. For a moment coalescing the leftist groups around the communist proposal of a "united proletarian front" even seemed possible. Then, however, everything quickly fractured again. The taste for fratricide, the appeal of calamity regained the upper hand and Matteotti was the first to jump back into bitter debate with the cruel brothers of the Italian Socialist Party. He accused them of effecting "the usual maneuver to unload on us, vile reformists, the responsibility of having divided and weakened the proletariat."

With the hope of a united front gone, the secretary of the Unitary Socialist Party abandoned the idea of abstention. In view of the breakup and disarray, with so many demoralized comrades and leaders prepared to compromise, to surrender, abstaining would have ended up being merely an evasion, a cheap way of dodging reality. Instead, the struggle had to be resumed, all-out, without giving so much as an inch, without retreating one step, on all fronts, even the electoral arena. On the eve of the elections, he also wrote to Turati, the gentle patriarch of humanitarian socialism: they had to toughen up, be more severe, claw out a space between majority and opposition, between fascists and socialists, between pure socialists and collaborationists, a space that no one would dare or be able to cross.

Matteotti wrote that to Turati, while to Velia, instead, Giacomo hasn't written for months. The last communication to his wife is an illustrated postcard from Venice, dated December 28, 1923. It depicts the flight of pigeons in Piazza San Marco. The message says only: "Greetings be well." Three words, not even a comma. The desert has swallowed up punctuation as well.

Not so much as a comma is missing, however, in the book that Giacomo Matteotti has just published: *A Year of Fascist Domination*. In his meticulous listing of the violent acts committed by the regime's squadristi, abuses and crimes perpetrated in the provinces while Mussolini, in Rome, pretends to be the nation's paterfamilias, every "t" is crossed. The clubbings, the fires, the killings are listed one by one, by the dozens, by the hundreds, by the thousands. Next to each a place, a name, a date, as on gravestones.

But the book that Matteotti worked on for months, consuming himself in the dizzying list, is already outdated as soon as it is published. Its scrupulously detailed pages had just come off the printing press when news came that in Reggio Emilia socialist candidate Antonio Piccinini, a printer by trade, had been killed. He'd been hung on a butcher's meat hook.

That's how it goes: behind the human tragedy is a greedy publisher. You've just published the complete volume when he already asks you to add a new chapter on the latest new crime. But Giacomo Matteotti, as usual, doesn't give up. In February he published the first edition of his innumerable denunciations, in March he is already working on the re-edition.

Nor does the secretary of the Unitary Socialist Party give up his scrupulous censure of the misappropriation of public funds. He is preparing a dossier which shows that the balanced budget presented by the Mussolini government to Vittorio Emanuele III, and countersigned by him, is a sham. Matteotti draws up lists of fraudulent appropriations to the detriment of the state that are no less detailed than those compiled for blood crimes. Here, too, the list is dizzying: private interests in the colossal reconversion of the industrial apparatus, billions purposely lost by tax authorities not taxing excessive war profits, privatization of entire strategic public sectors such as telephones, fraudulent bank bailouts, financial speculation, frauds against the national treasury. He notes them all, painstakingly, looking for documentary evidence for each of them, as if recording them one after the other could in itself guarantee compensation for damages, like a traveling salesman documenting his claim for reimbursement of expenses.

Now, from London, trade union comrades let him know that they have compromising revelations about the Italian government's secret agreements with Sinclair Oil, the US company that is securing a monopoly over oil prospecting on most of the Italian subsoil. An area equivalent to over 18,500,000 acres, one quarter of the national territory. A colossal kickback, it's rumored. Matteotti is already planning to leave for London at the end of April. First, however, there are the elections. In six days, April 6. First he must fight this other round in one man's fight against the world. Who will win?

The country cannot be said to be indifferent to the question. In the past few days newspaper circulation has increased, party sections are packed, and there are heated discussions in the bars. Political fervor is fueled, yet since yesterday evening people in the Campo Marzio district, where Giacomo Matteotti lives with his family, haven't talked about anything but that little girl. She was playing in the park at Piazza Cavour, not far from there, with her mother close by. Then the mother noticed that her daughter had disappeared. Two hours later a woman heard a child crying, crouched behind a hedge. She found her with her simple skirt ripped, and a brightly colored handkerchief tightened around her neck. Someone had seen a tall, slender, distinguished-looking man straighten his clothes and hurry off. But little Emma's condition did not allow her rescuers to pay due attention to the fugitive.

First of all, we must adopt a different attitude toward the fascist dictatorship than that which we've shown so far; our resistance to a high-handed regime must be more active; not yield on any point; not abandon any position without the most resolute, the most vociferous protests. All citizens' rights must be demanded; the law itself recognizes the right to self-defense. No one should be under the illusion that the prevailing fascism will of its own accord lay down its arms and restore a regime of lawfulness and liberty to Italy; everything it achieves propels it to new willful acts, to new abuses. That is its essence, its origin, its only strength; and it is that disposition that drives it.

Giacomo Matteotti, letter to Filippo Turati,
on the eve of the elections, April 6, 1924

BENITO MUSSOLINI

MILAN, EARLY APRIL 1924

He sleeps little, badly, a troubled sleep: his nightmare is empty urns. As April 6 gradually approaches, his anxiety grows. He does not fear a resurgence of the oppositions, nor a nudge of consciences, he's afraid of empty ballot boxes. His specter is mass abstention, the chilling surprise of a mild Sunday in April—an election Sunday, an Italian Sunday—on which the polling stations remain deserted. Everyone gone, to the shore, to the mountains, barricaded inside their living rooms, an entire nation that, disgusted by an overbearing power that it cannot oppose with anything but a violent fit of rejection, instead of taking to the streets, of raising the barricades, of openly voting against him, recalls his appointment en masse. A phantom nation. That's his bogeyman.

The Founder of the Fasci di Combattimento is not afraid to fight, he doesn't fear defeat on the open battlefield, the sudden revelation of that relentless hostility that arms the enemy's hand. What he fears is fear. The kind that gnaws at the soul, that eats at the heart of an entire people shut up in their homes after seven in the evening.

At this rate, the elections vigil turns into a constant alert. The supreme leader of fascism has his ear cocked and listens intently for news from the provinces. Each time the echoes of remote shouting inform him of a blatant violation of civil liberties on the Sarno plain, or a useless act of fascist violence at the Po delta, he flies into a rage, yells obscenities, then sends circulars to the prefects, ordering the most severe repression of any unlawful act. Nonetheless, the illegalities proliferate like bacterial colonies in rotting fruit. In the provincial capital cities the electoral battle takes place with an acceptable degree of orderliness, but in the smaller centers newspapers are seized and aggressions against opposition candidates are countless; in Novellara, in Frascati, in Venice, Prato and a number of towns in Brianza even priests are attacked. In many regions of the South and in the Po Valley, the petty provincial rases, headstrong and undisciplined, openly proclaim that they will not allow the candidacy of any list other than the fascist one; they ban socialist leaders from the cities, and go so far as to order electoral ballots to be handed in at the local fascio office.

When these news reports arrive, the prime minister renews the orders for the most severe repression. Earlier, De Bono, at his urging, telegraphed Milan's police chief, even ordering Albino Volpi's arrest if he continued to upset things on the eve of the elections. But then the Duce of fascism never finds the courage to impose the execution of those orders. He can't make up his mind. He wants to be loved by unanimous approval, he wants the people's consent, but he can't give up the forceps with which he has always delivered it. And what if the people, left to themselves, did not vote for him, if their love was not sincere?

Benito Mussolini spends the entire week before the April 6 elections in Milan, arriving at the wheel of a sports car he drives himself. Day by day his closest collaborators swallow the toxic pill of his discontent, his agitation: they put up with his outbursts against the parliamentary system, his irritation towards the fascist leaders who can't resist the "rapture of the parliamentary medal of honor," who can't avoid the electoral disease. They listen to him, dismayed, as the bitterness he carries inside him pours out in brazen public speeches in which he dreams of the establishment of special tribunals, an extension of full powers, speeches heaped with cosmic pessimism, universal contempt.

A lack of confidence in the human race is the obsessive theme of the "Preface to Machiavelli" that Mussolini writes for the April issue of *Gerarchia*, the journal edited by Margherita Sarfatti. The Duce recalls the pages of *The Prince* that he had heard from his father's lips during his adolescent years. He declares himself fully in agreement with Machiavelli's anthropological pessimism. Nations are governed by the sword, not with words. Individuals tend to continually evade, to disobey the laws, to not pay taxes, to not wage war. Power does not emanate directly from the will of the people. That's fiction. The people, left to themselves, are not capable of exercising sovereignty directly, they can only delegate it. Exclusively consensual regimes have never existed and, most likely, never will exist. Every armed prophet wins and the unarmed succumb.

Human beings are pathetic, more fond of things than of their own blood, quick to change their feelings and passions. The secretary of the Florentine Republic, and founder of modern political science, wrote that at the beginning of the sixteenth century, and Benito Mussolini, president of the Council of Ministers of the Kingdom of Italy, confirms it at the beginning of the twentieth century, on the eve of the elections: "Some time has passed, but if I were permitted to judge my contemporaries and the like, I could in no way soften Machiavelli's judgment. I would, perhaps, have to make it bleaker."

To escape his entourage of timid cowards and obsequious toadies, Mussolini finds refuge at the home of Margherita Sarfatti, who a few weeks ago was widowed. Although Rachele and the family are living nearby in the new apartment on Via Mario Pagano, he does not go there in the evening. Officially he sleeps at the headquarters of the prefecture with the excuse of overseeing the electoral battle, but in actuality he spends nights at his lover's place on Corso Venezia. The nervous tension, the manic revulsion for his fellow men, the melancholy view of human wretchedness have reawakened his erotic fervor, as often happens. Rachele, humiliated, takes the three children with her and finds comfort in Forlì with her sister Pina, stricken with tuberculosis, and herself the mother of seven children.

Her husband learns about it at the end of the funeral of Nicola Bonservizi, founder of the Paris fascio, a comrade from the early days, murdered by an anarchist while sitting at a cafe table. His casket is carried from the station to the headquarters of *Il Popolo d'Italia* and then from there to the burial ceremony. Mussolini follows along the route on foot under a lashing rain. Heartbroken, silent, he grimly takes part in the grandiose funeral for his old comrade-in-arms.

When the funeral procession is over, Cesare Rossi informs him of Rachele's departure. Historic tragedy mixes with conjugal farce amid the bird droppings at the Cimitero Monumentale. But there's not a moment's respite: Nicola Bonservizi's coffin has just been lowered into the grave when already four provincial delegates are asking for a meeting to talk about electoral trafficking. He shakes his head, turns to Rossi:

"This is the last time elections are held. Next time I'll be the only one who votes."

Collection and speculation re electoral incidents has already begun, which subversive newspapers are publishing in boldface to make an impression externally and internally. It is absolutely essential to 1) take all necessary preventive measures to avoid incidents 2) suppress them as quickly as possible 3) report them to the Ministry of the Interior, so as to identify nature and extent to defuse any conjecture [. . .]. It is absolutely imperative to prevent acts of vandalism against opposition newspapers in particular, to ensure that the national list emerges victorious from the elections. Let Cesare Rossi and the others know this.

Benito Mussolini, telegrams to all the prefects of the Kingdom and to the director general of public security, February 29 and April 4, 1924

It is decided that absolutely no list of any stripe will be permitted that is opposed to ours, even as a minority, and that measures deemed most appropriate will be taken against those that would promote abstention.

Agenda voted by the fascists of Moggio (Udine), 1924

During times of democracy's destruction, elections are a completely wrong yardstick with which to measure the balance of powers.

Ignazio Silone, leader of the Communist Party of Italy, exiled in France, 1924

MARGHERITA SARFATTI

VENICE, APRIL 1, 1924

THE XIV INTERNATIONAL Art Exhibition of the city of Venice is the first of the fascist era. As always, the gondolas, festively decorated, drift in procession on the basin of water between San Giorgio and San Marco. As always, the lopsided wisdom of the axe masters at the gondola workshop of San Trovaso has carved them from the wood perfectly unbalanced so that the gondoliers can steer them rowing on one side only. As always, artists meet at the Caffè Florian, ladies receive guests in the drawing rooms of their palazzos on the Grand Canal, and Venice, a museum of itself for almost two centuries, is the perfect backdrop for an art exhibition. This year, however, there are hierarchs in black shirts to receive King Vittorio Emanuele III in the garden of the Palazzo delle Esposizioni under the Lion of St. Mark.

In a certain sense, it is the first Biennale of her life for Margherita Sarfatti as well. She who was born in Venice, she who saw them all and has not missed a single one, not since her father, the prosperous Jewish merchant Amedeo Grassini—after founding the first vaporetto company, starting a financial group to transform the Lido into a tourist destination, becoming a city councilman and leaving the ghetto for Palazzo Bembo—took her as a young girl among the gentiles, who tipped their hats when they passed by.

Despite all this, Margherita is making her debut. She is exhibiting her painters of the twentieth-century group, the "Novecento," for the first time, in a gallery reserved for her. She is photographed among them, surrounded by well-chosen, thoughtfully arranged, judiciously spaced canvases; she appears tense, her shoulders hunched, dressed in a shawl and cloche, more petite than she is, the only female among six males, the only woman in a cultural world dominated by men.

Margherita is being put to a decisive test. Her conception of a new artistic objectivity—a return to order, a modern classicism centered on geometric composition, on cohesive design, on color harmony, on the pure motherhood of a young worker portrayed as a Renaissance Madonna by Achilles Funi—that conception will be displayed to the world alongside the pavilions of Japan, Romania and the United States of America, to the international delegations arriving at the dock of the Riva degli Schiavoni waterfront from Spain, Belgium, France, Holland, Hungary, Great Britain, Germany, and Russia. But the test that Margherita Sarfatti is subjecting herself to is also decisive for her conception of artistic power that is accorded equal status with political power, which speaks its same language, which forms a new constellation with it. The art critic is not the only one making her debut. Debuting is the "nymph Egeria" as well, the "dictator of culture," the "presidentessa"; debuting is the cultured lover of Benito Mussolini. Everyone has their rifles aimed, at one and the other.

Nevertheless, everything goes smoothly. There is no doubt that the works of the "Novecento" group are proficient, well selected, well displayed. Only Marinetti, during the opening ceremony, in the presence of the king, introduces some of the old disarray by interrupting Giovanni Gentile's momentum with a cry of "down with backward-looking Venice!" But by this time futurist chaos is a comic satire, and Marinetti relapses into a caricature of himself; everyone knows he's protesting because he hasn't been invited, and word has it that he will soon marry and start a family. The incident is most likely even welcome to the sovereign, who takes the opportunity to make an early departure from the gallery and its tedium. In short, the new order, decreed by Margherita Sarfatti and imposed by Benito Mussolini, triumphs. Yet for her it is a victory that smacks of defeat.

The first disappointment was occasioned, just before the inauguration, by the desertion of Ubaldo Oppi. Tall, blond, with a body sculpted in boxing gyms—perhaps the most representative painter of the group—Oppi accepted the invitation of Ugo Ojetti, art critic of the *Corriere della Sera*, to exhibit his paintings in a separate room dedicated to him. Then there was the malicious criticism: Giovanni Papini wrote about an art that was "soft and swollen like a bladder." Finally, after the event, came the withdrawal of Anselmo Bucci, the youngest of them all and the dandy of the group, beautiful as Lucifer.

Moreover, the year 1924 for Margherita had begun under an unlucky star. On January 18th, on the train bringing him home from Rome, Cesare Sarfatti had suddenly collapsed. He died five days later. After the numerous frustrations of his political ambitions, Margherita had just managed to get her lover to assign her husband the presidency of the Cassa di Risparmio bank in the Lombard provinces, but the poor fellow, stricken with inoperable appendicitis, hadn't even had time to enjoy the post. With her husband gone, just when she was finally free for him, her lover also deserted her. Just after Cesare died, Mussolini had publicly entrusted her with the legal responsibility for *Gerarchia*, which by now had become the official organ of the regime, but the priestess of fascist art found herself waiting for him in vain more and more often in the solitary rooms of sad hotels. That man always traveled on a double track, in love as in politics: the piazza and the palazzo; the squadristi and the ministries; the lover and the wife. No chance of shunting him over to the single track of a straight life.

Another failure, all in all. Yes, she had been able to teach him how to politely use a fish knife, but in the end, when he'd had to choose a Victory statue for his office in Palazzo Chigi, among the thousands of ancient marbles in Rome, the Duce of fascism had managed the improbable feat of selecting a fake.

For now, however, Benito Mussolini and Margherita Sarfatti are still seeing each other. In the days immediately following the opening at the Biennale, he goes to Milan, pretending to sleep in the prefecture; now that Cesare Sarfatti rests in the Jewish section of the Cimitero Monumentale, the prime minister, instead of staying at his own house, goes straight to the Sarfattis' palazzo on Corso Venezia. He is rabid, extremely anxious about the results of the looming elections, every muscle in his body intent on the conquest of absolute power. Margherita welcomes him, as always, devotes herself to him, soothes him, though evidently she fails to hide the discontent of a disappointed woman. So she talks about traveling again, exotic destinations, African deserts. Margherita's trip to Tunisia the previous year had been fruitful. After having had such a hard time getting Benito's permission to go, she managed to produce a successful book from it on her return. Now, by contrast, he's the one urging that she leave.

She sets off again but this time she doesn't get far. Arriving in Spain, descending the stairs of a luxury hotel with her luck in decline, the traveler falls and breaks her leg.

Such sad things around us—and so many of them—such a web of deceptions, I've suffered so much from all kinds of heartaches during this long, inauspicious year.

Margherita Sarfatti, letter to Benito Mussolini, 1924

How much worthier and grander art is, even in its most rudimentary expressions, than even the most brilliant politics.

Margherita Sarfatti, letter to Arturo Martini, 1924

ROME, MAY 24, 1924
PARLIAMENT OF THE KINGDOM, CHAMBER OF MONTECITORIO

FOUR MILLION SIX hundred and fifty thousand votes. Two Italians out of three voted for the national list of the Fascio Littorio. The Acerbo law provided for an inordinate award of majority to the list that exceeded 25 percent. There was no need for it: the fascist list received 64.9 percent of the yes votes. All of its 356 candidates were elected, down to the last one. Added to those are 19 elected representatives from a second national list. Even the turnout to the polls increased. The government of Benito Mussolini will therefore be able to count on an immense majority of 374 elected representatives in parliament.

There is no doubt: Italy, at first conquered by the Duce of fascism, has finally submitted to him. Even some of his most unyielding enemies recognize that Mussolini's victory is incontestable. In his journal, Piero Gobetti defines the liberal ruling class's acquiescence to fascism as a "masterpiece of Mussolinism."

The *Triumphus*. In Ancient Rome the Triumph was a solemn ceremony marking the greatest tribute paid to a victorious commander. After the electoral victory, Benito Mussolini is granted honorary citizenship in the "eternal city." Receiving it in the Campidoglio on the anniversary of its foundation, the Duce speaks, inspired by the highest honor. Since he was a boy—Mussolini reveals—Rome was an immense presence in the spirit with which he confronted life. He now bows to the secret that no analysis can unveil, that of a small people of peasants and shepherds who, little by little, were able to rise to imperial power and over the course of centuries transform the lowly village of huts on the banks of the Tiber into a gigantic metropolis, whose citizens numbered in the millions and whose legions dominated the world.

After the speech, as Mussolini watches a parade of trade union organizations, something extraordinary happens: a crowd that has become wildly excited pulls him away from his police protection and whirls him twice around the piazza.

The supportive newspapers keep printing the image of the father of the nation moved by his children's outpouring of affection, even in the weeks that follow. During a trip to Sicily, Mussolini promises that he will stamp out the mafia: "For a few hundred criminals to subvert, impoverish, and extort a magnificent population like yours must no longer be tolerated." On the hills of Florence, at the end of a conference of gravely wounded and disabled veterans, the former Bersagliere sits at the table with the battered soldiers of the trenches as evening falls on the grounds of the villa and casts the shadow of tragedy over their faces. To those who urge him to return to the city to perform his governmental duties, he replies: "I feel sad and quiet here, let me stay with you." To all Italians, in his first speech after the elections, the statesman, invested with the responsibility of his historic task, proclaims equably: "We want to give the Italian people five years of peace and fruitful work. May all factions perish, even the fascist faction, so that Italy may always be great and respected."

But the factions do not perish and not all of Italy is with Mussolini. The opposition parties have undoubtedly been decimated: the number of socialist deputies, compared to the previous legislature, has dropped from 123 to 46, the populists from 108 to 39 and the democrats from 124 to 30. Only the communists have gained something, increasing from 15 to 19 deputies. Among them is Antonio Gramsci, who enters the chamber replacing Nicola Bombacci, excluded from the lists. Yet an analysis of the vote, performed in the cold light of day on data coming from the Ministry of the Interior in the days following the intoxication, reveals that the fascist "long list" is a minority in the large industrialized regions of the North and in all their capitals, including Milan: the workers of the northern factories stubbornly voted against fascism. His triumph is due to the plebiscite of Central Italy and, above all, of the South, where until the march on Rome fascism was practically non-existent. It is the eleventh-hour fascists who delivered the country to Mussolini, it is a vocation for servitude on the part of those with little political education, the race to jump onto the winner's bandwagon. From Moscow where he fled, Giacinto Serrati, secretary of the Socialist Party, though defeated, calls for a vendetta on behalf of factory workers in Milan, Genoa and Turin.

Mussolini knows all this and is incensed by it. The idea that there are still those out there denying his triumph is intolerable to him. His exasperation comes to a head when he reads reports in the opposition newspapers about the intention to challenge the legitimacy of his election at the first session of the new parliament. Cesare Rossi, recently promoted to head the quadrumvirate that holds the party together along with its treasurer Marinelli, as always attests to the Duce's moods: "What the hell do they want? Still not convinced? Jesus, what do they want, to eviscerate me?" a fuming Mussolini shouts at him. The outbursts invariably culminate in profanity muttered in dialect: "*Boja de 'n Signur!*"—Bloody Christ!

Fascists are also spoiling Mussolini's triumph. The factions do not perish, not even within his alliance. Massimo Rocca resumes the revisionist dispute with Farinacci and the squadristi in the provinces continue their private acts of violence cloaked in political rationales. During a meeting with Ettore Conti, summoned to discuss some fiscal matters, the influential industrialist reiterates to the prime minister the citizenship's disgust for the blackshirts' continued vandalism. Mussolini shakes his head and strikes his fist on the back of the chair:

"Would you, Senator, be willing to have them face a firing squad for me?"

"I repeat my 'no,'" Conti replies. "Having sworn allegiance to the king, I would be willing to do so only at his command."

Mussolini explodes. "The vandals! The vandals! Well, I need those violent ones too!"

And that's not all. The hostile press mounts a ferocious campaign on what it calls the "oil scandal." On April 29th, the government signed the concession granting exploitation rights on Italian subsoil to Sinclair Oil, but a few days later Mussolini is personally forced to lie in a press release in which he solemnly ensures the non-involvement of the American company in the multinationals that hold the foreign trade monopoly of Italy's oil. The lie is obligatory: it is rumored that Giacomo Matteotti, on a recent trip to England, has obtained evidence of the underlying corruption.

Be that as it may, on May 24th, on the ninth anniversary of Italy's entry into the Great War, the parliament that emerged from the "triumphal" elections of April 6 is inaugurated. The date was chosen to mark the beginning of a new fascist era. The new era, however, is struggling to begin.

In protest against electoral irregularities, the socialists desert the chamber. Their empty benches, though few, leave a yawning chasm in the *triumphus* of Benito Mussolini, the leader who even now, in spite of everything, hates being taken for a man of the right. It is from the benches of the right, where his followers sit, that insults and threats against the deserters are being raised. Vittorio Emanuele III, King of Italy, ignoring the chasm, inaugurates the new chamber in triumphalistic tones, greeting the newly elected as "the generation of Victory." Benito Mussolini watches impassively from the government bench, arms folded.

The practice of non-resistance to evil is a disease no less grave than the petty politics of our country . . . The task of the oppositions is to intensify the battle, to keep up their intransigence, to provoke the regime, not granting it any respite . . . We will not be the ones to contest fascism its majority. We are modestly content with a future that we may not see.

Piero Gobetti, "After the Elections,"
La rivoluzione liberale, April 15, 1924

ROME, MAY 30, 1924
MONTECITORIO, CHAMBER OF DEPUTIES

"DEPUTY MATTEOTTI HAS asked to speak. He has the floor."

The murmuring begins as soon as the new president of the chamber, jurist Alfredo Rocco, gives the floor to Giacomo Matteotti. It starts with a muffled hum, like surf washing back, even before he utters a single syllable. The man who rises from the benches of the left, accompanied by a soundtrack of annoyance and loathing, is a solitary, virtually outcast figure.

In his four years in office, Giacomo Matteotti has delivered as many as 106 long, meticulous speeches, often packed with matters of finance and budget that no one, apart from him and a few others, understands anything about. His gaunt, run-down body, his rare smiles, the receded gums revealing the roots of his teeth, surely arouse the admiration of some, but for most of them, including many of his own party members, Matteotti is simply an irritating, nagging, rancorous obsessive.

His first topic is the list of names proposed for confirmation by the electoral council. The first interruption—caused by a shout from a right-wing deputy—comes after just three sentences. Matteotti ignores it:

"Now, against their confirmation we present this pure and simple objection: namely, that the governing majority list, which ostensibly obtained a count of four million plus votes, did not, in fact, obtain those votes freely . . ."

Immediately he is again interrupted by comments, clamoring, protests. The secretary of the Unitary Socialist Party is aiming at the big target: he has entered this chamber to challenge the validity of the elections right then and there, from his very first assertion. His next words repeat it as if reciting a fervent litany: "in our view, the result is essentially invalid," "no Italian voter was free to decide of his own will," "no elector faced with the question was free" . . .

"Eight million Italians voted!" fascist Carlo Meraviglia shouts at him. Francesco Giunta, standing up in the bench, attacks him with: "You're no Italian! Go to Russia, traitor."

The abusive slurs drown him out. Matteotti remains unfazed. He reminds them that the government had an armed militia to coerce voters. His relentless chant keeps harping on that point: "there is an armed militia . . ." (outbursts from the right, prolonged clamoring) "there is an armed militia . . ." (uproar, protests, shouting) "an armed militia composed of citizens of only one party that should have abstained and instead was in force . . ." The irritation of the 370 fascist parliamentarians, an overwhelming majority, overpowers the speaker. As the deputies' hearts pound in their chests and pressure dilates their arteries, the chamber of Montecitorio is pervaded by hints of blood.

Almost anyone, at this point, would revert to silence, but Giacomo Matteotti defies the storm and begins listing the violations. Signatures missing on the presentation of the lists, certifying formalities prevented by violence, electoral rallies denied to the opposition, seats dominated by fascist list representatives . . .

All hell breaks loose again. Interruptions, protests, abuse. Despicable, liar, provocateur. Slurs, protests, outbursts. Troublemaker, liar, contemptible! Matteotti pushes back: he professes his faith in mere facts. He is simply listing the facts:

"You want individual facts? Here they are: in Iglesias a certain Corsi was collecting three hundred signatures and his house was surrounded . . ."

Voices from the right: "It's not true, it's a lie!"

Bastianini: "That's what you say!"

Carlo Meraviglia: "It's a lie. You're making it up right this minute!"

Farinacci: "We'll end up really doing what we didn't do!"

Matteotti: "You'll be doing your usual business!"

Not even the crescendo of rage culminating in Farinacci's threats discourages him. When the shouting has quieted down for a moment, the socialist deputy resumes his list of abuses. He lays out the facts—he drives them home, doggedly. Just the facts. Facts are either true or false, they should not provoke protests.

Instead, after a few seconds, the shouting, the interruptions, the threats begin again. And they don't stop. The outbursts come from all sides, from Teruzzi, from Finzi, Farinacci, Greco, Presutti, Gonzales and numerous other fascists. Matteotti sits down, gets up again, objects that he hasn't finished. Amid Alfredo Rocco's frantic bell ringing, the fascists banging on the desks with clenched fists, the yelling and shouting, and the roars from the public crowded into the galleries, the endless stream goes on for hours. No one knows how long. Some estimate an hour and a half, some two, some as many as three. Time expands, gets entangled, goes around in circles cruelly, aimlessly. Rocco, as president of the assembly, enjoins the speaker to avoid provocations, as if he too feared for his life; he turns the floor back to him but urges him to use it "prudently." Everyone, friend or foe, implores Matteotti to finish. Matteotti finishes but not before he has reached the end:

"You who today hold power and strength in your hands, you who flaunt your power, should be able to observe the law better than anyone . . . if liberty is given, there may be errors, momentary excesses, but the Italian people, like any other, has shown that it is capable of correcting them itself. We deplore however the desire to show that our people are the only ones in the world who cannot rule themselves and must be governed by force. A lot of harm had been done by foreign dominations. Yet our people were picking themselves up and educating themselves. You are shoving them back down again."

Again the speaker is drowned out by shouts of threats and contempt. This time, however, he's finished. Giacomo Matteotti appears satisfied. His words of twofold opposition—against the enemies in the fascist government and against the socialist friends inclined to collaborate—have been pronounced. All the bridges have now been burned.

The unyielding antifascist sits down again, submerged by the uproar, and turning to his deskmate, tells him:

"I had my say. Now prepare my funeral oration." So saying, Giacomo Matteotti smiles, showing his long, protruding teeth, their roots exposed by gingivitis. Impossible to tell whether it's a joking smile or a nervous rictus.

Throughout the interminable 107th parliamentary speech by Deputy Matteotti, Benito Mussolini remained silent, seated at the presidency desk, making a show of indifference, as if the tempestuous wave that surged over the chamber could not reach his windward shore. For practically the whole time of the fracas, Mussolini seemed absorbed in reading the newspapers, making notes in pencil and tapping the lead point on the wooden desktop. When he was finally able to leave the chamber, however, parliamentary reporters said he appeared livid, his face tight.

"What's Dùmini doing, what's the Cheka doing?! It's unacceptable that after such a speech that man can still be walking around! *Boja de 'n Signur!*"

The Duce's angry outburst after Matteotti's speech set off waves of panic among those in his entourage.

Only Mussolini's closest associates and some of his family—his brother Arnaldo, Rachele, Finzi, Cesare Rossi and a few others—know the habitual fits of temper, the eruptions of rage, the moments of savage criminality that come over Benito Mussolini. Violence, for that matter, is the mood of the entire era, the law of the stratosphere in which the fascist planet revolves.

In fact, a few minutes after Matteotti's speech, amid the chamber's benches barely recalled to order by the clerks, a furious brawl breaks out between the fascists and the opposition following an insult by Francesco Giunta to the latter's exponents. Moreover, outside the hall, several journalists testify to Cesare Rossi, usually self-possessed, sitting at a table in the corridors of Montecitorio, all worked up and rattling off threats ("With enemies like Matteotti you can only let a revolver do the talking . . . if they knew what was going on in Mussolini's head, they would shut up immediately . . . those who know him should realize that from time to time he demands blood"). Finally, in the following days, the fascist newspapers print a succession of trivial insults and overt threats against the socialist deputy, in no uncertain terms.

Despite all this, Mussolini's intimates know that his enmity is tenacious but his rage is often ephemeral: they also know that these days "making life impossible" for an adversary is a leitmotif, a refrain, a death sentence and, at the same time, a figure of speech. It is up to the interpreter to choose which of the two meanings—literal or metaphorical—should be attributed to it.

Among Mussolini's intimates there is, unfortunately, also Giovanni Marinelli, the most despised of the fascist leaders. Physically inept in a group of violent brutes, precociously aged at forty amid a choir that exalts youth, incapacitated by devastating gastritis in a political party that has made vigor a religion, Marinelli clings to the enormous power conferred on him by his role as treasurer, exercising it with vindictive pedantry and miserliness. Above all the fascists themselves despise him, especially the squadristi to whom he deigns to grudgingly dole out money when they leave to stir up some violence that he would like to perform, but isn't able to. The party treasurer is by no means a mild-mannered man. With an acidic, spasmodic stomach and constant gastric distress, he suffers from an inferiority complex every time he sits down at the table; his septic moods cause him unrelenting bilious attacks, irritability, and spiteful envy. Giovanni Marinelli is, in a word, an ulcerous man who has made his ulcer into a world view. What's more, by all accounts, he is an obtuse man, loyal to his master like a blind man's guide dog.

For all these reasons, since the Cheka was created last January, Marinelli has jealously protected his role as its head, assigned to him by Mussolini and shared with Cesare Rossi. Incapable himself, he has become obsessed with the charge of command over men of action. And it is with this stolid, irascible, foolish retainer that the master vents his fury over Giacomo Matteotti's outrage:

"What's Dùmini doing, what's the Cheka doing?! It's unacceptable that after such a speech that man can still be walking around! *Boja de 'n Signur!*"

The schedule for the prime minister's appointments shows that, after an urgent meeting of the fascist directorate held at Palazzo Wedekind on June 1st, despite the fact that it's a Sunday, Benito Mussolini summons Giovanni Marinelli for a private talk in his office. The following day, June 2, 1924, he summons him again.

Italians have long been used to being deceived by everyone they placed their trust in; and now they'll be willing to believe only in someone who sheds his blood for them. Yes, for Italians to believe, they must see blood.

Giacomo Matteotti, early 1924

Deputy Matteotti gave an appallingly provocative speech that would have deserved something more tangible than the epithet "traitor" hurled by Deputy Giunta.

Il Popolo d'Italia, June 1, 1924

ROME, JUNE 7, 1924
MONTECITORIO, CHAMBER OF DEPUTIES

"ALL NIGHT LONG the victim, heinously murdered, lay there under the starry sky. The sun rose and climbed higher on the horizon and that little body remained motionless in its mangled nudity. The small innocent child lies with her head tilted to the left, her little arms clinging to the soil, her body naked, full of bruises: one tiny foot with its shoe on, the other shoeless. A clot of blood trickles out of the innocent half-open mouth."

The little girl had disappeared on June 4th, around 10:00 p.m., on Via del Gonfalone. Her name was Bianca Carlieri. The police searched for her unsuccessfully all night. Her raped body was found at 11:00 a.m. near the Basilica of St. Paul Outside the Walls.

Before noon, terror has already taken hold of the city with the sudden forcefulness of a cramp. Children are kept indoors, Rome's citizens call for justice. In Piazza Vittorio, a retired colonel, moved by the sight of his neighbors' daughter, barely escapes being mobbed by passersby. Rome has one million inhabitants. On June 6th, they are all at little Bianca's funeral, in body or in spirit.

This time, however, news of the crime against the little Roman girl appears in the national press. In its report, *Il Giornale d'Italia* uses the adjective "horrific" a good six times. The crime committed by the unknown perpetrator, christened "the monster of Rome," is a "horrific" crime. Its shadow already extends into lore. This time too, in fact, a tall, youthful, distinguished-looking man was spotted. *Il Corriere della Sera*, from Milan, sketches the elegant profile of "a man still young in appearance, dressed in gray." The man in the gray suit fills Italians' nights with new terror.

Under the political sky as well, a vaporous pestilence again weighs heavily on Rome. The violent reshufflings of the electoral battle, and Matteotti's harsh indictment, have stirred up the miasma of postwar hatred.

On June 3rd, in the hall of parliament, Roberto Farinacci shouts at Giovanni Amendola and the other opposition leaders: "We were wrong not to have you shot!" A few hours later, outside the chamber, the show of fascist solidarity ordered by Mussolini and organized by Cesare Rossi culminates in a manhunt. Socialist deputies are tracked down by hundreds of squadristi in the narrow streets of the neighborhood around Montecitorio.

Not at all frightened by this, as soon as he returns to the chamber the following day Matteotti again attacks the prime minister, censuring him for having granted amnesty to deserters in 1919. Compared to his usual pedantic nitpicking, he reduces him to silence with irony: "You certainly wouldn't want us to publish the complete critical edition of your works!" Another day goes by and on June 5th, at the meeting of the budget committee—a budget which the government, before the sovereign and the parliament, has declared to be balanced—Giacomo Matteotti, this man who reads a country's budget the way others read a novel, exposes the accounting ruse: his calculations show a staggering deficit of 2 billion 34 million liras. Each day the tension increasingly mounts. On June 6th, yet another furor erupts in the chamber between Mussolini and the extreme left groups. Enraged, the Duce vows to the communists that he will take an example from their Bolshevik idols: "In Russia you would have had lead in your backs! [Outbursts] But we have the guts for it and we'll prove it to you. [Applause, clamoring] There's still time!"

While the squadristi use clubs to vent their fury over the oppositions' criticism, a subtler, more toxic anxiety infects the fascist party leaders. It is rumored that Matteotti, during his trip to England, collected a dossier on the grave irregularities surrounding the oil concession to Sinclair Oil. The socialist deputy is said to be prepared to denounce them publicly during the parliamentary session on June 11th, scheduled to discuss the provisional budget. It seems he is in possession of documents that would be compromising for the regime and for the Mussolini family.

A telegram is sent to Washington from the ministry of the economy: information is requested regarding the alleged relations—publicly denied by the prime minister—between Sinclair Oil and Standard Oil. Please note that the information must arrive with the utmost urgency and under no circumstances later than June 10.

A cloud of rancors and fears obscures the sun, a malodorous mixture of oil by-products, relationships and bribes contaminates the soil. The regime's press attempts to attribute the miasma to the accusers. It crucifies Matteotti on a daily basis. His accusations are nothing but roaring, falsehoods, provocations—the fascist newspapers write—a jumble of excrement and secretions. In this drama of uneasy consciences, having reached this point, it doesn't even matter anymore that Matteotti has the compromising documents. What matters is the fear that they exist.

Things can't go on like this. Turati even writes as much to Anna Kuliscioff: "Too many of our people are tired of constantly clenching their fists, and ask for nothing more than a little relaxation, like the soldiers of our war, who sent bottles of wine from our trenches to the opposite trench, and vice versa." Turati feels his heart sink when he sees his comrades going around arm in arm with fascist deputies or joking with the ministers at the government benches. He views it as Matteotti does. The socialists are left with only one weapon: contempt. Implacable contempt. If that too were to be taken from them, they would be finished. Nevertheless, the leader of moderate socialism must recognize that this steady trickle cannot last. Matteotti's speech has left Mussolini with his back against the wall, the shady equivocation on which his government is based cannot continue. Now the prime minister is forced to choose: either the terror that Farinacci wants, or the indefinite adjournment of the chamber, until it's ultimately dissolved.

The most anxious of all is Mussolini himself. In the first year of his rule he has lived—and made his collaborators live—in a state of permanent alarm. The halfway solution of the march on Rome, the compromise with the old powers, the coalition government, the fascist minority in parliament have kept him in a constant state of instability and irritability. Now, the overwhelming political victory in the April 6 elections seemed to have cleared the field, freshened the air. And instead, the miasma again. When the prime minister takes the floor on June 7th to reply to the oppositions in the chamber, everyone expects an angry outburst of his violent temper.

Surprisingly, however, Benito Mussolini dons the brightly colored coat of the seducer and puts his best face forward. He gives one of his most brilliant, moderate, conciliatory speeches. No exceptional laws, no abuse of parliament, recognition of the educational role that the opposition could have. The register of his words is light, the tone joking, the feeling affable. The Duce appears serene again, ruler of the game, he speaks as if he had completely forgotten the Matteotti episode, as if the week of frenetic orgy that just passed were destined to remain the last.

Yet Mussolini's speech also resounds through Montecitorio's semicircular hall as candid, realistic, and coherent. He addresses the socialists directly. He speaks to them conversationally, not as enemies. With one hand he nails them to their responsibilities, urging them to examine their consciences: "We can't always absent ourselves, we can't always remain divided, we must say or do something, good or bad, there must be collaboration, positive or negative, otherwise we are condemned to being perpetually exiled from history." However, he offers them the other hand: for twenty months the opposition has been mired in a repetition of old, sterile polemics, cloudy protests, but perhaps, to be optimistic, it is possible to glimpse some sign of overcoming long-standing, aprioristic, negative positions. We'll talk again. Past rancors do not matter.

The Duce of fascism has barely concluded his conciliatory speech of June 7, 1924, when word already spreads: Mussolini wants to bring the socialists into his government. After all, he always wanted to be able to embrace his old comrades again. It seems he had tried before, in November 1922, after the March on Rome. At that time he failed. Perhaps he will succeed now, in June 1924. In the corridors of Montecitorio, people can breathe again.

Waiting anxiously if my presence urgently needed. Albino

Telegram sent by Albino Volpi in Milan
to Amerigo Dùmini in Rome, June 7, 1924

Please leave immediately stop Your presence needed to draft publicity contract stop Bring Panzeri and skilled chauffeur with you stop Regards. Gino D'Ambrogio

Cablegram sent by Dùmini (under a pseudonym)
to Albino Volpi, June 8, 1924, 1:00 p.m.

AMERIGO DÙMINI

ROME, JUNE 10, 1924

FOR AT LEAST an hour Giuseppe Viola has been writhing in the back seat like a woman in labor. He complains of searing spasms at the mouth of his stomach—"like being knifed," he says—and begs them to take him to the nearest pharmacy right away, in Piazza del Popolo. Around 4:00 p.m., Viola finally delivers a bloody vomit—dark and bloody—on the car's upholstery. The bolus of murky, grainy undigested food looks like coffee grounds. No one dares to read the future in it. Seen from there, the future would not be pretty.

Now the air in the Lancia Lambda has become truly unbreathable. The closed, limousine-type model, six seats, two exterior and four interior, two fixed and two movable, is so spacious that a sliding glass divides the passenger compartment from the driver's seat. Yet you can't breathe. For two hours, five corpulent adult males, stirred up and sated, bloated with food, engorged with wine and testosterone, have been burning up the oxygen of that confined space, breathing open-mouthed due to slow digestion, and blowing cigarette smoke from their tarred lungs. The car's compartment is heavy with burping, flatulence, and war recollections.

From the navigator's seat Amerigo Dùmini, the leader of the expedition, has forbidden any air exchange with the external heat of the early summer that has descended on Rome and on the world. The windows are raised, the blackout curtains lowered. No one must spot them boxed in there, they mustn't leave any witnesses.

Consequently, the mitigating influence of the silty river flowing alongside remains a mirage. The heavy sheet-metal auto body, hammered by the afternoon sun, is an asphyxiating bubble parked at the corner between Via Scialoja and Lungotevere Arnaldo da Brescia. From there, they are standing watch over the door of Via Giuseppe Pisanelli 40, where the target lives with his wife and three children.

The five men cooped up in the latest model from Vincenzo Lancia's car factory know how to wait. Long waits, before battle or before time in the prison yard, are part of their apprenticeship to life. The five men lying in wait in the Lancia Lambda—Amerigo Dùmini, Giuseppe Viola, Albino Volpi, Augusto Malacria, Amleto Poveromo—are all ex-Arditi and previous offenders for non-political crimes. They've all been in the trenches and they've all been incarcerated. Now that Viola has spit up his ulcerous blood and stopped moaning, they can light up yet another cigarette, dazed by the heat, wine and smoke, and resume reminiscing about when they spent nights along the banks of the Piave among the corpses of fellow soldiers, or on the lice-infested cots of the San Vittore penitentiary. The wait can't be much longer now.

Giacomo Matteotti is a methodical man; they've been surveilling him for days, they've studied his habits. When there's a chamber session, he leaves at 9:00 a.m., returns at 1:30, lunches, goes out again around 3:00 and doesn't return home before 9:00 p.m. Now that parliament is not in session, after lunch he regularly leaves around 4:30 to work at the library of the budget committee, taking tram number 15 from Piazza del Popolo. Always with that white envelope labeled "Chamber of Deputies" under his arm, the envelope they must take from him.

"Don't come back without that envelope," Giuseppe Marinelli, the party's treasurer, ordered them.

Amerigo Dùmini does not intend to disappoint him. Despite being a lousy skinflint—everyone knows this—Marinelli has been financing the good life for the entire crew since May 22, when they assembled at the Hotel Dragoni after registering with false names. For ten days they've had to do nothing but eat, drink and fuck at the party's expense. At lunch and dinner they usually settled in at Brecche's, or Al Buco, both offering Tuscan cuisine and as many flasks of Chianti as they wanted. Then they idled away the time until dawn in a lounge at Villa Borghese. One evening, the police broke in and nabbed Viola with a revolver. But Dùmini immediately had him released by Cavalier Laino, chief of staff at police headquarters. The good life came to an end in early June when Marinelli summoned Dùmini, telling him that the time had come.

At first they'd thought of doing it during a trip abroad. The police had issued a passport to Matteotti for that very reason. But chance had interfered: the train that was supposed to take the socialist deputy to Austria was the same train that Marinelli himself was to board to go to Milan. When he'd seen the whole gang on the train platform, he nearly had a stroke: "Don't even think of taking him now that I'm here!" he'd shouted at them, livid with rage. In any case, there was no sign of Matteotti.

So they decided to pick him up when he left his house. Filippelli, the editor of *Corriere Italiano*, former personal secretary to Arnaldo Mussolini, rented them the Lancia Lambda from a public garage. A car rental without a driver. The night before they parked it in the courtyard of Palazzo Chigi. Dùmini assured the carabinieri on guard duty that it was to be used for an important government mission. Everyone there knows him. They know that he works for the prime minister's press office. Then he had to telegraph Volpi, who meanwhile had returned to Milan, insisting that he return to Rome at once and bring some of his men. Volpi didn't need to be asked twice. They met in the Galleria Colonna for an aperitif, then went to lunch at Al Buco, and afterward Viola had started in about his duodenal ulcer.

Dùmini glances at the upholstery soiled by Viola's bloody vomit. He will have to have it cleaned before returning it to Filippelli. That guy is the type who notices every little thing.

His pocket watch reads 4:40. It's a silver Roskopf that keeps perfect time. Dùmini likes to say that he inherited it from a distant cousin who was a stationmaster.

The door of Via Giuseppe Pisanelli 40 opens. Instinctively, the waiting men lean forward, stretch their muscles, and buckle up their belts. For a moment they are taken aback: Matteotti is not wearing a hat. Something odd must have happened: for a respectable man to be properly dressed, even with that heat, going out into the street bareheaded is inconceivable. The socialist deputy has on a light-colored suit, white suede shoes and a matching tie. He is clasping the envelope under his arm. All according to script, except for the hat.

The second unforeseen twist of the day immediately forces them to improvise. Contrary to his habits, Matteotti, emerging from Via Mancini, crosses the Lungotevere and starts walking along the river. Perhaps he wants to take a look at the flow where, in his rare moments of relaxation, he likes to row against the current. But there are people on that side of the street: a carabiniere standing in the shade of a plane tree near Villino Almagià, several swimmers sunbathing on the stone steps leading down to the river, a street sweeper busy cleaning the pavement, and two little boys playing leapfrog and singing a tune as they run towards Matteotti.

Dùmini orders Viola to start the engine and stay in the car with him. The Lancia Lambda glides along the Lungotevere, passes the hatless man walking beside the river with a white envelope under his arm, then brakes and stops, as the doors open on both sides.

The first to put his hands on the deputy is Malacria, convicted of fraudulent bankruptcy, a former captain of the Arditi, son of Nestore, a valiant general. Albino Volpi, strangely reluctant, merely points the target out to his buddy.

The third surprise of the day is that Matteotti, yanked at, reacts. Malacria stumbles, falls to the ground. Volpi then leaps in but Matteotti, thin and agile, struggles with him as well.

Amleto Poveromo, a butcher in Lecco, moves behind them with his heavy step. He lands a single blow at Matteotti's temple, the sledgehammer to the skull with which he slaughtered animals at one time. Matteotti slumps.

Dùmini meanwhile has joined them. Four of them lift the inert body, one for each limb. The fourth unexpected turn of the day: the victim's resistance. Matteotti comes to and once more begins struggling. His captors start beating him again as they carry him. But he kicks like a madman. Where does he find the strength? Maybe the memory of the earlier abduction keeps him going, the time in the Veneto, his region, when, so they say, he had a club forced up his anus.

Finally they're in the car, the limo starts off, swerves, takes the Ponte Milvio, the bridge dear to lovers, and heads northeast at top speed towards the countryside, outside the city limits, the horn blaring to cover the screams of the kidnapped victim, like the siren of a fire engine racing to put out a fire.

Not even in the car, not even under the blows of three attackers, not even then does Giacomo Matteotti stop fighting. He resists. To the bitter end. With a kick he shatters the glass divider that separates the car's passenger compartment from the driver's seat. Dùmini, who is sitting up front and keeps turning around nervously, is hit right in the chest by glass shards. It wasn't supposed to go like this, resistance was not expected.

Matteotti, battered and beaten, does not stop yelling. Dùmini, turning again, leans over to silence him. The driver is forced to sound the horn again. The victim's shrieks destroy the indolence of an early summer afternoon.

Then, abruptly, the writhing ceases. The screams stop. Replaced by a gurgling, a strangled rattle.

Dùmini twists around again.

Giacomo Matteotti is white as a sheet, a bloody vomit spewing from his mouth. Albino Volpi is holding him close, his left arm around the deputy's shoulders, as if he were hugging a woman. His right hand, concealed by the folds of the light-colored jacket, plunges into the victim's side.

It was half past four. I was playing with my friends. Close by was a car that had stopped right in front of Via Antonio Scialoja. Five men got out and started walking up and down. All of a sudden I saw Matteotti come out. One of the men went over to him and punched him hard, knocking him to the ground. Matteotti called for help. Then the other four came over, and one of them hit him hard in the face. Then they picked him up by the head and feet and carried him into the car that then drove past us. So we could see that Matteotti was struggling. We didn't see anything else after that.

Renato Barzotti, known as "Neroncino," ten years old,
an eyewitness to Matteotti's abduction

ONE HUNDRED TERRIBLE HOURS

ROME, WEDNESDAY JUNE 11

"ALL RIGHT, I'LL take care of it. You, meanwhile, don't go broadcasting it."

Arturo Benedetto Fasciolo, private secretary, typist and personal stenographer of Benito Mussolini at Palazzo Chigi, is standing in front of his desk. On the mahogany desktop, halfway between the two men, one standing and the other seated, lies a wallet encrusted with dried blood. With a jerk of his arm, Mussolini takes possession of it. Still sitting, he grabs it, opens a desk drawer and tosses it in. He now knows everything. It's nine in the morning and the die is cast.

On his way home, the previous evening, Fasciolo spotted Albino Volpi in the Galleria Colonna, at the Picarozzi bar, the usual haunt for Roman night owls. The former Ardito joined him, told him everything, and handed him the wallet.

Now, coming out of the Duce's office, Fasciolo runs into Cesare Rossi. The Duce committed him to silence but for the stenographer, shaken, it's impossible to respect the instructions. As soon as he finds out, Rossi goes to look for Marinelli. The conversation between the two is heated. Marinelli, assailed by the fury of his de facto accomplice, tries to soothe him: "Calm down. It had to be done. Now don't get the Duce all riled up with your alarmism." Rossi rushes over to *Il Giornale d'Italia* and bursts into the editor's office. Filippo Filippelli, he who always stands aside from everything, who is inured to everything, who notices every little detail, feigns the nonchalance of a man of the world: the Lancia Lambda is well hidden in the garage of one of his managing editors. It's just a little soiled: Matteotti must have had a "bowel release," the man of the world adds with a smirk. Dùmini will be ordered to clean it up. Shortly afterwards, around lunchtime, the members of the gang meet with Marinelli at the Hotel Dragoni. The treasurer gives them 20,000 liras for the escape and instruction to leave the city after cleaning up the car. Before dark a somber criminal thread binds the men of state busily cleaning up blood and shit.

Velia Matteotti, who spent a sleepless night waiting for her husband, notified party comrades of his disappearance in the morning. An involuntary spasm of anxiety contracts the muscles of their thighs, beneath the skin. In the afternoon, Filippo Turati informs Anna Kuliscioff. He admits to feeling "horrific grief over Matteotti's fate," but says he is still unable to believe in a crime planned by the government. It seems unlikely to him. For this reason he hesitates to rush to the police commissioner. The risk is that of casting "a wave of ridicule" over everyone.

In the evening, when Rossi confronts the prime minister, Mussolini, according to his testimony, is said to have parried behind a sarcastic remark that, in a kind of perverse identification with the victim, attributes to him a page from the Duce's own reputation: "The socialists are uneasy in Montecitorio because since yesterday they haven't heard anything about their Matteotti. He must be with some whores . . ."

THURSDAY JUNE 12

THE NEWS SPREADS immediately after lunch. Rodolfo de Bernart, police commissioner for the Flaminio district, questioned the two custodians, husband and wife, of the building on Via Stanislao Mancini 12, adjacent to Matteotti's house, who, on the evening of June 9, the eve of the abduction, became suspicious of the Lancia Lambda that was patrolling the streets of the neighborhood. Fearing a round of burglaries, they recorded the license plate number.

Ingenuously dedicated to duty, De Bernart hastens to transmit the news to police headquarters. In a flash the news passes to De Bono and he conveys it to Mussolini.

"These guys actually rented a car from a public garage! Holy Mother of God! They could have at least pissed on the license plate, so the road dust would have covered it."

Cesare Rossi, having obtained a special appointment with the Duce after the afternoon newspapers begin hammering at the news, sees his face marked by consternation for the first time.

Benedetto Fasciolo, who meets with him shortly afterwards, reports the same impression. The previous morning he'd delivered Matteotti's wallet to him, now he presents him with his passport, received directly from Dùmini:

"Why did you take this?!" Mussolini protests. "By now all of Rome must know."

Nonetheless, Mussolini grabs the passport the way he had the wallet the day before and stashes it in the same drawer.

"I'll take care of it now."

Before dismissing Fasciolo, he inquires about the burial. He wants to know everything: the location, size and covering of the grave.

At 7:30 p.m. the prime minister confronts the parliament. He is received by the outrage and terror of men who now realize that one of them, a fellow colleague of theirs, can be attacked and abducted in broad daylight in the center of the Kingdom's capital. Mussolini shares their sentiment: the circumstances of the abduction indicate "the suggestion of a crime"—he declares—a crime that could not fail to arouse "the emotion and indignation of the government and of parliament."

Then, in front of 500 representatives of the people and the solemnity of the tragedy, Benito Mussolini lies shamelessly: "The police, in its swift investigations, are already on the trail of suspicious elements, and will overlook nothing that might shed light on the event in order to arrest the perpetrators and bring them to justice. My hope is that Deputy Matteotti will soon be able to return to parliament." At this very moment, the head of government knows the location, size and covering of the grave that holds the stabbed corpse of the man whom he hopes to see again soon. A blasphemy against the only deity who will not forgive him, the god of the dead.

The oppositions aren't satisfied either. The socialists declare that it is inconceivable that such an event could be dismissed in this way. Deputy Eugenio Chiesa, Republican, demands further explanations from Mussolini. Mussolini, however, remains seated at the government desk, motionless, his arms folded across his chest.

"Then he is complicit!"

The comment, which slipped out instinctively but which was spoken aloud, resounds in the silent chamber. Now that the word has been spoken, suspicion rises a notch on the scale of possibility.

As if wanting to lower it again by bringing down the man who uttered it, Giuseppe Bottai overturns the chair he's sitting on and leaps at Chiesa. A scuffle breaks out. President Rocco rings his bell hopelessly.

A few hours later, Amerigo Dùmini is arrested at Termini station while trying to flee up north. De Bono, chief of police, in defiance of every arrest protocol, drags him to a private meeting at the commissioner's office and has him hand over the suitcase packed with the victim's bloodied clothes:

"You must deny everything, deny everything. This is about saving fascism."

Amerigo Dùmini becomes prisoner 780/GSI (high surveillance and isolation) at Regina Coeli prison. For the time being he is the only one to pay for the crime, but he is promised an early release. Certain of impunity, he agrees. The other members of the gang are all still at large.

Meanwhile the Grand Council of Fascism, urgently convened, meets at Palazzo Wedekind. When the meeting adjourns, Rossi, Marinelli and Finzi gather secretly in De Bono's office at the Directorate-General of Public Security.

Rossi goes immediately on the attack: what's happening is crazy, they have to get out from under this cloud of suspicion, Dùmini's arrest is a dangerous charade. Marinelli justifies his actions of the previous days, pointing to intense pressure exerted from above since early June to liquidate Matteotti.

Irritated by the whining, Rossi comes out with it:

"Go ahead and arrest Dùmini and all the others, but do it as a pretense. Keep them locked up a few days, then let them go."

"Why?" De Bono asks, as if he didn't know.

"Because otherwise they'll squeal and say it was him who gave them the idea."

"Him? Who?"

"The prime minister."

Left alone in his office at the Ministry of the Interior, the police commissioner, one of the quadrumvirs of the march on Rome, an old general of the royal army, telephones the Duce of fascism from a private line:

"They're dumping the blame on you."

"Those gutless cowards want to blackmail me!" Mussolini yells. Then the line goes dead. A haunted night begins.

FRIDAY JUNE 13

RUMOR HAS IT that Dùmini castrated Matteotti's corpse and delivered the testicles to Filippelli, who fainted, horrified. Rumor has it that he delivered them directly to Mussolini instead who, laughing scornfully, tossed the trophy into a desk drawer with the passport. Rumor has it that the body was brought back to Rome, concealed in a hay wagon, and burned in an oven; rumor has it that it was thrown into the Tiber, that it was stripped of its flesh with acids and displayed in an anatomy studio, that it was made into soap, or sunk in Lake Vico. Yet another rumor has it that the socialist deputy's body was fed to the lions at the Villa Borghese zoo.

In the collective imagination, the fanciful imaginings about

Matteotti's disappearance have risen to the rank just recently occupied by the crime of the little girl raped and killed at St. Paul Outside the Walls by the mysterious "man in the gray suit."

The news of the abduction of a parliamentarian, in broad daylight, in the streets of the city center, violently shattered day-to-day life. The outrage is universal, voices of protest are raised everywhere, even among the fascists themselves; the opposition newspapers print one special edition after the other, yet readers remain avid for justice, their desire for revenge unsatisfied. The likely crime appears so perverse and odious as to shake up the entire system. Manifest corruption, the use of violence to eliminate political rivals, and the corrosion of ideals have suddenly become intolerable to everyone. Recriminations, disgust, threats, saber-rattling, wailing, remorse, a communal wringing of hands and generalized hair-tearing. All of a sudden that's all you hear and all you see, no matter where you turn. The abstract idea of Evil, bewildered, solidifies like a cast of rapid-setting cement around the figures of Amerigo Dùmini and his accomplices, unknown or on the run.

In the fascist camp it's "every man for himself." Another meeting of the Grand Council was held in the morning: it was "all against all." Defensive memos are prepared, Balbo rushes to Palazzo Chigi to demand "the immediate shooting of Dùmini," and the concealment of evidence begins, along with the dissemination of misleading clues, the wiping of traces, and diversionary smokescreen operations. The mud-slinging machine deliberately spreads false news, leading people to think that Matteotti has fled abroad, that he is holed up with a lover, that a few days earlier two killers from France's extreme right showed up in Rome, that a group of squadristi from Rovigo were on the deputy's trail.

The recoil of false news ricochets against the slanderers: Aldo Finzi, a fascist deputy from Rovigo, falls into the pit of suspects.

At 4:00 p.m. the prime minister goes to address parliament again but this time the chamber is all but empty. Though 370 fascist deputies sit dutifully at their benches, they are not enough to fill the crater left by the oppositions who decided to desert the hall in protest; they are not enough to fill the chasm opened by the presence of Velia Matteotti sitting up there in the gallery.

Mussolini promises to punish the perpetrators, condemns the abomination, he says he is moved, saddened, he says he is even prepared to enact "summary justice" if only he is asked. Then he protests that a crime so absurd, so injurious, has been committed against the core of the fascist revolution, rather than against the oppositions, leaving it deeply affected as a result:

"Only an enemy who for long nights had thought of something so diabolical," he exclaims vehemently, "could carry out the crime that today strikes horror into us and wrests cries of outrage from us."

Benito Mussolini asks that a single sheet cover the dead, all the dead, so that the dead may sleep without rancor. Then he declares parliament's summer session adjourned ahead of time and revises its reopening to a date to be determined.

The terrible day of June 13, the feast of Saint Anthony of Padua, is not over yet, however: Velia Matteotti has asked to meet with the prime minister. She showed up at the chamber that morning to beseech a couple of socialist deputies to accompany her to see Mussolini. Turati tried to dissuade her in every way possible, but she did not give in to his entreaties.

In the version reported by the regime's press, Benito Mussolini along with deputies Acerbo and Sardi receives the "poor woman" standing in the doorway of a room in Palazzo Chigi. As soon as Mrs. Matteotti crosses the threshold, he snaps to attention. When she bursts into sobs, he is moved, and consoles her firmly: "Signora, I want to return your husband to you alive. The government will do its duty exhaustively. We don't know anything positive, but there is still some hope."

Attorney Casimiro Wronowski, Matteotti's brother-in-law, describes a different scene. Velia, whom everyone already refers to as "the Widow Matteotti," accompanied by her sister Nella, waits, standing, in the anteroom for a clerk to inform the head of government of her presence.

Mussolini receives Velia Matteotti standing in this second version as well, but backed, virtually supported, by undersecretaries Acerbo, Sardi and Finzi.

Two women and four men face each other. Mussolini is shaking, Finzi hides his face with one hand. Velia asks that her husband, if alive, be allowed to return home and, if dead, that his remains be returned to her for Christian burial. Mussolini, stammering like someone searching for words, replies:

"I know nothing, signora; if I knew, I would return your husband to you, alive or dead."

SATURDAY JUNE 14

"MAY THOSE WHO should drown, drown to the last."

The words printed in *Il Popolo d'Italia* summarize the hopes and certainties of all the oppositions. Certainty of the ineluctable, and hope of being spared.

A wave of disdain and emotion is washing over fascism, a whirlpool of grumbling is sucking him to the bottom. Little by little, as details of the crime emerge and compromise the men in government, the newspapers run riot with scandalous revelations about their misdeeds of every kind: Aldo Finzi's trafficking in construction sites purchased at bargain prices with enormous profits, Michele Bianchi's shameless speculations on illegal emigration, and so on. The group photo that appears of the men surrounding Mussolini is that of a court of the Low Empire.

By contrast, the figure of Giacomo Matteotti ascends to the glory of a saint. His house on Via Giuseppe Pisanelli has already become a pilgrimage destination, hundreds of flower wreaths pile up at the site of the kidnapping, a kind of open-air mausoleum. The police step in to disperse the procession of the faithful on the Lungotevere, mounted carabinieri sweep away the flowers and break up the crowds.

"For now nothing can be done. Those guys completely fucked up. I'm powerless. De Bono is good for nothing. There's too much bad blood boiling over."

Those are the last words that Cesare Rossi hears an ashen Mussolini speak before the rupture occurs. The Duce appears stunned, dazed by the bombshell, paralyzed by the letdown. Giovanni Marinelli has just confessed that, five days after the abduction, he still has the formally signed receipts of the payments made to the killers before and after the crime. The treasurer of the Fascist Party justifies himself with the scrupulousness of a good administrator who files cash advances in perfect order. Then he buries his face in his hands and runs to destroy the proofs.

Mussolini shakes his head, and turns a glassy stare at a ghost on the horizon: he had always dreamed, preached, the historical necessity of surgical violence, of precise, exacting, inexorable savagery, and instead he finds himself with his hands smeared with feces and blood, a bestial crime.

If the chain of responsibility isn't broken, it will soon reach him. And so he breaks it, sacrificing his closest collaborators: Benito Mussolini asks for the resignation of Aldo Finzi and Cesare Rossi.

Aldo Finzi agrees, taken in by the promise that his self-sacrifice will be rewarded very soon with the interior ministry, as he is told. Cesare Rossi, on the other hand, reacts with a violent outburst: he protests his complete innocence, he declares that he must defend his honor, to his friends he calls Mussolini a madman. Rossi writes an official, sober letter of resignation, when finished, however, he delivers another confidential letter that is openly threatening. After sending the two letters, he goes into hiding.

Mussolini tries to pull himself together by playing the role of a head of state. He receives a visit from negus Haile Selassie, the emperor. But the statesmanlike behavior is of no use. *Il becco giallo*, a satirical magazine edited by Alberto Giannini, a brilliant journalist who had been clubbed by Dùmini and who for that reason had bravely challenged him to a duel, prints a toxic cartoon. In it the king of Ethiopia appears perched like a vulture on the shoulders of De Bono, the fascist police chief. He whispers in his ear with a conspiratorial look:

"You can tell me the truth: you ate him."

SUNDAY JUNE 15

SUDDENLY THERE IS a vacuum around Benito Mussolini. The orders to mobilize the militia that was supposed to defend the regime with drawn swords were just about ignored: in Rome only 40 percent of the soldiers responded, in Milan 20 percent, in Turin not a one. In Rome, on Corso Umberto, beneath the windows of Palazzo Chigi where the prime minister has barricaded himself in his office, pedestrians walk by swiftly, frightened, clearly taking pains not to look up at that balcony. In Milan, when news of Albino Volpi's arrest is brought to Giuseppe Viola, he declares to the friends who are still hiding him that if questioned in a trial he would want to speak only with Mussolini: "And then I'll throw myself at him and bite off a piece of his nose!"

No one knows his master's solitude better than a valet. Quinto Navarra met Benito Mussolini for the first time in Cannes in 1920, when he was in the service of His Excellency the Marquis Della Torretta, foreign minister at the time. On that occasion an unknown journalist had introduced himself, eager to interview the minister, and had handed him a calling card: "Benito Mussolini." Afterwards he had not seen him again until 1:00 p.m. on October 31st, 1922, at the Palazzo della Consulta, when Mussolini had by then become head of the government.

Since that day, Quinto Navarra has guarded the president's antechamber, as though living in a glass bell jar, and there he's seen Italy file past at his feet. For twenty months the faithful servant has heard his master's voice thunder from behind the closed door and seen ministers, generals, industrialists, squadristi and marquises come out with their heads bowed. One day Mussolini, in the mood to confide, told him:

"I'm sure if I slept all day, the Italians wouldn't ask for anything more. All they'd need to know is that I exist and that I might wake up at any moment. Admiration and fear are always somewhat related."

But now everything has changed, now only fear remains. In the last hundred hours it's been quiet as a tomb inside Palazzo Chigi. People in the streets took off their fascist badges and those in the ministry were doing the same. The gleaming rooms, which until a few days ago were teeming with obsequious individuals, gradually emptied out. Then this morning the antechamber was completely empty. If an avenger of Matteotti were to come up from the piazza with guns blazing, he'd find no one to stop him.

Tonight they are waiting for the king to return to the capital; the nation and Mussolini are once again in his hands. The Duce waits alone, in silence, in the Hall of Victories.

Quinto Navarra doesn't know what to do. He too remains alone, sitting in his place in the anteroom, resisting the temptation to flee, anxious and uncertain, forcing himself to observe the most absolute restraint. But the president hasn't called on him for hours, hasn't asked him to carry out any of his usual tasks or announce any visitors. On the other hand, there are no visitors.

Suddenly Navarra is summoned by the secretary to the presidency with an urgent dispatch for Mussolini. In these cases, protocol allows him to enter the master's room even without having been sent for.

Practically holding his breath, Quinto Navarra decides to open the door to the Hall of Victories. Inside the room, he sees something that he will never forget.

Benito Mussolini is sitting in his chair at his work table, a chair with a very high back, braced on both sides by two gilded wood uprights. At the precise moment when Quinto Navarra opens the door, Benito Mussolini, his eyes wide open, puffing and panting, is banging his bald skull right and left on the gilded uprights, like a rusty metronome inexorably beating time to mark its end.

The motive of the crime should not be sought in political reasons alone, but in the need to silence Deputy Matteotti who was determined to raise a scandal involving financial groups and their dealings with politicians.

Epifanio Pennetta, chief of the judicial police
during the preliminary inquiry at
the Matteotti trial, June 1924

Representing the widow and the Matteotti family I was present at the opening of Matteotti's desk drawer in the Chamber of Deputies, but all it contained was some paper with the chamber's letterhead . . . I then searched his house as well, I went through the drawers one by one. The only thing I found was a certain number of pages with large sums, subtractions, multiplications, and divisions noted on them. It was clear that they were all operations done to scrutinize the state budget. I found nothing more, which is why the story about compromising documents does not exist.

Casimiro Wronowski,
Giacomo Matteotti's brother-in-law

Mr. President,
From a series of indications and circumspect reports, I have the impression that you have chosen me and only me to be the scapegoat for the calamity that has struck fascism . . .

Well then, certain things require two people to agree to them.

I absolutely do not agree to go along with it . . . To come to the point: if I do not have proof, within a few days, of your awareness of the duties of solidarity not so much towards my person, towards my past, not so much towards my role as your collaborator and executor, at times of illegal actions ordered by you, but above all towards the elementary absence of reasons of state, I will carry out what I stated to you this morning and which during the day I have finalized . . .

And I don't need to warn you that if the cynicism which you have given terrifying proof of to date, complicated by the confusion that has affected you just when you should have controlled the situations created exclusively by you, were to lead you to order acts of physical suppression while I am in hiding, and in the unfortunate eventuality of my capture, you would be a destroyed man all the same and with you, unfortunately, the regime, because my long, detailed, documented statement is already, of course, in the hands of trusted friends who truly practice the duties of friendship.

Confidential letter from Cesare Rossi
to Benito Mussolini,
June 15, 1924

AT ANY COST

JUNE 16–26, 1924

A KING IS NOT a pig fattening, as Napoleon claimed. A constitutional monarch must know what is happening in his country. If a criminal prime minister, disapproved of by the majority of his subjects, sinks that country into shame, the sovereign, relying on the loyalty of the army, has a duty to put an end to the felonious regime by forcing the head of government to resign.

That is the gist of the message that Giovanni Amendola, on behalf of all the constitutional opposition groups, sent to Vittorio Emanuele III through the Count of Campello, his gentleman-in-waiting.

Vittorio Emanuele III, back from Spain, orders the Count of Campello to thank Giovanni Amendola for his staunch frankness. Then, on June 16th, he meets with Benito Mussolini, urges conciliation among political forces, upholds the need for a government reshuffling, and presses him to continue on the path of "normalization." In essence, despite the widespread outrage, the king of Italy, in continuing to respect the constitutional charter from a strictly formal point of view, reconfirms his confidence in the head of the government. Benito Mussolini rallies. The counteroffensive begins.

That same day, Mussolini convenes the Council of Ministers and obtains approval for his initiatives. To begin with, as a demonstration of his moderating goodwill, he takes a step back: he relinquishes the interior ministry in favor of Luigi Federzoni, a nationalist leader esteemed by conformist right-wingers. Then he dismisses Emilio De Bono, who proved inept and was implicated. He replaces him as police commissioner with Crispo Moncada, prefect of Trieste. Then, before the day is over, he summons Aldo Finzi to urge him yet again to reconsider.

After his initial assent to the request that he resign, feeling trapped, Finzi in fact contacted the *Corriere della Sera* threatening revelations: the hero of the flight to Vienna was willing to give everything for his country but not his honor. The mastermind of the crime was one man only, Benito Mussolini from Predappio.

An hour later, however, when the former interior secretary leaves the June 16 meeting with Benito from Predappio, he gives the impression of a terrified man. Finzi appears pale, agitated, and says he regrets his move towards the oppositions. The Duce has promised him that, as soon as he becomes arbiter of the situation, he will reinstate him in office. Then he dismissed him with:

"So long, Aldo, we understand each other." The words "we understand each other" have thrown the pilot's mind into a tailspin.

In the days that follow, Mussolini continues the counteroffensive. He orders the prefects of many of the provincial capitals to organize fascist rallies in support of the government. The prefects obey. In the piazzas, clubs are brandished again. Tullio Tamburini, the "great *bastonatore*," having come down to Rome from Florence leading the militia's 92nd legion, the so-called "Iron Legion," marches it through the streets of the center in battle formation. The most enthusiastic support, however, comes once again from the Po Valley and from Leandro Arpinati. Despite being bedridden as a result of a car accident, the ras of Bologna, loyal as ever, by June 19 has already assembled thousands of squadristi and three days later, on June 22nd, brings fifty thousand blackshirts from all over Emilia to the streets.

Justice, however, also follows its course. After escaping arrest, Albino Volpi is finally stopped at a hotel restaurant in Bellagio while having lunch before crossing the Swiss border. Filippelli, the editor of the *Corriere Italiano* who rented the car used for the crime, after a few days of brazen impunity, is intercepted by the coast guard aboard a motorboat headed for French shores. In the following hours, almost all the accused fall into the net, one after the other: Giuseppe Viola and Amleto Poveromo are arrested in Milan, Cesare Rossi, with no hope of continuing to run, turns himself in at Rome police headquarters on June 22nd. Finally it's Giovanni Marinelli's turn, indicted by various testimonies and by a telephone call on May 31st to the warden of Naples' Poggioreale prison in which he demanded the immediate release of one of the gang's men for a government mission. Marinelli, loyal as ever, retreats into absolute silence. Amerigo Dùmini, meanwhile, in the Regina Coeli prison—despite the fact that bits of upholstery and bloody clothing were found in his suitcase, along with the murder weapon and visiting cards reading "Press Office, Ministry of the Interior"—also continues to deny any involvement on the part of the fascist leaders and any murderous intention: Giacomo Matteotti, according to Dùmini, supposedly died accidentally during the scuffle, suffocated by his tuberculosis when a rush of blood was expelled from his lungs.

On the strength of all this, on June 24th, the head of government appears before the packed hall where the senators of the Kingdom are seated. He gives a moderate, skillful speech, its tone even-tempered and its register measured. Mussolini once again presents himself as a man of order dedicated to quelling all violence.

On June 25th he meets in private with Arturo Benedetto Fasciolo, his docile personal stenographer. Forced by Albino Volpi into being the messenger of the atrocity, it was Fasciolo who first informed Mussolini of the crime, and later, pressed by Dùmini into the role of errand boy, delivered the victim's macabre remains to him. Mussolini asks Fasciolo for his resignation as well. He demands loyalty and sacrifice from him also. He promises recompense to him too:

"If I save myself, I save everyone. Don't worry. The more confusion there is, the better."

On June 26th, the government obtains the Senate's vote of confidence with a large majority: 225 in favor, 21 against and 6 abstentions.

"A very important vote," Mussolini writes in his notes, "I would venture to say decisive. The Senate, at a difficult time, in the midst of a political and moral tempest, aligns almost unanimously with the government."

Mussolini is not the only one to sigh with relief over the senators' vote that saves him. Benedetto Croce, leading exponent of liberal thought, issues an interview in which he explains the reasons for his choice. After noting some criticisms, admitting a few regrets, and expressing some nostalgia for the good old days, the great liberal philosopher reiterates his decision to support fascism. Fascism, he says, is not an infatuation or a game, fascism has responded to serious needs and has done much good. Its benefits must not be allowed to dissipate and revert back to the slack inconclusiveness that preceded it. Fascism came to power amid the applause and consent of the nation, now its best exponents have the opportunity to confirm "the strong, healthy political element of which they are the bearers." The heart of fascism, Croce proclaims, is love of the Italian homeland, devotion to its salvation.

From the courts of Cremona, echoing the words of the distinguished Neapolitan professor, attorney Roberto Farinacci—who, it is well known, after having bought his high school diploma, got his law degree by force, by copying the dissertation of another candidate line per line—agrees, on Mussolini's suggestion, to join the team for the defense of Amerigo Dùmini, Giacomo Matteotti's killer. Only ten days earlier, the same proposal had met with his refusal. Now the regime is jumping in to defend the murderers.

To the prefects of: Alessandria, Mantua, Florence, Bologna, Piacenza, Treviso, Carrara, Perugia, Sulmona, Foggia, Catanzaro, Cagliari.

The crime against Matteotti, which was staunchly deplored by the entire party, has been appropriated by the oppositions as the pretext they were looking for to attack the government. We are faced with some kind of united antifascist front.

For the evening of Monday or Tuesday, order a rally of city and provincial fascists to be held in the town piazza, to solemnly reaffirm their confidence in the Government and in Fascism. MUSSOLINI.

Benito Mussolini, telegram to
the prefectures, June 16, 1924

The overall objective of my government policy remains unchanged: to achieve—at any cost, in compliance with the laws—political normality and national reconciliation, to screen and purge the party with untiring day-to-day vigilance, and to crush, with the utmost vigor, the last residues of an obsolete and ruinous illegalist conception . . . Let there be light and justice! Let the rule of law be ever more affirmed!

Benito Mussolini,
speech to the Senate, June 24, 1924

THE CLOUDED NATION

JUNE 27–JULY 22, 1924

"WE ARE NOT here to commemorate. We are gathered here at a rite, a religious rite, which is also the nation's rite. Our brother, whom I do not need to name because his name is evoked at this very moment by all men who have a heart, on either side of the Alps and beyond the seas, is not a dead man, he is not a defeated man, he is not a murder victim either. He lives on, he is here with us, and he is fighting. He is an accuser; he is a judge; he is an avenger. They cut him into little pieces to no avail. In vain did they disfigure his gentle and severe face. His members have been recomposed. The miracle of Galilee has been repeated. The tomb gave us back his body. The dead man has risen. And speaks. And I swear to him, on behalf of all of you, that his shade will soon be appeased."

Filippo Turati pronounces these words of sublimation for his murdered friend on June 27th before the assembly of all the opposition groups gathered there. As Turati speaks, many turn towards the entrance of Montecitorio's hall B, frightened, expecting to see the chopped up ghost of Giacomo Matteotti appear. Shortly before, at the start of the session, an awkward gaffe launched the séance-like atmosphere: the secretary, calling the roll of those present, was reading bureaucratically from the chamber's lists, and when he got to *the* name, he inadvertently called out: "Matteotti Giacomo?" After a moment of dismay and emotion, many people shouted: "Present!"

But all of Italy, these days, is leading a spectral existence, shaken and haunted by death. Starting with the oppositions, whose assembly, fertilized by Turati's words, gives birth to the decision to abstain from the work of the chamber until the shattered political and juridical order is restored. The indefinite abstention from parliament is immediately dubbed the "Aventino," in memory of other ghosts, of a previous secession, of a former Roman plebs, the one that withdrew in protest on the homonymous hill in 494 B.C.

The present secession, in the intentions of its promoters led by Giovanni Amendola, is meant to reject any "vulgar accommodation," and to intractably oppose the barbarism, but, in fact, it stakes everything on the universal outrage. It bets the entire kitty on the moral issue. As if, in order to be crushed, the fascist bloc, cemented by obedience to Mussolini and the complicity of power, weren't going to come out of a hammering battle shattered and defeated. As if outrage were enough to counter the truncheon. As if morality were a category of politics.

It's that way everywhere, in every office, in every club, in every bar in Italy. The most diverse people, united by the desire to get in touch with specters—starting with that of Giacomo Matteotti—gather in psychic séances in order to ask the spirits specific questions. But the questions go unanswered. Ghosts abound yet remain silent.

To honor Matteotti, tens of millions of workers across the country abstain from work. Mindful of the disastrous all-out general strikes of previous years, however, they do so responsibly, for only ten minutes. Nevertheless, the industrialists, the captains of economic Italy, do not speak out against the regime, considering the resumption of production and a balanced budget more advantageous than political liberty. Even the war veterans, however, gathered at a meeting on July 7th, distance themselves from fascism. A few days later, the injured and gravely incapacitated follow them in protest. But Gabriele D'Annunzio, whom all of them, ex-soldiers, wounded and disabled, look to as their natural leader, is unfortunately no longer a man of adventure, and has by now decided to devote himself entirely to literature: the state's purchase of the poet's manuscripts in gold—he being as always in precarious economic conditions—prior to a long series of subsidies, definitively appeases him. The short-lived antifascist outrage of the veterans, the maimed and the disabled therefore remains without a leader.

In Florence, meanwhile, on July 9th, thousands of armed fascists take to the streets. They seem to be signaling the arrival of the much-threatened "second wave," but then this surge also recedes, ending in a government reshuffle. Exit Gentile, Carnazza, Corbino. Enter Casati, Sarrocchi, Lanza di Scalea. And the eternal bureaucratic protocol swamps the wave.

The stock markets slide disastrously after news of the abduction circulates, but the king, like a "prisoner of war," breaking his oath on the Albertine Statute, signs a decree allowing the prefects to seize publications that spread news that is harmful to the nation. Having thus gagged the press, the markets' hysteria quiets down. The king's apathetic fatalism, on the other hand, sets the underlying tone for the spectral existence that is infecting his people. When a delegation of ex-combatants goes to him requesting urgent and drastic measures, Vittorio Emanuele III replies distractedly, changing the subject: "Today my daughter killed two quails," he informs them, with undisguised paternal pride.

Yes, the majority of Italians, horrified by the crime, would like to see the fall of fascism in order to decontaminate its ghost-infested houses, but then, towards dinner time, the demands of everyday life prevail. Morality is not among them. The nation is clouded, its sense of justice is listless and murky. The sense of rebellion is reduced to the morbid passion with which people follow news reports of the outrage.

In particular, theories about the elimination of the body proliferate: the fantasy of a pyre at the crematorium in Rome circulates among many, while others prefer ice to fire and imagine a freezing locker in the forensic medicine unit of the Polyclinic. Still others insist on the mysterious depths of Lake Vico. Divers explore it inch by inch, but the lake bed is empty, bereaved, forlorn. Nothing but mud and sludge are dredged from that mystery. Then caves, catacombs, and small abandoned cemeteries are zealously searched. The country's agitation is projected in a nightmare. Italy screams in its sleep, oppressed by ghosts that strangle any sense of liberation, as in a bad dream.

Even the existence of Benito Mussolini—the man who is at one with his body and the steely material with which, they say, it was forged—becomes spectral during these weeks. "There are two dead men," writes journalist Ugo Ojetti, "Matteotti and Mussolini."

After the brief blaze of dynamism in mid-June, the Duce of fascism, in fact, sinks back into apathetic inertia, scraping along in the shadows. Thereby allowing the controversy between revisionists and intransigents to resume within the party. Adding to those speaking for the latter now is a young Tuscan, a former war volunteer who calls himself Curzio Malaparte, and who founded a journal, *La conquista dello Stato* (The Conquest of the State). In it he upholds the popular, peasant, generous and unprejudiced spirit of provincial fascism, as opposed to the "Roman cesspool," and argues fiercely for releasing the intransigent action squads against Matteotti's mourners.

Mussolini lets him blather; he can't make up his mind. At the Grand Council of Fascism on July 22nd, the Duce is still wavering: he declares that revolution demands cunning and stratagems, asks for understanding and assistance, then states that he is also prepared for violence, if necessary. Meanwhile, the young attorney who has enthusiastically taken on Dùmini's defense urges him to retreat into obscurity, like a specter: too many people are talking about the accounts of those under investigation, about the interrogators, about the evidence; it's dangerous, he must refuse to talk about the matter, he must know nothing about the trial.

Benito Mussolini's private life also swings to extremes between brief bouts of euphoria and gloomy melancholy. Bianca Ceccato, his "little girl" lover, now the mother of his bastard daughter, is invited to Rome and spends a few days shut up in his apartment on Via Rasella, always at his disposal. At the height of his vanity, he reads her letter after letter from unknown admirers, then suddenly bursts into furious rants against his wife Rachele, who is said to be finally having an affair of her own with a man in Romagna. His wife's infidelity, added to the gall of that corpse dumped at his feet, causes Benito Mussolini, for the first time in his life, to have violent ulcer attacks. The doctors make him cut down on the orange juice he loves so much and forbid him to drink coffee. Quinto Navarra, his impeccable attendant, sees him lying on the carpet of the Hall of Victories one day, bent over double, twisted by the pain in his stomach.

The few friends who still go to see him describe a Mussolini obsessed with ghosts. At the end of July, having recovered from his car accident, Leandro Arpinati goes down to Rome with four comrades. Entering the deserted Palazzo Chigi, they have the impression that everyone has fled. Arpinati walks straight into the Duce's office, without waiting to be announced. He finds him haggard, a three-day beard, feverish eyes.

"The situation is intolerable: you can't stay in government with a dead man underfoot," the prime minister moans.

"Did you have him killed?" Arpinati asks him point-blank.

"No."

"So what does it have to do with you? Punish those who committed this stupid crime and stop thinking about it."

Benito opens up with Leandro, his loyal old friend: it's impossible not to think about it. Every evening he leaves around seven o'clock and on the way out there's always a small crowd watching him go by, silent and hostile. It's a nightmare. Matteotti's wife comes almost every day to ask about her husband. The first few times he received her, but now he no longer has the courage.

It's not true, it's another lie, maybe even a hallucination: Velia Matteotti, after that one time on June 13th, did not come back again. And yet as Mussolini confides in him, his friend Arpinati is dismayed to watch the Duce of fascism look around fearfully, as if she might reappear. That evening before returning to Emilia, the ras of Bologna orders his four squadristi to join the silent, hostile crowd and applaud when the Leader appears at the door. Mussolini is stunned—for weeks no one has applauded him—and smiles faintly.

It doesn't last long. Despite Turati's solemn promise, Matteotti's shade does not vanish. His ghost, unappeased, still prowls about the country. The nation does not get over it. It remains clouded. Will the persecution go on forever?

In his notebook, Benito Mussolini writes: "The body has not been found—Tension mounts—Accusations of foul play continue to spread."

There are two dead men, Matteotti and Mussolini. Italy is split in two, those who mourn the death of the one and those who mourn the death of the other.

Ugo Ojetti, July 1924

Too many people are involved in the trial and too many people come to talk to you about it. This is extremely dangerous! . . . And allow me, Mr. President, to give you some advice: when anyone comes to talk to you about it, you should claim ignorance of the trial and not allow anyone to talk to you about the matter . . . This is an indispensable necessity, to duly protect our personal responsibilities as well. I have presumed to give you such advice because I sincerely care about you.

Giovanni Vaselli, defense attorney for Amerigo Dùmini,
private letter to Benito Mussolini, July 1924

CHLOROFORM

JULY 22–AUGUST 7, 1924

"How are you?"

"How do you expect, my Vela?"

"Anything new?"

"Not a thing. By now, nothing surprises me anymore, not even the most absurd, the most heinous act . . . What pains me, besides, is that I have no idea what my so-called 'friends' think. The ones who betrayed me!"

"It will all work out, you'll see; but I urge you to stay calm, don't let your nerves get the better of you."

"It's not a question of nerves, I don't hate anyone, I don't hold any grudges! Unfortunately, destiny has played its card in favor of my enemies and if I lose the game, almost certainly, there's no chance of a playoff either!"

"But you always proved to be a skillful player, so you know that many games which seem to be lost at the start, end up being overturned at the last hand."

As attested to by wiretappings made by staff in charge of the president's private phone lines, towards the end of July 1924, it is once again Margherita Sarfatti who restores Mussolini's confidence in himself, in his skill as a gambler: never leave the table after a losing hand (as a twist of fate, talking to her intimately, the lover calls her by the pet name "Vela," which differs by only a single syllable from the name of Matteotti's widow). The same urging not to resign comes to Mussolini from Costanzo Ciano, the hero of the torpedo boats, who draws on his experience as a seaman: from the first time he went on board—Ciano reminds the Duce—he was taught "not to get off the boat when the sea is stormy."

And Benito Mussolini does not get off. For that matter, nobody forces him to do so. The king has reconfirmed his confidence, the oppositions' attacks are limited to journalistic controversy, and the judicial investigation, manipulated from above, does not touch him personally.

Amerigo Dùmini, installed in the VI wing of Regina Coeli with every comfort, continues to stick to the story of a beating that ended in tragedy, and to deny any responsibility on the part of Mussolini. The National Fascist Party administration pays off all the expense reports submitted by the illustrious prisoner and his cronies, without a peep: food brought in from an outside restaurant, suits of silk-lined English vicuna, pajamas trimmed with Astrakhan fur, stationery bearing the party emblem and the incredible letterhead "Arditi Fascist Group—Regina Coeli Detachment—Rome, Via della Lungara 29."

Dùmini is only moved to immoderation once when, at the end of July, a sworn statement by De Bono, "that old whore," seems to contradict his version of an unintentional crime. So then the Tuscan squadrista writes letters to Finzi blackmailing him and threatening to fight tooth and nail, against everything and everyone, at any cost, if he is deceived; later, however, Dùmini backtracks, regrets his outburst, and promises to go back to being "the good, loyal fascist he was before." In the end, for Amerigo Dùmini, Regina Coeli is a "prison without bars," and the pact with Mussolini holds.

Mussolini, therefore, feels he can weather the storm, and takes the party in hand again. Now recovered and speaking as fascism's Leader and head of government, the Duce conveys a new slogan and a new course to members of the national council attending the August 7 assembly in the Consistory hall at Palazzo Venezia:

"A German philosopher said: 'Live dangerously.' I would like this to be the motto of youthful, passionate Italian fascism: 'Live dangerously.'"

Then, having launched the dictum, he explains its meaning. We must be ready for anything, for any sacrifice, for any danger, but meanwhile we must acknowledge our mistakes. There's been a little too much fiddling around, too many commanders, too many knights. Instead, there should be pride in "reaching the goal unclothed," without the honorific frills and trappings. And unnecessary violence must stop: we must no longer say that we are ready to kill and die for fascism, but only that we are ready to sacrifice ourselves for our country. However, it is also time to put an end to revisionisms. These revisionists are people who love to bring up the rear to find themselves in the vanguard in the event of a reversal. Now, however, the revolution begun in October 1922 must be completed with the definitive overthrow of the decrepit democratic, liberal state. Fascism will not allow itself to be tried, except by history.

Nevertheless, having launched the slogan, what's needed most of all—since the battle is a difficult one, and because a split in the government majority must be avoided (Mussolini estimates nearly a hundred uncertain deputies)—is a very subtle strategy. The strategy is this: "We must chloroform—permit me the medical term—the oppositions and the Italian people as well."

It takes cruelty, of course, but the cruelty of a surgeon. No more alarmism, no more hysteria. You can beat a people, you can squeeze them with taxation, you can impose harsh discipline on them, but you can't trample on certain deeply rooted sentiments. You can't live under an apocalyptic sky day after day. The mood of the Italian people—the revived Duce assures the members of the Grand Council—is this: don't stress us every day saying you want to have firing squads. We've had enough of this. One morning, when we wake up, tell us you've done it and we'll be satisfied but, for God's sake, not this endless drip drip drip. Do whatever you want but let us hear about it later.

And besides, in a week's time it's the August holiday. This year *ferragosto* falls on a Friday. People will have three whole days to take their kids to the beach, to reunite with the old folks, with the dead, sitting around a table, in front of a plate of pasta, a bottle on the table, they'll have three whole days not to think about anything anymore, not to be aware of anything.

The truth is that members of parliament can only wait passively and non-parliamentarians can only vote for the agendas . . . In the end what do the oppositions do? Do they call for general or partial strikes? For demonstrations in the piazzas? Or attempts at armed rebellion? None of that. The oppositions engage in a purely journalistic debate. That's all they can do.

Benito Mussolini, speech to the
Grand Council of Fascism,
July 22, 1924

Let's try to avoid alarming the public, let's try to appear in our warrior guise, but only capable of certain necessary cruelty, a surgeon's cruelty. Let's not stress people's already tense nerves: in the end the people will do what we want them to do. Tomorrow a thousand determined individuals will govern Rome, tomorrow, if we act seriously, with the determination of those who have burned their bridges behind them and must necessarily move forward, the people would stand aside because, after all, humanity is still much as Alessandro Manzoni's landlord put it: "I don't meddle with the affairs of others."

Benito Mussolini, address to
the National PNF Council,
August 7, 1924

The blow was severe, stupid, unexpected. But I believe I will weather this storm: the most recent of the infinite number that were dumped on me by those who should have avoided them.

Benito Mussolini,
letter to his sister Edvige,
August 1, 1924

THE CORPSE

MACCHIA DELLA QUARTARELLA, AUGUST 16, 1924

A CULVERT, A LITTLE dog, a wild wooded area that had sheltered brigands. And so Italy wakes up from its atrocious nightmare.

While unblocking a gutter, Alceo Taccheri, a roadworker assigned to Via Flaminia, gets down on his hands and knees to check out the clogged sewer drain at kilometre post 18. There he finds a jacket with a missing sleeve, the piping where a pocket handkerchief is slipped encrusted with blood, over the heart. Looking around more closely, he spots something light colored lying on the ground. When he picks it up, he sees that it's the missing sleeve, with the lining turned inside out.

Ovidio Caratelli, a brigadier in the carabinieri, is in Riano Flaminio on leave at his family home. He knows the Macchia della Quartarella like the back of his hand—a dense, deep forest, a wild, impenetrable place—because as a boy he went on long hunting trips in all the woods of the surrounding area. Separated from the road by an imposing fence, with a profusion of tall trees and thorny undergrowth, the Macchia plunges into a deep ravine far within. But between the western edge and the ravine is the small clearing of an abandoned charcoal cellar, invisible from the road, buried by thick vegetation, and surrounded by brambles and oaks. It is from there, towards evening, in the lengthening of a summer twilight, that the carabiniere hears his dog barking. The dog is scrabbling around in the ground. By now, however, it's dark, best to go home.

The following day, the eager dog takes off on the run through the dense brush as soon as they catch sight of the Quartarella. The animal starts pawing around again, in the same spot as the day before.

The carabiniere pokes at the ground, covered with leaves and dry oak bark, and when the stick sinks into some soft topsoil, he kicks at it to see if it sinks some more. As if returning the kick, a nauseating stench of putrefaction rises from the earth. Almost immediately, the soil also exposes human bones and shreds of flesh, utterly crawling with worms. After he clears away more of the topsoil, the front part of a skull appears.

Giacomo Matteotti is already in an advanced state of skeletonization. Only a few soft skin-covered parts remain. He appears huddled up, squeezed into a pit that is too short. Only a coarse metal file stuck in the ground serves as a cross marking his burial. The tool used by his murderers to dig his grave.

The investigating magistrates note: Quartarella wood (opposite Via Flaminia at km post 23 from Rome, between Riano and Sacrofano), a shallow, oblong grave, from 0.40 m. to 0.75 m. wide, at ground level, with maximum central length of 1.20 m. and maximum depth of 0.45 m., located in a clearing formerly used as a charcoal pit, surrounded by brambles.

The medical examiner finds that the corpse must have been in the grave for a long time and that its dissolution took place there, by the natural process of decomposition, without the contribution of external agents; he further finds that the corpse, although complete and not having been mutilated, either in life or after death, must have been forcefully compressed into the superficial pit that was too small, dug hastily without proper tools. Presumably the killers had stamped on the body with their feet, then folded it like a book, the legs turned under the back, and finally covered it summarily with a bit of soil as filler. Two gold teeth, protruding due to the receded gums, confirm that these are the remains of Deputy Matteotti.

Given the lack of internal organs and specific lesions on the skeleton, and the absence of any other garments besides the torn jacket and the trousers already found, it is impossible to ascertain the precise cause of death. But hypothetically, and in consideration of the blood stain, spread internally and externally in the upper left anterior pectoral region and the homonymous axillary region of the seized jacket, it is quite likely that death occurred as a result of a puncture wound to the upper left thoracic-anterolateral region. A wound that bled profusely, from a blade-edged weapon. A single stab to the heart area.

Throughout the afternoon, the carabinieri sift through the surrounding soil in search of some other shred of flesh or bone remains. Before evening, however, the brigands' forest is already besieged by a crowd armed with flashlights, huddling at the edge of the woods. Among the first to arrive are the deputies of the Unitary Socialist Party. Filippo Turati staggers, and presses a handkerchief to his face, no telling whether to stifle tears or to suppress the urge to vomit due to the cadaverous stench.

Once again horror invades the world. The journalists have a field day. In the roars of the press, the meticulous accounts of the body being undressed, of the violence applied to it to forcibly squeeze it into an inadequate grave, hastily dug with a file, portray the desecration in Riano as one of the most "deliberately savage in history." The depositions of carabinieri captain Domenico Pallavicini and Ovidio Caratelli, the brigadier who found the jacket, also arouse skepticism: they contradict one another and some suspect that the find was manipulated.

But that doesn't matter now. Emotional shock waves, radiating throughout the country from a pitiable grave dug with a file and brought to light by a dog's nosing around, rouse the Italians from their midsummer torpor. During the night, in the streets of the capital, posters of Mussolini are retouched with splashes of blood-red paint.

The earth, therefore, returned the body of Giacomo Matteotti. The corpse, albeit with its few shreds of flesh, lays the ghost to rest. The nightmare is over. The end has begun.

I will spare you a minute description of the remains. Everything is reduced to nothing. There is no longer even a skeleton, only tibias, femurs, ribs, scattered bones and the skull.

Filippo Turati, letter to Anna Kuliscioff,
August 16, 1924

So many sad things around us, such a web of deceit . . . The discovery of this unfortunate corpse will silence the barking dogs and the chameleons who pay attention to them.

Margherita Sarfatti, letter to Benito Mussolini,
August 1924

PRECIPICE

AUGUST 21–DECEMBER 16, 1924

WHAT REMAINS OF Giacomo Matteotti is returned to the earth for the second time on August 21st. This time to his region: the funeral takes place in Fratta in the Polesine, at the wishes of his wife Velia, who refused Turati a "political" burial in the Verano cemetery in Rome.

The coffin's departure from Monterotondo station was, in any case, accompanied by the cries of a crowd of peasants, laborers and railway workers kneeling along the railway tracks, and met in Fratta by a similar crowd of tens of thousands of mourning workers, awaiting vengeance, justice, and retribution: "Vendetta! Viva Matteotti! Viva the martyr! Viva liberty!"

In Fratta Polesine, the place of his origins, the scene's central figure is no longer the young wife but the elderly mother. The battalion arrayed along the provincial road presents arms, the priest imparts the ritual blessing, then the bereaved mother, accompanied to the coffin, begins sobbing and ends with grief-stricken shrieks. With Giacomo, Lucia Elisabetta Garzarolo, commonly called Isabella, buries the last of her seven children, all taken from her by tuberculosis, by life and by fascism.

From this moment on, everything precipitates, everything comes apart. Italy is a country in mourning, siding with a mother's sorrow.

Fascism, once again reviled by the world, plunges back into the abyss of squadrismo. Already the preceding days saw deaths and injuries in the streets of Naples, but on August 31st, speaking at a meeting of Mount Amiata coal miners, Mussolini himself evokes the supreme violence: the socialists' clamor—he says—is annoying but they are perfectly impotent; the day they were to go from words to deeds, "on that day we will make them into fodder for the blackshirts' camps." As for the opposers who withdrew over the Aventino of their consciences, he isn't worried about them: "The abstainers will be in the wrong."

The violence summoned up by the Duce erupts a few days later, on September 5th, in Turin. A group of squadristi is waiting in the street for Piero Gobetti, the frail, young editor of *La rivoluzione liberale*; they beat him to a bloody pulp, causing him serious internal injuries; a small crowd, dismayed and guarded, watches one man's struggle against a dozen. But the attack in Turin is not the only one. Demonstrations, acts of destruction and incidents resume everywhere. Attributable to both sides. The escalation culminates on a tram in Rome where on September 12th a worker, Giovanni Corvi, kills fascist unionist Armando Casalini with three revolver shots, before his daughter's petrified eyes. From Cremona, Farinacci calls for ethnic cleansing of the oppositions: "If the broom isn't enough, a machine gun must be used." The fascist newspaper *L'impero* demands the concentration camp for the leaders of the Aventino boycott. The squadristi in the provinces implore Mussolini: "Duce, untie our hands." The "second wave" appears inevitable, incipient, a historical necessity.

Instead, the repudiation of fascism continues over the precipice. The first to act are the big industrialists who have supported it. On September 14th, the usual delegation—Olivetti, Conti, Pirelli—presents Mussolini with a petition that is equivalent to an ultimatum. Then the liberals make a move, assembled at a meeting at the beginning of October. They too distance themselves from the regime that they are still part of. Even the *Corriere della Sera* finally and openly attacks it. The judicial investigation also precipitates: Amerigo Dùmini, trapped by De Bono's deposition about Rossi and Marinelli's accountability, is forced to change his defensive line. On October 20th, he admits that he was working for the "Fascist Cheka" and that he had obeyed the orders of his principals. The injunction of the former police chief—"deny, deny, always deny everything"—no longer makes sense at that point. On October 28th, militia celebrations for the second anniversary of the march on Rome take place in deserted piazzas. Not even the war-wounded participate. From Gardone, Gabriele D'Annunzio speaks out as well, calling the Italy guilty of Matteotti's murder a "fetid ruin." Behind the scenes, plots are hatched to assassinate Mussolini. The National Fascist Party has shut itself in like a besieged fortress. Everyone is waiting for the order from the Aventino to storm it.

As it drops off the precipice, besieged fascism makes a last, toxic attempt to purify itself. On October 22nd, Emilio De Bono, already removed as police chief in June, is also forced to leave the command of the militia entirely in the hands of Italo Balbo. On October 25th, Don Sturzo is exiled to London. In Paris, during the trial for the murder of fascist Nicola Bonservizi, killed by a socialist exile, Curzio Malaparte produces an infamous false document that would pin the responsibility on Giacomo Matteotti's corpse. Even Luigi Pirandello, the greatest living Italian playwright, contributes to the attempt to purge fascism by acquiring a party card at the end of October. On November 4th, the anniversary of the victory, the regime, precipitating, attempts to fascistize the cult of the nation altogether. Mussolini kneels in front of the tomb of the Unknown Soldier while not far away, in Piazza del Popolo, the squadristi attack a nationalist procession led by Giuseppe Garibaldi's nephew. The attempt fails. Clashes between fascists and former combatants erupt everywhere. Mario Ponzio of San Sebastiano, a gold medalist for military valor, tears up his PNF card. He too joins the majority of Italians who continue to expect a specific political initiative from the Aventino to bring down the regime.

Meanwhile, on November 12th, even parliament, until then complicit, begins to repudiate fascism, pushing it over the edge. The agenda for the first day of work in the chamber, reopened after a very lengthy recess, calls for the commemoration of deputies who have died in recent months. The name of Giacomo Matteotti appears on the list. Communist deputy Luigi Repossi, having come down from the Aventine hill, forbids the fascists from taking part in the mourning: "Since the world began," Repossi shouts in front of them all, "murderers and those complicit with them have not been allowed to commemorate their victims!" The attack is vehement but no fascist dares to silence him. In the corridors of Montecitorio there are rumors of agreements among the main liberal leaders to oust Mussolini. Giovanni Giolitti, who at the first session is blatantly absent, takes a stand on November 15th, voting against a government proposed bill. Then he confronts Mussolini in the chamber over provisions that stifle freedom of the press. A few days later he is joined by Vittorio Emanuele Orlando, the "premier of victory." With each new vote, the government loses support. On November 24th the renowned playwright Sem Benelli announces his resignation: "Either fascism steps down or the state resigns," he declares. The majority crumbles, Mussolini's power shows cracks. Turati writes to Kuliscioff that by now "the succession is open."

On November 26th Italo Balbo also faces the precipice. Attacked by a newspaper for his role in the murder of Don Minzoni, the ras of Romagna filed a libel suit. But during the trial his former lieutenant Tommaso Beltrami exhibits a letter in which Balbo guarantees the perpetrators impunity after the crime. Mussolini demands his resignation. Thus the idol of the squadristi also falls. Fascism continues to plummet.

On November 30th, all the antifascist forces assemble in Milan. Huge popular participation, great excitement. At the center of the stage stands a large portrait of Matteotti garlanded with white and red flowers and green leaves. There are shouts of "Viva Matteotti!", shouts of "down with the assassins!" The investigating magistrates, having completed the preliminary phase of the trial, ask for an indictment not only for the perpetrators of the crime, but for Rossi and Marinelli as well. On December 3rd, Luigi Albertini, editor of the *Corriere della Sera* and senator of the Kingdom, passionately protests the abuse of law. A few hours later magnate Ettore Conti also takes the Senate floor against Mussolini: fascism has succeeded in the task of materially restoring the country, failing, however, at its moral restoration. Right after him, General Gaetano Giardino expresses the discomfort of military and royalist establishments being attached to the militia. On December 5th, the majority loses another 20 votes in the Senate. The social bloc that put Mussolini in government crumbles in the span of forty-eight hours. The bell tolls.

The day of reckoning appears imminent, the angles of attack multiply. On December 6th, Giuseppe Donati, editor of the Catholic daily *Il popolo*, presents a detailed allegation of De Bono's complicity in the crime. Questioned by the grand jury, De Bono confirms that on the night of June 12th, in a secret meeting at the Viminale, Rossi and Marinelli declared that they were carrying out orders from Mussolini. On December 16th, things reach the point where even a simple deputy, liberal Giovanni Battista Boeri, though elected on the fascist "*listone*," finds the courage to publicly contest Mussolini.

"Give back the mandate," the Duce of fascism shouts angrily at him, "given that you were on the national list."

"By entering the national list, I didn't think I was assuming criminal co-responsibility," Boeri rejoins.

La Stampa, Turin's liberal, antifascist newspaper, the only one that has never made allowances for fascism, issues a definitive ruling in the mild second-rank man's open rebellion against the totemic Leader: "The government has only one concern: not leaving. Only one fear: the sanctions of justice. A sense of uncertainty and anxiety is sweeping the country with no possibility of being stopped or remedied."

On the same day, in another newspaper, Filippo Turati reads that widespread anxiety as the state of mind that characterized the "crowds of the year one thousand," nervously awaiting a sign from the Aventino "of a decisive act, not clearly specified and therefore only terrible." Hoping to have reached the bottom of the precipice, although a few decades ahead of the turn of the second millennium, Italians hold their breath, waiting for the end of the world.

Of the same opinion as Turati, but more practical, Anna Kuliscioff replies from Milan: "It seems to me that it is time to precipitate matters."

SWAMP

ROME, DECEMBER 21, 1924

RAFFAELE PAOLUCCI IS a respectable person, a fervent patriot, an illustrious physician. A leading thoracic and abdominal surgeon, during the war he earned a gold medal for military valor by sinking an Austrian battleship with only a single partner and a single limpet mine, a 26-foot torpedo he built himself. On the evening of December 19, Raffaele Paolucci invited the "swamp" to his home.

Forty-four deputies of the moderate right—the fascism of "family men," those of the silent majority, those who are always in the middle between the two opposing ranks of maniacs, those whose civic conscience is horrified by every new act of violence though on the surface it barely ripples—gather in a Roman palazzo, in a setting of chocolate truffles and upper-bourgeois decor, to put an end to the chaos, to restore a peaceful climate, to promote conciliation, normality, the constitution. The objective of the deputies of the gray area, conventionally referred to as the "swamp," is to supersede the current government, by pushing Mussolini to break with the rases and align with the old liberals—perhaps making way for Vittorio Emanuele Orlando for the presidency—and persuading the oppositions to return to parliament. For days, Senator Pompeo of Campello, the king's gentleman-in-waiting, has urged them to do so.

To this end and with this charge from the Crown, the forty-four men sign a national renewal agenda: to free the nation from the excessive power of the rases, to avoid violence categorically, to entrust public order to the police, to crush "revolutionary second waves," to dismiss thugs, thieves, and the morally corrupt from every office, and to reform the electoral law by introducing the uninominal voting system.

It might seem strange that with the wolves at the door anyone would think about electoral reform but, in truth, a group of deputies elected to parliament thinks of nothing else. And as Raffaele Paolucci sees it, the uninominal system, providing for the election of only one deputy per district, subjecting every single candidate to the direct scrutiny of the electorate, should sweep away the political schemers, the trade union parasites, the hotheads, the thugs, and the lunatics. It should push Mussolini to yield to the liberals, the moderates, the king, and to decent people.

Raffaele Paolucci, however, is a man of honor, not a conspirator and, therefore, even knowing that this electoral reform has been talked about for months and that the Duce has always declared himself against it, after the meeting of the "swamp," he goes to the Leader to loyally report the results to him and apprise him of the wishes expressed by his parliamentarians. Mussolini listens to him attentively, yet Paolucci gets the impression that he didn't think he was sincere.

Raffaele Paolucci sees Benito Mussolini again the following day, in the Montecitorio chamber. He watches him approach the government bench and file a decree for the reform of the electoral system into a majority uninominal voting system, the very reform that Paolucci had proposed to him the day before and which Mussolini had spurned. No one knew anything about the decree; for now only two ministers have signed it, others will join them.

The honorable man, Paolucci, is astounded: by playing the card in advance, the political animal, Mussolini, hasn't thrown a stone into the swamp, but a bomb. The effect of the decree is explosive, the consternation enormous, the muddy water is shaken.

Once he gets over the shock of the masterful maneuver, Paolucci understands. Caught in a vise among oppositions, moderates, and squadristi, Mussolini with that one unanticipated stroke once again becomes master of the game: socialist, communist and populist oppositions, which owe a great deal to the proportional system, will be mowed down; the old liberal notables, who still enjoy a large individual following in their electoral fiefdoms, will appreciate the gift; the moderate fascists and reckless squadristi, both lacking a real electoral base of their own and elected thanks to the proportional flood tide, will now be at the mercy of Mussolini's blackmail. Behind closed doors, in his office, assigning or denying them a winning district, the Duce will be able to consign them to re-election or to oblivion.

Thanks to a simple reform of the electoral system, in short, Mussolini is back in the saddle. The liberal right, which until yesterday was ready to unhorse him, draws close again, attracted by the prospect of re-election. Threatened by the possibility of not being re-elected, moderate fascists, up till now tempted by the opposition faction, hasten to fall back in line. And so the swamp sinks back into its own sludge. For career politicians the only thing that matters is getting re-elected. The sky might be falling, they will not budge from their seats for anyone or anything.

The oppositions, meanwhile, are flushed out. In retreat on the Aventino for months, while Italy waited in vain for them to deal the final blow, they are now forced to attempt a sortie. Their most powerful weapon, perhaps the only one at this point, is still the accusation of murder. Indeed since the beginning of August Giovanni Amendola, leader of the Aventino secession, has been in possession of Cesare Rossi's account, written on June 15th. He sat on it for another three months, then, in mid-November, he transmitted it to Vittorio Emanuele III, hoping that the sovereign would be the one to solve the problem. Throughout the month of December, Aventino Italy has been waiting in vain. The king, as usual, did not lift a finger.

So Amendola decides to publish the report. The first extract appears in his newspaper, *Il Mondo*, on December 27th. In it fascism is exposed as a genuinely illegitimate state; the politician Mussolini is depicted as criminal by nature, the direct principal behind the violence; the man is portrayed as having the psychology of a felonious inside man, always careful to ensure an alibi for the day and time of the crime.

Yet, strangely, Mussolini has done nothing to prevent the publication of the account. He is even said to have encouraged it, that he forced the timing. "No confiscation, maximum visibility," he appears to have ordered. Could it be a fiendish calculation, could it be a craving for disaster, or could it be that the daily papers are called that because they only last a day?

In any case, the sensation raised by Rossi's revelations is once again enormous. The squadristi are champing at the bit, the fascist newspapers dismiss the disclosures as the usual babble, and the *Corriere della Sera* for the first time openly calls for the prime minister's resignation. It's back to butting heads again, back to wielding knives.

Once the first sensation of shock was overcome, the purpose of Mussolini's move was clear: to terrify the oppositions, but above all to crush the nuclei of the majority that showed signs of fanciful ambitions for independence. It must be said that Mussolini succeeded admirably.

Statement by Antonio Salandra, former prime minister,
on the proposed electoral reform law
of December 20, 1924

A few more weeks and then the oppositions, which feverishly kept on about the decedent, which exploited the deceased with the sadistic, exasperated fury of macabre sharks, which held the nation weighed down by a horrific nightmare, will be definitively swept away by simple human logic and the indestructible reality of the facts.

"A Festering Sore Not a Bombshell"
(commentary on the publication of Rossi's account),
Il Popolo d'Italia, December 30, 1924

When one is called into question regarding certain charges, one has a duty to appear before the law, waiving the prerogatives and immunities that power in effect accords.

In any other constitutional country in Europe a prime minister charged in this way would himself want to step down from the office to exonerate himself as a free citizen and, if he did not want to, he would be forced to.

Luigi Albertini,
Corriere della Sera, December 27 and 30, 1924

THE PACK OF HOUNDS

ROME, DECEMBER 31, 1924
PALAZZO CHIGI

THE SEVEN RED-BLUE Faber pencils, well-sharpened on both ends and perfectly lined up, are a bright spot on the extreme northwestern edge of the desk. The metal-plated square-tipped nibs with their thin slits are duly inserted into three different pen holders.

After the usual morning horseback ride at Villa Borghese, the Duce found his office in the Hall of Victories cleared of the unbearable flies thanks to the impeccable Quinto Navarra who, in accordance with his instructions, had abundantly sprayed the room with geraniol. The ever-present yellow leather briefcase, the same one he's always had, is placed on a coffee table, and the decrees authorizing police measures and press censorship are already signed on the desk. Even on this last day of the year, everything is in order in the prime minister's office as on every other day, all the details, even the tiniest, are meticulously seen to. Everything but the world: that, unfortunately, is recalcitrant, refusing to submit.

The morning newspapers, heaped in stacks on the desk, sweep the world's delirious disarray into the aseptic, well-ordered room. The liberal dailies demand Mussolini's resignation, the socialist tabloids demand his head, the fascists of the extremist alliance openly threaten him. In the first edition of the new year of his *Cremona Nuova*, Farinacci declares that the truncheon, temporarily stored in the attic, "must be dusted off and kept close at hand." In his journal

La conquista dello Stato, Curzio Malaparte, a second-rank squadrista, dares to caution the Duce: "whoever is not with us is against us," the fascist motto by antonomasia, also applies to the man who coined it, to Benito Mussolini himself, Malaparte roars. The headlines are explicit, insolent: "Fascism against Mussolini?" "Everyone must obey the admonition of integral fascism, even Mussolini." The accusations of the squadristi are precise, their hopes arrogant. Malaparte attacks him head-on, reminds him that "Deputy Mussolini, in addition to being appointed by the Crown, received his mandate from the fascist provinces," and the provinces, unyielding, don't want to listen to arguments: the revolution must continue, counter to all the compromising, lying, and dealing. And the squadristi are prepared to continue the revolution even without him.

Suddenly, the door to the Hall of Victories opens though he, inside, doesn't hear anyone knock. It is not the obsequious face and dutiful figure of Quinto Navarra that appear in the doorway. Instead, dozens of men burst in with a noisy, heavy military stride, wearing black shirts with medals of valor pinned to them. Some have daggers on their belts. As if to surround him while leaving him a way out, they position themselves in a semicircle around the desk of the prime minister, who remains seated.

The thirty-three militia consuls arrived separately and incognito from all over Italy, and were billeted at the militia barracks of the legion commanded by consul Mario Candelori. Then, in small groups of three, to avoid being noticed, they assembled in Galleria Colonna, opposite Palazzo Chigi. Now the consuls physically crowd around their Duce, who is surprised and irritated. They are led by Enzo Galbiati and Aldo Tarabella.

Mussolini has known both men for years. Galbiati, head of the Monza squad, is consul commander of the militia's 25th "Iron" legion, the man assigned to the defense of *Il Popolo d'Italia* during the march on Rome. Aldo Tarabella is a legend: captain of the Arditi in the Great War, specially trained in the use of the submachine gun, a new assault weapon, decorated for valor six times with three bronze medals and three silver medals, and a member of the original Milan fascio since April 1919.

Tarabella is the first to speak, offering the Duce his best wishes for the new year, the fourth year of the revolution. Mussolini, still assured, says he is annoyed to receive them spur-of-the-moment like that. The war hero immediately lays his cards on the table:

"Duce, we are here to tell you that we are tired of biding our time. The prisons are now full of fascists. Fascism is being tried and you are unwilling to take on the responsibility of a revolution. We will assume that responsibility ourselves and will appear before Judge Occhiuto this very day, who will be quite happy to lock us up in Regina Coeli. Either we're all in prison, including you, or we're all out."

Mussolini calls the soldier to order.

Tarabella, still standing, does not desist: it was he, the Duce, who ignited their hearts, who incited them against the socialist reprobates, he can't expect to pacify them now. At this point, the Duce must make up his mind to do away with the opposition and proceed with the revolution, or they will all turn themselves in as criminals along with him.

Mussolini falters. The soldier's *aut aut* hit him like a knockout punch to the jaw. The seated man looks around, glances at the daggers, does not see Tullio Tamburini, the "great *bastonatore*," tries to equivocate.

"How come I don't see Tamburini with you?" Mussolini asks.

"Because he's already on the march again, leading ten thousand blackshirts."

Tarabella accompanies his reply by handing Mussolini a signed letter in which Tamburini approves their initiative.

Mussolini plays for time, scans through the first few lines. He knows from the interior ministry that in Florence the squadristi from the Tuscan provinces are setting fire to socialist newspapers, raiding the barracks to free detained comrades, and sowing violence in the streets.

The Leader's peremptory tone abruptly changes, his voice softens, he tries persuasion, he asks for understanding, he raises his right hand to shield his body.

"They left me stranded . . . they dumped that corpse on me . . ."

"Duce, does it seem to you that a corpse is too much to pay for a revolution?!"

Tarabella's swift, merciless retort ushers a rush of low-pressure into the room. The air becomes electric, the silence absolute, convulsive, a reminder and presentiment of screams. A fly spared from extermination buzzes around frantically, beating its veined wings against the windowpane that imprisons it.

Mussolini stands up, his voice rising towards high, shrill notes as he again calls the captain to order: all of them, those militia consuls, are liable to sanctions for having left their posts without authorization. The Leader says he is pained, disappointed, by those soldiers from whom he expected blind obedience. Some of them, reprimanded, take a step back. A dispute erupts. Mussolini dismisses them.

Tarabella stays behind: "We stand at attention, Duce," he adds, "but we are slamming the door as we leave." The hero's assertion leaves behind a shattered man, with his back to the wall.

A few hours later, that same evening, the besieged man becomes an outcast. During the traditional reception at the Quirinale to celebrate the New Year, a solemn occasion attended by not only the members of the royal family, but everyone in Italy who counts, Benito Mussolini finds himself shunned in a corner of the great hall.

The Duce of fascism had to enter with the last bracket, after the knights of the Order of the Annunziata, senators, and deputies and was not greeted by either Giolitti or Salandra. He had to latch onto the company of some of his ministers so as not to remain a pariah.

Filippo Turati, who is present at the scene, considers him done for. He writes to his partner that all that's left is "the problem of finding a way for the Duce to step down."

The Duce, accordingly, has no other option than to gamble once again. He asks the king to sign a blank decree for the dissolution of parliament that he can use to threaten the deputies. The king refuses to sign it, making it dependent on obtaining a vote of confidence and the passage of electoral reform. So Mussolini then issues a desperate communication in which, bluffing, he announces that once the new law is approved, it will be possible to dissolve the legislature.

He spends the night before the reopening of the chamber alone with his seven red-blue Faber pencils, drafting the speech with which he will face the future tribunal. He sits at the same desk where the thirty-three militia consuls surrounded him like a pack of attack hounds.

The violent events in Florence, the decree prohibiting the publication of all newspapers on January 1st . . . are merely a maneuver linked to the ringleader to make himself look good to fascist extremists, in short a way of putting a dignified mantle on a demise already seen as inevitable.

Filppo Turati, letter to Anna Kuliscioff,
January 2, 1925

ROME, JANUARY 3, 1925
PARLIAMENT OF THE KINGDOM OF ITALY,
CHAMBER OF DEPUTIES, 3:00 P.M.

THE HALL OF Montecitorio is packed from the center to the extreme right, yet those few stubbornly empty benches of the left are enough to necrotize it like a myocardial infarction. Nonetheless, the secessionist deputies of the opposition are almost all present, hidden among the crowd in the galleries.

Down below, in the hemicycle, Francesco Giunta jokes with Alfredo Rocco at the presidency bench, Deputy Lanza of Trabia shouts "Viva Italy!" to which Farinacci shouts back "Viva fascism!" and the squadristi sing *Giovinezza*. Today in Italy's parliament there is joking, shouting, and singing, no one speaks.

For two days the country's ventricles have been fibrillating, and there's been a steady stream of rumors about the premier's resignation. The piazzas have resounded with antifascist clamoring, then when the buzz proved to be unfounded, they went silent again. The scene shifts from minute to minute, in a seesaw of pitiable passions; life is lived as in a film.

It is rumored that "He" is crushed, humiliated by the volley that has hit him, close to collapse; others maintain that the militia consuls inoculated him with the resistance bacillus. In any case, they are all waiting for Him with bated breath, as if awaiting an event capable of casting its consequences over the rest of an existence, of splitting life's natural cinema into a before and after.

A few minutes after 3:00 p.m., Deputy Mussolini enters the chamber from his usual door on the right, followed by deputies Di Giorgio, Federzoni and Ciano. He appears "scowling, his face dark," a reporter of the *Corriere della Sera* notes.

Dismissing the ritual applause of his acolytes with a wave of his right hand, the Duce of fascism takes his place at the bench of the presidency. When Deputy Rocco gives him the floor, in the most tense silence, Benito Mussolini adjusts his tie knot with a habitual gesture. Then he immediately goes on the attack.

A secession of opposition forces works if the opponent negotiates, but this man, with his back against the wall, now written off as done for by all his enemies, promptly shows that he will not stoop to bargain. His chair as prime minister is still a fortification, his words are openly addressed to his enemies.

"Gentlemen! The talk I am about to give cannot strictly speaking be classified as a parliamentary speech. I am not seeking a political vote from you, I've already had too many."

The speaker now picks up a book. It is the deputies' manual which contains the statute of the Kingdom. Everyone's attention is focused on the bound volume as though it were a live grenade.

"Article 47 of the statute says: the Chamber of Deputies has the right to bring charges against the king's ministers and to take them before the Supreme Court of Justice. I formally ask the question: is there anyone in this chamber, or outside this chamber, who wishes to avail himself of Article 47?"

It is an ostension. Benito Mussolini raises the book of democratic law to the parliamentarians like a priest performing the exposition of the consecrated Host of the body of our Lord Jesus Christ before the faithful.

Silence.

Just one.

All it would take is for just one person to speak up and he'd be done for.

Among the leaders of the opposition, seated at their benches or blending in with the crowd in the public galleries, there are men of courage. For years their day-to-day life has been trench warfare, they have endured constant threats, some have even been beaten a few times. All it would take is for just one of them to rise, to stand up on his own and make the charge, breaking party discipline, the circle of violence, pitting moral force against physical force, responding to the appeal of the future, executed in the present to be avenged by posterity, vanquished by life to be redeemed in history. All it would take is for just one man to stand up to ruin everything that "He" might still have to say, scribbled in a few notes, open to extemporization, on a sheet of loose-leaf paper.

No one gets up.

Only fascist adulators leap to their feet to applaud their Duce.

So the Duce forges ahead. If no one in that chamber dared to stand alone in accusing him, he, Benito Mussolini, will level the charge against himself.

And so his voice rises powerfully in the hall of Montecitorio, firing out one syllable after another. It was said that he supposedly formed a Cheka. Where? When? How? No one could say. If no one accuses him, he, then exonerates himself: he has always said that he is a disciple of that violence that cannot be expelled from history, but he is courageous, intelligent, forward-thinking; the violence of Matteotti's killers is cowardly, stupid, blind. Don't misunderestimate him by thinking he's such an idiot. He's never shown himself to be inferior to events, he could never even imagine ordering the absurd, appalling murder of Matteotti, he did not hate his implacable adversary in the least, he even admired him, he respected his determination, his courage, so similar to his own courage that has never failed him. And now he's about to give proof of it.

Benito Mussolini is silent for a few seconds, like someone having to reload his weapon. Then he plants his hands on his hips, juts out his neck and starts firing off syllables again, hammering out sentences in rapid succession.

For months there has been a vile, filthy political campaign, the most macabre, most necrophilic lies have been spread, investigations have even been conducted covertly. He has remained calm, kept the violence in check, brought about peace. And how did his enemies respond? By raising the stakes, aggravating the charges. The moral issue was called out, it was said that fascism was not a proud passion of the Italian people, but an indecent lust for power, that fascism was a horde of barbarians that had invaded the nation, a movement of bandits and marauders. By so doing, reducing everything to criminality, it was suggested that Italians never take anything as truthful, it was venomously insinuated that the sky, the earth, the air, color, sounds, smells are all just the deception of a malevolent demon, that the grand drama of History—youth's struggle against those in decline, the European continent's Mediterranean seafront launched towards the African landmass—should be written off as a banal, trite case of crime news. In short, all of creation was retracted, attributing it to the raving of an idiotic god spewing out strings of senseless phrases from the center of an unknown universe; it was argued that the world was nothing more than a perpetual fallacy governed by evil.

And, so, He, now, with his usual courage, He will oppose those who vilify life, the world, history:

"Well then, gentlemen, I declare here, before this assembly and before all the people of Italy, that I and I alone assume the political, moral and historical responsibility for everything that has happened. If more or less twisted words are enough to hang a man, out with the gallows beam and out with the rope! If fascism has been nothing but castor oil and clubs, rather than the proud passion of Italy's best young men, the blame is mine! If fascism has been a band of criminals, I am the leader of this criminal band!"

Once again, no one stands up to stop the son of the century. The chamber responds with a single roar, respectful, devoted, enthusiastic:

"All with You! All with You, Mr. President!"

Then he raises his chin towards the horizon, puffs out his chest, and sums it up. When two entities are locked in an unyielding struggle, the solution is strength. There has never been any other solution in history and there never will be. He, a strong man, promises that the situation will be spelled out "in all provinces" within forty-eight hours after his speech.

That ambiguous, prefectural expression—"in all provinces"—drops on the Chamber of Deputies like a tombstone. The session ends without discussion or a vote. The assembly will be summoned to reconvene by telegram.

Little by little, when the clamoring of the fascist ovations has subsided, the hall slowly empties. Benito Mussolini remains there alone for a long time, sitting at his presidential desk.

Listen to them. "Viva Mussolini! Viva Mussolini!"

They shout the name of the Leader because in a man's life a Leader is everything. Then, even before coming over to congratulate the Leader at the presidency bench, they sing *Giovinezza* again. They sing it because they're still young, and young men need to sing at the top of their lungs.

Look at them. Salandra and the other moderate dissidents still sitting behind their desks while the fascists, standing, prolong their ovations. Now, once the session is declared adjourned, they too gradually swarm towards the exit, muttering their pathetic disappointment. As the liberals retreat, Turati is still in the galleries, responding to the socialists' bewildered, questioning looks with reassuring, patronizing gestures. As if to say: "Don't be alarmed. It's the usual Mussolini, trying to scare the sparrows."

Look at them, listen to them, they don't understand what's going on. None of them. They don't see what I'm doing to them.

They will continue fighting, one side and the other, not knowing that they are already living in a house of the dead. Our men, the fascists in their black shirts embroidered with white skulls have always lived there, the others, who for centuries grew up with regard for human life, are unfamiliar with it. They wander through the night of the immense plain, groping and trembling, not even capable of following the instinct to fight. They don't understand, they don't see . . . blind kittens bound in a sack.

I have justified myself before history, but I have to confess: life's blindness concerning itself is heart wrenching.

At the end you go back to the beginning. No one wanted to shoulder the burden of power. I myself will assume it.